Harvest Moon

JUDITH SAXTON

Harvest Moon

St. Martin's Press ✎ New York

Library of Congress Cataloging-in-Publication Data

Saxton, Judith.
    Harvest moon / Judith Saxton.
        p.   cm.
    ISBN 0-312-15138-1 (hardcover)
    I. Title.
PR6069.A97H37   1996
823'.914—dc20   96-29248
                                             CIP

First published in Great Britain by William Heinemann Ltd.,
an imprint of Reed Consumer Books Ltd.

First U.S. Edition: January 1997

10 9 8 7 6 5 4 3 2 1

For Sylvia Turner,
who masterminded the Spanish side of the story,
with love and thanks.

For Sylvia Turner,
who masterminded the Spanish side of the story,
with love and thanks.

Acknowledgements

Firstly, my sincere thanks to Ken and Shirley
Bemand of Herefordshire, who made me so
welcome in their beautiful home, many aspects of
which I've used in the book, and particular thanks
to Ken, who sat down and went through the
hop-grower's year, blow-by-blow, with infinite
patience, explaining everything, whilst I scribbled
in my notebook.

Still in Herefordshire, thanks to the people of
Ledbury for answering nosy questions about their
town in the nineteen-thirties, and in particular the
lady in Ledbury Books & Maps, who guided me
with great success through her shelves and knew
exactly which books I should need most.

And thanks to the staff of the library service in
Coleford in the Forest of Dean, who advised me
where to find hopyards today so that I could see
for myself how the whole thing works.

Onto the Spanish side of the story. I am indebted to
Shirley Ball for explaining about Spanish names
and how to choose suitable ones, as well as for a
list of surnames typical of the various areas, and to
José María Sagaz for sending me a plan of Madrid
as well as sorting out which streets were called
what in pre-civil war Spain. And Lena Ball, who
was very young in the thirties, gave me a child's
eye view of the war – many thanks to them all.

One

John Hoverton woke as dawn lightened the sky in the east, and lay quietly watching the gradual return of daylight through the thin cotton curtains. Today, he reflected, was the beginning of the best time of all. Hop-picking time. Outside, the Herefordshire country-side would be waking up, but in Bees-wing Farmhouse, everyone still slept. Except me, John thought, and sat up on his elbow, glancing around him.

The room was large and lofty, with two rugs on the board floor, a washstand, a vast wardrobe and a chest of drawers. There were two beds, in the second of which John's foster-brother, Laurie Clifton, slumbered.

John grinned at the hump in the bed that was his friend, happy just because he and Laurie were under the same roof once more. Twice a year Sir George Clifton reclaimed his son for a while and John always missed Laurie badly, though his parents had done their best to keep him happily occupied. He had been counting the days to Laurie's return and crossing his fingers that Laurie would not miss the start of hop-picking. Late the previous evening Sir George had brought Laurie back to the farm and announced that he was off on a business trip. Then almost before the Hovertons had done exclaiming Sir George had simply waved a lazy hand at his son, grinned beneath his stained moustache at John, and walked out.

Ada Hoverton, having enveloped Laurie in a huge hug, sent him off to wash his hands before saying quietly to her husband that no doubt Laurie had been returned at such an odd hour because Cuffy's idea of a business trip was likely to be the sort of thing you'd be ashamed to do before a fourteen-year-old boy.

Bill had glanced uneasily at his son, but John was cutting himself a ham sandwich for supper whilst pretending to talk to his dog, Sasha, so apart from shaking his head at his wife Bill made no comment other than, 'That's as may be.' This was a remark, his son had noticed, that he used whenever he was lost for another retort. 'There's no real vice in Cuffy, as you're so fond of telling me, m'dear.'

John had long before realised that, when they wanted to pass a comment on Sir George without appearing to do so, his parents used the childhood nickname by which Laurie's father had once been known. Naturally he kept his knowledge a secret; and since his parents never said anything at all about Sir George in front of Laurie, that was all right. So John had continued to help himself to ham, sandwiched the slice between two rounds of his mother's homemade bread and began to eat, occasionally smuggling pieces of the meat under the table to where a hot pink tongue eagerly licked them off his carelessly washed fingers.

'No-o, but I wish he wouldn't take up wi' such ... but there, it's none of our business, Bill. Cut Laurie some ham, I doubt Sir George thought to give him supper before fetchin' him back here.'

John quite liked Sir George, though he didn't pretend to understand him, but he loved Laurie as he would have loved a twin brother. Laurie was a couple of weeks younger than he was but because Lady Clifton had died shortly after Laurie's birth the two boys had been brought up together. Sir George, with a child no more than fifteen days old on his hands, had been glad to hand his son over to the woman who had, before her marriage, been a valued parlourmaid up at the Place.

'I'll pay all the expenses for 'em both,' he had said gruffly. 'I know you'll see my boy right, Ada, and you can trust me to see you right.'

He had meant to pay handsomely, John had heard his mother say defensively more than once. But he'd no head for business, poor Sir George. So the monthly sums which were agreed for Laurie's upkeep – the Hovertons having said, rather stiffly, that they intended to pay every penny necessary for the upbringing of their own boy – never materialised. Everyone knew the Cliftons had a great deal of money, it was just not, Ada said wisely, negotiable. Look at all that antique furniture, she said, to say nothing of the oil paintings, the silver and glass, the wonderful old china – the Place itself! They would not lose by keeping Laurie with them until it pleased Sir George to claim him back and besides, there were more important things in life than money.

And although Bill Hoverton insisted on paying his own son's school fees, Sir George did pay up for what he called extras, though how or what with, no one liked to ask. Sir George drove the boys, in a large Rolls-Royce, to and from the exclusive boarding school they attended, paid for them both to go on school trips and to have extra coaching in maths and languages, bought their sports gear and kitted them out for such things as skiing and polo, pastimes which Bill Hoverton thought supremely unnecessary for two boys only just in their teens. But John was a natural athlete and Bill, recognising that his son was entering into a way of life foreign to his parents, agreed that, if Sir George was letting Laurie learn to ski and to muck about with a ball whilst on horseback, then his son should learn too.

Sir George was also responsible for some of the special treats which came their way – two weeks in the South of France last year, a wonderful weekend in London with visits to all the marvels of the metropolis before that – but money, as such, never seemed to appear. Ada handed out sixpence a week to both boys and Bill paid them for various tasks around the farm which contented them well enough. It obviously never occurred to Sir George that other children had pocket money, though from time to time, with great magnificence, he would tip them a quid . . . and as often, borrow it back to pay money owed in the village.

However, Bill Hoverton was a proud man and his farm was the envy of half the county; he needed no handouts from Sir George, who was slowly but surely running his once magnificent estate into the ground. Ada Hoverton, too, was only too delighted to have a couple of small boys around the farm instead of an only child. By the time Laurie was six months old the Hovertons thought of him as their own and would have fought to keep him.

There had never been any question of Ada and Bill providing John with a brother or sister; they had married late and been unsuccessful in their attempts to have a child until they had quite

3

given up and had resigned themselves to childlessness. And then, when Ada had been forty-one and Bill forty-five, John had been born. And four miles away as the crow flies and a fortnight later, Sir George's slender, delicate bride had given birth to a boy as well . . . and had died of milk fever before she had done more than request, in a failing voice, that her son be called Laurence.

'Poor gel; but she was like Sasha,' Bill Hoverton had once remarked in his son's hearing. 'Too nervy an' delicate for her own good, like. Now there's a dog as'll never take to the gun, not if I keep 'un a hundred years. Why, I'd no sooner put her in pup than I'd fly to the moon.'

Sasha was a red setter, beautiful, lively and totally brainless. She barked when she should have been silent, sat where she was when she should have been out retrieving the birds and ran for her life whenever a gun went off. What was more even indoors her manners were far from perfect. She stole food, sneaked upstairs and slept on the beds, widdled on your feet if you spoke to her in an annoyed tone. Bill, a practical man, would have put a piece of lead behind her ear, as he termed it, as soon as he realised she was gun-shy, but the boys loved her and pleaded so hard on her behalf that Sasha was now theirs – so long as they shut her up when the guns were in the neighbourhood and did not let her near Bill.

In termtime the two boys were always together, defended each other briskly from any threat, refused to refine their soft Hereford-shire accents, and took immediate revenge on anyone who hurt either of them. They wrote letters to their respective parents, Laurie copying John's one week, John copying Laurie's the next. Laurie was academically clever, John athletic. John was sturdy, fair-haired, grey-eyed and Laurie thin, dark-haired, hazel-eyed. Yet despite their differences they were still, somehow, a pair, immediately identifiable to their contemporaries as a formidable team.

So now, lying in bed and watching the light increase, John was aware of a double satisfaction; his brother was back where he belonged and very soon now the hop-pickers would begin to wend their way along the country lanes, getting ever closer to Bees-wing Farm.

John rolled over onto his side and poked an experimental toe out of the covers. The bedroom windows were open but it was still pretty warm in the room. Suddenly he was seized with a great yearning to be out of doors, in the cool of the early morning, with the sky lightening in the east and the farmhands and Bess, the collie, bringing the cows in for milking, starting their day. He put his feet down on the lino and winced; it was chilly. Still, nothing venture, nothing gain, and poor old Laurie had been stuck with his father for two whole weeks, whilst itching, of course, to be back here where his real life lay. So it stood to reason he wouldn't mind being woken up early; he'd *like* it, in fact. John considered a wet flannel but then remembered that a fight would only waste the best part of the morning and changed his mind.

Laurie seldom talked much about his stays at Clifton Place, save to say that the butler was a great gun and did his best to amuse his guest, but this time, because the stay had been longer, he was a bit more forthcoming.

'There never is much for me to do because they're all quite old, the staff, I mean, so I wander round the grounds on my own, mostly,' he had told John as they prepared for bed the previous evening. 'And when the weather's bad I explore the house; there's a good deal of it, I can tell you.'

'What does your dad do whilst you wander round? Does he talk to you much?' John had asked with only limited curiosity. It seemed rude not to show any interest. But Laurie only shrugged.

'Not much. He goes out straight after breakfast and he doesn't offer to take me – he's away on business, he always says. He isn't much interested in me, you know. Still, I'm back now, that's what matters. To tell you the truth, though, he was a bit chattier this time. He told me he hoped I'd marry a decent, ladylike sort of girl with money. He said we could do all sorts with a few more spondulicks; we could have hunters again, and a yacht . . . all sorts.'

'That's rum,' John had said, giving a jaw-cracking yawn. 'Who wants a yacht when we're miles from the sea? Hell, I'm fair wore out! And tomorrow the pickers arrive!'

'Oh yes, I'd forgotten. I wonder if Alfie'll be with them this year?'

'He's older than us; fourteen, getting on for fifteen, and if he's got a job he won't be back,' John remarked, burying his head blissfully in his pillow. 'And he'll have a job if I know Alfie – he'll be down the mines, I reckon.'

Alfie was a Welshman from the valleys, a small, square boy with enormously strong hands and arms and a capacity for swearing and downing ale which a good many older lads might have envied. The previous year John and Laurie had hung about with him, envying him his strength, his language and his speed at picking. They had gone lamping with him one night, though never on Hoverton land, John and Laurie had stipulated that. It had been great fun and enormously exciting, especially when Bob Halbert, whose land they were on, had all but caught them – his Alsatian dog had taken a chunk out of Laurie's trouser-leg before they had scrambled over a six-foot wall and dropped down the other side, breathless, laughing, Alfie with his little crook-legged cross-bred terrier tucked safely down his jumper and a fat rabbit swinging from one hand.

Still. That had been last year and right now, as John stood up, his main preoccupation was how to wake Laurie without a great fuss. He tried a shake, but Laurie merely grunted and burrowed deeper. So he tried heaving the covers off, and that worked, more or less. Laurie sat up, bleary-eyed, John let go the sheet, and Laurie heaved it up over his shoulder once more and sank into slumber.

'Laurie! It's daytime! Get up, you lazy sod,' John hissed desperately. His mother's remarks on the revenge she would exact if he did not let Laurie have his sleep out made him lower his voice still further. 'Come on, do you want to miss everything?'

'Yes,' came the reply from deep in the pillow. 'Bugger off, John, you know what Mum said.'

'Aw, c'mon, Lo,' John wheedled, changing tack. 'The pickers'll be arriving any minute and Dan and Elias will be getting the cows in. What's more, poor Sasha must be desperate to get outside – hear her whine? – because she knows what will happen if she puddles again.'

Had Sasha been barking her head off neither boy could possibly have heard; the ancient farmhouse walls were too thick and besides, the kitchen was at the back of the house, the boys' bedroom at the front. But the mere mention of Sasha brought Laurie's eyes resentfully open. He groaned and sat up.

'Damn, I forgot. If the stables have been cleared for the pickers of course Sasha has to be shut in the kitchen overnight. We should have sneaked her up here. Still, you could go and let her out.'

John walked across the room and pulled back the yellow cotton curtains, then bent to look out of the low window. A light mist was rising from the dewy grass and through the branches of the young silver birch which grew only six or eight feet from the glass he could see the gravel drive, the crescent of lawn which edged it, and the plank bridge over the tiny stream which led to the home meadow beyond. Through the floating scarves of mist he could make out three small, hunched rabbits grazing near the gate, as motionless as statues if you discounted their long, constantly twitching ears, and when he glanced up he saw a large cock blackbird see-sawing uneasily on an upper branch of the birch. It saw him at the window and began its shrill, rhythmic warning: *danger, danger, someone's about, someone's about!*

But there was movement. If he turned his head to the left and peered he could see the cattle being brought in for milking, moving with stately grace, Bess padding quietly along at their heels, Dan, with a cigarette in his mouth and his cap on the back of his head, bringing up the rear.

'What are you staring at?' a peevish voice from the bed behind him asked. 'Who's out there?' There was a definite creaking, a pinging of bedsprings. 'Is it the pickers? Have they arrived? Are they coming?'

'Look for yourself,' John said with rare cunning, and heard the patter of Laurie's bare feet as he crossed the floor. A shoulder was thrust against his, for the window was not only low, it was only just wide enough to accommodate two growing boys, and Laurie squeezed in beside him.

'Where are they? Is Alfie with them? I can't see . . .'

'Sold again,' John said smugly. 'Three rabbits, a blackbird – see? – and Dan bringing the cows in. But the gippoes could have arrived, they aren't dependent on trains or waggonettes or motor buses. And we wouldn't see them from here, anyway. Shall we go and take a look?'

'You're too bad, you lying blighter,' Laurie said, but he didn't sound really annoyed and when John turned to look at him he saw his foster-brother's eyes were bright and eager once more. 'All right then, now I'm awake I suppose I might as well get up. D'you think Mum will mind if we don't wash immediately?'

'Yup, because of the pickers coming,' John said briefly. He knew his mother wouldn't normally mind if they went out before anyone else was up and left their ablutions until later in the day. Then if she was in a good mood they would wash later in the kitchen or the back cloakroom with a jug of hot water straight from the stove, instead of having to use the washstand in their room and water which had stood all night. 'The kitchen will be like Ledbury on market day once they start coming in and being told where they're to sleep. Come on, the cold water'll wake you up.'

He went across to the washstand, stripped off his pyjamas and sloshed water from the cornflower-decorated jug into the matching basin, then seized his flannel, soaked it and applied it briskly but briefly to hands, face, neck and ears. Then he rubbed himself dry on the nearest towel and reached for his clothes.

'What about soap, young Hoverton?' Laurie said, his voice an exact imitation of a school prefect he and John particularly hated. 'No point in just moving the dirt around, boy . . . hey, don't throw water!'

The last remark was in Laurie's own voice again as John flicked the flannel at him.

'Bugger the soap,' John said, dragging his shirt over his head. 'The dirt's all gone, hasn't it?'

'Yeah, onto the towel, filthy features! Don't put my bags on, you lazy hound, find your own!'

John dropped the ill-gotten trousers on the end of the nearest bed and fell to his knees to peer underneath it. Sure enough his own trousers were there, richly enhanced with dust, but a brief shake soon cured that and he was dressed and shoving his feet into his slippers before Laurie had finished at the washstand.

'I'll go down and let Sasha out, shall I?' he suggested, but was not surprised by Laurie's vigorous shake of the head. It would not have been fair to steal a march on Laurie on such a day and the suggestion had not been made seriously, so he sat in the window embrasure once more and looked out whilst Laurie finished dressing and attacked his dark hair with the silver-backed hairbrushes his father had given him, using them alternately in a very professional way which had taken the boys long hours of practice to master.

Outside, the mist was lifting. If John peered through the thick foliage of the trees which surrounded the farm he could just catch a glimpse of the lane and presently, was almost sure he saw movement. He looked harder, then looked away and looked back quickly; yes, there *was* movement. Something, or someone, was moving along the lane and it wasn't the cows because they were in . . . it simply had to be the gipsies.

He said as much to Laurie, who came over to the window at once, but then shook his head.

'No, that isn't the gipsies; you know what a row they kick up, always boasting and bragging, hitting the kids, yelling at the dogs . . . we'd hear them from here, no question.'

'But they can be damn near silent,' John pointed out. 'When they want to be, that is. Dad said they're quiet as a fox in the woods at nights, that's why we lose chickens. They get right up into the farmyard and even the dogs don't hear them.'

'Yes, but . . . By God, John, you're right! See *that*?'

John, who had turned away from the window to argue, turned back in time to catch a glimpse of something brilliant, buttercup yellow through the screening trees. He gave a crow of triumph and jumped to his feet.

'It's a caravan! Come on!'

Laurie, stealing quietly down the narrow wooden staircase behind John, thought fleetingly of the contrast between this and Clifton Place. His father's home had a wide, curving staircase, carpeted in turkey red; the hall below was lit by a vast chandelier and tiled, the tiles scattered with rugs. There was a big brass gong, a number of animals' heads decorated the walls and the narrow windows were made of stained glass.

At Clifton Place Laurie slept in a room on the second floor which had once been a nursery – there were bars at the windows which he might have resented had he ever stayed there for more than a week or two, and blue and pink bunnies on the wallpaper. As soon as Laurie realised that his father never came near the room he had taken to embellishing the wallpaper and now he was quite fond of the result. All the rabbits near his bed wore goggles, sported moustaches and had curly pipes gripped between their teeth. They had bubbles coming out of their mouths which had very unrabbit-like sentiments written in them; some had sprouted odd haircuts. One of the rabbits – Fang, slayer of foxes – had been given a black highwayman's mask and his bubble now read: 'I shall rescue Freddy and his good mama from the foul keeper of Castle Drogue . . . with the help of ALLSOP!!!'

Castle Drogue was what Laurie called those parts of Clifton Place inhabited by Sir George, and Sir George himself was the 'foul keeper'. The good mama and Freddy had been the housekeeper, Mrs Platt, and her small son. Or rather the ex-housekeeper.

Other servants at the hall never seemed to stay long but the Platts had been there since Laurie had first been brought back to the Place at the age of ten, and Laurie had grown to value Freddy's company. The younger boy was fat and slow on the uptake, but he was still someone to hang around with.

'Why's she gone?' Laurie had asked the new housekeeper, a young, untidy woman with a loose mouth and a knowing smile. 'She was all right, wasn't she?'

The new housekeeper had shrugged. 'Dunno,' she said briefly. 'Never met 'er. Happen Sir George thought I'd suit 'im better.'

Laurie was forced to be content with that, since Allsop the butler, who knew everything, assured Laurie that there had been no outright argument.

'I believe Mrs Sutcliffe to be a personal friend of your father's. Apparently Mrs Sutcliffe needed a job and your father decided to employ her as his housekeeper. Mrs Platt will have no difficulty in getting another post, since she is a hard and efficient worker. Mrs Sutcliffe, on the other hand, is – is inexperienced.'

'But you shouldn't kick one person out and put another in,' Laurie said uneasily. 'You wouldn't do that, would you, Mr Allsop?'

Allsop had just smiled, but Laurie knew the older man agreed with him. He had always liked Allsop and admired him, too. Allsop, at least, seemed to be a permanent member of the house-hold; at any rate, he was always there, and Laurie had realised quite early on that Sir George could never have managed without him. Quietly, efficiently, he ran the household, saw to Laurie's wants during his brief stays and managed the servants, both outdoors and in. He kept Sir George happy, too – no mean task.

As for Sir George himself, Laurie tried never to put his feelings about his father into thoughts, let alone words. He found Sir George impossible to love, that was the trouble. His father blew hot and cold, took Laurie to stay at the Place and then ignored him, praised his excellent examination marks in the classics and modern languages and then told Laurie he would be better pleased to have a son skilled at rugger, or a first-rate mathematician. He told Laurie he was a bruising rider to hounds and then said John put him in the shade, left him far behind.

Laurie didn't mind *that*. It was true, and praise of John had always pleased him deeply. It was the way Sir George said it which made him uneasy, the sneer behind the words, and besides, Sir George seemed as indifferent to John as he was to his own son when they were together.

Then there was Laurie's painting.

'Cissy rubbish; only girls mess about with paints,' his father had growled at him when Laurie had shyly shown him the small watercolour which had won him much praise at school. 'You'll be boastin' about your embroidery next!'

The remark had stung; Laurie had gone up to his bedroom and given the keeper of Castle Drogue buck teeth and a squint. It had made him feel better.

But now, reaching the bottom of the farmhouse staircase and creeping across the tiny front hallway, the two boys bent simultaneously to listen outside the kitchen door. They had no desire to find Mum waiting for them, with a list of things they must do before they left the house.

However, silence greeted them. John turned and grinned, making a thumbs-up sign.

'Coast's clear,' he whispered hoarsely. 'In we go!'

The boys had envisaged making their way straight to the copse by Winford's acre because ever since they could remember, the gipsies had put their caravans and tents in the peculiar little

11

patch of ground with its masses of blackberries, dog roses and fringing hazel trees. They liked it because it was private, difficult of access and rich in things the women could sell – rosehips were picked and sold to those cottagers or townsfolk who wanted to make their own rosehip syrup but disliked the task of picking from the briars; blackberries were harvested too and the menfolk nicked any wood they could find for the manufacture of the clothes pegs which the old 'uns sold from door to door when winter came.

'There was a murder there once, that's why we don't cultivate it,' John and Laurie told anyone who would listen. Old Mr Pelham, Dan the farmhand's octogenarian father, knew more about the history of Bees-wing Farm than most and had told the boys this the first time they had asked about Winford's acre.

'Twas the murder,' he said ghoulishly. 'There were a cottage on that bit o' land way back in 'istory – in the seventeenth century, mebbe. Now Winford 'ad a daughter, a fine gel, an' the local lord o' the manor . . .' he leered at Laurie – '. . . an ancestor o' yourn, lad . . . wanted the gel.'

It was a rambling and repetitious tale but the boys enjoyed the bloodthirstiness of it – heads rolled, arteries spurted, various bits of people's anatomy were hacked off in old Mr Pelham's version of events – and were delighted, though surprised, when Bill Hoverton, consulted, said that for once old Mr Pelham was right; there had been some sort of skulduggery there once. Whether it was murder he could not say, it was too long ago, but skulduggery there had certainly been.

Not that ancient skulduggery had stopped any Hoverton from ploughing Winford's acre; no, indeed. They didn't plough it because it was too small to bother with, because it would be 'a turble job, turble', and because the ruins of the stone cottage were now so scattered as to ensure broken ploughshares should anyone try to cultivate the land.

So the gipsies knew they would have Winford's acre to themselves and besides, it was only separated from the farm by the copse which meant, curse them, that they could sneak up to the yard at night and help themselves to a hen unwise enough to roost anywhere but in the henhouse, to eggs in the nest, to washing left on the line, to just about anything not nailed down, Bill said grimly.

So when, having heard nothing but silence from the kitchen, the boys stealthily opened the door, they nearly died of shock when a voice said breezily, 'Hello, you two! Come to clean up after that bloomin' dog o' yourn? Well, you'm in good time, I was about to chuck she into the yard where no doubt she'd ha' found more mischief. So now you'm up an' about you can clear up after she . . . an' before you go out you might as well put the kettle on, make yourselves useful.'

It was Bill Hoverton, who must have let himself in through the back door just as they entered the room. He had his boots in one hand and was in the act of hanging his cap on the back door. The twinkling glance he sent them showed he guessed why they had come in so quietly – why they had come down so early, come to that.

The boys grinned at each other and entered the kitchen, where one glance at Sasha was sufficient to see that she had sinned. Jumping from paw to paw, her long ears swinging uneasily on each side of her comically worried face, she was trying to avoid treading in the spreading puddle by the back door whilst still endeavouring to imply that it was no doing of hers, that she had just found it there and was as astonished as they, that she was most awfully sorry, would never do it again . . .

'I'll get the mop, you put the kettle on,' John ordered Laurie. He was, after all, a fortnight the older. 'Best not let Sasha out, there's too much going on and by the size of the puddle, she won't be needing to go out again for a bit.'

It was a well-known fact that Sasha, unaccompanied by a calming influence, was capable of performing almost every wickedness known to a heedless and featherbrained dog. She would chase ducks and chickens, sheep and cattle. She would harass the cows in their stalls, the horses in their meadows, the other dogs, Bess and Nell, as they endeavoured to do their work. She pursued the postman, barking hysterically, and on the rare occasions when she saw a motor car, she attacked the moving wheels, putting herself in the gravest danger of a nasty accident. She loved to bathe in the stream, roll in cow-muck, attach burrs to her thick and shining coat – at least, when the boys were brushing her sleek coat and leg-feathering they swore she must have gone burr-hunting deliberately to have acquired so many – and to first devour and then bring up on the rug, unsuitable and disgusting objects. The only creatures she respected were the geese, who beat her up whenever she crossed their paths, and the pigs, who drove her out with squeals if she went into the old orchard when they were rooting contentedly under the apple trees.

'Kettle on the go? Make the tea, Laurie.'

'Doing it, Uncle,' Laurie called cheerfully. 'I'll cut some bread and butter it, shall I?'

Although he called Ada Hoverton Mum, lacking a mother of his own, he had always called Bill Uncle, which caused considerable mystification amongst casual acquaintances.

'Aye, lad. There's marmalade in the crock and some honey . . . might as well line our stomachs afore we start the day.'

'You started the day very early, Dad,' John commented. He had mopped the puddle away and was now rubbing the old quarry tiles with a cloth soaked in bleach. 'You must have been up before dawn.'

'Oh aye. Well, once the pickers arrive there's no rest for us. Still, we can't manage wi'out 'em, so no use complaining. That floor's clean now, surely? Then get a jug and fetch some fresh milk in, the men will be well on wi' the milking be now.'

'Right. I'll take Sasha, shall I? I won't let her run off.'

John took the big blue jug off the sideboard and slipped out into the yard, a hand twisted in the piece of rope which hung round Sasha's neck. Daylight was strong now, the sky a pale, clear blue overhead. When he looked above the pointed conical roof of the hop kilns he could see the hills, dark against the sky, their summits gilded already by the hidden sun. And somewhere, a bird was pouring out song in a cascade of sweet, clear notes – a lark, John knew, without even having to think about it.

Sasha tugged impatiently as they neared the cowshed but John clung onto the rope; he knew his dog. Later in the day she would obey a call to return if she was in the mood but first thing in the morning, when she'd been cooped up in the kitchen all night, obedience was too much to ask – or too much to expect, anyway.

14

'Right; then it's the cowshed, old girl,' John said, entering the gloomy building which smelt of warm cow, fresh dung and milk. Dan and Elias were halfway down their respective rows of animals already, the milk hissing into the galvanised pails. Elias, who was nearest to the doorway, cocked a knowing eye but did not pause in his steady tugging at the long, pink teats.

'Want some milk? Come on 'en, I'll put it straight into the jug for 'ee.'

John went over, bent and held the jug inside the bucket; the milk continued its steady hissing hail until the jug was brim-full and then John removed the jug carefully so as not to spill a drop and Elias redirected the jets into the bucket once more. Sasha, who had been watching with the keenest interest, not even trying to pull away, whined hopefully; she adored milk. Elias took the hint; he squirted some in her direction, trying to score a direct hit on Sasha's round, golden-brown eyes or her whiffling black nose, but despite his efforts the dog managed to catch most of the jets in her mouth and then, when the flow ceased and Elias returned to his work, licked her milky whiskers with great satisfaction and pranced towards the doorway, tugging impatiently at the rope.

'Thanks, Elias; see you later,' John said. 'No use pulling my arm out of its socket, greedy; Mum won't give you anything else, that milk will have to last you till dinner.'

It wasn't so easy crossing the yard again with a full jug of milk and Sasha bounding to left and right as she explored all avenues for food or fun, but John managed it without spilling a drop or releasing the dog. He went into the kitchen, slammed the door behind him, put the milk down by the teapot and then reached for his slice of bread and butter. He knifed honey out of the jar onto the bread – his mother would have told him some home-truths about manners if she had seen him – and then began to eat whilst Sasha, released, sat and waved a feathery paw hopefully in his general direction.

'Want some tea?' Laurie said, finishing his own bread and honey. 'I think I'll have milk; I love it all foamy, like that.'

'I'll have milk too; it'll be quicker,' John said thickly through a full mouth. 'If we're going to Winford's acre and then down to the hopyard we can take Sasha. She'll run off some energy that way.'

15

'We'll start picking at daybreak tomorrow, most likely,' Bill said, eating bread and honey at a great rate. 'You can tell the gippoes that, if they've arrived. And Dan will be down the yard, checkin' on this and that. Tell him to come up for breakfast, would you? Come to that, you'd better come back yourselves.'

'Don't want brekker after bread an' honey,' John objected. 'Besides, if the gippoes have arrived we'll likely hang about down the acre for a bit. We thought we saw 'em in the lane, didn't we, Laurie?'

His father shrugged and poured tea, hot and black, from the pot into his large tin mug. At breakfast he would have a cup like everyone else but now, with his wife still upstairs, he could have the mug he preferred and tea so strong that the spoon, he said, stood upright in it.

'Dunno if they're here yet, but they won't be long, they're always early, and they know how I like things done. Old Mrs Smith will be up here to report before I've had time to get down to Winford's. I'll say one thing for the old gal, she rules 'em with a rod of iron, makes sure they behaves as well as a gippo can; knows I wouldn't have 'em, else.'

'Right. When'll the Welsh arrive?'

Bill glanced up at the clock which ticked calmly away beside the great, blackened oak dresser. He wound that clock once in twenty-four hours, adjusted the weights, put the hour on in spring and took it off in autumn and stopped the chime when there was a death in the family. All these things his father before him had done, and his father before that. The clock was probably as old as the farmhouse itself, an ancient grandmother clock, the walnut-wood case polished by generations of Hoverton wives, the tiny sailing ship which rocked away the seconds as accurate and bright as the day it had been made. Now, it showed seven forty-five.

'I've told the fellers to take the haywains down to Ledbury around two this afternoon. Mostly they'll be here around 'leven but they can either wait or walk – or catch the bus or hire one of young Tilley's motors, if they'm minded.'

'And the Brummies?'

Bill grinned tolerantly at Laurie. Both boys knew that he regarded the folk from Birmingham as the best pickers because they weren't as union-conscious as the Welsh, and enjoyed the countryside more, being less accustomed to it.

'They'll arrive, likely, at one o'clock, or soon after, which is why the wains be goin' into town for two.' He cocked his head. 'I think I hear a footstep – that'll be your mum, comin' down to cook brekker.'

The boys dived simultaneously for the back door. Mum could always use an extra pair of hands and they wanted to watch the gipsies make camp, so making themselves scarce was their best hope.

In their eagerness to get away the boys almost slammed the back door behind them but now it opened again and Bill appeared in the doorway. 'Take thy dratted animal,' he roared and pushed Sasha into the yard before closing the door once more.

Sasha bounded joyfully out, her grin at its broadest, her pink tongue lolling in anticipation of fun to come.

'Oh lor . . . but I suppose she'll be all right if she's got the worst of her early morning bounce over,' Laurie said, grabbing for Sasha and missing her completely. 'Calm down, old girl, or you're for the barn. Heel now – *heel*!'

Sasha was always surprising them and now she dropped to heel as immediately and obediently as though she had understood the threat. The boys grinned at each other.

'She's not as dumb as she seems,' John said wisely. 'Come on . . . quietly now, old girl.'

They crossed the farmyard and climbed the stile into the home meadow just as the sun showed red over the shoulder of the nearest of the hills.

For three days the pickers worked from dawn until dusk and John and Laurie worked amongst them, getting to know new people and greeting old friends. Alfie was there; he would start work in the pit at the beginning of October, he told them, but he was free for now. He and his pal, Dewi, were hellbent on earning good money from the hops, though – they were now into poaching in a big way and wanted to buy one of the skinny, sly-eyed lurchers that the gipsies usually had at heel.

'With one o' them dogs we could 'ave Sunday dinner every day o' the week, mun,' Alfie told them. 'Times is 'ard in the valleys; the bosses lays a feller off soon as look at 'im. But a rabbit in the pot is a rabbit in the pot.'

This was unanswerable logic but as John said to Laurie, later, there were some landowners so mean they grudged a rabbit to their own farmhands let alone to hop-pickers, so Alfie and Dewi had best look out.

'Oh, well,' Laurie said tolerantly. 'They want the dog for poaching in the valleys, not round here, Dewi said so. Come on, let's take a look in the kiln.'

As they strolled down the gently sloping hill, walking carefully between the pickers, stopping whenever they saw someone they knew to exchange a few words, John marvelled again at the industry around them and at his own pleasure in it. He loved picking hops, and enjoyed giving a friend a hand for half an hour, but now it was high noon and the sun was scorching down on pale cheeks, necks and arms so most of the women had donned headscarves and the men wore handkerchiefs tied at each corner to protect their pale skin from burning. One skinny, freckled girl had incautiously tied back her mass of reddish hair, however, and John saw that the nape of her neck was a deep and raw-looking scarlet. He nudged Laurie.

'Gosh, look at her neck, it's like raw beef! She'll be laid up in the morning if she doesn't cover herself. Shall we tell her?'

Laurie shrugged. Very soon now, he reminded John, the women would produce bread and cheese and bottles of tea and work would be suspended whilst everyone ate. Mothers were protective towards their kids and when the family met for their food no doubt the redhead's mother would tell her she was burning. But John, though he took the point, was worried nevertheless. The girl had been picking with a grim determination which the kids almost never showed – not even Alfie and Dewi picked like that – so perhaps she would not go to her mum for her food. Although Ada Hoverton always provided potatoes, cheese, homemade bread and plain cake, with chunks of fatty bacon every now and then as a treat, leaving each family to prepare and serve the food how they wished, the pickers mostly had their main meal in the evening, when dusk had fallen and they could no longer pick, making do

18

with a snack at midday. It would not be a great loss, therefore, to work through the short break, and there were always a couple of buckets of clean water at the edge of the yard with a tin mug beside them for anyone who wished to quench their thirst.

'It's all very well to shrug; it wouldn't hurt to mention it to her, she's only a kid,' John pointed out. 'Mum told me some of 'em aren't with their own mothers, they come with aunts and such. I can imagine what her neck feels like now, but by tonight she'll be in agony. Remember when we first went skiing and didn't realise that we'd burn with snow on the ground?'

He turned, with Laurie trailing behind, and went back to where the red-haired child was still stripping hops off her bine and into the crib with blackened, sticky fingers. As he watched her a trickle of perspiration ran down the side of her face and dripped off her small, pointed chin. She raised her arm to brush the sweat away – and winced. She had felt the tug on the delicate skin of her neck.

John stepped forward and just as she finished with her last bine he caught hold of her arm. 'Look, kid, if you don't . . .'

She gave a small, muffled shriek and stepped back sharply. John, who had been leaning towards her, was caught off balance and knocked into the crib and the crib tipped. Hops, light as air, fell and bounced delicately onto the stripped bines, disappearing into the sea of foliage like a grain of sand in a desert.

'Oh my Gawd . . . look what you bloody well done, you clumsy bleedin' yokel!' The small girl's pale face had flushed to a delicate shade of pink but even as John began to apologise, Laurie moved forward.

'Don't you talk to my brother like that,' he said indignantly. 'It was an accident, a blind idiot could see that. You're a nasty little vixen, you mind your manners or you can pick up your bloody hops yourself.'

'No, it was my fault,' John began, 'But I was only . . .'

The girl lunged at them, both boys dodged – and the crib went right over, scattering hops to the four winds. The girl gave a shriek and charged down on them like an avenging angel, all white-hot fury and flying, brilliant hair. Her weight caught John squarely amidships and, caught off balance, he went flying, considerably hurting his knees with the force of his descent. The girl promptly began to punch and kick with all her strength whilst yelling abuse at the top of her voice.

'You wicked bugger . . . you'll pick up every one of them bloody hops or I'll tell the farmer on you,' she shrieked venomously. 'That's a mornin's work that is . . . go on, git started!'

Laurie started to laugh. 'What a temper,' he said jeeringly. 'Well, go and tell the farmer, then – Mr Hoverton's only our dad, so he'll take your side against his own son, naturally!'

'Look, I'll pick them up . . .' John was beginning when the girl suddenly went white as a sheet and, before their horrified eyes, sank slowly down onto the piled-up bines.

'She's fainted,' a motherly woman picking a bit further up the row announced. She flung her bine down and came towards them, face red and angry-looking. 'That's your bullyin', you *young gennelmen.*'

'Sarky old bag,' Laurie muttered quietly. Aloud, he said, 'It wasn't us, missus, it's the sun. She's got sunstroke, her neck's red-raw – you her ma, then? Why isn't she wearing something over her head?'

'She ain't nothin' to me, she's just a kid what the Brummies brung along,' the woman said. 'She were wi' Bea, earlier, mebbe Bea's 'er aunt or some such. Dear Gawd, lads, Bea won't care if you're farmer's sons or not, she'll crucify you for this carry on. Foxy's a bleedin' good picker for a young'un.'

'Foxy? What's her name, then?'

The woman shrugged and bent over the child. 'Foxy, din't you 'ear?' she said impatiently. She smoothed a hand over the child's hot pink forehead and frowned at Laurie. 'Oh aye, you'll cop it for this!'

'It wasn't our fault,' Laurie said, whilst John, visited by inspiration, ran for the nearest bucket of water and brought it back, leaning heavily to port. Sasha, who had taken no interest in the proceedings so far, promptly got excited and ran with him, jumping up and barking. 'We didn't do a thing – it was her. She's got an evil temper, that one.'

'How can you say that, when the poor li'l . . .'

'This'll do the trick,' John panted, hefting the bucket. 'Soon bring her round, don't you fret.'

'Don't you go 'alf-drownin' . . .' the woman began warningly, but it was too late. The bucket was heavy and John tipped it with enthusiasm. The red-haired girl got it not just in the face but all over, so that her thin, greyish cotton dress was soaked and her hair hung in rat's tails. Sasha tried to lick some of the water off but Laurie pulled her back as the girl began to make an awful gurgling noise. Just as John was beginning to wonder rather apprehensively whether someone could drown on dry land she sat up groggily, spouting water like a whale, wheezing . . . crying. You couldn't see tears, of course, for the flood, but you could tell she was crying by the odd shapes into which her mouth was pulling itself and by the helpless way she sat there, soaked and shivering, staring blindly round her and rubbing half-heartedly at her water-beaded lashes.

John couldn't bear it. He had seen at a glance that she was a tough kid, not the sort to break down and blub, and now she was crying from sheer weakness and because he'd hurled water at her and nearly drowned her. But he hadn't meant any of it, he had only meant to warn her of the dangers of sunburn. He squatted down beside her and took out his handkerchief. For a wonder it was neither filthy nor wrapped round something unsavoury. He mopped her cheeks gently and she neither cursed nor swore nor tried to hit him but simply sat there, seeming unaware of his ministrations.

'You've had a touch of the sun, little'un, that's all,' John told her in his gentlest voice. 'We didn't mean to knock the crib over, either of us, we were just messing about. Now come on, let's clean you up a bit, we'll see to your hops.'

The woman, seeing that the child was conscious once more, returned to her own crib and Laurie crouched down too. He peered into the wet, dirt-streaked face now so near his own. Sasha, not to be outdone, joined them, peering into the girl's face as though she, too, would have offered comfort had she only known how to speak.

'We're really sorry,' Laurie said with surprising feeling, for he usually had little patience with what he termed 'kids'. 'We were messing about, John and me . . . we'll pick the hops up, as many as we can, and if we can't pick them all up, because some will be spoiled, you know, we'll pick more and fill your crib in a trice. Just you sit there and watch us.'

The girl sniffed and knuckled her eyes hard, then glanced first at Laurie and then at John. Her eyes were very large and greenish-grey and fringed, John saw, with thick, very straight white lashes. He thought of Aggie, his father's favourite brood sow, who had lashes just like the child's, then hastily dismissed the thought as unkind. Besides, the kid was looking up at him, beginning to smile.

'Did I 'urt you? I were just so cross . . . I want me Auntie Bea to bring me agin, so I'm workin' like a perishin' navvy. Who's you, any'ow? And what's this daft lummock doin', a-sniffin' at me?'

John grinned at her. 'The daft lummock is Sasha, our dog. I'm John Hoverton and he's Laurie Clifton. We're foster-brothers. Who are you?'

'Foxy Lockett,' the girl said. John could almost see her self-confidence and aggression returning by the second. She pushed strands of wet red hair off her face, struggled to her feet and as John, too, stood up, she began to salvage some of the spilt hops. 'Me Auntie Bea brung me. I'm the best picker she ever had, she telled me so.'

Sasha, losing interest, went and sat in the shade of the bines. She kept glancing meaningly in the direction of the farm – Sasha always knew dinnertime. Laurie was putting the spilt hops back into the crib so John went over to pull down another bine. Then he turned to the girl.

'Yes, we thought you were a good picker when we passed earlier, Foxy. And it was my fault the hops got spilt, but all I was doing was trying to tell you that your neck was sunburnt and you should put something over it. Even untying your hair would help. Red-haired girls can't stand very hot sun, or at least red-haired boys can't so I s'pose girls are the same. There's a fellow in our school who fainted on the cricket pitch one day last term – he's a redhead.'

'I can untie me hair but I ain't got nothin' to put over me neck,' Foxy said, reaching up wincingly to untie the piece of hop-string which had kept her hair back. Released, the rich, wavy mass of her hair almost obliterated her small, pale face. 'Me Auntie Bea never said nothin' about wearin' a hat or leavin' me hair loose. Won't me neck just go brown, like Auntie Bea said the rest o' me would?'

'No. Your skin's very fair,' John explained kindly. 'Look, stay there until we've filled the crib, then come with us. My mum's ever so good, she'll put something soothing on your neck and give you some dinner. Then we'll come back and pick some more.'

Foxy raised her eyes to his face and stared at him very hard, as though trying to see through the offer to the reasoning behind it. Then, suddenly, she smiled, a three-cornered smile which showed her small, white teeth. All her woe seemed to have dissipated and now she just looked like a scruffy, tough little girl again, neither the avenging angel who had attacked the boys nor the doleful weeper.

'Oh . . . I wish I could, but Auntie Bea won't like it.'

'Well . . . when do you have your dinner? I'll go along and tell her you're having dinner with us, today.'

'I don't bother wi' no dinner,' Foxy said. 'I'd rather pick.'

'No wonder you passed out,' Laurie put in. He frowned down at her. 'There's no sense making yourself ill, you know, and I bet your Auntie Bea has something to eat. Picking's hard work, you need to keep your strength up. Come on, John, give us a hand and we'll fill the crib, then take Foxy . . . is that your *real* name? . . . along to Mum.'

'Everyone calls me Foxy.' The girl abandoned her rescue attempt on the spilt hops and pulled herself down another bine. She came alongside the crib and began to pick, her sticky black fingers incredibly quick and neat as she stripped the bine. 'Soon fill this 'un, then I wouldn't mind a bite, I tell you straight. I ain't never seen the farm . . . you won't tell no one? Only Auntie could send me home if I does anything wrong, see. An' – an' this ain't like nothin' I ever see'd afore.'

'Oh, you mean you aren't allowed to go up to the farm,' John said, light dawning. He remembered that there was a rule about only one member of each picking group visiting the farm. 'But it's all right for you to come with us; we invited you and it's our home, you know.'

'Good,' Foxy said blithely. It was clear that whatever her earlier feelings, she now trusted John. 'Don't stop pickin', feller, or we'll never fill this bleedin' crib!'

*

Foxy was astonished by the farmhouse. She knew the long row of timber and corrugated iron sheds called the barracks because the pickers from the Black Country were billeted there, and she had a nodding acquaintance with the big barn where the Welsh had their quarters, but the farmhouse itself was forbidden ground. Only those in charge of each small band of pickers were supposed to go up there, and Auntie Bea, charging up of an evening to argue the rate, ask for a pennyworth of milk or a few extra potatoes, was not likely to invite a child to go along, especially a child like Foxy, who was only here on sufferance. On trial, Foxy supposed.

For Foxy had been living with her father's mother until Auntie Bea had suddenly appeared in their midst ten days ago. She had marched into the filthy hovel where Foxy was trying to light a fire to cook the potatoes she had just peeled, and looked around her disparagingly. She was a tall woman, black-haired and gaunt and she seemed, to Foxy, exceedingly clean and amazingly neat. She was wearing a black cotton blouse, a grey striped skirt and a pair of cracked boots and from her lowly position Foxy could see that Bea also wore striped stockings, gartered above her knees. She made Foxy think of teachers, school attendance officers, people in authority. But as soon as Bea spoke Foxy realised that here, in this unlikely guise, was her guardian angel.

'You Mrs Grant? Harry Grant's ma?'

The older woman, who had been nagging Foxy to get the fire lit so that they might eat, stared up at the intruder from her seat on the couch.

'What if I am?'

'I've come for me niece.' Bea's eyes scanned Foxy for a moment, then she nodded. 'That's 'er. I'd know that red'ead anywhere. I'm Bea Lockett, Vonnie's sister. Oh aye, she's Vonnie's daughter, any fool can see that.'

Foxy, open-mouthed, continued to stare. Niece? What could the woman mean? For as long as she could remember Grandma Grant had told her that she, Foxy, was a foundling, dumped on the charity of Grandma Grant, a nuisance, an expense, a nobody. So how could she be this woman's niece?

'She's a foundling,' Grandma Grant said defensively. 'I been good to 'er, so I 'ave. Brung 'er up, fed 'er, clothed 'er, kep' 'er decent . . .'

'She's skinny as a rail an' that rag she's wearin' ain't clothes,' Bea said derisively. 'I on'y just found out where she were, so now I'm takin' 'er. She's me sister's gal – tell that, easy as easy.'

Foxy was shrewd enough to know that she was useful to Grandma Grant in many ways, but she was not prepared for the older woman's response. Grandma surged to her feet, heaved Foxy to hers, and clasped the girl to her large and strong-smelling bosom.

'Me son's kid, you'd not dare tek me son's gel,' she declared dramatically. 'Poor Harry's gorn, now the kid's all I got left. Foxy, tell 'er you won't go!'

Foxy detached herself from Grandma with some difficulty. She gave Bea a long, hard stare.

'Why d'you want me?' she asked. 'You don't know me.'

'Vonnie were me favourite sister,' Bea said readily. 'An' I'm goin' hop-pickin', over Hereford way. A feller tole me he'd seen you, said our Vonnie died of a fever when you was a littl'un. Said the old gal . . .' she jerked her head at Grandma Grant, '. . . din't look after you too good. 'Sides, I run a boarding 'ouse t'other side o' the city wi' my mum. We could do wi' an 'and.'

Foxy nodded; it sounded reasonable. She knew what hop-picking was, kids in school talked about it, but she assumed that the reason Bea wanted her was to help with the boarding house in her absence. It seemed fair enough to her, and besides, any escape from Grandma Grant could only be for the better. Grandma wouldn't let Foxy go to school nine days out of ten and she had grown to dread the words, 'Not today; I can't spare you today,' which so frequently occurred during termtime. Foxy loved school, the one orderly and interesting event in her otherwise slavish existence, for Grandma had long decided that Foxy should run the house, do the shopping and generally look after her. School came a poor second to Grandma's general comfort.

'I'll come,' Foxy had said, therefore. 'How long'll I be gone for?'

'For good,' Bea said. 'If we get along, that is. Suit you?'

Foxy looked up at her benefactress, at the strong, fierce face, the clean clothing, the amazingly white and even teeth, and grinned.

'Suits me,' she said. 'Shall I bring me blanket?'

So now, having been brought to Bees-wing Farm to help her aunt with the hopping, she suddenly found herself in seventh heaven. Auntie Bea fed her, provided her with clothing and a bed-roll and asked of her only a fair day's work at the picking and a hand of an evening. It behoved Foxy, therefore, to be cautious for fear she might annoy or offend her guardian angel.

So Foxy continued towards the farmhouse, walking between the two boys, deciding that if Bea suddenly appeared she would maintain that John and Laurie had forced her to go with them. It sounded unlikely, but not as unlikely as it would if she said she had been invited to visit the farm. Foxy often lied and knew everyone else did, too, but she had the strangest feeling that John and Laurie would not think highly of this, and already she wanted their friendship. She felt strongly that no matter what she did, if she was friendly with these two boys they would save her from Bea's most awful threat – to pack her off home without a penny piece. Not to Grandma, she had made that clear, but to the boarding house in the stuffy backstreet just behind the railway station.

The boarding house had seemed like heaven to Foxy at first, but now banishment from Bees-wing was the most awful punishment that Foxy could imagine, because already she was deeply in love with the countryside, the work, the whole way of life. Whilst she industriously picked, in fact, she was trying to work out a plan by which she could stay here for always. So far it had eluded her, but you never knew. When one door closes another opens, her teacher at school said from time to time. Foxy had long ago decided that this was just wishful thinking – but if, as the door closed, you could get your foot to it and give it a good old kick . . .

It was strange, though, Foxy thought, that the beauty, which had her gasping half a dozen times a day, seemed to pass the others by. Sunrise over the Malverns, sunset behind the Welsh hills, dew shining like diamonds in the grass, the river soft and brown beneath dimpling rain, the hops deep green against a blue sky, all these glories were simply taken for granted by pickers and locals alike. But not by Foxy. At school they were occasionally given powder paints and water . . . if only I could paint the hills and the sunsets, Foxy yearned, I'd be so happy! But she had never been able to manage paints. They weren't like facts, which could simply be fed into one's memory, or sums, which were, to Foxy, a matter of simple logic. The ability to appreciate beauty had been given to Foxy in abundance, the ability to reproduce that beauty on paper had not.

And now, in addition to all the other wonderful things here, she was seeing the farmhouse itself. Built in a hollow, with the long hop fields stretching up the slope at the back and the brook winding around the front and forming a natural boundary between garden and farmland, she had never seen, or dreamed, of a house more beautiful. The roof was made of warm golden-grey tiles patched with lichen and cushions of moss and the house itself was stone-built, old, the windows small and deep-set, the virginia creeper which covered one side already darkening to red. And it was huge! Foxy hung back for a moment the better to admire but John hung back too, so she had to keep up; she had no intention of letting a boy think she was afraid. Boys, in her experience, rarely pitied the weak but preyed upon them and Foxy had always let it be known that she was tough and mean. What a blessing there had been no boys other than these two about when she had fainted, or whatever it was she had done. These two, being farmer's sons, were obviously different from the boys she had known previously – these boys had been kind, it turned out they hadn't even meant to tip her hops over.

'Come on, then.' That was the fair-haired boy – John, that was his name. She liked him. He seemed dependable, somehow. Sensible. He had a fringe of very clean, straight hay-coloured hair falling over his brow and his eyes were grey and steady. He looked strong – Foxy tended to avoid strong boys, as a rule – and was clearly older than she, but she found she did not fear his strength. Perhaps it was because he was a country boy, but she did not think he would deliberately hit someone smaller and younger than himself. And he must be at least fourteen, she would ask when she knew him better.

They crossed the yard and entered a large, empty kitchen. Foxy looked round appreciatively; now she was here she might as well see all she could. There was a stone sink with wooden draining boards each side, a big table, several chairs with ladder-backs and cushions on the seat part. There was a big black cooking range with a couple of saucepans bubbling on it, the steam whisking away to the rafters overhead, and all sorts of pretty things – a deep windowsill by the back door with beautiful plants in pots crowding each other, a shelf full of what looked like cookery and gardening books, a rocking chair, a clock with a blue-enamelled face, a rag rug made of gaily coloured materials.

'Where's Mum?' Laurie said. 'I'll give her a shout.'

He went over to another door, opened it and put his head out. His shout was a loud one – his voice echoed. A hallway, perhaps, Foxy guessed, without very much furniture in.

'Mum! We've got a guest!'

Foxy, alarmed at the description, tried to shrink out of sight behind the nearest rocking chair but John shook his head at her just as the kitchen door was pushed wide and a woman came through. She had greying fair hair and a round, fresh-complexioned face and she was smiling over a pile of what looked like sheets.

'Goin' to get these washed,' she said briskly. Her blue eyes fixed themselves on Foxy's wet red head. 'Hello, who's this?'

Foxy bobbed a little half curtsy; she couldn't think what else to do. Shaking hands was clearly out of the question since Mrs Hoverton – she thought the lady must be Mrs Hoverton – had her arms full.

'Mornin', missus,' she said. 'Your boys said to come – I've burned me neck.'

Mrs Hoverton put the sheets down on the draining board and wiped her forehead with the back of her hand. 'Burned your *neck*, love? How did 'ee do a thing like that?'

'It's the sun, Mum,' Laurie chipped in. 'She went all faint, like. We thought you might have something soothing . . . and we asked her back for a bite of lunch with us.'

'Spuds is on,' Mrs Hoverton said. She dumped the sheets in the big stone sink. 'Soak these, would you, boys, while I take a look at the littl'un's neck?'

John and Laurie charged for the empty buckets and disappeared into the yard, clanking. Mrs Hoverton came over and parted Foxy's hair gently, then tutted.

'That's nasty, m'dear. Now there's a lotion in the pantry which might give you some easement... shan't be a mo.' She disappeared through another doorway which Foxy had not previously noticed and came back presently with a large brown glass bottle. 'Here we are! Hold your hair up and stand still whiles I spread it on.'

The liquid was deliciously cool and, Foxy thought, soothing. She held her hair out of the way but when she would have let it go Mrs Hoverton shook her head. 'No, no, my love, I'll just tie it back wi' a scrap o' ribbon and lay a clean cloth over the burn to keep off the sun. In a couple of days you'll be fine.'

'Thanks, missus,' Foxy said. 'You're their mum, aren't you?'

'That's right. And who might you be?'

'I'm Foxy Lockett, Bea Lockett's me aunt,' Foxy said promptly. 'Your boys was kind to me – they filled me crib.' She did not mention that they had first emptied it – it had been an accident, after all.

'And now you'll have a bite,' Mrs Hoverton said. 'We won't wait for the men. Get the table laid for three, boys.'

'It's a bit early . . .' John was beginning, but on receiving a glare from his mother, mumbled off into a random remark about fetching the ginger beer from the dairy. 'Mum makes gallons, so we drink gallons,' he told Foxy. 'Ever had ginger beer?'

Foxy shook her head. She'd heard of it, but at home the kids, she told John, drank mostly water.

'Do you more good,' Mrs Hoverton said, overhearing. 'Laurie, if John's getting the ginger beer you can get the meat pie out of the lower oven. There's two, fetch out the small one. I'll drain the spuds.'

Laurie, who was thinner and slighter than John, and quieter, too, bent over the oven. He took the pie out armed with a thick cloth and Foxy felt water rush to her mouth. Meat pie! And the spuds were steaming hot and smelt wonderful – would they really give her some, a bit of the pie, even? Auntie Bea fed her pretty well, but cautiously. At mealtimes her portion was never enough to fill her up.

'Sit down, the three of you,' Mrs Hoverton said presently. 'Come along, you'll want to get outside o' your grub before the men come in for their share. You pour the ginger beer, lad.'

John glugged ginger beer into three short, thick glasses. It foamed, then settled. And Mrs Hoverton put before each one of them a plate of food which would have satisfied Auntie Bea herself. Foxy stared for a moment, then grabbed her knife and fork and got to work. The pie was wonderful, the potatoes buttery, and the cabbage was nicer even than it was raw. Foxy had sneaked a few cabbage leaves when she skirted the field on her way to the hops in the early morning, but she had never tasted it cooked before and she liked it. She said as much through a full mouth.

'This is the best grub I ever had in all me life. I wish I had it every day!'

'You'd get sick and tired of it if you did,' Laurie observed. 'Mind, Mum makes the best meat pie ever – but you should taste her roast beef and Yorkshire puddings.'

'Mebbe she will, one of these days,' Mrs Hoverton said. 'There's no need to rush, Foxy, the grub won't run away.' She looked at Foxy's rapidly emptying plate and slid another couple of potatoes onto it. 'What do they call you in school, me love? Not Foxy, surely?'

Foxy shrugged and finished her mouthful. She speared another potato but did not stick it straight into her mouth. She felt beautifully full already and her plate still had food on it!

'I dunno. They calls me Florence at school, but that ain't me proper name, it's just that the teachers don't like Foxy. Grandma Grant – I lived wi' her, in Brum, afore Bea found me – she tole me my mum jus' called me "our kid", which ain't much help. So I's Foxy, you see.'

The potato, slippery with butter, was jammed in sideways. Mrs Hoverton closed her eyes for a moment, then opened them again.

'Well, Foxy it shall be, then. How does your neck feel now, me love?'

'Oh, much better. I'd forgot it,' Foxy assured her hostess. 'I ain't never had food like this afore, missus.'

'Well, no, because it's difficult to cook a meat pie over a brazier, but I'm sure Mrs Lockett is an excellent cook under her own roof,' Mrs Hoverton said. 'No doubt you have meat pie at home, Foxy?'

'Nah, ain't never tasted it afore,' Foxy said promptly. 'I were only wi' Bea four days, then we come here. Grandma uster git bought pies from the corner shop but I ain't never had one. Grandma Grant, she give me an 'ome but not much else, that's what I reckon now. It's rare good wi' Bea, I tell you.'

'So Grandma Grant gave you a home? Is that because your mother died?'

'Nah, she din't die, she went orf,' Foxy said. She finished her food and leaned back, then leaned forward again and picked up the glass of ginger beer. She drank and the stuff fizzed up her nose and prickled her tongue. It made her laugh, then sneeze. 'Grandma Grant was the feller's mother what my mum went orf with – I think. She got landed, so when Auntie Bea said she wanted to take me hopping, she should ha' been glad to git shot o' me. On'y I were useful,' she added reflectively. 'Still, she'll find someone else, I reckon.'

'Well, you've got a month here, to get fatter in,' Laurie said. 'You'll have to eat all you can – how old are you, Foxy?'

'Twelve. How old are you?'

'We're fourteen,' the boys said together, then laughed. Foxy laughed too, though she didn't know why. She supposed that it was because she had a full belly and was happy.

'Oh ah, older'n me, then. But I ain't goin' back, though Bea's good to me. I likes it here.'

'But you're too young to work, yet, me love,' Mrs Hoverton said gently. 'And children have to be with their parents, or . . . or guardians. They can't just leave. That's running away and if a child runs away it ends up being took home by the police – or taken to the workhouse, of course.'

'Why can't I just leave?' Foxy asked, her eyes bright with interest. She did not intend to waste her time worrying about policemen or workhouses. 'Grandma Grant kept sayin' how good she were to gi' me a home but I were allus hungry, often cold, she made me do all sorts o' work . . . I'd rather live on the perishin' streets than wi' the ole lady. Come to that, what's wrong wi' the workhouse?'

'They boss you about and won't let you roam,' John said suddenly. 'They wouldn't let you come hopping either, Foxy. If I were you I'd stick with your Auntie Bea in Brum. She's all right to

31

you, isn't she? And Mum's right, you aren't old enough to move away and earn your living yet.'

Foxy finished her ginger beer, sneezed, then pushed back her chair. She smiled up at Mrs Hoverton.

'Thanks,' she said simply. 'That were wonderful. Mebbe I'll not think o' leavin' Brum just yet, then. But I'd best be gettin' back or Auntie Bea will have me guts for garters.'

The boys had finished too and stood up as she did.

'We'll come back with you and get your hops weighed and put in the book, then we're going to cart sacks to the kiln for a bit,' John said. 'See you later, Mum.'

Mrs Hoverton watched the three children hurrying across the yard, then turned back to the table. She cleared it, relaid it for the men, and wondered about Foxy Lockett. She had known better than to feed a strange child with the farm workers, who would have resented it and might have taken it out on the child, but for herself, she approved of Foxy. She had very little to do with the children save if she went down to the barracks at night for a chat with some of the women, but it struck her that Foxy was the sort of child who would keep her eyes open in company and would pick up nice manners and the correct way to do things quicker than most. She had eaten fast, to be sure, but she had not tried to speak with her mouth full nor had she used her fingers. She had overfilled her mouth once, but had coped remarkably well with the large potato on that occasion. Either someone had taught her table manners or she had kept her eyes open, Mrs Hoverton concluded. And she's bright as a button, that's easy to see. I wonder whether it might be possible to find her somewhere . . . ? But no, not at twelve and with this Grant person in the background. Would Bea keep her in the Birmingham boarding house? It seemed probable – the child herself accepted that she would stay, and to send her back would be a great shame, because she was obviously very under-nourished and generally ill-used. Even with Bea, Ada Hoverton concluded, she wasn't getting enough food.

She thought about Bea Lockett though and decided that it would be sensible to have a word with the other woman. She had known Bea for years and had always thought of her as hard but fair; she probably didn't realise that Foxy was half-starved, but if Ada Hoverton pointed it out and offered to give the family double rations surely then Bea would see that Foxy was allowed to eat her fill?

As her mind worked, so had her hands. The table was cleared and relaid, the potatoes in the big pan pulled back over the heat, the big jugs of cider, kept under the sink to cool, brought out and placed on the sideboard. Presently, just as her knife sank into the second and larger of the two meat pies, the back door opened and her husband and the men came in, talking, taking off their dusty boots, going over to rinse their hands in the bowl of water, poured ready for them.

'Lads been in? Good, good,' Bill said. 'The pickers will be havin' their grub but Wilf's still cartin' and they can give 'e a hand.'

'They've found a friend,' his wife remarked, dishing up. 'A little girl – a redhead. She had sunstroke and her neck was badly burned so they brought her to me.'

'Oh ah? It ain't like the boys to waste their time on li'l girls,' Bill remarked. He took his place at the table and pulled his plate towards him. 'Smells good, m'dear.'

'I don't think she's an ordinary little girl,' Mrs Hoverton said, spooning potatoes onto the plates. 'A real character, that one. She's Bea Lockett's niece I believe.'

'Mrs Lockett?' To his wife's amusement Bill actually shuddered. 'Oh ah, that's one who never gives up wi'out a struggle. She knows the rate and what it's worth for ten, fifteen years back. Should lead a union, that one. Handsome woman, though. Dark.'

'Unmarried, too; Mrs is a courtesy title. And she's also six foot in her stockinged feet, passionate, determined . . . but neither a liar nor a cheat,' Ada said cheerfully. 'You could have worse against you, me love.'

'Oh ah? Well, wait'll she's up here demanding more cheese or potatoes or cheaper milk, then see how you feel.'

'I'd give 'em,' Ada said quietly. 'That child was nowt but skin an' bone, Bill. Made me ashamed. Seems her aunt don't give her too large a share of the grub that's going.'

Bill shook his head, squared his elbows and began to eat.

'You'll settle it,' he said confidently. 'Pass the mustard, Elias.'

*

That night, when the boys had gone to bed and the Hovertons were thinking of following their example there came a knock on the back door.

'I'll go,' Ada said, getting to her feet. She and Bill were sitting in the front room, Bill doing the books whilst Ada knitted the boys socks. 'It's bound to be one of the pickers with a grumble. Better I go; you finish off here and then we'll go up.'

Ada went to the door and opened it and there stood Bea Lockett, her face a trifle grim. She did not wait to be invited in but stepped into the kitchen and stood opposite Ada.

'Scuse me, missus, but I come for a word,' she said. 'It's about me niece, young Foxy.'

'Yes?' Ada said, beginning to bristle. Just let Bea say a word wrong . . .

'She says someone give 'er meat pie an . . .'

She got no further. 'That child, Mrs Lockett, is grievously under-nourished,' Ada said. 'I fed her because she needed it and if you've got anything to say as to why you haven't fed her properly I'd be glad to hear it.'

'Aye, that I have. If you find a starvin' pup, Mrs 'Overton, an' feed the little blighter wi' meat and two veg, what d'you reckon'll happen, eh?'

'It'll scour,' Ada said. 'But . . .'

'Aye. And I've been feedin' me niece careful, like, gradually buildin' 'er up to a proper size 'elpin' o' grub. And then someone comes along an' gives 'er meat pie an' what 'appens? Ever since, Mrs 'Overton, the poor little bugger's been either throwin' up or perched on the lavvy. See?'

'That isn't necessarily the meat pie; she had a touch of the sun as no doubt she told you. And furthermore, Mrs Lockett, the child told me she doesn't eat at midday and when you're working hard I believe everyone should have a meal at midday,' Ada said, hearing the defensive note in her own voice with some horror. She rallied a little. 'You've no right to take food for your pickers and then not pass it on to the child.'

'No right?' Bea Lockett swelled with righteous wrath. 'You tell me I got no right when you've damn' near poisoned 'er wi' meat pie? I can't get 'er to leave off pickin' at midday just for food, so

I've stopped tryin'. I feeds all the rest wi' bread, cheese, pickles, milk . . . but them as won't come . . .'

'My meat pie was certainly not poisoned,' Ada said sharply, cutting across the other woman's sentence without a qualm. How dare this woman criticise her good, homecooked food! 'If you think you can insult me with impunity, Mrs Lockett, just because the child was half-starved and grateful for a square meal . . .'

'Yeah. Well.' Mrs Lockett had the grace to look a little ashamed. 'Reckon I got me rag out for no real cause, Mrs 'Overton, 'cos I don't want no one thinkin' I'd let a kid go short. 'Tweren't the pie, exactly . . . an' any road, she'll be awright tomorrer. We've been here four days; I reckon, in another week . . .' she grinned suddenly, revealing her large white teeth. '. . . In another week she'll put away any victuals she's give wi'out no 'arm comin' to 'er.'

'Good. And when she goes home . . . ?'

'I'll keep 'er by me. She ain't goin' back to the ole devil I found 'er with, that's what we've decided, me mum an' me,' Bea said gruffly. 'She's a clever kid, young Foxy. Top o' the class at school they told me when I went there, on'y the ole devil scarce ever let 'er attend classes. Aye, I'll keep Foxy wi' me.'

'Good. And Mrs Lockett, if there's anything I can do to help I'd be happy to do so. She's a brave little girl.'

'Thanks, Mrs 'Overton, I'll 'member that. And now I'd best be gettin' back or they'll be wonderin' why I'm so long away.'

'Thank you for calling, Mrs Lockett,' Ada said primly, and found to her own surprise that she meant it. She was glad the two of them had cleared the air and glad, too, that Foxy would not be deserted when she returned to Birmingham in October.

Two

Foxy sat in her corner seat, watching the September countryside go slowly by, whilst Auntie Bea, in the corner opposite, crocheted a length of lace, her favourite pastime at present. Beside them, Bea's sisters and sisters-in-law chatted and her nieces, Liz and Nell, at fifteen quite experienced hop-pickers, discussed, in low tones, which of the lucky local lads would receive their favours, this year.

Foxy did not have to ask herself who she would favour, however. Ever since the day, five years ago, when John and Laurie had taken her up to the farmhouse to have soothing lotion spread on her sunburn, she had spent September picking hops in the daytime and going around with John and Laurie in the evenings.

Her life had changed radically – had it been the hop-picking which had changed it? Certainly she had gone back to Birmingham that first October almost two stone heavier and a great deal healthier – and, as Bea had promised, she had never returned to her slavery at Grandma Grant's house, either. Bea simply said that the Locketts had claimed their own and that in future she would live with them.

Foxy had offered to go round to the Grants' place and explain, but Bea said it would not be a good idea; she would do any explaining necessary. And off she went and back she came, and never a word did she say as to what had happened, save that all was agreed. Foxy was to live with Bea and her old mother in the boarding house which the two women ran between them, and would help Bea with her small dressmaking business by delivering completed orders and learning to measure up and to hem, tack, and sew on buttons.

'We'll expect you to 'elp wi' the boarders, and to give an 'and wi' me dressmaking business,' Bea had said gruffly when Foxy had tried to thank her. 'I know you ain't 'andy with a needle, but I'll teach you to sew on buttons an' that. An' you can deliver orders, stuff like that. But you won't be overworked an' you'll attend school regular an' be treated fair. Your ma was me favourite sister.'

And under the new regime Foxy blossomed. She sat the scholarship to the local Girls' Grammar School and passed; she told Bea that it did not matter, she did not have to go and would be quite happy to begin to look for work, but Bea grinned at her and said she would go whether she liked it or not; they were proud of her and wanted to see her do well. Foxy reminded Bea that the uniform was expensive and that though there was a generous grant for books and travel to and from the school it did not cover the smart navy blazer with silver cord trimming, the pleated navy skirt and the cream and navy striped blouse.

'And I'd need more'n one blouse, very like,' she added desperately. 'And boots, o' course.'

'I'll make the clo'es,' Bea said. And did. She was so clever with her sewing machine that parents who saw Foxy's beautifully fitting skirts and blouses asked where she had had them made, and this brought more work for Bea – well-paid work, too.

And school itself was a tremendous success. Foxy was clever, soon popular, even good at games. Because she was clever she realised right from the start that the best way to fit in, at first, is to be exactly like everyone else, so she worked at her accent until she talked just like the other girls – better, if anything. Because they liked games she tried very hard, though at first she thought tennis and hockey a waste of time, and soon she was playing for her year and enjoying every moment of it. She and Bea plaited the mass of curling, chestnut-coloured hair into two long tails tied with narrow navy ribbon and Foxy joined the local free library, discussed books, saved up her pennies for a seat at the cinema now and then, even began to read the headlines on other people's newspapers on the tram going home from school.

A year ago, what was more, Bea had married. Ned Baxter was an elderly machine-worker in a shoe factory and he and his wife had been good friends with Bea for years. When Lil died, Ned took to calling more often, and it was no surprise to anyone when he proposed and Bea accepted.

Foxy liked Ned, but she began to distance herself from the couple a little. School was satisfying and she had some good friends, but she was growing up, beginning the first tentative moves towards the biggest move of all – leaving home. And still, the high point of her year was September. Without fail, on the first of that month Foxy, Bea and various Lockett relatives set out for the hopyards of Herefordshire.

'It's me 'oliday,' Bea said if anyone asked. 'The only 'oliday I'm likely to get – and we make a tidy penny an' all, eh, Foxy?'

They did. Bea was, she told anyone who would listen, a great believer in a fair wage for a fair day's work. When the rate was low the hops should be easy picking, but alas, it was not always the case. Sometimes the farmers reduced the rate for other reasons – a bad run of disease earlier in the season, a poor yield, perhaps even high expenses in some other aspect of farming. Bea always marched up to the house, colour high, lips set in a grim line, and usually came back with either additional money or possibly payment in kind; a sack of free potatoes to take home when October came, or one of the big farmhouse cheeses, or even a bacon flitch.

And for Foxy, turning each year further from childhood and towards the young womanhood for which she yearned, the farm meant very much more than a holiday or extra money. It was still magic for her – beauty so unbelievable at first became expected, but that did not make it one whit the less beautiful. She loved everything about it and whilst she was there she lived life to the full in a way that she found impossible in Birmingham. Every year she and assorted gipsy boys, Welsh boys, Brummy boys, went scrumping for apples in the surrounding orchards. John and Laurie couldn't come, of course, because it was thieving no matter how you dressed it up, but Foxy did not intend to turn down a sport of which she had speedily become fond. Though she was fitter – and fatter – she was still the best climber of trees around, and could go high into the branches like a little monkey, there to throw down her booty to those earthbound mortals waiting around the foot of the tree. And then there was poaching. She, who loved all animals and hated to see the little rabbits torn by the dogs, still never missed a poaching expedition, and here John and Laurie joined them.

'We don't set traps or snares, but everyone's got a right to bag a rabbit now and then – or a trout from the stream, or a duck,' Laurie said airily. 'We really ought to try the estate some time; my dad's in France next week and I don't suppose he'd mind losing rabbits any more than Uncle does.'

They didn't try the estate though, because as John said, what Sir George thought might not be what his keepers thought and anyway, the countryside round the Hoverton farm was overrun with rabbits, the streams swarmed with small, sweet brown trout.

'I'm glad when someone nabs the rabbits,' Bill Hoverton told the three children as they ate bacon, eggs and fried bread. Foxy had been asked in for breakfast, and was absorbing every word the farmer said along with the food since she felt herself, when she was with John and Laurie, to be a part of the family. 'Because rabbits do a deal o' damage to the crops. But not every farmer feels that way and rabbits are supposed to be the farmhands' little extra. Still, there's plenty for all, worse luck. And I daresay I shan't miss the odd trout.'

Bill Hoverton had taught John and Laurie fly fishing when they were seven and was proud, now, of their prowess. Foxy saw her friends were looking rather glum because the gipsies tickled for trout with great success, but they could scarcely complain – the gipsies were fishing for food, not sport, and Foxy knew that Ada and Bill had long ago impressed on the boys that they were privileged and should help those less fortunate whenever the opportunity arose. Which meant, in this instance, that the gipsies must not be begrudged their trout.

And Foxy enjoyed the picking as much as the pastimes because she could dream as she picked; fingers black and sticky snatched the hops from the bines in one smooth, oft-repeated movement, her crib rapidly filled, she could go off in her mind anywhere she liked, could relive last night's poaching expedition, or imagine tomorrow night's scrumping, high in the windy boughs of a big old apple tree, scratched, breathless but triumphant as she tossed the big, sweet-smelling fruit down to the small figures below her.

'You're gettin' a big girl now; a grown woman, near enough,' Bea had said last night, as they packed the hop box with all the cooking utensils, bedding and odds and ends they would need over the coming month. Ned said he was too old to live in the barracks and stayed home to mind the house and keep the boarders happy. 'You've just turned seventeen; when I was your age I'd been workin' for Heffners for two year, just about. Any time now you'll say you're too old for the hoppin'.'

'I shan't,' Foxy assured her. 'But I do feel guilty at going back to school in October. I ought to get a job, you know I ought.'

Bea had shaken her head. 'No, that's short-sighted thinkin', that is. If you stay at school, get your 'igher school certificate, mebbe even go on to one of them college places, you'll earn a deal more'n if you just settle for a factory or a shop . . . you'll earn more'n they do in offices. You get educated, gal!'

Foxy knew it was good advice, knew she would almost certainly take it, too. She had discussed with her teachers what she should do and with one voice they advised her to stay on, to try for a university place.

She had gone home and told Bea, said that, if Bea thought it right, she would like to try.

'You can get a free place, if you're clever enough and don't have rich parents,' she said earnestly. 'Oh Bea, I'd like to try! Imagine me, at Oxford or Cambridge!'

But higher school cert came first. It looked as though she would be spending every penny she earned on books for the next couple of years, which made – she had hugged herself – hopping an essential as well as a pleasure. She had no other means of making so much money in so short a time.

And now, sitting in the train and dreaming through the window, she wondered about John and Laurie. Their ways were to part for the first time since they were born, since John did not want to go to university and Laurie's father was insisting that Laurie should go. For Foxy, university was still two years and a tough examination away but for John and Laurie it was here and now. Sir George had insisted that both boys should have six months on the continent, perfecting their French, and though John had come home at the end of that time Laurie had gone on to Spain for a few months and had come home speaking the language as well as he spoke French. Their decisions on university had been made the previous year – now she would see whether any minds had been changed.

'What good's a degree in modern languages, or politics, or history, to a farmer?' John had said last year, when the three of them had been discussing their futures. 'It's all very well for you, Lo; your father went to Cambridge and his father before him and besides, you're heir to a great estate, you'll have other people to do your farming for you. But I need practical experience more than I need even more book-learning.'

Foxy had never seen the Clifton estate, but she knew about it. Mrs Hoverton sometimes told the children stories about her time as a parlourmaid before her marriage. She described the huge house, the multitude of servants, the wonders of the orangery, the peaches and nectarines which grew fanned out on the walls in the kitchen garden. So Foxy knew it was a wonderful place, and gazed enviously at Laurie when he talked about spending a few days there. He was seldom there for longer, but as she understood it, a great house was not much fun for one boy, on his own.

'I'm not really interested in the land,' Laurie had said offhandedly, when John had suggested, the previous September, that Laurie might also do well to get practical experience of running the estate. 'As you say, the farms are all run for us, and Father has a bailiff and gardeners and things, I believe. But I don't know any more about it than you do; Father talks about stocks and shares, the value of antique furniture, pictures, old silver . . . it's all double-Dutch to me. And what's more he doesn't seem interested in the land himself. The truth is, Johnny-boy, that farming's in your blood and it isn't in mine – if I took over Cumber Farm, which is the nearest to the house, it'ud go bust in a week. So I'll please the old boy and spend the statutory three years up at Cambridge having a good time and meeting people, and then we'll see. I'd be bored to tears just managing an estate which someone else could do much better, so I'll either join the diplomatic corps or the army or marry an heiress, I daresay. Then I won't have to manage the estate, will I?'

That had ended the discussion in laughter but Foxy had seen real unhappiness in Laurie's eyes and had, all in a moment, understood the importance of choice. Laurie will be Sir Laurie one day and he's rich as rich, but he has no more choice over what happens to him than I did at Grandma Grant's, she thought. How odd, I never thought that the rich and titled could ever be pitied, but I do think John and I are luckier than he. John desperately wants to farm, and I can pick and choose within certain limitations, but Laurie must do what is best for the Clifton estate.

And now, rattling nearer the beloved country with every turn of the wheels, the train hurried on through the summer counties and the aunt nearest Foxy reached into her basket, producing a bag of homemade toffee.

'Not long now,' she observed. 'Want some stick-jaw, Foxy gal?'

'Thanks,' Foxy said, accepting a chunk of the sweet, sticky stuff. 'I wonder who'll be driving the cart? Bet it's either John or Laurie.'

'They'll both come,' Bea said. 'Wonder what they'll set the rate at, this year?'

'Wonder what Foxy will look like, this year?' John, driving the pony cart, addressed his friend lightly. 'She's seventeen . . . can you imagine that little kid is actually seventeen? Quite grown up!'

'She was looking better last year,' Laurie said. 'Rounder . . . she was starting to get tits.'

'Vulgar bugger,' John said cheerfully. 'Bosoms; she was starting to get bosoms. I like Foxy, though I don't know why. She's certainly no beauty, and her figure has been compared unfavourably to that of a hop-pole. So when you think of Sarah, and Nina, and Lucy . . .'

'Farmers' daughters, all creamy skin and big bosoms and lovely peachy bottoms,' Laurie agreed with a half-groan, half-laugh. 'Huntin', shootin' and fishin' girls. Girls who look good on a raw-boned chestnut gelding, girls with voices you can hear a mile away, girls with faces like the hunters they mount. Whereas Foxy has rather a nice little face. Figures come as girls get older, they tell me.'

'She'll be here in a minute and we'll see for ourselves whether her figure's arrived,' John reminded him. 'And we'll see the others, too . . . Flossie, Rebecca, Lilly . . .'

'Ah, Floss,' Laurie said dreamily. Flossie was a Welsh girl with coal-black curls, sparkling dark eyes and a weakness for anything in trousers. Laurie had danced with her at the village hop last September and had told John, in strict confidence, that she had grabbed him through his trousers and tweaked his old man whilst he was kissing her. Whether this was supposed to be encouraging he could not say but he assured John it had had the opposite effect. 'A total squelch, like a bucket of cold water,' he told his friend. 'Everyone says she's a goer, but if so, that was a funny way to show it.'

'Ah Floss indeed,' John said now. 'What about Lilly, then? I got my hand up Lilly's skirt in the flicks.'

'And got your thigh pinched,' Laurie said. He had seen the bruise.

'Considering we're the most eligible bachelors for miles around, Lo, we're having a bit of difficulty at losing our virtue, wouldn't you say? Dad says leave the farmers' daughters alone or it's shotguns to the church door, Mum says leave the hop-pickers alone or she'll personally castrate us ... and the gipsies won't let us near their girls. What are we supposed to do? Stay virgins for the rest of our lives?'

'We could pretend we were saving ourselves for marriage,' Laurie said, grinning hugely at the thought. 'Actually, I'll probably break my duck at Cambridge. They say clever girls are wild to experience everything, including the love of a Good Man. But you, you poor soul, you're doomed you are. No crumpet for you until you've taken it up the aisle.'

'I haven't really tried yet, apart from Lilly; and that was more what you could call a spur-of-the-moment thing. Unfortunately it wasn't *her* spur of the moment, or perhaps the pinch was like Flossie's grab; meant to encourage but having the opposite effect. I apologised, you know, said I hadn't realised where my hand was. She laughed.'

'We ought to stick to much younger girls,' Laurie said after some thought. 'The truth of the matter is, John, that Flossie and her crowd are too bloody knowing. They expect a feller to get on with it, and we ... well, we're still trying to find out what "it" is!'

'Yeah, you've got a point. Fellers say you start with kissing and go on from there, but where? I mean cuddling is so *close*, you can't get your hands anywhere interesting because she's pressing up against you. Oh hell, we ought to ask Foxy; she's a girl and we know her better than most.'

'I don't think it's the done thing to ask one female how to get other females to come across,' Laurie observed. 'Besides, Foxy's as inexperienced as we are, I'd swear to it. Although she's getting tits, she's still a skinny little wench; not even the randiest fellow has made a pass at Foxy. And if someone did she wouldn't know what to do about it.'

'Hmm. Well, everyone's got to start some time, so why not start with Foxy, who we know and like? She won't mind, I bet, if we explain.'

'Oh John, honestly! What do we say? Can I put my hand up your skirt, because the other girls won't let me? That's ten-year-old stuff!'

John drew the horse and cart to a halt outside the station, then leaned over and thumped his friend's shoulder.

'Shut up, you dirty-minded blighter! We say we want to know just what girls expect us to ... we explain that we've still not ... no, perhaps that wouldn't do. But Foxy must have the sort of feelings we have, I mean all girls must, mustn't they? Blokes do, all the time ... yet the fellows at school manage to get their end away with all sorts of girls during the hols, no problem.'

'John, you are a simpleton! Have you told everyone in our class that you're a virgin still?'

'Well, no, but ...'

'Have you given them to understand that the lovely Lilly was eager for your attentions and that you continued them up to the point when she was screaming for more?'

John laughed. 'I get your drift; no one tells the truth, eh? They all lie like crazy to hide the fact that they're as innocent as us? Is that it?'

'More or less,' Laurie acknowledged. 'Except that innocent isn't the word I'd have chosen – ignorant, perhaps. Hey up, is that the train?'

It was. The boys got down off the cart and looked across to where the travellers were already descending from their carriages and hurrying across to the guard's van to reclaim their hop boxes and other belongings.

'I say, was that Foxy? I saw a mass of red hair, anyway. If it was her, she's better than she was. Come on, let's go and give her a hand with her luggage.'

'Remember what Mum said about killing us if we meddled with the pickers,' Laurie reminded his friend. 'Foxy's a picker, or she will be if it suits Mum to call her one. Come on, bustle about, tie Dobbin up and we can go and give Foxy a smacking kiss, all in the cause of us becoming more at ease with the fair sex, of course.'

John tied Dobbin up and the two of them strolled through the small, dusty booking office and out onto the platform. It thronged with hop-pickers, their boxes, their baggage, their kids. John glanced along the platform, first in one direction, then the other. He pulled a face.

'Foxy's not here, she must have missed the train, we'll have to . . .'

Laurie gripped his arm. 'No, she's just getting down; see?'

Foxy jumped down from the train and came towards them, grinning from ear to ear. She wore a neat blue shirt-blouse tucked into a navy skirt and her hair was loose, restrained only by a navy-blue Alice band. Her clothing was simple enough, but nothing could hide the fact that she was finally beginning to develop a figure.

Laurie nudged John. 'I told you so; she's getting 'em,' he breathed into his brother's ears. See? Well, *something's* pushing against that blouse, anyway; I suppose it's them.'

'Shut up or she'll guess we've been talking about her,' John mumbled. 'She really is growing up, though. But she's still thin. I like a girl to be . . . oh, hello, Foxy, we've driven the cart down to meet you. Can we help with your luggage?'

'Last year you were gangly boys and now you're young men,' Foxy said when they had settled themselves in the cart. She was sitting on the driver's seat between John and Laurie, very squashed, whilst Bea and the others were crammed into the cart behind them. The luggage had gone in the haywain with one of the farmhands. 'It's not fair, I'm always two years behind you no matter how I try! Oh, I know I look a bit older with my hair like this but I'll plait it when we arrive, it'll only get in the way, else, but

I don't seem to be growing up anywhere near fast enough. Now you two . . . well, your shoulders have got awfully broad, and I bet you shave now, Laurie . . . that really does make you seem older.'

'We're all older,' Laurie said. 'Besides, it isn't your hair – well, not entirely – there's your – your figure.'

Foxy felt her cheeks grow warm. At first she had felt ashamed of her figure, had announced that she was getting fat and would have to eat less, only Bea and her mother, Trixie, had laughed at her.

"'Tain't fat, you foolish li'l wench, 'tes your woman's body come to you,' Trixie had said, as though a body had marched through the door, kicked out Foxy's skinny frame, and taken its place. She cackled. 'An' very nice it is, too. You'm a purty thing, Foxy Lockett.'

'I'm *not*,' Foxy had replied, scandalised. She had no time for pretty things: prettiness, in her view, was just a waste of time. Unlike cleverness and efficiency, it got you nowhere. What was more, since her face was still thin, her eyes still green and her hated lashes still white, she knew she was still plain little Foxy Lockett. 'All I am is a bit rounder, and it'll slow me down and get in my way. Is the – er – fatness all part of the belly-ache and my monthlies, then? I might have known it wouldn't just end there.'

Trixie had cackled again. 'There's other girls waitin' for their monthlies to start, wantin' nice figures to int'rest the fellers, but you moans an' says you'd rather be a skinny, plain little thing. You doesn't know when you're well off, Foxy.'

And Foxy had not known, until she got off the train and walked down the platform and spotted John and Laurie, waved, began to run . . . and saw their faces change at the sight of her. Admiration was a new thing to her and she realised now, sitting between them on the driver's seat, that she liked it. No one had even pretended to admire the skinny, aggressive Foxy, or not her looks, anyhow. But here were two boys who knew her, were her friends, and they were treating her rather nicely – they smiled, they glanced quickly at her blouse and then away again . . . she decided, all of a sudden, that it might not be so bad after all, this growing up. She could never make up her mind which she liked best, John or Laurie, but it was good to see them both glancing at her as if – oh, as if they really liked what they saw. But even though it was rather nice, she realised that she did not want their friendship to alter, she wanted things to go on as they had always done. So she hastened to behave in her usual forthright manner. With sharp elbows, she dug both boys simultaneously in the ribs causing them to give a simultaneous squawk.

'Well? What's been happening this year? Are you going to university with Laurie, John, despite saying you wouldn't? What's the rate been set at per bushel? Are the hops big? Will the picking be easy? Are we still in the barracks?'

'Your elbows haven't changed, they're still sharp as knives,' John said, rubbing his side. 'No, I'm not wasting my time with more education, I told you last year. As for the rate and the picking, we don't know ourselves yet, but you'll be in the barracks as usual, of course . . . oh, and Mum says would you like to come in later for a spot of supper and a chat.'

'Thanks, I'd love to,' Foxy said at once. 'Aren't you going to ask if I'm on course for my higher? Well, I'll save you the trouble. I'm doing nicely, or so the teachers say.'

'Sorry; we're too stunned by your beauty to say much,' Laurie said with a grin. ' "That's Foxy, looking like a human being," I said to John, but of course he's difficult to convince.'

'Yes, I said, "that's not our Foxy, she's got frizzy ginger plaits and a figure like a hop-pole," ' John assured her. 'Who are you really, young lady?'

Foxy giggled. 'Don't be a fool, John. *Are* you going to Cambridge with Lo?'

'No, I'm definitely not. But it looks as though you'll be there in another year. Clever old Foxy – shall I give you a big, sloppy kiss? I mean, we're old friends, wouldn't you say? And I do need the practice.'

'You'd bloody better not try,' Foxy growled, seriously alarmed. No one had yet tried to kiss her and she didn't want anyone doing so, either. From what Auntie Bea had said once you started kissing it got to be a habit and Auntie Bea had told her it was either education or kissing, you couldn't have both. Well, she'd said something on those lines, anyway, and to Foxy, there was no contest. She wanted to get educated, to get a good job and to get rich. In that order, from necessity, but from choice it would have been money first, so that she could live in the hop country all her days and never go back to the city.

'Perhaps, in the circumstances, a handshake would be more welcome,' Laurie interrupted silkily. 'Or would you bite the hand that fed you as well, Foxy?'

'Your mum feeds me, not you,' Foxy pointed out. 'I'm glad you're definitely going to Cambridge, though, Laurie. So what'll you do, John, when October comes?'

'Farm. Plough, reap, sow, dip sheep, harvest apples . . . all the things my father does now,' John said with deep content. 'There's so much to do here, so many things I've wanted to see tackled. I'll leave Laurie to chase after academic rewards and pretty girls in caps and gowns.'

'He won't get many academic rewards if he's chasing after girls,' Foxy said shrewdly. 'But you're awfully clever, aren't you, Laurie? Though you try very hard not to sound it.'

'I'm not clever, but I get by, and I do enjoy learning languages,' Laurie admitted. 'Anyway my family have always gone to Cambridge so I can't let Father down. I'm looking forward to it, in fact. Ah, we're coming up to Boulger's place; if you want to take a look at his hops we'll slow Dobbin down and you can stand up and peek over the hedge.'

'I'll stop for a moment by the gate and everyone can look,' John said, more practically. He turned in his seat. 'Now coming up to Boulger's, Mrs Lockett; take a look,' he advised Auntie Bea. 'Our hops are big this year, we've had a good summer, so his will probably be similar.'

They reached the gate and he slowed the horse. Foxy stared down the tunnel-like rows with pleasure and pleasant nostalgia. How she loved it, all of it! The work, the smell of the hops on her hands, even the prickly leaves and the harshness of the hops themselves. Big or small, easy or hard, hop-picking was what she liked doing best in the world. Teachers at school pointed out that she had not done an awful lot, that there were things which she would enjoy far more than picking hops once she had sampled them, but this she found difficult to believe. Hopping, and the countryside, quite simply made her life worthwhile.

'It should be easy picking,' Auntie Bea remarked, having had a good look at the lofty, lush foliage and the heavily hanging hops. 'That means the rate will be lower, seemingly. Can't see whether the growth's even all over, but likely 'tes.' She heaved a sigh and settled back in her seat. 'How's your ma, boys?' she enquired. 'Been keepin' well?'

The barracks welcomed them, or so it seemed to Foxy as she lugged her belongings into their own particular partitioned-off room. She had a bag of her own this year, because Bea had decided that at her age she should own a decent dress, a skirt and some blouses which were not part of her school uniform.

'You're a tidy shape now, and won't change much, I reckon,' she had said. 'So I'll mek the stuff to last.'

She had, too, and Foxy was proud of her beautiful clothes and did not intend to ruin them by wearing them to pick hops. But there were the weekly dances in the village hall; it would be fun to wear a pretty dress for that. And then she was asked up to the farm on a fairly regular basis, and the boys took her with them to the cinema in Ledbury from time to time, so her dress would not be wasted.

'Where's the straw pallets?' Bea demanded, staggering through the doorway with one end of the hop box whilst her favourite sister Nonny and Nonny's daughter, Liz, giggling, shared the weight of the other end between them. They always messed together since each room could sleep four pickers. Nonny and Bea were fond of one another and Foxy quite liked Liz, who was willing, though none too bright. So now, with the hop box in position and Bea rolling up her sleeves to get on, Nonny and Liz exchanged a quick glance and made themselves scarce – tactfully, since Bea liked to arrange the room herself and did not appreciate Nonny fluttering around and trying to interfere.

Foxy found the pallets piled, as usual, in one corner of the room. She had brought a blanket and a thin pillow, too, since if she slept on the straw she got a rash on her cheeks and neck and now she put out the pallets, got the pillow out of the hop box and laid it tenderly on top of her bedding. Tomorrow she would put on her hop clothes – a brown cotton frock, much-darned, much-stained – and would keep her nice travelling skirt and blouse and her other things rolled up in the blue striped holdall until such time as she needed them again.

'If you're up to the farm for supper I'll finish up the sandwiches for mine,' Bea decided aloud, bustling around making the place seem homely. 'But they won't stretch to Nonny and Liz, so I'll boil up some spuds, fry a piece o' bacon . . . that'll do us.'

Bea had packed four folding stools and a scarlet checked tablecloth in her box and now she produced these items, stood the stools up and spread the cloth over the wooden table. She hung a framed print on one of the lime-washed walls – a child with its arms round a huge St Bernard dog – and placed a glass flower vase carefully in the exact centre of the table. Tomorrow it would be Foxy's job to pick wild flowers for that vase and to see that fresh ones were brought in whenever the ones in the vase faded.

Foxy had always brought with her a limp and faded cushion and now she watched with satisfaction as it was produced from the depths of the box. On many a long evening, while the adults drank and sang round the fire, perched on chairs, boxes, or sprawled on the ground, she had cuddled up on that cushion, eventually falling so sound asleep that she had not even roused when Bea had carried her – and her cushion – back into their barrack and slid her onto her straw pallet.

But now . . . I wonder if I ought to have brought that cushion, she wondered uncertainly. I'm seventeen now, too old for that sort of nonsense. But the fact that it was there did not mean she had to sit on it, so she helped her aunt to get out the cooking pots, the crockery and cutlery, and the line which they would string up under the jutting corrugated-iron roof – and it jutted as much as four feet – so that their washing stood a chance of drying even in the rain. Each barrack was almost like two rooms, or perhaps one room with a deep verandah outside it was a better description. If it was fine or very hot folk would live and eat out on the 'verandah', but in wet weather or when it was chilly the inner room was best.

There was no door on the barrack but each year Auntie Bea brought a red baize curtain which she hung on a heavy, rattling old pole across the top of the door. The curtain was pulled at night and when it rained heavily or was unbearably cold, but since the barracks did not have windows it was not practical to sit in the room during the day, and indeed, farmers who were paying workers to work would not have been best pleased had they found them doing any such thing.

Bea straightened up from putting the groceries she had brought in a box beneath the side bench. She was red in the face and puffing slightly but she smiled brightly across at her niece.

'Well, ain't that nice, gel? Real 'omely the place looks when us've got a few of our own things about, eh? I'll put me cats out on the ledge when I've done me cooking.'

Auntie Bea had a collection of china cats of which she was extremely fond. She particularly liked marmalade cats and had at least a dozen china examples, but when, three years ago, Foxy had pleaded that the marmalade cat on the farm had had kittens, one of which could be hers, Bea had reacted with great firmness.

'What, one of they dirty, squalling ginger beasts? No indeed,' she had said roundly. 'We don't want no more mouths to feed nor messes to clear up. *China* cats is one thing; *real* cats is another.'

In vain Foxy had protested that cats were clean: only china ones, Bea said grimly, and shelved for ever Foxy's hopes of a pet.

But on the farm you did not need a pet because the animals were all around you. Farmyard cats, thin and quicksilver-fast as they hunted mice, begged for milk, jumped into your lap for a cuddle. Dogs, the two black and white working collies, who grinned and wagged but did not bother with the pickers, and daft Sasha, who lolled about everywhere, bounded into barracks and wailed when she was ejected, stole anything left on a low shelf and loved to sit by the brazier and lick the hand which stroked her smooth and silky side. Lambs, reared on a bottle, running towards you with a hopeful baa-aa whenever you appeared. Horses hoping for sugar lumps, pigs rooting for acorns, grinning at you with their merry little eyes, accepting anything you gave them with a liquid snottling snort.

'Stop dreamin', Foxy,' Bea said now. 'If you ain't off up to Mrs 'Overton yet, you can go an' get me some water.'

There was a pump in the farmyard but Mr Hoverton always provided a big barrel of fresh water each day between three or four families, so Foxy took a bucket and went out of their room and along the row of barracks to where the barrel stood. There was a round tin bowl beneath the small tap so that the earth didn't get wet and puddled when someone made a mess of filling their bucket. Foxy moved it to one side and stood her bucket beneath the tap. She filled it nearly to the brim, turned off the tap and lifted the bucket out of the way, then replaced the bowl without spilling a drop. Then she carted her bucket back into their room where Auntie Bea was peeling potatoes and Auntie Nonny and her daughter Liz, returning from their visit, were telling Bea how nice everything looked.

'Good; wash the spuds I've peeled, Liz. And Nonny, find me up a pan what'll 'old enough spuds for three,' Bea said briskly. 'You going off now, Foxy? Don't be late back, it's been a long day.'

'I won't be late,' Foxy promised blithely. She hesitated, wondering whether to just brush her hair, take a look at her reflection in the piece of mirror which Bea propped between the marmalade cats on the shelf . . . but then she decided against it. Bea was a shrewd old bird and Nonny knew a thing or three. They would soon jump to conclusions – albeit the wrong ones, of course – if they saw her apparently prinking and preening before the glass when she was going up to the farmhouse for supper.

So she pushed her hair back over her shoulders and set off, feeling the old, familiar excitement as she crossed the pickers' yard and rounded the corner into the farmyard proper.

It was just the same; or was it? The two sheepdogs ran to meet her, hackles up, ears pricked, then recognised her and relaxed with flattened ears and furiously wagging tails. They fussed round her, leaving a generous number of black and white hairs on her skirt, then began to shepherd her across the yard and over to the back door. They were not allowed in, but lived, she thought, in hope of a quick visit to the kitchen and the delights that they were sure waited within. She always tried to save a titbit for them; poor dogs, just because they were good and trustworthy they were kept in the yard whereas naughty, disobedient Sasha lived with the family – and off the fat of the land, too.

She knocked briefly on the kitchen door and opened it. Rather to her surprise the whole family was assembled, Mr and Mrs Hoverton, John and Laurie. And someone else, someone she did not at once recognise. A tall, red-faced man with thinning grey hair and a prow of a nose. He reminded her of someone but she could not think who.

She had interrupted something, she realised it immediately. John was flushed and Laurie was pale, and Mr Hoverton, a man of few words, had actually taken the pipe out of his mouth and was speaking as she stopped short in the doorway.

'Of course, Sir George, if that's the way it has to be,' he was saying. 'But the lad'll be in Cambridge in a month or so; wouldn't that be time enough? We need every pair of hands we can get, come hop-pickin'.'

'I'm damned sorry, Hoverton, but I'm afraid it won't do,' the red-faced man said. Foxy now realised that this must be Sir George Clifton, Laurie's father. 'It ain't like me to spoil sport, as ye know, but I need my son to speak to the trustees for me. There's things that need to be done . . .'

Sir George made a quick, impatient gesture with one huge hand and Foxy noticed that the hacking jacket he wore had leather elbow patches and leather round where the cuffs had been. Boys at the grammar school only put leather patches on their blazers when they couldn't afford new ones, but Laurie's father was a sir; surely he could not be hard up? And then she remembered that Mr Hoverton sometimes wore a jacket with leather elbow patches and everyone knew farmers were rich as Midas, golden touch and all, so that was all right.

'What can I do in a month, though, Father? I've got my place at Cambridge, I've worked hard this summer . . . it's only a month, damn it!'

That was Laurie, sounding defensive, almost querulous. Foxy realised that he had shed his warm Herefordshire accent for a moment and appeared to be imitating his father's clipped vowels.

'And we won't be together, except for the vacs, whilst he's in Cambridge, sir,' John said, speaking for the first time. 'It will seem strange . . .'

His voice tailed away. Plainly, he had noticed the impatience in Sir George's face, the way his fingers constantly drummed against his tweed-clad thigh. Laurie's father, Foxy could see, was not used to having his pronouncements questioned.

'It is only a month, John, as you say,' Sir George said abruptly. 'A month is no time at all, so why quibble? Why not just accept that I need Laurie and leave it at that? As for you, Laurence, I think the worse of you for shirking your duty – and your duty is by my side,' he added in an almost threatening tone.

'Very well, then, Sir George, if it must be, it must be.' That was Mrs Hoverton, her very placidity comforting because it made Sir George's request seem natural, not threatening. 'I take it we'll be havin' Laurie back for the Christmas vacation?'

'Well . . . no, Mrs Hoverton.' Now Sir George sounded definitely apologetic, and also rather guilty. He rubbed the side of his nose with a finger like a pork sausage and cleared his throat uneasily. 'It's time the boy faced up to his responsibilities, began to learn how the estate's run, what will be required of him when . . . when I'm no longer here to do the job myself. Of course he'll pop in from time to time, there's no doubt of that I'm sure, but . . . he'll be living at Clifton Place in future.'

Foxy looked across at Laurie. He caught her eye and pulled a face, then winked, a quick, almost furtive flutter of one eyelid. Then he turned and addressed his parent.

'All right, Father, I think we get the picture. No doubt you'll explain to me in due course what's brought about this sudden change of heart. But I can't pack and come right away, I've far too much stuff here. I'll get my things into boxes and come at the end of the week. Can you bear to wait until then?'

'Tomorrow. I'll come back for you tomorrow,' his father said grimly. 'As for explaining . . . damn it, boy, you'll reach your majority in less than two years and you have no more idea of how to run an estate than a babe in arms! You've been coddled here . . .'

Mr Hoverton had put his pipe back in his mouth. Now, with slow deliberation, he removed it. 'What were that, Sir George? Did I hear you say we'd *coddled* your son? As I recall . . .'

Sir George broke in, his face now flushing so darkly that it could have been described as purple. 'No point in coming to fisticuffs, Hoverton. I've a right to say where my son shall live until he's twenty-one, and I say he's coming back to Clifton Place. Is that clear?'

No one spoke. Mr Hoverton put his pipe back in his mouth and stared ruminatively across at Sir George. Mrs Hoverton tightened her lips but went on staring down at the rag rug on which she stood. The boys, both now pink and angry-looking, glanced at each other, then away.

Foxy, hovering, suddenly decided to take a hand. Otherwise, she thought wildly, we'll still be standing like this tomorrow morning, and we've hops to pick! She stepped forward, into the kitchen, into the tensions and the hurt and the bewilderment which were emanating from the Hovertons and Laurie. Only Sir George seemed to feel none of it; all that emanated from him, Foxy thought scornfully, was a stupid, pig-headed determination to have his way.

'I've come for supper, Mrs Hoverton – thanks for inviting me. Can I do anything to help you get the meal? I see you've not laid the table yet, nor . . .'

'Ah, Foxy, love, I didn't see you there.' Mrs Hoverton beamed across at her, and then, as though released from a spell, turned to Sir George. She said with perfect politeness: 'And now, Sir George, since I can see you've finished your little talk, I really must begin to prepare supper. I won't ask you to stay for I can see you're far too busy; good evening, sir.'

'Twas good of you to call,' Mr Hoverton added, when Sir George said nothing. 'We shall see you in the mornin', no doubt.'

'No doubt,' Sir George mumbled. He waited until Foxy was clear of the doorway, then strode through it. In the yard, he turned. 'Laurie, I'll be here at ten; be sure you're ready.'

Five people watched in silence as the tall, thick-set man strode across the yard and out of the farm gate. When he had gone the collies, who had followed a couple of yards behind, stiff with suspicion, came running back and settled themselves by the door, tongues lolling, eyes beaming. Sasha emerged from behind Mrs Hoverton's rocking chair – she hated arguments of any description – and came over to sniff at Foxy and lick her hand.

'Well, that's that,' Laurie said, breaking the silence. 'Mum, Uncle, I'm awfully sorry . . . I'm sure he didn't mean . . .'

'Don't worrit yourself, Lo,' Mrs Hoverton said. She began to bustle about the kitchen, checking the oven, peering into a pan bubbling on the stove. 'Oh dear, Foxy, I'm afraid it won't be much of a supper tonight, since the spuds are boiled to a mush and the beef's dried up. But there's nothing wrong wi' the apple pie and the cream's fresh from the dairy this morning. Who's going to lay the table for me, eh?'

'I will,' both boys chorused, making Foxy laugh; they were not keen on such mundane chores and normally they would have unhesitatingly given the task to her; it was clear evidence of how much the argument had upset them both that they were prepared to lay the table for supper.

'It's all right, boys, I don't mind setting the table,' Foxy said, therefore. 'I'm so sorry I barged in when you were – were busy, but I did knock.'

'So you did, dear,' Mrs Hoverton said placidly. 'And a good thing, too. Well, Lo, I daresay you'll visit us now and then until you go to university, eh, lad? Only we'll want to know how you go on, and 'tesn't that far away.'

Laurie, getting knives and forks out of the dresser drawer, began to say that of course he would visit them, but Mr Hoverton shook his head.

'Nay, lad, do as thy father wants,' he said. 'We've served our purpose, that's clear. 'Sides, though I took offence when 'e said we'd coddled you, for we've done no sich thing, mebbe we've done things what don't accord with the Clifton family way. If Sir George thinks you're best away from us for a while no doubt he has his reasons. I wouldn't want to encourage a man's own son to go against him. Stay away a whiles, lad.'

'We'll see,' Laurie muttered. 'Damn it, Uncle, I'm *nineteen*, I'm not a child! No one should dictate to me without explanation.'

'You'll have your explanation; it's just that your father didn't see fit to explain to us as well,' Mrs Hoverton put in. 'And nor he should, as Mr Hoverton said. Now let's stop talking and get on with this supper. And then, Lo, you'd best go upstairs and throw your good clothes into a bag. We'll send the rest on by carrier, or perhaps John here could bring them over to Clifton Place? What d'you think, Bill?'

'Best wait and see,' Mr Hoverton said. 'Is that beef ready to carve, Ada my love? Because if so, let's have it out of that oven and on the table, pronto!'

*

Foxy walked back to the barracks after her meal in a very thoughtful frame of mind. She had always assumed Sir George to be a loving father, as interested in Laurie as Mr Hoverton was, but the scene she had watched earlier had made her doubt it. Sir George had deliberately treated the Hovertons badly, riding roughshod over their feelings. She'd not realised that there was any question of Laurie going back to the Place to live and thought that this must have been the first time Sir George had mentioned the matter, either to the Hovertons or his son. And he had done so not in the manner of someone who was conscious of the obligation the past nineteen years had put him under, but as one asserting a God-given right and one determined to force the issue, what was more.

Aren't the rich odd? Foxy said to herself as she walked. It was almost as though Sir George wanted to make enemies of the Hovertons, wanted to take Laurie away so that it would be difficult for his son to take up his old relationship with the family at Bees-wing Farm. She could not imagine why Sir George would do such a thing but then she knew very little about any men, particularly the rich and influential.

She reached the barracks and saw that the open fire over which meals had been cooked, beside which beer had been drunk, was no more than ash. It was late, then. She slipped through the curtained doorway and fumbled her way to her bed; it would not do to wake the others, they would start work tomorrow as soon as it was light, everyone needed their sleep during September.

Foxy undressed in the dark and climbed onto her pallet, then plumped up her pillow and lay down. Things were going to be very different, with Laurie up at the Place; she would miss him badly, she knew. But growing up is one change after another, she told herself, pulling the blanket up round her ears. All Sir George had done was start the changes going a little earlier than they would otherwise have done. He's spoiled the relationship between himself and the Hovertons too, of course, her thoughts continued, but that wouldn't affect Laurie, would it? Surely it would not?

But Laurie was sensitive, took things hard. She had always known it. He would hate what his father had said to his foster-parents, and would brood on it. Sir George was an old fool, Foxy concluded at last; he would live to regret how he had treated them, she was sure of it.

And then, because she was worn out, she put the whole matter out of her head and speedily fell asleep.

Laurie couldn't sleep. He had eaten his meal – the beef had been dried up as predicted – and drunk his cider and afterwards he and John had flirted experimentally with Foxy and walked her home to the barracks, but now, tucked up in bed with John already snoring in the bed next to him, he could only wonder miserably why his father had behaved the way he had done.

Fancy coming the heavy father like that over a measly month! It simply did not make sense, because God knew his father had been happy enough to send him back to Bees-wing after all of his brief stays at the Place. I don't believe he likes me at all, Laurie told himself in the early hours, when sleep would not come. So what does he want with me? And why now? Why, even when he had been at the Place, his father had always kept him in the house and grounds, he had never taken him to see friends, or tenants even.

'As though I was something to be ashamed of,' he had once said lightly to John. 'As though he didn't want anyone to know he had a son.'

The result was, of course, that Laurie knew about the bailiff, the gardeners and the tenants from Mrs Hoverton's stories, but had scarcely met any of them save for the redoubtable Allsop and the constantly changing indoor servants. Oh, he saw an old man digging in the borders, another leading the donkey which was pulling the mowing machine over the huge lawns, young men in the fields who tugged at their caps when they saw Sir George, sometimes a figure at the front door, but since he was never introduced to any of them, he still had no idea who such people were.

But at least he knew Allsop; the butler had made sure of that. On the very first occasion that Sir George had brought Laurie to the house, when he had been no more than five, Allsop had stalked into the breakfast parlour one morning, when Sir George and his son were eating eggs and bacon, and introduced himself.

'I am Allsop, your father's butler,' he said, holding out a thin, dry hand. 'How d'you do, Master Laurence?'

'I'm very well; and how are you, Mr Allsop?' Laurie had piped. He had been very impressed by Allsop's height and his air of competence. And ever since that day, whenever Laurie visited Clifton Place Allsop had gone out of his way to make him feel welcome. Even Sir George had not tried to stop Allsop talking to Laurie, taking him about; clearly he dared not. The butler, obviously, was a man to be reckoned with.

And now that Laurie came to think of it, it was four whole years since he had actually stayed overnight at the Place. He and John had twice accompanied Sir George to a villa in the South of France where they had stayed for two or three weeks, and the three of them had gone once to the races, twice on a shooting trip, twice to a ski resort, but he had not stayed at the Place once in that time.

The thought was so strange that he sat upright in bed, staring at the hump in the other bed which was John. Had his father really been ashamed of having a son? Or had he just been ashamed of Laurie? But the old man had seemed pleased enough, Laurie reflected now, when he came to school and found Laurie in the cricket team, or swimming for his house, or winning a tennis match. Of course he was nowhere near as good an athlete as John – but he knew himself to be academically very much cleverer. Sir George said he was proud of Laurie's brains, too, but Laurie had always thought that was eye-wash. The old man wasn't too bright himself and resented a brainy offspring.

'There's somethin' damned un-English about brains,' he had once mumbled upon being given Laurie's latest glowing school report to read. 'I'd sooner you played rugger for your house – be more natural, in a Clifton.'

'But I do, Father,' Laurie had said. He knew himself to be fireproof because the Hovertons had been delighted and they were the ones who mattered, to him. 'So does John.'

'Oh . . . John. Different kettle of fish.'

And that had been that.

I really didn't care, Laurie remembered now, because it never occurred to me that he'd expect me to move into Clifton Place whilst he lived. He must know, and acknowledge to himself, that he doesn't like me at all. Why make us both miserable, then, by throwing his weight about and insisting that I live with him?

And why, for God's sake, after nineteen years, had he deliberately turned on the Hovertons, more or less refusing an explanation of his conduct, saying that Mum and Uncle had 'coddled' him, knowing, as he must, that this would be thoroughly offensive?

I wish I knew him better, Laurie thought gloomily, staring out of the window at the night sky and the stars, twinkling faintly in its dark arch. I wish I knew him at all, come to that, because I don't. I didn't want to, I didn't think knowing him was at all necessary. All right, he fathered me, but Uncle's more my father than Sir George . . . and Mum . . . well, she's my mother. Thinking it over now, he was pretty sure that Sir George had deliberately been rude to the Hovertons to cause a breach. So that Uncle wouldn't want him back, even if he wanted to come. He thanked God for Foxy's timely arrival, though he wondered whether, if she had not put her oar in, he might have found something to say to aid his cause.

Because it was his cause. The Hovertons were his beloved family and the thought of abandoning them at hop-picking time was abhorrent to him. They all worked so hard, and he had been determined to pull his weight and more this coming month, knowing in his heart that it would probably be the last time.

He knew, of course, that he was growing away from Mum and Uncle, that apart from the vacs he would probably not return to Bees-wing to live. It happened to most young people, though perhaps not to farmer's sons. In fact, had his father just let him go off to university and then suggested – not ordered, suggested – that his son should in future live at Clifton Place, Laurie suspected that he would have accepted the need without fuss, that the Hovertons, too, would have understood.

But it was the way he had done it! Refusing to explain, simply ordering, riding roughshod over the two people to whom he had most cause to be grateful. It was the action of an extremely stupid man – or an extremely devious one.

Sadly, Laurie concluded, after more cogitation, that Sir George had acted with considerable cunning. Because though I would have left of my own free will, I'd never have gone happily to Clifton Place when Bees-wing and the Hovertons were waiting to welcome me, he told himself. I'd have visited Father and lived with my family, as I've always done. But now, after the things that have been said, it will be difficult to come back to Bees-wing. Uncle was mortified, and he's a proud man. Oh what a hellish mess! And no doubt Sir George is sleeping the sleep of the just, telling himself smugly that he's done the trick, that I won't ever return to Bees-wing once I'm living at the Place.

Well, he can forget *that*, Laurie told himself, lying slowly down again. There is no way, no way at all, in which I can be stopped from visiting Mum and Uncle, let alone John! Why, John and I are as close as brothers, closer than most because we're friends, too. I couldn't simply disappear out of their lives and I won't let them disappear out of mine. I'll wake John, tell him what I think my father was up to when he came round this evening, and we'll plan how to get round it.

But John was snoring and Laurie was beginning to feel sleepy at last, as though with his partial solving of the mystery of his father's behaviour he had quieted his over-active mind. The morning will do, Laurie told himself, turning away from the fading starlight and closing his eyes firmly. In the morning we'll have plenty of time to talk.

He overslept, of course. After a disturbed night it was only natural, but it meant that he and John washed and dressed at breakneck speed, Laurie suddenly afraid that, if he was not ready and packed by ten o'clock, his father might re-enact the scene of the evening before all over again.

But even so, as the two of them packed and sorted their clothing and possessions Laurie found time to tell John what he suspected and John, after the briefest of pauses for thought, agreed.

'Though I can't see the sense in a feud, myself, I suppose he might want to keep you away from us peasants now we've served our purpose,' he said, grinning and ducking as Laurie aimed a blow at his head. 'Ah well, he'll soon discover the dreadful truth, I suppose.'

'What truth is that?' Laurie asked, knowing what was expected of him.

'Why, that you've become a peasant too,' John said cheerfully. 'He'll expect upper-class manners and bearing and he'll get Farmer

Giles impersonations all over the place.'

'Serves him right,' Laurie said. 'I've a good mind not to go to Cambridge, just to spite the old bugger.'

'You know you're dying to go, if only to break your duck,' John said. 'Is this shirt mine or yours?'

'Mine, you peasant – get your earthy hands off it! That shirt's got my monogram embroidered in the neck.'

'It's mine. Thought as much,' John said, chucking it carelessly onto his chest of drawers. 'Why do I have so many pairs of underpants?'

'Oh Lor', because I've been putting mine there, too . . . look, just give me half of what's there, because underpants are underpants.'

'Here you are, then. Only don't nab my binoculars because they're newer than yours, and keep your filthy aristocratic paws off my ski boots because they won't fit you, not even if you did a Cinderella on 'em and sliced off all your bleedin' toes.'

Laurie sniffed. 'My ski boots, as it happens, are perfectly adequate for my purposes and I've already slung 'em in the bag so I'm not likely to fancy yours. What about goggles, though? Did you break yours or did I break mine, or did you break mine?'

'You have 'em,' John said, suddenly sober. 'I don't suppose I'll be needing them again; there isn't much skiing done on your average hop farm. And we'd better get a move on, because in another twenty minutes your father will be here and I wouldn't like to be responsible if you're not ready and waiting on the doorstep, like the good little lad you are.'

Sir George had brought the chauffeur-driven Lagonda and arrived late, deliberately, so that Laurie was watching for him. He didn't get out of the car but wound down the window and, whilst the chauffeur went round and put Laurie's bags in the back he opened the door and bade Laurie abruptly to 'Hop in, we're late.'

There was no one to see Laurie off because they were all either busy or up at the hopyard so Laurie cast one last loving glance around him and then climbed into the car and sat stiffly on the polished leather upholstery, looking straight ahead of him as the big car swung onto the road.

'Well, my boy!' Sir George sat back in his seat with an assumption of ease. 'I'm sorry if I was a bit abrupt with the Hovertons, what, but the time has come for you and I to talk alone, without folk listening who've got nothing to do with our family.'

Sir George had made no attempt to introduce his son to the straight-backed individual who drove the car and there was a glass panel between driver and passengers, but even so Laurie cast a meaning look at the back of the man's head. 'We aren't alone here, either, Father,' he pointed out. 'And the Hovertons have been my parents since before I can remember. I couldn't possibly cast them off and nor, I think, could they stop . . . stop regarding me as . . . well, as a member of their family. You shouldn't expect it, you've been happy enough to make use of them all . . .'

'No, no, I didn't mean . . . But you must take your rightful place . . . oh dammit, this is not the moment . . . we'll talk later. Tonight, perhaps, when . . . no, not tonight, but this afternoon. Yes, this afternoon! We'll have a sandwich and then we'll sort things out. Does that appeal? What? What?'

'I want to talk, naturally,' Laurie said slowly. 'Why not this morning, Father? Why not the moment we get back to Clifton Place?'

'I've business appointments,' Sir George said after a short but pregnant pause during which Laurie said to himself, *he doesn't know how to answer!* 'Naturally, a man in my position has many calls on his time . . . this afternoon will suit me better.'

'Right. And what am I to do this morning?'

'Oh, unpack, settle into your room, make sure you've got everything you need,' Sir George said vaguely. 'You'll find plenty to do, plenty to do.'

And presently the house hove into view and Laurie found that he was looking at it with new eyes. Suddenly, it seemed, it was to be his home, as the farm had been his home all his life so far. He noted the odd little turrets, the gothic windows, the ancient trees espaliered against the warm Cotswold stone of the walls. He admired the dovecote and its golden weathercock, the sweep of the drive, the great trees whose branches met overhead.

The lawns, though . . . they were not in good shape. Mum had kept the grass cut at the farm, the boys giving a hand when they could, and these lawns, which he remembered as once being green velvet sweeps, were more like badly tended hayfields. And the drive, which had been thick with golden gravel, was pitted with holes and infested with weeds. Laurie turned to his father.

'What's happened to the lawns?'

'The lawns?' Sir George looked puzzled. 'Happened to them? What should happen? I don't understand.'

'Nor do I,' Laurie retorted. 'Lawns are meant to be cut and watered and generally looked after. The grass on that lawn . . .' he pointed, '. . . must be a foot high.'

Sir George laughed without much humour. 'Oh, I see what you mean. That's why I decided you must come home. Things are getting out of hand.'

Laurie's eyebrows shot up.

'You're bringing me home *to cut the lawns*? I don't believe it!'

'What? What?' Sir George said testily. 'Cut the lawns? What on earth are you on about? I begin to wonder, boy, whether you're all right in the head! Cut the lawns, indeed; as if I give a tinker's cuss about the lawns.'

Laurie was about to make a sharp retort when it occurred to him that there was absolutely no point in having a row over lawn-cutting, particularly as his father seemed suddenly to have become totally obtuse. Or had he always been so? A short holiday acquaintance with the man who had fathered you began to seem like a very bad idea, but it wasn't my fault, it was his choice, Laurie reminded himself. Still, we really do need to know each other, and if I'm going to give the relationship a chance, I have to listen and listen hard when he eventually does decide to talk to me. So a soft answer, in this case, is called for.

'No, of course lawns aren't important,' he said soothingly, therefore. 'I was only trying to make conversation, Father.'

Sir George grunted. 'I see. Well, you're in the Chinese room, with your own bathroom and dressing room. I'll show you up there, see you know the ropes, then we'll meet for luncheon in the crimson salon. Remember it, do you?'

'No, Father,' Laurie said as the car crunched to a halt before the massive front door. 'It's over four years since I visited the Place last, and I was only here a few days then.'

'Never! Why, you must have been since . . . and surely then it was for two or three weeks, not just days? Why, you've stayed here on several occasions, I have a distinct recollection of one particular occasion when you were here for a whole hunting season and . . . but never mind that. Hudson will bring your bags in.'

'I can manage them . . .' Laurie began, for he only had two bags, both of which were light enough for him to carry. Then he shut his mouth firmly. There I go again, he thought ruefully, contradicting him, making him aware that I'm a person in my own right, that I can pick and choose . . . and I can't, of course. Not here, not yet. Better go along with him until I find out just what is going on.

Three

The Chinese room was certainly unusual, or at least unusual compared with what he was used to at Bees-wing Farm, Laurie reflected, after his father had thrown open the door, mumbled something about important business and left him to it. The chauffeur had brought Laurie's bags as far as the foot of the stairs, then Sir George had seized one, Laurie the other, and they had carried them the rest of the way themselves. So much for letting the chauffeur carry them, Laurie thought wryly as he shut the door behind his father, who was making for the stairs once more at a cracking pace. He didn't want to stay with me a moment longer than necessary. And not a lackey to be seen in the hall, either . . . not that he minded. A lifetime of carting his own bag had at least accustomed him to the task!

Now, having closed the door, he took a long look around him. The first thing that struck him was that the room had the chilly, unlived-in air of a museum piece despite the fact that sunshine was falling through two of the four pairs of long, narrow windows which overlooked the unkempt lawns and the sweep of parkland beyond. Because it was an octagonal tower room it was full of light, the walls papered, predictably, with a Chinese-style wallpaper upon which tiny oriental ladies strolled over elaborate bridges or languished under weeping willows. Against one wall stood an extremely imposing canopied bed curtained in faded yellow silk which matched the long curtains on either side of the windows and the flat, worn cushions which were placed upon the wide stone sills.

To a chance observer the room would look bare, but Laurie realised that there was a reason for this; the room contained no washstand because of the adjoining bathroom, no wardrobes or clothes chests because of the dressing room. Nevertheless, it seemed odd not to have a cupboard or two, a few shelves for books, the clutter of two boys – no, two young men – living in one not very large bedroom which he had known all his life.

But he must try not to judge everything here by Hoverton standards, so he continued to look around him. Three of the windowless walls had doors in – he had entered the room through one, the other two would be the dressing room and bathroom – but the fourth was bare save for three pictures. One was a small portrait in oils of a young woman, dark-haired, dark-eyed, pretty in a dated, Victorian way, Laurie thought. The others were water-colours and Laurie, a keen watercolourist himself, went closer to examine them. One showed Clifton Place with the magnolia in bloom and beds of roses under the mullioned windows. It was a pleasant picture, well-executed, but pretty rather than either interesting or striking. The second watercolour held his attention for longer, though, perhaps more because it was a scene which had long been familiar to him rather than for its artistic merit.

The painter had depicted a hopyard in September at the height of the picking and had managed to catch the scene so well that Laurie felt he could smell the hops, feel the hot sun on the back of his neck. In the picture a man on stilts was cutting the bines down for the pickers and the bines were falling, in rich profusion, round the base of the plants and round the pickers who stood waiting for them.

I bet those pickers were real people, Laurie said to himself, with his nose not six inches from the glass. That old fellow has a look of Alf, and the boy's got a spotted scarf round his neck just like the one old Simpson always wears. I wonder who painted it? I wonder whether Father still grows hops anywhere on the estate? I hope he does – I might be able to give him a hand; I don't know much about estate management otherwise, though.

Stepping back from the picture, Laurie turned his attention to the rest of the room. The floorboards had once been polished but now they were just clean and bare, though there was a rug on the floor so that whoever slept in the fourposter would not have to get straight out onto chilly boards. The bed itself seemed soft – Laurie gave it an experimental poke – and had a couple of rather thin blankets, worn but crisply-ironed cotton sheets and a yellow silk counterpane spread across it.

It was a pleasant enough room what with the sunshine, the pretty paper, the yellow silk curtaining, yet somehow it made Laurie feel sad. Laurie was not a particularly imaginative young man, but he felt that the room had known a deal of suffering, that the walls had resounded more often to the sound of sobs than to that of laughter. Yes, there was something . . . he walked over to the bed again and sat down on the yellow silk counterpane. Immediately he felt a coldness creep over him, and jumped hastily to his feet, staring rather wildly around him.

He returned to look at the pictures and found himself smiling. Whoever had done the paintings had known what they were about and had enjoyed painting them. And when he walked over to the windows the view of the garden was delightful, there was even a late blossom or two on the magnolia which framed two of the four windows. Surely there was nothing wrong with the room, it was simply that he had never liked fourposter beds and felt chilly at the thought of actually sleeping in one.

His father had told him to settle in so he had better unpack his bags, and that meant finding the dressing room. He threw open the nearest door and a bathroom with a lavatory at one end met his gaze. He was used to modern flush toilets at school though they still had an earth-closet at the farm but he walked over to have a better look. Should he try it out? Why not? John would be impressed – a lav all of his own! He piddled thoughtfully into the blue and white porcelain bowl – real willow pattern this time – pulled the chain and the lavatory flushed. Then he walked over to the window, which had a different view to that from the tower room, and gazed out. He saw flowerbeds which had once been bright with roses but were now overrun with grass and weeds, and little box-edged paths green with moss and neglect. Puzzled, he returned to the bedroom and pushed a window open. Leaning out and looking sideways he saw a high wall with various fruit trees trained against it, unpruned, running riot. A green-painted garden door set in the high wall showed almost more wood than paint, and the gravel itself, now that he looked closely, was weedy and neglected.

Laurie frowned; what had been happening over the past few years? When he had come here as a child, the well-groomed splendour of the gardens had been something to be proud of. Now things had definitely changed, and for the worse. He could not understand it, but he would undoubtedly find out. He was going to live here, wasn't he?

Moving back from the window, he went to the enormous handbasin and turned one of the huge taps. Cold water gushed; he turned it off again and went to put the plug in so he could have a wash, but couldn't see a plug anywhere. Shrugging, he turned the other tap on anyway. More cold water, so the word *hot* on the tap was a bit misleading. But perhaps it was like school, where hot water was only available in the evenings and very early mornings. He rinsed his hands, splashed water on his face, looked round for a towel. No towel. Oh dear. He dried his hands on his trousers and returned to the bedroom, then went and opened the other door. This was the dressing room, down three quite steep steps, which was a surprise since the bedroom and bathroom were on the same level.

Laurie got his bags and touted them into the dressing room where a close-packed mass of furniture met his gaze. There was a narrow bed, a huge chest of drawers, and a smaller one, a shoe-rack and a clothes horse set up before the empty grate. There was a dressing table, a long mirror, a ladder-backed chair, an easy chair upholstered in the faded yellow silk of the bedroom, a roll-topped desk, a nest of small tables, several footstools . . . this little room was as over-furnished as the bedroom was bare. And why the single bed, for God's sake?

Still, now that he was living here he would find out. He began to unpack his bags, stuffing underwear and socks into the drawers and opening the wardrobe to find some coat hangers so that he could hang up his shirts, trousers and jackets.

Nothing met his gaze apart from an empty rail. He hadn't thought to pack coat hangers because he had been in such a devilish rush when it came to the point. Never mind, he could put most of his stuff in the chest of drawers, and lay the trousers carefully on top. And when he opened the next drawer down in the big chest he discovered some towels, and took them through to the bathroom with a small sense of achievement. A hand towel and two bath towels . . . that was better! Before he knew it the place would begin to look more like a fellow's bedroom and less like a museum.

Having unpacked he went back into the bedroom and over to the windows once more. As soon as he entered the room he realised that in the vicinity of the fourposter, it was actually physically colder than the cosy little dressing room. An uneasy chill seemed to emanate from that great bed, as though it were no keener to have a peasant like himself sleeping there than he was to bed down in it. To show himself it was just imagination he went over and sat on it, then wriggled round and lay down. He immediately felt sure that something sinister was on the canopy above his head, about to drop on him. A truly horrible feeling. With an uneasy shudder he sat up, swung his legs over the side, and got off the bed. You're a fool, Laurie Clifton, he told himself. It's just a bloody bed, that's all, it can't hurt you. Why, the worst it could do is fall on you in the night, I suppose.

Immediately he remembered a story by Edgar Allan Poe in which a young man was almost pressed flat by a bed. He had always thought it a stupid story; now he wasn't so sure. He could almost hear the clanking down below (or up above) as someone who wanted to do away with the Clifton heir began to work the crushing mechanism.

Fairy tales, he scolded himself, walking over to the window and sitting down on the nearest windowseat. From his perch he examined the view, telling himself to forget melodrama and begin to face facts. There was certainly a magnificent view – beyond the rolling parkland he could see woods, meadows, pinky-red plough, and beyond that again the blue hills rearing up against the clear and sunny sky. He tried to identify something he knew, but was unable to do so. He was a good way from Bees-wing Farm, several miles, though Clifton land almost touched Hoverton acres in several places. He wished he could see Cumber Farm from here, he remembered walking up to it once with Allsop, the lady had given him milk and new-baked scones. Seeing a homely, muck-strewn farmyard would have eased his sense of strangeness, but he could see no houses at all, just the parkland, the trees and the distant hills.

Presently, Laurie got to his feet and glanced at his wristwatch; not yet time to go down to the crimson salon for this sandwich his father had spoken of. He hoped it had been a figure of speech; he had been too late and too distressed to eat a proper breakfast, now he could have eaten a horse had it been offered. He strolled across the bedroom and went into the dressing room again. Nice little room – welcoming. He wondered about the roll-topped desk; secretly, he had always rather fancied having a desk of his own, and this one, for all he knew, might have a hidden drawer, and the drawer might contain an important document or something which would lead to a treasure, buried years ago, perhaps, by some Cavalier Clifton, hiding his gold from the Roundheads. He could imagine the newspaper headlines . . . *Heir to the Clifton millions finds documents missing for centuries.* Something like that, anyway.

The roll-top refused to answer to his touch but when he tried the small key which protruded from the tiny drawer it fitted. He turned it and then pulled upwards. The lid rolled back, revealing a leather-bound blotter with a sheet of faded pink blotting paper already in place, a thick pad of cream-coloured writing paper, a packet of envelopes and a pot with several old-fashioned pens in it. Bottles of blue, black and red ink were lined up, all of them old though one or two were still unopened, and there were other things, too. A rubber, grey on one end, white on the other. Rusty paper clips in a small cardboard box, drawing pins in another, rubber bands in a third. Then there was a selection of pencils, ranging from soft- to hard-leaded, mostly well-used. A pad of sketching paper, each page a different colour, and a small, much-used box of paints. Laurie settled himself in one of the ladder-backed chairs and examined his finds carefully. Curiouser and curiouser; the stuff was so old, and not just a year or two, either. The paints in the small, black-japanned box were dried up water-colours which had cracked with disuse. But, with careful handling, they might come into their own again.

Laurie closed the box and examined the lid. J.A.T. had been painstakingly scratched on the shiny surface. J.A.T.? It had plainly not belonged to a Clifton, so what was the box doing in the desk? Then it occurred to him that his father might have picked it up secondhand . . . but no, that was stupid; Mum had told them many times about the vast amounts of furniture up at the Place, all of it old, most of it valuable. Sir George would have no possible reason to buy a secondhand desk and since Sir George had shown distaste whenever Laurie mentioned painting it was unlikely that he would ever have acquired the things in the desk, even as a small child. If he ever was a small child, Laurie thought bitterly. I believe he was born with a moustache and thinning hair, with a purple nose and a loud, arrogant voice.

No, the paints and pencils must have belonged to some long-ago visitor and been left after that visitor departed. If they were useful to him, well and good, he would use them as of right. If not, then he could throw them away easily enough.

Satisfied on that score, Laurie went through the rest of the desk, but apart from some ancient stationery and a great many more pencils, all much-chewed and well-used, it was empty. Laurie got up from his chair and went over to the sash window which looked out on the same view as his bedroom, but a bit further along. He heaved the sash up and stuck his head out. Here, the enormous magnolia tree shared the available space with a yellow climbing rose still in rich blossom and with a silvery-grey branched wisteria. Laurie guessed that, in spring, the scent of the blossoms would pour into the room when the sun shone on them. A nice way to wake. It had already occurred to him that it might be more sensible if he actually slept here, in the dressing room.

There was no doubt about it, he did not care for the bed in the Chinese room. Probably it was one of those rooms which Charles the First had slept in. Probably it was haunted; that would be just my luck, to have a haunted bed, Laurie told himself, then jeered at his own faint-heartedness. Hadn't he and John always longed to see a ghost for themselves? Why was it so different, then, just because John was a few miles away? Why did the thought of a ghost-hunt no longer intrigue him?

It was a question that he did not particularly wish to answer, so he surveyed the dressing room instead. He would take some of the furniture out, make up the little bed, and kip down here happily enough. He didn't like the thought of that great, dusty canopy hanging over him whilst he slept, and knew he would never willingly pull the curtains closed around him. There were curtains at the windows if he wanted privacy. Not that he would – there was no more chance of being overlooked here than on the farm.

What about the servants, though? It would be a chore, humping the bedding from one room to another morning and evening, and he saw no reason why he should do it. He would simply tell the servants that he did not like the fourposter and intended to sleep in the dressing room. What business was it of anyone's, come to that, where he chose to sleep? His father would probably growl all sorts of unpleasant remarks, say he was a ninny, but from the way he had shot out of the room earlier he was unlikely to be doing much visiting. And a determination not to sleep in the Chinese room was growing. There were a thousand good reasons why a person should prefer one room to the other. He would tell anyone who enquired that he, Laurie, was used to small, cosy rooms and did not like large, imposing ones.

He went back into the dressing room and was about to start shifting furniture when he happened to glance at his watch . . . and gave a yelp. Time for this sandwich . . . and it had better be a figure of speech or his father would have to lock the kitchen door against him!

Laurie made for the stairs.

It wasn't a figure of speech, but neither was it one sandwich, it was a plate of them. They weren't dainty, either, but were made up of great doorsteps of bread with cheese and pickle in some, ham in others, cold chicken in the rest. When Laurie got down to the crimson salon – his father had shown him where to go before taking him upstairs – the sandwiches, on an enormous silver salver, were in the middle of a long, highly polished occasional table, flanked by a bowl of apples, another of ripe tomatoes, two glasses and a jug of what looked like cider.

Sir George was sitting in one of the wing chairs beside the empty grate and eating enthusiastically; he waved a half-eaten sandwich at his son and spoke thickly through his mouthful: 'Come along, grab a seat and get going; I've had a head start on you! D'you drink cider?'

Laurie, who had been brought up on it, repressed an urge to say *do pigs fly?* and sat down, murmuring that he would be grateful for a drop.

'Help yourself,' Sir George said. 'You might pour me a glass.'

Laurie complied, then took a sandwich and bit into it. It was good, the bread freshly made, the ham cut thickly. He helped himself to a tomato and began to enjoy the picnic. He grinned at his father and Sir George grinned back, at ease for the first time, Laurie thought, since he had marched into the Hoverton kitchen the previous evening.

'Well? Good, ain't they?'

'Prime,' Laurie agreed. 'A bit of all right, Father. I'm hungry . . . thirsty, too.'

'So I see. Get to it, then.'

For ten minutes or so there was complete silence save for the happy sound of food being vigorously chewed and drink being swallowed. Only when the silver salver was empty did Sir George utter once more.

'Well? Like the room, do you?'

'It's very grand,' Laurie said. He leaned back in his chair and surveyed the cider in his glass. It was strong, stronger than the stuff Uncle gave him and John, the glow from it had spread from the top of his head to the tips of his toes. He considered telling his father that he intended to sleep in the dressing room and opened his mouth to say something to that effect, when Sir George spoke.

'Good, good. Now I'm a blunt man, boy, not given to fancy statements. I said I'd tell you why I wanted you here, and tell you I shall. The truth is, Laurie, that I've somehow managed to outrun the carpenter a trifle.'

Laurie had never heard the expression before, but he got the gist of it. 'Do you mean you've over-spent, Father?' he said innocently. 'But I don't know what I can do, my allowance hasn't been paid for years.'

For a blunt man, Sir George did not appear to take kindly to an equal bluntness in his son. He frowned across at Laurie, biting his lip under the short, military moustache he favoured.

'Your *allowance*? What's that got to do with anything, eh? This isn't just a piddling little allowance, this is money for the future of the entire estate, money which at present I just don't have.'

'Why not?'

Mum would have said he was being rude, Uncle would have smiled behind his hand. John would have uttered just the same words. And the 'blunt man' was looking decidedly shifty.

'Why not? Damn it, boy, what sort of a question's that? The upkeep of this place alone, the money for improvements, the stables, my hunters . . . it's a constant anxiety, as you'll find out for yourself one day, though not too soon, I trust. What I'm trying to tell you is that I need a substantial sum of money just to continue . . .'

'How much? And for what purpose?' Laurie said inexorably. 'And what did you say about a trust, yesterday? I think you have to give me the whole story, Father, otherwise how can I possibly understand you? I've been brought up to plain speaking, so don't be afraid to speak plainly.'

Sir George had gone alarmingly purple. Now he breathed noisily down his huge nose – in, out; in, out – and then reached across, picked up an apple, and took an enormous bite out of it. 'Help yourself,' he commanded. 'I need about a thou, I suppose.'

'A *thousand*? Do you mean a thousand *pounds*?'

Sir George, mouth extended with apple, nodded. Laurie leaned forward and took an apple for himself, but did not start to eat. Instead, he stared very hard at his father.

'And the money? I take it there's a trust in my favour, otherwise you wouldn't have brought me home. Right?'

'Well now, that's being rather . . . I don't like your attitude, boy, and I tell you straight . . .' Sir George choked, swallowed, reached for the cider, poured himself another glass and took a long pull. 'Yes, there's a trust,' he said, when he could speak once more. 'And you're the beneficiary, naturally. You were her only child, after all.'

'Her? Do you mean my *mother*? She left me money? But I've always understood that she wasn't rich at all, that she came from quite an ordinary family. It can't be much money, surely, Father? Not enough to – to pay a debt like a thousand pounds!'

Sir George shrugged. He did not look happy. 'It ain't a debt, exactly, m'boy. Thing is, I was brought up to do things *right*, if you follow me. And I've done things right all m'life. My man of business, Hawkings, told me years since to cut my coat according to my cloth but I couldn't do it. Couldn't let people think we Cliftons were on the slippery slope. So I sold what I could . . .'

'Not land, Father?' For the life of him, Laurie could not help sounding scandalised. Mr Hoverton's view of anyone who sold land had been made extremely plain. 'You didn't sell *land*?'

'They wouldn't let me,' Sir George said gloomily. 'What difference would it have made, eh? The Cliftons own half Herefordshire, if you're unable to farm it because you haven't the money why not sell some of it off? But Hawkings was clear on that score; no sale of land allowed . . . as though I were a child instead of a man in the prime of life.'

'Then if it wasn't land, what was it?'

'Oh, stocks, shares, that kind of thing. And a bit of old silver, some paintings. There was a nice little seascape, in oils, and a portrait by someone who's apparently collectible. All in all it kept me going for the best part of six years. But it's gone now, which is why I'm saying to you, m'boy, we've got to break that damned trust!'

'All right, I understand that you've no money,' Laurie said with what patience he could muster. 'But what, precisely, do you want the thousand pounds *for*? If you aren't in debt . . .'

'I owe wages,' Sir George said, looking hangdog. 'There's repairs to cottage roofs, drainage . . . And I've got to feed my hunters, run my cars . . . In short, m'boy, I need the money to live.'

'I see,' Laurie said. 'You mean to live in the style to which you've become accustomed, I suppose.' He tried not to sound as bitter as he felt. What on earth had his father been doing with the money from the estate? He remembered the Hovertons telling him many years ago that quite apart from the money the estate made from the sale of its own resources, because the Cliftons owned so much property they also took in huge sums in rent. And Bill Hoverton had talked about money which had been invested in a variety of different ways, all of which had made the estate richer yet. 'Look, Father, if I have as much as a thousand pounds coming to me and we can break the trust, how long will that last you?'

Sir George mumbled something about only the poor having to be as financially aware as Laurie seemed to think him and Laurie, with a sigh, remembered something else Mr Hoverton had once told them.

'Money breeds money,' Mr Hoverton had said. 'That's why I'm always tellin' you boys to put a bit away whenever you can. That's what your Mum and me do, anyroad. I know you won't need to save, Laurie, but John here does, so you can learn the lesson between you.'

So now Laurie looked severely at his father across the width of the crimson salon. 'You don't know how much you spend in a year? Look, Father, if we've got to go and see this Mr Hawkings to try to break the trust . . .'

'For God's sake, boy, stop acting like a tenant farmer and remember you're my heir,' Sir George said testily. 'He's Hawkings to you and me, not *Mr* Hawkings.'

Laurie had been leaning forward in his chair, trying to understand his father's dilemma whilst having a shrewd suspicion that he understood only too well. Sir George had squandered the money and would continue to do so unless someone put their foot down and he imagined that Mr Hawkings, in spite of any representations which Laurie himself or his father might put forward, would make sure that the trust was just that, and that the money stayed where it was until he, Laurie, reached a suitable age. But now the older man's words, and the sneer with which he pronounced them, suddenly proved more than he could stomach. Laurie jumped to his feet and strode to the door, fists clenched, brow set in a scowl.

'I'd rather be a tenant farmer who doesn't owe a penny to anyone than a member of the so-called landed gentry who hasn't even paid his dependants their wages,' he said, his voice thick with anger and disgust. 'I'm not staying here where I'm only wanted for any money I might bring in. I'm going home!'

He would have rushed out of the room and out of the house, except that Sir George surged to his feet, made the most awful, rumbling, choking noise deep in his throat, staggered, and then fell heavily across the table, which tipped sideways beneath his considerable weight, spilling Sir George onto the carpet where he lay on his back, mouth open, eyes turned up, making a very unpleasant snuffling sound.

Laurie turned and crossed the room in a couple of strides, then bent over the older man, all anger forgotten.

'Father? What happened? Are you all right?'

There was foam on his father's lips and the whites of his eyes showed whilst the skin of his face twitched and jerked as though it had a life of its own. He was moaning, and still breathing so heavily that it sounded more like a snore.

'Father?'

Laurie's alarm was real. He didn't like the look of the old boy at all, he had better find help. He looked around and spotted a long bell-pull in the corner by the door. He ran over to it and tugged frantically, then returned to his father's side. He saw that Sir George's normally ruddy colour had drained away and that he was clenching his teeth, his lips drawn back. Hastily he slid an arm under the older man's shoulders, lifting him into a semi-sitting position. Then he reached for the cider and began to splash it, none too carefully, into Sir George's ashen face.

Footsteps hurried across the hallway. A man appeared in the doorway and Laurie felt relief wash over him in a great tide; he was no longer alone, in fact the man before him was far more likely to understand his parent's collapse than anyone other than a medical practitioner. He even managed a watery smile as the man came swiftly into the room.

'Allsop, it's you – thank God! Look, my father's collapsed, can you fetch a doctor, please? And is there someone who could help me lift him onto the couch, fetch hot bottles or whatever one should do? He – he seems to be having some sort of a fit or seizure.'

Rather to Laurie's surprise the butler looked exactly as he had done six years earlier, neither older nor more frail. And to Laurie's enormous relief he did not seem unduly ruffled by finding his employer stretched out unconscious on the Turkey carpet. Indeed, he came and looked down on Sir George for a moment, coolly put a thin hand on his employer's forehead, and then said: 'I'll fetch a servant, Mr Laurie. And I'll send someone for the doctor. Then I'll get his existing medicine, which may well be sufficient to bring him round.'

'Existing medicine? I didn't know he wasn't well, even. And can't you ring for the doctor? It would be quicker, and I do think he's probably quite ill.'

'They've cut the telephone off, Mr Laurie,' the butler said quietly. 'But the Becketts only live at the end of the drive; they'll ring through to the doctor for us and he'll be here as quickly as he can. Sir George has collapsed before, though not, perhaps . . .' he eyed the overturned table and his employer's grey countenance, '. . . not perhaps quite so violently, Mr Laurie. I'll send someone to help you get the patient onto the couch whilst I search in Sir George's room for his tablets.'

He was as good as his word. A young man in his stockinged feet came shuffling in presently and he and Laurie got Sir George onto the sofa and covered up with a couple of blankets which a maid brought down from upstairs. And presently the butler returned with a glass of water and some small blue tablets. Laurie heaved his father, whose head, lolling horribly, showed that he was still unconscious, into a sitting position, and helped Allsop to force a tablet and some water between the clenched teeth. And after a few moments Sir George's grim face relaxed and the snoring sound which had so worried his son eased. When the doctor was ushered in, he was able to tell them that Sir George should be all right in a week or two, with rest and the medicine he would prescribe.

'It looks worse than it is; he's suffered a slight seizure, but it's happened before and he's made a good recovery,' the doctor said comfortably. 'Forgot to take his medicine, I daresay, in the excitement of having you home, Mr Laurie. So in future, you put the tablets in his hand twice a day and all should be well.'

'You may be sure I shall,' Laurie said fervently. 'I was frightened out of my life!'

The doctor grinned and nodded. 'Aye, it's a frightening business, illness, whether it be your own or another's. And now let's get him up the stairs and comfortably tucked up in bed. He'll be back on his feet in less than a month, I'm sure of it. Are ye back for good, lad, or just for a holiday?'

'I'm off to university in October, sir,' Laurie said, evading the question. 'I'd be much obliged if you could tell me exactly what's wrong with my father – he seemed very ill, to me.'

'A patient's health should be confidential, between him and his medical practitioner,' the doctor warned, but Laurie could tell he spoke automatically, and had no intention of remaining mum. 'Your father, however, is a sick man. It's my belief that he's suffered a number of minor strokes – he's always been a big eater and a hard drinker, he pushes his body to extremes – but since he won't go into hospital or change his lifestyle, there isn't a great deal I can do about it. I've prescribed some tablets, which help, as you saw, but so would a quieter life. But there, we all go to damnation in our own way . . . I'm sorry, lad, I didn't mean that, precisely . . . I'll call again tomorrow.'

With the doctor ushered off the premises and his father soundly sleeping, Laurie played with the idea of going quietly back to the Hovertons and explaining what had happened and why he had been press-ganged into leaving them. But he knew his father could have him brought back and might well take revenge by being particularly unpleasant to the Hovertons and anyway, it seemed a pretty mean sort of trick. Hitting a man when he was down wasn't Laurie's style. Besides, I probably won't be able to give him the money he wants, and even if I could, I don't think I should, Laurie told himself, making his way slowly back across the huge hallway. Because I don't think he'd pay wages with it, or mend cottage roofs or improve drainage or anything like that. I think he'd never quite know where it had gone, and neither should I. It isn't as if it was even Clifton money, because it belonged to my mother and I'm very sure she'd rather I had it when I was older and could use it the way she meant it to be used – for the good of the estate.

But right now, he must find Allsop and they must talk. God knew when the man had last received any wages, but at least he was still here. Judging from the number of servants he had seen when the butler had gone to fetch help, very few of the others had stayed the course. One little maid, the gardener who had helped him lift Sir George, and a large lady with a rather vacant face who said she was the cook; that was the sum of the once impressive staff of Clifton Place.

Laurie went through the green baize door which shut the servants' quarters off from the rest of the house and followed his nose to the kitchen. Sure enough, the gardener, the little maid and the cook were sitting round the table whilst Allsop, in an apron now and carving a joint of meat with a very large knife, lectured them.

'The boy is young and won't, perhaps, see that his father cannot be trusted to . . .' he broke off, his eyes widening slightly as he caught sight of Laurie hovering in the doorway. '. . . Ah, Mr Laurie, I didn't realise you were about to join us.'

'It doesn't matter; I am young, of course, but I'm beginning to see a lot of things,' Laurie said. He pulled out a chair, turned it with its back to the table and straddled it, leaning his chin on the back. 'Go on if you please, Mr Allsop; I think I need to hear what you are about to say.'

'Yes. Well, perhaps you're right, Mr Laurie, perhaps the time for keeping our own counsel and praying for a miracle is indeed past. The truth is that Sir George does not have a feather to fly with and the reason he's lost so much money . . . well, I hesitate to say this, Mr Laurie, but your father has no head for figures and he – he's very fond of the horses, to say nothing of . . .'

'But surely he couldn't lose all his money on hunters, could he?' Laurie said, horrified. 'I know he has a good stable . . .'

The gardener stifled a laugh, then looked horrified and ducked his head, a tide of crimson flooding his face and neck. The little maid bit her lip and looked frightened and the cook frowned down at her folded hands. Mr Allsop permitted himself a small, tight smile.

'No, Mr Laurie, not hunters, racehorses,' he said. 'Sir George is a betting man. I understand when you and he go off to the South of France he spends a good deal of his time in the casino, but unfortunately he isn't particularly lucky either on the tables or at the track. In short he loses vast sums.' He paused, then added, in a lower tone: 'And should your father manage to lay his hands on – on any sum of substance, I fear it would go the same way. He would tell himself he was recruiting the family fortunes, but, alas, should he by some miracle win, he would speedily lose it all in some other game of chance.'

'The casino! So that was where he went,' Laurie muttered. 'Mr Allsop, I want you to know I had no idea until today that things were in the state they are. But I think perhaps you and I should have a talk. When you've finished your meal perhaps you could join me in – in the crimson salon?'

'I'm carving for supper, Mr Laurie, not for immediate consumption,' the butler said rather reproachfully. 'We had sandwiches earlier. Mrs Waughman was asked to do them for the salon, so she did them for the servants, too.'

'Yes, of course. Well, I'll see you in a few minutes, then,' Laurie said getting to his feet. 'Um . . . I'm going to do my best to – to see to things whilst my father is unwell,' he added over his shoulder.

Back in the crimson salon he sat on the windowseat, staring out over those long, ragged lawns and suddenly realised that this time the previous day he had been preparing to go down to the station with John to meet the hop-pickers. He had been wildly happy, excited, ready to take on the world, in fact. And now he felt crushed, bewildered and lonelier than he had ever felt before in his entire life.

If only John were here! Or Mum and Uncle, always ready with quiet commonsense, with good advice. But he was not quite alone; there was Allsop, who would be with him shortly, and the man of business his father had spoken of – Hawkings, that was it. Once he had spoken to them perhaps things would become clearer.

'Are you very lonely, John? Do you miss Laurie very much?'

Foxy looked across at John as she asked the question and the two of them continued to drop hops industriously into the crib. Ever since picking had started, John had spent at least a part of each day picking with her; he said it was so she would have money to buy the books she needed when she went to university, but Foxy thought, without conceit, that he did it for companionship. Whatever he might say, life must be very different up at the farmhouse without Laurie.

And now he was looking back at her, with the faintest of frowns creasing his brow. He had a nice, freckled, tanned face, the whites of his eyes whiter than you would have believed possible, his fair hair burnished to platinum by the September sun.

'Missing him? Yeah, course I am. Odd, isn't it? I knew he'd have gone in October, anyway, I was prepared for that. But to go now, with everyone so busy over the hops, just didn't seem natural. So I expect to see him, I wake up in the mornings and look across the room . . . and his bed's empty. But I'm not lonely, because you're here. So it's a mixture, really.'

'But you aren't with me all the time,' Foxy pointed out. She finished stripping her bine and reached for the next. 'You're only with me evenings, and a bit of each day.'

'Oh, sure. But three's an awkward number, wouldn't you say?'

Foxy stared. 'An awkward number? It never has been, it's always been the three of us, and your mum and dad. Why should it be different now?'

John shrugged, finished his own bine and hauled in another one, but did not immediately start to pick. 'I've been telling myself that now we're older, three of us could have been a bit difficult. If we'd been friendly with another girl, so that there were four of us, it might have been different, but . . . haven't you enjoyed our evenings, then, since Laurie left?'

He sounded faintly injured. Foxy hastened to reassure him.

'Yes, they've been lovely, and your mum and dad have been wonderful to me. But they're sad, John, and so are you, a bit. And I am – I miss Laurie as well, worse than I thought.'

'Ye-es. It's the not knowing, that's been the worst. I mean why hasn't he come back, or rung up? Why don't they answer the phone at Clifton Place, for that matter?'

Foxy, who had gone into the village with John to ring Clifton Place from the public call box, shook her head, as puzzled as he. They had tried and tried until the operator had got quite cross with them, but they had not managed to get through.

'Mum and Dad are waiting for Laurie to phone just to tell them he's all right,' John continued. 'It's not like him because he must know they'll worry and he's usually better than me over things like that. What's more, I thought he'd be back in twenty-four hours yet here it is, four whole days, and not a word or a sign of him.'

'Why don't your mum and dad phone, then?' Foxy asked, then immediately regretted the question. 'No, don't answer that – how could they? The way Sir George's behaved has made it difficult for them to do anything other than wait, I suppose. But probably it's hard for Laurie, too. Why, he might have been taken off to London . . . that's possible, isn't it, John? I remember him talking about a London house, saying how big and gloomy it was. Yes, that's probably it.'

'I wonder if you're right?' John said reflectively. 'Tell you what, why not put it to Mum this evening, at supper? It would cheer her up just to think it was the reason, I believe. It really isn't like Laurie not to get in touch.'

'Oh, am I invited to supper tonight? Lovely, thanks very much, I'd be delighted,' Foxy said. 'Your poor mother has a guest every evening now!'

'She's used to cooking for four; she says you're welcome any time,' John said absently. 'Tell you what, Foxy, why don't you and I take an evening off when we finish here and go for a bike ride? If we pedal like hell we could reach Clifton Place before it's dark. We needn't go slap bang up to the front door – after the way Sir George behaved I'd not like to do that – but we could skulk around, keep our eyes peeled. I'm sure we'd catch a glimpse of Laurie; we might even manage to have a word.'

'I thought you didn't miss him?' Foxy said teasingly. 'We could give it a try, though. No harm done if he wasn't about. Tell you what, why don't we tell Auntie Bea and your mum that we want to see a flick so we're going in to Ledbury? That way they won't worry if we're home late.'

'Bright girl,' John said approvingly. 'Look, can you carry on by yourself for a bit? Only I'll go up to the house and tell Mum now, and then we won't have to wait for supper. We'll get some chips as we go through the village.'

'Sure,' Foxy said stoutly, only slightly dismayed at the thought of missing one of Mrs Hoverton's marvellous meals. 'Who's paying? If it's me I'll make do with chips but if it's you why don't we have fish, as well?'

John, turning away from the crib, grinned at her over his shoulder. 'You are nothing but a stomach on legs, girl,' he said. 'And mean as hell, considering I'm picking for your profit. Still, I can run to fish and chips for two, if that is madam's pleasure.'

Foxy smiled gratefully. 'Thanks, John. Only picking's hard work and I only had bread and cheese and an apple for me midday's. And the apple was hard.'

'If you nicked it from the high orchard it would be,' John called back as he trudged up the long, sloping tunnel beneath the bines. 'They won't be ready for the best part of a month – stick to the low orchard, you silly scrumper you!'

Foxy giggled and watched him out of sight, picking industriously all the while. Any minute now the crib would be full and Len, who was supervising the weighing and filling in the owings book, would be coming for it. It was a grand crop, which meant that the picking was easier so one was paid less per bushel, but even so she should have done pretty well today. John wasn't as fast as she but it was a close-run thing, and seeing her slogging away always put him on his mettle. She knew that he often dropped by, intending to chat and to pick for twenty minutes or so and ended up scarcely speaking but picking like a robot for three or four hours.

One day I'll make it up to him, she thought vaguely now. And one thing I know – you wouldn't catch Laurie picking like a professional, or letting John pick like one, for that matter. Laurie would flirt and tease and pick for ten minutes, but he was as likely to lie on his back on a pile of empty bines, gazing up at the blue sky and talking a lot of rubbish about film stars, motor cars, or aeroplanes as he was to do anything useful.

So if Laurie were here, I wouldn't have earned as much money, Foxy concluded, as Len and his equipment came into her row. Ernie was with him; Ernie would see fair play, because if one of the farmhands was feeling a bit mean he would push the hops down so hard that you needed half as many again to fill the pocket, and Ernie would soon put a stop to that. He had been hop-picking for seventy years and knew all the tricks; even Auntie Bea gave him best when it came to an argument, though Ernie wasn't one for quarrelling. He simply stated the facts as he knew them and waited for the opposition to come round to his point of view; which usually happened quite quickly.

'Right, now, Foxy. My, that crib's fairly squeakin' wi' hops.' Ernie scooped out a handful and held them lovingly, close to his face. 'You'll mek a bob or two this year, girl.'

'Hope so,' Foxy said. 'Start shovellin', Len!'

They picked hops until it began to get dark and then John and

Foxy hurried round to the stables. The boys had always kept their bicycles in the tack-room and Foxy was well-used to riding with a crossbar so she just pulled her skirt above her knees and tied it in a knot so that it would not get in the way.

'Trousers would be easier,' she said wistfully as the two of them mounted the bicycles in the yard. 'Good job it's darkish.'

'Yup, you're right there; I'd be fighting off the fellers if they could see you properly,' John agreed, eyeing her with a grin. 'Have you ever heard the expression, *she's got legs all the way up to her elbows*, Foxy?'

'No, I haven't,' Foxy snapped. She could feel her cheeks beginning to warm. Why did young men always have to be so personal? 'It don't make sense, John Hoverton, so don't talk foolish.'

'I'm merely telling you you've got lovely long legs,' John pointed out righteously. 'That's a compliment, you daft hen.'

'If that's a compliment I'd rather have a few insults,' Foxy assured him, beginning to pedal hard as they turned into the lane. 'When'll we get the chips? Going there or coming back?'

'Going, you want me to say,' John observed. 'Tell you what, why not chips going and fish coming back? Then we'd have something to look forward to.'

'The shop might be shut by then,' Foxy said, having given the matter a second's thought. 'Besides, I'm hungry *now*.'

'Oh ah? Yes, I'm peckish myself, but I didn't waste time when I went back to the house earlier, you know. Whilst Mum was finding me up some money for the flicks I whipped into the pantry and nicked a damned great slice of egg and ham pie. Fancy a bit?'

'Where did you hide it?' Foxy asked suspiciously as John slowed his bicycle and dismounted neatly. 'In the filthy pocket of those filthy bags?'

'My bags are pristine; they're my cinema-going best ones,' John assured her. 'And the pie is wrapped in greaseproof paper anyway.' He heaved at his trouser pocket and produced two well-wrapped slices of his mother's famous egg and ham pie. 'Well? Do you want some or shall I scoff the lot?'

'I'd better have a piece, I don't want you to make yourself ill,' Foxy said with watering mouth. She really was starving! 'Did you bring some pickle?'

'Pickle? Dear Lord, woman, I'm not a – a mobile Lyons, you know! But I did swipe a couple of tomatoes . . . here, grab.'

Foxy grabbed and together they munched pie and bit into the bright red, juicy tomatoes and presently, much refreshed, Foxy was brought to acknowledge that perhaps it would be better, after all, to save the fish and chips for the ride home.

'Because it is getting dark,' she agreed as they rode through the quiet lanes. 'And as we've never been to Clifton Place, we'll probably have to reconnoitre a bit. I expect there's a lodge keeper and gates that get locked at night and all sorts.'

'Yes, there is. Mum's told us about it often enough,' John agreed. 'But we can't get the bikes over the wall, so we'll have to get in by one of the proper entrances. Apparently it's a couple of miles from the wall to the house and we really can't afford the time to walk it.'

'I hope you know the way,' Foxy said presently, with some apprehension, as they turned from the lane onto a proper road. 'Are you sure we go to the left?'

'No, not certain,' John said cheerfully. 'But all these huge old houses have more than one entrance, don't they? We're bound to find the wall soon, and a gateway. Once we do that we can decide how to get through without alarming the guard.'

'This is not a *Boy's Own Paper* adventure,' Foxy said severely. 'Ah, that must be the wall. I wonder if they have Sherlock Holmes-type hounds roaming loose in the grounds?'

'Stoopid! Ah, we're in luck – a gateway! And it's open!'

'So that's the house! Gosh, it is a size, isn't it? No lights to be seen from here, though . . . I've a good mind to go up to the front door, knock as hard as I can, and demand admittance!'

Foxy, keeping as close to John as darkness and Laurie's bicycle would permit, gave a small shiver. Exciting though it had been to find Clifton Place, to sneak in past the lodge, to extinguish their lamps and cycle slowly up the long, potholed drive, she was still finding it an eerie experience. The lodge, for instance, had been deserted, which had startled them both. Mrs Hoverton had often told them about Phoebe Manus and her son Peter who lived in the lodge and opened the door whenever a rider shouted or a car hooted its horn. But although she and John had prowled all the way around it not a light had shown, nor had there been any sign of life in the dark, dreary rooms. Even a bicycle lamp, daringly shone into what must have been the kitchen, had failed to reveal so much as a table or chair within, though there were some pretty sizeable cobwebs stretching across the window embrasure.

And now they were actually within twenty or thirty yards of the house itself. They could see the turrets outlined against the stars, the mullioned windows, the great tree which grew up and spread out its branches beside the imposing front door.

'John, I do think I was right, I do think they must be in London,' Foxy said nervously, pulling at his arm. 'There can only be servants in, that's why there aren't any lights round here. Do let's go home . . . or we could telephone from the village, I suppose.'

In the faint starlight, she saw John shake his head, saw his mouth tighten into obstinacy.

'No. Laurie's in there, I'm sure of it. Or if he isn't there'll be someone who knows where he is. Come on, dump your bike and we'll go up and take a look.'

It was a pleasant enough night but there was a breeze; it's that which is making my arms gooseflesh, Foxy told herself defensively. I'm not frightened of a witchy-looking house, particularly if Laurie really is in there. And John's right, we've come a long way, we really have to find out just what's going on. Nevertheless she leaned her borrowed bicycle reluctantly against the nearest tree, untied her skirt and then clutched John's arm . . . so that they wouldn't bump into each other or get separated, of course, for no other reason.

Together, and slowly, they made their way towards the towering bulk of Clifton Place.

Laurie was sitting in the kitchen, with Allsop, companionably polishing silver and talking, whilst outside the night pressed against the windows, held at bay only by one lamp and a couple of kitchen candles.

'If we sell the knives and forks . . .' Laurie was beginning, for the talk, as always, was of raising money, when Allsop cocked his head on one side and held up a hand for silence.

'It's your father, Mr Laurie,' he said after a moment, rising to his feet. 'He's trying to ring his bell.'

Already, in five short days Laurie had been amazed at the rapport between the two men. The butler had never said he despised his master, Sir George had never said that he had little regard for the older man, but Laurie was sure that each regarded the other with a fair degree of contempt. Yet old habits die hard; he, who should have felt at least a filial affection for Sir George, never heard the bell tinkle, the slurred, mumbling voice call. Allsop, who was held in little regard, could hear not only the voice, the bell, but frequently knew when Sir George was trying to ring or call, as though he could read his master's mind.

'I'll go, Mr Allsop,' Laurie said now, jumping to his feet. 'You go on with the silver. Shall I take anything up with me?'

'It's Allsop, Mr Laurie, just plain Allsop,' the butler said reprovingly. 'Well, if you're sure, I can't say I relish doing the stairs yet again this evening. Don't forget, all the medicines are on the small table by the door including the brandy, so you've no need to carry anything up. And it's just a drop on a teaspoon if he demands spirits.'

'Right,' Laurie said, realising even as he said the word that he would not know what his father was demanding but determined to do his bit for once. Because apart from doing what he could to help the butler and to keep his father company, he had done very little. The doctor came daily, Mr Allsop and Mrs Waughman between them did most of the nursing and Laurie mooched about the house, helped the overtaxed general handyman to look after Sir George's two remaining mounts, and sat with his unresponsive parent for long hours at a time. 'Shan't be a tick, then.'

Mr Allsop nodded and reached for the salad servers; Laurie took a candle off the kitchen mantelpiece and went out of the room, along the passage, passing a great number of doors on the way, and into the main hallway. He crossed the tesselated floor and mounted the stairs two at a time, reaching his father's lamplit room – a tower room, like his own, only on the other side of the building – just as Sir George managed to knock the bell he had been trying to ring onto the floor.

'It's all right, Father, I'm here,' Laurie said, standing his candlestick down and bending to pick up the bell, at the same time touching his father's hand reassuringly. The doctor assured them that Sir George heard every word and understood every word too, but Laurie could not tell whether this was so or not and thought a touch must be comforting. 'It isn't time for your medicine – or did you want the chamber pot?'

He hoped devoutly that his father wanted no such thing, since he knew very well that he could not possibly do whatever Allsop did on those lines, but Sir George shook his head impatiently and gestured crossly, making a quite distinct noise which was almost a word.

'Irewess,' he said. 'Wanna ireless.'

'A drink?' Laurie said at random. 'Would you like some beef tea, Father? Or some of Mrs Waughman's lemon barley water?'

His father's eyes bulged and the thick, untidy eyebrows drew close over the huge, bulbous nose.

'Ge' Allsop, idiot,' he said with astonishing clarity. 'Ge' *Missa* Allsop.'

It was the *mister* that did it; the implication, even from this sick man, that he, Laurie, was somehow inferior, a peasant. Laurie smiled at his father with all the sweetness at his command and sat down on the end of the bed.

'No, Father, I'm afraid Allsop's busy; you'll have to make do with me,' he said. 'Now speak slowly and carefully and I'm sure I'll manage to make out what you're trying to say.'

It was probably cruel, but he felt better for having said it, and oddly enough, after one strangled snort of rage and frustration, his father almost smiled. At least, the expression which crossed his mottled face was rather more pleasant than any Laurie had seen on it for five days.

'Ri,' his father said. 'Lissen, boy. Wanna ireless set. Wanna ire . . .'

'Got you, sir,' Laurie said at once. He was not a cruel person and this time, because Sir George had not been in a rage at his own slowness, the words were clearer. 'You want a wireless set. There's one in the kitchen but the batteries are rather low; is there another set anywhere?'

Sir George had sat forward when he spoke and now he leaned back against his pillows, obviously considering.

'Mm, mm, mm . . . 'tudy,' he said at last. 'Set in 'tudy.'

'In your study? Right. I'll fetch it up. Anything else, sir?'

His father actually grinned; lopsidedly, but it was a real grin. 'Sma' branny.'

'Right.' Laurie got off the bed, measured a small amount of brandy into a glass and held it for his father, who sipped it awkwardly, clearly finding it difficult to drink when only one side of his mouth would obey his commands. 'I'll be back in a minute, sir.'

He picked up his candlestick and made his way downstairs, going at once to his father's study. Though he had had little opportunity to explore the house he had decided that he must learn the whereabouts of all the principal rooms and was able to go straight to the leathery, tobacco-scented, brandy-reeking room. He had already scanned the walls – photographs, in silver frames, of his father at various high points of his life, though no wedding photograph – the furniture – leather-topped desk, one revolving chair and one carver, a small drinks cabinet, bookshelves – and the carpet and curtains – turkey patterned former, balding velvet latter, but now, by the wavering light of his candle, he looked more closely and discovered a heavy, walnut-fronted wireless set on top of one bookcase. Damn, it was a big, heavy thing, he'd need Allsop at the very least to help get it up the stairs and into his father's room.

It was at this point that Laurie saw the ghost.

He had been holding his candle high, scanning the room, ignoring the long windows which, in daylight, would have shown the side garden, or rather the multitudinous weeds and brambles which now constituted the side garden. But having found the wireless set he stood his candle on the desk and went towards the bookcase, which was on the same wall as the two mullioned windows. And saw, swimming uneasily towards him, a small, white face framed in what looked, at first glance, like a number of thin but lively snakes and flanked by another face . . . a two-headed ghost!

Laurie uttered a faint squawk and stepped backwards, cannoning heavily into what he had thought of as the visitor's chair, a solid oak and leather carver which hacked him in the ankles as painfully as it could. And the weird, wavering face was split by a ghoulish grin, the snakes writhed . . . and it was – good God, the snake-woman was Foxy and her companion was John!

Relief, embarrassment, sheer joy . . . they all battled for first place as Laurie recognised the other two and strode across to the long window. It opened after a sharp struggle – Laurie did not intend to be beaten by a mere window – and he gestured the other two forward, for they had slunk back into darkness as soon as he began to tussle with the pane.

'John, Foxy, just you come in here! Whatever are you doing? Haven't you heard of doors, or knockers? Oh God, I'm so bloody glad to see you I could bloody weep! Can you climb in? I know there's a side door but . . . oh great . . . come on, Foxy dear love, over the sill with you!'

He and John between them bundled Foxy over the sill despite her hissed protests that she was quite capable, thank you . . . ow, that hurt, you silly fool . . . and a minute later the three of them stood in the dim, candlelit room, ruefully regarding one another. Laurie was the first to speak.

'Well, who's going to explain this midnight visit? You damned nearly gave me a heart attack, incidentally, putting your ugly mugs up against the glass like that. I thought, for one horrible moment, that you were family ghosts, out to get me.'

'We might as well be ghosts for all the notice you've taken of us since you left,' John pointed out. 'Mum and Dad are worried, though they try not to let on. And Foxy and I phoned and phoned . . . why didn't someone answer, even if you weren't around?'

'Umm . . . it's been cut off,' Laurie mumbled. 'A – a misunderstanding, I believe.'

'Oh! So you can't make calls either, I suppose?'

'That's right. Look, John, tell Mum and Uncle that I'm most terribly sorry, but something's happened. My – Sir George – he's had a stroke. I'm not much of a nurse but I'm doing my best with – with what help I can get from the – the servants. Only as you can imagine I'm in a bit of a pickle one way and another. He can't speak very well and when he does speak I don't always understand him so I'm still not absolutely sure why he wants me to live here. And I can't come home whilst he's like this, it would be a pretty shabby thing to do.'

'Jesus! I'm sorry, Lo,' John said, looking as uncomfortable as he probably felt, Laurie thought. 'You should get hold of a real nurse, though, shouldn't you? Only everyone's too busy at hop-picking to do much else.'

'The doctor said he'd be on his feet again in less than a month; well, that was what he said at first,' Laurie said. 'He comes in each day though, and he did say, this morning, that he hoped it would be a lesson to the patient to take his medication and that it was only by the grace of God that he hadn't killed himself.'

'What did your father say?'

Foxy was eyeing Laurie with open curiosity. It was plain she was remembering the scene in the farmhouse kitchen, Laurie thought ruefully. No use pretending that his father had accepted a criticism so total with meekness!

'I think he said that the doctor was a silly old bugger who couldn't cure a cow with croup,' Laurie admitted, with the beginnings of a grin. He had not understood the furious, garbled shouts at the time but Allsop had translated for him once they had left the bedroom and anyway, Laurie had got the gist of the meaning from his father's red-faced, pop-eyed countenance. 'He really hates being crossed, even though he's still quite ill.'

'I can imagine,' John said drily. 'What were you doing in here, anyway? You looked as if you were searching for something – *not* buried treasure, old feller?'

Laurie grinned again, but agreed that buried treasure, of late, had not been much on his mind.

'It was the wireless set,' he explained. 'Sir George wants it, I was just wondering how the devil I was going to get it all upstairs when your faces appeared at the window. Well now, here's a thought! John and I can carry the set and the batteries if you can manage the accumulators, Foxy. I'll take the stuff into the room in three lots, it's just the stairs that I need help with.'

'Yes; I don't think he ought to see me,' John said thoughtfully. 'I can't imagine it would exactly aid his recovery. Still, we can carry the set easily enough – if you can't manage the accumulators, Foxy, one of us will run down and fetch them up.'

'I can,' Foxy said stoutly. 'Disconnect them and I'll go first, then if I flag one of you can give me a hand.'

So thus it was that the three of them, heavily laden, mounted the smooth, shallow curve of the staircase with their various burdens. Then, at Laurie's whispered instructions, John withdrew into the shadows outside Sir George's bedroom door whilst Foxy flung it wide so that Laurie and the wireless set could enter.

'He'll think you're a maid; he's the sort of man who never actually looks at servants,' Laurie assured her. 'He won't have looked at you the other evening, either. He'll just have thought you a farm worker of some description.'

'I am,' Foxy said stoutly. 'I'll look as like a maid as I can, but your beastly bicycle chain has oiled my legs rather.'

Laurie grinned. 'The old boy won't notice your legs, maid! Come on, then. You open the door.'

The door creaked open and Laurie, with the set in his arms, marched in. He put it down on the small table, pushing aside the medicine bottles in order to do so, and pulled it nearer the bed so that his father could reach the knobs.

'There you are; I'll just get the accumulators and plug everything in, then you can listen to – well, to whatever's on, I suppose.'

From the bed, Sir George's bloodshot eyes swivelled across the set. He mumbled something, but Laurie, heading back to the hall for the accumulators, did not catch what it was, and when he returned his father was lying with his eyes shut, either dozing or simply resting.

Laurie found the Home Service, which was relaying a classical music concert from somewhere, turned the volume down and put his father's small brass bell within reach. He carried the glass of cloudy barley water over to the bedside and checked that all was as it should be. Then he spoke softly: 'All right, Father? Nothing else you want? Then I'll leave you.'

He crossed the room, opened the door, which Foxy had tactfully shut behind him, then glanced back. The face on the pillow had not changed, the eyes remained shut, the line of the mouth grim, down-turned. But the heavy, blunt-fingered hand on the top sheet was, very slowly, tapping out the melody. Laurie nodded to himself, then left the room, pulling the door to behind him.

Outside, his friends still lurked; John looking guilty, as though his mere presence here was some sort of sin.

'Come to my room for a bit,' Laurie said, not quite knowing what else to say. 'You've not met Allsop, but I'd rather you came more openly to meet him for the first time; he's a stickler, is Allsop.'

'Allsop?' That was Foxy, wide, sherry-brown eyes enquiring. She looked more interested than guilty, Laurie realised thankfully, but of course she had no one's unspoken disappointment to contend with. She did as she liked, did Foxy.

'Yes, Allsop. He's my father's butler. He's an awfully decent chap and knows no end about the Clifton family. He can handle my – my father, too, which is more than I can. Look, this next door is my room; I'll leave you there whilst I just go down and tell Allsop I'm going to bed, then I'll be straight back.' He began to open the door to the Chinese room, then paused and glanced at his friends. 'There's a bottle of fruit squash in the small cabinet by my bed and a tooth-glass somewhere near the handbasin, if you're thirsty. I'll be as quick as I can, but Allsop's bound to ask what Father wanted that took me such an age.'

'Don't be too long, Lo; we've got eight miles or so to cycle when we leave here,' John said. 'And we've not had anything to eat, either. I don't want to miss the chip shop.'

'I'll get you food,' Laurie said eagerly. All at once he realised that he did not want them to leave at all, he was enjoying their company tremendously. It was such a relief to have John near . . . and Foxy was a love, he thought her a pretty and delightful kid. 'Will bread and cheese do? There's probably other things but I'm not sure what I can nick without Mrs Waughman noticing. She's the cook.'

'Gosh,' Foxy said, awed. 'A cook, a maid, a butler . . . bet you don't know you're born, Laurie.'

Laurie threw the door wide and gestured them inside. 'Take a look,' he said. 'Oh . . . I'll just light a candle or two, then I really must go.'

He walked over to the mantelpiece and lit two candles, handed a candlestick to each of his guests and left the room. Halfway down the stairs it occurred to him that he really should have sufficient faith in Allsop by this time to know that the older man would have taken John and Foxy in his stride, would probably have invited them into the kitchen for a bite of supper.

But it was too late now, he had decided how he would behave and for the time being he would go along with the fiction that he was happy with his father, and that he was going to stay at Clifton Place for the rest of his life. But sooner or later, he would confide in Allsop and explain that he had to go home, to Bees-wing Farm and the Hovertons. He was sorry for Sir George, but damn it, the man had virtually ignored him for years, he did not deserve the sort of consideration which he had impatiently denied to the Hovertons. As soon as the old man's fit again, I'll go back to Bees-wing, he promised himself. I'll make my peace with Uncle and tell them how awful it is here and we'll be comfortable together once more. Uncle won't send me away, not when I tell him what's been going on.

Immensely cheered by the thought, he hurried on down the rest of the flight.

'Jeepers, what a place!' John held his candle up and watched the shadow of the great bed dance around the room, the long curtains move in the breeze from a half-opened window. 'What d'you think, Foxy?'

'It's grand, like a museum, but not a bit like someone's bedroom,' Foxy said slowly. She, too, looked slowly around the shadowy room. There seemed to be quite a lot of furniture just standing around, not seeming to fit in with its surroundings at all. It was probably elegant and beautiful furniture, she could not really see it clearly by candlelight, but it definitely did not look as though it belonged. 'Tell you what, John. I wouldn't sleep in here for a fortune.'

'Why ever not?' John reached out and took the hand that wasn't clinging grimly to the candlestick. 'Scared of ghosts? Or Laurie?'

Foxy sighed and shook her head reprovingly. 'Why should I be scared of either? It's – it's just that it's so big and shadowy and – and different. And those doors!' she shuddered briefly. 'They give me the creeps. Where do they lead, d'you suppose?'

'Well, not to dungeons, because we're on the first floor. But actually, I do agree: it isn't exactly cosy. Poor old Lo, sleeping in that creepy, Edgar Allan Poe bed night after night! I'd keep imagining that a vampire was lying across the canopy, just waiting for me to drop off so he could drop off – and suck me dry whilst I slept.'

'John, you have a vile mind,' Foxy said roundly, trying to back even further away from the yellow silk bed. 'Shall we go home, now? I've just realised I'm not hungry at all, not even a little bit.'

'Let's take a look in here,' John said. He opened the nearest door and grinned as Foxy squeaked and retreated nearer to the door through which they had entered the room. 'Gosh, don't you want to see the mouldering skeleton or the bats? No, stoopid, I'm just kidding, it's all right really, it's only a bathroom. With a lav, too, if you'd like a free pee.'

'Are there spiders?' Foxy quavered, inching closer. She held her candle up and peered. 'Well, that's smart! Fancy Laurie having a whole bath to himself, to say nothing of the handbasin, and a lovely blue and white lavvy!'

'Told you,' John said complacently. 'I suppose the aristocracy like to stay in their own rooms . . . no, their own suite of rooms, rather than having to prowl down the corridor like the rest of us. Or I suppose they could use jerries with a coat of arms on the side, and get the skivvies to empty them,' he added thoughtfully.

'This is nice,' Foxy said approvingly. She and her candle had gone right into the bathroom and now she crossed to the handbasin and ran one of the taps, splashing a hand under the stream. Then she sat on the lavatory, running an approving hand round the mahogany seat first. John laughed and she glared at him, jumping to her feet. 'I'm just testing it for feel, you fool! I wouldn't *use* it; that would be rude. I say, I really am thirsty; what did Lo say about a bottle of fruit squash?'

'Oh . . . in the cabinet by his bed, which must mean that nasty great cupboard thing,' John said, opening the large, ebony bedside cabinet. 'No, there's nothing in here but dust. Why don't we try the other door?'

'I don't think we ought; suppose it leads to someone else's room and they're in bed?' Foxy said uneasily. 'Oh, John, don't . . .'

'It is another bedroom,' John said, having ignored her strictures and opened the remaining door. 'There's a little bed, just a single, and a couple of chairs which look quite comfy, and a lovely roll-top desk. And there's pictures – do come and look, old girl.'

'I like this room,' Foxy said presently, as they explored. 'It's small and cosy and – and friendly, somehow. That other room . . .' she shivered, clutching her arms as though she were cold, though it was a warm night, '. . . it gave me the creeps, no kidding. I say, if I were Laurie I'd sleep in here.'

'I think he does,' John said. He had opened the small cherry-wood bedside cabinet and extracted a glass and a bottle of squash from its depths. 'He didn't think to tell us, but it's obvious now. I suppose he uses the big room to sit in, or for his painting, like a studio or a study.'

'If he does, he's got sense,' Foxy said. She sat down in one of the chairs and stretched her feet out towards the imaginary warmth of a fire. 'It would be all right in winter, to have a fire in your room. Was there a fireplace in there?' She pointed to the door which led back into the Chinese room.

'Course. A huge one. And a damned great oil painting of some old misery above the mantel,' John confirmed. 'Want first slurp?'

'Aren't there two glasses? No, of course, there wouldn't be. Yes, all right, I'll have first go, because I'm still dreadfully thirsty. I say, John, wouldn't you love to see the rest of this place? Not taken round by horrible old Sir G or a servant, but just left to explore on your own? I bet you could play a wonderful game of sardines here.'

'What was that song about the old oak chest?' John said, heading for the bathroom. He ran water into the fruit squash, then returned and handed it to Foxy with a deep and mocking bow. 'Milady's champagne! Don't sip, get it down you, I want a go next.'

'The mistletoe bough, you mean,' Foxy said, handing him back the empty glass and wiping her mouth with the back of her hand. 'That story of the girl who plays hide and seek and then can't lift the lid of the chest . . . oh John, how could you? We've got to cycle miles through the dark, remember, and you won't like it much if I keep clutching you!'

'We neither of us mind the dark, not outside,' John said, returning to the bathroom and raising his voice to a shout. 'It's just . . .'

He stopped speaking.

'What? What were you going to say, John?' Foxy asked. 'Don't just stop in mid-sentence or you'll make me scared to leave this room! John?'

Silence. From here Foxy could hear the tap running clearly. But nothing else, not the splash of a glass being filled nor the sound of John's footsteps as he returned to her across the Chinese room.

'John? Don't fool about . . . John?'

The candlestick stood on the bedside cabinet and Foxy stood up suddenly, making the flame swirl and dip, and grabbed it. Her heart was beating so hard that when she glanced down she could see her breast leaping to its rhythm. She held the candlestick up so that the light fell through the open doorway into the Chinese room and began, slowly and tremblingly, to move across the room after it.

In the doorway she paused; a breeze, cold and sharp, made the candle flame waver and lean sideways just as a shadow lurched towards her, the draught of its coming almost extinguishing her candle's flame so that for a moment she could see nothing. And then a body brushed against her. Hands, wet and chilly, gripped her upper arms painfully hard for one moment, then were abruptly withdrawn as John spoke almost in her ear.

'Sorry, old girl, a draught blew my bloody candle out,' he said. 'Yours almost went as well, but I see it's recovering.' He held his smoking but flameless candle next to hers until the wick caught. 'The bathroom door must have swung shut behind me so I couldn't see a blasted thing until I got it open and saw your light flickering away. I hope Lo isn't going to be long, though. I'm devilish hungry and as you said, we've a long way to cycle.'

'John, you gave me such a scare . . .' Foxy was beginning when the far door opened. Laurie's head poked round it, a candle held high.

'You two okay? I've got some grub and another candle. We can sit on the bed and eat . . .'

'We really haven't time . . .'

'I'm really not hungry . . .'

The remarks burst from two throats simultaneously. Laurie looked from one to another and Foxy, at least, waited for him to ask what was up. But Laurie just opened the door wider and gestured them past him.

'All right, we'll eat downstairs, in the kitchen. Everyone's gone to bed, even Mr Allsop. Come along, there's the bread and cheese, some excellent pickled onions and plenty of milk – I could make us a cup of tea, the fire's still in.'

'Oh . . . well, we'd like to see the kitchen and have a bite, but we really mustn't be long,' John said as they descended the stairs. 'Lo, why don't you come back with us? You said yourself that you were no nurse and . . . and this isn't exactly a home from home, is it?'

'I can't,' Laurie said in a low voice. 'But it'll be Cambridge soon enough. The old man still wants me to go to university and I'm pretty keen to go, myself. What's more I'm hoping I'll be able to come back to Bees-wing for vacations.'

'Right. Thought it wouldn't hurt to ask,' John mumbled. 'Lead on, Macduff!'

Four

The impromptu meal in the kitchen at what proved to be after ten o'clock at night should have been fun, but somehow, though Foxy did her best, it wasn't. Laurie, she thought, was uneasy because he was afraid that someone would catch him entertaining friends of whom his father disapproved. But why on earth was John so – so prickly? He didn't laugh at Foxy's jokes, he didn't seem to listen whilst Laurie was telling them about Mr Allsop, the cook, the gardener's boy who had helped him when his father had had his attack. He kept looking at the door, then he would twist round in his seat and start to say something, and stop short. Foxy couldn't understand it, and she didn't like it, either. It was not at all like John, who was normally even-tempered, sensible and above all, kind.

But when at last she asked him if anything was the matter he just stared at her for a couple of seconds and then said, 'We're going to be most awfully late, that's what. And I don't want to lie to my parents because I never have, but if I tell them where we've been there's bound to be bad feeling.'

'We'll say the film finished late; or I'll say I had a puncture,' Foxy said cheerfully. She had no particular aversion to telling a lie, particularly if it saved trouble. 'You won't have to speak at all if you'd rather not, I'll start talking the moment we step over the threshold.'

'Mum and Uncle will be in bed, most likely,' Laurie said. 'Damn it, John, you're a bloke and taking a girl to the flicks, not five years old and coming home from someone's birthday party! Besides, why shouldn't you visit me? We've known one another all our lives, surely that counts for something?'

'Ye-es, and I know Dad never bears a grudge, but he was hurt, Laurie, because you didn't get in touch, tell us what was happening. I did suggest I might phone or call, and he almost bit my head off. Said you were a young man and could make your own decisions and if you'd decided to steer clear of us then that was your business. So if I say we've been here he'll make me feel – oh, disloyal, I suppose.'

'Oh, dear Lord, what a mess,' Laurie said, clearly dismayed by John's words. 'I never would have hurt or upset Uncle – do you think you could explain, John, about the old man's seizure, or stroke, or whatever? Only I'd hate Uncle and Mum to believe ill of me.'

'We might as well be hung for a sheep as for a lamb,' Foxy said, when John did not reply but continued to look dubious. 'I know you don't like to lie to your parents, John, but it is in such a good cause, so why don't I say we met Laurie at the flicks, and he told us about his father? Isn't that a good idea?'

'No, because it would seem pretty bad to go to the flicks whilst my father was at home, ill or maybe dying,' Laurie put in. 'If only I'd written a letter! But I didn't have a stamp and besides I was so sure I'd get away, be able to tell you myself what was happening . . . look, if I write a note now, could you take it? I'll address it to the whole family and you can tear it open and then hand the sheet inside to Mum. Would that do?'

'Better than nothing, I suppose,' John said after the silence had begun to lengthen embarrassingly. 'But make it quick, Lo; we haven't got all night.'

'Thanks, John,' Laurie said gratefully. 'I'll not be a moment.'

He left the kitchen to reappear a few minutes later with an envelope and a sheet of paper in his hand. He waved the paper at them both, then folded it and stuck it in the envelope, licking the flap down and stamping his fist firmly on it.

'There! I've explained, begged them to let you come over if only for an hour or two, and said I'll visit just as soon as the old man's fit to be left. Will that do the trick, d'you think?'

'Hopefully,' John said. He took the letter, stuck it in his trouser pocket, and caught Foxy's hand. 'C'mon, kid, let's start out. We'll be picking hops at the crack of dawn tomorrow.'

'Wish I was coming with you,' Laurie said wistfully, following them across the starlit yard. 'Where are the bikes?'

'Down the drive a piece; leaning against a tree,' Foxy said. 'Oh Lo, it's horrible leaving you here. Do take care of yourself and come and see us soon!'

'It's horrible being left,' Laurie admitted. 'I feel like begging a seater from you and damn the old man! But I have to stay, you know I do. Here, Foxy, let me hold the bike while you mount, I don't want my precious Raleigh scraped.'

He held the bicycle, Foxy mounted, wobbled a bit and was away, riding down the drive close to John. She turned and waved once, then began to pedal in earnest as John began to draw easily ahead.

'John, wait,' she panted. 'Don't race, I'm too tired, though I'm as keen to get home as you are.'

John sighed but slowed. 'Right. But try to keep up, Foxy. I have a feeling my parents are waiting for us and if I'm right we're going to have to do some pretty nifty explaining!'

Laurie watched the two figures until they were out of sight, then turned reluctantly back towards the house once more. It had been so good to see them again. And Foxy had understood, her eyes had softened when she looked at him. He did like Foxy; not that it was any use his liking her. John was clearly smitten, had always been fond of her. John likes looking after people, and he's never forgotten the little lost kid in the hopyard, Laurie told himself. Dear old John, he'd scarcely noticed as Foxy's self-confidence and aggression grew. To John, Laurie was sure, she was still the little lost kid – though with certain obvious additional attractions, of course.

But now he thought, John had not been quite the fellow he knew and loved; he had been strange, almost unfriendly. Not at first, at first he had been his old self, but after . . . damn it, after he had left them in the Chinese room for twenty minutes or so it had seemed as though John could not wait to get away again. Was it because he sensed that Laurie's friendship for Foxy was beginning to change, as his own friendship had changed? Or was it something else? Could it possibly be the Chinese room itself?

The Chinese room. Had they stayed in there? Fool that he was, it had not occurred to him to tell them to go through into the dressing room which he thought of, now, as his bedroom. He had never slept in the state bed but always in the small single one in the dressing room. He continued to use the Chinese room, painting at a table in the window, reading in a chair similarly placed so that he could see the glorious view over the park whenever he glanced up. But he always tried to avoid walking too near the bed, even on the sunniest day. It was not imagination, he was sure of it, now. Sadness, fear, too, emanated from that bed.

But Foxy had been fine, her usual self. And girls were supposed to be more susceptible to atmosphere than fellows. He frowned over it, trying to remember what had been said. Remarkably little, now that he thought about it. He had not asked his friends their opinion of the rooms and they had not vouchsafed such a thing. But they had found the fruit squash and drunk some, which meant that they had realised he slept in the dressing room and that they had found and used the water out of the bathroom. No, he couldn't blame the room, or the bed rather, for John's coolness. It must be that he was more deeply entangled with Foxy than Laurie had supposed; keep off the grass, in other words.

At this point he re-entered the house, took his candle from the hall table and climbed the stairs. He crossed the starlit landing and opened the door of the Chinese room. It was weird how the room itself seemed to welcome him, so long as he did not actually go too near the bed. But he walked steadily, not looking around him, ignoring shadows, flickerings, the soft sibilance of the silken bed-curtains moving as though in a breeze, though the windows were all shut.

He went straight to the bathroom and shut the door, then stood his candle on the shelf above the handbasin. He washed, changed into his pyjamas, cleaned his teeth, brushed his hair, filled a glass with water and reclaimed his candle. He shielded it with his hand as he slipped out of the bathroom door, across a couple of feet of the bare boards, and into the dressing room. Once there he shut the door firmly, put his candle on the bedside cabinet, got into bed and said his prayers.

Here, in the narrow bed in this cosy, ordinary little room, Laurie felt safe. He could not hear the old man's shouts or his tinkling bell and in any case Allsop had said from the first that he would be personally responsible for Sir George's well-being during the hours of darkness, so Laurie did not try to listen. Instead, he recruited his strength for the day ahead with total abandonment to sleep.

And despite his worries over what had made John curt, almost unfriendly towards him, whether it had been the way he himself had looked at Foxy or, indeed, the way she had looked at him, he felt better than he had done since leaving Bees-wing Farm. They had come to visit him and would come again; he was no longer quite so completely alone. For a few minutes he ran over the letter he had written in his mind, but then weariness overcame him. He slept.

'Why were you so cross, John?'

Foxy's voice was low, pensive, but John knew her of old. There was no more persistent girl on the face of the earth than Foxy Lockett when she had the bit between her teeth. He might deny crossness, feign ignorance, but she would nag and nag and nag . . .

'Oh, Foxy, don't start! I wasn't cross, exactly.'

'You were quite horrid to Laurie. You know you were. And it isn't like you.'

In the windy darkness, pedalling steadily, their bicycles eating up the miles, John grinned to himself. She was a dear, was Foxy Lockett. He had always liked her but now he realised she was desirable, as well. She pretended to be hard-nosed, tough, but underneath she did try to think of others, hence the rider: *and it isn't like you*. He knew she was right, too, knew that in the normal course of events he would never have let Laurie know that the Hovertons were truly upset over his behaviour. So why had he done it? Because he had been thoroughly disturbed by what had happened in that wretched Chinese room where Laurie did not sleep? He supposed, grudgingly, that it had been that. All he had wanted to do was flee from the place, but Foxy must not be terrified for no real cause and anyway, it was stupid. Imagination. Yet all he had wanted to do in the kitchen was to rush out into the night, slamming the door of Clifton Place behind him, preferably for ever.

'John? What happened in the Chinese room?'

There, she had said it, and now, John thought, he would have to tell her. Because it had been nothing, not really.

'Nothing. Not really. Only my candle went out.'

'Yes, you said. When you were running water. You grabbed me. Your hands were cold and wet.'

'That's right. Sorry if I scared you, but the candle going out gave me a bit of a scare too, to tell you the truth. It wasn't as if it was draughty . . . well, I suppose it must have been, but I hadn't noticed it till then. I was shielding it with my hand and next thing I knew, puff, and it had gone.'

'I saw a sort of shadow,' Foxy said pensively. 'Near that horrible old bed. And there was a draught; I felt it. It made goose-bumps all over my arms.'

'Yes, I know. Too much imagination, that's what was wrong with us. But it was a bit like being in a museum when all the people have gone home, wasn't it? And that bed – well, it was all shadows. I kept thinking that there was someone hiding . . . but I knew it was just imagination, of course.'

'Yup,' Foxy said cheerfully. 'Or ghosts.'

'Ghosts! Honestly, Foxy, we don't believe in ghosts, we've said so a thousand times!'

'I know. But when I was in that room, near that bed, I could kind of feel unhappiness. Perhaps it was Laurie's, I don't know, but it was there, John, and I believe you felt it too. So aren't I just glad it's Laurie who's going to be the heir to all that! Oh, isn't it wonderful that it's not you or me?'

There was a short silence whilst they turned, at last, into the lane which led to the farm. Then John said: 'Poor old Lo though, Foxy.'

'Yes, poor old Lo. But if he really hated it, if he sensed whatever it was like we did, he could change his room. I mean there are dozens of rooms, he said so, and only the servants, who live upstairs in the attics, and Sir George and Laurie himself, in the whole place.'

John was starting to reply when suddenly Foxy swerved and their front wheels grazed for a second, making both machines wobble uncertainly.

'Oh John, look at that! Now we're for it!'

'What's up?' John said, putting out a hand to right her bicycle and pulling them both to a halt. 'I'm not a bloody owl, girl, I can't see where you're pointing!'

'Lights! There's lights in the farmhouse! Oh damn, damn, damn, now we're going to have to think fast!'

When Auntie Bea shook her niece's shoulder next morning Foxy was so tired that she tried to turn over and go back to sleep, but Auntie Bea was having none of it.

'You was out gadding till the small hours, now you'll suffer for it,' she said grimly. 'There's still 'ops to pick, Foxy, an' you're going to pick 'em. Come on, get out o' them blankets.'

Foxy sat up and glanced towards the doorway. The curtain was pulled back and she could see a milky mist slowly rising from the ground, a man, wading through it as though it were really milk, a child making the mist swirl as he stirred vigorously at it with his arms flailing like windmills. The sky overhead was colourless, but if she craned her neck she could see, faintly, the palest blue. It was going to be a fine day.

'Come on, gel, don't just sit there staring out o' the doorway like an eejit! Get yourself moving afore I gi' you a clunk round your lug.'

'I'm still half asleep, Auntie Bea,' Foxy protested. 'Did you know about Mr Hoverton?'

'What about him? Did he give young John a telling off for keeping you so late?' Bea chuckled. 'Thought he might, though the lad's the apple of his eye. And what did the boy say to that? Did 'e flare up, tell 'is old feller where to get off?'

'No, you've got it all wrong. When we got back to the farm last night the doctor was there. Mr Hoverton had had a bad fall; he'd been up on the stilts, taking a look at the topmost bines, when he came over dizzy like, and fell. Mrs H sent for the doctor and he got the ambulance; they wanted to take him to hospital in Gloucester but he wouldn't go till John got home. So of course everyone was fed up with us . . . and we didn't mean to tell anyone where we'd been, but after the ambulance had taken Mr Hoverton off to hospital John went and blurted it out. Still, at least his mother was the only one who heard.'

'Where 'ad you been?' Bea said curiously. 'Look, I'll mek the breakfast for you today, though it's your job be rights. You get yourself out o' that bed an' tell me about last night at the same time.'

Foxy thanked her aunt and began to explain to Bea just what had happened after they reached the farm. And what a night it had been, now she looked back on it! It had been a nerve-racking experience just walking into the kitchen, nervous and ill-at-ease, to see Mr Hoverton lying on what looked like a door, with his legs strapped to it and his normally ruddy face grey with pain.

'At last! John, they're tekin' me into Hereford, to the big hospital, not to Ledbury. Now here's what you'll have to do . . .'

The list of instructions which followed had been carefully thought out but Foxy, listening, could not imagine that John was taking it all in. So many different things to do! Sheep to be dipped against various ailments before winter set in, apples to be picked, packed and despatched, the herd of Hereford cattle to be milked, fed and watered. And the hops! The rate now being paid, what might be paid in the coming weeks, especially if the weather should change, how to check the hops early each morning for any sign of disease, from red spider to the dreaded downy mildew, the weighing of the hops, the temperature in the drying chambers, the buyers who would be coming round . . . the list seemed endless and endlessly complex to Foxy.

'The men know about most of this,' Bill Hoverton was saying, his voice grown husky and breathless, clutching his side where what might possibly be a broken rib or two stabbed him when he spoke. 'Dan's a first-rate worker and he's been with us years, so's Elias . . . Harry. But they've never worked for themselves, they've always waited to be told how, when, where. That's your job for a few weeks, son. D'you think you can handle it?'

'I'm sure I can, Dad,' John said sturdily. 'They'll let me come into the hospital each evening, just to check with you that I'm doing it right, won't they? And the men won't let me down.'

'No, the men won't. I worry most about the bloody pickers,' Bill said fretfully. Foxy knew that Bill Hoverton prided himself on never swearing, and saw John's eyes widen with surprise. 'They're the ones who can make trouble if they choose. Let 'em see who's the boss, lad, don't let 'em get away with a thing. If you're soft with 'em they'll break you – never forget that.'

'I won't, Dad,' John said gently. 'But most of 'em are decent enough folk. When they see I'm managing alone they'll be as fair as they can and if they aren't, I'll see they regret it, not me. Now do let the ambulance people take you away. The sooner you're there the sooner you'll be back here again.'

'That's no more'n the truth, sir,' one of the ambulance men put in. 'You've got a nasty compound fracture there, the sooner it's treated the less time you'll spend on the ward. And time's money, especially in farming.'

'Aye. And specially at this time o' year, when we're harvesting hops,' Bill grunted. 'All right, we'd best get going,' he clicked his fingers. 'Ada! You'd best stay here, give the lad a hand wi' planning tomorrow. You'll come and visit me, first thing?'

It was gruffly said, but Foxy realised it was really a plea. Bill, a healthy man, had probably never been in hospital in his life and had no desire to go now. But since needs must he was making the best of it.

Ada stepped forward and took his hand, then bent and spoke to him. 'I'll be in first thing; I'll get a lift wi' the milk lorry,' she said. 'Just you get better, William, and don't worry about how we're going on. Our John's got a good head on his shoulders and I know a thing or three. Goodnight, William, love. They'll tek good care o' you for us.'

'Goodnight, my dear. John will take care of things whilst I'm . . .'

But the ambulance men had grown tired of waiting. One seized the front of the door, the other the rear, and they whisked Bill out to the waiting ambulance.

'So you see, no one would have asked us where we'd been,' Foxy ended as she ate the fat bacon sandwiched between two rounds of bread which Auntie Bea considered a good breakfast for someone about to start work. 'But when the ambulance had gone Mrs Hoverton looked at the pair of us, and tears came to her eyes. "I just wish Laurie were here to help out," she said, and John said, "Laurie's got troubles of his own, Mum. Sir George has had a stroke. He'll be laid up for a good while and Laurie's playing nurse."

' "My! So that's where you were, you young varmints!" Mrs Hoverton said. "Ah well, no harm done, then. I'd begun to wonder . . ." and she looked very hard at me, Auntie Bea, though I really don't know why, and then sort of shrugged and changed the subject.'

'She'll 'ave been wondering whether the pair of you'd done something foolish, something you'd be ashamed to talk about,' Auntie Bea said placidly. 'I would, an' all.'

'Like what? Going to the flicks?' Foxy asked, genuinely puzzled. 'It was a bit sneaky to go round to Clifton Place, but we were really worried, all of us. It isn't like Laurie not to get in touch, and Mr and Mrs Hoverton – well, they were hurt as well as worried, Auntie Bea. It was as if Laurie had gone back to his posh house and rich father and cast them off. He hadn't, of course, but that was how it seemed. So anyway, I don't know what Laurie had written in the note he sent but Mrs Hoverton read it, and then she had a little weep and John was wonderful, he put his arms round her and said: "There there, you mustn't cry, Mum, you should be glad Laurie didn't mean to upset you." Only she did cry, and then she pulled herself out of John's arms and said: "Bless me, whatever was I thinking of, I must make the pair of you a hot drink and a sandwich and then we must all go straight to bed, for like it or lump it, there are hops to be picked in the morning." '

'And back you came, and straight into your blanket, and snorin' fit to bust five minutes later,' Auntie Bea finished, standing up and beginning to collect the dirty crocks. 'Come on, we're already late, get that tea down you and let's go an' pick 'ops, like the missus said.'

Sir George was still confined to his room when Laurie was packing his possessions to leave for Cambridge, but he was a great deal better and Laurie had no compunction about leaving him. Allsop was a tower of strength and though he seemed well aware that Sir George was not an admirable man, he still held him in sufficient affection or respect, Laurie did not know which, to do his best for his irascible employer.

To Laurie's pleasure, Mr Allsop had arranged to have the telephone reconnected after Sir George was taken ill.

'A cheque arrived for barley which the estate sold to a firm of Scotch whisky manufacturers, I believe. The crop was of high quality, I remember Sir George remarking on it. So I sent the money on to Mr Hawkings, Mr Laurie, and he's going to see it's used for the benefit of the estate. I said I thought the telephone absolutely essential with Sir George ill, and he has agreed to pay the reconnection fee out of it.'

That was excellent news; not only did it mean the estate was in touch with the rest of the country, it enabled Laurie to ring John and his Mother and meant that they could ring him, too. He had been horrified to hear of Bill Hoverton's fall and had insisted on a rush visit to the hospital, though his reception there was a trifle cool. But he told John that he understood Uncle's feelings and by the time he left he felt that the breach had been healed, though he knew that Uncle was still very angry with Sir George.

And in the weeks since that first visit to the Place, Foxy had made a point of coming over and keeping Laurie company in the long, lonely evenings. She had been a tremendous help to John of course, throwing herself wholeheartedly into the business of farming, but Laurie really appreciated the way she somehow managed to find time to come and see him. She could only visit him after dark, when work in the hopyard was finished, but then she was a real little brick. She doggedly begged lifts, bicycled, once she had ridden on the back of Reggie Pilling's motorbike, she had even walked, and each time she came she spent at least half an hour with Laurie.

It was an enormous help. Together, they discussed most of the things which puzzled or worried Laurie, from the overgrown gardens to the dusty, neglected house. And they talked about other things, too. About their aspirations, what they wanted to do with their lives, the careers they would eventually follow. And Laurie watched Foxy's small, lively face and listened to her frank opinions, her good sense, and reminded himself constantly that this was John's girl, that to him Foxy must simply be the best friend a fellow could have.

'I don't know what I'd have done without her,' Laurie had told John the night before he began his packing. He had telephoned Bees-wing, as he did at least once a day, for a few words with John.

'The old boy's getting better every time I see him, and consequently more difficult, but Foxy takes my mind off him. He's still hell-bent on breaking this damned trust, incidentally, but Mr Hawkings says it's unbreakable. I can't get a penny of the money until I'm twenty-five, but Sir George just says he doesn't intend to wait years for what is rightfully his and keeps on and on at me.' He sighed deeply into the mouthpiece. 'It doesn't make our relationship any easier.'

'But it's not rightfully his,' John protested. 'It's yours, Lo. It was left to you, not to your old man.'

'I know. But it is quite complicated. I can't explain over the telephone, but next time we meet I'll have a go.'

Presently, having sent his love to Mum and Uncle, Laurie returned to his room and his packing. As he worked he wondered how he could possibly explain the trust to John, when he found it so hard to understand himself. He could remember his own puzzlement barely a week ago, sitting opposite Mr Hawkings in the former's study in Church Street, when his father's man of business, as Sir George always called him, began to try to tell Laurie about the trust and all that it meant.

'I don't know how much you know about your mother, so I shall start right at the beginning and you must stop me if I'm covering old ground,' he said. 'Your mother was Jennifer Tyrell, the only daughter of Frederick Tyrell, a yeoman farmer. They owned Cumber Farm . . . you'll know the place, I'm sure, since it is now the home farm for Clifton Place.'

'I didn't know any of that, it's all news to me, but nevertheless I don't see what it has to do with the trust,' Laurie said. 'If my mother was a farmer's daughter then she could scarcely have been rich. The trust must be at least £5,000, judging from what Sir George has said to me.'

'It is more than that, but if you'll just let me explain, Mr Laurie . . .'

'Sorry, of course I will. Do carry on.'

Mr Hawkings looked down at the top of the desk for a moment over the top of his pince-nez, and then continued.

'Your mother was twenty-four when she married Sir George; scarcely a young girl. As you say, farmer's daughters are not usually wealthy, but Frederick Tyrell was the eldest of a family of three boys. One of the boys moved to Gloucester and he and the family lost touch. Your grandfather worked the farm, and the other brother, Albert Tyrell, went into cider production. He became very successful indeed but never married, and when he died – he was only in his fifties – he left all his money to his elder brother, your grandfather, who, in his turn, left it to his only child, Jennifer.

'So the money's got nothing to do with my father? Nothing to do with the Clifton family, really. Only my mother died when I was ten days old, so I suppose Sir George took it for granted that he would inherit. Indeed, if she'd not thought of the trust the money would have gone to Sir George quite legally, wouldn't it?' He felt like adding, *Indeed, she scarcely knew me*, but that sounded ridiculous.

Mr Hawkings smiled.

'Lady Clifton was advised by me to put the money in trust for her son. Sadly, her father died and left her the money when she was expecting you and she was clearly not strong. She never had a chance to enjoy using so much as a penny piece of her inheritance.' Mr Hawkings glanced quickly at Laurie over his spectacles, then quickly away again. 'The fact is, Mr Laurie, that your father is – is not a good manager. He doesn't understand the value of forward planning, nor . . .'

'He squanders his chink,' Laurie said smoothly, earning a snort of amusement from the man opposite.

'Yes, indeed. Your mother knew it by this time, and wanted to see that you had some money of your own. She sent for me and between us we drew up the trust. I imagine that because she was herself twenty-five she chose that as a suitable age for you to inherit the money . . . twenty-one might seem more usual, but she already knew that Sir George might use his persuasive powers to – to – '

'To get the cash,' Laurie supplied.

'Exactly. Though she had no idea that Sir George would send you away to be brought up by the Hovertons. I believe she thought that, by the time you reached the age of twenty-five, you would be sufficiently conversant both with the – the weaknesses of your

113

father's character and with the running of the estate to use the money in the best way possible.'

'I see,' Laurie said slowly. 'But my father thinks the money is his by right, and wants me to break the trust so that he can use it.'

'Naturally Sir George would find the money useful. And you cannot break the trust. I know, I drew it up. You must tell him that the money cannot be reached and persuade him that it's possible to live very comfortably upon the rents, the incomings and the revenue from his stocks and shares. Tell me, how do you get along with your father?'

'I don't know him very well, and neither of us likes the other very much,' Laurie said truthfully. 'Sir George only saw me two or three times a year until deciding, less than a month ago, that he wanted me to move into Clifton Place with him. But to be frank, he doesn't care for me at all, it's plain he's only interested in breaking the trust.'

'I fear I guessed as much, which was why I asked you to come into Ledbury, to my office, rather than attending on you myself, up at the Place. Mr Laurie, we must work together to try to keep the estate solvent until you come into your trust money, and that means, to an extent, that we must – must try to keep Sir George's expenditure within bounds. Mr Allsop and I meet from time to time . . . we've had limited success only, I fear . . .'

'I'll do my best,' Laurie said uneasily. 'In a way, I wish my mother hadn't left me the money. It's brought me my father's enmity, which isn't making my life any easier, and I'm going to Cambridge in less than a week; hopefully, once I've got my degree, I'll be capable of making my own way in the world.'

'I'm sure, but the estate is in very poor shape,' Mr Hawkings murmured. 'Farms need repairs, cottages are falling down, farm machinery has been allowed to rot or rust away. I'm hoping – we're all hoping – that you'll do your best to set the place to rights when you inherit your mother's money.'

Laurie grinned. 'As a future owner of Clifton Place I have responsibilities, you mean,' he said. 'Oddly enough, I love it already, but I wish I'd known my mother. I don't even have a photograph; I don't believe Sir George does, either.'

'She was very like you to look at, as regards colouring,' Mr

Hawkings said. 'Haven't you seen the self-portrait?'

'Self-portrait? Of my mother? Do you mean she painted?'

'Yes, indeed. She was quite a considerable watercolourist. The self-portrait used to hang in the drawing room, but I suppose Sir George has taken it to his own room now. You might ask him . . . it's a first-rate likeness.'

'So she painted,' Laurie said slowly. 'I say, were her initials JAT? Because if so, I've been using her paint-box, amongst other things. I found it in my room, when I arrived.'

'That's right, Jennifer Tyrell; her middle name was Allen, which was her mother's maiden name; the Allens were a respected family locally and I imagine they wanted the name carried on. And yes, you might well find her paint-box in the house, and some of her paintings, though a good few were sold after her death. I daresay Sir George did not care for the reminder of his loss.'

Or they were worth a bit, Laurie thought uncharitably, but did not voice the thought aloud. Instead, he said, 'Suppose we just sort of *bent* the trust then, Mr Hawkings? You said there was quite a lot of money. Sir George has asked me for a thousand.'

'As I was saying, the trust cannot be broken, nor should you endeavour so to do,' Mr Hawkings said heavily. 'I can see I must be as frank as you have been, Mr Laurie. Money given, or lent, to Sir George would be money thrown down the drain. I have had the greatest difficulty in persuading him that he should not sell up half his possessions since they are part of the estate. Over and over I've told him that the scion of a noble house owns nothing, because he merely holds it, during his lifetime, in charge for his children and his children's children. Unfortunately, this is not an aspect of nobility which commends itself to your father. He has never had the pleasures of fatherhood nor its responsibilities, preferring to leave your upbringing to the Hovertons, so now he cannot see you as his successor but rather as someone whose mere existence denies him access to the money his wife willed elsewhere.'

'Oh!' Laurie said hollowly. 'What would happen were I to die before my twenty-fifth birthday then, sir?'

'Without issue? Then the money goes to the eldest of your second cousins. Your mother was determined that your father should not lay hands on any of it, not because she did not feel affection for him but simply because she knew he would squander it. Once you come of age, however, the money is yours to do with as you wish. It is my hope – and was your mother's, I'm sure – that you will spend at least some of it for the benefit of the estate.'

'Right,' Laurie said. 'Then if I was killed, there would be no advantage to my father in the fact.'

Mr Hawkings' eyebrows rose to where his hairline would have been had he not been balding. He stared incredulously at Laurie whilst Laurie, who had spoken without serious thought, felt his cheeks grow hot. Then he tutted.

'Really, Mr Laurie! But your death would benefit no one save that second cousin, wherever he may be, as things stand. Sir George will undoubtedly grow fond of you, and will speedily understand that trying to break the trust would help no one. With two of you working at it, indeed, I hope to see the Place brought back into profit long before your twenty-fifth birthday,' he said in a rather self-conscious tone. 'And now you must catch your bus, but if you need me, please telephone at once. I will do anything I can to help.'

'I will, and thank you for your frankness,' Laurie said.

He was grateful to Mr Hawkings for telling him about his mother and about the trust. He liked to think of her, painting away in the window of the Chinese room, if that was where she had painted. It seemed likely – the light was excellent there and it was quiet and comfortable.

Yet he had decided to change his room, because ever since John and Foxy had come visiting, he had been more conscious than ever of the great, yellow silk fourposter. He wasn't afraid of the sadness which emanated from it, but he found it disturbing. And why should I stay here, when there are a dozen or more rooms, equally large and equally comfortable? he asked himself. The bed in the dressing room is too small for comfort, I'd be better off painting in the Chinese room, but sleeping somewhere else.

'I don't want to continue sleeping in the Chinese room,' he told Allsop. 'I find it extremely depressing. What other rooms are available? And I want a suite, I've grown used to having my own bathroom.'

Allsop glanced shrewdly at him.

'You don't like the Chinese room? Nor I, Mr Laurie, I've not felt comfortable there since . . . well, for many years. But your father suggested it, possibly because he thought . . . but no matter. What do you think of the ivory room, then?'

'You aren't comfortable in there either? Why, Allsop? Is it haunted?'

Allsop shrugged. 'It's an old house, Mr Laurie. It wouldn't surprise me. Shall we take a look at the ivory room together?'

The ivory room had no dressing room but it was a pleasant, sunny room with a bathroom adjoining. It had cream-washed walls, several attractive watercolours of the estate as it had been some years earlier, and the same view as the Chinese room, since it overlooked the front of the house. Laurie loved it on sight, he loved the fact that if he leaned out of his casement he could look into the walled vegetable garden which he intended to make good as soon as he could, and could also see into the lane which separated the Place from the home farm. The home farm, or Cumber Farm as it was now called, had come back to the estate when Jennifer Tyrell had inherited it, but the present tenant was old, lazy and ill-tempered. When he snuffs it, Laurie thought, I'll take over that farm and earn some money by my own hard work. And once it's up and running I'll put a manager in and I'll be able to lean out of this window and check that he's not shirking.

So Laurie lugged all his favourite furniture through from his tiny dressing room. A comfortable double bed graced the ivory room and Laurie was happy to sleep in it, undisturbed by shadows, flickering or otherwise.

So Laurie packed in a glow of contentment. He was about to leave the house which, in a way, had felt more like a prison, though in recent weeks, with his father gradually improving and the relationship between himself and Allsop growing closer, he had begun to appreciate the beauties of house and estate. He was also about to plunge back into the world of other people his own age, with the added challenge of a whole new way of life to take up. And as it was growing dark there was a good chance that Foxy would turn up presently, to tell him all the news from Bees-wing Farm. She did not come every evening of course, but since tomorrow was his last day there seemed a good chance that she might arrive. He wished John might come too – he had done so a couple of times – but as the month drew to its close and the number of bines left to strip shrank, John grew busier and busier. What was more a week of rain, which had done Laurie's three new rose bushes the world of good, had held up the pickers so there was a rush now to get the hops off the bines before the month's end.

When the doorbell rang he guessed it would be Foxy, and knew his guess had been correct when he heard Allsop's deep, dignified tones and a girl's higher notes. He shut his case, picked up the clothes which needed attention and hurried from the room and along the upper landing, breaking into a run as he reached the stairs.

By now, Foxy and Allsop were on good terms, though Allsop had never said openly that he liked Laurie's young visitor. But that was not Allsop's way; he seldom voiced either approval or disapproval of anyone save the occasional servant, but his opinion was usually implicit in his actions. On Foxy's third visit Allsop had stalked majestically into the study bearing a tray of hot chocolate, a fruit cake and some shortbread and had used, moreover, the delicate Sèvres china. Now, after many such visits, he invited Foxy into the kitchen to drink her chocolate, and listened indulgently to her chatter.

So it was no surprise to Laurie to reach the bottom of the stairs in time to see Foxy and Allsop disappearing through the green baize door. He hurried after them and Foxy, hearing the baize door crash shut after him, turned, smiling.

'Laurie! Mr Allsop said you were packing so we were going to have a cup of tea whilst we waited for you to finish. Mrs Waughman is heating the irons to press some of your clothes, so we knew you'd be bringing them down.' She grinned wickedly at him. 'Want me to have a go with the iron? I'd have your trousers with dear little pleats from knee to ankle in no time.'

'I'm sure you would,' Laurie said as the three of them entered the kitchen together, Allsop holding the door for the younger couple. 'But I think we'll leave my ironing to Mrs Waughman if you don't mind.'

He had long ago discovered that Mrs Waughman was a trifle

simple, but she worked hard and well and though she was rather slow, she got through her work eventually. She and Allsop were the only resident staff members though from time to time giggling girls appeared to 'help out' as Allsop put it, and a variety of ladies, mostly well-whiskered and well-muscled, too, were to be seen scrubbing floors, shifting furniture, and attacking the rugs, hung on a line across the yard, with a strangely shaped instrument known simply as a carpet beater.

Mrs Waughman, standing at the ironing board, turned her blank face towards them and blinked a dozen or so times. It was the nearest she ever got to a smile but Laurie smiled back anyway.

'Did you hear that, Mrs W?' he said cheerfully. 'You iron magnificently, so I beg you to keep young Foxy here away from my clothes, she doesn't have your touch.'

'That's right, Mr Laurie,' the cook replied. 'Evenin', Miss Foxy.'

Foxy loved being called Miss and smiled at the cook. 'Evening, Mrs Waughman. I'll put the kettle on, shall I?'

'I'll do it,' Allsop said, bustling forward. 'Sir George will be wanting a cup of something presently. Why don't you go and show Miss your new rose bushes, Mr Laurie? You can take the stable-lantern and I'll have a snack put up by the time you get back.'

'Dismissed,' Laurie said with a laugh as he and Foxy strolled across the yard and out under the side arch which led, eventually, to the front of the house. 'I don't know if I mentioned it, but Mr Hawkings is paying me a small allowance from the estate so I splashed out with some of it and bought three rose bushes. It's a small start . . .'

'I think it's good of you to spend your own money on the place,' Foxy said. Laurie had told her about the trust and she disapproved deeply of Sir George's efforts to have the money for himself. Now, she slipped her hand into the crook of Laurie's elbow and tried to match her stride to his. 'Once you're twenty-five, though, and can use your inheritance, you'll have it beautiful in no time.' She laughed. 'Mr Allsop will see to that; he really does love Clifton Place.'

Laurie stared at her; in the faint, shifting lantern light her face looked elfin, a touch mischievous. His heart gave an uneven bump;

there was something very sweet about Foxy – John's girl. Hastily, he burst into speech. 'Does he? He's never said so . . . in fact I've often wondered why he stays here, because he doesn't like my father very much and I'm sure he wasn't paid for ages, though Mr Hawkings has the wages in his own hands now.'

'I'm sure it's because the Place is his home and he loves it,' Foxy assured him. 'He's a strange old fellow, though. I never quite know what he's thinking. Ah, I believe I can see your roses . . . hold the lantern a bit higher, would you? Yes, that's them . . . who did all the work? I say, you've even put horse-manure round the roots!'

'It's one thing we've plenty of,' Laurie told her. 'Actually, I wanted to dig the ground and put them in myself, but Hector would have been hurt. Allsop said so. He said Hector had been here a thousand years and had just about fed the household from the kitchen garden and if I was prepared to lose him over three rose bushes . . . so I stood by watching jealously whilst Hector put them tenderly in the ground, and congratulated him on his expertise. He's a nice old chap but I think young Cyril does most of the heavy work. Hector must be eighty.'

'And he's been here even longer than Allsop,' Foxy mused. 'I wonder how old Allsop is, Lo? It isn't the sort of question you can ask anyone, I suppose, but I'd love to know. He's got an ageless face, I think.'

'I believe he's in his late fifties; a year or two older than Sir George, that's all,' Laurie said. 'Want to take a closer look at the real roses – I mean those look a bit like sticks, wouldn't you say? But we've pruned and dug and now the old roses are beginning to emerge. Hector says next spring they'll be a picture.'

He swung the lantern again, directing its beam on the beds which had been cleared of weeds and brambles with the old roses, pruned down to no more than eighteen inches high, looking, Laurie suddenly realised, just like dead sticks. He glanced rather guiltily at Foxy – there are few things more boring than a rose garden when the blooms have either finished or not yet arrived – but she murmured appreciatively so Laurie told her that this one would be pale pink, this a deep crimson, that this one was yellow and had a wonderful scent . . . all the time aware that Foxy's curly mane of red hair was close enough to touch, that the lashes lying on her cheek as she examined the roses were darker than he remembered, that if he took a step sideways, as if by accident, he could take her in his arms . . .

But he could do no such thing, of course. It would spoil the friendship between them, to say nothing of what it would do to the relationship which he and John shared. So he told her the names of most of the roses and talked a little about the excitement growing in him because by this time tomorrow he would be in Cambridge, starting his first term there.

'We'd better go in now, or Allsop will wonder what's become of us,' he said presently, taking Foxy's elbow to steer her past an uncleared tangle of brambles. 'Hector's promised to keep an eye on my roses and Allsop will do the same for the house. Until my father's up and about, that is.' He sighed and Foxy, her hand clutching his arm as they made their way across the wilderness which was the garden, looked enquiringly up at him. Her face was just a pale smudge but he could see her mouth clearly, the lips just parted . . . Hell and damnation, he needed a woman, that was his trouble! He'd better find himself one before he made a fool of himself. 'Oh, well. Perhaps now Sir George has been so ill he'll be different.'

'Has he really got no money?' Foxy asked rather timidly. 'I mean you say Mr Hawkings is paying wages, giving you an allowance, so surely Sir George must have some money?'

'When I said something similar he sort of snorted and said: 'Peanuts!' and I suppose, if you've been used to an almost unlimited supply of the stuff, what's coming in from the property and so on doesn't seem much. But the doctor says Sir George won't be riding for months and months, if he ever does again, so we've sold the hunters and all the hacks. The doctors don't want him to go abroad, either, or to live in London for months, as he used to. He needs a quiet life, without fuss or excitement. Even the motor car and the chauffeur went because Hawkings says we can hire if we need motor transport, and Allsop told me my father was the world's worst driver and would probably have killed the pair of us if we'd just tried to manage without the chauffeur.'

'Gosh,' Foxy said. 'I'm beginning to feel quite sorry for your father, Lo. He's going to be made to be sensible whether he likes it or not.'

'That's it. Sometimes I think it's wrong of me to go to Cambridge, particularly to do something as useless as a degree, but Allsop thinks it's a good idea. He says it will give Sir George time to get used to the fact that he has a son and to learn to live with his disability. The stroke affected his right side and his right arm and leg aren't very good, now. And his sight's affected, too. So you see I'll have to come back here in the vac, even if there are things I'd rather be doing.'

He must have sounded wistful because Foxy leaned against him and squeezed his arm. Laurie squeezed back, tentatively. 'But you can always pop over to Bees-wing, especially once your father is up and about,' Foxy went on chattily. She could not have noticed the squeeze, Laurie concluded sadly. What an idiot he was, to read anything into Foxy's natural warmth and friendliness other than . . . than warmth and friendliness.

'Yes, you're right; of course I can pop over any time.' The lantern, held high, illuminated the yard and the kitchen door as well as Foxy's bicycle, leaning against the post. 'I'm going to cycle over tomorrow afternoon in fact, just to say goodbye to – to everyone. I expect Uncle will be up to his eyes in the hops, but . . .'

'John will, but Mr Hoverton's not doing any physical work yet,' Foxy reminded him. 'He does the books now, but not much else. I know he only broke bones, Lo, but he's been very poorly. I hope you really *will* come.'

'Well, I will,' Laurie assured her. 'To tell the truth I've tried once or twice since visiting Uncle in hospital, but something always comes up so I can't get away. You'd be astonished, Foxy, at how busy I am now, with Sir George up in his room all the time and doctors and things coming and going.'

'Lo, wait.' They were just inside the yard when Foxy jerked at Laurie's sleeve, hauling him to a halt. 'Is it your father who stops you coming? Or Mr Allsop?'

Laurie opened his mouth to reply, then paused. He frowned down at Foxy for a moment. 'Well, Mr Allsop usually reminds me of something I ought to be doing for my father, or the estate,' he said slowly at last, keeping his voice low. 'But I'm sure he's not trying to keep me from the farm, Foxy! Why should he? He's said often enough that the Hovertons could not have been better or kinder to me had I been their own flesh and blood.'

'I don't know why, but I've sometimes thought he doesn't much want you coming back any more than Sir George does,' Foxy said thoughtfully. 'There are a lot of mysteries in this house, Laurie, and I don't just mean the Chinese room.'

'Oh, that! I guess the way I felt about the Chinese room was nine-tenths loneliness and one-tenth vivid imagination,' Laurie said. 'But I didn't know I'd told you why I changed my room, Foxy.'

'You didn't. And it wasn't your feelings that I meant when I mentioned the Chinese room. That first night, when we came over here, something happened to John in the Chinese room – well, it was in the bathroom actually. But I think it came from the Chinese room . . . and I really think I saw something. Or someone.'

'Me, coming to fetch you,' Laurie said flippantly. 'Or did it have its head tucked underneath its arm?'

He put an arm round Foxy's small, supple waist, pretending to pull her towards the house, but she ignored him, her face very intent and serious in the growing dusk.

'I tell you I did see something; it looked like someone bending over the bed,' she said slowly. 'I never told John, but that was what I thought. Someone bending over the bed in a threatening sort of way.'

'And what did John think he saw? The same?'

Laurie's voice was no longer flippant; a seriousness which he could not avoid had crept into his tone.

'I don't know, we never talk about it. But his candle was blown out and Laurie, it wasn't draughty in that room, really it wasn't.'

'It was a windy night,' Laurie said obstinately. 'It must have been, for the candle to blow out.'

Foxy sighed and let him pull her towards the back door. 'Yes, you're probably right,' she said. 'Let's go in and see what Mr Allsop's got for our supper. I'm starving!'

John was walking across the yard to the cowshed, his rubber boots squelching in the mud, when the back door opened. His mother stood, framed in it, the cheerfully firelit kitchen behind her, the icy-cold, rain-soaked yard before. She gestured to John.

'Come in for your breakfast, lad! There's a letter for you, postmarked Cambridge.'

'Good old Lo, making sure my brain doesn't atrophy, but I was just going to see if the fellows were managing the milking,' John explained. 'I'll come in when I've done that, if they don't need a hand, that is. Dad's driving into Ledbury later, to buy feed, and I'd rather like to go with him. We could do with some day-olds and it's about time I changed my library books.'

'I've just been over to the cowshed and they're nearly done,' Mrs Hoverton said. 'I wouldn't mind coming in to Ledbury, I could do with some new shoes, something sturdy, for the winter. But if you're both going, perhaps I ought to stay here after all. Unless you think Dan can cope?'

John chuckled and walked across the yard towards the open door. 'He can always manage.' He took off the sack which he had draped across his head and chucked it into the kitchen ahead of him, kicked off his rubber boots, then unbuttoned his waterproof and hung that on the back of the kitchen door. 'Thank God the rain held off for the hop-picking! But it's been bucketing down ever since.'

'Oh nonsense, a bit of rain never hurt anyone,' his mother said, picking up the soaking sack with a tut of disapproval and spreading it out on a ladder-backed chair by the stove. 'And besides, we had a real summery October, and November wasn't too bad at all, though we had some nippy mornings, I grant you that. Now when you've settled, I'd just like to remind you of something.'

John padded on stockinged feet across to the table and sat down. It was good to be in the warm, not to feel the rain trickling down the back of your neck and up the sleeves of your waterproof every time you reached high. And the smell of breakfast – sausages, bacon, eggs, fried bread – was sufficient to bring the water rushing to his mouth. Mum had baked yesterday so the bread would be new, she would cut thick slices because you can't, she always explained, cut dainty off a new loaf.

'Well? What have I forgotten?'

'It's Christmas in two weeks, that's what. And that means Laurie could be coming home any time now.'

John's heart did an excited flip, then righted itself. 'Ye-es, Mum, but to which home? His father's still a sick man, according to the stories we hear at the market.'

'That's what I want to talk to you about. Laurie writes to us, of course he does, but I don't think he's likely to forget what your dad said to him when he came over to say goodbye before leaving for Cambridge. It upset him; I could tell.'

'It really did,' John agreed. His father had told Laurie rather coolly that though of course he was always welcome at Bees-wing as a visitor, he did not wish to supplant Sir George in Laurie's affection and thought it best that Laurie should spend his time, in future, up at Clifton Place. Laurie's face had gone quite white, and it had taken John the entire ride back to Clifton Place and a couple of hours hard talking when they arrived to make his friend see that it had been Bill Hoverton's pride which had spoken and not his heart.

'Then do you think he'll not come home to us? Do you think he will go to Clifton Place?'

'Let me open my letter,' John said, evading the question. The truth was, he thought it would be very difficult for Laurie to slip into his old life at Bees-wing Farm after the break, even if his conscience – and his father – would allow it. Laurie was revelling in Cambridge, loved the lectures, the company, the social life, so what they had to offer at the farm would seem poor indeed in comparison. What was more, Laurie's father, though no longer confined to his room, seemed to be a changed man. He no longer rode or drove or interfered with the life of his tenants. He stayed on the property and did not go up to the London house nor abroad. Rumour had it that his wild, profligate spending had stopped, too. Perforce, perhaps, but he had not again begun to sell either furnishings or land and even half-crippled, John reasoned, he could have managed to do that if he had had the will.

'Well? What's he say?'

John looked up from the letter. 'He says he'll only be home for a few days himself, not for the full month. He's got a job of some

125

description, he doesn't say what. He says if he has time he'll pop in.'

Mrs Hoverton's shoulders sagged. 'There! He took your father seriously – I was afraid he would. Still . . .' she brightened, '. . . if he does come, I'll do my best to explain.' She was dishing up now, sliding two fat, orange and white eggs onto a thick round of golden-brown fried bread. 'He's good as a second son to me,' she added, pushing the plate across to John, 'and like a brother to you, my lad.'

'Better; I'm fond of him,' John said, and his mother smiled properly this time, the sadness vanishing from her face.

'Aye, brothers don't always get on, do they? Write back, love, and tell him to visit us soon. Ah, here come the men, the milking's finished, then. I'd better get back to the stove.'

Five

It was a fine May evening and Laurie, feeling solitary for once, had decided to get his bicycle out and ride up Gog and Magog. He was heading for Wandlebury, where there was an iron-age hill-fort, abandoned by man hundreds of years ago and now thickly surrounded by trees and the soft green grass which flourishes on the chalk hills around the city. Here, Laurie told himself, he would sit and eat the cheese and pickle rolls he had bought from a shop in Market Street, whilst he studied a particularly obscure piece of Spanish literature on which he was supposed to hand in an essay the following day.

He reached the foot of the hill and dismounted, deciding to push his machine rather than pedal up the steep ascent. It was a marvellous evening; he was walking up a narrow lane, thickly hedged on either side with hawthorns in full, creamy-white blossom, and puffs of the scent of the may reached him with every breeze. What was more the sun shone gold and warmed his cheek and apart from bird-song there was the sort of silence which you only find, Laurie thought, in the heart of the English countryside.

He missed Bees-wing, and John, and their life together badly, far worse than other people realised, though he was popular with other undergraduates and had plenty of friends of both sexes. A wet bob, he rowed, swam, took pretty girls out on the Backs in a punt, showed them how neatly he could guide his craft through water traffic, then moored under the friendly green-shading willows, kissed, caressed . . .

It was a lovely life and Laurie enjoyed every moment of it, but he thought about Foxy a lot. She had somehow managed to get under his skin without him being aware of it at first, then John had stepped in and made a play for her, and he had lost his chance. He ought to forget her, simply choose one of the delightful girls he had taken out, and let John court her. *If I'd kissed her, even, I'd probably think no more about her than I do about other girls I've kissed*, he told himself. *It's just that I've never so much as cuddled her . . . God, I'm pathetic!*

Yet he knew very well he would do nothing which might cause John to distrust him, because the loss of John's constant companionship was an ache inside him. There were times when he had felt tempted simply to go over to the farm and move back into his old bedroom, let Sir George curse him and Allsop show disappointment, so long as he had his real life back. But it was impossible to spend more than the odd hour or so at Bees-wing whilst Uncle Bill was determined never to be accused of luring him away from his natural father and continued to treat him with stilted politeness. Knowing, now, that Sir George had deliberately engineered the quarrel so that the Hovertons would feel diffident about allowing him to return to them, Laurie put the blame where it belonged and, accordingly, disliked his father with growing intensity. It was, he knew, a dislike which was entirely reciprocated. He and Sir George were anathema to each other and no longer bothered to hide it when they were alone. But at least, during termtime, Laurie could know himself well-regarded and did not have to guard his back.

Because he had been brought up in the country, however, Laurie found Cambridge itself, though the most beautiful city, rather restricting, confining. Despite being glad to be away from Sir George he did miss the rolling parkland, the orchards and meadows around Clifton Place. He missed Allsop, of course, and his hack, Rum'un. Mr Hawkings had countenanced the buying of the grey gelding because Laurie had earned the money working in the Post Office over the Christmas vac; the estate, Mr Hawkings said, could still feed and shoe a horse for the heir. Laurie would have liked a dog of his own to take the place of Sasha but was too wary of his father even to make the suggestion. He would have to leave the animal at the Place during termtime, that was the trouble, and though his father had said, almost approvingly, that Rum'un wasn't a bad buy, though a trifle short in the back, Laurie was only happy to leave the horse during termtime because Rum'un went down the road to the village, where the Crisp family kept him, meat for manners, until Laurie returned once more.

But you couldn't do that with a dog; dogs liked their own place. And Laurie was by no means sure that Sir George would behave well to a dog owned by a son he disliked so intensely.

'Sir George likes a gun-dog,' Mr Allsop had said reflectively, when Laurie asked him if his father was a dog-lover. 'But he's of uncertain temper; when we had a gamekeeper he kept the dogs in kennels by his cottage. Sir George didn't have the patience. That's why there are no dogs in the house at present.'

But now, pushing his bicycle up the increasingly steep incline, Laurie was not thinking about dogs, or Allsop, or Sir George. He was not even thinking about John, or Foxy, who hoped to be coming to Cambridge herself the following year. He was thinking about the bottle of beer – well-warmed by now – pressing against his hip and the cheese rolls and apples nestling in his bicycle carrier. He ought to have been thinking about Spanish literature, but unfortunately it had not crossed his mind since he began his ride; he was hungry and thirsty and extremely happy and hot, and was simply longing, in a very uncomplicated and delightful way, to reach his destination.

Presently he wheeled his bicycle in among the beautiful beech trees and came to a halt, panting slightly, by a large, rather overgrown pond upon whose surface a family of ducks were disporting themselves in the slanting sunlight. It was a sylvan scene. The ducklings, little balls of cream and brown fluff, were paddling along busily in their parents' wake, trying to imitate the actions of their elders. Birds sang and swooped, a swallow darted past, beak gaping after flies, brick-coloured breast almost touching the water as it garnered itself a feast.

Mesmerised, Laurie stood very still for a moment, then sighed and set off through the trees once more. He would reach the hill-fort before he stood the bicycle against a convenient tree or wall and got out his food and the beer; then he would sit on the grass with his back against another convenient tree or wall and dream, and eat, and drink warm beer . . . he might even do some work, later.

He came up out of the trees into a round glade, grassy and

sweet-smelling. Above him the sky's blue seemed softer, the sun's gold brighter. He sighed with pleasure, leaned his bicycle against a tree, and walked forward, across the daisy-scattered grass. This was perfection! Deep countryside, birdsong, sunshine – and solitude.

It was then that he realised he was not, in fact, entirely alone. On the opposite side of the glade was another bicycle, and the owner, or someone he presumed to be the owner, was sitting on a patch of grass with her back resting against a tree, her hands over her face and a great quantity of long, curly dark hair falling forward across her shoulders.

She was crying.

Laurie stared at her and for a moment he felt inclined to turn quietly on his heel and sneak back into the trees again. If he did that he might still salvage his peaceful evening, but if not . . .

The girl gave a smothered sob and lifted her head. A pair of huge, black eyes gazed across the clearing at him, huge black eyes set in a small, pointy-chinned face. Right now her eyes brimmed, her cheeks were wet with tears and because she had been about to cry again her mouth had pulled itself into a very odd shape indeed.

Despite the difference in colouring, her tears reminded Laurie sharply of Foxy at their first meeting. He remembered how defenceless she had been, how totally unprepared for the tears. This little girl, trying to pull herself together and look away from him, was suffering just as Foxy had suffered so long ago.

But the girl before him was undoubtedly very pretty and very, very young. Laurie's heart might not have been stirred had she proved to be elderly, with a beak of a nose; truth must out, his peaceful evening would not have been well lost for such a one. But for a slender, curvaceous, dark-haired maiden with a small, straight nose, a kissable mouth and those huge eyes . . .

Laurie got out his handkerchief – clean, thank God, in fact still in the square into which the laundry had ironed it – and held it out towards her. She began to shake her head but he crouched down on the grass and put it straight into her small, though distinctly grubby, hand.

'Come on, wipe your eyes and blow your nose and you'll feel a lot better,' he said in what he fondly thought to be an avuncular tone. 'And then tell me what it's all about.'

The girl scrubbed vigorously at her face and then blew a trumpet blast down her nose. Then she scrambled to her feet, pushed her hair back over her shoulders and said, in a wobbly voice still showing definite signs of distress: '*Qué?*'

'You've wiped your eyes and blown your nose, so you must have heard me,' Laurie pointed out. He took a comb from his pocket and offered it to her, but this, apparently, was the wrong thing to do. Her eyes brimmed over once more and she shook her head, saying: '*Lo siento, señor . . .*'

'You're Spanish!' Laurie said. He beamed at her. 'How very strange; and I've come up here tonight to study Spanish literature and do a translation of what I suspect to be a very long and very boring poem. Well, you may help me, if you like!'

He spoke in Spanish, and the girl stood up straighter and actually smiled at him, revealing very small white teeth and a deep dimple at the side of her red-lipped mouth. She was wearing a white blouse and a long navy-blue skirt, both garments looking rather the worse for wear and dusty, but even to Laurie's untutored eye they were of good quality and very well made.

'You speak Spanish so very well, *señor*! But oh, I am so homesick, so dreadfully homesick! My parents wanted me to study English, to be a good student and do really well, which is why they sent me here. They hope I will marry a young man in the diplomatic service – such a one needs a wife who speaks English well. Only – only the other girls are not kind to me, they laugh at my accent, they make fun of me . . . and I am so, so unhappy!'

'If they laugh at you then they are fools,' Laurie assured her. 'It is no doubt just jealousy, *señorita* . . . by the way, allow me to present myself. I am Laurence Clifton, but my friends call me Laurie. I'm in my second year at King's College and I'm studying English and European literature. You have only just begun, I take it?'

'Oh yes, onlee just! Zis is my first monz in England,' the girl said, in heavily accented English. She sighed and reverted to her native tongue. 'Most other girls at my school are French, which is why they don't like me very much. But I speak French well, really I do.' She gave him a dazzling smile and changed to English once more.

'Eet is onlee English I spik not so good.'

'And your name?' Laurie asked hopefully. When she smiled like that he forgot her dirt-streaked face, the woebegone expression which it had worn when first he saw her, and wanted only to take her in his arms and comfort her.

'I am Evodia Cristiana Miryam de Salvorini y Rodriganez,' the girl said, lifting her chin. When she had first stood up, her head had just reached as far as Laurie's chin but with the rapid recitation of her name her back straightened and something of arrogance flitted across her small, tear-stained face. 'My familee are ver' important – *muchas importante, moy grande*. In Spain, of course,' she added rather more humbly. 'Here, I am nozzing.'

'You are a very pretty girl, a charming young lady,' Laurie said. 'And your English isn't at all bad, considering you've only been here a matter of weeks. Here, let me comb your hair back, you do look rather untidy, you know.'

He produced the comb again and she looked up at him doubtfully, biting her full lower lip with the small white teeth. But he combed the thick, tangled locks with care and presently said: 'There you are, all tidy and neat again! And now, Señorita Rodriganez, I trust you won't be offended if I ask you to share my supper and help me with my essay on your countryman's poetry?'

It surprised a chuckle out of her, and another of those sweet, tilted smiles. 'Your supper? I see no supper, Señor Clif . . . I forget it already! But I would like to help you with your essay; what is the poet's name?'

'You must call me Laurie . . . say it after me . . . "Laurie". There, isn't that an easy little name? And don't you have an easy little name that I might use, because Señorita Evodia de Salvorini y Rodriganez is quite a mouthful. What do your friends call you?'

She cocked her head on one side, looking like a kitten about to pounce. 'Is it right that I call you by your first name? There is so much that is strange to me . . . but my mother calls me Mirri, and so does my nurse. Now, Laurie . . .' she shot another glance, half shy, half coquettish, at him through long, curling lashes. 'Tell me what you are studying.'

'There are several poets actually, who have to be studied, and a couple of novelists, too. Two of the poets are twentieth-century chaps – Manuel Machado is one and García Lorca is another.'

'Ah, Lorca . . . yes, I can help you with his work, I've studied it myself,' the girl said. 'And the novelists?'

'Cervantes, naturally. And Ramón Pérez de Ayala. *Troteras y Danzaderas* is one title, I recall.'

'I will help you with that, also,' Mirri said decidedly. She smiled hopefully up at him. 'Ah, I am extremely hungry and also thirsty; where is this supper? May we eat first and study next?'

It made him laugh and he took her hands, squeezing them slightly, releasing them immediately when she tugged against him. He knew better than to retain her hands far less hug her, though he found himself very much wishing that he might do so. He had been studying Spanish literature for two years and knew quite well that a high-born Spanish lady would have to be betrothed to a man before he so much as held her hand. But he was an ignorant Englishman, so possibly, if he played his cards right, he might be given a little more liberty.

And presently they made themselves a nest with the wall at their backs and Laurie got out the bottle of beer and the cheese and pickle rolls and they had quite a feast, sometimes jabbering away in Spanish, now and then in rather more stilted English, drinking from the bottle turn and turn about since Laurie had neglected to bring a cup in his carrier.

'Tell me about yourself, and try to do a little bit in English now and then,' Laurie said presently, when the food was finished and the sun was a red ball in the west, the shadows of the trees around their dell long and blue with incipient dusk. 'Where is your language school? Where do you live in Cambridge?'

Mirri considered, then began to speak.

'In Cambridge my school is on Sidney Street. It is the Miss Honeyford Language Academy – do you not know it?'

Laurie, watching her face as she frowned in the effort to get it right, shook his head. 'Don't think so. Whereabouts on Sidney Street?'

'Nex' door to the pastry-cook,' Mirri said after prolonged thought. 'Ze one wit' ze . . .' she broke into Spanish, '. . . the wiggly, greenish glass in the tiny little window panes. I think it's called Hanniman's . . . something like that, anyway.'

'Oh yes, I'm with you now,' Laurie said. 'And where do you live? Do you have rooms over one of the shops?'

'It is a residential school,' Mirri explained, again after thinking quite hard. 'All the young ladies live at the school, only not in the building on Sidney Street; the schoolhouse as they call it, is on Earl Street. Really, it is three houses made into one.'

'Well, in future you must be happy there, and remember that you are going home to Spain soon enough. You will soon begin to speak excellent English if you meet me often and help me with my work, I'll make sure of that, and once your English is as good as your French your time here will be up . . . so enjoy it!'

She was gazing up at him, her eyes following every movement of his lips, a little pout and a frown of concentration marring her brow now and then if she did not perfectly follow the carefully enunciated words. How wonderful it would be if she adored me, Laurie found himself thinking. And why should she not? Already, he adored her, was prepared to do anything, promise anything, if only they might meet again.

'Well, Mirri? Will you help me, and let me help you?'

'Oh, yes, if it is not wrong,' Mirri breathed. 'The other girls are all older than I am, you see . . .'

'How old are you?'

'I am sixteen,' Mirri said proudly. 'A woman! Very soon I shall be betrothed to someone of sufficient status. I am a Rodriganez, my father's heir, one day I shall be very rich, very important in my own right, so naturally I must marry someone equally rich and important.'

'Here in England we call that boasting,' Laurie said gently. 'If you speak like that to the other girls in your school, Mirri, it is no wonder that they aren't kind to you.'

Mirri shrugged. 'They are common little French girls,' she said scornfully. 'They want to learn English so that they can get good jobs in the big offices in Paris. I want to learn English because my papa thinks it one of the social graces to speak a language well.' She looked at Laurie's face and drooped penitently, all the scorn falling away at once at the sight of his disapproval. 'You don't like that I speak the truth? I'm sorry, I don't understand.'

'Nice girls don't call other girls common,' Laurie explained.

'Nice girls are sorry for those less fortunate then themselves. If you have a great deal of money and a high position, then it is your duty to treat those less fortunate with all the more consideration and respect.'

'Is it?' Mirri said. 'Not in Spain it isn't. In Spain we say the truth.'

Laurie sighed. This was going to be an uphill struggle, but he had a feeling, every time his eyes fell on that so very kissable mouth, that it would be worth every steep step.

'Right. Then say the truth and have no friends, or learn tact and have friends. Which is it to be, Mirri?'

She pouted, but he could see she was thinking. 'What is tact?'

It surprised a shout of laughter out of him and she laughed too, her eyes almost disappearing as she rocked with mirth.

'Oh, Mirri, tact is saying you like someone's dress when you don't, or pretending you don't mind doing something for someone when you would much rather not.'

'Ah. In Spain we call this lying.'

'Perhaps. But I think, since you are doomed to spend a good deal of time with a group of "common girls", you would do well to learn tact. It oils the wheels of ordinary intercourse, you will find.'

'Oh? What means that?'

'Mirri, you little devil, I'm sure you know perfectly well what I mean, you just want me to tie myself into knots trying to explain. I'm very sure you've seen your papa telling your mama or your aunt that blue suits her when you know she looks better in green, or pink.'

She smiled up at him, but this time she nodded slowly.

'Ah, yes, this I understand. Very well, I will be tact. And now should we start to cycle back? I do not ride a bicycle good, you will find.'

Ten hilarious minutes later Laurie realised that she did not ride a bicycle good at all, in fact she did not ride a bicycle. She managed quite well on the straight but did not seem able to turn the wheel without immediately falling off. He now realised why her skirt and blouse were dusty, her hands grubby; doubtless they had met the ground every time she turned a corner, and there were a good few corners to turn between Gog and Magog and Earl Street!

'Whose bicycle did you borrow?' he asked at length, catching

135

her handlebars just in time to prevent another fall. 'I admire your courage, little one, that last tumble must have hurt.'

Mirri, wobbling upright again, bestowed her sweetest smile on him. 'It does hurt; my knees have no skin on them and there is much blood,' she observed dispassionately. 'And the bicycle is mine, truly. I told my papa that I needed a bicycle and he sent me a money order to buy one. He must have thought I knew how to ride it, but very soon I shall, of course. It is just when the wheel turns . . .'

'You go straight,' Laurie finished. He hauled her machine to a halt. 'This is absurd, the streets are no place to learn to ride a bicycle. Do you know Parker's Piece, Mirri?'

'No,' his companion panted, trying to wrest her handlebars out of his grasp. 'Let go, I can do it!'

'No you can't! It's getting dark, you'll have an accident. We'll both walk, and push our bicycles; how will that be?'

'But we'll be dreadfully late,' Mirri said. With the sinking of the sun in the west it had grown decidedly chilly and she shivered pathetically, looking hopefully up at him. 'I'm *muy frío* . . . ver' cold, I mean.'

'Here, have my blazer,' Laurie said, removing the garment and throwing it round her shoulders. 'Is that better?'

She snuggled into the jacket, warm from contact with his body. 'Much better . . . only I'll still be late.'

Laurie smiled sweetly at her and put his arm gently about her waist. 'We'll walk quicker like this,' he said untruthfully. 'Left, right; left, right! We'll be back in Earl Street in no time, just you see. And since tomorrow's Saturday I'll come and stand outside your schoolhouse at about ten o'clock in the morning, and we'll go over to Parker's Piece and I'll give you a lesson in riding a bicycle.'

'I don't need a lesson,' Mirri murmured, cuddling confidingly against him. 'Oh, this is so nice and warm!'

'Yes, isn't it?' Various comments chased through Laurie's mind but he dismissed them all. This odd Spanish girl was special to him, he knew it already. He would not blot his copy book by stepping out of line, he would, for once, take things slowly because otherwise he might well lose her altogether. 'Not much further now, *chica*.'

Mirri slowed her pace. Laurie slowed his, too. They sauntered like lovers, affectionately entwined, up to what she called the schoolhouse, then Laurie gave her one last squeeze and let her go.

'Goodnight, Mirri,' he said softly. 'Don't forget, I'll be out here at ten o'clock tomorrow morning and we'll go along to Parker's Piece and have a practice. And then I'll take you somewhere nice for luncheon.'

Her face was white with exhaustion but her eyes glowed and her smile was full of anticipation. 'Really? Oh, that will be so nice, Laurie. Until tomorrow!'

He watched her out of sight, then mounted his own bicycle and began to pedal slowly back towards his college. She was a darling, was Mirri Rodriganez, a cuddly, spirited, brave little darling, and he was going to woo her and win her, no matter how hard it might be nor how long it would take. He would put his brief, insubstantial infatuation with Foxy behind him and concentrate on this delightful girl.

It was only as he was climbing into his bed much later that night that something else occurred to him. Her parents were rich, upper-class Spaniards, set in their ways, proud of their daughter. She was an only child and they had a town-house in Madrid, a property by the sea in Alicante and an enormous estate outside Seville where they bred horses and fighting bulls. She had told him all this in her chatty, inconsequential way and he had listened indulgently, thinking how nice it all sounded, never realising, until now, that the high-nosed Spanish aristocrat who was her father might refuse to consider for one moment the suit of the penniless son of an impoverished estate, even if he would be Sir Laurence one day.

It should have daunted him, stolen his peace of mind, but somehow it did not. I'm already beginning to fall in love with her and she's well on the way to loving me, he told himself. And if there is one thing I have learned tonight it's that Señorita Evodia Cristiana Miryam de Salvorini y Rodriganez is a girl who likes her own way and is accustomed to getting it. I don't see why, between us, we shouldn't pull the thing off, get round her parents, and be together.

And on that heartening note Laurie fell asleep.

*

Foxy had worked like a slave to get her scholarship, and get it she did. She intended to do a degree in English and told anyone who would listen that she meant to be a teacher. And so she did, but she also meant to teach somewhere in Herefordshire, so that she might, by sheer force of personality, somehow get her heart's desire – a farm like Bees-wing.

'Farmer's sons marry farmer's daughters,' Auntie Bea had said warningly when Foxy had first revealed her dream. ''Tain't often they goes outside the family for a bride, so to speak. Still, there's farm workers; they needs wives and they ain't so fussy as them wi' money an' property. You'll do good, Foxy lass, even if you has to lower your sights a bit.'

But in the sixth form, Foxy discovered she had a natural talent for languages, and decided to do French as a second subject with her English. She got her scholarship without any trouble, if you didn't count months of eye-wateringly hard work, and in due course, one sunny October day, she set out for Cambridge and the place she had won.

In the rough and tumble of an enormous all-female college she was, for a couple of days, out of her depth, lost. Miserable, too, because she had somehow expected everyone, pupils and staff alike, to be overcome by her cleverness, by the fact that she had won a scholarship. But she soon realised she was not unique; she was surrounded by clever people. What was more, the dresses and skirts which Auntie Bea had made for her looked pretty ordinary beside most of the garments sported by her classmates.

So, wandering along King's Parade on a chilly Saturday morning early in the term, walking without intent, she was astonished and delighted to be hailed by a voice she knew.

'Foxy, is it really you? Well, you made it – I always thought you would! Come and have a coffee in Auntie's and tell me where you are and who you're sharing your rooms with and how life's treating you.'

'Laurie – oh, Lo, I'm so desperately glad to see you,' Foxy squeaked, and cast herself into his arms, to their mutual embarrassment two minutes later, when they had hugged and separated, to stand, pink-faced and beaming, side by side on the flagstones. 'It's – it's all quite different from how I thought it would be. No one seems to have noticed me at all and we have huge classes in a sort of theatre place – they call them lectures and no one cares if you go or don't, there's no roll-call or anything – and only one girl's said a word to me so far and she's got a drawly voice and lots of wiry fair hair and I'm frightened of her, she knows so much!'

'I don't believe it, Foxy. You, frightened? Just box her ears and pretend you're both ten years old and you won't have a qualm,' Laurie said. 'Gosh, you were a fierce little beast then – I've got the scars to prove it.'

'Yes, I know, but I had to be, then. And even now . . . oh Lo, they talk about their daddies and their motors and their summers in the South of France and they all seem to know each other. An awful lot of them come from some girls' school down on the south coast that I'd never heard of, there isn't one girl from Brum, let alone from my old school. If I wasn't even more scared of Auntie Bea than I am of those girls I'd cut and run, honest to God!'

'You sound like my friend little Mirri,' Laurie said wistfully. He took her arm. 'Come on, in here . . . grab that window table, sweetie, just shove your way across whilst I have a word with the waitress.'

Comfortably settled in the window table with coffee cups beside them and a luscious cream cake each, the two smiled at each other with mutual contentment. Foxy saw a tall, good-looking young man with a sensitive face and curly dark hair. She knew, from constant worried sessions before her own mirror, that he saw a thin-faced, freckled redhead with grey-green eyes and thin, darkened brows. She hoped that all the girls from her classes were walking past the café and envying her because she was with such a good-looking young man but guessed, ruefully, that not one would mention him to her even if they were out there this minute. I'm not one of them, she reminded herself ruefully, and never will be.

Presently, with the cake half-eaten and the coffee well down in the cup, she leaned across the table and spoke directly to her companion.

'Laurie, what am I to do? I've never cared before that I'm different, but – but I do care, now. It's as if I had a glass wall round me that I can't see but they can. They're never going to be friendly with me, really they aren't.'

'They will, Foxy. Have you joined any groups or circles or clubs or whatever?'

'No. I wouldn't know how.'

'You're so good at all sorts of games, why don't you join a badminton club, for instance? D'you play squash?'

'Never heard of it,' Foxy said. 'I've heard of badminton but I don't know what it is. And I can't afford things, Lo. Especially not equipment. The scholarship pays for my room, my books and my education, obviously, but it doesn't shell out for things like the latest skirts and whatever you need for badminton or squash.'

'Racquets. Look, my racquet will probably be all wrong for you, too heavy, that sort of thing, but I'll lend you one and I'll take you down to the badminton club. And I'll introduce you to a few of the chaps – just so you know someone – and before you know it the girls will be running round in circles trying to get pally. It's hard for the girl undergrads to meet fellows, because quite a few of the chaps prefer town to gown. They think they'll come across with less fuss, I'm ashamed to say. But it'll work to your advantage, really, because there isn't so much competition. And I'll introduce you to my Mirri, when she comes back.'

'Comes back?'

'Yes. She returned to Spain for the summer vac and she hasn't come back here yet. I think she's rather special, Foxy, and I've missed her dreadfully. She came over here to learn English at the Miss Honeyford Language Academy on Sidney Street – we've only known each other since we met last May, but I think both of us realise that – well, that we were made for each other.'

'Gosh,' Foxy said inadequately. She stared at him; was this her old friend talking? He had always seemed fairly indifferent to girls, certainly he had never shown the slightest interest in her, though she had thought him romantically handsome when she was younger and had even dreamed of him from time to time. 'And when does whatsername come back here?'

'Señorita Evodia Cristiana Miryam de Salvorini y Rodriganez; Mirri for short,' Laurie said cheerfully. 'I don't know and I'm beginning to get worried. Only this is my last year, Foxy, so if the worst comes to the worst and she doesn't come back to do another

140

term, then I'll go over there as soon as I get my degree. I've got her address, we do write, but . . .'

'But what?' Foxy said as the pause lengthened, eating the last bite of her cream cake. 'That was delicious, Laurie, thanks ever so.'

'Well, I can't write to her home because her father would open the letters and she would be in awful trouble,' Laurie explained in a rush. 'They're terribly old-fashioned and strict, her parents. And she is only sixteen . . . well, she'll be seventeen in March, but that's a long way off yet.'

'Gosh,' Foxy repeated. 'How does she get your letters, then?'

'Oh, I write to the home of one of the servants and the maid hands the letters over on the sly; for a price, probably. Which is all right whilst the family are in Seville, but when they go to Madrid or Alicante . . . well, we've not looked that far ahead yet. I expect we'll work something out.'

'I'm sure you will,' Foxy said comfortingly. 'Well, I do hope I meet your Mirri one of these days, Lo, but in the meantime, I'd be most awfully grateful if you would take me around a bit, introduce me to people. Because otherwise I'm sure I'll throw myself off Magdalene Bridge in sheer despair.'

Laurie laughed. 'I felt like that when I first arrived, too, and I knew a great many people. So it's a date, is it? We'll go along to the badminton club together this evening and I'll introduce you to a few of the chaps, and then tomorrow you must make a bit of an effort yourself. This girl with the wiry hair – what's her name?'

'Emily Bruce. Only I imagine she's a dreadful bore as well as being awfully clever, since she's been forced into speaking to me. I don't think she knows anyone else either, you see.'

'Then remember she's as lonely and lost as you, no matter how loudly she drawls,' Laurie advised. 'Finished your coffee? Let's be moving on, then. And remember, always look as if you're enjoying yourself. Join in conversations, smile, offer to help if someone's lost or has dropped their books.' He looked extremely smug. 'That was how Mirri and I met – she was crying because no one would speak to her, and I lent her my hanky and gave her some good advice . . .'

'And she's staying in Spain rather than returning to England for more advice,' Foxy said, grinning, and dodged his swipe. 'Oh come on, let's get this over with; where's the badminton club and what does it cost to join?'

'Emily, are you coming or aren't you? Only I've got some shopping to do; I need a packet of tea and some more sugar. Oh, and a loaf. And then I'm probably meeting Laurie and I may bring him back for coffee and toast. Can't run to cakes, not this month. So if you're coming, get a move on!'

It was a cold February morning and there was snow on the court which stretched between Foxy's stair and the college itself. Almost unmarked snow, furthermore, because as yet very few people had walked across it though the path which led round the edge of the grass was slightly more disturbed. Foxy, standing by the window looking down at the wintry scene, turned back into the room and raised her brows impatiently at her friend. Emily Bruce was as clever as she looked, but she had proved to be a good friend. She was shy, occasionally witty, usually reliable. She did not have a boyfriend, what was more, so she and Foxy were a good deal together though Foxy knew that half of Cambridge thought that she and Laurie had a thing going.

Much they knew. Laurie's Spanish girl hadn't come back to England, though she assured him earnestly in her letters that she had done her best to persuade her parents to allow her to return.

'But they only say my English is now good, and there is no longer a need for more education,' she had written plaintively soon after Christmas.

I told them about your kindness and how much I liked you, dear Laurie, and they grew agitated. My mother and my grandmother hissed to each other in corners when they thought I was far away, and held little meetings with my father and my Uncle Hesiquio, a man I dislike very much. Now they want me to meet the son of Uncle Hesiquio's sister-in-law whose horrible name is Ulises de Kassorla, because they say we are much alike and would get on well together. We are not alike, Laurie, he is a hombre both boring and a little frightening to me. They plot a marriage, I know they do, but they cannot understand that I do not wish this wedding. My mother says that to be almost seventeen and not betrothed is shameful; I say this is not the rule in England and she spoke unkind to me. And though I have not yet spoke with this hombre *I have seen him. He has a black brow and a nose most big. Also his nostril are hairy and his inside ears, which I much dislike; I do not wish to meet this* hombre, *far less to marry with him.*

Foxy's lips had twitched as she read this, but she had not smiled. She could see Laurie's anguish and understood that, to him, Mirri's odd way of expressing herself no longer seemed odd. It seemed just right, as Mirri herself seemed. And she felt sorry for the girl, so far from the man she believed herself in love with, possibly being forced into a distasteful marriage.

'You'll have to wait until the summer, when you've got your degree, and then go straight over to Spain and try to talk sense into the parents,' Foxy had said, handing the letter back. 'But Laurie, there's an awful lot of unrest in Spain just at present, isn't there? I'm sure Mirri will be safe enough, but I'm not at all sure you would be.'

'Oh, I'd be fine,' Laurie had said carelessly. 'My Spanish is pretty good, I'd probably pass for one of them in the dark. And I won't need to be there long, only long enough to steal Mirri away and marry her.'

Foxy's eyebrows had shot up. '*Marry* her? Isn't that a bit extreme? You only knew each other for a couple of months, you've been parted already for the best part of a year . . . wouldn't it be wiser to . . . '

'We'll see,' Laurie said, but Foxy had known that he was just nipping a disagreement in the bud. He had already made up his mind what to do and would do it no matter how sensible the arguments against such a course might appear. And Foxy, knowing she would feel the same in his shoes, smiled, wished him good luck, and changed the subject.

But knowing how he felt did not stop her worrying; she was sure he hadn't known Mirri long enough to have fallen in love. It's infatuation, that's what it is, she told herself. He's deeply unhappy over Mr Hoverton's rejection, he's lonely at Clifton Place without John or me or any of his friends, and so he's simply imagined

himself in love with the first girl to give him any real encouragement. What a mess it all is – but fortunately, she's out of sight, and
very probably, by the time he finishes his degree, she'll be out of
mind, too.

'I don't know that I want to go out at all in that snow,' Emily said
now, having apparently thought about the shopping trip and
decided it wasn't a very good idea. 'But I like Laurie; he's nice to
everyone, wouldn't you say?'

'Well, he's nice to us,' Foxy conceded. 'He's awfully clever, too. I
wonder who he gets his brains from? Not his father, he's thick as
pigshit.'

Emily's fair brows shot up and Foxy clapped a hand guiltily
over her mouth. 'Why do I do it?' she said aloud. 'I've got rid of
my Birmingham whine and forced myself to forget all the bad
words I used as a kid, so why can't I do the same with farming
talk? But of course when I think about Sir George I remember that
dreadful scene in the Bees-wing kitchen the September before
Laurie started at King's. And that, apparently, makes me talk like a
farmer.'

'I bet Laurie never talks like that,' Emily said rather stiffly. She
was a clergyman's daughter, an only child, and was frequently
shocked by the most ordinary remarks. But if she was as pure as
she pretends she wouldn't know what pigshit was, Foxy told
herself wistfully, and then she wouldn't be shocked by my
mentioning it.

'Laurie used to talk just like John,' Foxy told her friend. 'I know
he's the son of a knight – well, I think Sir George is a knight,
though I'm not a hundred per cent certain – but he was brought up
on a farm from the time he was ten days old, I believe. I haven't
offended you, have I, Em? You know I don't mean to do it, it just
sort of pops out.'

'Well, pop it back in again,' Emily said severely, but she smiled.
'Was Laurie's mother clever, then?'

'Dunno. She died. But no one's ever said she was bright. Laurie
told me she was a painter; she was pretty good, too. But you paint
by instinct, brains don't matter, and though Sir George did come to
Cambridge I don't think he ever got a degree. In fact the only
brainy member of the family isn't a member of the family, and

144

that's Allsop, the butler. Believe it or not, he once let slip that he was at Cambridge too, and got an honours degree in Natural Sciences.'

'Hmm. Laurie finishes in June, I suppose? We'll miss him next year, won't we? Especially you.'

'I shall, because he's doing his year out then, you know, his fourth year. He told me last time we talked that it isn't obligatory, he'll get his BA anyway, providing he passes the exams, but it's advisable. And of course he's doing it partly because of Mirri and partly because of his painting. He's always longed to go to Paris and this will be a wonderful opportunity. I thought, actually, that I might go over to France in the long vac this year – care to come too, Em? Only Sara Osborne says her sister went last year and had a spiffing time. They picked grapes so they were paid as well, and some people go and dig up archeological remains, though I don't think they get paid for that. It's awfully good for your French, and I'd enjoy it no end, particularly if you came along as well.'

'I'll see,' Emily said vaguely. 'You can't imagine picking grapes in the hot sunshine when there's snow on the court, can you! Is that your thickest coat, Foxy? Oh, I'll come with you, I can't bear to frowst in here all day, and perhaps we could take some bread for the ducks.'

'The Backs may be frozen,' Foxy said, tidying away her books. 'I'd love to skate on them, wouldn't you? I remember someone telling me a story when I first arrived about an undergrad who skated from the Backs right out into the fens, it took him all day, and I thought how grand it would be to do that. Not that I can skate . . . but I'm sure I could learn.'

'It probably won't last,' Emily said hopefully. She hated the cold. 'Do you have a scarf?'

'I have Laurie's,' Foxy said proudly, producing it from the drawer in the dresser and wrapping the colourful length of wool twice round her neck so that the ends dangled below her waist at the back. 'He gave it me and bought himself another one because he said it was all the rage for a girl to wear a boy's colours. I don't know whether King's approve, but it's done my standing some good. Are you ready? Come on, then, let's go.'

They clattered down the stairs and told the porter that they were just going shopping and would be back shortly.

'How's the screws, Mr Bledoe? This isn't the weather for aching bones,' Foxy said, pausing by his cubbyhole. Remembering his sweet tooth she added: 'Tell you what, we'll buy you some chocolate bickies and you can eat them when you brew up – it'll help to keep the cold out.'

The porter, a fatherly sixty-year-old, thanked Miss Lockett, advised his 'young leddies' to stick to the pavements so's their tootsies didn't get soggy, and watched them tramp straight across the court with an indulgent smile. That, he thought, was the young ladies for you – heedless of their own comfort but interested and concerned about the comfort of others. From what he'd heard, those who looked after the young fellows didn't get chocolate biscuits for their tea, nor kind enquiries after their arthritis, either.

'He's a nice old boy,' Foxy remarked as they went into the Maypole to buy their groceries. She gave a little skip. 'It's going to be a nice, cosy sort of day today, Em. First there's this brisk walk through the snow, and we'll have to go down to the Backs, just to test for skating. Then there will be coffee and toast with Laurie, and I'll let him read my latest letter from John and if Mirri's written, he'll let me read that. After that I suppose you'll be off to the library to do your research, and I won't see you any more until nine or ten o'clock, but I shan't be lonely because Laurie will very likely suggest that we have lunch together and do a flick, or wander round a museum – the Fitzwilliam for choice – depending on the state of our pockets. No, the state of his pockets because mine are always empty. After that it'll be tea and toast in his rooms, and talk round the fire until bedtime.' She hugged herself. 'Lovely!'

'Lovely for you, but what about Laurie?' Emily asked. 'Is he still hankering after that Spanish girl, Foxy, or is he going to settle for you?'

Foxy sniffed. 'He's still thinking about his Mirri, though I'm sure I don't know why, when it must be obvious to everyone that he's not going to get any encouragement in that direction – and she's only a kid, anyway, she isn't seventeen until next month. But as for settling for me – well, chance would be a fine thing.'

'You've got a soft spot for him, and I think he has for you, too,' Emily said calmly as they joined the small crowd around the counter, waiting to be served. 'I think you're two of a kind, myself.'

Foxy sniffed again. 'You don't understand, dear Emily. I like Laurie very much, but then I like John very much, too. And Laurie doesn't think of me as a girl, you know. Just as a friend. And since that's how I think of him, it suits me down to the ground that he's in love with Mirri.'

They were getting near the long wooden counter now and the middle-aged shop assistant in his brown working coat said good-bye to the elderly lady he had been serving and leaned towards them, his eyes brightening as they fell on the two well-wrapped, rosy-cheeked figures.

'Yes, young ladies? And what can I get you this morning?'

The courtyard was green and cool. In it the fountain played, the fish swam leisurely in the depths of the pool into which the fountain splashed, the white kitten, sitting on the fountain's rim, gazed gravely down at the rippled water. On three sides of the courtyard rose the grey stone walls of the house with narrow windows peering out through vine leaves and bougainvillea petals. The fourth side was just a tall blank wall into which was set a pair of elaborately gilded wrought-iron gates. The gates showed only the beginning of a dark passageway which led to the roadway beyond.

Mirri was sitting in the windowseat of the room which, according to her mother, had been the children's nursery when she herself was a child, looking down into the courtyard. There were thin bars at the windows, painted white. They looked innocuous; they were not. Through the open window Mirri could see the white kitten lean forward and put out a paw ... touch the water ... hastily draw back. As she watched a slight breeze from a passing vehicle in the roadway outside stirred the purple petals of the bougainvillea, touched the tall, formal irises which grew on the margin of the pool so that they quivered, caressed the falling fountain's drops so that, for a moment, the lacy water was thrown casually towards the white kitten, making it blink and shrink back.

Mirri turned away from the window with a frustrated sigh. If only she had never mentioned Laurie's name to a single member of the household! If only the treacherous Beatriz had kept her promise never to tell about the letters! The Granada house was one she had never mentioned to Laurie because she herself did not know they owned a house here. Perhaps they had not owned it, perhaps they had merely borrowed it to hold her a prisoner . . . oh, but she would go stark, staring mad if she spent much longer in the wretched place!

Mirri got to her feet and walked, slowly and deliberately, across the room and over to the door. She turned the door-knob and the door swung open, silently, on well-oiled hinges.

'You are *not* a prisoner, foolish little one,' her mother had said with her sweet, cold smile, smoothing a hand across Mirri's hot forehead in what seemed like a gentle, affectionate caress. Silks and satins, smooth, lush velvet, hiding the steel beneath! 'You are free to come and go as you wish, but of course a young girl like you, not even betrothed yet though you are a month past seventeen, cannot wander the streets of a great city alone. If we were at the villa in Alicante, or at the ranch between Seville and Cádiz, then it would be a different matter, but here, or in Madrid, you cannot be allowed to roam like a street urchin.'

'Send me out with Beatriz,' Mirri had begged at the end of the first week, not knowing then of the maid's treachery. 'She will look after me as she has always done, since I was small. I've not seen her once since we arrived at this horrid house and she is supposed to be my maid!'

'Ah, do you mean you no longer consider her to be your little letterbox?' her mother had said, even more sweetly. 'Not the bringer of letters which an unmarried girl may never receive from a young man? Fortunately, Beatriz came to her senses and gave one of the letters to your papa; he was horrified by what he read, he feels he can no longer trust you. I've assured him he's wrong, that you learned strange ways in Cambridge, but he thinks, until you are betrothed to some pleasant, suitable young man, you are best kept safe, within these walls.'

And so it had gone on, for weeks. The charms of Ulises Kassorla, the handsomeness of him, the fortune at his command, the very fact that he, too, owned a great property where fighting bulls were bred, had been constantly reiterated, until Mirri had realised that she would have to at least pretend to give way a little.

Scowling and reluctant, therefore, and determined to be as difficult as possible, Mirri had come down from her prison into the lofty reception room with its cool tiled floor and its wonderful collection of brilliant, vivid pictures, when Ulises and his mother were partaking of a little light refreshment. A warning glance from her mother had banished the scowl; if you must do a thing, do it properly, she adjured herself and had been, if not welcoming, at least polite.

'He was enchanted,' Señora de Rodriganez exclaimed afterwards. 'He thinks you a paragon amongst young women, he says you are perfection personified! Oh, my darling, can you not like him a little bit, for my sake? Believe me, I am not at all enamoured of keeping my own little girl virtually a prisoner. But your papa is an old-fashioned man. Writing and receiving letters of which we knew nothing . . . that was not good behaviour, was it?'

Honesty forced Mirri to agree that it was not good behaviour.

'But Laurie is so nice, so kind, so good; if only you had agreed to meet him,' she cried despairingly. 'You don't understand, Mama, what it is like to be kept from someone you – you are truly attached to!'

'But he is a foreigner,' her mother said, as though pointing out that he had two heads. 'Such a marriage would be impossible, quite impossible. As for Ulises, dearest, no one is trying to force you to marry him, but we do want you to meet young men other than . . . than foreigners. You know no one, and your papa and I want you to meet young people your own age. To meet Ulises is just a beginning.'

So Mirri had been polite to Ulises and his mother, had laughed at his shyly told jokes and handed the plates, even giving him a coquettish glance through her long lashes as she did so.

'He's probably not too bad,' Mirri had admitted grudgingly after the Kassorlas had left. The tufts of hair in his ears and nostrils seemed to have vanished, but the huge nose and the beetling black brows were still much in evidence. She supposed that he had plucked his nostrils and inner ears – she winced at the thought – but he had probably only done it to impress her. Once he had her married he would doubtless grow hairy once more and she would wake one morning to find herself staring up a cavernous nostril from which abundant black hairs curled forth. 'But I could never love him, Mama.'

'Oh, love! Love comes later, *querida*. I did not love your father when first we wed because I did not know him at all. Things were much stricter then, we had very little chance to get to know one another. I doubt we had exchanged more than half-a-dozen sentences in our lives. But later . . .' she rolled her cold dark eyes ceilingwards in a manner which caused Mirri's stomach to clench with disgust. It was such a false gesture, somehow, coming from a woman like her mama. '. . . Ah, later, what a man! What a husband! Yet, *querida*, if I'd had my way I would never have married him.'

Beatriz had not reappeared; she probably would not dare, Mirri thought crossly. Just because my money ran out and I could no longer pay her a large sum for each letter . . . I wonder if Mama knew what I was spending my money on, and that was why my allowance failed to materialise at the end of February?

But now, with the door standing open, Mirri hesitated in the doorway. True, she had been free to leave her room once she had expressed her sorrow for behaving deviously, although her sorrow came mainly because she had been found out, but the house was so secure! The windows mainly overlooked the courtyard and were extremely narrow and barred. And the courtyard itself, though one could look out through the gates, was secure unless one had a key to the padlock which kept them closed.

Still, in the courtyard she would have, at least, the illusion of freedom.

The long flight of stairs curved graciously from the upper landing to the black-and-white tiled hallway with its palm trees and ferns in pots, watered lavishly by the maids twice a day. Mirri descended slowly – there was no point in hurrying – and for some reason, halfway down the flight, she remembered that day on Parker's Piece, the way they had laughed, the way it had rained, flattening her hair, making the bicycle even more unmanageable.

Oh, Laurie, Laurie! Her parents would never realise it, but now Laurie, and Cambridge, stood for freedom, for the wind on her face, the rain pattering down, and for the speeding bicycle, with Mirri perched on the saddle, mistress, at last, of this unpredictable steed.

Spain was the unnatural warmth of a centrally heated house in the winter and the cruel, searingly humid heat of summer. It was being watched and followed and spied on, ordered about, shut up in her room to read the papers because a well-educated young lady should understand current affairs. It was swift journeys between one city and the next shut up in a large, luxurious limousine with her parents on either side of her, like gaolers, and every window sealed shut. It was rattling the wrought-iron gates to see if the padlock was still secure, waking in the night and stealing round the darkened house, hoping, always vainly, that someone had left a door unlocked, a window unbarred. What she would have done had she discovered an escape route she did not know, she just longed, with all the passion of her passionate heart, to escape. To feel once more the wind and rain on her face, to run and to walk . . . to know the total freedom which she had known, alas so briefly, in the city of Cambridge.

She crossed the hallway, opened the big front door and slipped out into the courtyard. The kitten, eyes widening, got unsteadily to its feet, dropped off the fountain's rim and ran towards her, tail straight up in the air, eyes fixed on her face. Its purr was like a motorbike engine, its little warm body, vibrating against her legs, took her mind off her troubles for a moment. She bent and picked it up, held it against her face, whispered lovewords into the pricked, furry ear.

'Little one, you are so small and skinny you can slide out through the gates and the bars . . . you go where you will when you will. Nothing and nobody can stop you.'

Inside her head, an insidious little voice began to whisper. *How long can you keep this up, Mirri? Because Mama and Papa aren't going to give way easily, not over a matter like this. You can't get to Laurie and he can't get to you, so why not pretend really hard that you've changed your mind and will marry 'someone suitable' after all? Marriages don't happen all in one moment, time will be taken. And you'll get your freedom back, Mama more or less promised you would. They'll take you to Alicante and you can walk on the beach, paddle in the sea. Or they might even take you to the ranch, where you could ride again, and walk for miles without anyone objecting. You don't have to mean it, just tell them you want to see Ulises again and in a few more weeks . . .*

She had done her best to get a message through to Laurie, though, for all her parents' care. She had realised as soon as they descended on her, brows black, lips tight, that something was up and had scribbled a note, attached it to one of her gold bangles, and thrown it out of her bedroom window when a small boy had been passing by. This had been in the Madrid house, before she was so strictly chaperoned. The note told Laurie not to write again, that all was discovered. She had not known where they were taking her so she could not tell him, her one thought had been to stop the correspondence until she was again in a position to answer his letters. And since her father had said nothing about more letters arriving she supposed that the boy had not simply run off with the bangle, but had posted the note as she had asked.

She sat down rather hard on the fountain's rim and turned to look at the fish; they weren't free, but they didn't know it. They raced and dawdled as they wished, lurking under the lily pads one moment, sending themselves, with a flick of the tail, into hiding by the irises the next. Presently, she found that tears were forming in her eyes and running, unheeded, down her cheeks.

She was deeply unhappy and could see no way out of her dilemma save to give in, and if she gave in, she might as well do it now as later, because even if she did manage to escape how could she get to England with no money? And she was under age, they would set the *guardia* on her, she would speedily be caught and handed back to her even more outraged parents.

The tears were flowing in earnest now, fairly raining down her cheeks, and when a hand fell on her shoulder she was so busy with her weeping that she scarcely moved, save to shrug impatiently at the fingers gripping her flesh like a prison warder intent on preventing an escape.

'*Señorita*, don't be so distressed! Whatever is the matter?'

She looked up, through tear-bedewed lashes. A man stood there, his expression concerned, looking down at her. He wore a dark suit and a white shirt, black, shiny shoes, a maroon tie. She did not know him, but registered almost without realising it that he was very good-looking and that the hand on her shoulder no longer felt like a prison warder's.

'Oh, *señor*, I'm so sorry, I didn't realise . . .' she scrambled to her feet, feeling like an untidy schoolgirl, unprepared to come face to face, in her own courtyard, with a handsome stranger.

He held out a hand and took hers in a warm grip. 'I'm the one who is sorry, *señorita*, I did not mean to frighten you; my name is Cosme Barador and I came to the house on business, to see your papa – I take it you are Señorita Rodriganez? I was about to leave when I saw you sitting there . . .' he smiled down at her, '. . . looking like some beautiful princess out of a story book. I'm ashamed to say I desired hotly to see if your face was as delightful as the rest of you, so I touched your shoulder . . . will you forgive me?'

'Of course,' Mirri said, trying to dry her eyes with the backs of her hands and pretending to yawn as she did so. 'I was nearly asleep, *señor*, you must forgive me! But you won't be able to leave the house until I've fetched someone to unlock the gates for you; I'm afraid I don't have a key.'

'I don't think the gates are locked, since I came through them not an hour ago,' her companion said gravely. 'Shall we see?'

He strolled towards the gates just as Señor Rodriganez came out of the house and stopped short.

'Ah . . . Cosme, I see you've made the acquaintance of my daughter Miryam. I was about to unlock the gates . . .'

'In that case, Señor Rodriganez, since this is my first visit to Granada, I wonder if I might have the company of your delightful daughter for an hour or so? I am anxious to find the Alcaiceria; I have a commission from my mama to visit a certain shop . . .'

'My daughter does not know the city at all well and her mama is unable, at present, to chaperon her,' Señor Rodriganez said with assumed regret. 'So unfortunately she can be of no possible help to you.'

Señor Barador shook his head; he was laughing, his eyes glinted down at Mirri. 'I don't need a guide so much as a person of taste, *señor*,' he explained. 'I shall hail a taxi; the driver will know the quickest way to the Alcaiceria much better than either of us. No, it is when I reach the shop that I need some assistance. My mother has prevailed upon me to buy, for my youngest sister, a traditional dress for a fiesta . . .'

Mirri held her breath. What would her father say to that? Truly, without being rude, he could scarcely refuse!

'I . . . see. Well, *señor*, as you are an honoured friend, if you will take good care of my little one . . .'

Mirri could hardly believe it; her father was about to say she could go! She realised she had stopped breathing and was gripping her hands into fists, imploring God, the fates, her father, anyone, to let her go.

'You could not be more careful of her yourself than I shall be,' Cosme Barador promised solemnly. 'I will take her to the Alcaiceria with me, and when we have chosen the fiesta dress perhaps the *señorita* would enjoy a glass of wine and some cakes? And I will, of course, accompany her back to your delightful *casa* once our pleasant expedition is over.'

'Very well,' Señor Rodriganez said reluctantly. 'She – she is a good girl, my little one, and precious to us. You won't be late?'

'I will bring her back before dark.'

'Go, then.' Señor Rodriganez turned to his daughter. 'Do you want a coat, or a jacket?'

'No thank you, Papa, I'm quite warm enough,' Mirri said, punctiliously polite. If he was to change his mind now she would surely die! But he did not. He walked with them over to the gates and unlocked them, then swung them open.

'The gates won't be locked again until dusk, but if you are a little late, ring and someone will come,' he said. 'Enjoy yourselves.'

Señor Barador tucked Mirri's hand into the crook of his elbow and smiled down at her. 'We most certainly shall,' he murmured. 'Off we go then, *señorita*!'

'Off we go!' Mirri echoed gaily. Her fingers on his arm were light as air, light as her heart, as her step. Free, free, free! And with a handsome and delightful young man, too!

Señor Rodriganez went back across the courtyard, through the front door, and into the lofty reception room where his wife was lying back in a winged chair, desultorily reading a novel. She looked up as he approached and smiled at him.

'Well? How did it go? Was she scowling and furious with you, as I said?'

Her husband smiled smugly, then sat down on the arm of her chair and took the book from her hands. He turned it over to read the cover. 'What rubbish you read, my dear,' he said mildly. 'As for fury, there was no such thing. I told you, a little guile is worth a great deal more than threats and punishment. But we tried it your way first since you were so sure it would work and did we change her mind? Did we break her indomitable spirit? Of course we did not, because she's a Rodriganez, and we Rodriganez are obstinate as any mules, every one of us!'

'So? What did you do and why are you looking so unbelievably pleased with yourself, *querido*?'

'I did nothing. Almost nothing. But I brought young Cosme to the house and explained the situation, said I wanted him to befriend the child, to behave naturally, to be kind to her. And I might add, my dear, that he took one look at her as she came down the stairs, quite unaware that we were watching, and was delighted with the idea. She is a very pretty girl, with something more, a sort of coquettish sweetness which is – well, very fetching.'

'So you introduced them, and . . . ?'

He laughed. 'I said I used some guile, Marcelina, and I meant just that. I made him wait – he was anxious to meet her – until she had dissolved into tears, sitting on the fountain's rim in the courtyard, and then I sent him to her. I told him to say he'd been visiting me on business and was about to leave when he caught sight of her. And it worked, my dear, like a charm. When he asked leave to take her to the Alcaiceria to choose a special dress for his youngest sister I looked disapproving, but gave my consent reluctantly, in the end. To give Cosme credit, it would have been difficult for me to refuse without seeming churlish. They left arm-in-arm, delighted with one another, and will return, I promise you, already a little in love. He is an outstandingly handsome boy and she's a little jewel. You mark my words, in a few months we'll be arranging a wedding, and one far more advantageous than the marriage with Ulises could ever have been.'

Six

Bees-wing Farm,   *25th July 1935*
Nr Ledbury,
Hereford.

Dear Laurie,

I'm feeling distinctly left out! First you bugger off and leave me so you can go and be lord of the manor and a model student, then Foxy gets her university place and works like a beaver all year and then tells me she's spending the vac treading grapes in France to improve her French and earning money at the same time. And now, with the bines swarming up the wires and everything happening – we've been making hay, cutting barley, shearing sheep, spraying apples, cosseting hops of course – all the usual tasks of the farming year, you simply drop me a line to remind me that you're off to the continent, and you won't be coming back until after hop-picking because you've got to get down to the study of French and Spanish medieval literature! I ask you, do you expect me to believe that tissue of lies? It's some bit of skirt, isn't it? You did mention a girl, but then she stopped appearing in your letters and I thought that's it, the old sod's after something a bit more willing. Some juicy young first-year from that girls' coll., where Foxy goes, all dewy eyes and big tits, who will only be yours if you take her somewhere exotic.

Well, I suppose, if I were in your shoes, I might find young big-tits a bit more exciting than old Granny Smith and Alfie, a-pickin' of them 'ops. But I do have the consolation of Lily, Rebecca and Flossie, to name but three. Farmer's daughters, dear Laurie, are Friday's children every one – now work that out, you clever sod!

I like getting your letters though, so don't stop writing. It gives me a taste of the wider world ... Foxy writes a natty note too, though her writing is appalling, God knows how her tutors (or are they tutoresses?) manage to decipher it. She is chattier than you (always was) but skates over many things I'd like to know and homes in on the boring stuff, like her class-marks, the splendours of her college, and her friend Emily, who must be the dullest girl in the world. So I'll send this to Paris and when you move on, just let me know the new address and I'll tell you all the latest gossip. What gossip there is, with you not here to set tongues wagging. The Clifton family certainly get their share of local attention, wouldn't you say?

I'm glad Allsop writes but it's sad that your father doesn't drop you a line. Is it that he can't be bothered or is it because of his disability? Mum says he still can't use his right arm or his right leg properly and I imagine he's right-handed? Dad and she are well, by the by, and would send their love if they were around to do so, but they've gone into Ledbury to buy Dad a new tweed jacket. He slung the old one on the tractor one hot day, or thought he did. Apparently it hung down between wheel and workings and got slowly chewed apart ... Dad laughed like a drain when he pulled out what was left but Mum burned with a slow and righteous fury and at this very minute is probably forcing him to spend money on a new one. She says he had the old one thirty years; many would doubt this but I believe her. Dad is tight as a tick (and you and I know how tight that is!) over what he would call splashing out money on luxury items, though he'll spend a small fortune on a new tractor without a second thought.

Where was I? I seem to have rambled somewhat. Well, what I really meant to say is how differently we might have parted almost four years ago had we known we wouldn't meet up again – all three of us, I mean. Foxy went on coming back until this year, when apparently she could not resist the lure of the grape. She does need to earn money, and in France she can earn it all summer, not just the one month, which is a good enough reason for being away I suppose. But you didn't even come over when you were home whilst the hops were being picked. Each year we told each other, Foxy and I, that you'd be sure to turn up, but either you were up to your eyes in holiday work, or you'd taken your father off somewhere to see if a couple of weeks abroad, or down in Devonshire, or up in Scotland, would improve his health.

We missed you. We'd been quite a successful little group, the three of us. *The three witches, three little pigs, three blind mice . . . and us three.*

Anyway, that's all water under the bridge now, and I see I'm in for a lonely September. Apart from gipsies, Brummies and the Welsh, of course. They'll all ask after you, and Auntie Bea will tell me how well Foxy's done and how clever she is . . . but it's not the same. I'm too busy chivvying the pickers now to help with one particular crib, but whenever I walk down between the rows and smell that very English smell and hear the voices, sometimes cooing, sometimes clacking, I'm glad my lot in life has fallen here. I don't even envy you she of the enormous potentials . . . but do come home one day, Laurie! We've grown up, but not apart, surely? I realise September and the hop-picking is out, but later, perhaps? Come over for a day or so at Christmas, I'm sure your father and the marvellous Allsop (never met him but Foxy tells me things) could manage without you – they have to do so whilst you're at college, after all.

Your affectionate (just) friend,

John

Du Vallière Vineyard,   *24th August 1935*
France.

Dear John,

I'm tempted to write in French, just to show off, but since you wouldn't understand my brilliant, colloquial chatter I suppose there's no point, and anyway I'm much too excited. The weather is absolutely wonderful and the grapes not only look a bit like hops, they taste a great deal better! I gobbled and gobbled the first day, then I had the well-known tummy upset (and a vineyard on a hill miles from the shacks where we all sleep is no place for a case of galloping runs) so now I am more mature. Like the wine. We work tremendously hard all day and sing and carouse all evening and sleep like logs or pigs or anything else famed for its ability to snore the clock round all night.

Emily couldn't make it after all, so I've palled up with a girl called Felicity who is from a red-brick university (Aberystwyth) poor dear but is great fun and assisting me to have fun too. What is more, she is luckier than me. She has very dark hair and her skin browns beautifully but never never freckles and she certainly does not burn. When I got over the tummy upset I proceeded to roast myself to a crisp – actually, the colour of my skin was anything but crisp, it was a repulsive raw-bacon shade. I hurt dreadfully, John, and felt dreadfully sorry for myself, and crept around afraid to smile in case my flaming red face cracked and fell in half, for there was no moisture left in my skin and my eyes felt half-baked.

But I recovered. Well, I'm writing to you, aren't I? I managed to get myself as far as the river one afternoon and dropped into a nice deep pool (I heard the water sizzle as I struck, truly I did!) and I stayed under water with just my head poking out for all of an hour. When I got out I was still a nasty purply plum colour and wrinkled like a prune from being under water, but I began to think I might live. I felt ashamed though, that so many seasons hop-picking had not taught me that redheads burn. Only at Bees-wing I had you and Laurie, your mum and Auntie Bea all watching over me, telling me off if I didn't cover up when the sun was strong. And here everyone was working in as little clothing as they dared and it would have seemed so sissy and despicable to drape myself in long-sleeved blouses and lengthy skirts. So I cast doubts aside and suffered for it.

But though feeling much better, I don't look it, since I am now peeling. Wet wallpaper has nothing on me, my skin comes off in long, delicate strips, like snakes' skin does, and if you try to hurry it it HURTS, so of course you go around looking like a birch tree in autumn and hoping no one notices and they all do.

'Been in the sun too long?' they coo, eyeing you with secret joy because they are all smooth and tanned and you look such a sight. 'Better luck next time, dear.'

That is the girls. The boys don't say anything, they just hurry off to find someone who won't scream with anguish if they put a companionable hand on her shoulder.

You say in your letter that Laurie's here somewhere, but it's a big country, John, and if he's doing something about medieval literature I don't imagine he'll come to the vineyards to do his research. He was so kind to me my first year, and at the beginning of the second, too, but what with my exams and his we've hardly met. I don't want to embarrass him by tagging after him the way I admit I did when we were kids – you were both awfully patient with me. So I haven't gone out of my way to see Lo in Cambridge, though I've glimpsed him once

*or twice in the street but never when I could go over and say hello. I am
either on a bus or a bicycle and usually in a mill of traffic whilst Laurie,
also on a bus or a bicycle, goes past on the other side. We met at a May
ball earlier in the year and danced a bit, which was lovely. We talked
about the farm, and you, and Laurie's worries over the estate, and the
girlfriend I never met, but of course that was just a chance meeting and
may not happen again until next year, if then. I don't really understand
this extra year of study you say Laurie's doing but take it that he will
come back to Cambridge to get his degree next summer? But though I
may glimpse him from time to time, it's you and Laurie who don't see
much of each other any more, which is a dreadful shame. Our little trio
had such fun, didn't we? I felt very close to you both, quite a part of the
family. Still, there's always the vac, if I come hop-picking next
September, that is. As you know I'm doing a nice, straightforward
English degree with French as my second subject, so I might spend the
long vac next year in France again. A friend (Felicity, actually)
suggested we might go to Spain and pick sultana grapes next year but I
don't fancy it; there's so much poverty in Spain and from what I've
read in the papers there's trouble brewing there so perhaps it will be
France again. Only next year I'll try to get back for the hops, honest I
will. It's my best thing.*

*Yes, she says, coming back to the point, it is odd that the three of us
haven't met up since Laurie left. But we'll make it one day, I'm sure. I do
think it's difficult for Laurie to come back to Bees-wing after what your
father said, and you know Laurie. He spends a lot of time pretending to be
terribly sophisticated and so on, but underneath he's just as easily hurt as
the rest of us.*

*Tell you what, we ought to have a pact; we all write to each other,
though Laurie and I don't as much, because of exams and things I
suppose. Well, you're the pointed bit at the top of the triangle, John, the
important bit that the other two lean on. (You can tell I'm not reading
mathematics, can't you???) So you must write formally to us both,
issuing the sort of invitation we can't refuse, to have a reunion, possibly
somewhere mutually convenient. Not Bees-wing Farm; why not somewhere in Cambridge, for instance, during termtime? When Lo comes back
from his tour of foreign parts, I mean. I'll drop you a list of possible places
if you're interested in this scheme. I'd suggest meeting in my rooms but
people might talk – not one but two handsome young men . . . etc. etc.*

What do you think? I know how busy you are, up to your eyes in hop-pickers, with all the worries on your shoulders now that your father has handed the hops over to you, but it's an idea, isn't it? Think about it and let me know. I'll be back in Cambridge in October so write to me there rather than here – the postman probably does call but I've never seen him and the name Lockett gives the locals a good many problems without asking them to deliver mail to it!

I'll miss your letters, John, so make sure there's a big fat one waiting for me when I get back to Blighty,

With love from

Foxy

17 Rue Richelieu,   *3rd September 1935*
Paris.

Dear John,

Thanks for your letter and sorry, sorry, sorry! Not just for missing countless hop-pickings because you do know how awkward it has become for me to spend time at Bees-wing, but because I swore I'd come over before I left. But then the chance came up to have a month in Paris staying with a friend from King's, whose father actually owns a flat on the Rue Richelieu, and as you can imagine I simply couldn't miss this chance, and what a chance it's been! Your apocryphal Miss Big-tits isn't here (alas) but a great many other things I care about are. Including a fellow student, tall and willowy with blonde hair cut in a pageboy, very large blue eyes and a penchant, she tells me, for men with titled parents – what could be more convenient? To tell the truth, I'm not here for academic purposes, though I shall probably stay on and write my treatise (essay indeed; I am no longer in the upper sixth, Hoverton!). No, I'm here for pleasure and the pleasure is painting. Never was there a city which cried out to be painted like this one does. The Seine is wonderful, the Madeleine more so, the street markets . . . well, I could paint the street markets for a year and never get bored.

What is more, there are others, like me, who simply want to paint what they see. Only they are, for the most part, a great deal more talented, and are happy to pass on to a beginner any tips which might prove useful. I know I'm just a dabbler, but how I enjoy it, though the end result always disappoints me. What I see with my eyes isn't what my brush portrays, or it isn't usually. But just occasionally I manage to get at least part of a painting right, and then it's marvellous, the sense of achievement, of having put down on paper a fleeting moment . . . can't explain but I bet you understand, you aren't the Philistine you'd like us to believe are you, old son?

I know just what you're thinking – how can I find Paris beautiful when I was brought up in the most beautiful countryside in the whole of England? Rolling hills, gentle valleys, the Forest, the view from our bedroom window . . . the list is endless. But Paris is different; it's quite a small city really and it is crammed with artists. They say there's something special about the light, but I don't know that. All I know is that I feel at home here. At school my painting seemed something of which to be slightly ashamed; my father absolutely hates to see me with a pencil and a sketch-pad. He was supposed to love my mother dearly, but she painted . . . one is bound to wonder, or this one is, at any rate. I know that if I married a woman with any sort of talent and she had a son who shared that talent, no matter on how small a scale, I'd be delighted, surprised, proud . . . not annoyed and embarrassed. But there you are, that's Sir George for you. He's better, incidentally, much stronger. Allsop wrote; said Father had demanded that someone get him a horse. Good old Cyril went out and borrowed a hack from the Richardsons a couple of miles down the road (Sir George would have died if he had known the nag was merely borrowed) and the old man rode for an hour, grumbled that the horse was a slug, and came home very full of himself. So long as he doesn't start wasting the readies again, that's all I ask, but Allsop and Mr Hawkings are on my side so perhaps, between the three of us, we'll keep expenditure and income down to Micawber-like levels. You know, income nineteen shillings and ten pence, expenditure nineteen shillings and eightpence – result, happiness. Income nineteen shillings and tenpence, expenditure nineteen shillings and elevenpence, result misery. That's what I mean.

You say Foxy's in France; good for her, wish we might meet up, but I don't plan to go rushing off to the vineyards, not with all Paris at my feet (or rather, in front of my eyes). I've not met her since the May ball though I've seen her a couple of times, usually on that old boneshaker of hers or with that awful little prig she goes around with. Don't see her with fellers

162

yet, I'm glad to say. I wouldn't approve of Foxy having a serious boyfriend, she's one of us. I just hope she doesn't get entangled with some awful froggie fellow; Frenchmen, so far as I can see, are strutting, self-satisfied and greasy with poor complexions and enormous egos. The French girls are all right, but not a patch on our wenches. I never appreciated what marvellous, milky, rosy skin English girls have until I came over here. I should say British girls – remember seeing that girl Sîan bathing in the river very early one morning? Gosh, I'll never forget, her skin was like pearl. Beautiful. I could paint her now, I can see her so clearly in my mind's eye; and don't think 'filthy beast', because us artists are above that sort of thing.

Incidentally, you mentioned a girl in your last letter, said I didn't talk about her any more. I still care for her, but she's gone back to Spain. It's complicated – her parents are hidalgo Spanish, to them I'm a peasant from whom they must guard their daughter – but I've been very patient, and when I go on to Spain I'm going to try to get in touch. I don't hold out much hope, because her letters stopped coming; she may well have met someone else, someone more suitable, but I'd never forgive myself if I didn't try to see her, hear from her own lips that I'm no longer important to her. So don't be surprised to get a letter with a Spanish postmark.

Where was I? Oh yes, I was saying I wasn't likely to see much of Foxy over here. Nor I am. But I'll look her up in Cambridge when I go back. I'm doing my practical work now and when I've completed that I'll be back at Clifton Place for a bit and then off to Spain. I don't know where yet, John, but it's idle to pretend that I can stay within spitting distance (sorry) of my father. We simply don't like each other, can't see eye to eye, and I absolutely refuse to be nagged and shouted at and bullied over that bloody trust. I'm afraid I've made it clear enough that I won't shell out in three years' time, far less try to break the trust now for his benefit. When he was really ill he didn't mind so much but now that he's getting better he minds – God, how he minds. I've promised Allsop I'll go home for a couple of weeks at Christmas because it's very unfair to leave him with Sir George and all the misery of it for twelve months out of the twelve, but we're going to have to have a talk, Allsop and I. I've never admitted I can't live there whilst Sir George does, but I'll have to tell Allsop, see what he says. Perhaps if I moved out of the hall, down to the lodge? It is empty, and there are empty cottages, too, which I could use. I'm not kidding myself that the old man would like it, but he wouldn't have much choice. I'm twenty-two now, I'll be twenty-three by the time I get my degree (if I get it; there's many a slip . . .) and I won't allow the old boy to push me around then, believe me.

Anyway, at the moment I'm having my last taste of true freedom. This time next year I'll be clerking it in some office (only joking; whatever I do it won't be an office job) or sailing halfway round the world on a tramp-steamer. Now that really does appeal. Care to join me, Johnny, before you're too old to want to get your leg loose, you old sobersides, you? We could have some fun, the two of us. Think about it: the salt breeze in your face, exotic shores, lovely ladies (naturally) and all that goes with such things. I dare you, Hoverton, to cast aside farming just for six months or so and come adventuring with me!

Take care, you randy old sod, you, I'll try to pop in at Christmas.

Yours etc.,
Laurie

Bees-wing Farm,   2nd November 1935
Nr Ledbury,
Hereford.

Dear Laurie,

Thanks for your letter; glad you were enjoying France so much when you wrote, and hope you bring home some pictures for us to admire. Sorry I haven't replied sooner but no one writes letters in September anyway, not if they live on a hop farm, they don't! And October has simply flown by, so much to do! But we're well into our work now and so I'm answering your letter whilst I've got a quiet moment. It's evening, of course, Mum is crocheting a bedspread – she never does things by halves – and Dad is listening to a classical-music concert on the wireless. Well, he's pretending to do so, really I suspect he's sound asleep but it wouldn't do to rag him about it. He really loves classical music.

Mum sends her love and Dad says to tell you he's fighting fit again, the leg has mended properly at long last and he's taking the management of the farm firmly back into his own hands. It's idle to say I don't mind because of course I do, I'm only human, but I don't mind much. And I'm still overseeing the hops, which is gratifying, especially since it makes more money from less acreage than any other aspect of the farm.

Of course I've found it a trifle hard having to get permish, as we used to say in school, every time I want to fart, but there are compensations; it's great to have Dad on top form again for one thing and the responsibility, the waking up in the night and worrying, have just disappeared as if they'd never been. And Dad's being very understanding over my feeling that we must get mechanised and we have a good, modern tractor, a Massey Ferguson, and we're going to go shares with a combine next year. What's more we now use pricier seed for the barley, wheat, etc., since I decided to have a go with the superior stuff when I was in charge and Dad has had to agree, albeit reluctantly, that the bigger outlay resulted in a far better and more valuable crop.

We had an excellent hop season this year despite a touch of downy mildew right at the top end, where Dad cut the elms down a couple of years ago. I told him at the time if he thinned that hedge too much he'd let all sorts through from Fairbrother's place . . . but it probably wasn't that, I believe it's carried on the wind or some such thing. I keep meaning to look it up, but we're always so busy.

Anyway it didn't affect the crop since it was only half-a-dozen or so plants and we've dug them up and replaced them. Dad thought spraying would be good enough but the hops are my pigeon so we bought new cuttings. Better safe than sorry – we got over three hundred pockets out of our acreage this year, so you know it was a good one, and the brewery buyers had quite a brisk little auction, which is always to our advantage.

It sounds stupid to say I miss you more at hop-picking, but it just happens to be true. We had such fun as kids, and it was a time when we were never apart. And then of course there was Foxy. Never was there a better climber; when I'm in the orchards now, at the top of a ladder, picking into one of those big enamel buckets, I often think of Foxy shinning up with her skirt tucked into her knickers, and throwing the best fruit down to us. She used to get scratched and bruised, her hair was always getting caught up, but she didn't give a damn. She was a right'un was Foxy! Still is, I guess. This was the first hop-picking she's missed since she was twelve – remember her then? A skinny, sarky,

165

bossy little beast . . . and she got a sunburned neck and we made her cry . . . can't remember how, just remember feeling a brute and trying to make it up to her by taking her up to the house to Mum.

Still, at least she writes regularly. She enjoyed her French trip but doesn't see herself going over again, not for a while, and certainly not during September again. She enjoyed the contrast, she said, but still missed Bees-wing like hell. Well, she didn't say hell, but you get the gist.

So another hop season is successfully over, and we're starting again. Ploughing, sowing, weeding, spraying . . . good job I love it! But one of these days I'll kick over the traces and go off with you and that's a promise. Dad actually said I ought, what do you think of that? So you see, one of these days . . .

But in the meantime, there's Christmas. I can't tell you how good it will be to have you here again, actually at Bees-wing. We've never moved your bed you know, so all you have to do is turn up and leave the rest to us. Take care, old son,

Yours etc.,
John

King's College,   20th February 1936
Cambridge.

Dear John,

Oh God, Johnny, I ought to throw my hat in first, even before I write a word, but I swear on the Bible and on everything else that I simply couldn't help it, couldn't get to Bees-wing. Christmas was the giddy limit, not like Christmas at all – you must have heard the rumours? My clodhoppers never even touched the ground – to be blunt, there was quite a rumpus back at the old stately home. Father, feeling better, suddenly decided to make a break for it and you wouldn't believe how far he got; all the way to London and into some wretched club to which he belonged at one time. No details, they wouldn't interest you, but he managed in five days to do the sort of financial damage that would have taken me, had I decided to go on the binge, at least a year.

Allsop, mouth tight and brows close, went in pursuit and then telephoned me that he'd found the old man but couldn't shift him. It's most awfully awkward because Sir George is an elderly man and as he took considerable pleasure in informing me, I'm a brainless, ball-less stripling with ink instead of blood in my veins: that was one of the least offensive epithets he bawled at me during our subsequent encounter. By God, John, but he was shifting the readies! I saw red, literally, for the first time in my entire life when Allsop, without an emotion crossing that ideal-butler countenance, told me the sum Sir George had already lost. Let alone what he'd spent on various fripperies.

But one glance at the old man's purple, bulging-eyed countenance told me that I wouldn't be able to shift him either unless I used violence, so I resorted to cunning. I went up to his room with a bottle of single malt (that's extremely good whisky, I'm informed by Allsop) and encouraged him to take a gargle or two. I had to pretend to drink as well, but the more he drank the less he noticed that I wasn't, if you see what I mean. And when he was comatose I got hold of Allsop and we assisted him down the stairs and into the back of the Riley. I drove him all the way home to Clifton Place – he was vilely sick twice, we had to stop and hold his head out of the window – and then we put him to bed in the old nursery at the top of the house (it's got bars on the windows) and locked the door on him.

All the way home in the car, incidentally, we kept on telling each other that we could be thrown into gaol, very likely, for kidnapping, but I can't say it seemed to worry Allsop overmuch and I have to admit it worried me not at all. I could quite see that I should have to have a talk with the old boy and I was dreading that, but I didn't repent of having carried him away from London, not a bit of it. The old fool had been gambling on tick, buying on tick, even eating, sleeping and drinking on tick, and what enraged me was that people had let him do so because he told them that his son would cough up. Me, pay for his confounded pleasures when, thanks to him, I've scarcely a feather to fly with!

The trust is big, though. Lots of spondulicks, as the fellows at school would have said. But since I can't get at it, we have to soldier along on what the estate can bring in. It is heavily encumbered, Mr Hawkings says, and I think this means the old man's mistakes have to be put right just as his debts have to be paid, but I'm going to make sure any new debts are disowned. I won't let him ruin all of us. It's an awful thing, John, when you discover that the man who sired you is not only dishonest, stupid, sly and a liar, but nasty as well . . . bit much, eh? Plus he hates my very guts with the utmost venom because the staff stand by me and won't let him escape, Allsop won't connive with him to fool me, and I won't – can't, but he sees it as won't – break the trust.

So where does that leave me? I spent the entire Christmas break first seeing that my father didn't escape from the nursery and jolly off back to London, and then talking reason to him. I talked till I was dry and bored and furious with myself as well as him, and then Providence stepped in. He had another stroke, not a bad one, just a slight one, but it was enough to knock him off balance again. I felt a trifle guilty because of the whisky I'd encouraged him to drink (the doctor told me that a small whisky was good but that downright drunkenness was not), but you can't make an omelette without breaking eggs, the end justifies the means and all roads, they tell me, lead to Rome. In other words, I 'ad to do it, your ludship, I 'ad no option. I wasn't around when he had the slight stroke but Allsop was, which was lucky. He understands the old man and his medicine far better than I ever could. I don't really know what happened, except that Allsop rang for the doctor and by the time I got back (I'd been into Ledbury to buy some stuff for the staff since we'd missed out on Christmas thanks to good old Sir G's jolly jaunt) they were saying, rather wearily, that he would doubtless live to worry everyone sick once more and could be brought down from the nursery since he wasn't well enough to escape again.

The doctor asked where we intended to put him and Allsop suggested the Chinese room because it's awfully convenient for nursing a sick man; the nurse could sleep in the dressing room and make full use of the bathroom. But I couldn't agree to that, there's something about that room which worries me still. It sounds silly, but there's a desperate sort of sadness there, I've always been conscious of it, and even the old man, who has the hide of an elephant, might possibly be uneasy. So Sir George was put back in his own bedroom, which has a bathroom though no dressing room, and when I left again, seemed settled once more.

I've written to Mum and Uncle Bill apologising and trying to explain, only it's difficult because your dad said he never wanted to hear Sir George's name again and since the old man was my chief *reason for not coming over . . . well, there you are. Only don't let them blame me too much, John old fellow. I'm really not responsible for the sins of my father . . . except that I am, of course.*

One other thing which has been bothering me is that I've still not had my talk to Allsop about not wanting to live permanently at Clifton Place when I come down in June. Do you think I should tell him? Only it's so unfair on him – Allsop, I mean. But I'm sure the old man will live for years yet and I can't spend my life being the most hated gaoler in town! So I'm going to tell Allsop that I won't make any demands on the estate, that I'll earn my own living by the sweat of my brow etc. etc. (and abroad, if I possibly can, only I needn't say that to Allsop) and advise him to abandon the old place and the old man while he still can. Not that I can see him doing it; he must be very fond of Clifton Place to have stayed for so long when the old man didn't pay him and is such a pig, and he has been endlessly good to me. In short, he stuck with the status quo for years when he could, I'm certain, have got a very much better butlership (is that a word?) elsewhere. Certainly any other employer would at least have paid him! So I doubt he'll abandon ship yet awhile, no matter what I say, but I feel he must at least be given the opportunity.

I've done a lot of thinking about this wretched trust, incidentally, and I've come to the conclusion that I have absolutely got to be a long way from Sir George when I'm twenty-five or he'll have the money out of me somehow. I realise I may have to gazette him discreetly, in fairness to all the people who'll let him punt on tick and run up debts in the starry-eyed belief that his loving son will bail him out, but I can do that from a distance. When he's gone, it will be a different story; then I can go home and take up my responsibilities with a fair chance of success. I know I shouldn't say such a thing and I wouldn't to anyone else, but between ourselves John, that's how my mind is working. Until then, the more distance there is between us the merrier we both shall be.

So all being well, I'll come back in June to pick up my hard-earned BA, and then I'll go off again, to lead a life of profligacy and pleasure far from Clifton Place and my extremely unrevered parent. But before I go I promise and swear that I'll come back to Bees-wing Farm, if only for the briefest of brief visits. After all, since I intend to abandon the old man and the ancestral pile there will be no reason why I can't spend a couple of hours saying goodbye to old friends. And also to mere acquaintances, such as yourself!

Cheerio for now, old bean, give Mum a smacking kiss from me,

Yours etc.,

Laurie

PS Forgot to tell you I bumped into Foxy in the street the other day and suggested we go to Auntie's, in St Mary's Passage, for coffee and a cream cake, which invitation she briskly accepted. She's turning into one of those clever, lively girls who throng the streets of Cambridge, usually with a good many young men in tow. I wouldn't say she was conventionally pretty, but she's certainly got something – and her figure is greatly improved. Well, she's got one, no longer can she be compared unfavourably with a hop-pole. She's a good kid, I like her immensely and know you do too. If you didn't, old boy, I might have a go there myself! She says she'll pick hops next year, come what may, couldn't bear another year away from all of you. Said – a trifle graciously – that she had missed me, too, and would be sure to look me up next autumn. I told her I wouldn't be there and she said, without a blink, in that case she would certainly call on Allsop, for whom she had a great affection. That set me back a bit, I always thought she rather liked me. Still, can't win 'em all and as you know I'll be hotfooting it after my own particular little peach any time now. By next June I may very well be married – imagine that, old John!

Must go and do some work, but take care of yourself, and write when you have time, reading your letters is almost as good as walking up the hopyard and into Long Acre.

Bees-wing Farm,   10th April 1936
Nr Ledbury,
Herefordshire.

Dear Foxy,

Didn't we have a nice time? Aren't you glad you decided to accept my invitation to help on the farm for your Easter recess or whatever they call it? I hadn't realised how lonely I had been, with you and Laurie gone, until suddenly there was Foxy Lockett herself, standing on the doorstep, one hand raised to knock. And me shambling across the kitchen on my way to the shippon, opening the door, and standing staring, no doubt with my chin touching my knees, because I never really thought you'd come, not with so much work to do for your degree. It was a real bolt from the blue ... but you know all that because I must have mentioned it once or twice whilst you were at Bees-wing!

You're going to make some farmer a wonderful wife, I trust you know that? You've got the knack and I don't see why a degree in English literature shouldn't come in useful even on a farm. You could teach, I imagine. Or be a writer for a newspaper. Or a novelist, if your fancy led you in that direction. Or you could just be a farmer's wife, the most beautiful, talented farmer's wife ... shut up, John, I can hear you say, you're doing just what we promised we wouldn't do. No ties, no strings, no promises. We're awfully young, you're saying, and I'm still only halfway through my degree, I must finish it, I must show everyone that they were right to give me the opportunity ...

You are such a darling! I'm older than you, so I know a darling when I see one and I know how I feel, even if you aren't quite so sure yet. Mum and Dad loved you when you were a kid so they'll love you again, especially when I tell them that you've agreed ... Well, you haven't yet, but you will, won't you? Oh Foxy ...

Sorry. Sorry-sorry-sorry! I know I promised. Only I'll never walk through the hopyard in spring again without remembering that night, the full moon, the young hop plants just beginning to climb, the mist just beginning to form between the rows, the breeze wafting across and bringing us the unforgettable scent of the primroses on the bank ... and the funny little noise you made when I tried to kiss you, the feel of you in my arms.

You felt lovely, Foxy. All the poetic words, lissom, supple, tender, soft, that was how you felt. In my arms you were a part of me, a part that had been missing and had come home. You belonged there, I knew it; I find it hard to believe you didn't know it too. And your skin smelt of apples (had you been scrumping in the apple loft, you bad little girl, you?) and your hair of the dark red roses which grow under the dining-room window. I was so happy; kissing you was the most wonderful ... but I promised, I mustn't forget. You're right, of course. You aren't twenty-one yet and I'm only two years older and we've got all our lives before us. I don't know what you mean about my

171

parents – they'll love you as much as I do, it's just that Mum had somehow got it into her head that I was going to marry a farmer's daughter; the Fairbrothers' one and only, you know. But I've never been other than slightly friendly with her and though I suppose it's possible that I might meet someone else then it's equally possible that I might fly to the moon. There's only one Foxy Lockett and she's the . . . sorry, sorry, sorry!

Change the subject, then. At once. Immediately. Very good, ma'am, if that's what you want, if you don't wish to be reminded of moonlight, and soft lips touching . . .

I wish Cambridge was nearer but at least, with Dad back in command, I can get time to write. You'll come and see us in the summer vac? Of course you will, you'll come and work here again, you said you would. At this rate, you'll be seeing the whole of the hop-year, from the moment of putting in the little new plants to the cutting down of the bines for the pickers. And you'll learn about sheep, shearing 'em, dipping 'em, helping them to lamb . . . you'll love lambing, my . . . you'll love lambing, Foxy. Mustn't forget the rules, must I? And you'll love seeing the new calves born and persuading them to suck your fingers in a bucket of milk instead of their mother's teats. It's all such fun and it's all ahead of you. Like life, Foxy.

But it's bedtime and I just want to walk across the yard and into the lower orchard and check on the hens. In the spring a young fox's fancy lightly turns to thoughts of a chicken dinner, so we have to round the hens up or we'll find ourselves one short. Goodnight, dearest little Lockett, and write soon,

Yours as ever,
John

Cambridge. 15th May 1936

Dear John,

I'm back. I didn't write from Spain because I was pretty down, and that's the understatement of the year. I haven't said anything to anyone else, but you'll only have to clap eyes on me to know something's happened, and anyway, I've got to tell someone.

I tracked Mirri down rather cunningly I thought. I intended to do the rounds, but then it occurred to me, when I reached Madrid (where

172

the atmosphere was so tense that a touch on the shoulder had you spinning round and reaching for an imaginary pistol – the Spanish are so volatile that they all behave as if they were armed even when they aren't), that I might easily discover what I wanted to know by guile. So I booked into a horrid, hot little boarding house place and then I had a good look round. I didn't go up to the Rodriganez house until the second day and then I went and skulked and listened in all the usual places for gossip or for any news of the family. I gathered that they had left the house some months ago but no one seemed quite certain where they had gone so after a decent interval I went and visited the house myself, as though I had a right there.

An old man with rheumy eyes and seamed, dark skin answered my knock. I said I'd called to see Señor Rodriganez on business but had been told he was out of town; I had news, I said significantly, which the señor would be most anxious to hear.

Safe enough, with Spain buzzing the way it was and probably still is. The Popular Front, with Azaña at its head, may have won hearts and minds amongst the people, but I must admit I feel very uneasy. They've released prisoners, many of whom should have been released, of course, but what about the child molesters, the murderers, the men of violence who kill for killing's sake? They're out as well, and though the clergy may have been dilatory so far as the poor were concerned, burning the churches down along with a good few monasteries hasn't exactly reassured anyone as to the rule of law.

But I digress; back to my questioning of the old porter in Madrid. The old fellow said at once, 'They're in Granada, at the house of the señora's family.' I clapped a hand to my head and said very well, I would hire a car and go there at once, and he gave me the address; just like that! It did occur to me that Mirri and her mother might have been sent elsewhere, but I didn't think it likely.

So off to Granada I went. It's a beautiful city but I never even got inside the Escorial, which I've wanted to see all my life, because on my second day, I saw Mirri.

I found the house; what a grim pile! It took me several hours just to get round the back and make absolutely sure which windows belonged to which house because Spanish houses are built like fortresses. In order to visit the family legitimately I would have had to open a pair of wrought-iron gates, walk down an extremely dark passage which led under the humber housing which fronted their casa, and then ring a huge bell outside another pair of cast-iron gates. I would then be admitted – or not – into an Arabian nights courtyard, all tinkling fountain, palm trees and enormous earthenware bowls in which scarlet and pink geraniums and more exotic blooms fought for attention. Across the courtyard I would have gone, up three white marble steps, to a vast, blackened front door which would have swung open to reveal a marble hallway and a wonderfully ornate stairway.

I don't know where it would have led though, because I never got inside the front door, but I'll tell you what happens.

It was the following day, while I was still planning my strategy. I didn't fancy going up to the house to see her father on business because I knew very well I couldn't keep up that sort of pretence to Señor José de Salvorini y Rodriganez. I was in a small café, eating a Spanish omelette, drinking red wine and planning my strategy. I was so happy, John, because I knew I was near her – the casa wasn't more than ten minutes' walk away.

And then I saw her, trotting past the window. She had her arm tucked into that of a young man and she was chattering away, glancing up at him through her lashes, almost dancing along the pavement. I knew it wasn't her father, though I've never met him, and she doesn't have a brother. Spanish girls are so strictly watched over that I knew he must be someone of whom her parents approved, but even so I would have run after them, begged a word . . . only I hadn't paid for my omelette or my red wine. And by the time I'd done so they were out of sight. But I didn't despair because I knew there was only one way back into the fortress; she must pass along the narrow cobbled street with vines and climbing plants to reach her home. If I lay in wait there at least I could speak to her, snatch a word. No doubt the young man to whose arm she clung was a Spaniard, hopefully one who did not speak English. I would manage something.

So I loitered up and down the street for what seemed like hours – it was hours, two hours and ten minutes to be precise – and then along they came, only in a taxi this time. It stopped right outside the gates and Mirri got out, her arms full of the most beautiful white lilies. I could smell them – I'll never like that scent again. Heavy, sweet, it hung in the street for moments after the young man had hurried her inside.

I moved forward as she got out of the taxi as though I hadn't noticed her and said, 'Mirri! I must speak to you!'

She was astounded; her eyes and mouth rounded, she went very pale, then she blushed fiery red.

'Laurie! Oh, Laurie, I thought I'd never see you again!' she said – in English, of course. 'They locked me up for months . . . I wanted to write but they've sent my maid away . . . I've been so unhappy!'

The man with her gave me one look and simply hustled her away. I stepped forward, of course, and tried to catch hold of her, but she said, 'Don't! Oh Laurie, don't make trouble!' and I saw that it would be useless. The servants must have been waiting for her, the wrought-iron gates opened, the couple were ushered inside . . . I moved away and heard him questioning her about me. We'd been speaking English, of course, and clearly it wasn't a language he understood. Mirri, bless her, fobbed him off with some tale of a schoolfriend's brother . . . and then they were making their way down the passage, their voices growing fainter and fainter, and the gates had clanged shut behind them.

I didn't know what to do, John! And in the end I decided the honest approach might be best. The following day I went up to the gate, rang the bell, said I wished to speak with Señor de Salvorini y Rodriganez, and was let in as far as the courtyard. The servant went indoors – he shut the big front door behind him so there was no chance of sneaking inside – and presently a tall, dark-haired, cold-eyed man came out. He knew me at once.

'Mr Clifton, you are not welcome here,' he said, in almost impeccable English, he has only the slightest of accents. 'My daughter is not for the likes of you; she is betrothed to someone of her own class. You must leave at once or I'll have you thrown out.'

I was taken aback, his voice was so full of hatred and disgust, but I just said, 'Where is Mirri? Why can't she speak for herself?'

'She's gone,' he said, still coldly, not as though he cared about her one bit. 'She was happy enough here, she had some freedom, at least, but because of you we've had to incarcerate her elsewhere. And she'll stay locked away until she's safely married. And now, Mr Clifton, you are in my country, not yours. If you don't leave my daughter alone I'll have you whipped to within an inch of your life. Her, too, if you persist.'

John, I wanted to hit him; but there was no point. He had the upper hand because I knew, as soon as he said it, that he had moved Mirri and *that another time I'd have a harder job to find her. He would have had me whipped – and Mirri, no doubt. He would have enjoyed it.*

So I hung around for a couple of days, just to make sure Mirri really wasn't there, and then I headed for Blighty. What else could I do? I came home because I could see that my presence would only get her into trouble, and anyway there seemed no way to find out where she was or how I could help her. Poor little thing . . . I couldn't forget how happy she had looked, hanging on the young fellow's arm, nor how unhappy and scared she had become when she recognised me. Finally, I decided that leaving was best for both of us, that she wasn't for me and I would have to acknowledge it.

And now all I have to do is pass my finals and get my BA and I'll be all set to start a career of some description, until such time as I'm needed to run the estate, that is. So as soon as my feet touched British soil I decided to snatch a weekend at Clifton Place. I wanted to talk to Allsop about bringing my father up for the 'do', and as you may have guessed I still hadn't admitted I wouldn't be coming home to take up the reins again yet because there is so little I can do until I come of age.

So I rushed home, talked to Allsop, who told me the old man isn't really up to a trip to Cambridge (well-hidden relief on both sides, I fancy) and then hopped into my old jalopy and arrived at Bees-wing halfway through my first Saturday morning home. And you, you rat, were in Scotland! Didn't you know farmers are meant to stay on their farms? Have you no sense of occasion? I know I hadn't warned you, but it was rather a spur-of-the-moment decision. So it was a bit flat, though Mum and Uncle Bill were absolutely spiffing to me. We talked about the old days and about the future and they said you had a young lady only it was a secret and asked if I had one.

I'd come specially to weep on your shoulder, but you weren't there so it was stiff upper lip time for me whilst you entertained yourself in the land of the pine and the haggis. Or should have been, but Mum knows me so well . . . so in the end I told your parents a bit about Mirri. I also told them that it was a lost cause and Mum was really marvellous. She told me, amongst other things, not to jump to conclusions, that if there was a way Mirri might still find it, because Mum – could she be prejudiced? – could not imagine any girl not falling for either you or me.

She made me feel ever so much better! She said that even in Spain the old ways were giving way to new and with the country in such a state of turmoil I might easily find that Mirri's parents would be glad to see her safe in England in a few months! She said go back then, go straight up to the front door, and ask to speak to Mirri's mother this time, because mothers love their children, they can't help it, and her mother will want what's best for her. She made it all sound so simple that she had me smiling again in no time and telling her all the good things about Mirri − her sweetness, the funny things she says because her English still isn't perfect, I even told them what a little terror she can be.

And then I told Mum about the family attitude, which seems to be rather rough on anyone not, like the Rodriganez clan, stinking rich. They cling to the old ways, which I gather means eating a peasant a day and trampling a couple more underfoot, and although Mirri says it is a wrong attitude, she can be pretty thoughtless about others herself. The waitresses in Cambridge did not like the way she expected them to jump when she said jump . . . and she told me the other girls in her school were common, because they would have to work, one day.

I even told Mum what Mirri had said in an unguarded moment of truth: that in Spain only pigs eat potatoes and only peasants eat pigs! So you see she is a bit of a snob, it's the way she's been brought up. But I would soon charm it out of her. Personally, I don't mind being called a peasant by someone as beautiful as Mirri, provided she doesn't try to stop me eating bacon and enjoying roast spuds on a Sunday.

So that was what I came all the way over to Bees-wing Farm to tell you, Hoverton. I meant to bare my soul to you and you weren't there! And though I still get most awfully depressed at times, I can throw it off whenever I remember Mum's advice − leave it a bit and then go back and try again.

I asked Mum about Foxy and she got a bit tight-lipped and said that whilst Foxy is a dear child and a good friend, she wouldn't like to think that you would consider, even for a moment, marrying outside the farming community. She muttered about Nina Fairbrother, but I said I didn't really think you were smitten in that direction . . . still, she seemed to think you'd got your eye on a farmer's daughter, somewhere. But somehow, I got the feeling that she thought you really did like Foxy rather too much and if so, I'll shake your hand and tell you you've got a good 'un, there. I'm not saying she's right for you, because I've not been with the pair of you often enough to tell. She's grown pretty, has Foxy, though not as pretty as my little Spanish onion . . . am I in love? It feels perilously similar. I'd quite decided that I would never fall in love and it seemed to me a good thing, because there are so many complications. But when it hits you, brother, ducking and weaving get you nowhere. That little arrow bites hard! So I'm going to try my luck again because if you ask me there'll be a really bad disturbance in Spain quite soon. I'll bide my time, but I think of Mirri all the time, see her in my mind . . .

God, how unbearably twee, destroy this letter, eat it or burn it or tear it into a million bits and chuck it to the four winds! I really meant to tell you that Allsop was shattered to hear that I wasn't coming back to Clifton Place until after the old man snuffs it. I was quite touched, to tell you the truth. There were tears in his eyes! Yes, you may well say that the tears were caused by the thought of being shut up for years with the old man, but I don't think it was entirely that. We do get on rather well; he's a tower of strength, he has a nice sense of humour, and to tell the truth I feel a rat, abandoning him.

But I'm going back after the degree ceremony, just for a couple of weeks. I'll tell the old man that I've taken a job abroad for a year or two, and I'll nip over to Bees-wing and we'll have a chat; you can tell me about you and Foxy (if Foxy it is) and I'll tell you all over again about Mirri and you can advise me how best to go about getting her back here.

I haven't actually taken a job abroad yet. First I shall get Mirri out of it, by hook or by crook, then perhaps we'll live in Paris for a bit, so I can paint. Note the 'we', Johnny-boy. I was a fool to let myself be sent home with my tail between my legs; we love each other, I'm sure of it and love jolly well will find a way.

And having made up my mind to try again, I keep having this feeling that life is going to be a lot of fun for the next few years, and when I'm twenty-five, I can reel in the trust and start living responsibly. I haven't said, but the old man looks to me as if he's going downhill fast. Allsop says that planning what he'll do with the trust money when he gets his hands on it is all that's keeping him going . . . he can forget that! I won't change my mind because I dare not; it's going to be hard work putting right all the wrongs as it is without the old man chucking my readies about the way he did his own.

See you soon, then – don't dare go up to Scotland again! Uncle Bill said you'd gone on a course at some agricultural college there concerning stock breeding. Farmers do not go off on courses, they leave that to under-graduates, don't do it again, boy, or it'll be six of the best!

Take care, you old son of the sod,

Laurie

Bees-wing Farm,   *2nd June 1936*
Nr Ledbury,
Herefordshire.

Dear Laurie,

We're not tremendously lucky in love, are we? Yes, I do fancy Foxy, but she's determined to get her degree and equally determined to plough her own furrow until then. I do think she likes me, but it doesn't make any difference, she says we must wait. What's more, she was bitterly hurt by Mum's and Dad's attitude; they've always seemed the epitome of kindness to her before and having them suddenly turn against her (that's how she sees it) has been very painful. For me too, of course, but I know them well enough to realise that it will pass, once Foxy and I are a fait accompli. And in the meantime, I have to try to be patient. But it's not much fun.

It's not much fun having Nina F thrust down my throat morning, noon and night, either. Nina insists on pursuing me whenever the opportunity arises and would much enjoy marriage, I'm sure. The fact that I just can't bring myself to be anything but normally friendly hurts her, but as I told Mum, it's scarcely my fault if the silly girl decides to have a crush on me which I clearly can't reciprocate.

So here we are, the pair of us, in the soup. But my course is easier and more straightforward than yours; all I have to do is wait until Foxy has her degree and then we'll marry, come what may. Dad would never disinherit me, he and Mum would just make the best of it, and in time they would come round, I know they would.

But poor old Lo, I don't envy you! But I'm sure Mum's right and if you go back in a while and speak to Señora de Salvorini y Rodriganez – Gad, what a mouthful – or this time simply leap in and kidnap your Mirri, then you'll be on your way to living happily ever after. It does occur to me that Mirri is probably a Catholic and you're a Protestant,

179

albeit a rather lackadaisical one, but I daresay that won't bother either of you? It may have worried the parents rather more than your Englishness, though. Catholics don't like their children marrying out of the church, I believe.

I'm sorry I wasn't around to have my shoulder wept on, but I'll be here now for months, probably. It will be good to see you, it's been far too long.

Yours affec
John

Clifton Place   *6th June 1936*

John – can you come? My father died this morning.

Laurie

Seven

John had been working in the stackyard, perched on top of a load of hay which he was forking down to the men below, when Cyril, the gardener's boy from Clifton Place, had come puffing into the yard on his ancient bicycle and delivered Laurie's note.

'Letter for Mr John,' Cyril had shouted breathlessly, bringing his bicycle to a wavering halt. He looked uncertainly round, plainly not knowing master from man when all were in shirts and shabby corduroys. One of the farmhands indicated John, balanced on top of the stack, and Cyril shouted up to him: 'Can 'ee come down out o' that, sir? Tes an important letter.'

John had come down off the stack, wiping the sweat off his brow with the back of his arm, and taken the letter. He had not been particularly alarmed; he and Laurie were to have met for a pint at the pub in the village when work finished and he assumed the note would cancel their meeting. He felt a trifle impatient with his old friend and more than impatient with Sir George, who was usually the cause for Laurie cancelling engagements. He tore open the white envelope with his name on and read the note inside.

'*John – can you come? My father died this morning. Laurie.*'

John glanced across at the messenger, then round at the farm workers, all tactfully going about their business. He should have expected something of the sort the way Sir George went on, but somehow he had not. Even so he did not have to consider what he would do, he knew that he would go, and at once. Laurie needed him; that was sufficient.

'Dan, can you take over here? I'll be away for the rest of the day, probably. Harry, you'd better continue with the stack . . . oh, can one of you find my father presently, when you've unloaded the cart, and tell him someone's called for me and I'll be in touch when I can? Oh, and . . . give Dad this note.' He handed it to Elias, who stuffed it into his grimy trouser pocket. 'I'll take the Sunbeam, it'll be quicker.'

'You're off to Clifton Place then, Mr John?' Elias asked. 'Gone to Mr Laurie, have you? Shall I tell the master that?'

'If you would. There's – there's a bit of trouble.' John turned to Cyril, who was scarlet in the face from his bicycle ride through the heat of the day. 'I'll give you a lift back, Cy. You can leave your bike here and pick it up another day.'

'Thanks, Mr John, but it ain't possible. The telephone's gone wrong, seemingly, so I'm to ride on to Ledbury and . . .' he lowered his voice, '. . . fetch the undertaker. The doctor's there now.'

'The telephone's gone wrong again? But Mr Laurie said a bloke from the telephone company had come in and put the instrument right.'

The boy nodded. 'Aye, he did that a week gone, and we ain't to say Mr Laurie no more, he's Sir Laurence now. Mr Allsop said to 'member that. And Mr Allsop said the telephone seemed to 'ave gone wrong agin, but he may've been mistook. It ain't workin', anyhow.'

'Right. You go on your way, then, and I'll drive over to the Place.'

John ran from the stackyard into the farmyard and over to the door. He entered the kitchen breathlessly, to find his mother placidly making scones, her ingredients spread out round her. She raised her eyebrows at his sudden appearance.

'Someone had an accident? I can come in a moment if . . .'

'Yes . . . no, not an accident. Mum, Laurie sent a lad over with a note, their telephone's gone for six again. His – his father died earlier today. He wants me.'

'Dear God! But Sir George can't be much more than fifty-five or six! What was he doing? I suppose he come off that great roan of his and broke his neck? Oh no, someone said it had been sold after his stroke.'

'I don't know anything other than that he's dead, which is what Laurie put in the note,' John said patiently. 'I must go, Mum, Laurie really needs me.'

'Yes, of course you must, lad. No point in me running on. You go

182

off then, love, and drive careful. I'll not put you out a dinner.'

'I can't ring you to let you know when I'll be back, but I'll send someone down to the neighbours and ask them to phone from there, if I'm going to be late for supper,' John said. He was washing at the sink, not wanting to waste time going upstairs. He soaped his hands, face and neck, then rinsed them, turned to the little piece of mirror over the sink and began to tidy his hair by combing the hay out of it with his fingers. 'I probably won't be long . . .'

He was heading for the back door when his mother stopped him.

'John, you look a scarecrow! Put on something decent for the love of heaven! A clean shirt . . . some respectable trousers . . . a decent pair of shoes . . . your black lace-ups . . .'

'No time,' John called over his shoulder. 'I'll borrow some clobber off Lo, if I have to.'

The door slammed behind him.

Mrs Hoverton watched her son go across the yard, then returned to her task. She had made one batch of scone mixture but decided to make a second; the men were always hungry and a buttered scone went down well. She poured flour into her big yellow bowl, added just a touch of sugar, then began to rub in the fat, letting her thoughts wander. And, inevitably, they wandered to Clifton Place, to Sir George, and to Laurie.

She had loved Laurie from the first moment she had seen him, a tiny, sad-looking little monkey of a baby whose mother had died only a few hours before. Sir George had thrust him into her arms with a mumbled explanation and left the house, promising to return as soon as he could. And she had popped the scrap of humanity into the old-fashioned cradle where her own placid blond son had been lying.

'This is a little feller what's lost his mum, our John,' she had whispered. 'He's come to live with us for a bit, an' you'll have to take good care of him 'cos you're two whole weeks older'n little Laurie, here.'

And John had taken care of him, though Laurie was by no means a milksop. Taken care of him until now, rather. Now both boys were beginning to make their way in the world, to turn outwards instead of, in. Ada had known it would happen, but losing Laurie so abruptly, the way they had, had hurt her. And sometimes, looking at John's fair head bent over a letter which she knew must be from Foxy, Ada had felt again the pain a mother feels as the silver cord stretches, stretches . . . as the child fights to tumble into the great world for the second time in its life, only this time the child tumbles away and not towards the parents who have given him that life and have spent their own lives teaching him to live without them.

She worried about John, because he was his father's son through and through. He could only be happy farming the land, and it should be his land, Bees-wing Farm. But he needed a good wife by him, the right sort of wife. Ada came from farming stock and she knew that a wife can make or break a farm. An idle slut, like Ginny Tickett from over Brampton Abbotts way, could do endless harm.

Ginny was a city girl, from Hereford. She had caught Benny Tickett and reeled him in like a silly trout, dazzled by her peroxide hair, her long, slender legs, her pretty, doll-like face. She settled into her husband's small farmhouse and proceeded to buy in every morsel of food they ate; she couldn't cook, no one had ever taught her and she had no wish to learn. Benny had to employ someone else to milk the cows, to cultivate the vegetable garden whilst Ginny spent his money like water, even buying herself a car so she could go back to the city three or four times a week. She didn't bother to lock up the henhouse each night so there were no eggs and the fox got the hens, she forgot to feed the pigs, went off gadding when she should have been in . . . and worst sin of all, she had given birth to three girls, each one as empty-headed and giggly as herself.

Foxy was a city girl. Hadn't she burned her neck raw the very first time she entered a hopyard? What was worse, she was clever. She was at Cambridge University, filling her head with a lot of bookish nonsense, when, if she truly intended to be a farmer's wife, she should have been doing something practical. Cookery lessons, sewing lessons, learning how to manage on a small budget, forgetting all this nonsense about a career. A farmer's wife *had* a career, it was looking after her husband at first and then their sons . . . sons, not daughters . . . and it was making the best bread

184

for miles around, cooking the sort of meals which would line a hardworking man's ribs, knitting him thick scarves, feeding his hens and using the eggs, feeding the pigs, driving the pony and trap, not yearning after a scarlet sports car when your husband had difficulty finding the money to pay his feed merchant.

Foxy was a nice little girl, though, the kinder side of Ada's nature reminded her. You liked her so much, then.

But then I thought Laurie was sweet on her, Ada's not-quite-so-nice side replied firmly. Then, she wasn't a threat to my John. Foxy would do very well for Laurie, he needs a wife with brains, someone who can look good. John just needs a homely girl whose father owns land.

Still. If the worst comes to the worst and they marry . . .

I'll tell him they can't; there's pretty girls, farmers' daughters, who'd give their right hand for a smile from my boy. He must choose one of them.

Ah, but human nature can't always help itself, Ada's kinder side interpolated. You wouldn't want to break your boy's heart?

Ada, kneading her scone dough so vigorously that the poor scones had no chance of rising but would have to be served as biscuits, shook her head at herself. Of course she wouldn't want to break John's heart, but he was only a foolish young man, after all. Everyone knew what young men were after and either Sarah, Nina or Lucy would be only too delighted to give it to him, once he'd agreed to marry one of them.

Vague recollections of a saying her father had once used – *all cats are grey at night* – entered her head. It would be all right, she'd simply warn John off and push a farmer's daughter at him. As for Foxy, she was welcome to her career and anything else she wanted so long as she let John Hoverton be.

Ada began to roll out her scone dough. Later, when she got the scones out of the oven and found them flat as pancakes, she would lay the blame where it belonged. On Foxy, for – temporarily – making her hand as heavy as her heart.

John hurried across the yard and into the shippon. The Sunbeam was parked against a bale of last year's hay. It looked like a beast about to eat and John, grinning, swung the starting handle and heard the engine begin to purr, then got behind the wheel, slammed into reverse and shot out into the yard. A quick turn and the car was bouncing across the potholes in the lane, then onto the road. The roof was down and the wind tore at John's hair, drying the sweat on his brow, giving him a feeling of holiday totally out of tune with his mood. He remembered uneasily that Laurie had come home specifically to tell Sir George that he would be living and working abroad for the foreseeable future; suppose the news had brought on another stroke?

But now . . . what exactly would Laurie do now? Stay? Go? He would inherit nothing from Sir George but debts . . . oh, this is stupid, John told himself crossly, I can't possibly know what will happen until I've seen Laurie so it's a waste of time and imagination trying to guess. Accordingly he drove the rest of the way singing loudly to himself, only stopping, guiltily, as he swung into the estate between the tall wrought-iron gates.

As he got out of the car the front door shot open. Laurie almost dragged him into the house and over to the study.

'John, thank God, I was beginning to feel I'd go mad if I couldn't talk to someone! Sit down, old boy. I'll ring for the maid – Allsop and the doctor are up there with a sort of midwife woman who lays people out – and she'll get us something to eat.'

'It doesn't matter,' John said, sinking into the visitor's chair and watching whilst Laurie circumvented the big old desk and took his place behind it. 'I can last without food for an hour or so, you know.'

Laurie ignored him, tugging so impatiently at the long, embroidered bell-pull that John wondered if it would come apart in his hands. Most of the furnishings of Clifton Place made him feel like that. But it remained all in one piece and remarkably quickly a small, shabby girl in a grubby apron made her appearance.

'Yessir Mr Laurie?'

She had clearly not made the connection between Sir George's death and his son's inheritance of the title – not yet, at any rate. And Laurie was far too distracted to notice, or care, John thought.

'A sandwich or something, please, Carrie.'

The girl gave a sort of bob and left the room. Laurie leaned back in his chair, sighed deeply, then stretched and yawned.

'Dear God, what a day, and it's scarcely past noon! Now look, I'm going right back to the beginning, which was last evening, right?'

'All right,' John said soothingly. 'Just you tell me what's been happening here; do I take it Sir George died of another stroke?'

'Yesterday evening,' Laurie said, not answering the question, 'I decided I would tell my father that I should be leaving in about ten days. As you know I'd told Allsop, but I hadn't broken it to the old boy. I knew he didn't really care one way or the other but I guessed he'd make some sort of fuss once a definite date was set, so I'd been putting it off. There's still quite a lot of work to do on the estate, but I reckoned I could get through most of it in ten days.'

'Got you,' John said, when the pause stretched rather. 'And then . . . ?'

'Oh well, I told him and he grumbled a bit and then said that since I'd decided, like the rat I am, to desert the sinking ship, he presumed I had made financial provision for him? Just like that! I could almost like him for his cheek, except that . . . oh, confound it, the poor old bugger's dead, I mustn't . . .'

This time the silence looked like being a permanent fixture. Laurie stared out across John's shoulder as though he were seeing a ghost and John looked at his friend's strained white countenance and thought of that other Laurie, the one who had lived so happily at Bees-wing Farm with the Hovertons until he was nineteen years old and about to go to university . . . and who had been dragged off on that September day four years ago, never to return. Sir George, John thought bitterly, was responsible for that change in Laurie. Because of his demands and his profligacy Laurie had been forced to become hard, to stay away from Bees-wing, to learn to dislike the man he knew he should love.

'And then . . . ?' John prompted again, when Laurie continued to stare into space. 'You told Sir George you would be leaving in a fortnight and . . . ?'

'And he asked me to reveal my plan for breaking the trust and putting him in charge of sufficient money to keep body and soul together. I told him that if he didn't splash the stuff about he should be able to manage on what came in from the rents etc., and he began to shout about a thankless child being sharper than a serpent's tooth . . . that sort of thing. So I got up and went through to the dining room for dinner. He didn't come with me, but I know how he can sulk, so I ate my meal and went round the estate – it was a lovely evening. I left the old boy to Allsop, who can usually manage him.'

More silence. This time John let it stretch and finally Laurie sighed, yawned again, and said: 'Where was I?'

'You went for a walk and left him to Allsop.'

'Yes. And then at eleven o'clock, when I was sitting in here doing the books, he came stumping in. It surprised me because I thought he was in bed but I pushed the books aside and greeted him as nicely as I could. He looked very much better; he smiled at me, a thing he seldom does, and for a mad moment or two I actually entertained the hope that he had realised, at long last, that there's no point in these constant quarrels and his equally constant airing of his unfavourable opinion of me. But I suppose he was smiling because he had spent the intervening hours since our last encounter working out a plan, and it had come to him at last. Pleas hadn't worked, threats hadn't worked, so he would combine the two; carrot and stick.

'He was very sensible and friendly at first; reminded me that the money which my mother had put in the trust should have come, in the nature of things, to him since he was her legal husband. Told me that if he had just sufficient for his needs we would all pull through, that he would run the estate sensibly, would see that expenditure didn't exceed income. I said I was sorry but I really had done my best; the trust was unbreakable.

' "Right, boy," he said, still quite calm and friendly. "I've not had much of a life, what with your good mother dying on me so young and having all the responsibility for you with none of the pleasures of fatherhood. If you can't see your way to breaking the trust then I'm sure I might just as well be dead. If there's truly no way round it then I shall top myself and make you a good deal happier, though no richer, I fear."

'That really infuriated me because I knew, or thought I knew, what an empty threat it was. The old boy clings to life and I don't blame him, I'd be the same. But anyway I told him not to be foolish, said that in a relatively short while now the trust would end and we would be able to get the money, but he'd gone all sulky on me by then, kept looking at me under his eyebrows the way a tricky old bull looks at you before he charges. And then he just shot his chair back and started reviling me. I really admire his grasp of invective, there wasn't much he didn't call me, and when he was almost howling with it he sort of grabbed at his throat, turned the most baleful glare on me, and stamped out of the room, still muttering under his breath.

'Scenes like that have happened often enough, God knows, but I was still shaken by it. Not by the suicide threat because I didn't think he'd ever do that, but by the fact that he'd bothered to make it. So I footled around downstairs for a bit and then went up to my room. I didn't look in on him or anything like that, just went straight to bed. And straight to sleep, too.

'I woke at six or so; old habits die hard. I still keep farmer's hours, and very handy it was when I was studying. I never gave the old man a thought, I just went straight downstairs, to the kitchen, got myself a sandwich and a cup of tea and went out to the stables. We've got a couple of horses now, nothing fancy but good nags, and I wanted a ride, wanted to get away. The row the previous night had left a nasty taste in my mouth and I thought a good gallop would set me to rights.

'I tacked Hannibal up and we went round the park fast, then turned into Hangman's Wood. We made our way through the trees, with the smell of honeysuckle all around us, and out onto the banks of the lake. Well, I call it a lake but it's probably really a very long, winding pond, and very choked up with iris and reeds, too. But it's most awfully pretty, with willows leaning over the water, and two little rustic bridges, and a great many dragonflies zooming across the reed beds. It's a beautifully secret sort of place, I've spent hours there and never seen another living soul.

'I dismounted there, because I wanted to dawdle by the water, and looped Hannibal's reins up so he wouldn't tread in them and let him graze for a bit and went over to see if I could spot a carp. The lake was stocked once and although it's gone to wrack and ruin there are still half-a-dozen carp. Big fellows, gold, orange, silver.'

'I didn't know you had a lake, or even a large pond,' John

murmured into the silence. 'I'd like to go up there, sometime.'

Laurie shuddered. 'I don't think I'll ever want to go up there again. Anyway, I walked out onto the first bridge and looked down into the water. And the old man's face looked straight back at me! You'll think I'm mad, but for a moment I thought he was behind me, leering over my shoulder, that it was his reflection I could see just below the water.'

'Only it wasn't, of course. It was him. Dead.'

'How horrible,' John said in a low voice. 'And you think he killed himself?'

'I don't know! What I truly believe is that he meant me to think he had tried to commit suicide but something went horribly wrong. And now he's dead and he didn't want to die, I know he didn't. He's only fifty-five though he seems – seemed – very much older to me; Allsop's fifty-eight and he seems years younger than Sir George most of the time.'

'Poor Lo. But none of it was your fault, there was nothing you could have done! He hated you and never let you forget it, he wanted money you couldn't provide . . .'

'I know. Oh yes, I know. But John, what in God's name do I do now? I inherit nothing but debts from the old man and the trust still won't come to fruition until I'm twenty-five. Somehow, I've got to keep this place going on the rents for the next three years . . . and in the back of my mind there'll always be the suspicion that if I'd handled it differently, if I'd promised to try to break the trust . . .'

'Stop it, Laurie,' John commanded, seeing tears starting to form in his friend's eyes. 'There was no love lost between you and though you wished him no harm, he was a terrible burden. Through no fault of yours – no fault, Lo – Sir George is gone and you're left to struggle on alone. You'll do it a great deal better if you put all thoughts of guilt out of your mind.'

'That's what Allsop said,' Laurie muttered. 'Well, I shall do my best because I owe it to the estate, but – oh, John! What about Mirri, and getting her out of Spain? I was sure I could get a job in Madrid and either persuade her parents that we were right for each other, or simply steal her away . . . how can I do that if I'm all wrapped up in the estate?'

'What's to stop you doing both, you idiot?' John said bracingly. 'Sort Clifton Place out whilst you're waiting for the situation in Spain to be right for your interference . . . you think the Nationalists will start making life difficult for the ruling classes, I take it? And since the Rodriganez are clearly members of that class, then when they take a tumble you can rush in and grab Mirri either with or without parental sanction. Is that it?'

'Yes, that's what I plan to do,' Laurie said, brightening. 'But that's for the future; for now I'll have to concentrate on the estate, which means seeing Mr Hawkings in the morning to find out what's what. And there's still no money to do all the things that need doing!'

'You'll cope,' John said energetically. 'Besides, now that your – now that Sir George has gone, you'll have as much help as I can give you. I won't deny I found it difficult to come over here while he was alive, after the way he treated Mum and Dad, but now . . . well, whenever Dad can spare me I'll be happy to do what I can. You've got the home farm back, Dad was telling me. Why not start with that?'

'I could have a go,' Laurie said. There was a knock at the door and then the peculiar shuffling push of someone endeavouring to open it without much success. John jumped to his feet and went over and flung the door wide. The girl Carrie, complete with a heavy tray, stood there, mouth open, surveying them both. Since she seemed incapable of actually getting over the threshold John took the tray from her.

'Thanks, Carrie,' he said, as the girl turned away. 'This all looks rather splendid!'

'Doesn't it?' Laurie said absentmindedly as John stood the tray down on the desk between them. 'Mrs Waughman's a treasure as a cook, though pretty damned odd in other departments. What she calls her rough bread is out of this world . . . but you can taste it for yourself.'

He cut several thick rounds off the cottage-style loaf, added generous wedges of cheese and speared some pickles. He divided the food between two plates and handed one to John, then poured coffee from the tall jug into two brown pottery mugs. John took a large mouthful of bread and cheese and nodded approvingly; the bread was coarse, but it had a flavour all its own which blended well with the rich orange double Gloucester.

'First-rate,' John said through his mouthful. 'I really like the bread; what's in it?'

'God knows. Oats, I think, and grain of some sort. It *is* nice, isn't it? Even the old man . . . sorry.'

'For the love of Mike stop apologising every time you mention your father!' John said with some exasperation. 'You don't really think he committed suicide just because you couldn't break the trust, do you? Personally, I think he went up there to sulk . . . don't scowl at me because I'm putting into words what you're thinking . . . and fell in. He might quite easily have been drunk, you know.'

'Stop it, Hoverton,' Laurie said, but without much conviction. 'Do you know, it had crossed my mind . . . but at eight in the morning?'

'No. Last night, you fool. Surely it must have occurred to you that he probably fell in last night?'

There was a longish pause whilst Laurie considered this. Then, ruefully, he shook his head. 'It hadn't. I don't know that it's occurred to anyone, yet. Look, perhaps I'd better see how Allsop and the doc . . .'

Someone knocked briefly on the door and opened it. John swung round and saw a tall, heavily built man with pince-nez perched on his nose, hovering in the doorway.

'Oh, Sir Laurence . . . I'm so sorry, I didn't realise you had company, I just wanted a word . . .'

'Come in, Dr Pready,' Laurie said quickly. 'You've known John Hoverton as long as you've known me and you can speak freely in front of him, we – we're like brothers.'

It was odd, John thought, that this was the first time either of them had ever used the phrase, much used by others. It touched him that Laurie, even after a break of four long years, could still trust him so completely. Yet he knew that, had the positions been reversed, he would have felt exactly the same.

The doctor entered the room and held out a square, well-manicured hand. 'Nice to see you again, Mr John. Last time was when you and Eggy crashed heads in the playground at the village

school – little devils, you were. Sad that the circumstances ...
hmm ...'

'How d'you do, Dr Pready,' John said as they shook hands. He gestured the doctor into the visitor's chair and pulled out another for himself. 'Now, are you sure you wouldn't rather be left alone?'

'Don't be daft, John,' Laurie said impatiently. 'Now, Dr Pready; what do you want to say to me?'

'I've sent for an ambulance, Sir Laurence, to take your father's body to the mortuary, because I fear there will have to be a post-mortem. I don't think he drowned, I believe that death was caused by another stroke which toppled him into the water, where I understand you found him. But Mr Allsop has impressed upon me the importance of making quite sure.'

'Naturally,' Laurie said. 'I suppose you've no idea how long he was in the water, Doctor?'

'Not yet. But as soon as we have sufficient information you will be informed, Sir Laurence, so that funeral arrangements can be made.' He paused, shooting a quick, sideways glance at John. 'Mr Allsop was telling me that there had been a slight disagreement and that in the course of it Sir George made a wild threat to do away with himself. If it's any comfort, Sir Laurence, there was absolutely no sign ... I'm sure the pathologist will confirm ... In short, accidental death, in my opinion, is almost bound to be the verdict.'

'Thank you,' Laurie murmured as the doctor struggled to his feet. 'I'll ring for Allsop; he'll see you out.'

He tugged the bell-pull and the study door opened so promptly that John suspected Allsop must have been outside with his ear to the keyhole.

'Show the doctor out, Allsop,' Laurie said, sounding very much in charge of the situation. John really admired him; Laurie seemed to have banished all his doubts and fears and was already settling into his new role as Sir Laurence Clifton of Clifton Place.

Mr Allsop bowed. 'Certainly, sir. Dr Pready ...'

The two men disappeared and John closed the door behind them and then returned to his seat opposite Laurie.

'Gosh, what a business. I say, Lo, is there anything I can do to help? We could walk round Cumber Farm if you like; farming is

193

something I do know about. You could tell me what happened to your tenant just for a start.'

'Drink and loose women, from what I've heard,' Laurie said, grinning. 'He was an old reprobate, Stan Coleman, and his sons were worse. He had three and they all ran out on him so there's no question of passing the farm on to one of his children. No, it's reverted to the estate and though it's very run-down I think we could make a go of it. I could put a manager in . . .'

'Look, Lo, you *do* know a bit about farming; why don't you have a go at running it yourself? A few years ago, I grant you, it wouldn't have been worthwhile, but now there are crops which can bring in a tidy sum – if you spent the summer ploughing and the autumn planting, you could be making a decent profit next year. And wouldn't it be better doing that than taking some poorly paid job on the continent, far away from . . . well, from us and your responsibilities?'

Laurie sighed. 'I'll talk to Hawkings and Allsop and then I'll let you know what I decide. But you're right, walking round the home farm would be a lot more sensible than just sitting here feeling . . . oh, feeling a complete dead loss. Come on!'

The two of them had gone over Cumber Farm, and after twenty minutes or so John's interest and enthusiasm had infected Laurie. Together, they pulled swathes of grey hay out of stacks, jumped into empty silage pits to examine the state of them, rattled the bars of the pig-pens and pulled faces over the thistle-ridden pastures, the neglected meadows. Even the grazing cattle were poor doers, their hips sticking up like clothes hangers, their skin patchy.

'I'd sell this lot off if I were you,' John said at one point, indicating the remains of the Coleman milking herd. 'They're all old as the hills, you'd do better to buy in new stock. As for the land, you might as well plough the lot and re-seed the pastures, judging from what we've seen so far. I don't believe any of this ground's been treated or manured for twenty years, if not more; I wonder why your father didn't evict him years ago – I bet he never paid rent? Still, we'll never know now. If you take it on it'll be hard work, Lo, but it's a tidy enough place, or will be, when you've brought it into good heart once more. Well worth the trouble, if you ask me.'

'You sound almost envious,' Laurie said, laughing. 'If only I could get at the trust money, though. This place needs money spending – the house is a wreck, even the damned roof leaks!'

The house had been the worst shock. Poultry had wandered freely in all the downstairs rooms, or so it appeared from the mess everywhere, and John doubted that fires had been laid or lit for several years. The grates were broken, the chimneys blocked with nests and dead birds and the smell everywhere was indescribable.

'Oh, but you won't need the house,' John reminded him quickly. 'Not for years yet, anyway. Even if you did get a manager in, he needn't live in the house. As you say, it would cost a fortune to put it right.'

'In a couple of years . . .' Laurie was beginning when John stopped short, frowning down at his feet in their sturdy rubber boots.

'Hang on, don't say anything for a moment. I'm thinking.' After a pause, he looked up, his eyes bright. 'Borrow!' he said.

'Borrow? Borrow money, do you mean? Because I don't know anyone with the sort of money . . .'

'No, you fool . . . well, yes, in a way, I suppose. You're the one with money, Lo! I don't see why you can't borrow on your expectations. Remember your father doing it, when he went up to London that time? You were sick as a dog about it and of course it wasn't his money he was promising to pay back with, but he did get chink out of people, you said he did.

'Well, yes, but the situation isn't quite . . .' Laurie said uncertainly. 'It doesn't make sense, to ask if I can borrow the money that will be mine anyway, in a couple of years. But now you've said it, I can see what you mean. I wouldn't be borrowing my own money, I'd be borrowing from a bank and Mr Hawkings would send them details of the trust so that they would know their money was safe.'

'Only it might not work, because they might realise that, if something happened to you, the cousin wouldn't pay up,' John said belatedly as they hurried back to Clifton Place. 'Still, it's worth a try, don't you think?'

Laurie stopped dead and turned to stare at his friend. 'Worth a try? You're bloody brilliant, Johnny-boy! It even helps me with Mirri because I won't have to tell her I'm penniless for a couple more years, I can tell her we've got money right now! Like a fool I was so busy wanting to be twenty-five that I never even thought of using a bit of intelligence to get what's mine, but now that I can see it . . . John, you're a jolly old genius, d'you know that? You're the tops, you are. Come on!'

He broke into a gallop and John hurried along in the rear. 'I'm not certain, Lo,' he cautioned breathlessly as they burst into the kitchen some ten minutes later. 'I may have got it wrong, it was just that I seemed to remember . . .'

'Allsop! Where the hell is Allsop?' Laurie fired the question at Mrs Waughman, who was placidly rolling out pastry, then burst out of the room without waiting for her answer. His shout of 'Allsop!' echoed round the room and Mrs Waughman, looking dazed, said: 'He'm in the 'all, is Mr Allsop. A-talkin' to the tellyphone feller.'

'Thanks, Mrs Waughman,' John said soothingly. 'I'll just go and tell Laurie where he is.'

'Sir Laurie,' Mrs Waughman reminded him reproachfully. 'Or do that just be for servants, Mr John?'

John laughed and hurried out of the room in the wake of the impetuous Laurie. 'I don't know, Mrs Waughman,' he called over his shoulder. 'I don't think it matters much, though.'

He closed the door of the kitchen behind him and hurried along the passage and through the baize doors into the hall. There stood Allsop and a man in uniform, plainly the representative from the telephone company. Laurie was hovering impatiently in the background.

'I daresay a bird got entangled,' the official was saying as John came within earshot. 'Tes the sort o' thing that don't 'appen more'n once in thirty years. Anyway, I've put it right, you're connected again, and you won't 'ave no more trouble.'

Allsop sniffed. 'We'd better not,' he said roundly. 'Of all the times for telephonic communication to be cut . . .'

The man saw Laurie and tugged at his cap.

'Beg pardon, Sir Laurence, I didn't see you there . . .' he was beginning, but Laurie gestured impatiently at him.

'It's all right. I gather you've mended the telephone so thank you for your trouble . . . he dug into his pocket and came up with a handful of loose change. 'Buy yourself a drink. Now, Allsop, if I could have your attention . . . it's about the trust. John and I were discussing what I should do, and he seemed to think . . .'

The house on the Barrio de Salamanca was almost unbearably hot. Mirri, shut up in her room, sometimes thought she might die of the heat, and of the almost unbearable boredom. But it was her own fault. If only she had been sensible, gone on pretending . . . but after actually seeing Laurie she had not felt able to dissemble. He was too important to her.

'I don't want to marry anyone but Laurie Clifton,' she screamed at her father as she was hustled across the marble-tiled floor and up the shallow stairs to her room. 'Why won't you listen to me? Papa, at least ask him to call . . .'

But he had locked her in her room and an hour later her mother had come in, pale and furious.

'You will come with me,' she had said in a low, grating tone. 'What a wicked girl you are – your father has told me all about it. Misbehaving with that Englishman, flouting our wishes, screaming like a fishwife so that the good young man we had hoped . . . ach, but you are intolerable, spoilt, selfish . . .'

They had bundled her into the car and driven off, at dead of night. No chance to leave a message, no chance even to speak to a servant. She had been brought to the Madrid house and here, in the stifling heat, she had stayed. Here there was no cool courtyard, no pleasant room with a window, albeit barred, through which a breeze might enter. She was locked into a tiny, airless box-room with a slit of a window at ceiling level and a servant's pallet bed. She was in disgrace, her mother informed her icily, and would remain in disgrace until she agreed to marry, without further fuss, either Ulises or Cosme Barador.

'That's ridiculous! I only met Señor Barador once,' she had protested with spirit, on the only occasion that she and her parents had met in the salon for what her mother had termed 'a sensible discussion'. 'He cannot want to marry me, nor I him.'

The salon was large and airy, with light-coloured drapes and comfortably upholstered chairs, but Mirri did not care about her surroundings, all she cared about was convincing her parents that she would not change her mind. As she spat out her defiance her father stepped forward and quite deliberately hit her, twice, across the face. He was breathing hard down his nose and a white line had formed round his mouth and Mirri fell back into the chair, a hand to her throat. She knew her father to be a violent man but he had never before laid a finger on her.

'Papa . . . how dare you hit me?'

'I told that – that puppy that I'd have him whipped within an inch of his life if he tried to get in touch with you, and then when he stared at me, I told him I'd whip you, girl, if I had more nonsense,' her father said between gritted teeth. 'He left, then, with his tail between his legs. Now will you have some sense and do as I say or will I be forced to beat you into submission?'

Mirri's mother murmured what might have been a protest, but Mirri saw that her dark eyes were glistening strangely and suddenly she felt very alone. She sat down on the chair and looked up at her father, looming over her.

'Would you rather I said I would marry either Señor de Kassorla or Señor Barador simply to keep my skin whole?' she asked huskily. She had bitten her tongue when her father's hand had lashed her face and now she was tasting the salt of her blood, feeling it trickling down her split lip and across her chin. 'Is that what you want, Papa?'

He reached down and pulled her to her feet; she tried to resist but doubted if he even noticed. He was strong, dominant, unused to anyone disagreeing with him, let alone defying him. Between his hands she shrank from him, hating the cruel, patrician face, the sweat beading his brow, the heavy scent of the hair oil he favoured. But she dared say nothing; the fingers digging into her upper arms were bruising the tender flesh deliberately and she knew, suddenly, that he was enjoying this, would enjoy bending her to his will.

'I – want – obedience,' he said harshly. He shook her, hard, between words. 'You – will – obey!'

Mirri tightened her lips but said nothing. What was there to say? If she defied him he would beat her; if she agreed to marry the man of his choice then at least he would leave her alone, he might even stop locking her up and bullying her and watching her like a cat watches a mouse. Yet she could not bring herself to deny Laurie.

'I don't want to marry anyone,' she said in a small, weary voice. 'Mama, tell him!'

Her mother looked uneasily up at her husband. 'José, if the girl does not wish for marriage . . . she is only eighteen, after all.'

Her husband spoke without looking at her; his black, glittering eyes were still fixed on Mirri's, as though just by his glance he could dominate her, force her to obey him.

'How old were you when we married, Marcelina?'

There was a pause, then his wife said, with marked reluctance, 'I was eighteen, José, as you well know. But that does not mean . . .'

'Good. What was good enough for you and I is good enough for this spoiled brat.' He pressed Mirri down into the chair, pushing with unnecessary force so that her shoulders creaked with pain. 'You will remain in your room until you agree to marry Kassorla or Barador. Be thankful, you little slut, that you have any sort of choice, because if they knew the licence we had allowed you, if they knew you'd been carrying on with an Englishman . . .'

'I didn't . . .'

He hit her again, twice, a quick, ferocious left and right slap which made her head rock violently. Then he caught her arm and heaved her to her feet.

'Up! Back to your room!'

She had been there ever since. Meals came twice a day and her father came each night. He wanted her word that she would cease defying him. As each long day crept by, every hour seeming more like ten, Mirri decided to give in; what was the point in defiance when her father had the whip-hand? But when he stalked into the tiny room, dwarfing it still further with his height and breadth, she could not give him the satisfaction of admitting defeat.

'Well?' he would bark at her.

She did not even have to speak; perhaps, if she had, she might have cracked, agreed. As it was, she simply shook her head and watched the door crash shut.

She longed for Laurie; at the end of the first week she even longed for her mother, though she knew that Señora Rodriganez would be powerless against her formidable husband. But clearly, her father had forbidden anyone but himself and his man to enter the room, and his man, Pérez, was a creature of few words. Lank, pale, listless, he came in the morning with soup and rolls and in the evening with a dish of paella, or a salad and some beef. She drank bottled water, hating its flat flavourlessness, and relieved herself in a chamber pot which Pérez emptied and returned to her once in twenty-four hours.

I'll give in, or pretend to give in; there's no shame in it because he could keep me here for ever, until I died, she would tell herself about an hour before her father came to the room. This time, I'll give in. But at the very last second something strong and obstinate and probably stupid in her nature would prevent the words from forming and he would go away, unsatisfied.

She lost track of time, of the days, weeks . . . had it been months? She was given a bowl of water, a tiny piece of soap and a towel to keep herself clean. She stopped bothering once or twice, but then self-regard stepped in and she washed once more. She brushed out her hair, sang to herself, told herself stories.

She thought that she would go mad.

'Foxy, there's a letter for you!'

Foxy heard Auntie Bea's voice and groaned; this was the first morning she had had a chance to relax since coming down from Cambridge and someone had been cruel enough to write her a letter! But most of her letters came from John, and a letter from John lit her day, so she rolled out of bed and padded to the door. She was wearing a long cotton nightie but she got the dressing gown Auntie Bea had made her off the door and slipped into it – Auntie was strict about not appearing before the boarders in a state of undress – then hurried down the stairs.

In the kitchen, Auntie Bea was cooking breakfasts and Great-aunt Mary was dishing up. Auntie Bea gestured to an envelope lying on the table and Foxy picked it up and slid it into her pocket. Then she began to help with breakfast preparations. Normally, during vacations she came down early every morning and helped to cook, but because this was the first day of her holiday she had been told she might lie in. But having woken, she might as well help.

Presently, in a lull, she pulled the envelope out and studied it; not John's handwriting, but Laurie's, which was almost as good. So she shoved the envelope back into her pocket and continued to help with the breakfasts until Auntie Bea pushed the limp hair back from her face and announced that they had finished.

'Only the fam'ly to feed now,' she said. 'Go up an' git dressing, gal, then we can eat.'

Foxy was only too happy to obey. She hurried up to her room, slit open the envelope and scanned the first page eagerly. As she had suspected it was from Laurie and he was back at Clifton Place.

She began to read.

Clifton Place,   *21st July 1936*
Herefordshire.

Dear Foxy,

Thanks for your kind letter after Sir George's death. I'm getting stuck into work on the estate, though the home farm's a bit of a problem. There's so much work and though John's been very good Uncle Bill isn't getting any younger so John's needed at home from time to time and will be there constantly once September arrives. Hop-picking waits for no man, as you know. So John and I were discussing it the other evening and John mentioned that you and he – well, that you would like to see more of each other. But he also said you wouldn't be coming for the hopping this year, because of a certain coolness between you and Mum. To be honest, dear Foxy, he would love to have you at Bees-wing but for the moment at least that isn't possible. Personally I think Mum and Uncle are being downright daft, but that's parents for you.

So I said if you'd come to the home farm that would seem to solve both our problems and John fell on my neck (a slight exaggeration; but he did look pleased!) and blessed my name and so on. So how about it, old girl? Usual rates plus a bed and your grub. John swears you'll be running the place by autumn and I must say it would be marvellous to have someone in charge I could trust.

Because Foxy, old bean, I shall be going off to Spain quite soon. Thanks to John's brilliance in suggesting it, I've managed to borrow some money, using the trust as security, so I'm able to afford a trip abroad, and also able to afford to pay someone to take care of the Place for me. As you'll realise from reading the newspapers, anarchy seems to be reigning in Spain, with one half of the country intent on wiping out the other half. I can't stand by and see Mirri involved in a civil war whilst I'm safe here in Herefordshire and the atrocities being committed are beyond belief. That any so-called civilised country could do the things they've done . . . but it's almost impossible to separate truth from fiction, which comforts me a bit.

So if you could come it would be an insurance against my having to flit suddenly, and another pair of hands would be a lifesaver. I'd expect to be back before October, well before. It would just be a rush in, grab, rush out job, you see.

So will you come? John will keep his eye on you, give you any help you need once I'm gone, and Allsop is ever-present and will doubtless look on you as a daughter and take great care of you. I feel mean having to ask such a huge favour but if you carry it to its logical conclusion this could easily be a life and death situation – Mirri's life or death. And that means mine, too.

Well, that's it. Hope all's well with you – and that you'll answer my frantic call. See you soon, I hope,

Love from Laurie

'Foxy, what you doing up there? Your grub's on the table.'

Foxy flung the letter on her bed, whipped off her dressing gown and nightie and slammed herself into her clothes. Then she ran down the stairs, very pink and hot, and burst into the kitchen where the family was placidly eating breakfast.

'I'm awfully sorry, it was the letter, I had to read it before I could get dressed. Auntie Bea, I do have a holiday job during the hop-picking after all. Laurie wants me to work on Cumber Farm, keep an eye on things whilst he goes off to Spain.'

'He's not a-goin' to fight in this 'orrible war?' Auntie Bea said incredulously. 'There's boys gone from Brum, but they're all communists, Mr Roper says. Young Laurie's a sir, he can't go doin' things like that!'

'He isn't. Do you remember me telling you about his girlfriend, the Spanish one? Well, he's going to try to get her out of Spain.'

'Ah,' Bea said. She cut fresh bread and arranged it on the grill pan. 'But will she want to come?'

Foxy stared. 'Of course she will. She and Laurie are in love, Auntie Bea, they want to get married and spend the rest of their lives together. Just like . . . well, just like anyone else who's in love.'

'Hmm,' Auntie Bea said. 'I've always 'ad a lot o' time for Mrs Hoverton. Till now.'

'Yes, well,' Foxy said uncomfortably. She had never told Auntie Bea that Mrs Hoverton did not approve of her friendship with John, but the older woman had guessed how matters stood when Foxy had returned from her Easter vac noticeably silent as to what had transpired. And when Foxy had admitted she would not be going to Bees-wing for the hop-picking that had sealed the Hovertons' fate in Bea's prejudiced eyes. 'You can't altogether blame Mrs Hoverton for wanting the best for John, though, Auntie. I remember you telling me ages ago that farmers' sons married farmers' daughters. By and large, that is.'

'Aye, by and large. Still, you're young, you've plenty o' time. What's this job for young Laurie, then? If there's one thing I do know, it's who grows hops and who don't, and the Cliftons don't.'

'Read the letter,' Foxy said, mindful of the toast. She handed the letter to her aunt, pulled the grill pan out and stood the nicely browned rounds of bread in a toast-rack. 'And Auntie, don't let how the Hovertons feel about me affect the way you feel about them. Because it isn't *me*, precisely. It's not personal, I mean.'

'Mebbe not,' Auntie Bea said. She had finished frying now and leaned against the sink, perusing the letter slowly and carefully. When she had read it all she sighed and took a round of hot toast from the rack still waiting to be taken into the dining room. She spread marmalade thickly on it and bit, crunched, swallowed.

'Well? What d'you think I should do, Auntie?' Foxy asked, seeing that Auntie Bea was not going to give an opinion unasked. Not that Foxy would have dreamed of turning such an opportunity down; ever since the previous April she had longed for her next meeting with John, though she would have died rather than tell him so. And now a chance to be together was being handed to her on a plate, which meant, amongst other things, that Laurie approved of John's choice. I must go, Foxy thought wildly, I have to go! But still she waited anxiously for her aunt to speak.

'Do? You'll do as you think fit, o' course,' Auntie Bea said at last, having chewed and swallowed her second bite of toast just to show Foxy that she was not to be hurried. 'But if it were me, I'd go. Young Laurie's a good lad an' it's plain 'e needs you. And what's more you'll 'ave me, jest down the road.'

'Eight miles isn't just down the road, but I'll go – I'll telegraph – no, I'll go to the corner box and telephone,' Foxy said joyfully. 'I'll tell him I'll arrive by the first train tomorrow! Oh, Auntie, I know I said I'd find a job in Brum this September, but I shan't have to, after all.'

'You'll do better wi' Laurie, and you'll be nearer us,' Auntie Bea said gruffly. 'You're a good gel, Foxy. You deserve a bit o' luck. Now go an' get dressed, do, afore someone begins to think this ain't a respectable boarding 'ouse!'

When Mirri's door shot open in the early hours of the afternoon she was lying on the tiny, narrow bed in a stained crêpe de Chine underslip and nothing else. She sat up, a hand flying to her mouth. Her next meal should not have arrived for three hours at least and her father's daily visit always came after she had finished the meal. Pérez had been in earlier in the day and had gone, as usual, without a word exchanged between them, carrying away her chamber pot and her washing water. So who was this, disturbing her siesta?

It was her father. He jerked his head at her.

'Up. Your mother's not well and I'm – I'm busy. She's in her room. See to her.'

He did not wait to see if she was going to obey him but turned and disappeared down the stairs. Mirri jumped off the bed immediately and ran into the corridor, leaned over the banisters, watched.

Her father hurried across the marble-tiled hallway and out of the big front door. He was shouting instructions to someone she could not see and though he tugged the door closed behind him it did not quite latch. She could see that it had bounced back, that a thread of bright light separated door from surround. Without giving herself time to think Mirri shot back into her room, grabbed her dress and dragged it on. She looked wildly round her for a weapon in case she was stopped but the only thing remotely resembling one was her hairbrush so she grabbed that and ran out of the room and down the first flight of stairs.

Her mother's room was on her right, but she did not even glance in that direction. Her mother had a personal maid, a dozen servants, she did not need a daughter no matter how unwell she might feel. She had not once come to Mirri in all the weeks or months of incarceration; now she could whistle for her daughter. Mirri set out, down the next flight of stairs and into the marble-floored hallway.

The house was quiet, though there was considerable bustle outside. Mirri could hear a hum of subdued talk coming from the servants' quarters and guessed that once they realised her father had left they would come out, but his temper was legendary; not a maidservant would venture to cross his path when he was in a hurry or annoyed about something.

So the time to escape was now, this minute, whilst the front door was not quite shut. Without a thought for her bedraggled appearance, the fact that she had neither shoes nor stockings, Mirri pushed the front door open and peered out and just as she did so there was a sharp *crack*, as though someone had dropped a large glass dish from a great height. Mirri, who had once done just that, flinched at the sound, flinched, also, because when her father had slapped her face – left, right – it had sounded like that, too, the second slap almost an echo of the first.

What could it have been? Not that it mattered, what mattered was the whereabouts of her father. Peering round the door with all the caution of a mouse on the look-out for a cat, Mirri saw that the barrio was crowded with people and there seemed to be some sort of argument going on. There were shouts, yells and raised voices, but because Madrileños are always shouting, laughing, calling out, Mirri thought little of it. Instead, she looked anxiously up and down, expecting to see her father striding away from the house, hailing a taxi, climbing into the long-bonneted car which had brought them here from Granada. Or worse, of course, waiting for her nearby, to pack her ignominiously back to her prison cell.

But he was nowhere to be seen. Commonsense told Mirri that he must have leapt into a taxi and driven off, but some electric excitement in the air, some intensity of feeling, made her look again.

Then she saw him. He was lying on the pavement. His head was turned slightly to the left, and there was a dark, round hole in the middle of his forehead. A thin stream of blood had started to run across his brow. Mirri looked again. Pérez stood over him, a smoking pistol in one hand; he was haranguing the crowd, shouting something about a traitor, about the *señor* setting out to join the Nationalists ... about how the man had treated his servants, his own child ...

He's dead; my father is dead, Mirri thought. She had no time for any other thought. At any moment Pérez might look up, see her, aim his pistol for the second time ...

She slid out of the door and down the steps whilst Pérez was still talking excitedly. She went, barefoot, along the hot pavement, and dived down the first little alleyway which opened up before her. She was horribly thirsty and her feet did not take kindly to padding barefoot but she knew that she must get as far away as possible from her home. Suppose her father was not dead? Suppose it was all some clever act, to trap her into believing him gone? So she hurried, taking every turning as she reached it until she was thoroughly lost.

Presently, she emerged into a tiny, stiflingly hot square. It was deserted save for a thin tortoiseshell cat with only one eye and a well with a tiled canopy, a creaky wooden bucket on a rope and a wooden cover. A well meant water; Mirri's mouth, dry from excitement and heat, longed for water. The cover on the well could soon be removed; Mirri tugged it off and began to lower the bucket into the cool, dark depths. Then, when she heard and felt it strike water, tip, sink, she hauled it up. It was surprisingly heavy but she managed it – just. She and the thin young cat took a drink. Mirri, who once would have been disgusted and horrified at the thought of drinking from a common well let alone sharing with a common cat, merely thought that no drink was ever more delicious.

When she had drunk her fill she sat on the well-coping, under the shade of the tiles, and wondered what she should do next. She had no money, no shoes, no home, for she would never return to the Barrio de Salamanca. Even with her father dead – and

206

commonsense, beginning to return after the rest and the long, cool drink, assured her that he had indeed been dead – it was no place for her. Señora Rodriganez had shown precious little interest in her only child until her defection and then with what cruel indifference had she handed Mirri over to her father's tender mercies! I owe them nothing, Mirri reminded herself. Now it is me that I must look out for. I wonder what I should do next?

She looked down at the cat, winding itself round her ankles, its one bright, round yellow eye staring unblinkingly up at her. It was a very young cat, no more than a kitten, really, and she felt that they were two of a kind. She put out a hand and stroked the small, hard head, smoothed the big, pricked ears. The cat began to purr ferociously loudly, sounding like the big old sewing machine with which Mirri's nanny, Leá, had once made all her dresses, smocks, coats.

'Little *tuerto*, little one-eyed cat, will you come with me?' Mirri asked as the small thing jumped onto her lap and began to settle itself comfortably there. 'Will you catch me mice for my dinner and sing me songs so I can sleep easy on the pavement at nights? I will call you Leá, after my old nanny, and you shall be my very own little cat. We'll share everything, and when I have my own place again, you shall share that, too.'

The cat seemed amenable and presently Mirri got to her feet, tucked the little animal under her arm, and set off. But no longer at random. This time she knew where she was going. She would find her nanny, who had been pensioned off on Mirri's thirteenth birthday. She had wanted to visit her on several occasions but her mother, perhaps jealous of her child's deep affection for a servant, had forbidden it.

'You are a young woman, Mirri, not a child,' she had said crossly. 'You must learn to stand on your own two feet and not rely on an old peasant woman whose sole claim to your affection was that of spoiling you and letting you have your own way. Besides, she won't want a reminder of her time with the Rodriganez family. She has a good pension and thus the means of leading a pleasant, independent life. Leave well alone.'

Mirri, to her shame, had done so. But now she was free, she could, within reason, go where she wished. And Leá would help her, if she could. So with the cat under one arm and hope in her heart, Mirri padded back across the square and plunged once more into the maze of alleys. People were beginning to emerge from their houses, rubbing their eyes and yawning after their siestas. Shops were opening, but cautiously; Mirri realised that the civil unrest which had resulted in her father's death was a far more widespread thing than she had imagined. Shut away, not even able to speak to a servant, she had had no idea that things had reached such a pass, but now, with the city all around her, she began to notice things. The first of these was that, with her filthy bare feet, stained dress and tangled curls, no one took the slightest notice of her. They thought her one of themselves – and who was to say they were wrong? I have been one of the oppressed in truth, for weeks and weeks, Mirri reminded herself, trudging along the dusty streets.

And when presently she strayed back into a more fashionable area of the city, and found herself briefly on the Calle de Velázquez, she could see that most of the fine houses were closed up. The wealthy and influential, who were naturally on the side of the fascists, had fled because ordinary Madrileños were, she knew, mostly Republicans and outnumbered the fascists by many thousands. But that did not tell her why her father had stayed; perhaps he had remained out of a misplaced belief that he would be allowed to go about his business regardless of politics, perhaps he had simply not bothered to fly from the despised poor of the city. But whatever the reason, his arrogance had been repaid by a bullet in the head.

After a while, however, Mirri realised that she would have to ask the way to Leá's street. Knowing the name of it was simply not going to be enough. So she accosted a boy of about ten and asked him for directions. He grinned at her, revealing broken and blackened front teeth, and answered in a strong local dialect that she should turn herself around, take a left and a right, continue along that road until she reached a certain taverna, and then she would see a narrow alley to her left, which was the place she sought.

It sounded simple, but it was the best part of an hour before Mirri finally found herself in the narrow alley, standing before a green-painted door and waiting for her knock to be answered. She heard shuffling footsteps, then a querulous voice cried, 'Who is it?' and upon her answering that it was Mirri de Salvorini y Rodriganez the door was promptly flung open and the woman who had cosseted and made much of Mirri for the first thirteen years of her life peered, gave a deep, throaty gasp, and then held out her arms.

'My child! Why, how tall you are, and how very pretty, I scarcely recognised my nurseling! Come in, come in, and tell me why you've come down here, to this poor part of the city. You're not with your mama or papa?'

Mirri slipped into the narrow, dark passageway and gave her old nurse a hug and kissed the softly wrinkled cheek.

'Oh, Leá, it's so good to see you again! I'll tell you everything, but it's a long story and I'm famished – I escaped from the house soon after noon, and I've been searching for you ever since. Do you have a biscuit or something?'

Leá Roldán dabbed at the tears which were running down her cheeks. She was a small, sturdy woman, and though her black hair was streaked with white, she had a youthful air, perhaps because she had spent most of her working life with children.

'Escaped? what's this? Oh, my darling, don't tell me you crossed your papa? But no, you were always such a good child, you never gave me a moment's anxiety, you were so sweet, so biddable . . . but come along in, of course you must have food – a biscuit, indeed! You shall have some wine, some freshly baked sweet rolls and a piece of my apple cake. Come into the kitchen, then we can talk whilst I prepare a tray.'

The kitchen was dark and narrow, but it seemed wonderfully homelike to Mirri and for the first time for months, she felt safe and amongst friends. She sat down in a chair and Tuerto hopped out of her arms and followed Leá over to the food cupboard. The little cat watched gravely as the old woman began to produce the rolls, a cake, cups and saucers. Mirri watched too, peacefully, no longer anxious, and presently she found herself sipping a glass of wine and eating a roll whilst the little cat, at her feet, attacked a saucer of scraps with great enthusiasm.

'Now, my dear,' Leá said, sipping her own wine. 'Why have you come to me? And why so dirty, so shabby?'

'It's a long story,' Mirri warned her. 'And if you're to make sense of it, Leá, I'll have to start more than two years ago, when Papa decided to send me to England, to learn to speak English as well as he did. He didn't consult me, of course, but I wanted to go and oh, Leá, I'm so glad I did! Because . . . but there, I'm jumping the most important part again, I knew I would. Papa enrolled me with the Miss Honeyford Language Academy on Sydney Street, Cambridge. I was to board there for a year and you know Papa, Leá; he did not care that I spoke almost no English, he just said one learned best from necessity. So off I went, in the care of a very upright lady who was going to England as governess to a family of small girls.'

'England! Oh, my dearest, no wonder you fled – so cold, so wet, so far from your dear homeland!'

'I reached England, and went on to Cambridge, and at first I was very unhappy there because the girls at my school were rude and unkind and besides, I knew no one, no one at all. Then, one evening, I decided to borrow a bicycle and ride into the countryside because I could see it was very beautiful, and I was homesick. And I climbed into the hills, which are called Gog and Magog, I don't know why, and when I got to the woods I sat down in a clearing . . .'

When the long, involved story was finished Leá sat and stared almost unbelievingly at Mirri.

'And he's dead? Your papa is really dead? Well, he has been served out for daring to lock an innocent child up for weeks and weeks and for no sin other than that you would not promise to marry a young man you scarcely knew. And your poor mama? Don't tell me she's dead, too? Ah, this wicked war, where will it end?'

'Are we at war? I suppose it's the people against the fascists – I guessed something of the sort must have happened, though I've not seen a newspaper for weeks. But Mama isn't dead; so far as I know she's still at the house in the Barrio de Salamanca. Papa said she wasn't well but I didn't stop to see her, I just fled. She never helped me at all, never came near me all the time I was locked away. She was always indifferent to me, only interested in Papa and their life together. I felt I owed her nothing, after such neglect.

Besides, I can scarcely go back to the Rodriganez house after this.'

'Indifference to one's child is a sin,' Leá said definitely. 'But perhaps it was fear of your father, a frightening man, which led her to pretend indifference? And it might be easier to get news of her than you think. I have a great many friends, no doubt one of them will tell me what is happening to the Señora de Salvorini y Rodriganez. But what of you, my love? What will you do? You can't spend the rest of your life in my little home, it isn't suitable for the likes of you. And besides, I do not have only myself to consider. I have a – a young lady living with me.'

'I didn't know, but will that matter, Leá? Will the young lady mind if I stay here for a little while? Because I don't have any money at all, and I don't suppose you've got much, either. But if I can get a letter or a message to Laurie I'm sure he'll come for me, take me back to England. And until then, couldn't I stay with you? I'll work, if you can find me work, and when he comes, Laurie will repay you for any money you've spent,' Mirri said eagerly. She could not bear the thought of being sent away from this cosy little house and its well-loved owner. It represented the only safety she felt she had ever known, save for that brief period in Cambridge with her love. And surely a young lady lodger could scarcely object if her landlady took in someone else?

'I don't know about work, *chica*, but if you'd like to stay then I'm sure we'll settle down very comfortably,' Leá said after a moment's thought. 'My young lady is called Jacinta; very likely you will get on well with each other. We will settle down no doubt, the three of us. Three women, after all, should be friends. And then there's your little cat.'

'Oh, Tuerto, I call her that for I can scarcely call her Leá, now,' Mirri said drowsily. She gave a huge yawn and smiled apologetically at her hostess. 'I'm so sorry, Leá, but I'm terribly tired. Is it nearly bedtime?'

Leá smiled reminiscently and surged to her feet. 'The number of times you've said that to me, little one, desperately hoping for another few minutes of play! Yes indeed, what you need, now, is a good night's rest. I've a little pallet bed which I can sleep on and you can have my big one. Jacinta is in my tiny spare room.'

'I wouldn't dream of turning you out of your bed, I'll have the pallet,' Mirri said at once. 'I could sleep on a church spire I'm so tired, the pallet will be wonderful.' The little cat, curled up on the rug at her feet, got up, stretched and began to purr. 'Will it be all right if Tuerto sleeps with me? Only she'll keep bad dreams at bay.'

'Of course she may, the little darling,' Leá agreed. 'Come along both of you and I'll tuck you up. And I'll let you lie in in the morning.' She bent down and picked the little cat up, stroking the small, multi-coloured head. 'And you, little lady, can just keep a weather eye out for mice, because you must earn your keep, you know!'

'I'm sure Tuerto will eat your mice for you,' Mirri said ten minutes later as, clad in an enormous nightgown belonging to her hostess, she climbed between the sheets on the little pallet along-side her nurse's big brass bedstead. 'But I do hope she doesn't lay her catch out on my pillow during the night! Oh by the way, Leá, what does Jacinta do? She might be able to find me work. And how did you come to meet her?'

Leá hesitated, then smiled. 'Jacinta is my daughter, little one,' she said softly. 'It was not known that I had a child; your mother would not have allowed me to remain as your nurse and I needed to work, so I never told her. As for work, you will see for yourself in the morning.'

'Oh, Leá,' Mirri exclaimed, sitting up in bed. 'I never even knew you were married! But that is just like Mama – she did not think other people's lives were in the least important compared to her own and she seldom talked to me anyway.'

'I was never married,' Leá said tranquilly. She had been standing by the bed holding the cat, but now she put Tuerto down on the coverlet and watched as the little animal curled up at the back of Mirri's knees. 'Jacinta is, however, a very great blessing. Good-night, my child.'

'G-goodnight, Leá,' stammered Mirri. 'But don't go yet, you've puzzled me so much! All these years you've had a girl of your own yet you were better than a mother to me. Tell me, is – is Jacinta my age?'

'No, she's a little older. She was born a year before I came to the Barrio de Salamanca to take care of you for your parents. She is always up early and away from the house betimes, but I promise

212

you, you will meet her some time tomorrow. Oddly enough, Jacinta has a little cat, black as night with bright green eyes. She calls it Pepper. Your Tuerto will be company for Jacinta's little one.'

Tuerto gave a small miaow and cast a one-eyed, golden glance up at her little mistress as though well aware that she had been the subject of conversation.

Leá chuckled. 'That cat's a knowing one,' she remarked. 'You needn't catch mice until tomorrow, puss. Sweet dreams, both of you.'

'G'night,' Mirri murmured; and was asleep before the door had closed behind her nurse.

Eight

It was a brilliant summer's day when Foxy arrived in Ledbury. She had expected Laurie to meet her off the train but to her joy, it was John who was standing at the platform's edge as the train rolled in, John who seized her suitcase, kissed her, squeezed her, dropped her case on his own toe, kissed her again . . .

'Foxy! My dearest girl, I'm so bloody grateful to Laurie for asking you and to you for agreeing . . . I swear I'll do anything I can to help you, if Laurie does go off, though it's seeming less and less likely. He's not heard a word and with a civil war raging the situation is pretty dire. He might do more harm than good, that's what I think. And he's getting very absorbed in the estate, particularly the home farm, because it's the one thing his father never interfered with, though old Coleman, the last tenant, did his best to run it into the ground. Is this little case all you've got? Bless me, the girl travels light! I brought the trap because it's slower than the car so it will take us longer to get back. And I ride over to the Place most mornings so if I'd taken the car someone might have asked questions. Not that I care if . . . oh come on, let's get going!'

He marched ahead of her; Foxy watched him with love and apprehension. She had not expected to feel like this about him, not all trembly and soft and – and *giving*, somehow. He had recently had a haircut, not a good one, and his lovely, hay-coloured hair stuck up at the back in an endearing little hedgehog tuft. She had noticed a cut on his chin as he kissed her – even the little whisper of cottonwool attached to it seemed infinitely appealing.

Foxy Lockett, what in God's name is the *matter* with you? Foxy asked herself desperately, trotting along in the rear and smiling distractedly at various people who called out greetings as they passed. You know what you've always said – no nonsense until your degree is in the bag. Well, if this isn't nonsense, and pretty soppy nonsense at that, I don't know what is. Pull yourself together, girl, and remember that you've got to keep John at arm's length or all your lovely plans could well go for nought.

And it wasn't just that, either. It would scarcely endear her to Mr and Mrs Hoverton if she mooned round after John like a lovesick calf. She wanted to marry him, she loved him, but she was far too canny to go at it like a bull in a china shop (like John would, for instance). No, that was not the way. It was for that reason she had decided not to go to Bees-wing for the hop-picking; it would put her in a difficult position. Instead, she must work on the Hovertons until they were on her side, saw her as a suitable mate for John, and then she would be accepted, taken in. She had no intention of marrying John and seeing him disinherited by furious parents. Auntie Bea might say they'd never do it, but who could tell? They were mortal fond of Laurie, even Mr Hoverton was, though he'd been badly hurt by the way Sir George had treated them. If the chips were down who was to say that they wouldn't hand over the farm to Laurie, if John married to spite them? For that was how they might well see it if their beloved only son married a penniless nobody from Brum in the teeth of their stiff opposition to the match.

So Foxy had decided to treat John circumspectly – and started when they reached the trap. John slung her suitcase into the back and then tried to give her a hand to get aboard, only Foxy told herself she knew a trick worth two of that and jumped up onto the driving seat, moving along to give him room.

'Thanks for meeting me, John,' she said as he clambered up beside her. 'But remember what I said; no strings. Want me to drive?'

'No, thanks. I want to get us back to Clifton Place in one piece,' John said rudely, but his words were rendered void by the loving smile in his eyes. 'Why's your hair done like that?'

Foxy, who had spent a tedious half hour plaiting it into one long, thick tail and then folding it under and securing it with a great many pins, shrugged. 'Makes a change, don't you think? Besides, it's tidier.' She meant to leave it at that but some horrible little imp

215

worked her voice for her and she heard herself say, in a rather injured tone, 'Don't you like it?'

'It's very nice, but I prefer it loose,' John said. There was a wealth of fondness in the ordinary words and in the glance he shot her, but Foxy took no notice and John slapped the reins on the horse's neck. 'Geddup, Bess!'

Bess, who had been drowsing, put on a good act, flicking back her ears, swishing her tail and setting off at a smart trot which presently became her more usual amble. She did not enjoy swift movement in the midday sun and besides, she was eighteen and had worked hard all her life. No doubt she felt an easier pace would ensure she saw twenty.

'I won't hurry her,' John remarked as they began to leave the town behind them. 'I want this journey to last for ever!'

'Don't be daft,' Foxy said with some asperity. 'You'd pretty soon get bored, sitting up here on this hard seat with the sun beating down. Anyway, I want some dinner.'

'No dinner yet,' John said. They were in a shady part of the road and he drew the trap into the verge and loosened the reins. Bess thankfully dropped her head and began to graze. John turned to his companion. 'No dinner until you've thanked me nicely for coming to meet you when I've so much to do. How about a nice cuddle? Because that brief, chilly little kiss you gave me on the platform has scarcely done more than whet my appetite.'

Foxy scowled. 'John, you know we shouldn't. Do drive on, I really am hungry.'

'Me, too. But first . . .'

He drew her into his arms and Foxy, who was longing for his kisses, struggled sharply. 'Do stop it – suppose someone comes by?'

'Don't give a damn,' John said against her hair. She had somehow relaxed against him despite her words. He tilted her chin and his mouth came slowly down over hers. Conversation stopped. Foxy, knowing she was being a fool, strained against him, felt his hands begin their hypnotic movement across her back, pulling her closer still, felt his mouth moving on hers . . .

'Afternoon, Mr John, sir.'

The voice jerked them apart, red-faced, breathing hard. Foxy, feeling not only foolish but also absolutely furious with John, spun round in her seat and glared down at the intruder. Dan, in shirt sleeves with a ragged old jacket slung over one shoulder, stared back at her; Dan, who had known her ever since her first hop-picking, who had known John all his life. He was grinning knowingly but so terrible was Foxy's scowl that the grin was wiped from his face in an instant, to be replaced by a look of spurious apology.

'Oh, tes you, Foxy. I thought it were . . . were someone else. I'm that sorry, m'dear, to intrude . . .'

'There's no need for sorrow, Dan. Just keep your mouth shut and no one need be sorry,' John said crisply. 'I was – was just – I was just – '

'Words fail him, Dan, as you can tell,' Foxy put in as John stuttered into silence. 'And words had better fail you, an' all. Want a lift? We're going to Clifton Place.'

'Not back to Bees-wing? No, course not,' Dan said. He looked pleased with himself. 'I'm 'ere legal-like, I'll 'ave you know. Got signed off wi' that bad cut I done last month. Oh aye, Doc's signed me off, so I'll be back to work before we start pickin' the 'ops. You might tell your dad, Mr John.'

'And I might not,' John said, recovering a little of his self-possession. 'I'm going to forget I saw you, Dan, since I am *not* here legal-like. My parents think I'm at the home farm, putting a new roof on the big barn. Which is what I've been doing all morning and shall be doing all afternoon.'

'Got it, Mr John,' Dan said. 'Trouble is, what about Foxy here? Do the missus know she'm at the Place?'

'No, I don't think she does; and if she finds out, I'll know who to blame,' John said, looking grim. 'Just remember, Dan, that one of these days a lot of people are going to be dependent on me for their livelihoods. You amongst 'em.'

'Oh aye, Mr John,' said Dan placidly. 'I 'on't split on you. Now I'd best be gettin' on. Good day to you.'

They waited until Dan had gone round a bend in the road and then John sighed deeply and laid a light arm along Foxy's shoulders. She shifted uneasily but did not push him away. They were in trouble, and would have to talk.

'Foxy, my love, you know my parents don't approve, I don't have to spell it out, do I? It isn't you, they're fond of you, it's just the blooming land. If I took a shine to Nina Fairbrother then of course the two farms would combine.'

'But not whilst Mr and Mrs Fairbrother were around,' Foxy pointed out. She sighed deeply and snuggled against his shoulder. She did not mean to, but suddenly she wanted the comfort of nearness. 'And they're both younger than your parents, so I don't see why it makes any difference, really.'

'They want it for me; the fact that I don't want it for me doesn't really come into it. It's for future generations of Hovertons, Dad would say, and Mum would talk about grandchildren, and their heritage . . . but they'll come round in time, I promise you. When they see it's you or no one for me they'll come round.'

'Oh, sure. I'll be thirty-eight and you'll be forty and we'll still be waiting,' Foxy said, only half laughing. 'Your father's a patient man, John. I remember your mother saying that his patience was one reason he was a good farmer, because he was prepared to lie low through the bad times and wait for the good.'

John laughed too and gave her a squeeze. 'It won't be that long, I promise you,' he assured her. 'Despite longing for me to fall in love with Nina they want my happiness. When they see that you *are* my happiness they'll give in. I promise.'

'But if you're not going to tell them I'm in the neighbourhood then how will they ever believe we're in love?' Foxy demanded. 'People who love each other want to be together. And anyway,' she added pettishly, 'I'm not sure I am in love. Oh, it's all so difficult!'

'I'm not going to tell them yet,' John said after a moment's thought. 'But you're right, I'll have to tell them in the end. Only I can't bear it if they make excuses to keep me away from the Place, I'll have to ignore them and then there'll be trouble, ill-feeling . . . I know, when you've gone back to Cambridge I'll tell them you were here.'

'That's the coward's way out,' Foxy said severely. 'Why can't they just let us find out for ourselves how we feel? If we saw a lot of each other, went around together, we might easily discover we'd both made a mistake. If you ask me, John, they've more or less pushed you into saying you love me just to show them they can't go on treating you like a kid!'

'No! Foxy, that's a black lie.' John's normally smooth brow was marred by a heavy scowl. He pushed her away from him and clicked to the horse. 'Geddup, Bess! No point in staying here whilst little Miss Lockett denies how we both feel. Anyway, you don't have to have anything to do with me even if we are both up at the Place. We'll both have our jobs to do. You can avoid me easily enough if that's what you want.'

Foxy's temper flared. Just because she'd flicked him on the raw with a home-truth he had to hit back – it was clear enough, now, that his affection for her was simply put on to annoy his parents.

'I'll do my work, don't worry,' she said tartly. 'And I won't seek you out, you may be sure of that.'

'Nor I you,' John said grimly.

For fifteen minutes or so the two of them were frostily silent. Foxy sat on the hard wooden seat and looked straight ahead of her, at the dusty lane unwinding. Now and then she glanced at the rich hedgerows with their burden of wild roses and pinky-gold honeysuckle, or down at the verges where foxgloves nodded their freckled faces. She was determined to remain furious with John – it would make things easier, in some ways – but when they passed a hopyard, clinging to a gently sloping hill, she caught her breath and turned to him, their quarrel forgotten.

'Oh, John, how well the hops are doing! They've already . . .' she broke off and glanced uneasily up at him. He was smiling. He reached out and put one broad, tanned hand over both hers and after a moment she smiled back at him. Quarrelling was silly when two people liked each other as much as she and John did.

'Darling Foxy, aren't we stupid?' John said, rubbing his thumb gently across her knuckles. 'Besides, we're both right. We should be allowed to pursue our friendship at our own pace, and so we shall. We'll take no notice of disagreements or watchers, we'll just be good friends and – and love one another. Agreed?'

'Not the last bit,' Foxy growled, instantly suspicious. 'It's no use saying I'm sure when I'm not. Besides, you know you . . .'

'. . . promised,' John finished for her, pulling a face. 'All right, leave the last bit off. We'll just be good friends. Can you agree to that?'

'Yes. Yes, of course.' Foxy heaved a sigh. 'That's better, I hate being cross. And you did see those hops? Are ours that high yet?'

'Easily. It'll be a grand crop this year. Going to come over to Bees-wing and have a chat to the pickers when you're free of an evening? Your Auntie Bea will be there, I daresay.'

'How can I, when I'm not supposed to be here?' Foxy asked impatiently. 'On the other hand, if I don't visit Auntie and the other pickers they'll think I've gone all snooty on them. Oh, John, isn't life difficult?'

'Yes, it is sometimes. But I think you should come, no matter what, because it would be a natural thing to do. And Mum and Dad will see that you're not putting yourself deliberately in my way – I shan't say you've been working for Laurie for a while – so it'll give you a chance to meet Mum and Dad on – on the old terms. Are you game?'

'If Laurie really doesn't need me in the evenings,' Foxy promised. 'And – and if your parents don't snub me the first time they see my face. I can come over and have a meal with Auntie Bea and Nonny. I might even stay overnight, give a hand with the picking, if your parents seemed not to mind.'

'What, in the barracks? After weeks of queening it at Clifton Place?' John turned the trap between the gate posts and the ruined lodge and they began to traverse the considerable length of the neglected, weedy drive. 'Well, it's up to you, sweetheart. I wonder what room Laurie's got ready for you?'

'Not the Chinese room, I trust,' Foxy said. She gave a brief shiver despite the heat of the day. 'Isn't it odd, John? Whatever happened was years ago, when we were nothing but a couple of children, but I don't think I could sleep in that room to save my life!'

'You should be so lucky! The Chinese room, indeed! You'll probably be in one of the attics, with the servants.'

'I don't mind,' Foxy said contentedly as the trap and its occupants emerged from the trees and swerved round the front of the house, diving under the arch which led to the stables. 'It's going to be all right, isn't it, John? All of us, the three of us, I mean.'

'All right? Of course it is. And it'll be the four of us, if Laurie can get in touch with his little Spanish onion!'

Foxy enjoyed working for Laurie, even after she realised that most of the other members of staff, possibly including Mr Allsop, were under some considerable degree of misapprehension.

'They think Laurie's keen on me,' she told John late one evening as the two of them, having worked hard at their different jobs all day, met for a stroll around the home farm's acreage in the gathering dusk. 'I was really embarrassed when I realised from the winks and nudges and nods that Mrs Waughman has somehow got the impression that I'm in line for the next Lady Clifton. I mean, me – can you imagine anything dafter?'

'He's an attractive bloke and you're a very pretty girl,' John said rather lugubriously. 'At one time, I used to think . . . but anyway, if I didn't know about his little Spanish onion I'd probably do a bit of wondering myself. What did you tell the old girl when she revealed her wild surmise? Did you cut her down to size?'

'She didn't mean it nastily, but I said it was all rubbish, of course. That I wasn't going to marry anyone for years and years because I was going to have a career, instead. And I reminded her, blushing, that I sleep up in the attics, whereas Laurie, I suppose, has a room on the first floor.'

'And what did she say to that?'

Foxy giggled. 'She really annoyed me, only Laurie explained that she's simple, so I shouldn't have been cross. She said a man can go to bed in one place and wake up in another and no one the wiser save those two! So of course I told her pretty sharply that anyone prowling round the house near my room would get more than he expected and she just stared over my shoulder and said, "That's what they allus say, I reckon. Do you want a sausage wi' your egg?" '

'Cheeky old witch,' John muttered. He eyed Foxy broodingly. 'Is that why Laurie put you in the attic, so that there wouldn't be talk?'

'No, it wasn't like that, it was my decision in a way. In fact, he offered me any room I cared to pick so I took an attic. I won't say it had occurred to me that people might talk because it hadn't, but

I've never fancied any of the bedrooms at the Place, not since that business in the Chinese room. And as it turns out it's a good job I did. In order for Laurie to sneak into my room he would have to come up a steep flight of jolly noisy, uncarpeted stairs and then to tiptoe past Allsop's room. And there's a creaky board just as you come through my door which would wake the dead, I imagine. But Mrs Waughman has the housekeeper's room, downstairs, because of the rheumatism in her knees, so I suppose she wouldn't realise that I'm as safe, up there, as in a chastity belt.'

'You could go down, though, I suppose,' John said thoughtfully, shooting her a mischievous glance. 'I mean you know where the squeaky boards are so you could avoid ... Hey! I was only thinking aloud, no need to get violent!'

Foxy, pink-faced, gave him another hard punch on the muscle in his upper arm. 'I'm not interested in Laurie and he isn't interested in me; remember? All I want to do at nights is sleep, despite everyone else's fantasies.'

As she spoke she turned out of the lane and leaned for a moment on a mossy gate, thoughtfully eyeing the sloping meadow beyond. 'John, do let's be serious for a moment and remember what we're supposed to be doing! I've been meaning to ask you, what was in this meadow before the Colemans let it go?'

'Dunno,' John said, giving it a cursory glance. 'It's been derelict for as long as I can remember. Why?'

'Because it looks like a hopyard; the hedges are high, and if you look very closely you can see where the hop rows once were. Don't you agree? The rows ran north to south, too, or they did, once.'

'Reckon you're right,' John said, having scrutinised the meadow with rather more interest. 'But the whole place is out of kilter; it might take years to get it producing properly again.'

'It wouldn't! Laurie could do it easily in a year, and then he could make some money, because the hops do make money, don't they, John? There's a kiln at the back of the home farm, too, though it's not been used for goodness knows how long. He could have a go, couldn't he?'

'Yes, if he could be bothered,' John said. 'But he's got an awful lot on his plate, Foxy. Still, it's definitely a thought.'

'Why isn't it a good idea? Why just a thought?' Foxy said hotly. 'I don't see . . .'

'Because there's more to hops than planting them and eventually reaping them,' John said patiently. 'There's accommodation for the pickers, for a start. Then you need cribs, stilts, poles, pockets . . . no end of equipment. Then you'll want a team of good men to work in the drying room, men who know what they're doing, not just ordinary farm labourers, and it costs money to buy sulphur, and coke for the burners. Then there's spraying, tending, weeding . . . it isn't something you can go in for lightly.'

'Oh,' Foxy said, rather deflated. 'Oh, all right. But we might just suggest it to Lo, mightn't we?'

John put his arm round her and kissed the side of her face. 'Poor little chicken, we'll suggest it to Lo, of course, but don't blame me if he turns it down flat.'

Foxy, still annoyed that her idea had been so promptly squashed, rubbed vigorously at her cheek. 'Stop it, no silliness, we agreed, didn't we? Isn't it a blessing that the orchard isn't too bad? You said prune back in the winter, but at least there's fruit on the trees.'

'Aye, and the cider growers aren't too fussy, so he should get a decent price, though some of the fruit is rather small. And don't keep rubbing at my kiss or you'll make a hole in your cheek and then where will you be?'

Despite herself Foxy chuckled and John promptly caught her by the shoulders, swung her round, and kissed her properly, on the mouth. But just when she was beginning to feel all swoony and willing, as she put it to herself, he put her gently away from him, kissed her on the tip of the nose, and turned back towards the home farm.

'All right, I know. No silly nonsense,' he said. 'Let's get back to the house; if I miss another of her suppers my mother is going to start getting suspicious. In fact I ought to kidnap Laurie and take him home, too. Which would mean you would have a lonely supper, little Miss Lockett.'

'I don't mind,' Foxy said, but she could not stop herself from sounding wistful. The meals up at the Place were very good but the kitchen at Bees-wing still wore a rosy glow for her. She had been so happy there, had felt herself to be such a part of the family, and now, just because John liked her, she had been cast out. It really wasn't fair.

'Well, I don't suppose Laurie will come,' John admitted as they turned their steps towards the house. 'He works on the books in the evenings and he said last night he's still got a long way to go before everything's sorted. I'll deliver you to the kitchen and get off, tonight.'

'All right,' Foxy said. 'Laurie's getting a delivery of slates in the morning; he's re-roofing Cumber Farm – old habits die hard, I keep forgetting that it's just the home farm, now. Anyway, he's got two lads coming in and I'm going to use the old slates from the house to patch up the pigsties. I say, John, couldn't we use the pigsties for the pickers, if we went in for hops, I mean?'

'We? If you want people to jump to conclusions you're going the right way about it,' John said as they crossed the lane and dived through the low doorway in the big wall which separated the house from the home farm. 'I doubt if the public health people would approve . . . or aren't you going to keep pigs any more?'

'I'll ask Laurie,' Foxy said. 'I say, is that your horse I can hear?'

John had a showy bay gelding called Lightning. It had white socks and a white star on its forehead and was cursed with a quick temper as well as a fair turn of speed, and right now, judging by the din, it was trying to kick the stable door down.

'Oh damn, I believe it is,' John said, dismayed. 'What on earth's got into the creature? Mind, I left him in the paddock, someone must have brought him in. Good of whoever did it, because I don't fancy trying to catch him now – hasn't it got dark quickly, tonight?'

'It's because we were talking and not thinking about the time,' Foxy said, rather dismayed to realise that darkness had fallen and they were hurrying up the lane by the light of a huge harvest moon. 'Oh John, you shouldn't ride back at this time of night, anything might happen.'

'Nonsense! But what on earth's up with Lightning?'

Another frantic clattering and a shrill whinny had them breaking into a run: they clattered into the stableyard and stopped short, panting. There was Laurie, leaning over the stable door with a lantern in one hand, trying to placate the animal which raged to and fro within. He turned at the sound of their footsteps.

'Hello ... this chap's in an awful rage, John. Why did you put him inside? He doesn't seem to care for being confined in a stable not his own and the grass in the small paddock's awfully good.'

'I didn't,' John said, beginning to frown. 'He was out when we left. Anyway, ask around, see who brought him back, and tell them not to do so again, would you? He's a tricky blighter, and I've got to ride him six miles or so before I get my supper.'

He went over to the door, spoke soothingly to the horse, then slipped inside. A moment later he led Lightning, saddled and bridled, out of his stall and across to where Laurie and Foxy still lingered.

'He was tacked up,' he said in mild astonishment. 'Someone must have borrowed him – no wonder he was in such a state. He's sweating, look.'

'No one could have borrowed him,' Laurie objected, beginning to frown too. 'No one here can ride. Are you sure you didn't ...'

'Of course I'm sure,' John said impatiently. He was hopping round on one foot, trying to mount. 'I'd never leave a horse in the stable tacked up and anyway, Foxy and I were ... hey-ey-ey!'

He had reached the saddle and the moment he settled in his seat Lightning gave a squeal of rage and set off like a mad thing across the yard, heading for the archway onto the drive, with John bumping in the saddle like a beginner, one stirrup flying free, the reins still loose on the gelding's neck. In the moonlight his face showed white and strained as he tried to keep his seat, pull steadily on the reins, find the stirrup. Foxy's heart did a double somersault; he would be thrown and the yard was cobbled, the drive pitted with holes!

'Get out of the way, Foxy!' Laurie roared and tried to push Foxy clear as she dived for the horse's mouth, then grabbed for the reins himself, but neither of them stood a chance. Lightning was away on the instant, John ducked under the arch and even as they watched they saw the saddle begin to slip.

'My God, he wasn't tacked up at all,' Laurie shouted. 'The girth's loose ... come on!'

'I don't know what happened, I only know I could have broken my back,' John said crossly half an hour later, when the panting, sweating Lightning had been incarcerated once more in the stable and he, Foxy and Laurie were sitting on the mounting block, drinking cold beer. 'I can't imagine why anyone would want to half tack a horse, can you?'

'I think it was someone not used to horses,' Foxy said. 'I don't know much about them, but I've seen you put the saddle on and tighten that strap thing that goes under the belly, and then dig your knee into the poor animal's stomach so that the air comes whooshing out and you can pull on the strap and do it up tighter. I reckon someone tried to be helpful, knowing you wanted to get an earlier start tonight.'

'Yes, but what made him go wild like that?' Laurie said uneasily. 'He set off like a dervish!'

'There was something uncomfortable under the saddle, perhaps a bit of straw digging in, or dirt or something,' John said. 'He screamed when I landed in the saddle and then again when it started to slip. Still, I'm alive and kicking, only do put the word around that no one's to touch him in future, would you?'

'Of course. Only . . . I'd feel a lot happier if I knew who did it,' Laurie said, twisting his beer mug until the foam swirled up almost to the brim. 'John, you weren't exaggerating. You could easily have been killed.'

'Yes, but I wasn't,' John said briskly. He slid off the mounting block and stood his empty mug down beside him. 'I'm off now. He's had his cooling-off period, I bet he'll be quiet as a lamb this time.'

And he was, apart from a bit of eye-rolling when John started to tack him up.

'Wish that horse could talk,' Laurie said as they waved John off. Lightning minced delicately out of the yard and they heard him trotting away down the lane. 'Lightning knows what happened – but he's the only one. I'm completely in the dark.'

'And me,' Foxy admitted. 'Still, no harm done. Let's go and ask Mrs Waughman to make us some supper – I know I shouldn't be hungry, but I am!'

Laurie woke in the middle of the night for no reason that he could put his finger on. It was as though someone had whispered his

226

name, called him. But though he sat up and peered into the darkness he knew at once that he was alone in the room.

Accordingly he lay down again, but still, niggling away in the back of his mind, was the strange affair of John's horse. He had asked Mrs Waughman whether she had noticed anyone in the yard but she told him she had been boiling up bones to make broths and jellies and not only was the kitchen full of steam but she had been far too busy to glance outside.

Allsop, questioned when he came back into the kitchen for a late supper, said that he'd decided it was time the chandelier in the front hall was cleaned. Since this involved some brave soul with mountaineering tendencies swinging themselves out over the gallery rail, capturing the chandelier and reeling it in until it was close enough to unhook from its chain, he and young Carrie had been fully occupied all evening.

'Carrie fetched the chandelier over and I unhooked it and then we got young Cyril to give us a hand to bring it downstairs. It's pure crystal and wrought-iron, extremely heavy. We brought it down to the butler's pantry and I've been doing the droplets with warm, soapy water ever since,' Allsop said. 'Why, Sir Laurie? What happened while I was away? Nothing bad, I trust?'

'Someone brought Mr John's horse in from the side paddock and tacked it up. Only they didn't do it properly and the saddle slid round when he mounted; he could have broken his back,' Laurie said grimly. 'I realise that whoever did it was only trying to be helpful, but I'd like to know who it was, nevertheless.'

Mr Allsop tutted disapprovingly. 'A dangerous thing to do. But I can't help you I'm afraid, being as how I was in the hall or the butler's pantry all afternoon. I imagine it must have been one of the farm workers, they being more at ease with horses than the indoor staff. Mr John wasn't hurt, I trust?'

He sounded genuinely concerned. Laurie shook his head.

'No, he was all right. He's a very good rider, and he was able to stop the horse after it had bolted about half a mile down the lane. Still, I'd be obliged if you'd ask around.'

'I'll do that, sir. And now, Mrs Waughman, what have you got for our supper?'

So now Laurie lay in bed staring into the dark and trying to think what had woken him. He went over the day's doings in his head but could not find a good reason. The incident with the horse had been upsetting, but not, surely, enough to steal his sleep? He slept excellently, always had done.

Shrugging, he turned on his side and was almost asleep again when he realised that he had not thought about Mirri once since the incident with the horse. He had been too busy puzzling over the mystery, because it was such a strange thing for someone to have done, not a sensible or responsible action at all, and it had put Mirri right out of his head. And now, suddenly, she was back in his thoughts, a picture of her as he had last seen her in his head. He smiled at her; she smiled back. And on the instant, he thought: there'll be a letter in the morning. And then, without giving the matter further thought, he simply rolled over and went back to sleep.

Morning dawned bright and sunny. Laurie washed, dressed and ran downstairs. He was not going to think any more about the horse incident; they had been lucky, no one had been hurt. Now he would concentrate on the day ahead.

He and Foxy breakfasted in the kitchen these days. There was absolutely no point in going through to the breakfast parlour when they could equally well eat sitting round the scrubbed kitchen table. And Laurie was still farmer's son enough to enjoy a collective meal during which they discussed the work before them that day. This morning Foxy was down before him, talking to Mrs Waughman.

'I've collected most of the eggs,' she was saying as he entered the room. 'I took them through to the dairy but there's enough for breakfast in the basket still.'

'Morning, all,' Laurie said and Foxy turned and grinned at him.

'Morning, Laurie,' she said cheerfully. 'I've got the eggs and I've milked my four cows and later I'll go and give Keith a hand with the churns. Is there anything else you want me to do before I have breakfast?'

'No, nothing,' Laurie said, returning her smile. 'It's a lovely day, isn't it? I'll come and help with the churns, and by the time we finish the fellows with the slates should be here and we can start on the roof.'

'Speak for yourself; I'll do most things but clamber about on roofs I will not,' Foxy said decidedly. 'I'm not keen on heights . . . oh, morning, Mr Allsop, I didn't see you by the door.'

'That's because I wasn't here until this minute, Miss Foxy,' Allsop said, giving her his most fatherly smile. 'I heard the postman pushing the letters through the box so I went into the hall to collect them. There's quite a few for you, Sir Laurie, and a couple for me and one for Miss, here.'

'Mine's from Auntie Bea,' Foxy murmured, taking the pink envelope. 'She's over at Bees-wing but we've been so busy I've not got away once to visit her. I must write to her tonight. My goodness, I hope yours aren't all bills, Lo!'

But Laurie wasn't attending. He was staring down at the letter on top of the pile. The envelope was white, or rather off-white, the ink faded, but the handwriting was as familiar to him as his own.

Mirri! He had thought he would receive a letter today and so he had, it was here, in his hand! He tried to open the envelope and to his astonishment his hands were shaking so hard that he couldn't manage it. He sat down at the table and Foxy picked up the breadknife and passed it to him with an encouraging smile. She had obviously noticed his perturbation, but he would be all right in a moment, once he'd got over his first heady excitement.

He breathed deeply a couple of times, glanced at the rest of his mail, then returned his attention to Mirri's letter. He picked up the breadknife and insinuated the tip under the envelope's flap. He pulled it along and the envelope opened cleanly. He took out the two thin sheets of paper within and spread them out beside his plate.

Mrs Waughman was dishing up, Mr Allsop was bringing the laden plates over to the table. Laurie thanked him absently but his eyes never left the page before him. She had written in Spanish, and briefly, but he devoured every word, then turned back to the beginning and read it all again.

Dear Laurie,

My parents brought me to Madrid but I got away. My papa is dead and my mama has left the city without me. I am at present living very happily in a small alley in a poor quarter of the city – I don't know how well you know Madrid, but it is above the Manzanares – with my old nanny, Leá, and her daughter, Jacinta. I was going to ask you to come for me, but it would never do; Madrid is not easy to reach and the war is everywhere. Besides, I don't know for how long I shall remain here because Jacinta and I are doing an important job with the military and it may take us away from the city at any moment.

So do nothing, my dearest Laurie, until you hear from me again. When I feel that it is right for me to leave I'll try to get to Santander or Gijón, if this is impossible I will let you know where I am to be found. A few weeks ago I thought I would be perfectly happy only if you came for me, but now I know better. I am doing a good job and I am of use to my country. We will meet again, I know it in my heart, but until then, I love you and think of you always.

Your Mirri

Laurie could not believe what he was reading – she had not given him her address, had not even told him the full name of the woman with whom she was staying; and why? Because she was happy and of use to her country – she, who had kept him in a state of dithering anxiety ever since his unsuccessful attempt to steal her away, last spring!

For a moment he was so angry that he saw nothing but a red blur before his eyes, then it cleared and he saw Mrs Waughman, ponderously bringing her plate over to the table, Mr Allsop, eating his own food whilst peering through his rimless glasses at a letter he had received, and Foxy . . . watching him, her eyes soft with anxiety. Only Foxy knew, guessed, that the letter was important, and suddenly all that mattered was to get Foxy to himself for a moment so that she could be told about the strange letter, could comfort him, advise him.

'Get your breakfast eaten, Laurie, and we'll go and fetch the churns,' Foxy said. 'Want some more toast to help the egg down?'

He stared at her. Egg? What egg? She interpreted his glance and pointed, with her knife, at his plate. He looked down and saw an egg, untouched, two rashers of bacon, a sausage, some fried tomato . . . Quickly, be began to eat, shovelling the food in with the help of a round of toast. No one was taking any notice; whilst he ate he re-read the letter, his anger and impotence gradually growing. How could she do this to him, the little wretch? She was happy and busy so what did it matter, to her, if he was miserable, worried for her? And just what did she mean, *an important job with the military*? Spanish girls did not join the forces; but she might be working in an officers' canteen, he supposed vaguely, or possibly as a nursing assistant in some hospital or other. Grinding his teeth, he thought how he would love to rush over to Spain, find her, give her a good spanking, tuck her under his arm and carry her back to England. But he would stand about as much chance of finding one small girl in the backstreets of Madrid, lacking an address, as the proverbial needle in the haystack. Dear God, there must be a way, though – if only he could think straight!

Mr Allsop said something about the letter he had just read; it was from an old employee, interested in working for the estate again. Laurie said that Mr Allsop should invite him over for an interview and hastily began to open the rest of his mail. Bills, an advertising gambit from a feed merchant, a note from Mr Hawk-ings saying they must meet in the next few days. He pushed the letters into his pocket and let his eyes rest once more on Mirri's brief epistle.

She must have known what she was doing, that was the rub. Little monkey, she must have realised she was making his life difficult by not mentioning her nanny's surname nor her address. And Madrid was the capital city of Spain, whilst she was there she was in great danger. Already air power had been brought into play, though it stood to reason that the fascist forces, who controlled the air at the moment, were unlikely to start bombing Madrid which, from what he remembered, was full of the wealthy and privileged. No, the threat to his love would come from the Republicans and they, surely, would have their hands full without making war on young ladies? But another glance at the letter – which he already knew by heart – confirmed that she did not intend to stay there. She would be moving on, she had said so. Perhaps to Gijón or Santander, two ports from whence ships plied regularly between Spain and Britain.

'Ready, Lo? Then we'd better make tracks.' That was Foxy,

scraping the last piece of toast round her own plate, finishing her tea, getting to her feet. 'Thanks, Mrs Waughman, that was delicious.'

She went out of the kitchen, holding the door for him. Laurie followed, Mirri's letter gripped in one hand. He followed Foxy blindly across the yard, round past the stables, through the door in the wall, across the lane and into the home farm. Two milk churns stood on the roughly made wooden table outside the cowshed. The milk lorry came to the end of the lane, the farmer was supposed to get the churns up there rather than asking the lorry driver to come down and turn in the farmyard.

'Laurie? You all right? You looked pretty ghastly back there for a minute. Want to talk now, or later? Only we don't want to miss the milk lorry and it'll be along in twenty minutes or so.'

'I'll get the cart,' Laurie said at once. 'No, you go and tack the pony up to the cart, I'll roll the churns across to you.'

Foxy nodded and very soon the churns, in the back of the small cart, were joggling down the lane. They reached the stone trough with the block beside it and Laurie manoeuvred the churns onto the block. Then Foxy said gently, 'Come on, Lo, what's upset you?'

For answer, Laurie fished the letter out of his pocket. 'Listen to this,' he said bleakly. 'I could smack her, but – oh, Foxy, what the devil am I to do now?'

Foxy listened as Laurie translated the letter for her, then glanced uncertainly at him.

'Can it be true? Can she really be doing important work, work so important that she doesn't want to leave all that danger and – and everything? And with the army, too! You know her very much better than most, Laurie. Does she yearn for excitement? Is she prone to exaggeration? Could the important job be a flight of – of fancy?'

'I don't know,' Laurie said helplessly. 'I knew her for a little over two months, Foxy, and in that time she was busy learning English and I was trying to get my degree. She's an arrogant little thing in some ways and remarkably down to earth in others. I suppose she's doing some sort of job connected with the armed forces which she enjoys and believes to be useful. I remember Mum telling me about the VADs in the last war – they were often girls from excellent backgrounds who had never so much as washed their own gloves and they found themselves working in filthy hospital wards in France, fighting infection, bombed by the enemy, bossed about by nursing sisters who despised them. And Mum said they loved it, most of them; the ones that didn't, left.'

'Right. So you think she really is doing an important job and that she really is happy. What about danger? She doesn't mention it.'

'No, because she's in Madrid. I only visited the city once, briefly, and of course I went straight to the area where the Rodriganez family live. I've been following the war news in the papers, though. The capital is held by the government forces – the Republicans – and presumably the fascists will try to take it eventually. Not that they call themselves fascists, I don't suppose. Do you know what General Franco's army is called?'

'Don't know and don't care,' Foxy said promptly. 'Yes I do, though, I read it in the paper the other day. They're the Nationalists. And from what I've heard, the army aren't all on their side by a long chalk. They are pretty evenly divided.'

'I don't much care either, to tell the truth. But I've got to get Mirri out of it! It's all very well her saying that she's doing important work but there have been such mad killings. Did you hear about the model prison in Madrid? They killed fifty prisoners because of a massacre somewhere or other, a sort of mad reprisal.'

'Like the people of Liverpool burning down shops and houses belonging to folk with German-sounding names in the last war,' Foxy agreed. 'We did it in modern history at school. Awful. And persecuting German governesses.'

'Worse,' Laurie pointed out. 'Well, that's it. Personally, I'd like to go over there and join the Republican army, help the Spanish people to fight for their independence. Don't shake your head at me, Foxy love, I know it isn't on, but if you'd seen the way the peasants are treated by the landowners and Spanish upper classes . . . don't worry, I know there's a job I must do here, I won't run out on you! But I reckon I can get to Madrid and back in three weeks if I really push myself and if I'm not back, Foxy, you'll stand by me and look after things, won't you? Only it's plain as the nose on your face that if I don't go now, whilst Mirri's still in the capital, I may never find her. Are you on? I'll have a word with the staff and with Allsop. He's a treasure, he'll do everything he possibly can to help you and he'll see you're kept in the picture even whilst you're in Cambridge. What do you say? Are you on?'

'Of course I'm on, as you call it,' Foxy said uneasily. 'You told me when I came that there was a possibility you might have to leave me to it. But Lo, I really do have to go back to Cambridge in October! I would stay if I could, but . . . well, I've worked so hard for this chance I can't just let it slip away, not even for you and your estate!'

'I know, and I wouldn't ask it of you,' Laurie assured her. 'Just do your best to get the home farm off the ground, there's a good girl, and I'll be back in no time. Allsop and Hawkings, between them, will manage till I get back. I'd like a word with Hawkings, so if you wouldn't mind telling the chaps with the slates what wants doing I'll get off into Ledbury at once.'

'But not in the pony cart,' Foxy observed. She slid off the block and waited until Laurie joined her, then they set off back up the lane together. 'I do hope you find your Mirri, Lo – it will scotch all the rumours, for a start.'

'What rumours? Oh, you mean that you and I . . .' Laurie chuckled. 'Be thankful, my girl, it's meant that Mum and Uncle Bill are now looking upon you with a softened eye.'

Foxy looked up at him, her clear grey-green eyes dancing. Laurie swallowed; though he was deeply in love with his Mirri he had to admit that Foxy had something about her . . .

'Do you really think so?' Foxy shook her head sadly, smiling at him. 'Honestly, how can they possibly believe that you and I . . . but it's what they want to believe, I suppose. And if it means I can see John without unpleasantness then I suppose I mustn't grumble.'

'Let them think anything they like. When I bring Mirri back in triumph then they'll have to think again,' Laurie said cheerfully. 'Come on, let's get a move on. I want a word with Allsop before I drive into town.'

'Dig, Mirri, dig! One day soon we'll be using these trenches so the deeper we get them the better! Presently, we'll stop for a drink and a rest, but not until we're down another foot.'

Mirri, in her dirty overalls, dug her spade into the unyielding clay and smiled at Jacinta as she used every ounce of her strength to pierce the sod. Perspiration ran down the sides of her face, tickled her neck, soaked into the front of her dusty overalls. She was longing for a drink, for a rest, yet she had seldom been happier. If she looked over the edge of the trench she was digging she could see, stretched out before and below her, the scorched plain of La Mancha. It was a desert with nothing but a couple of ruined windmills and a few tatty umbrella pines to break its bleak monotony – and the dusty road which stretched to the distant horizon.

This was Spain, her country. For years she had loved it without knowing she did, now she loved it passionately, with every fibre of her being, because it was under threat and because, for the first time in her life, she could do something positive to help. She was one of Spain's children, deeply concerned and involved in her country's fate; she had thrown off the shackles of her upbringing and could fight for this land, these people. Perhaps, she thought, she might be asked to die for them. And when you are eighteen and see things in black and white, feel the pure fire of rage burning within you over injustice, treachery, then to die for an ideal seems a marvellous thing.

'That's it, put your back into it,' Jacinta said. She wiped the sweat off her brow with a dirty wrist and left dust on her forehead. 'My, but you're right about one thing; it *is* hot!'

'I'm digging, I'm digging,' Mirri said, suiting action to words. 'Won't it be good when winter comes, though? Then, digging will make us warm; now it bakes us like lizards.'

Jacinta wrinkled her nose and dug her own spade ferociously into the hard-baked earth. She was a pretty girl with the black, curly hair and smooth olive skin which hinted at Moorish ancestry, but the light in her eyes and her way of expressing herself was all Spanish.

'Ha! Madrid has nine months of hell and three months of winter,' she said, quoting the old proverb. 'And winter can be hell, too, out here on La Mancha. Don't invite it in too soon, little sister.'

'I wasn't, but inviting it won't change a thing, and you must admit, digging is not a pastime for the heat,' Mirri pointed out.

'Oh, Jacinta, I wish I was strong, like you!'

'Ah, you mean strength of muscles; but what you should yearn for, Mirri, is strength of purpose, and that you can have for the asking. Your trouble is you have no strong convictions to keep you going, unlike myself.'

'I have,' Mirri said, putting a booted foot on the shoulder of her spade and driving it viciously into the iron-hard earth. 'Oh, not *political* convictions, I grant you that. It isn't that I haven't tried, either, Jacinta. I've read books and pamphlets and listened to the officers and the councillors and everyone else who talks so incessantly about the need for this war and the reasons behind it. I agree that it's time the people of Spain had a say in their destiny. But that doesn't make me a believer in some of the things they allow others to do. I don't think the end justifies the means for either side.'

'But what about the vines? You started to tell me something yesterday . . .'

'Ah, that was Pablo; even in his uniform you can see he's been denied food more often than he's been given it. He told me that in Andalusia, where he was born and raised, the landowners grubbed up their vines after the Popular Front won the election simply so that there would be no work for the labouring masses. Why, they even had posters made which read "You voted for the Republic; let the Republic give you work and fill your bellies, for we will not!" If that isn't true evil, real wickedness, then I don't know what is. To deny a man work, a child bread!'

'Well, there you are! Your heart, little sister, is in the right place and I respect you for it. But you say we should not hit back, not take revenge when we may against those who oppress us, and with those words I cannot agree. A child learns not to touch fire when it is burned; the fascists will learn to leave the people alone when they see their homes destroyed and their property confiscated.'

'I'm not talking about burning churches or taking a pot shot at some rich old general who's made people's lives a misery,' Mirri said, digging steadily. 'I'm saying that random violence is pointless, because when certain people find themselves sud-denly powerful they kill innocent people without even the pretence of a trial. Look at the *paseos*; mostly the men carrying out those – those killings are Russian *tchekas*, not even Spaniards, and Sergeant Cortal told me that some of the bodies which his men were told to bury after Manuel Lacorte had done one of his "Dawn Patrols" were those of women in nightdresses and young children in pyjamas. Not the most convinced Republican can think that is right!'

The *paseo* murders had horrified many people both older and wiser than Mirri. Russian communists and leaders of the left, mostly fanatics who enjoyed killing for its own sake, would simply seize any passerby, bundle him into a car, take their victim to a quiet spot and there 'execute' him. The act alone seemed to give relief and satisfaction to the perpetrator, but only until the next time.

Jacinta, however, dismissed the *paseos* with a wave of the hand. 'Madmen; political unreliables. They would commit such acts under any circumstances, given the opportunities and the weapons. No regime can entirely stamp out such people but in time we shall, at least, control them.'

'Well, until that happens I don't want to call myself one of them, though I'm happy to wear a uniform and fight for my country,' Mirri said firmly. She glanced proudly down at her stained blue overalls. 'And I'll use my gun on the enemy if they attack our city.'

'If! Who holds Madrid holds Spain. It's when, not if, little sister.'

'Oh, I don't deny they'll *try*,' Mirri said quickly. 'They have to try, naturally. But we've got a strong army, a good navy, even an air force. The filthy fascists won't be allowed within ten miles of my good little gun.'

'Hmm. Maybe not. And your good little gun, my child, is old and none too reliable, so don't wave it around near me.' Jacinta squinted at the great brass sun above their heads, then put down her spade. 'Thank God, it's past noon, we'll go back to the huts. Imagine a drink of cold beer, and a good slice of bread and goat's cheese.'

'Imagining it is all we'll do, then,' Mirri said ruefully, clambering, not without difficulty, out of the trench. 'The water's never cool, we aren't even offered beer, and the last time I saw really fresh bread I was locked up in my father's house on the Barrio de Salamanca.'

'Here, give me your hand and we'll run down to the huts,' Jacinta said as she, too, emerged from the trench. 'Wouldn't it be wonderful if a flash flood somewhere up in the mountains had filled the river, so that we could bathe? Oh, how I loved to bathe when I was a small child, visiting Alicante.'

'Why, did you come to Alicante when Leá did?' Mirri asked, as they hurried, shoulder to shoulder, back to the primitive huts which were the headquarters of the trench-diggers. 'I don't remember ever seeing you there.'

'No, of course you didn't. I could not be acknowledged, remember? Your parents never knew I existed or my mother could not have kept her job. But sometimes she took you to the beach and my grandmother took me, and no more than a dozen or so yards separated us.'

'Why didn't you come over and play with me? I wish you had,' Mirri said wistfully, as they reached the door of the hut and ducked under the lintel to go inside, into the relative cool, for the huts were stone-built. Here, great jugs of tepid wine and water awaited them, and rough loaves of the local peasant bread.

'Why? Because I didn't exist, little sister,' Jacinta said matter-of-factly. She pushed her way through the overalled women and picked up a rough pottery mug. 'We'll drink first, eh? As for not existing, I didn't mind, I understood. And there were other children; I could play with them. Indeed, I was luckier than you because you scarcely spoke to other children, did you?'

'It wasn't allowed,' Mirri muttered. 'Well, look at that! Did you know we were to have cheese today or were you just guessing?'

On the rickety wooden table, flanked by the water jugs and the loaves, was a platter of creamy goat's cheese. Jacinta had poured water into two mugs, now she picked up a knife and hacked two hefty slices off the nearest loaf, then dug the same knife into the cheese and smeared a generous amount on the bread.

'I didn't know. I just wish there were figs, too,' Jacinta said wistfully, making Mirri give a shout of laughter. Heads turned towards her, mouths curving into involuntary smiles.

'What's funny?' Inma asked. She was tall, willowy and aristocratic, with pale blonde hair and long-lidded blue eyes. Inma's grandfather had been a Scandinavian. Inma was the exact opposite of her best friend Josefa, a short, dark-skinned peasant from Asturias, and now the two of them came over to where Mirri and Jacinta stood. 'Come on, Mirri, share the joke, we've not had much to laugh about this morning. The bloody earth's so bloody hard my spade-handle snapped just before noon. I could have cried.'

'I was laughing because Jacinta said there would be cheese, and there was, so she said she wished there were figs . . . and she looked round hopefully, as though she thought she might have wished them into being,' Mirri explained. 'We can buy some in the market when we go off duty though, if Jacinta longs for them so. Now shall we take our food outside? We might find a patch of shade somewhere . . .'

'And Sergeant López might smell of roses instead of goat's turds,' Josefa remarked cynically. 'Still, we can't stay in here; it's too crowded for one thing and for another, it's getting terribly hot. Just think, in another four hours or so we'll be marching down the Gran Via, going off duty. And it'll be cooler, because it'll be evening. And I've met a lovely young man, all dark eyes and interested hands, who admires girls in uniform and talks of free love. What about that, eh?'

Mirri smiled. Jacinta did not approve of young men and she thought free love disgusting, or so she said when asked. But Mirri had seen her dimpling and glancing up under her lashes at a certain army captain.

'Your young man sounds very little different from most young men, Josefa,' Mirri said now as the four of them moved back into the pitiless sunshine. 'But I'm not like Jacinta; I approve of free love, provided it's kept in reasonable check.'

'If it's kept in check it isn't free,' Inma said. 'Besides, I don't want some man telling me what to do before I've enjoyed a bit of freedom. It was bad enough being ordered about by my papa and my eldest brother, but to have a lover ordering one about – a man to whom one is not even related – must be very unpleasant.'

'Then don't go falling in love, my aristocratic little nanny-goat,' Jacinta said with spirit. 'Because that's what happens when you fall in love. Though just having free love is different, I suppose, provided you don't have babies, too.' She jumped up

239

onto a ruined wall and shaded her eyes with one hand as she glanced around her. 'Ah, there's a patch of shade with no one in it under that old olive tree. Quick, girls, let's get there before someone else spots it!'

Hurrying along, with her watered wine sloshing in her mug and her food tucked into her overall pocket, Mirri looked at her companions and knew one of those moments of total, blissful happiness which only affect the very young. Comradeship, watered wine, some bread and a patch of shade, she thought: what more could any human being ask?

Nine

On his last night in England, Laurie, restless and worried that he was not doing the right thing, asked Foxy if she would go out walking with him.

'We can take a last look round and I can tell you what's happening,' he said quietly. 'And I might as well confess that I don't believe that I will be back here in a few weeks. It's taken longer to arrange the sea crossing and so on than I would have believed, to say nothing of setting all to rights on the estate. But never you mind that, Foxy, the place will run itself if necessary. Only if you can tell John what needs doing I'm sure he and Allsop between them will manage. And there's always Hawkings.'

Foxy agreed she would do her best, but September was nearly over and she would only be in Herefordshire another week. Cambridge waited for no man – nor woman, either. She went on to promise that she would spend Christmas at the Place, if Laurie himself was not back by then.

She only made these promises because she knew that Laurie was a lot more worried than he would admit, and not only about Mirri. The responsibility for his employees whose living came from the estate weighed heavily on him and he dreaded returning to find the good he had done come to nought. To be sure there wasn't much he could do about the tumbledown cottages, the ruined acreage, until the trust came to full fruition, but the home farm was coming on nicely. The roof was half finished, a plasterer had made the downstairs rooms habitable and when they had had the chimneys swept and the rooms thoroughly cleaned it would be a decent little home for any man. Even the pigsties, under Foxy's care, had begun to look respectable enough to put pigs in. Nothing had happened about the hops for the simple reason that there was, as yet, neither time nor money, but Foxy clung to the hope that, in a year or two, hops would flourish once more in that long, sloping meadow with its high, wild hedges.

So now, in the blue September dusk, she and Laurie walked. Down the drive, along the road, and into the autumn-scented woods. Once there, they sat down on a damp log by a little stream and Laurie lit two cigarettes, handing one to Foxy. They smoked in silence for a moment. Foxy inhaled smoke luxuriously and watched as Laurie began to blow smoke-rings into the quiet evening air.

'You blow smoke-rings very nicely. Now tell me what you've brought me all this way to say,' Foxy said rather sharply at last. She ground out her own cigarette and buried the stub in the soft leaf-mould at her feet. 'It must be something you'd prefer that Allsop didn't hear, though heaven knows what it can be!'

'It isn't; not exactly, anyway. But I've not told him about Mirri, at least not that she means something to me. I couldn't.'

Foxy stared. 'Why ever not? You're not worried that Allsop would disapprove because she isn't English, are you? He thinks the sun shines out of you, Laurie my lad; what you says, goes.'

'Ye-es. But he's a funny old boy in some ways. I definitely got the impression that he wasn't too keen on a Clifton marrying a foreigner. And then there's the – the misapprehension.'

'What misapprehension?' Foxy asked, as the silence stretched. 'Poor old Allsop, and I've always thought him sharp as a needle.'

'So he is, generally. Oh Foxy love, you aren't going to like this!'

'Go on,' Foxy said grimly; she was beginning to have an inkling. 'Surprise me.'

'Well, back in the summer, when you and John wanted to see a bit more of each other, and people started saying on the q.t. that you and I had a thing going . . . remember that?'

'I didn't say it; I said I didn't have anything going with anyone,' Foxy said with spirit. 'It was Mrs Waughman started the rumours, I think.'

'Perhaps. But we didn't deny them, did we?'

'No-oo, but what's that got to do with anything?'

'I've arranged with Hawkings and with Allsop that, in the event

242

of my not being around, you shall have a sort of power of attorney over the estate. And they leapt to the conclusion that you and I were – were fond of each other.'

'Me, to have power of attorney? Oh Lo, why not John?'

'Because I knew they wouldn't buy that. But saying I wanted you taken care of, that you knew what I'd got in mind . . . well, it satisfied both of them, I could tell. And Foxy, it's no skin off your nose, or mine either, for that matter. Because if I come home with Mirri then they'll see for themselves that they got hold of the wrong end of the stick. And if I snuff it out there, then I'd sooner you did your best for the estate until my wretched little second cousin once removed, or whatever he is, puts in an appearance. I've always been fond of you, old girl, and I trust you, too.'

'But I can't take your place!' Foxy said, really horrified. 'I don't know enough – I'd get torn to pieces by all the legal business and by your second cousin's family, I expect. Oh Lo, don't ask me to do it!'

'Too late. And the family would be grateful to you for helping out. But you can refuse,' Laurie said. 'Only, Foxy, I don't *intend* to snuff it out there, I mean to come back, with Mirri if I possibly can. And you'd be doing me the most terrific good turn, honestly. And – and there isn't anyone else, you see.'

'All right, I'll do my best,' Foxy said gruffly, and Laurie turned on the log and pulled her roughly into his arms. He sighed, and his breath stirred her hair in the stillness.

'You're a brick, a real darling,' he said. 'And John's a lucky beggar. If it wasn't for Mirri I'd give him a run for his money, dangle my title before your dazzled eyes . . . oh, Foxy, I'm scared! It's such a huge undertaking and I'm not really the aggressive, warlike type. I don't think I could kill anyone, but if they try to shoot me, or Mirri, I'd simply have to hit back. And suppose I can't find her? Suppose I muck the whole thing up?'

'You won't,' Foxy crooned, hugging him. 'I know you aren't aggressive, but you're brave and true, which is what counts. It may take you a bit of time, Laurie, but you'll come back, triumphant, with your Mirri. And I'll do my very best to see that you've something to come back to, as well. And I'll think of you all the time, and pray for both of you.'

'Thanks,' Laurie said. He kissed her cheek, then, clumsily, her mouth. He loved the feel of her, pressed against him, and told himself, as he held her, that it was a good thing he was in love with someone else... because he could never compete with John. 'You're one of the best, old Lockett. Don't know what I'd do without you; I'd trust you with my life, so leaving you in charge of the estate is easy.'

'Good,' Foxy said. She stood up, then held out her hands to him. 'And I take it you want me to pretend, to Allsop and the others, that you and I have an understanding?'

'Do you mind? Of course you do, but you know I wouldn't ask you to deceive anyone. Just let them assume and before you know it I'll be back in the saddle again. Oh, you'd better tell John, otherwise he might pursue me with intent to murder! John's the steady, reliable type and steady, reliable types only fall in love once, but they fall hard. Still, with Mum and Uncle Bill being so unreasonable, pretending that you and I are all but engaged will soothe savage breasts over at Bees-wing.

Allsop was cleaning the silver, sitting at the kitchen table with his precious pieces spread out round him and the little dish of pink liquid to his right, when there was a knock on the door.

'Come in,' Allsop called, suspending operations for a moment with the silver fruit bowl in one hand and the polishing cloth in the other.

The door opened and Davy Walsh, whose mother came up to the Place twice a week to clean, came hesitantly into the room. He was a cherubic-looking urchin of twelve or so and now he grinned at Mr Allsop and glanced round the kitchen.

'Come to tell thee what I sin jes' now, Mr Allsop; awright to fire ahead?'

'Shut the door, Davy,' Mr Allsop said, imperturbable as ever. He got up and checked that the door into the passageway was shut, then returned to the table, pausing by the pantry door to take a substantial egg and potato pie from the shelf. 'I'll cut you a piece of this for when you've finished talking.'

'An' a bob, Mr Allsop,' the boy reminded him. 'Yo' said a bob iffen I watched all week, an' so I 'ave.'

'And a shilling,' Mr Allsop said, gravely inclining his head. 'Come along now; what have you seen?'

'Mr Laurie an' Miss Foxy, a-huggin' an' a-kissin', up in 'Angman's Wood,' the boy said triumphantly. 'They done all sorts, Mr Allsop, what you'd niver b'lieve!'

Mr Allsop permitted himself a small smile. 'Would I not, Davy? I was not born fifty-nine years old, you know – which means that I, too, was young once.' He fished in his trouser pocket, brought out a handful of loose change and then deliberately selected a shiny florin. He held it up. 'Would this satisfy you? Plus the pie, of course.'

'Ho, yis, Mr Allsop,' the boy said, his eyes shining. 'Any time you want an eye keepin', you jes' call for me, sir!'

He took the money and the pie and let himself out, back into the yard. Allsop watched him cross it, cramming pie into his mouth, and smiled again. Not a bad boy, young Davy, and he had only confirmed what Allsop had suspected. Ever since Miss Foxy had come to Clifton Place, Sir Laurie had seemed happier, more relaxed. There was romance in the air from the start, Allsop told himself serenely, returning to his silver-polishing, and in my opinion he's made a good choice. She's a working-class girl but she's bright and she's brave, she'll do very well for him. Aristocratic blue blood thins with the generations, nothing wrong with an injection of good red working-class blood from time to time.

He didn't altogether understand the boy rushing off to Spain, though. Of course every red-blooded young man wants to fight a war, but Mr Laurie – Sir Laurie – knew he had responsibilities here, and he was not the sort of boy to disregard his duty. Mr Hawkings had not wanted him to borrow money from a bank against the trust, so he had lent him several sums, enough to keep the estate going and to get the home farm back into good heart, and the boy had seemed settled enough. And then one morning a letter had arrived from Spain, and Mr Laurie said he had to go. A friend was in trouble, he said.

Friendship. Mr Allsop shook his head indulgently and continued to polish the fruit bowl, paying particular attention to the handles, which were a couple of lion's heads, holding rings in their mouths.

Rings! That reminded him. Ten days ago, Laurie and the girl had gone into Hereford together; they had not said much, but when they returned they had exchanged bright glances and he had found them several times whispering in corners. Sir Laurie tried to tell me he'd been booking a cross-channel passage, but I do believe they plighted their troth then, Allsop told himself, working up a marvellous shine on the lions' aristocratic noses. I don't understand all this Spanish business, but the young will have their flings and Sir Laurie has friends there. No doubt it's a whim, and he'll take a look round and then come home to his true love. And once the boy reaches twenty-five the trust comes to an end and Sir Laurie will have control of his money and will be far too busy to go rushing off anywhere. And they'll be able to marry, too, make it all legal.

The fruit bowl was like a mirror, so Allsop put it on the Welsh dresser and picked up a vast tureen, liberally decorated with bunches of grapes and intricately carved vine leaves. He dipped his toothbrush into the pink mixture and began to brush. It was a pity Sir Laurie was so set on going away, but Allsop had no doubt that the experience of war, no matter how brief, would help Mr Laurie to appreciate his home and his own country. Mr Laurie – Sir Laurie – was young enough to see war as glamorous, but that wouldn't last. Allsop could remember the trenches all too well. But sunny Spain and helping a friend was exciting, or it sounded so at any rate. He decided, magnanimously, that he did not grudge the boy a bit of excitement. Then he turned his attention back to the task in hand; taking care of the Clifton silver.

When Sir Laurie and Miss Foxy returned from their walk, holding hands a little self-consciously, he was able to greet them with all his usual blandness.

'Ah, just in time for a nice cup of hot cocoa before you go off to bed. You'll want to be up early, tomorrow, sir.'

At two in the morning, Foxy, sleeping soundly, was rather startled to hear someone walking softly across her bedroom floor. She opened her eyes and peered in the patchy moonlight, and it was Laurie, very pale and hollow-eyed.

'Foxy? Are you awake? I couldn't sleep, because there was

something I totally forgot to say to you.'

'I'm awake now,' Foxy said ungratefully. 'Couldn't it have waited until morning, Lo? I'm dead tired, and tomorrow's an early start again.'

'No it couldn't, because my train leaves early, so I'll be off at the crack of dawn. Mr Allsop's driving me into town, too, so that means no opportunity for a quiet word. It's now or never, m'dear!'

'Oh, go on then,' Foxy said resignedly. 'What was it?'

'I'm going to give you the home farm; it'll be a sort of dowry for you. I'm not being cynical but I do think it will make you far more acceptable to the Hovertons, because quite a lot of land goes with it. And – and I want you to have this. It was my mother's.'

He held out his hand. In the middle of his palm, a small ring sparkled up at Foxy; two tiny diamonds and a dark stone, in the moonlight she could not see what it was.

'Oh, Laurie, Cumber Farm's a wonderful present, but I couldn't take your mother's ring! It – it's probably an heirloom or something.'

Laurie shook his head. 'No, the heirloom's a big, three-stone diamond which has been in my father's family for generations. This is just a little ring my mother wore because it was her mother's. Please, Foxy. You've done an awful lot for me and I'd like you to have it. Wear it, too. It will add weight to – to our story.'

'On my *engagement* finger?' Foxy asked, scandalised. 'Oh, I couldn't possibly – that would be living a lie!'

'No, not on your engagement finger,' Laurie said, chuckling. 'On your right hand, if you like. But I thought if you wore it on a chain round your neck, people would guess I'd given it to you. But if you'll just wear it . . .'

'. . . Everyone will draw their own conclusions,' Foxy supplied. She sighed. 'Yes, I'll wear it. Thanks, Laurie. And in another week or so the hop-picking will be over and I'll be able to see John officially before I go back to Cambridge. And good luck for tomorrow. Give me a kiss goodbye, dear Lo.'

They kissed with gentleness and, as Laurie went to turn away, Foxy realised he was crying. She gave a little exclamation of distress and caught hold of his hand. He looked down at her, his eyes very dark. He's unhappy and afraid, Foxy told herself, he's going back to his bedroom and he won't sleep a wink, because he's going into the unknown. Poor old Lo, it must be awful to be a fellow, to have to do things which scare you because it's your duty, to be prevented from doing what you'd really like to do, because men are supposed to be the strong and silent ones.

He was an artist, she remembered belatedly, pulling him down to sit on the bed. She had always known he was sensitive, now she knew he was very brave, too. It was far braver to go into a country at war for the sake of a pretty girl you had only known for two months, than to go because you wanted to fight someone.

'Foxy? What is it?'

She stroked his hand, then pulled back the covers.

'You'll never sleep if you go back to your own room, you're too tense and het up,' she whispered. 'Lie down with me and we'll put our arms round each other and talk, and perhaps we'll even cuddle a bit. And before you know it you'll be sleeping like a baby.'

'I can't, Foxy, it wouldn't be fair. Anyway, I won't die if I don't sleep all night.'

But he stayed sitting on the bed, and turned towards her.

'Laurie, you're giving me the home farm, it's tremendously kind and generous of you. Can't I give you a night's sleep, and a cuddle, in return? It's little enough, God knows.'

He sighed, then rolled into bed beside her. She cradled him in her arms, trying to soothe away his worries, stroking his forehead, gently kissing the side of his neck.

Presently, she felt him begin to relax. He sighed and put his own arms around her.

'Dear Foxy . . . go to sleep and I'll sleep, too.'

Presently, rather to Foxy's surprise, his breathing deepened. She had pushed the little ring onto the third finger of her right hand – it fitted her as if it had been made for her – and now she stroked it lovingly. A dear little ring – and the home farm! She had never dreamed of such a gift because landowners, she knew, seldom wanted to sell land, let alone give it away. But Laurie had always been generous, and he knew how important it was to her that the Hovertons should accept her, if she and John married. To bring them land was the one sure way to their farmerly hearts, and though she wished they could have loved her for herself, she was a realist. Cumber Farm would make all the difference, when the time came to declare their love openly.

Presently, despite her excitement over Laurie's gift, despite the strangeness of having Laurie in her bed, she slept. And dreamed of wars, of death, of violence, so that she cried out in her sleep. Even in her sleep she knew herself comforted, and slept again, more deeply.

She woke as day dawned to find her bed empty; had she dreamed that Laurie had come to her, that they had lain together all night in loving comradeship? But then she saw the little ring on her finger and remembered that, one day, the home farm would be hers.

Smiling, she slept once more.

The creaking of the stairs in the night had woken Allsop, who had always been a light sleeper. He listened as the footsteps slowed on the landing, heard a door softly open . . . heard more footsteps. He heard bedsprings creak, and softly, two voices.

Surprisingly, he felt a deep and dreadful sense of guilt; it was fair enough to make sure that Sir Laurie was truly in love with Miss Foxy by setting young Davy to spy on them, but to listen to their love-games from his own warm bed seemed, to Allsop, to be a very real betrayal.

So he rolled over and pulled the pillow down over his ears. And presently, slept.

'I'm tellin' you, man, young Foxy Lockett's goin' to get young Clifton! Aye, they were kissin' an' cuddlin' an' worse in the wood t'other day, an' on the marnin' arter 'e left, she wor wearin' a ring . . . diamonds an' a ruby. Mrs Huggett what's bin 'elpin' to clean up at the 'ome farm seen it wi' 'er own eyes!'

John was in the stable, saddling up Lightning, when he heard Elias telling Dan the tale in the yard outside. For a moment he just stood motionless, whilst the most frightening, sickening rage and disgust enveloped him. Gossip, gossip, backbiting, rumour . . . was his love never to be free of it? Just because she was living under Laurie's roof . . .

'Well, the lad's gorn orf to Spain, be all accounts. My nephew, young Reggie, 'e's gorn an' all. Mind, 'e's a strong union man, Reggie. Says 'e's socialist, but 'e talks communist, if you asks me. So young Foxy's mekin' 'ay whiles the sun shines, eh? Most of us 'ad the odd roll in the 'ay by the time we was Mr Laurie's age, so if she's got 'is ring on 'er finger, she'll likely be Lady Clifton yet . . . an' why not? She'm a nice little gal.'

'Oh ah, she'll do awright, will Foxy. Clever, 'er is. She's at Cambridge, they tell I. Gotta be clever to go there, especially since she'm a gal.'

'Ah. Worked out that if she lay wi' the lad, 'e'd wed 'er sooner than let shame come to she; I do calls that clever. I'm mortal glad my Sal . . . oh, sorry Mr John, I didn't see you there.'

John was leading Lightning and the two men, rather red about the gills, tried to move away but John was not seeing them disappear before he'd had his say.

'Hang on, you two. Ever heard of slander?'

'I've 'eard of it,' Dan admitted cautiously after a longish pause. 'Jest about, I 'ave.'

'Good. Then don't talk utter rubbish about a decent kid like Foxy, right? And don't repeat spiteful gossip as if it were gospel truth.'

'Sorry, Mr John. But she do be wearin' a ring on 'er finger, Mrs 'Ugget seen it. An' she were wi' Mr Laurie . . .'

'Sir Laurie to you, Elias,' John said crisply. 'You saw her, did you, man? With your own eyes?'

'Well, no, but . . .'

Then you're simply passing on gossip and rumour as though it were the truth.' John shook his head pityingly and mounted his gelding. 'Dangerous thing to do, as well as pretty nasty. Get on with your work, now.'

'We're on our way 'ome, Mr John,' Dan said with a touch of defiance. 'Finished for the day, see?'

'You have? Well, I want a dozen or so bales of hay brought over from the Dutch barn to the loft. See to that before you go, please.'

Neither man answered him but they turned as one towards the Dutch barn.

That'll take them an hour or so, John thought with mean satisfaction as he swung Lightning out of the yard. Serve them right for daring to sully Foxy's reputation. But his plans for the evening were in tatters. The hops were almost over and he meant to see them finished before visiting Foxy again, but he would have to go to the Place, now, instead of checking with the men in the drying kiln, examining the finished produce, so to speak. It had been an excellent crop, though; he could not remember a better. As for the stupid gossip Elias and Dan had been exchanging, he did not believe a word of it. What had struck him most forcibly, however, was that the men said Laurie had left for Spain, and his foster-brother had not even phoned to say goodbye. Oh, he'd known Laurie was leaving for Spain very soon, and had been vaguely against the idea, but he had been putting off arguing him into staying for a variety of reasons. Perhaps he had not realised fully how very dangerous such a trip could be until recently. He'd read some dreadful newspaper reports about the war, and this morning the paper had been full of the shooting of an English-woman a few weeks earlier; the usual innocent bystander, no doubt, but dead, nevertheless. Laurie wanted to go and fetch that girl Mirri, so he'd be an innocent bystander too – but surely he'd have more sense than to risk getting embroiled?

If anyone goes, it ought to be me, John told himself, turning Lightning out of the farm lane and onto the road. I'm a good shot and I was in the OTC at school – I was an NCO by the time we left. Old Laurie wasn't interested in playing soldiers, just used to slope off with his drawing pad and let me get on with it. Laurie's a dreamer, an academic, so it's all wrong that he's going to Spain. But I assumed he'd probably change his mind, try to get word to the girl instead, through our embassy, perhaps.

But if the men were right . . . resolutely, John turned his horse's head towards Clifton Place. No harm in just making sure . . .

'He's really gone? Well, thank God he doesn't plan to join the army – I take it he doesn't plan to do any such mad thing? Foxy, I can't believe he's really left without a word to me – we've always been so close and he must have known I'd not approve. The country's at war, for goodness' sake, and . . .' John broke off and grabbed Foxy's hand, pulling it towards him. 'For the love of God, that ring on your finger, girl . . . where did you get such a thing? I heard two of my men gossiping, but I thought . . .'

Foxy had been going round the home farm when John had ridden into the yard. She was examining the newly whitewashed pigsties, the clean though empty kitchen, the well, working properly, the brand-new bucket on its length of rope just waiting to be lowered into the water. In short she was gloating over what would, one day, be hers. She had not been prepared for John's outrage over Laurie's leaving without saying goodbye, nor for the way his eyes glinted with anger when they fell on the ring on her finger. Two tiny diamonds flanked a round, glowing ruby, set in gold. She thought it pretty, doubted it was very valuable, enjoyed her possession of it.

'Laurie gave me the ring. It's all right, John, it isn't valuable, it's not an heirloom or anything. He gave it to me for looking after the place whilst he's away . . . I mean I'm going back to Cambridge, we agreed that, but if he isn't back by the Christmas vac I'm coming down here again to run things whilst I'm able. And again at Easter, if he's not back, and again next summer, only of course he'll be back long before then. As for his not ringing you, I think he was afraid you'd try to persuade him to drop the idea.'

'I would have, of course. And you shouldn't accept valuable gifts from men if you don't intend to marry them,' John said in a low voice. 'The trouble with you, Foxy, is that you want to have your cake and eat it. You want this great career of yours, yet when Laurie snaps his fingers you come running, because he pays well and because he gives you presents.'

The unfairness of the remark almost took Foxy's breath away; for a moment she just gaped at him, then she began to fight back.

'How *dare* you tell such wicked lies, John Hoverton! You wanted me to work for Laurie so that you and I could see more of each other, you know you did! And what's wrong with his giving me a ring, anyway? He says it isn't valuable and he would know, wouldn't he? And he's gone to Spain after that Mirri girl he's always talking about, so he certainly wasn't giving me a ring for any – any ulterior motive, if that's what you think!'

'That's what people will say,' John muttered. 'You know how villagers gossip. And it's not very pleasant for me to hear the woman I love linked with my best friend.'

'Oh, phooey,' Foxy said scornfully. 'That's all rot, John, and you know it. Besides, your parents will feel much happier if gossip reaches them that I'm all but engaged to Laurie, you know they will. They'll stop talking about disinheriting you if there's no question of you marrying me, which should please you!'

'Let them disinherit me; I can't just unlove you because of the way they feel,' John said savagely. 'I'd find a job – you say you want to teach, so we could both earn. You mean more to me than Bees-wing, I swear it.'

'Oh, John, if that's true then why are we quarrelling?' Foxy sighed, leaning her head against his tweed-jacketed shoulder. 'You know I don't care for Laurie, except as a friend, and you know I care very much indeed for you. And think how awful I would feel if you lost Bees-wing through me! Besides, Laurie had a marvellous idea before he left. You'll never guess what it was.'

'What was it?' John said grudgingly after a pause. 'I suppose he intends to marry you and then divorce you so you can marry me, because Lady Clifton could scarcely be a bad match for a mere Hoverton!'

'Not quite,' Foxy said. She rubbed her head against his shoulder, then turned and put her arms round him. She kissed his chin, his cheek, then his mouth. He resisted at first and then began to kiss her back, wildly, hotly. She purred beneath his mouth, then tugged at his arm, 'We can't talk here, someone's bound to come along, and besides it looks like rain,' she whispered. 'Come to the hayloft, it's nice and private and I'll tell you what Laurie said.'

Together, hand in hand, they ran over to the barn and climbed up into the hayloft. They flopped down in the hay and Foxy said triumphantly: 'Laurie's going to give me the home farm for my very own, as a dowry, when he gets back from Spain. He says your parents can't say I'm just a hop-picker if I'm bringing Cumber Farm to the marriage.'

'He can't do that,' John said uncertainly. 'He can't give away land; not even for our sake.'

'Well, he can. He can't give away land from the main part of the estate because it's entailed, but Cumber Farm is different. It belonged to Laurie's mum, apparently, so he owns it outright.'

'He shouldn't give land away,' John repeated stubbornly. 'I can't let him do it . . . it isn't right.'

'Let him? Just you try to stop him! And anyway, he's promised it to me, not to you, and I'm not grumbling. After all, I'm going to work for it. Because if he isn't back by March I'm giving up my degree and I'll act as his deputy at Clifton Place until he does return. Oh John, don't be cross, give me a cuddle.'

She moved against him, unwittingly seductive, and suddenly Laurie, the home farm, the diamond and ruby ring, were all forgotten. John slid his hands under her shoulders and pressed her onto her back in the soft hay, kissing, persuading, murmuring her name. And Foxy, sensible Foxy, who wanted her career, a respectable marriage and the good things of life, forgot everything but John, the violent, tender, thrilling feelings aroused by his touch, his warmth and nearness.

'Foxy,' John breathed presently, when they were lying breast to breast, warm and supple and eager amongst the hay. 'Do you love me, my darling girl?'

'Oh, so much,' Foxy moaned, arching herself against him. 'Oh, I love you more than anything . . . more than anyone.'

'And do you want me?'

'Yes, I want you very much,' Foxy whispered. 'Oh John, love me, please love me!'

He hesitated for the merest second and then she felt him move over her and saw, above the silhouette of his head, a ray of moonlight coming through the ancient roof slates, and told herself it was not too late to be sensible, to change her mind, to make him leave her.

But it was too late for both of them. She could no more deny him than he her. Love seized them, carried them to the heights and then into the still, gentle waters of fulfilment. Tired but happier than they had ever been, they lay, then, in each other's arms and murmured endearments and promises never to be parted, never to quarrel again. Impossible promises.

Foxy stood on the platform as the train chugged in, the wind of its arrival stirring the piles of crisp autumn leaves which had already fallen from the trees at the far end of the platform. She had done everything she could to ensure the smooth running of the home farm and of the estate whilst she was gone, she just hoped it was good enough. Mr Allsop, who had driven her to the station, cleared his throat.

'I'll put your case aboard for you, Miss Foxy. I shall keep you informed by letter as to what is happening on the estate, just as though you were Mr Laurie himself. Sir Laurie, I should say. And you'll be back in December?'

'I certainly shall, Mr Allsop. And don't forget, if there's anything I can do to help you've got the telephone number of my college, and my address. Though Mr Hawkings will probably cope with most problems.'

'That's right, Miss Foxy. But the winter's a quiet time, we're not likely to have problems for the next few months. To tell you the truth, I feel very much better about Sir Laurie now that I know Mr John's on his way to join him. Those two were always close.'

'Yes, that's true,' Foxy said. 'John's always taken care of Laurie, ever since they were children. Goodness, isn't the train crowded? I do hope I manage to get a seat.'

She and the butler got aboard the train and Mr Allsop stowed her case on the string luggage rack above her head. Then he solemnly shook her hand and told her to take care to work hard, and to keep in touch with either himself or Mr Hawkings.

'I will, Mr Allsop,' Foxy said soothingly. 'It's only a ten-week term, so I'll be back in no time, just you see.'

He nodded, pressed her hand and glanced round the carriage. Foxy, rather touched, realised he was checking over the other passengers as suitable companions for her, but as luck would have it there were only four people in the compartment besides herself and they were all women. Foxy had managed to get a windowseat and she smiled round at her fellow-passengers, all of whom seemed pleasant-looking. Mr Allsop seemed satisfied that no one was likely to annoy her, anyway, for he climbed back down onto the platform and then slammed the door shut. Foxy let down the window and leaned out.

'Thank you for driving me down, Mr Allsop,' she said. 'If you hear from Mr Laurie, could you drop me a line and tell me what he says?'

Mr Allsop gave her his small, discreet smile. 'I daresay Mr Laurie will write to you rather than to me,' he said. 'I'd be very obliged, Miss, if you would communicate the import of such letters to me; I am – very fond of Mr Laurie. He has not had an easy time of it and though I shall try not to worry, it will not be easy. He's a true gentleman.'

'I know,' Foxy said, thinking of Cumber Farm. 'I'll either write or phone, Mr Allsop, every time I hear. Ah, we're about to leave, I think.'

She was right. The guard whistled and waved his flag, the engine hooted and they were off, hurrying away through misty water meadows, woods golden with autumn, hills purple with heather. Foxy settled down in her seat and let her mind go back over the events of the past few days.

She had scarcely believed her ears when John had telephoned to say that he had put his name down to fight in Spain and would be leaving the following day. It seemed such a mad, unnecessary thing to do . . . and to tell her over the telephone after what they had shared seemed like a slap in the face, deliberately administered.

But John had dispelled that feeling, at least.

'It's Laurie giving you the home farm,' he had said. 'He never knew his mother, but he thought a lot of her and he's had it dinned into him that you don't ever sell or dispose of land since he was toddling. To do something like that for us . . . and he's no good as a fighter, he never was. Even at school he hated scrapping and wouldn't join the OTC. Called us mindless louts, I recall. So I can't just let him go off alone to find that wretched girl, and the only way to get over there is to join up, so I've joined. Oh Foxy, I love you so much!'

'Can't you stay?' Foxy had quavered. 'I'm afraid for you, darling.'

'I have to go,' John said miserably. 'I'd never be able to hold my head up again if I let Lo down. But as soon as I've found him, and he's found Mirri, we'll come back. I swear it.'

'But Laurie said you'd advise me over farming matters,' Foxy said wildly. To have given herself to John and to have him snatched from her seemed too cruel! 'What will I do when I'm stuck, John?'

'You'll have to ask my parents,' John said with a hint of laughter in his voice. 'They're going to have to accept you, Foxy love, whether they want to or not, because they won't have me, or Laurie, to fall back on. They said they'd disinherit me if I married you – well, now they'll find out how it feels to have someone you love turn away from you, and perhaps they won't be so keen to threaten, in future.'

'Perhaps they may like it,' Foxy said mournfully, making John give a crack of laughter.

'No fear of that,' he said bracingly, however. 'They'll miss me like the very devil and you'll be a link. You will write? I'll send you an address as soon as I've got one.'

'Of course I will,' Foxy said stoutly, though her heart gave a doubtful thump. How was she going to bear it, separation, responsibilities, no more delicious lovemaking? 'You'll write too, won't you? Laurie sent a card when he landed, but that's all, so far.'

'I'll write each day, but I may not be able to post them that often,' John said. 'Be good, sweetheart. And miss me, because I'm going to miss you hellishly.'

'Good,' Foxy said shakily. 'Come back soon, then. Soon as you like. And bring Laurie and his l-little S-Spanish onion.'

John laughed, but his mirth sounded as shaky as Foxy's voice.

'I will, darling. Take care.'

And that had been it, because they had agreed that it would not do for John to come down to the station to see Foxy off, nor would it have been politic for them to have met openly, when they now knew that it was just a matter of time before Foxy was as acceptable to the Hovertons as any farmer's daughter.

And now Foxy, leaning back in her corner seat and watching the countryside jog past, found herself feeling really sorry for the Hovertons. They were nice people, it was not their fault that they were old-fashioned about things like marriage ... and she was only a hop-picker, after all. And through no fault of their own they were losing their only son for a time, to a war which was none of their business, which did not interest them in the least. Laurie was dear to them of course, but he had already grown away. When he had been forced to move in with his father the silver cord which had bound him to the Hovertons had stretched and stretched . . . it might not have broken, but Foxy was sure that the Hovertons had given up all claim to the boy they had reared as their own. They loved him but did not really understand him, and were proud of him in their way, but not in the same way that they were proud of John.

Still. If it had not been for their prejudices they could have talked to Foxy, shared the letters from John when they came, discussed the situation with her. As it was, they would be cast on their own resources, and Foxy was pretty sure that neither Ada nor Bill Hoverton had the slightest idea of what was happening in Spain.

The train-wheels clickety-clicked over the points and the woman sitting beside Foxy remarked to the compartment at large that she was goin' up to London to see her daughter Polly, who had recently wed a very pleasant gentleman who worked in Harrods which was, she understood, quite a big shop.

Foxy said that she was going back to Cambridge to start her second year as a student of English literature and had to change not only trains but also stations when she reached the capital. The passenger nearest to Foxy in age, a girl in her early twenties, said that she, too, was studying, though in her case it was shorthand and typewriting at the Underwood business school in Regent Street.

Conversation became general and Foxy, in discussing her future plans and how a degree might influence them, was able to forget, for a while, that her dear John was far away and heading for danger the like of which they had neither of them ever encountered before.

But when she had crossed London and got into the Cambridge train thoughts of John and the danger into which he was heading returned at once, for Spain was the subject of conversation in her carriage. One girl had a brother fighting there, another a dear friend. They knew all about the conflict, the reasons for it, what each side was doing, and gave their opinion freely over the rights and wrongs of it all. Foxy tried not to listen, to detach her mind, but it was impossible, and pointless, too. She knew well enough that when she reached Cambridge, she would find herself amongst a great many people who would admire John for what he had done

258

and would be able to discuss with her what was happening in war-torn Spain even more intelligently than her travelling companions. I may feel I'm better not knowing, she told herself, as the women chattered, but that's head-burying, and head-burying never did anyone any good. Besides, he's well on his way by now, he might even have arrived . . . oh dear God, keep him safe! Guard my good, solid Herefordshire boy for me while he fights for what he sees is right!

And then, conscience-stricken, she added a prayer for Laurie, that he might find his little Spanish onion and come home safely, too.

Laurie came down the dry-baked track onto the dust of a small, steep road. Above him the sky was brilliantly blue, the sun baking hot. Before him was the town of Badajoz, his present destination. He was a long way from Madrid still, but the country was at war and a civil war, which sets brother against brother, means that no man can safely be neutral; if you are to get anywhere, you must take sides. And the side you take, Laurie realised, must be the one which is strongest in your particular area. Here, in the town which he was approaching, he knew it was the Nationalists because they had fought a great battle here a week ago and taken Badajoz, so he would exhibit sympathies without actually joining them if he could possibly help it; his main object was to find Mirri and not to fight in a war which was no concern of his.

But he imagined that Mirri, with her freely expressed contempt for the peasants, would naturally support the landowning, governing classes. Since it was these classes who supplied the money and made up, in the main, Franco's Nationalist army, he supposed vaguely that if he took any side it ought to be the Nationalist one. But somehow he hated the idea. He had travelled extensively in Spain in his year off after school, long before meeting Mirri, and had been appalled by the condition of a good three-quarters of the population. Abject poverty and gruelling work on land as barren and hard to cultivate as any he'd seen was no way to live. Indeed, the peasants' lives were scarcely more than a mean, grudged existence from the day they were born to the day they died, and the people who had been in a position to improve the situation were indifferent to anything but themselves and their own comfort. Oppressed by the ruling classes, treated with cruel contempt by the church, the Spanish poor had been ripe for an uprising for many years and now that it had come Laurie had a sneaking hope that they would win, in the end.

He had thought, when he set out, that getting to Spain would be simple; he would say that he wanted to join the army, he would say he had relatives there, he would say anything if it meant he could get to Madrid before Mirri left the city. He had planned to buy a passage on a Spain-bound ship, but he had not taken into account the Non-Intervention pact. A good many European countries were completely ignoring it – from guarded comments in the newspapers Laurie realised that Germany and Italy were sending both men and equipment to the fascist forces – but others, Britain in particular, were holding back. Without being an accredited newspaperman, therefore, he would not get to Spain by ship.

But young men are resourceful and Laurie was no exception. He went to France, then took ship to Portugal, where, he was assured, the border would not be particularly closely guarded. The Portuguese, far from being neutral, were in deathly fear of the insurrection spreading, of their own peasants rebelling against the misery of their lives, and consequently did everything in their power to aid the fascist forces.

'You might have difficulty getting from Spain to Portugal,' a friend in Paris told him. 'But from Portugal to Spain is a different kettle of fish. No one will try to stop you jumping from the frying pan into the fire, dear fellow.'

Laurie had reached the small town of Elvas the previous day. The place hummed with rumour and Laurie, who spoke excellent Spanish and had soon picked up a sprinkling of Portuguese, learned from the landlord of a tiny inn facing the main square that there had been a great battle just over the border, that the Portuguese international police had prevented refugees from crossing into their country, had actually repatriated those who had made the crossing.

'But isn't that illegal? What about the right of asylum?' Laurie had asked, shocked. 'Even fighting troops are entitled to asylum!'

'They weren't fighting troops; they were people like us, ordinary people. They sent them back knowing they went to certain death,' the bent little innkeeper told Laurie, his seamed face angry, his eyes ashamed. 'Women and children . . . the wounded, the old . . . back they went.'

'Why?' Laurie asked helplessly. 'Why did they do it?'

The old man shrugged. 'Oh, they were only peasants, landless men,' he said bitterly. 'They can't make a fuss, poor folk such as they. But that Franco . . .' he spat neatly, '. . . he is wicked and powerful. Our masters see they would perhaps suffer if they extended clemency to the enemies of such a one.'

'But – but you said women and children, and the wounded,' Laurie stammered. 'Surely a man such as General Franco would not call women and children his enemies?'

'Anyone who raises a hand against him, or thinks a thought he does not share, is an enemy,' the old man said. Behind Laurie, feet scuffled in the dust as someone entered the dark little bar and the innkeeper raised his voice, saying immediately: 'But I can assure you, *señor*, that a bed for the night, the best bed in my house, will cost you only a few centavos . . . for that you may have a meal, too.'

So Laurie had spent a restless night in a bed shared with bed-bugs, fleas and other similar livestock. He had got up as dawn broke at last to reconnoitre the steep, white-walled fortress town perched on the hill no more than ten miles or so from the Spanish border. He walked quietly up the narrow streets until he found a wall with a fig tree growing below it from which vantage point he could see the line of a river, gleaming in the pale dawn light, the frontier post and beyond it, Spain. He could also see that it was perfectly possible to cross into Spain without passing a post if one took to the fields, the little hills and the scrubland where the cork oaks grew. If one waited till nightfall it would be plain sailing. He had learned from the innkeeper that the town of Badajoz was in the hands of the rebels, or the Nationalists as they now called themselves. They had murdered innocent civilians, according to the innkeeper, but Laurie had heard of the killings on the Republican side and guessed that of the cruel and terrible atrocity stories which had filtered out of Spain, each side had done its share. He must not let such things deflect him from his purpose, which was to find Mirri and get her to safety before joining the struggle.

Because, having seen for himself how things were, he rather thought that he would not return to England just yet. He would take a hand. Others were beginning to flock to the aid of the Republicans and Laurie's conscience said that he, too, should be one of them.

He had realised, too, that in order to find and rescue Mirri he must question people, behave in a friendly fashion to those he might secretly despise and must at least appear sympathetic to the Nationalist cause when it was politic to do so, even if he hated everything about them. Not that he did; he told himself there must be faults on both sides and decided he would do his best to remain impartial, at least until he'd got Mirri safely to England.

So Laurie spent the whole day in the small, fly-ridden town. He lunched on stale rolls, tomatoes and a piece of beef with which he could easily have soled his shoes, had a siesta under the olive tree in the town square and gave most of the food to a mongrel cur which was covered in sores and clearly starving. Then Laurie professed a desire to go early to bed in order to move on at an early hour.

'You'll cross the border,' the innkeeper muttered uneasily. 'If they catch you they'll kill you, señor. They don't care if they kill a few English. Who will know, or dare to tell? You'll be just another unidentified body.'

'I'm going to get an early night,' Laurie said, ignoring the words. 'Thanks for your good wishes; I'll leave at dawn so I'll pay my shot now, then I won't have to disturb you tomorrow.'

But by midnight he was out of the inn and making his way slowly and cautiously over open countryside, towards the border. Despite the fact that autumn was almost over the night was mild, the stars blazing overhead. At one point he walked into a herd of sleeping pigs but they seemed to bear him no malice and he went on more cautiously, not stopping to rest until he could see Badajoz below him, curiously silent, seemingly peaceful.

He slept when he judged he had come far enough, curled up by a crumbling dry-stone wall, and was woken by the sun and by a great thirst which he slaked, presently, when he reached the Guadiana river. When he had drunk his fill he climbed up the bank and crossed the bridge which led straight into the town. There were men in the grey uniforms of the Nationalist army standing around, one picking his teeth with a sharpened matchstick, another reading a letter, but no one took any notice of him. I don't suppose they have much trouble keeping people out, Laurie thought with grim humour; they're guarding the gates to keep people in.

The atmosphere in the town was thick with fear, heavy with dread. It hung in the air, showed itself whenever two people passed, each avoiding the other's eyes. Laurie knew he could not go long undetected as someone not of the town, but every time he tried to approach ordinary townsfolk they turned aside, disappeared. He might be dangerous – a spy, or just someone who would bring the wrath of the fascist army down upon them.

In other towns he had gone to an inn but here the inns were closed and shuttered, not open for business. He wandered around and arrived at the bull-ring in the white-hot heat of noon and smelt burning; from above the walls smoke drifted lazily upwards and presently Laurie asked a passing soldier what had been happening. The man told him that after the battle the defenders of the town had been brought to the bull-ring and machine-gunned; women as well as men. Now the bodies were being disposed of, because there were too many of them for even the largest grave.

Later, he talked to another man, a grey-clad soldier who stood with his rifle at half-cock, chewing on a stick of tobacco, who confirmed that even now anyone suspected of being a Republican was brought here and shot. The sickly stench of burning flesh and an almost palpable cloud of fear and disgust hung around the bull-ring, making Laurie turn on his heel and hurry away, sick and trembling.

By the afternoon Laurie was beginning to feel like a leper and danger crawled on the back of his neck. He could be shot at a whim . . . whatever was he doing here? He had hoped for news of Mirri and the war but it was pretty plain he would not get it in a town still suffering from the horrors of a siege and then the mass shootings. One black-clad woman, her eyes still dull with shock, told him that the Moors fighting for the Nationalist forces had killed indiscriminately once they breached the walls, even their own supporters, who had run out waving their fascist ribbons and been mown down with the rest.

At some stage Laurie had found one of the red and yellow fascist ribbons and put it through his buttonhole and thus armed he had tried to find out whether any of the soldiers knew if there were any women fighting or working with the army, but they had no idea, merely shrugging and saying that war was for men. As the sun was beginning to slide down the sky he spoke to a young Phalangist, strutting across the *plaza* with a gun in his hand, and explained he was searching for the De Salvorini y Rodriganez family, but the young man, though he had heard the name and knew the family to be good monarchists, could tell him little other than that.

'Spain isn't a safe place to be neutral in,' he said quite kindly, when Laurie had told him he was betrothed to the daughter of the Rodriganez family and wanted to ensure that his future wife was safe. 'If you truly love her, *hombre*, then you should fight for her. Go to the offices of the governor; there are people there who might help you – if you join us.'

Laurie said he would take his friend's advice and walked purposefully away, but not towards the offices of the governor. He had heard that the main part of the army had moved on to another battle area and until he knew where Mirri was he could not afford to become a tiny cog in that great machine, sent hither and thither at General Franco's whim. The men he saw around him were merely keeping Badajoz subdued and would not need another conscript – not that he could do any good by remaining in this terrible town.

When darkness fell, he thought about leaving, but now he could see that the innkeeper's words were no more than the truth. Getting in had been relatively easy; getting out would be a great deal more difficult. But not impossible, Laurie thought reflectively, remembering the tobacco-chewing guards, the bridge over the great river, the stunned lassitude of the people of Badajoz. Few if any of them had the heart to try to escape. They would accept whatever fate threw at them now, and besides, where could they go? Portugal would send them back under guard, watch them shot. The rest of Spain was no safer than Badajoz itself. So they would stay because they had no choice.

But I shan't, Laurie told himself grimly, slipping like a shadow down a narrow *calle* littered with the debris from damaged and abandoned buildings. I'll get out of here and go on searching if it's the last thing I do, because I must find Mirri!

There were three of them, in the end. They had met up, of all places, on Gloucester station and after a casual conversation had realised they were all heading for the same destination – Spain. There was John Bellingham, known as Jack, John Franklyn, known as Frankie, and John Hoverton; three farmers' sons in their early twenties with the warm accents of Gloucester and Hereford, a strong sense of right and wrong and the unselfconscious confidence which was the result of happy family life and first-rate health.

Jack was a socialist and knew little about the war other than that once more the privileged were trying to impose their will on the poor. He thought this a bad thing and wanted to stop it, but above all, he wanted a war, a chance to prove himself and, as he ingenuously put it, to have some fun as well.

Frankie, on the other hand, knew all about the war and still wanted to put his oar in. He was indignant that a government elected by the people and of the people should be threatened by the rich; in Frankie's eyes the ruling classes had lost the game and had promptly decided to change the rules. The game must be won by them or they would take it by force. This, he assured the other two, was the thin end of the wedge. If the fascists found it worked in Spain then it would be tried in other countries, too. It behoved everyone who loved justice and liberty, therefore, to fight against the rebel Nationalists led by General Franco.

'And the Germans and the wops have come out on the rebels' side, so naturally we should oppose them,' he told his two friends. 'Good thing there's three of us; we'll stick together, watch each other's backs. Got a girl, back home?'

John admitted he had, Jack that he hadn't.

'Best to be fancy-free,' Frankie observed. 'Spanish girls are damned pretty. You'll be writing home every other day, I suppose?'

John, thus addressed, nodded sheepishly. 'Probably. But I'm here because my friend Laurie's here too. He's trying to find his Spanish girlfriend. He's not . . . not involved at all.'

He found he could not explain their closeness, the fact that he and Laurie had shared all their battles from the moment of their birth, just about. Nor could he explain, oddly enough, that Laurie might well not join the fight. He found it hard to say that Laurie was not aggressive, was really an academic type, not the sort of person to join an army. But if he's forced to join up in order to find the girl he'll simply not survive without me, John found himself thinking over and over as he and his new friends crossed France by train and on foot. He'll be brave and he'll obey orders, but . . . oh, hell, he'll get himself killed, and I can't allow that!

They reached the Pyrenees without being either helped or hindered although most people probably realised where they were bound. However, the three of them were self-sufficient and all spoke reasonable schoolboy French though Frankie was the only one of them with excellent, idiomatic Spanish.

'We'll start out at dawn tomorrow,' Frankie told them as they stood in the window of the tiny inn in the foothills where they had elected to spend their last night before beginning the ascent. 'It may take us a couple of days, but we'll make it easily.' The three of them eyed the peaks stretching away into the distance measuringly. 'Good thing it's not winter, though. I wouldn't fancy climbing that lot in winter. As it is, I reckon it'll be pretty bloody cold at night.'

'We've got sleeping bags,' John pointed out. 'And there's bound to be water in the mountains, isn't there? We'd best buy bread and some cheese tomorrow; that'll see us through.'

'Trust you to think of your belly, John,' Jack said. He was dark-haired with a ruddy complexion, always smiling. 'It'll be goat's cheese, that's the rub. Still, I daresay there's not much point in dreaming of double Gloucester. Do the Spaniards eat goat's cheese, too?'

'Bound to,' John said, snorting on a laugh. 'Come on, let's get some rest; mountain climbing's hard work for three fellows from the heartland of England.'

It took them four days in the end, because they went wrong, twice.

But they did find water, their bread and the despised goat's cheese lasted out, and one sweltering noon they found themselves ambling through the foothills and heading for the village which, Jack assured them, was the one they had planned to arrive at. Jack seemed to have an in-built compass and on each occasion when Frankie had insisted on a change of direction against Jack's advice they regretted it.

So now they made their way down into the village. John was nervous, feeling as though unseen eyes watched them every step of the way, but the other two strode out, apparently without a care, so he hid his own apprehension as best he could. Frankie was whistling, Jack's hands were driven deep into the pockets of his trousers and he was gazing idly ahead so John threw back his shoulders and hummed a tune beneath his breath. It was only later that he realised it was the *Marseillaise*.

The first bombs had fallen on Madrid at the end of August, but no one was killed, though three people were injured. Mirri, Jacinta, Josefa and Inma were out at University City manning the trenches so saw and heard little of the actual explosions and Inma, who listened to the wireless each night, assured them that it was just an experiment, something which would not happen again.

'Franco is filth, but not a liar, surely?' she said. 'I heard on the wireless that he had said he would never bombard Madrid because there are innocent people living there who must not be exposed to such danger. Besides, it's a most beautiful city, he cannot want to destroy the most historic and ancient buildings in Spain.'

By and large the others agreed with her, though Josefa was less sure. 'A man who let the Moors loose on his own countrymen would do anything,' she said darkly. 'However, you are probably right. It would not look good in the eyes of the world to bomb Madrid, especially after his promises, made publicly.'

But the authorities decided to take action and the girls were told to put aside their guns and dig air-raid shelters.

'I'm a soldier, not a gardener,' Mirri grumbled, hefting her spade on their first day at the task. 'First it's trenches for the defence of the city, now it's air-raid shelters for the defence of the citizens . . . and then it's bill-poster, nanny, general dogsbody . . .'

'We're doing this in order to relieve men for active service,' Jacinta pointed out. They were working in a small park in the city centre and children played and shouted only feet away from them. 'Just dig and stop grumbling. Besides, Josefa said army rations were making her fat; digging will put a stop to that!'

Josefa, digging, grunted. 'We're probably doing it for nothing,' she observed. 'But our time will come. The rebels won't leave Madrid, they dare not. Sooner or later it will be hand-to-hand fighting on the barricades and then we'll look back on digging shelters and wish we were digging them again.'

'Oh, you!' Mirri said. 'Whilst we've got our rifles we won't need to fight hand-to-hand.' She had already dug down about four feet and jumped out as she spoke, wiping the sweat out of her eyes and smearing dirt across her forehead, gesturing to the hole she had dug. 'Is that deep enough, do you think? I mean, if they crouch . . .'

Jeers greeted this remark so Mirri, grinning, jumped back into the trench and started digging once again, throwing the loose earth out of the hole and occasionally into the trench next door. Jacinta, who was already five foot down and going deeper, did not appreciate this bombardment.

'Stop it, Mirri, or I'll start shovelling dirt in on top of you,' she announced. 'Chuck it somewhere else, will you?'

'Sorry,' Mirri said cheerfully. She stood up and dug her fists into the small of her back. 'Isn't digging a spine-cracker? By the way, did you know some of the men have been given the wrong ammo for their rifles? They've been swopping around, trying to get it right. I wonder if we ought to check ours?'

'Dig,' Jacinta said grimly. 'Dig, little sister, or I shall personally shove your ammunition somewhere extremely painful.'

Mirri giggled and bent to her task once more. Josefa called out that her trench was six foot deep already and she could no longer get out of it unaided. Inma went off to fetch the short ladder which was used for just this purpose. The sun beat down and a small girl in a pink dress came over to them with a bag of oranges.

'For you,' she said, giving the three militia girls a sweet, three-cornered smile. 'From Pepita.'

'Thank you, Pepita,' Mirri said, returning the smile and taking the bag of oranges. Her mouth watered at the sight of the luscious fruit. 'How delicious, and we are so hot and tired!'

'My mama says you are her-o-ines,' the child said without self-consciousness. 'And my brother Luis says you are very pretty!'

'We're just doing our duty to the Republic,' Jacinta said, but Josefa, climbing out of her trench with the aid of the ladder, added, 'Your brother sounds a gentleman; and you, Pepita, are every bit as pretty as us, and a heroine to bring us oranges.'

The child bobbed a curtsey and ran off to where a tall, grave-looking woman awaited her. The diggers abandoned their work and scrambled up, with varying degrees of difficulty, to sit on the piled-up earth.

'Oranges!' Inma said longingly. 'Bless the child, I can hardly wait. Chuck us one over, Mirri.'

Mirri complied and very soon the girls were gobbling the fruit as fast as they could.

'That was wonderful,' Jacinta said at last, carefully burying her orange peel in the mound of dry and crumbly earth. 'Back to work! I wonder what the Republic will ask next of us, though? Not more digging, I trust!'

It was evening and the sky was clear. In the west the winter sun was sinking, red as an orange, and above the great city of Madrid the stars were pricking out. Mirri was just thinking that the worst was probably over for the day when she saw the tiny silhouettes of the enemy's aircraft coming out of the setting sun. More! As if they hadn't suffered enough today already. She hesitated; should she dive into a shelter or continue on her way? The shelters they had so grudgingly dug were, in fact, of little use in the face of the sort of bombardment which Madrid had been suffering for the past three or four weeks. Relentlessly, unceasingly, the German aircraft came out of the blue, dropped their bombs, went. They were out of range of the Republican guns and the great red crosses on the hospital roofs appeared to mean nothing to them. The rules of war – of common decency – were clearly unknown either to the fascist rulers or the German pilots who so unerringly targeted those least able to defend themselves.

They bombed indiscriminately – or perhaps not so indiscrimi-nately since hospitals and railway stations were definitely targeted, as were the more crowded slum areas of the city – and they seemed to need neither sleep nor respite for it was mid-November, the cold which gripped the great plain of La Mancha gripped Madrid also, and yet the skies remained clear and the bombing went on.

Mirri was returning to headquarters to sign off her shift, but she had assumed the raids were over for the day: now she realised she had been too optimistic. She was still wondering what best to do as she emerged into the Carrera San Jerónimo and saw Inma, plodding wearily along the pavement ahead of her. Mirri broke into a trot; they were both, she guessed, making their way to headquarters to sign off before returning to their billet in Leá's house; whatever they decided to do they might as well do it together.

She reached Inma and linked her arm with her friend's.

'See the planes? Another wave coming over and we've not got over the last lot yet. I hate them so – I've just come from the children's home, or what was the children's home, rather. It must have been an awfully big bomb. We dug and dug . . . we found two alive but I doubt they'll stay that way. They were . . . terribly injured. Look, ought we to go back to . . .'

A bomb, dropping near at hand, caused both Mirri and Inma to duck, but though the blast rocked the building against which they stood, it was too far away to do more.

'Had we better get into a shelter?' Inma asked.

'Do you know, I feel safer in the trenches on the edge of University City, waiting for the Nationalists to attack, or with the girls defending the Segovia Bridge, than I do in a shelter,' Mirri confessed. 'There, at least you can see the enemy and fire at him. At least you're *doing* something. The fascists are there, you can almost touch them, but when planes come over . . .' she shivered. 'I'm glad I'm a militiawoman and not a civilian,' she ended.

'Yes, but what about trying to reach a shelter?' Inma said impatiently. 'Where's the nearest entrance to the Metro?'

'I don't know,' Mirri said doubtfully. 'Besides, if we run to a shelter just as a bomb drops we'll be as dead as if we'd never moved a muscle. Cellars are safest, or the Metro of course, but I don't know where the Metro comes up round here and anyway, it will be full to bursting tonight.'

'Right; we'll shelter here until the planes go away,' Inma shouted above the drone of the engines and the whistle and crash of falling bombs. She caught hold of Mirri's arm and towed her into a deep doorway. 'They'll run out of bombs soon, and then we can get back to our quarters. Dear God, look at that!'

At the end of the street a water-main had been hit. A huge fountain of water soared skywards just as a building, which must have been struck at the same time, slowly began to fall to earth. Somewhere, a dog howled, the howl cut off so abruptly that both girls involuntarily shuddered. A child cried, sobbing out its fear as the hellish noise of the bombardment continued but moved a little further away.

'One comfort is it can't get worse,' Mirri said as dusk gradually turned to night and the noise slowly faded into silence. 'They can't bomb us in the dark, so at least we're safe at night. And now we'd best go back to our quarters and get what sleep we can. Because they'll be back some time tomorrow; at least we always know they'll be back.'

'And we're due in the trenches in a couple of hours,' Inma said wearily. 'I wish I had some warm gloves . . . it gets freezing down in a trench when it's so miserably cold. And the sergeant shouts at anyone who looks like dozing off . . . I'm sure I really will fall asleep one of these days.'

'If you do you'll wake to find yourself being raped by a huge black Moor,' Mirri said. 'That 'ud warm you up!'

'It wouldn't. They bayonet you first,' Inma said grimly. 'Do you think Leá will have a hot drink ready for us? I could kill for a cup of strong coffee.'

'She might; rations are still getting through even though the fascists have got over the Tagus,' Mirri said. 'We're holding them, despite everything. We're going to win, Inma.'

'What a relief to know you have faith in us,' Inma said sarcastically. 'Oh thank heaven, we're almost home – and Jacinta's ahead of us, did you see her wave?'

'I saw someone wave . . . was that Josefa with her?'

'It was. So we've all survived, so far. Come on, Mirri, or they'll drink all the coffee before we even reach the door.'

*

271

A couple of weeks later, in the early afternoon, incendiaries began to rain down on Madrid. By mid-afternoon the Hospital San Carlos, the Madrid District Hospital and the Central Red Cross Hospital were in flames. The great Puerta del Sol was burning and the icy wind from the Sierra blew the flames into yet more joyous and destructive life, sending the inferno roaring along all the main thoroughfares, gobbling up houses, shops, places of worship, historic buildings, everything.

Mirri, Jacinta and Josefa were fire-fighting, but it was a useless exercise. No sooner had they beaten the flames in one quarter than they sprang up in another, and all the while the bombardment from the skies went on. Darkness came unnoticed, because the black, oily smoke which overhung the city had long ago hidden the sun.

'Mirri, it's me – someone's just told me the Metro's been hit,' a voice called and Mirri, looking round, recognised Inma, her face blackened by soot, her long fair hair thick with it. 'There'll be no shelter there any longer for those without cellars to their homes . . . hundreds are dead.'

'And hundreds more will die if we can't put the fires out,' Mirri sobbed, as she and Jacinta beat frenziedly at the flames roaring through the Red Cross Hospital. 'If only, if only we'd been able to guard against this!'

Inma disappeared into the gloom and Mirri and Jacinta laboured on, sweat streaking their dirty faces, their limbs slowing as exhaustion attacked them.

'And all our digging was for nought, little sister,' Jacinta said half-humorously when at last they stepped back, exhausted, knowing that here, at least, the flames had won. 'None of our shelters could defend anyone against a raid like this.'

'They'll be deeper dug next time,' Mirri said, trying to sound defiant. 'Oh, but the poor patients, Jacinta!'

'I know. And the bloody planes will be back very soon. They'll return to wherever they get their fuel and their bombs from, and they'll come back to finish off what they've started.'

'I suppose. The only good thing about it is that the fascist troops have drawn back a little; they're afraid of being killed by their own bombing, no doubt. What's more, if we can't quench the fires, there isn't going to be much of Madrid left for them to take.'

Mirri was staring up into the evening sky as she spoke, scanning it for the evil black shapes of the aircraft they had grown to dread. Suddenly she shook Jacinta's arm.

'Look! Up there!'

'What? Are they back so soon? I can't see . . .'

'Oh, Jacinta, we're saved, we're saved! This will stop them!'

The two girls were standing in the gutted street, gazing sky-wards, and even as Mirri spoke Jacinta felt, on her face, the first tiny, chilly specks of rain.

'They can't fly in thick cloud or really bad weather,' Mirri shouted, as they made their weary way back to Leá's house. She raised her voice above the sudden howl of the tempest, for the rain was coming down in earnest now, long silver rods of it, beating on the bloodstained paving stones, the charred rubble in the roads, on their pale, exhausted faces. 'Winter's come at last, and it'll save us! Oh thank God, thank God, for the rain!'

Laurie had not known that Spain could be so wickedly, bitterly cold. He was living as best he might in a small village, eyed doubtfully by the residents but suffered to remain there because he was a foreigner, and because he had come here for the sake of a girl.

'Her name is Mirri Rodriganez,' he had said constantly as he travelled across the country. It would not do to give her full name, to brand her a member of the ruling classes. 'She lives with her parents in Madrid and we are betrothed. I want to take her back to England, to have her safe.'

'The fascists won't believe you,' he was warned, over and over. 'They say there is no such thing as a neutral; if you are in Spain you must take sides. Even the communists – you can understand it – need to know whether you are Republican or Nationalist. Spies are everywhere.'

But this village was tiny, unimportant. It was perched high on a crag in the Sierra de Gredos, above the plain of La Mancha, and no one wanted to claim it. Fighting over it would have been impossi-ble, surrounded as it was by natural cliff walls, and the young men of the village had left, presumably to join the army. The remaining elderly inhabitants who remained just wanted to be left in peace.

What was more, the snow and ice, to say nothing of the biting wind, cut the village off completely. There was no point in labouring up and down the narrow, winding track which led down to the villagers' sandy, stony little fields because no crops would grow there until spring warmed the earth once more. Beasts were gathered inside the walls, food, which had been laboriously garnered throughout the summer, was eked out, and the villagers simply tightened their belts and waited for winter to pass. As, Laurie told himself, I must.

So now, Laurie sat on an outcrop of rock above the village and watched an eagle soar on the bitter wind which whined and howled uneasily around the crags and envied the bird its ability to spread its wings and cross the snow-covered plain almost as quickly as the great black aeroplanes which he occasionally saw as they passed overhead. He had heard that the rebels had sworn not to bomb Madrid so presumably the planes were dropping propaganda material; he imagined so, anyway. Laurie was sure that no Spaniard, however depraved, would bomb his own capital city or allow another to do so.

When winter's iron grip eased he meant to go on, to cross the plain below him and get to Madrid. He knew there was a possibility that his love would have moved on, but surely he would be able to get news of her? She had run away from home, she had said so in her only letter, but with the country in such a state of upheaval, surely by now she would have run back? Her parents had the house in Madrid, another in Granada, another in Alicante . . .

'They told me you were up here. They said you'd welcome news from Madrid. You're English, they said.'

Laurie was so startled that he nearly fell off his perch; he had grown used to speaking in Spanish, to thinking in Spanish, so to be addressed in English was astonishing enough, let alone to be found here, in this high and lonely place.

He swung round and surveyed the speaker; a man of middle height, dark-haired, with a square, pugnacious face and small, twinkling eyes. He looked English and certainly sounded it, and what was more there was something about his face which was familiar, though Laurie was sure he had not met the man before. And what on earth was he doing here?

'Who the hell are you?' Laurie said bluntly. 'And how did you get here? The village is cut off in winter.'

'Climbed. Crawled the last couple of hundred yards,' the man said cheerfully. He stuck out a large, spade-shaped hand. 'Pietro told me there was another Englishman staying here, so I thought I'd come over and say hello. I'm Andy Griffiths; I was in Madrid trying to discuss tactics with the Republican bosses, but it's like talking to ill-mannered children. They're so keen to make sure they're all equal that they automatically disagree with whatever the other says, they can't take decisions, they issue contradictory orders . . . so I came away. I was pretty damn disillusioned, if you want the truth. What a way to run a war!'

Laurie shook hands. 'Nice to meet you, Andy. I'm Laurie Clifton. You mean you've recently come from Madrid? But it's miles away . . . I want to get there but it's impossible whilst this weather holds. I wonder, can you tell me what's happening in the city? I've heard rumours, of course, but no firm news.'

'Well, the frontal assault carried out by General Varela and his troops on the city failed completely. We threw everything we had into its defence, although privately some of our generals are saying that Madrid is nothing but a millstone round our necks, and though the enemy did get in briefly, we pushed them out again. But rumour has it that the Germans and Italians have told Franco they'll acknowledge him as Spain's leader if he takes the city, which is a big incentive. Unfortunately, it's an equally big incentive for us to hang on . . . apart from the Republicans not wanting to lose face, of course. I suppose Franco assumes other world powers will follow Germany's lead and acknowledge him as Spain's leader if he takes the city, though I don't think they would. So the fighting goes on and Madrid, for better or worse, is still in Republican hands.'

'I see. That's good, I suppose, but I'm not really interested in the war, I'm . . .'

'Not interested in the war? My dear fellow, if the fascists win this war it'll mean the end of Europe as we know it, certainly the end of France and Britain. If you're a man of principle you must take sides, you can't just stand by and watch the people's legal government strangled, the people's will deliberately flouted. If you'd been in Madrid whilst the bombs fell, day in, day out . . .'

'Bombed? But Franco said . . . he promised . . .' Laurie stammered. 'You never mentioned bombing, you simply said the assault had failed. Dear God, my girl may be in there! Were many killed? Injured?'

'A great many; maybe thousands,' Andy Griffiths said quietly. 'Still not interested in the war, Clifton? Strange how everything comes down to individuals, in the end.'

'Yes, I hadn't thought of it like that,' Laurie said. For the first time he felt ashamed of his lack of interest in the rights and wrongs of the conflict. 'But it's my girl who matters. She's only young, it's not fair that she should . . .'

'Suffer? Die, even? Is it any fairer that the fascists shot a fifteen-year-old girl in Saragossa because she picked up a fallen rifle in the street? That they killed women and children and the elderly, four thousand of them, in the bull-ring at Badajoz, after the siege? That they drenched the mayor of a small village in petrol and shot him until he burst into flames? You'd let all that happen, I daresay, just to save a hair of your girl's head?'

'No, of course not . . . Well, but . . . I don't know,' Laurie stammered. 'I was at Badajoz just after the – the massacre. It sickened me, but I'd be no use, I'm no soldier! I've never even held a rifle, let alone shot one. All I'd do is get myself killed and what good would that do to anyone, especially my girl?'

'It depends how many fascists you took with you,' the older man said quietly. 'I'm sorry, I shouldn't have said half the things I did, it wasn't fair. I'm a professional fighter pilot and I feel my skills, such as they are, are being wasted by quarrelling, self-righteous elderly men who don't know one end of an aeroplane from another.' He had been squatting down beside Laurie, but now he stood and gestured to the village below them. 'Come along, we'd best find shelter, there's a snowstorm coming across the plain. Once we're under cover you can tell me about your girl and what you need to know about Madrid.'

'So you think that if Señorita Rodriganez stayed in Madrid she must either be there but in hiding, or she's got out since the bombing started?' Laurie said later as the two of them sat in the straw-strewn stable where Laurie had been sleeping, sharing a meal which consisted of half a loaf of unleavened bread and some rough but potent red wine. 'But why, man?'

'Your friend is a gently reared girl of good family,' Andy said resignedly. 'I can't see such a one doing any sort of job for the Republicans. If you hadn't said she was doing important work I'd have assumed she was lying low, keeping her head down and just waiting for the Nationalists to arrive, but you said she had a job . . . so she must be working for the fascists, and in the unlikely event of her still being in Madrid, all she can be is a spy.'

'A *spy*? But that's deadly dangerous! If she's caught . . .'

'She would be executed at once, of course,' Andy Griffiths said with calm deliberation. 'There are spies on both sides, but many more on theirs. Our people find it difficult to infiltrate the fascist army because they're very much more professional. They don't have enormous numbers of men dedicated to the cause, as we have, but they do have a great many highly trained modern officers, and an unbelievable amount of equipment. And they've got the Huns and the Eyeties with them, of course.'

'Don't we have the Russians?' Laurie said diffidently, not realising that he had said 'we' until it was out of his mouth. 'And there are the International Brigades.'

'Yup. I'm one of them, I suppose, though fliers are somewhat different. Look, Clifton, I'm going to level with you. If you join us, I can put out feelers, try to find out about Señorita Rodriganez. If I find her, then I can make sure she's treated as well as possible . . . sent back to England, if you like. If you don't join us, I can't make any promises at all; for all I know, man, you might join the fascists!'

'No,' Laurie said definitely. 'Not after Badajoz.'

'And even if you don't join them, what do you think would happen if they picked you up? There's no such thing as a neutral, not any more. It would be straight up against the nearest wall and bang! Which would scarcely help the *señorita*.'

'But what good would I be to you?' Laurie said helplessly. 'You know nothing about me, but I assure you . . .'

'You speak very good Spanish and French, and if you wonder

how I know . . . well, I saw you staring at me out there . . .' he waved a hand with a chunk of bread in it towards the wooden door, outside which the storm raged. 'We've never met, but I know all about you, Sir Laurence!'

'Who . . . What . . .' Laurie stammered. 'You *do* look familiar, but . . .'

'Remember Bertie Griffiths, in your class at school? He's my kid brother.'

'Good God, the times Bertie's boasted about his big brother . . .' Laurie leaned over and seized Andy's hand. 'Hello, Andy! But I still don't know what's going on.'

Andy laughed. 'Your progress has been charted pretty well from the border, my dear fellow. Then we heard from one of the locals that there was an Englishman up here, asking about a girl, and I had a hunch it might be you. So I said I'd pop in on my way back to my airfield. I've a lorry waiting at the foot of this confounded mountain, I only hope it'll start when I reach it again. So you see, if you want to hitch a lift . . .'

'Couldn't you get me to Madrid first?' Laurie pleaded, but already the thought of being with his fellow-countrymen once more was tempting. 'If I could just see Mirri for myself, make sure she's safe . . .'

'I'm coming away from . . .' Andy broke off, staring. 'Mirri?'

'Her real name's Señorita Evodia Cristiana Miryam de Salvorini y Rodriganez,' Laurie said, reeling off the name with the familiarity of one who has been saying it, like a creed, a dozen times a day. 'But everyone calls her Mirri. Mirri Rodriganez.'

'Is she small and dark, with dimples? And . . . and a little scar, shaped like a crescent moon, just beneath her right eye?'

'You know her? Oh dear God, not because you've – you've found her body?' Laurie stammered. 'Is – is – is . . .'

'She's alive and well and she served me at dinner last night,' Andy said. He was grinning. 'She's one of the militiawomen and they do work damned hard. They dig trenches, man them with rifles at the ready, shoot as coolly and steadily as a man when the need arises, get civilians into shelters when raids start . . . the work they do is endless. Those young girls are wonderful! And last night your young lady tipped a tureen of soup into my neighbour's lap, which is how I know her name, because the other girls were all shouting at her, saying Mirri was a dreamer, Mirri could aim a rifle but not a tureen of soup, that sort of thing. And I noticed the little scar because when she blushed – and she blushed divinely, old fellow – it went blood-red and was very obvious. But hang on a moment, if she's spying for Franco . . .'

'She's not! She may be well-born, but she loves her country and besides, how could she possibly spy for anyone? If she works as hard as you say she'd scarcely have the opportunity and I don't suppose she gets much classified information, digging trenches and pouring soup over officers,' Laurie said hastily. 'Why, if she's been a spy she could have gone over to the enemy when they were attacking, very probably. Look, I know Mirri, none better. She's straightforward, she'd never pretend. Andy, old boy, if she was in Madrid a couple of days ago then I must get a move on, I must go to her, it may be the last chance I get!'

But Andy was shaking his head. 'No, you'll have to deserve to go to her, old bean. In fact, if you'll come back with me now and do as we ask, I promise you that your girl will be looked after, got back to England too, if that's what she wants. But we need you, Laurie. We need you badly.'

Laurie stared into the depths of the red wine. He swirled the drop that was left round in his glass, then looked up at his companion. He felt a grin bisect his face; action at last, no more of this hole-and-corner business which he had grown to hate!

'What must I do to join you, then? A part of me has longed to stick my oar in, to have a go at the buggers, but whilst Mirri was in danger . . . you're sure she'll be looked after, sent to my home in England if she wants to go?'

'I'll see to it as soon as I can get back to Madrid,' Andy said cheerfully. 'Look, drink the rest of the wine and then try to sleep. First thing tomorrow we'll make our way down to my lorry and set off. I'll be your sponsor, so to speak, and I'll see you get to officer training school and become useful, not just cannon fodder. And when you're due for your first leave, I'll make sure you get to Madrid and at least spend some time with your little Mirri.'

Ten

By the time Foxy came down from Cambridge for the Christmas vac she was beginning to feel almost a part of life at Clifton Place.

It was mostly Allsop's doing, of course. He wrote to her every time the cow coughed, Foxy thought indulgently, and of course she wrote to him every time she got a letter from John, because John's letters were full of the sort of war-news which interested Allsop, and she wrote when she received letters from Laurie, too, though since she could not write back – Laurie had not yet got a permanent address – she found his letters rather frustrating.

And there was no doubt about it, no matter how fascinating her lectures might be, life at Clifton Place rivalled them. She was warmly interested in everything that went on and looking forward to doing her stint there over the Christmas holidays. She wondered if Laurie had found his girl yet, but it didn't seem likely, which might well mean that she would be needed there at Easter, too.

Cumber Farm needed her, she felt, almost as much as she was beginning to need it. She found herself dreaming in lectures, wondering whether she ought to invest in more sows, or what about increasing the milking herd? As yet it consisted of one cow, Lucille, who was in calf. If she had a heifer, then they would keep it, which would mean they had a two-cow milking herd eventually. But if they bought in . . .

So it was an impatient and excited Foxy who climbed off the train and climbed up into the trap, driven by Horace. Horace was old and taciturn but not even his lukewarm greeting could take the beam off Foxy's face.

'Horace! You are kind to fetch me; can you give me a hand up with my case?'

Horace, muttering, climbed down and together they heaved the case aboard, their breath steaming in the freezing air, their feet slipping on the iced-over puddles.

'There we are! All aboard, Horace, and we'll be back before you know it. How's the home farm looking?'

Horace admitted that it looked all right, so far as he could tell, and clicked at the pony, and very soon they were driving along between the winter-bright hedges, with the pony slipping every now and then and Horace keeping its head up and jerking on the reins.

They reached Clifton Place and Horace insisted on driving right up to the front door. Foxy was still arguing that they should go straight to the home farm when the door shot open and Allsop's beaming face appeared, with Mrs Waughman hovering in the background.

'Oh Mr Allsop, it's lovely to see you looking so well,' Foxy called, getting carefully down from the trap. 'But I told Horace he ought to take me to the home farm, because . . .'

'What a suggestion, Miss Foxy – why d'you think we keep the Place aired through, and a fire in the best spare? There's good food on the table three times a day to say nothing of clean sheets on the beds, and flowers in your room. You're Mr Laurie's deputy, remember, and Mr Laurie would be very angry indeed if you did not stay here, at least whilst he's away. When he comes home of course . . .' he gave her his small, secret smile, 'it will be a different story.'

Foxy made a token protest, but she was pleased to fall in with Allsop's plans. The Place was beautifully warm and smelt of cooking and polish; the home farm, despite the care she and Laurie had lavished on it, would be cold, lonely and probably damp.

'Now come along, Miss,' Mrs Waughman said as Foxy entered the hall, pulling off her red tam o'shanter and hanging her coat on the hall stand. 'Mr Allsop will take your case up, you come along o' me. There's tea in the pot and a nice apple cake just out o' the oven. You'll want a bite after that journey.'

It was a wonderful welcome and Foxy soon settled back into the house as though she had never left. She did her farm work clad in a pair of blue denim overalls which had once belonged to Laurie, and her housework in a voluminous white apron lent by Mrs Waughman. The home farm, when she visited it, was clean and spruce, but there was scarcely any furniture in it and the chill struck Foxy to the bone. Allsop was right, she would be much better off at the Place.

In her absence the work had gone well; walls which had crumbled away had been built up, pigsties had been made good and now housed fat pink baconers and one huge sow with her litter. Simon Fletcher, old Fletcher's eldest lad, was proving to be the stuff of which farm managers are made. He went quietly about his work, and Allsop said approvingly that no one had ever got bigger yields from the wheat and barley crops than young Fletcher had.

'He's talking about buying good young stock this spring,' he told Foxy. 'He'll want a talk with you, naturally, but I'm sure Mr Hawkings will see that you get the money if you agree that a milking herd would be a good moneymaker.'

'I do. We've got young bullocks for fattening, I see,' Foxy said. 'Simon's a very real asset, Mr Allsop. We must encourage him.'

It was three days before Christmas when John's latest letter arrived. Foxy had had her breakfast with Allsop and the other staff in the big, warm kitchen, but as soon as the post arrived she took it, and a couple of rounds of buttered toast, through to the study. There, sitting in solitary splendour behind the big desk, Foxy opened the long brown 'forwarding' envelope which had the Cambridge postmark on it, a frisson of excitement and love chasing down her spine. Would he say he was coming home, wanted her so badly that he could no longer remain away? But when she got the letter open, he said none of those things. He told her he and his pals were now in a little village in Murcia called Madrigueras where they were being kitted out and turned into a fighting force.

We have khaki battledress, heavy boots, tin hats like the ones the French wear, and wonderful, brand-new rifles. The rifles have fixed bayonets which is a bit awkward, but no doubt we'll get used to them in time. And it's so warm here in the south, my darling girl! I can imagine you, out in the fields – you'll be back at the Place by the time you receive this – with icicles hanging from your nose and ears, whilst we're still picking oranges!

Learning to use our weapons is interesting, especially since they have a kick like a bad-tempered mule, but I am getting the hang of it. And when we aren't drilling, practising with our weaponry or wriggling up hills on our stomachs to attack an imaginary enemy, we're in the largest house in the village (ex-fascist, of course), which has been commandeered for our use.

It's a big house, but empty. No furniture, ornaments, carpets, nothing. It's been looted, of course, but no one is supposed to say that since Republicans do not loot. For my part, I can see the people are so miserably poor that in sheer self-defence they have to loot, so I'd be the last one to blame them.

Food is not too short but it's horrid, my love, absolutely horrid! It seems to be mostly rice and beans and has to be cooked over open fires, which none of us are much good at. I was a boy scout, but I blush to admit we never burned unseasoned timber, which is all there is, here. And the water shortage is appalling. It comes from a small fountain and we queue and queue and queue, just for sufficient to cook in. We can – and do – drink the local wine, which is much nicer than water, though there can be problems. We aren't used to it and us Herefordshire lads spent the first night rushing wildly down to the latrines which have been dug and most of the next day regretting the previous night. We were naked and must have caused some raised eyebrows, but the locals are awfully good and put up with us, our perpetual need for water and our occasional bouts of Spanish stomach – and less occasional bouts of drunkenness – with great good nature.

We drink with them, in the local bar. Once, there would have been little dishes of food scattered over the counter – tapas, *they're called – to eat whilst you drink, but not any more, alas. It's a poor village at the best of times but with troops billeted on them – and there must be more than 500 of us – they have to conserve their food as best they can.*

There are a few girls, but we don't have much to do with them. Frankie was smitten with one young Amazon who rolled her eyes at him and gave him oranges – there are plenty of oranges – but one day, in mid-conversation, she stamped on a frog. Frankie was outraged. *Killing for killing's sake is not a nice thing, he told her, and added that the frog had never hurt anyone and she had killed one of God's innocents. He told us she roared with laughter and walked away . . . 'She was a nasty girl,' he said when we, too, roared with laughter. So that was that. He has to pick his own oranges now.*

Yesterday a crowd of new fellows arrived; they were tired and dusty, and told us they had come straight from the Córdoba front and had come to give us combat-training which would be more useful than the textbook stuff we had done so far. Too right, as our Australian friends say (we have two Aussies in the battalion, grand chaps both). We'll do a month to six weeks with them, we're told, and then we'll be posted to a front ourselves, though we don't know which one.

Must go now, my darling girl. Think of you all the time, dream of you in my arms. Be good. Be true. Work hard. Love me as I love you.

Your own John

Having read the letter through twice, Foxy sat quietly in the big chair in front of the enormous desk and just thought about what she had read. John's face, tanned, his hair bleached even fairer by the hot and foreign sun, swam before her eyes. She had not known she loved him until they had held one another, but now she was conscious of her love all the time and of the need to express it, too.

She would write to the barracks at Madrigueras, but he had said he would be moving on. To the front. If that meant a battle she would pray for him even harder than she did now . . . and she would write anyway, tell him all her news. He would be delighted to hear that everything was going well at the Place in Laurie's absence, and also interested in the improvements they were making at the home farm. But he must not write to her here too often, and it looked as though she would be back again for Easter. She knew that one reason why Allsop was so helpful and co-operative was because he believed that she and Laurie had a thing going, and though loth to deceive him, she realised that for Laurie's sake if no one else's, she must foster the impression that she and the master of all this decayed splendour were more than friends.

So she wrote her letter to John, but could do nothing about Laurie. He had written twice, brief notes, but had been unable to give her an address in Spain to which she might write. He had promised to send an address as soon as he could do so but in the meantime promised he would drop a line whenever the opportunity occurred.

'I could do with some more money; or something negotiable,' he had written in his last note. When I'm settled I'll get you to send me something.'

Foxy's heart bled for him, but there was little she could do. She knew that the Hovertons sent John parcels whenever they could and had done so herself, filling a small cardboard box with cheap but sustaining food and odd bits of clothing – knitted gloves for the cold weather, a box of good chocolates, some dried fruit, apple rings, sultanas, prunes, and of course, cigarettes. John was very grateful, talked enthusiastically about the pleasure the parcels gave but poor Laurie, who had still not reached the Republican army, had no such comforts.

Still, no doubt he would arrive, sooner or later, at the International Brigade Headquarters and join them, find John or be found by him. Foxy knew that Laurie had professed interest in the war only to the extent that he must get Mirri out of it, but she was sure that, once there, Laurie would be like John and want to fight the fascists. Besides, John, too, would be spending as much time as possible searching for the man who was the nearest thing he had ever known to a brother. They're bound to meet up soon, Spain can't be *that* enormous a country, Foxy told herself. And got resolutely to her feet. There was work to be done before they could enjoy Christmas, and she needed to persuade Allsop that they should send at least two of the pigs for slaughter. Allsop had grown fond of the pigs and despite knowing that they were baconers, kept trying to gain a respite for them.

'Not before Christmas, Miss Foxy,' had been his last plea. 'Let them enjoy Christmas, at least.'

But they needed the money in order to feed other pigs, so Foxy headed for the kitchen, her letter shoved well down inside her brassière, determined that she would not only take the pigs to their cruel destiny, but would tell Allsop, firmly, that there were a dozen geese which should go into Ledbury too, to brighten the Christmas tables of others. In order to steal a march on him, in fact, she went out of a side door and found one of the farmhands.

'Get two of the fatteners and a dozen geese into the pony-cart; I'm going into Ledbury presently,' she said. 'It's going to upset Mr Allsop, but we'll get a good price for them at the Christmas market and we really can't hang on any longer. We need the money!'

'Very good, Miss Foxy,' old Ned said, heading for the pigsties. 'Give I forty, fifty minutes and they'll be ready for 'ee.'

Foxy repaired to the kitchen and told Allsop, with unaccustomed briskness, that she would be taking stock into Ledbury in about an hour and would he kindly remember that Mr Laurie was in farming to make money, not to rear pets.

'Very well, Miss Foxy,' Allsop said, chopping dried mint on a large board with an evil-looking carving knife. He was proud of his mint sauce and swore he used a recipe more than a century old. 'But I'll be downright glad when you start growing hops – no one can grow fond of a plant!'

Foxy grinned. 'You'll probably be begging me not to pull up a cabbage by the roots, this time next year,' she observed. 'I wonder if I might have a sandwich or two, Mr Allsop? Only I doubt I'll get back in time for lunch and I feel very out of place at the White Horse, which is where Mr Laurie always went.'

'You could try the Central Café,' Mr Allsop observed with a twinkling glance at her. He swept the chopped mint into the palm of his hand and transferred it reverently to a small jar, then added a spoonful of sugar and some liquid from a dark bottle. Shaking his concoction vigorously he added, 'Or the Temperance Hotel, of course.'

'I don't believe it's there any more,' Foxy said loftily. 'Anyway, I'd rather take sandwiches.'

'That's fine, then,' Mr Allsop said. He went to the kitchen door and shouted. 'Mrs Waughman?'

A faint, echoing cry indicated that Mrs Waughman was '. . . in the drawing room, 'avin' a go at this yur dratted fireplace'.

'Miss wants a packed luncheon,' Mr Allsop shouted. 'Is it all right if I use the cold pork?'

There was a brief pause and then Mrs Waughman appeared in the doorway, with a smut on her forehead and the light of battle in her eyes.

'You don't want to go mekin' sangwidges, Mr Allsop, not when I's around,' she said reproachfully. ''Sides, if you'm takin' the pigs in, Miss, I daresay you won't fancy pork?'

Foxy, a little green around the gills at the thought, made noncommittal noises.

'Right, Miss. Then I'll do you cheese an' pickle wi' one of my apple turnovers for afters. Will that suit?'

'I'll tell Mr Carruthers to put the horse up,' Mr Allsop said, when Foxy had agreed that Mrs Waughman's packed lunch sounded delicious. He headed for the back door and presently could be heard calling for the pony cart. Though quite capable of giving a farmhand a terrific dressing down, he always used their full names when addressing them. Not for Mr Allsop the casualness of Christian names, of calling the workers Dan, Elias or Harry. Formality, he would probably have averred, made for a better relationship between master and man. 'I often wish, Miss, that Sir Laurie had taught you to drive the car, not that it would do you much good now, with pigs and geese and such. Still, one of these days perhaps I can give you a few lessons. For when he comes home, you know.'

'That would be lovely,' Foxy said demurely, imagining all too clearly Laurie's horrified expression should she turn up outside the station, driving his precious car, to welcome the conquering hero home. 'But for now the cart suits me fine. Ah, you've done my sandwiches, Mrs Waughman. Many thanks. I'll probably be home before tea.'

'Cart's yur,' Mrs Waughman remarked as Foxy took the packages from her and stowed them in the pockets of her thick winter coat. It was actually Laurie's thick winter coat but Allsop was sure his master would have insisted on Foxy using it, had he been able to do so. 'I could do wi' a couple pounds of mincemeat, Miss, if you 'appen by the Market House. And I could do wi' a Christmas card or two . . . in fact, six, if you could oblige me.'

'I'll nip into Tilley's and get us both some cards,' Foxy said. 'After I've done all my other business. See you later, Mrs Waughman.'

She slipped out into the yard where Dapple, the pony, stood between the shafts in a cloud of his own breath. Ned had a dozen geese ready for dispatch and was just tying down the netting over the pigs. One of them squealed – it had probably been trodden on – but Foxy hardened her heart and Allsop, coming out of the back door to help her into the cart, sighed heavily.

'That was Lion, the one who squealed,' he informed her accusingly. 'The other is Tiger.'

'Yes; well, don't you ever dare name the pigs again,' Foxy said crossly, as she got onto the driver's seat. 'It wouldn't have happened, only you've been feeding them from time to time. Cheerio!'

Foxy whipped up the pony and turned the cart into the lane. It was a very cold, sunny day and the wind of her going stung her cheeks and tore at her mane of red hair, teasing it out from under the tam o'shanter she had pulled well down on her head. Looking around her was sheer bliss; the verges were grey with frost where the sun had not reached them but where it had, every blade was diamond-dropped and in the hedges scarlet berries and dark green holly shone as the frost was melted by the sun's wintry warmth.

As she neared the town she met other vehicles; some motor cars, but mostly horse-driven carts, like her own. People called out to her, greeted her, and Foxy felt warm and glowing. At home in Birmingham you knew folk in your own street but once outside your area you were a stranger; how different it was here, in this beautiful country town!

With a slight pang of conscience she took the pigs along to the cattle market in Bye Street and saw them into a pen, dropped the geese off at the poultry section, then swung the cart into High Street and drove down towards the Market House. Pony carts were parked all along the left-hand side of the street, under the bare-branched trees, so Foxy pulled Dapple over and jumped down. She tethered the pony near a smart trap owned by Mrs Fairbrother, who was attaching her pony's nosebag and told Foxy placidly that she'd come to the right place for a bargain, for had she not herself, only moments earlier, bought a beautiful leather handbag for a mere five shillings? Foxy admired the handbag, congratulated the older woman on her bargain and then headed, her purse in her hand and her basket on her arm, down towards the stalls. She dearly loved any market, but a Christmas market was always particularly good, especially when she had Mrs Waughman's commissions to execute and a few small Christmas gifts to buy.

And presently, her basket full, Foxy gave herself up to the pleasure of the morning. This was her first visit to Ledbury Christmas market and she was loving every minute of it! The stalls were doing good business, the customers were satisfied, children shrieked and played up and down the busy street and red-faced farmers stood, legs spread wide, in the middle of the carriageway, indifferent to passersby, looking – and probably acting – as though they owned the universe. Gaiters gleaming, laughter loud, the dogs at their heels subservient but well-tended, the farmers looked successful and supremely self-confident.

And I'm a farmer too, thanks to Laurie, Foxy thought. I could have gone to the pub and eaten lunch with them – but I'd rather have my sandwiches in quiet woodland, with the sun on my hair and a stream tinkling by. She spotted Bill Hoverton with Bess by his side, slapping someone on the back, shaking hands, making a deal.

Now for it, Foxy thought. Now to see how he'll behave when I walk slap-bang up to him and ask him if he's keeping well. Suppose he snubs me? Suppose . . .

But she should know better than to fear a middle-aged man, and one, furthermore, who had fathered her lover! So with her chin in the air and her shoulders well back, Foxy marched towards the farmers.

'Good morning, Mr Hoverton, and how are you? And Mrs Hoverton? I had a letter from John yesterday . . . Oh, I'm very well, thank you. Going back to Cambridge in two weeks, but very well indeed.'

Despite all their marching, rifle practice, grenade drills and map-reading, John, Jack and Frankie realised that they could not become experienced soldiers except in the field, so when they were told, very early one dark morning, that they would leave Madrigueras next day, they were apprehensive as well as excited.

'Where will we be going?' more than one brave soul asked, only to be told, laconically, that they would know soon enough. So they said their goodbyes to the local people and climbed aboard a fleet of lorries next day at dawn. The lorries were open so John sat on his kitbag and watched the greys and browns and blacks of the landscape begin to sharpen as the light increased, watched a gold line suddenly rim the nearest mountain, saw the pale gold disc of the sun climb, with infinite slowness, over the ridge. And suddenly there was sunlight, and colour came with it; rich chocolate browns, tender greens, pale yellows, passionate reds. John nudged Frankie.

'We're arriving; there's a railway station!'

'Yes, they'll be sending us on somewhere else,' Frankie said. When the lorries stopped he went and talked to a peasant leading a thin, weary-looking cow along the track. He came back to them, grinning.

'This is Albacete. We're going to be entrained for Villarrubia de Santiago, which is just east of Aranjuez. From there, we'll wait and see.'

'Who told you? That old fellow with the cow?' Jack asked suspiciously. 'How come he knows when we aren't allowed to be told?'

'Because a railway line's a railway line, and only goes to certain places, and probably his son drives the train,' John said. 'And if we're going to the front, well, that'll be the best dropping-off place.'

'Well done that man,' Frankie said. 'Wonder where we'll sleep, tonight? It'll be cold later, I reckon, all crushed into a bloody train. Let's see if we can find something to drink.'

'We shouldn't leave the station,' Jack said doubtfully. 'Should we?'

'Train doesn't leave till dusk,' Frankie called back. 'I wonder if they grow oranges around here?'

At dusk they climbed aboard the train. It was blacked-out so they sat virtually in darkness and dozed, sang songs, swore at feet which kicked out, elbows which collided with knees. Early next morning the train eased its slow, creaking way into a tiny station and they were told to disembark and line up for a march.

290

It was a glorious morning, the sky pale blue, the sun apparently determined to outshine the previous day's efforts. As John watched, a flight of white pigeons wheeled and soared against the blue, their wings gilded with the sun. 'Doves of peace,' he said to Jack, standing beside him. 'Pretty, aren't they?'

'Wish those pigeons would come near enough to shoot,' was the unromantic reply. 'It seems years since I tasted poultry.'

'Pigeons aren't poultry, and anyway they're doves,' John pointed out. 'You are an unromantic bugger, Jack. I bet, if you'd been in that ark, the poor dove wouldn't even have got off the deck, olive branch or no olive branch.'

'Noah and his sons were vegetarians and I'm not,' Jack said. 'Oh, Robbie's shouting at us; best get moving.'

They marched out of the tiny station yard and up a long, dusty road. Above them, pink in the sun, reared a mountain range.

'Where's that?' John said, gesturing. 'Not the Pyrenees?'

'You're right there; definitely not,' Jack assured him. 'You've got no idea of geography, have you? They're the Sierra Pingarrón . . . can you hear anything?'

'Thunder,' John said after a moment. 'Damn, we're going to arrive wherever we're going soaked.'

'That's not thunder, that's the guns,' Frankie put in. 'And I can see a village ahead.'

'Guns? Where's the noise coming from, then? I can't see any action and we're quite high up, here.'

'It's coming from the mountains, the sierra,' Frankie said. 'Ah, the column's heading for the village, the first few men have turned in to the main street.'

'Guns,' John said quietly. 'It sounded just like thunder, to me.' But already he had noticed the difference, was making a mental note of the sharper cracks of artillery, the booming, muffled thud of the cannon. He turned to Jack, who understood maps, knew about plans. 'I know you say those are the Sierra Ping-something-or-other, but where are we? Why should the battle be here?'

'We're not all that far from Madrid,' Jack said, after a moment's thought. 'They say the Nationalists want to cut off Madrid's supply routes and gradually surround the city, so I suppose we're here to stop that. So far as I can recall, the road between Madrid and Valencia runs along here and it's an important route, what you might call a main artery, in war or peace. Our side must know how important it is to keep it open for the Madrileños.'

'I see,' John said. 'I wonder if Laurie's here? He wants to get to Madrid; he thinks Mirri's there.'

'If he's here you stand a good chance of meeting, then,' Frankie said equably. 'Although I don't imagine he'll want to be this far from the city if he's searching for his girl. Still, you never know, we might get furlough in Madrid . . . if there's any city left standing, that is.'

'Yes, it's been bombed, of course,' John agreed. 'But they're still fighting. Like we'll be, shortly.'

They swung off the track and into the village; a small, mean place where poverty seemed stamped on the very stones of which the rough little houses were made.

'What's this village called?' Frankie said in Spanish, addressing an old woman, leaning against the trunk of an olive tree even older than she.

'This is Chinchón,' the old woman replied and John realised, with a little thrill of pleasure, that he had understood both question and answer. They were gradually beginning to understand quite a lot of spoken Spanish.

'And are there many troops here?'

'Aye, many. Here the soldiers come to rest,' the old woman told them. 'For a little while you will rest here too, before you go to die.'

The three young men looked at each other, then at the old crone.

'Thank you, mother,' Frankie said politely. He turned to his friends. 'Poor old girl, she's just wishing us luck,' he said.

John grinned at Jack. 'He might have fooled us once, but not any more,' he said. 'We understood every word, eh, Jack?'

'Wicked old witch,' Jack grunted. 'Ah, we're stopping here . . . my God, do they expect us to sleep in *that*?'

'That' was a stable, recently occupied, judging by the smell, and far from recently cleaned. The straw was filthy and the walls were blotched with what might have been manure – or blood.

'Thank God for our issue blankets,' Frankie said devoutly. 'I'm kipping down outside!'

He led the rush to the tiny square and its stunted olive trees.

By the time Foxy came down from Cambridge for the Easter vac, she knew, with a stab of real dismay, that she was pregnant.

She had suspected it for some time and when her grey skirt ceased to button, she had to accept what had happened to her. She was going to have John's baby and he was far away, fighting another man's war in that other man's country. He had joined the army, so he could not simply throw everything up and return to her side and anyway, she knew that he had not yet found Laurie. Luckily she was not showing much, she might be able to do another half a term before anyone noticed, but she did not think it was sensible. She intended to stay at Clifton Place whilst it was still possible to disguise her condition, working as Laurie had asked her to do. And then to go home to Auntie Bea in Birmingham and give birth to the child amongst friends. Laurie would thus get his money-worth, John would know that she had remained true to her trust, and once the child was safely born she would have it adopted so that she might return to Cambridge and complete her degree.

She did not intend to mention her condition to either boy, though she wrote to them regularly. Since Christmas she had received five letters from John and three from Laurie. John called her his darling girl, Laurie addressed her as Foxy dear. To the uninitiated, both could be seen as love-letters, which was probably as well.

So Easter came and back Foxy went, with her large case, to Clifton Place. She thought this time that she must insist on living at the home farm but, once more, Mr Allsop vetoed the suggestion.

'Don't even suggest it, Miss Foxy. Why, you've got the telephone here, the study in which to work, myself to organise and assist and the redoubtable Mrs Waughman to cook and clean. In fact, I think we should suggest to Mr Laurie that young Simon Fletcher moves into the home farm for the time being. He's engaged to be married, you know, and he doesn't want to live with the old people when the knot's tied.'

Foxy could scarcely object without either telling Allsop that Mr Laurie had promised the home farm to her, which would, obviously, make him suspect that the romance between herself and his employer could not be a fact, or admitting that she was pregnant.

So she moved into Clifton Place at once and told Allsop nothing.

It was fun to be back. To Foxy, there was nothing so delightful as working in the garden on a blustery spring day when she could admire the daffodils nodding in the breeze under the study window as she raked a winter's supply of dead leaves off the rose-beds. Then she had to feed the spindly-legged calves – there were two – from a bucket of warm milk, or dig over a patch of kitchen garden and then crouch on the damp earth, sprinkling cabbage or carrot seeds along the row and then placing the cloches tenderly in position. With the new grass coming and aconites a golden carpet in the wood, with the birds flirting and courting and the vixen howling for the dog fox, her own pregnancy seemed colourless and unimportant; indeed, it was hard to remember that she *was* pregnant. Her head knew she was, of course, but her heart did not really believe in the baby, so she never paused to wonder whether the hard work she did around the farm was good for the child and indeed, she was sure it must be good for her, so well and happy did she feel. She was sure she was not showing, anyway. Her thickened waist was hidden beneath her aprons indoors and her overalls out, and apart from that, she was pink-cheeked and healthy-looking. So Foxy pushed her condition to the back of her mind and decided to enjoy the Easter recess and then see whether she could fool the university authorities for a further term.

Had it not been for her decision to go into Ledbury so that she might buy a clutch of day-old chicks, to increase her flock after one of her broody hens had only managed to hatch six out of the twenty or so eggs she had been crouching over, she might have kept her secret very much longer.

She had harnessed Dapple to the small cart, discussed with Allsop whether White Leghorns or Rhode Island Reds laid the most acceptable eggs, and agreed to order some serviceable linoleum for the home farm kitchen. She had swung herself up onto the driving seat preparatory to leaving, when Allsop came hurrying into the yard.

'Oh, Miss Foxy, I could do with some more candles, would you get me a box? The six-inch ones will be sufficient. Here's the money.'

He stretched up towards her and Foxy stretched down towards him and as she took the money, something very odd happened. She felt a curious sensation, as though some part of her, perhaps a muscle in her stomach, had suddenly decided to wriggle and jerk independently. It made her hold her breath for a second, then glance down at herself, puzzled. What was it? What on earth could have done *that*?

Mr Allsop reached up and touched her knee. She glanced down at him and he was smiling very smugly.

'He kicked out, didn't he?' he said. 'I've been wondering when he'd make himself felt and it was just now. I'm not saying hard work's a bad thing, Miss Foxy, but you'll want to take things a bit easier over the next three or four months.'

Foxy was so startled that she could only stare. Who had kicked out? And why, for God's sake?

'It was the child,' Allsop said in his usual quiet, forthright manner. 'The child kicked you – didn't you know babies kick whilst still in their mother's bodies, Miss Foxy? I remember how surprised Lady Clifton was when young master Laurie first made himself felt. And just now you felt the child kick, I saw it in your face.'

'Oh! I – I don't . . . What an odd idea, I really don't . . . Good gracious, I'm going to miss all the best chicks if I don't hurry! I'll see you later, Mr Allsop.'

Foxy whipped up the pony and turned the cart into the lane. She did not look back but she knew that her cheeks had flamed hot whilst she stammered and stuttered and grew obviously more and more agitated. She tried to concentrate on her driving, to ignore what had happened, but she could not. Allsop knew! She had done nothing, absolutely nothing, to give her secret away. She had been sick once or twice first thing in the morning, but had made very sure that no one knew about it, and anyway, that had been earlier in the month. How the *devil* had Allsop discovered that she was pregnant? This would complicate things horribly, for suppose he thought it only right to tell her to leave? After all, as he would no doubt tell her with the utmost reasonableness, a pregnant woman could not be as useful to the Clifton estate as one who was not burdened with a child.

It was a glorious day but the previous night had been cold so there was a heavy dew. The grass was grey with it, until the sun reached out and touched it into a million diamonds, and above Foxy's head, in the pale blue sky, puffy white clouds kicked up their heels and raced across the heavens as though they, too, were affected by springtime.

Foxy, however, was not, at first, able to appreciate the day. She was too busy making wild plans. She would deny her condition, laugh lightly, tell Allsop he really must keep his imagination in check. Or she would go back to Birmingham and somehow find an abortionist who would rid her of the child. This led, not unnaturally, to her imagining vivid and terrible scenes; backstreets, blackened kitchens, unimaginably horrible instruments which would be thrust within her . . . and blood, pain . . . death.

She swung into High Street, and drew the pony cart to a halt. She jumped down, tethered Dapple, and set out to do her shopping. People called out to her and Mrs Hoverton, also shopping, came over in a natural and friendly fashion and told Foxy she was looking bonny; hard studying suits you, dear, she said, and Foxy told her she had come to buy chicks and asked Mrs Hoverton which ones she favoured and felt very odd when the baby moved again, because it was as though it knew its mother was talking to its grandmother, and had involuntarily waved.

'Get a score o' Rhodes an' a score o' Leghorns, m'dear,' Mrs Hoverton advised, as though she had never suggested, to her son, that Foxy Lockett was a townie and no better than she should be. 'A mix be good, in my 'sperience.'

And after that things began to come into perspective a bit and it no longer seemed the end of the world that Allsop knew her secret. I won't try to get an abortion, it would be a wicked thing to do, Foxy thought, and immediately felt relief and pleasure, in equal measures, rush through her. She smiled as she picked out her two score of day-old chicks and popped them into the cart and climbed up onto the driving seat again. It was a lovely day, a marvellous day, she was glad she was alive and glad that she was carrying John's baby, too.

Birth happened all the time, it was a natural thing. Today was market day and she was surrounded by birth – piglets, calves, lambs, chicks. She, too, would have her baby and, somehow, she would manage. Her life was not over, it was only just beginning, and a baby should enrich life, not take away from it.

Mind made up, Foxy climbed up onto the driving seat and headed towards Clifton Place once more. It was only as she turned into the drive that she remembered she had forgotten Allsop's candles.

Driving back to town to fetch the candles was a nuisance, but at least it gave Foxy some additional thinking time. And having thought, Foxy decided she would have to make a clean breast of it to Allsop, especially since he already knew she was expecting a child. She would say nothing about her child's father, but she would admit her pregnancy. So as soon as she got back from her second trip to Ledbury she handed the pony and cart to Ned and carried the chicks and her basketful of shopping into the kitchen. She and Mrs Waughman discussed how the chicks should be reared for a few minutes – a score to the erring broody hen, the rest indoors for a few days – then Foxy asked where Mr Allsop was hiding himself.

"'E's gone over to the 'ome farm wi' the pig-bucket,' Mrs Waughman told her. "'E was talkin' about 'avin' more pigs, till you took yourn to market last Christmas, Miss Foxy. Now 'e's not so sure 'e could stand it, though 'e says as 'ow pigs is pleasanter than folk in some ways.'

'Oh dear, I expect that was a dig at me,' Foxy said remorsefully. 'I'll keep him away from the fatteners in future, let him fuss the breeding sows. I want a word with him though, so I'll go over.'

She found Allsop, having emptied his bucket of scraps into the nearest sty, leaning on the wooden fencing and surveying Lily, the larger of the two sows. He turned as Foxy approached.

'Ah, you're back, Miss. I trust you had a successful shopping trip? You got your chicks?'

'Yes, thanks. Mr Allsop, I don't know how you knew, but you're absolutely right. I'm expecting a baby, though I don't think it will be born until June or July.'

He smiled at her, properly this time, a wide, delighted smile. He looked much younger when he smiled broadly, Foxy thought.

'Well, Miss Foxy, I guessed it, of course, but it wasn't tactful of me to say so, nor, perhaps, very kind. However, you've clearly come to terms with my knowing and you may be sure I shall do everything possible to safeguard you and the child. You will not want to bruit it abroad just yet but people will have to know, in due course. Tell me, Miss, you and Mr Laurie did not marry, I suppose, before he left for Spain?'

'No,' Foxy said. Least said soonest mended here. 'No, we didn't marry. It was just . . . he was going away . . .'

'Quite, quite,' Mr Allsop said soothingly. He glanced at her, then gave her his small, rather tight smile. 'But a son . . . I'm sure it will be a son . . . will bring Mr Laurie back quicker than anything else could. There's a good deal of truth in the saying *Love is of man's life a thing apart; 'tis woman's whole existence.* But Sir Laurence cannot fail to be delighted . . . an heir so soon, and he's only a boy himself. He'll realise, you see, that having fathered one child so easily he can father others. Sir George, as you may have guessed . . . but we won't go into that. Let me just say that I'm very happy for you, Miss.'

'Thank you, Mr Allsop. But – but people are going to be cruel about the baby. They'll say he's a bastard. So perhaps to call him Laurie's heir is not quite accurate,' Foxy pointed out.

Mr Allsop actually flinched when she said bastard, first shaking his head dolefully and then suddenly smiling, nodding portentously.

'I won't have a word like that used about a Clifton. I shall tell everyone that you and Mr Laurie were secretly married before he left for Spain. If necessary I shall produce documentation to prove the truth of my allegation. Then, when Mr Laurie does return, it will be easy enough for the two of you to marry – you could go to Scotland, to Gretna Green – now wouldn't that be romantic, Miss Foxy?'

'Ye-es, but I don't see how you can produce documentary proof,' Foxy argued. 'That would be impossible, surely?'

'Nothing's impossible,' Allsop said reprovingly. 'I shall forge a marriage certificate; nothing easier. I shall say you were married in . . . let me see, shall we say France? No, better not . . . we'll say

Southampton. That's far away, no one's going to check, anyway. It isn't as if the child were about to inherit the estate because the estate is Mr Laurie's, and anyway, the child has more right to it than anyone apart from Mr Laurie himself, of course. The estate can't go to Mr Laurie's second cousin, I'm sure you realise that, only the money in the trust. So if something dreadful did happen your baby would have every right to inherit.'

'But if that did happen, people would believe I'd lied to gain advantage, to get the estate,' Foxy pointed out uneasily. She did not like the sound of all this forging of marriage certificates. 'Is it really necessary, Mr Allsop? I can't stop you forging documents if you want to do so, but it makes me very uneasy.'

'And you mustn't be made uneasy, not in your condition, Miss Foxy,' Allsop said at once. 'We'll not talk about marriage or certificates or anything else either, unless the need arises. Do you feel better, now?'

'I do,' Foxy admitted. 'Thanks, Mr Allsop. Oh, and one more thing. I don't have an address for Mr Laurie, not a firm one. He's moving around all the time, it seems. So I can't tell him about the baby.'

'Oh! But you've had letters . . . you've written back . . .' Allsop said, his expression shocked. 'I had no idea, Miss . . . what a terrible worry for you!'

'Yes, it is,' Foxy said and it was no more than the truth; she worried about Laurie as much as she worried about John. I was more or less brought up with them both so naturally I want them both to be safe, she told herself defensively now. 'But John has joined the International Brigade and writes regularly – he's doing his very best to find Laurie. I'm sure it won't be long, now, before I get an address.'

'He could be anywhere, in any sort of danger,' Allsop said, in a low tone. 'I had no idea, I felt sure . . .'

His voice trailed away. Foxy hastened to comfort him. 'I heard two weeks ago, and he was all right then, but running short of money,' she said. 'He hasn't joined the military, he's trying to find a friend of his. Someone he knew at Cambridge and has a great fondness for.'

'That's like Mr Laurie,' Allsop said approvingly. 'I daresay the young fellow was one of the Spaniards he stayed with when he was in that country in '32, before Cambridge? He became very friendly with one particular young man, I remember him mentioning it.'

'That'll be it,' Foxy said, mentally crossing her fingers and reflecting that one little lie speedily embroiled one in a morass of untruths. 'Of course he wants to fight, I'm sure he does, but his first duty is to his friend. I can't help hoping that when they meet up Laurie will realise that he's not a trained soldier and will come home.'

Allsop looked a little doubtful, then sighed and turned away from the pigsty. 'It's getting chilly,' he said reprovingly. 'We'd best be getting back to the house, Miss Foxy. You – you'll let me know next time you receive a letter? I would like to write to Sir Laurie myself, when you've got a firm address.'

'You won't tell him about the baby? Only it would be awful if something happened and he came home for no good reason.'

They were entering the kitchen; Foxy saw Allsop's eyes darken with dread. She remembered someone telling her, once, that Lady Clifton had had a miscarriage before she had Laurie. But she did not want Allsop boasting of her condition to anyone, not yet. There were those who might put two and two together – Auntie Bea, for one. Best to keep quiet all round, then.

'You shouldn't talk like that, Miss Foxy, but you're quite safe. I'll tell no one until it becomes necessary. Now go and change out of your good things whilst I give Mrs Waughman a hand with supper.'

'Whoever thought we'd be taken to the front in lorries?' Frankie looked at the old vehicles rumbling back the way they had come, then turned to his companions. They had reached the village when dawn was breaking and now, after a brief sleep, they had been woken as the sun rose for some food and drink before making their way to their positions. 'Where's the river, anyway? I thought Robbie said we were to take up our position on the east bank of the river?'

'It's over the hills,' Jack said. 'Isn't it quiet?'

It was a beautiful morning. Sunshine flooded the small village square and somehow, when two men brought huge jugs of coffee round and a woman followed with supplies of ensemada, the sweet rolls which the troops already valued, it was difficult not to feel a mood of holiday encompass them. It was already quite hot on the plains but the air up here in mountain country was cool and fresh, the food and coffee good; what more could a soldier ask?

'It's a bit too quiet,' John said uneasily, however. 'We could hear the guns two days ago. What's happening?'

But no one knew, so they continued to eat and drink in the sunshine until Robbie came and gave the order to leave the village and begin to climb the hill, in battle formation this time.

'Leave any gear you don't need behind,' he said. 'You'll probably be back here by nightfall.'

'Are we doing all right over there, then?' someone asked.

Robbie grinned, a flash of white teeth in a sun-bronzed face. 'Don't know; just passing on orders. Forward!'

Presently they reached the first mountain top and saw the valley below them, with the river sauntering between high banks.

'We've had to pull back,' a weary officer told them, making his way past them. 'The Nationalists charged us earlier, at sun-up. That was why the barrage stopped, because the enemy didn't want to shoot their own troops as they advanced. But we won't fall back again. Take up your positions here; there are trenches which we left behind as we advanced, you can use them.'

The day seemed never-ending. Their company, too, were forced to retreat and Frankie had a word with a wounded Spaniard, dragging his way back through the lines to find a dressing station.

'What's happening up in front?' Frankie asked. 'Why were we given the order to retreat? We've not so much as laid eyes on the enemy yet.'

'I'm told your machine-gunners have been given the wrong ammunition,' the Spaniard told Frankie. He was using a fence-post as a crutch and his trouser leg was stiff with dried blood. 'So there are no machine-guns to support your fire. And for some reason there's no aerial cover so there's no chance of a strike from above.

But they've brought the right calibre ammo up now, only the wrong stuff has to be manually removed from the belts and replaced, which is taking time.'

'The enemy must have realised we've no machine-guns,' John said, rubbing his sweaty face with a filthy hand. 'I wonder how long we can keep them back without more support?'

The wounded soldier shrugged and began to heave himself along again, grunting with pain every time he took weight on his wounded leg.

'God knows, *amigo*. God knows. But I'm out of it for a bit, thank the Lord.'

The day wore on; birds sang in the olive groves, small animals went about their business. John marvelled at the way ordinary life went on as the troops fired, rushed forward, were forced to fall back again. And again. John, Jack and Frankie stuck together, and as the enemy came over the ridge above them they managed to reach the shelter of an olive grove, where they sniped from behind the trees as a hundred or so Moorish soldiers from the Army of Africa came pouring down the hillside, howling their battle-cry. They sounded like wounded wolves and looked twice as big as any men had a right to look. John felt the palms of his hands wet with sweat but he steadied his rifle and fired at one of the huge black men, saw the soldier sway, then crumple. He fired again; another fell, then another. Beside him, Frankie and Jack fired steadily, stopped to reload, fired again. Stopped altogether as the last screaming soldier passed them.

'We'll have to wait till dark and then make our way back; the enemy are between us and the village,' Frankie said presently. 'Try to sleep.'

He curled up in a hollow and the other two joined him, John aware suddenly that he ached all over and was suffering from a sore throat and an enormous, unquenchable thirst. He said as much to the other two.

'I'm the same,' Jack said. 'Think of the coffee we left this morning – I could drink a gallon of it now.'

'Me, too,' John said longingly. He rolled onto his back and gazed up through the silver-grey leaves at the blazing blue of the sky. 'I'd fight an army of Moors for one cupful.'

'You may have to,' Frankie observed. 'Try to sleep until dark.'

'Too tired; too tense,' John assured him. 'Still, we can rest, I suppose.'

Two minutes later they were all three sound asleep.

Later, they knew that the enemy must have decided to make a big push, having realised that for some reason the Republican machine-guns were out of action. They re-formed, charged . . . and were met with blistering machine-gun fire. John, Jack and Frankie, considerably refreshed by their unplanned siesta – unplanned by their officers, at any rate – watched the sudden retreat of the enemy in the dusk and hastily made their way back to their own trenches.

'We've lived to fight another day,' Jack commented as a runner brought their belongings up from the village square below. 'God bless my dear blankets – it's cold once darkness falls. And God bless whoever brought up the coffee!'

'It was cold,' John said from beneath his own blanket. 'Still, mustn't grumble; even cold coffee's better than none at all.'

Above his head the sky was full of blazing stars and, oddly, he felt good. Simply surviving, being alive, was a sort of triumph, and with his thirst quenched and his hunger satisfied, he gloried in it. Just before he slept he thought of Foxy, so far away, back at Cambridge now, reading her beloved English literature. Waiting for him. Loving him. He realised, with a stab of shock, that though he could see her in his mind, he no longer ached for her. Between them, war had stretched its cruel, cold talons, touched him with pain, horror, a little pride. Secretly, he had wondered if he was brave enough to fight, if he would run when the guns began to boom. Now he knew he was all right. He was in this for a confusion of reasons, but he wouldn't back out now, wouldn't retract until he'd gone the distance. England, home and duty wasn't just hundreds of miles away, it was part of a different existence. Until he had come to terms with this war, he would not be able to think of Foxy or his own country in quite the old, carefree way. The fellow she loved isn't the fellow I now am, John told himself dreamily. I'm being proved in the fire of adversity . . . I hope to God it doesn't devour me.

*

Almost as soon as the Republican army had accepted Laurie as a recruit, he was told that he would go, for officer training, to the nearby town of Tarazona de la Mancha. It was a small but pleasant town and the barracks, which were only large houses requisitioned by the army after their fascist owners had either fled or been killed, were very overcrowded, but they were full of young men of about Laurie's own age, several of whom were English, and after months of slogging across Spain on his own, scarcely daring to talk to anyone save in the most casual manner, talking easily to people who thought as he did seemed like heaven to Laurie.

And everyone was friendly. Most of the other young men were battle-hardened, but that did not stop them from envying Laurie his command of the language and taking him into their circle. They were put into companies and stayed that way and very soon Laurie was learning his craft. Everything was covered. Tactics, battlefield conditions, map-reading, the way one organises a front . . . all these things were taught and taught well.

Gunnery was a headache because Laurie, who was not mechanically-minded, had to take a machine-gun to pieces and then reassemble it in the dark. This meant blindfolded and Laurie and the others spent many frustrating hours streaming sweat with a handkerchief around their eyes whilst they fumbled with the smaller parts of the Maxim in total bewilderment. But by the end of the course there wasn't one man who could not have stripped down and reassembled his own rifle and a machine-gun in his sleep.

One of Laurie's first acts in Tarazona was to write to Mirri; he felt it was safe to do so now, because he was a Republican soldier and as such knowing him could not harm her. Her reply put him in seventh heaven; she was well, she still loved him, she was working very hard for the Republican cause as were her friends Jacinta, Josefa and Inma and she had dug miles and miles of trenches and she had killed a great many fascists with her beloved gun.

'My gun is magnificent and I am an excellent shot,' she wrote complacently. 'But one's bullets cannot reach the planes which bomb and machine-gun, which I would dearly love to destroy. But killing fascists and those dreadful Moors who scream so when they attack is good. *Salud*, dearest, dearest Laurie; I love you very much,' she ended. The letter, many times read, crumpled and stained, was in the pocket of his jacket and would stay there until the next one arrived. He hated the thought of her so much as firing her gun, but told himself that she was probably exaggerating. He could imagine her, eyes squeezed closed, bringing herself to pull the trigger, but not doing anything so unladylike as aiming the thing. And besides, he knew, now, how a rifle kicked, turning your shoulder to one enormous, aching bruise. No delicately reared girl could stand that for long, so she must be exaggerating, his little darling.

And even when he heard, on the grapevine, that Andy Griffiths had been shot down and was in enemy hands, he did not despair. Andy had promised to look after Mirri and was now unable to do so, but Laurie was in touch with her himself now, and Mirri seemed happy and quite capable of taking care of herself.

He even wrote to Andy, care of the Red Cross, to tell him that all was well, both with him and with the young lady of whom they had spoken.

And he wrote to Foxy, of course, giving her the barracks as his address, and received three lovely fat letters back. Foxy had not gone back to Cambridge after Christmas, she had decided that the home farm and Clifton Place needed her more than she needed her English degree.

'I haven't given it up, I've asked for a year out and my tutor's agreed,' Foxy's letter said. 'Allsop is also writing and sends his best regards. We have packed you two parcels; don't know when they'll arrive but it should be quite soon after the letters. Oh, and John's in Spain, too, did you know? He's with the International Brigade as well and searching for you. I'm sure you'll meet up any time now.'

John was in Spain! It gave him such pleasure to know that John and he were in the same country, fighting the same war. Even his desire to see Mirri soon no longer seemed so terribly important. He had explained to Foxy in his letter that because Mirri's father had been a fascist she was now in some danger, so he had joined the Republican army in order to safeguard her.

'Friends with some authority say they will keep their eyes on her and make sure she comes to no harm from either side, so far as they are able,' he had written. 'I feel dreadfully guilty because until I told them she was Salvorini's daughter they did not know and

305

had been treating her as just another Republican girl who wanted to work for her country's freedom. I jeopardised that. But I am making reparation – and enjoying it very much so far. Though I've yet to see fighting, of course.'

And now that things had changed – Andy could no longer take care of Mirri for him and he knew she was in no danger from the Republicans – it did not seem worthwhile writing and explaining all over again. He would keep his letters simple, and just say that he intended to bring Mirri home when he could.

Now, he was sitting in one of the classrooms with the rest of his company, sweating over a battle plan. Position your troops *so*, your machine-guns *so*, your reserves *so*. Dig trenches fifty yards behind your front so that if the enemy break through and your men fall back, they have something to fall back on, somewhere to recover whilst your reserve troops take up the attack and you plan the next move. He was scowling over the best position for his machine-guns (not too near the front in case the enemy tried to capture them, on rising ground if possible so that they could fire over your own troops) when he noticed a fat and drunken bluebottle lurching down the windowpane beside him. It was buzzing in an infuriating way and Laurie took his sheet of paper and endeavoured to guide the bumbling creature up and through the open half of the window and into the heat and sunshine of the square outside. As the bluebottle obligingly clutched the paper and Laurie tilted it, he saw a movement outside the window. Three young men were coming towards the house; one was tall and dark, another tall and fair, the third slight, with mid-brown hair. The middle one . . .

'My God!' Laurie was on his feet regardless of the stares of his fellow students, the outraged glare of his tutor. 'My God, it's John!'

Their courses only overlapped by a couple of weeks, but John and Laurie made up for lost time whilst they were together. They never stopped talking, they read each other's letters, they discussed, with pleasure, both what was happening at home and how they would write, no matter how busy, what the difficulties.

John watched Laurie in class and decided he had underestimated his foster-brother. He had forgotten how easily Laurie had taken to being in charge at Clifton Place, and this must have stood him in good stead. At any rate Laurie planned strategy, drilled a company, took lightning decisions, could aim and fire his rifle fast and accurately and seemed to have no worries over either his personal safety or his ability to command a number of semi-trained soldiers.

'I did some preliminary work with the company that I'm going back to command,' he explained to John, 'and they were all good fellows. I'm putting my back into this because I want to do right by them. Simple as that. Besides, it will be far easier to get Mirri out if we're in the ascendant.'

John realised rather guiltily that he had not really considered Mirri, not since hearing Laurie say she was safe and working as a militiawoman in Madrid. But it did occur to him that for someone who knew where his beloved was, Laurie certainly wasn't falling over himself to get to her. Not any more. We're two of a kind, John thought ruefully. Now I'm away from Foxy, though I'm sure I still love her and so on, there isn't that hot urgency of need for her. And I don't mean the physical things, either. I yearned to be near her, I thought about her, dreamed about her ... now I dream about a decent English Sunday dinner, or a hot bath when I've been slogging through Spanish mud in winter, or a cold beer when we're sweltering in some airless little town on the plains somewhere. And if I long for anything it's for the sight of the sun sinking over the Welsh hills, or rising over Malvern.

He felt rather ashamed, rather guilty, because Foxy's letters were a delight to receive, so full of information, chatter, humorous incidents. He wrote back as lightly as he could, but he was increasingly aware that his heart wasn't in the letters. But he loved her – didn't he? He'd always loved her – hadn't he? He refused to accept that what he had felt for Foxy might have been infatuation coupled with the natural lust of a young man working closely with a young woman.

Still. It would work out, once they got home. And meantime he was still on the course and enjoying it. So he waved Laurie off, knowing that the only thing they hadn't discussed was his relationship with Foxy and Laurie's with Mirri. And telling himself that no man worth his salt thought much about a woman when he was fighting a war.

And almost believing it, too.

Eleven

Laurie had been listening to a news bulletin on a crackly wireless set up at HQ, and returned to his company to give them bad news.

'Bilbao has fallen; they were starved out, the port blockaded, there wasn't even any water for the poor buggers to drink, so what else were they to do but give in? The army fled, they say . . . but it's easy to talk about fleeing – we've been forced to withdraw time and again because of the Nationalists' superiority in numbers and weapons. But where, in God's name, do we go from here? The Basques are superb fighters but they're losing the will to win, even the belief that they might do so. The industrial north is going down like a pack of cards.'

'They'll send us to Santander,' Piggy Bates said. 'Right up on the coast . . . we could get home from there!'

The yearning in his voice might have made Laurie laugh, except he felt the same yearning himself from time to time; oh, to be home again! He found himself imagining that homecoming over and over. He would get off the train at Ledbury station, which had never seemed particularly beautiful before, but which now wore a golden glow. He would jump into the trap and drive slowly through the town, waving to friends leaving The Feathers and having a look at the shops on High Street. He would tether the pony then in order to wander round the Market House, nip into Tilley's for a few presents to take home, then, back in the trap once more, he would drive towards the clock tower seeing, on his right, the dear old church lengthily dedicated to St Michael and all the angels, with its square tower surmounted, so oddly, by a tall thin spire. Then he rather thought he would get out of the trap once more and go for a stroll down Bye Street to take a look at the cattle market, ask farming friends how life was treating them, before he drove down the Homend, out of town and onto the road which led to Clifton Place.

And once there, he would examine the gardens and the home farm, before going indoors to give Foxy a hug, to shake Allsop's hand, to walk across the big old kitchen on his way to the study. And once home he would never be discontented, not he; he would paint one day, dig the garden the next, examine his stock the next . . .

'Yes, we might easily be sent to Santander,' he agreed now, wrenching his mind back to the present, to the summer heat of Spain. 'Only I'm due a spot of leave and I've cadged a ride in a lorry, going to Madrid. Our CO wants a word with the generals and he says there are always one or two high-ups in the city, so I said I'd go too. Which means, if we are sent to Santander, I'll have to join you later.'

'You've got a girl in Madrid, haven't you, sir?' Corporal Andrews said with open curiosity. 'She's a local, isn't she? Some of 'em are real 'ot stuff.'

There was a subdued mutter of amusement. Andrews, a tall, chunky young man with sandy hair and eyes like gooseberries, had managed to find himself pretty little Spanish girlfriends wherever they were posted and boasted that, under his blandishments, they had proved far from reluctant to take him to their hearts.

'Yes, I've a girlfriend there,' Laurie admitted, grinning at his corporal. She's joined the militia so I think "hot stuff" may be true, though not quite in the sense you mean it. It will be good to see her again.'

'Ooh, them militiawomen! Can't resist a gal in uniform,' Bert Flowerdew began to say, then caught Laurie's eye and subsided.

'Quite, Flowerdew,' Laurie said. 'So don't think I'm running out on you; it's just a spot of leave.'

It was a hot and sticky night, and scarcely a breath of wind was coming through Foxy's bedroom window, though she had left it as wide open as it would go and kept the curtains drawn back.

She woke, at first, because of the heat. Sweat was channelling down between her breasts and her stomach felt horribly extended, as though it had been blown up with a bicycle pump and could not, now, do anything but burst. Cursing herself, she swung her legs out of bed and immediately wanted to spend a penny. Because of her size her bladder was constantly being squeezed so when she wanted to go it was an immediate need. Beneath the bed was a cheerful blue chamber pot embellished with red roses; Foxy produced it and then had a tussle with her nightgown which, though it was only made of flimsy cotton, was still too long for comfort in heat such as this, and very much too clinging. It clung lovingly to her damp legs and had to be physically wrenched away, so by the time she was able to use the pot it was almost too late.

I really shouldn't sit on it, not now I'm so vast, Foxy told herself, sitting nevertheless. She had a secret, terrible fear that one day she would be forced to summon assistance, her bottom having become irreversibly stuck, by some sort of suction, to the chamber pot. Or worse, suppose she sat and it splintered? She would feel such a *fool*! She could just imagine the sort of remarks the nurses would make at the hospital as they tweezered daggers of porcelain out of her bum; they might be amusing but they wouldn't do a thing for her dignity.

But the chamber pot was equal to her weight and to the suddenness of her assault, as well. She always tried to be discreet, remembering that Allsop or Mrs Waughman might be awake and prowling the house, but it was getting less and less possible. Now, she gushed fiercely and then stood up, her knees creaking a double protest; they didn't like being bent out at right angles but neither did they much enjoy having to bear her new, extended weight.

Slowly, upright and more or less in her right mind, she pushed the chamber pot back under the bed with a cautious toe, then sat down on the edge of the mattress. What a nuisance to wake in the middle of the night, baking hot, and then have to lug your newly stupendous body from one position to another. If she lay down now heartburn would attack her, as sure as her name was Foxy Lockett. If she sat up, she would probably get cramp.

Then, unexpectedly, she felt the pain. Not an ordinary sort of pain, the sort that came because you'd been lugging yourself in

310

and out of bed, on and off chamber pots; nor the sort that meant you'd overeaten or eaten something which disagreed with you. It was an odd, dragging pain.

It was in her back, what was more, not in her stomach. It wasn't particularly bad but it was persistent. It would come slowly, stay for a few minutes, then die away, grumbling. And just as she thought it had definitely gone this time, that she was safe to go back to sleep, it would come again. Nag, nag, nag, weak at first but growing stronger and stronger, it clawed at her lower spine, only to fade once more as she began to resist it.

Sighing, Foxy sat up and reached for the candle she kept beside the bed. She fumbled for the matches, lit the candle, stared at the alarm clock's round, complacent face. Two a.m. No need to get up for another four whole hours ... what on earth was her back doing, waking her at this hour?

She lay down again but left the candle burning. It couldn't be the baby, because everyone had told her that first babies are always late, and according to her shaky calculations and the nurse's slightly more accurate ones, this baby should not put in an appearance for another week at least. And anyway, babies didn't start in your *back*, for God's sake, they started in your belly, everyone knew that. The pain, Foxy believed, was caused by the baby trying to get out, not trying to burrow through to your bleeding spine!

It was wind, that was it. Wretched wind. Heartburn would doubtless follow, then cramp, then an urge to revisit the chamber pot ... Sighing crossly, Foxy closed her eyes. A false alarm; one of the farm labourers had a wife who'd had four or five false alarms before the baby was actually born. Yes, it would be a false alarm. But she still did not blow out the candle.

An hour or two later she sat up again, feeling sweat trickle down between her breasts though it was no longer as hot. She slid out of bed and padded across to the window, then pulled her nightie over her head in a couple of savage movements. Outside it was still dark but dawn was coming; she could see a lightening in the sky to the east and the stars which had shone so brightly earlier in the night seemed to be paling as dawn approached. And as she stood there, hot, cross, tendrils of hair sticking to her forehead, she felt the blessed relief of a slight breeze. The dawn breeze, she supposed, turning back into the room once more. Oh, nakedness was good when you were so very large and so extremely hot! Foxy felt a little better. She supposed, vaguely, that it really could be the baby, because her periods had always been erratic and she hadn't really started counting dates or making guesses until well on into the New Year. And it was no good writing to John and asking him because for one thing he probably wouldn't get the letter until the baby was quite old, and for another, she was certain he would have no more idea than she of the exact date of their union.

She sat down on the edge of the bed and wondered what to do, even as the pain came again. She scowled, but reached over and lit the candle. The flame flickered, no longer warm or reassuring but frightening, because she was not ready to have a baby, not right here and now. A nurse was arriving in a week, someone to keep her company, to tell her what to do when her pains started . . . and now here she was at four in the morning, alone and bloody scared, for God's sake!

I'm not! her mind said sharply as soon as the thought had entered her head. I don't frighten easily, I'm Foxy Lockett, she's always faced up to things. And anyway it won't be the baby, it'll be wind, or eating too many raspberries when you were picking them for Mrs Waughman to make jam, or . . .

It's the baby, of course it is; you'd better fetch help, a little voice said spitefully. Stop grabbing at straws and face facts! Foxy tried to fight back, remembering the number of times the doctor had told her that first babies were always late, but something told her that the little voice was right on the dot this time; this time it was the real thing.

Five minutes ticked by. Six. She was beginning to relax when the pain struck; boing, boing, *boing*! It had her out of bed and halfway to the door without even realising it. She snatched her cotton dressing gown off the hook on the back of the door and tied it round her with shaking hands. Then she tugged the door open, perspiration running down her forehead and stinging her eyes. Her heart was beating like a drum and she felt downright terrified; it would have to start early, and in the middle of the night what was more. Allsop had insisted on a resident nurse and she had teased him, said he was an old woman, but inside, she had been thankful. And now the wretched woman was miles away and wouldn't come unless she could get away from her present employer early. It'll be the village midwife, Foxy thought. Oh well, she's delivered lots of kids – she delivered John and probably Laurie, too. So long as she comes soon!

On the landing she paused and, after only the smallest of hesitations, turned in the direction of the Chinese room. Why she did so she could not have said, she just had a strange, restless feeling that she would like to have a look around. Doing something, anything, was preferable to remaining in her room counting pains and feeling sick with fright.

She pushed the door open. The room was bathed in the pale grey light of pre-dawn and the windows were all closed, yet Foxy thought she could smell roses. Odd, Foxy thought, walking into the room. She checked the windows, but they were all tightly shut and the smell of roses, faint but sweet, persisted. Was it on the bed? She went towards it, then hesitated; for months and months she had carefully avoided coming in here because of what had happened when she and John had been waiting for Laurie that night so long ago. In fact, she realised, she had not set foot in the room since. And yet now, the feelings which she had associated with the room were completely gone. She had talked it over with John and, later, with Laurie, and they had both said sadness seemed to surround the bed. But here she was, standing right by it, and all she felt was a pleasant sort of calm. Highly daring, Foxy laid a hand on the bed, then sat down on it. The pain came, clawed, went. Foxy breathed deeply, something her book on childbirth had advised but which she had completely forgotten until this moment, and then actually lay back on the bed, rustling the yellow silk of the counterpane. She waited. It felt . . . right. She checked to see if the bed had been made up but it wasn't, the yellow silk counterpane was laid directly onto the feather mattress. Yet she had such a strong feeling that this was a good place to have a baby in! She remembered stories of cats and dogs seeking out a good place to give birth and sticking to it, no matter how inconvenient it might have seemed to their owners. That was how she felt, that she would give birth here or nowhere!

The trouble was, the bed wasn't made up and the pain was coming again and no one knew she was in here. She had better telephone for the midwife and then wake Allsop and Mrs Waughman. If there was one thing she did want, it was the company of another woman, she realised. Someone who could tell her if she was doing the right thing, someone to help, advise.

She left the room reluctantly, turning in the doorway for a last look. The room smiled gently back at her; I'll look after you, it seemed to be saying. I'll keep you safe.

What poppycock I've been thinking, Foxy told herself severely as she padded heavily down the stairs. I really am quite mad – it must be the baby coming, it's addled my brains. She reached the hall and picked up the telephone receiver, paused, then replaced it on its rest. She would wake the others first, then perhaps Allsop could help her to make up the bed in the Chinese room and Mrs Waughman could sit with her until the nurse arrived. Whilst clearly no nurse, Mrs Waughman was at least another female, she might have some idea . . .

Across the hall Foxy went, and into the short passageway which led to the housekeeper's room where Mrs Waughman slept since her legs could not manage the stairs on a regular basis. Foxy pattered to the door and knocked timidly. There was no sound. The pain struck again; boing, BOING, *BOING*! Suddenly the calm which had descended on Foxy in the Chinese room deserted her. She banged on the door with both fists, then kicked it for good measure.

'Mrs Waughman, it's me, Foxy. I've bleedin' well started having this damned child, and I want you out here *now*!'

There was a thump and then a muffled shout from behind the housekeeper's door.

'I'm a-comin', Miss Foxy, don' 'ee fret, now.'

Almost simultaneously a voice said coldly, right in Foxy's ear: 'There's no need for bad language, Miss. You'll be right as rain if you just quieten down a trifle.'

'Oh goodness, you nearly gave me a heart attack,' Foxy gasped, spinning round to stare, open-mouthed, at the butler's austere figure. Even clad in a maroon towelling dressing gown he managed to look spruce, and Foxy, clutching her own gown round her huge stomach, felt sluttish to say the least. 'What are you doing here, Mr Allsop? You should be in bed!'

'I heard you thumping around and coming down the stairs like a ton of bricks,' Allsop pointed out. ''Twas enough to waken the dead, Miss. Have you telephoned for the nurse, yet?'

'Not yet,' Foxy admitted, remembering the time she had spent trotting round the house and never thinking to call Allsop down from his attic. 'I'll do it ri . . . ouch!'

Forgetting to stay calm and breathe deeply, Foxy bent double, one hand flying to the small of her back.

'Aha, so your little gentleman has decided it's time he put in an appearance,' Allsop said, and Foxy thought – hoped – that she could detect some worry in his usual unruffled tone. 'Come along, Miss, up the stairs and back to bed. I'll telephone for Mrs Bottomley and send her up as soon as she arrives.'

'I'm not going back to my room,' Foxy said fretfully. 'I want to have this baby in the Chinese room and the bed isn't made up. Could Mrs Waughman do it?'

'Well . . .' Allsop was beginning cautiously when Mrs Waughman emerged bashfully from her room. She had managed to dress, more or less, though her hair hung in two thin little plaits on either side of her large face and her mouth had the sunken look of one who has forgotten to pop in her top and bottom set.

'Marnin', Mr Allsop, Miss Foxy,' Mrs Waughman lisped. 'Did I oversleep? Is you wantin' yous brekfusses?'

'Not right now, Mrs Waughman,' Foxy said soothingly, though her stomach heaved at the thought of breakfast. 'I was wondering if you could give me a hand to make up the bed in the Chinese room?'

'Before *brekfuss*?' Mrs Waughman said incredulously. 'Surely you'll 'ave your brekfuss first, Miss Foxy?'

Foxy stifled the urge to scream and shake the older woman and embarked on an explanation but Mr Allsop was having none of it. He waved a hand at her, commanding silence, and then spoke decisively.

'Teeth, Mrs Waughman.'

Mrs Waughman clapped a guilty hand over her mouth and shot back into her bedroom, to reappear moments later with a bright porcelain smile.

'Sorry, Mr Allsop; now what did you want, Miss?'

'It's four in the morning, Mrs Waughman, and Miss Foxy is in labour,' Allsop said smoothly. 'She needs the bed making up in the Chinese room, which is where the family always give birth. Can you help her, please?'

'Course, Mr Allsop,' Mrs Waughman said comfortably. 'I'll do it meself, though. You 'ave a sit-down, Miss Foxy.'

She stumped across the hall and began to mount the stairs. Allsop advised Foxy to take through into the Chinese room anything she might want, such as books or a glass of water, and then took the telephone receiver off its rest. He was speaking to the operator as Foxy began to follow Mrs Waughman up the flight, now and again clutching her stomach whilst the candle-flame bobbed and swayed.

Below her in the hall she could hear Mr Allsop speaking into the telephone. 'Yes, I want the midwife, Mrs Bottomley,' he said authoritatively. 'You say she's at Meadows Lea? Then I shall ring off and ask the operator to connect me with Meadows Lea at once.'

Breakfast time came and went. The midwife didn't arrive; she had gone to Meadows Lea farm to attend a middle-aged woman who was expecting twins. Her mother, who minded the phone for her, said her daughter might be away some considerable time and when Allsop phoned the farm and showed considerable perturbation, he was reminded by a bland Mrs Bottomley that first babies were always late, always slow to arrive, and was Miss quite sure it wasn't a false alarm?

Allsop relayed this information to Foxy, now snugly ensconsed in the big fourposter in the Chinese room with a jug of Mrs Waughman's homemade lemonade, some dry biscuits and a number of rather treacly romantic novels close at hand. Mrs Waughman, it appeared, enjoyed her romance secondhand and was eager to share her supply of reading matter with Foxy.

'Mrs Bottomley says false alarms aren't uncommon with a first child,' Allsop said apologetically. 'I told her this was no false alarm, Miss Foxy, I said it was the real thing, but even so she can't get away at once. Mrs Stanghow's having a difficult time and the nurse doesn't think she ought to be left yet awhile.'

'I'm not having big fun, either,' Foxy said crossly. 'I don't think Mrs Waughman's ever delivered a baby and I bet you haven't either, Mr Allsop. And I don't intend to start trying to deliver my own kid . . . I'd make a muck of it.'

'I quite agree,' Mr Allsop said with a slight shudder. 'I did tell Mrs Bottomley in no uncertain terms that you needed someone here, and she said all right, her assistant might attend, but I should have to drive into Ledbury and fetch her when the time is ripe. I'm afraid I put the telephone down so abruptly that the girl from the exchange rang back, asking me whether I'd meant to cut the connection or whether I'd dropped the instrument in error.'

'She was listening, of course. Then it'll be all round the village by lunchtime . . . *ouch!*' Foxy said. 'And all round Ledbury by teatime – ouch, *ouch!*'

'Don't worry, Miss Foxy, there won't be any nasty talk, not once I tell people that you're really Lady Clifton,' Allsop said complacently. 'I'll say we don't want it talked about, of course, which will mean they'll all tell each other, in strict secrecy, just what I've said. And we're only jumping the gun by a few months, because that war can't last for ever. And once Mr Laurie knows he's got a son . . .'

'Or a daughter; I feel sure it's going to be a girl,' Foxy panted, trying to be brave and keep her shouts down to a minimum. 'I'd *like* a girl; I *will* have a girl!'

Allsop gave her an indulgent smile. 'Of course you'd like to have a girl, Miss Foxy, and so you shall. Next time you shall have a girl if that's what you want, but this time . . .'

The words *stupid old fart* formed themselves tantalisingly behind Foxy's firmly closed eyelids and begged to be spoken aloud but she tightened her lips against them. Allsop was only being concerned, it meant a lot to him that Laurie should have an heir, so why spoil things for him? They would know soon enough, but suddenly she was almost certain that she was about to give birth to a girl. It would be worth all the pain just to prove Allsop wrong, she decided; it would be worth having a squirrel come to that, because he would be so very annoyed.

At the thought, her eyes shot open. Allsop was smiling gently, rearranging the things on her bedside table. He had brought her a

317

couple of books up from Laurie's rather old-fashioned library and a small vase with her favourite rosebuds. Foxy felt ashamed.

'I don't really want to have a squirrel, Mr Allsop,' she whispered. 'But I'd like an aspirin tablet, if you don't mind fetching me one.'

Allsop smiled down at her. It was a very loving smile.

'Anything you say, Miss Foxy,' he said softly. 'Anything you say.'

Time passed slowly, on leaden feet. Lunchtime and the midwife arrived simultaneously and Foxy shouted rude things at Mrs Bottomley when that person pulled back the bedclothes, took a cursory glance at Foxy's oddly pointed stomach, and said there was no hurry and that she would come back later.

'I want to get it over with, I want it out!' Foxy said sharply, through the wave of pain which was engulfing her. 'Do something, can't you? You're the bleeding nurse!'

'Look, Miss Foxy, poor Mrs Stanghow's not so young, an' it's twins,' Mrs Bottomley explained, obviously deciding to take offence neither at Foxy's tone nor her language. 'She 'on't be long now, then I'll come back yur on the instant, but you b'aint even at the pushin' stage, yet. 'Ave your waters broke?'

'I don't think so,' Foxy said doubtfully. 'Couldn't you make them break? If it would speed things up, I mean.'

'There's a time for everything,' Mrs Bottomley said comfortably. 'They'll break, in their own good time. You try to 'ave a bit of a nap whiles I deal wi' Mrs Stanghow, Miss Foxy.'

'Nap?' Foxy screeched after her departing back. 'I can't nap when my guts are being pulled out of my . . .'

The door closed. Firmly. Foxy tottered out of bed and across to the door, circumnavigating the chamber pot as she went, determined to have the last word.

'. . . Out of my innards,' she finished defiantly as she hurled the door open. 'I need help, Mrs Bottomley, not a bloody lecture!'

'The only person who can 'elp you is yourself,' the nurse called up the stairs. Foxy longed to throw the chamber pot at her, but she might well need it all in one piece later. Instead, she hung on to the newel post and called pathetically down to Mrs Waughman to bring her some more lemon barley, before tottering back to bed.

She didn't really want a drink but she did want company. Even surrounded by the calm of the Chinese room she still felt she would be happier with some female companionship.

Presently, Mrs Waughman surged in with lemon barley water and a spoonful of honey. Foxy thanked her listlessly and watched her leave without a murmur. She seemed to be floating on a sea of pain and all she could do was put up with it and wait. The men in Spain, fighting for the poor and downtrodden, must suffer worse pain, she reasoned, and tightened her lips against the involuntary cries which wanted to escape.

By teatime, Foxy had drifted into the grey half-world which all women in labour know. She was aware, as the day lengthened, that people came and went, whispered over her, left her, but it was not until well into the night that the pain changed, bringing her out of her trancelike state.

This pain was quite different from those which had preceded it. It arrowed through her, no longer simply hurting but demanding something of her, though she was not yet quite sure what it wanted. Foxy pushed herself into a sitting position just as the door opened a crack and Allsop slipped into the room. He looked grey and worried.

'Ah, Miss Foxy. I've just rung the doctor again; his wife tells me he's at the cottage hospital, operating on a young fellow with a burst appendix. And Mrs Bottomley won't be free for a while yet, she's working to sa . . . I mean she's still with Mrs Stanghow. But there's Mrs B's assistant. I'm to pick her up in the car when you . . . you feel the need.'

'I think you'd better fetch her right away,' Foxy said between gritted teeth. The pain was giving her no rest, it was continual, yet it wasn't such an awful, dragging business now. 'I think the baby's starting to get born, Mr Allsop.'

'Right. I'll tell Mrs Waughman to boil water, fetch towels, scissors . . . she'll be up presently,' Allsop said distractedly. 'I'd best be off, Miss.'

He left the room and Foxy tried to tell her body that it must not keep bunching and growling at her because she did not want the baby to arrive before Mrs B's assistant did. But her body took no notice and suddenly she realised that the pain wasn't really pain at all, it was a command, an order. Push, it said, push! And Foxy, knowing she had no option, obeyed.

It was exhausting work but much more satisfying, somehow, than simply lying and enduring. Foxy could not have said how much time had passed but she knew she was winning, knew that the baby and she together were making it happen. She was no longer conscious of the heat of the day fading, the cool of evening beginning to come gently in through the open window. When she obeyed the pain and pushed, the room blurred before her eyes with the intensity of her effort, and when the pain eased she panted like a dog and rested, grateful for any respite, no matter how short.

'Push, baby, push,' she found herself chanting as the cycle continued. 'Push, little baby, help me to get you born!' And then, because she was frightened and alone, she added: 'Oh, I *wish* someone would come!'

And someone did. Foxy was lying back on her pillows, trembling, taking great breaths, when the door opened and the nurse came towards her. Young, dark-haired, efficient-looking, with a friendly smile and a blue dress. Foxy, looking at the other woman's face, was sure she knew her, but then in a village you tend to meet most of the inhabitants at some time or other.

'Hello,' she said rather weakly. 'I'm awfully glad you've come.'

'Well, dear, I shall do my best to help you, but I think you're doing very well by yourself,' the nurse said, placing a cool hand on Foxy's hot brow.

'Oh nurse, am I doing the right thing?' Foxy asked anxiously. 'I keep pushing because the pain says to push, but I don't know if I'm doing it right, and then when it tells me to stop, I just do as it says. But it's been going on for ages now . . . I think I'll split in half if the baby doesn't come soon but I'm sure I'll die if I stop pushing!'

The nurse laughed. 'Everyone giving birth feels like that,' she said. 'You're doing exactly the right thing, you're a very clever young mother, and I believe your baby will put in an appearance any moment now. Ah, I can see you want to push again; don't let me interrupt such good work . . . it won't be long now!'

Reassured, Foxy put her heart and soul into the next few pushes.

She sweated and strained and even sobbed once or twice, but she knew she was winning. And then, when she really did think she was going to split in two, there was a wonderful, slithery feeling and the pain which had goaded her faded away in the most natural manner imaginable.

Foxy lay with closed eyes for a moment, then opened them and heaved herself up on one elbow. The door was swinging open and Mrs Waughman's large, untidy head appeared. And there, on the sheet between Foxy's legs, was a red, wet, glistening creature . . . her baby!

'He's come!' Foxy said. 'He's come! Oh, thank God that's over and he's born at last. Where's the nurse?'

'She'm scrubbin' up to 'elp bring 'im into the world,' Mrs Waughman said. She came forward and picked up the child, then smacked it, twice, on its small, pointed bottom. The baby took a deep, indignant breath and wailed and Foxy giggled. She felt so happy! It was over, she had her baby, and he had breathed, cried, was wriggling in Mrs Waughman's grasp.

'Is it a boy or a girl?' she asked, pushing strands of wet red hair off her face. 'Oh, it's a boy, I can see now. Where's that nurse, though? There's things to do, cutting cords and so on, she should be here when I need her.'

'She won't be a moment . . .' Mrs Waughman was beginning when the door opened again and Mrs Bottomley surged in. She looked tired and drawn, her usual high colour quite gone, but she smiled at Foxy and bustled over to the bed.

'Well done, Miss Foxy – a dear little son for . . . for you. Lay him on the bed, Mrs Waughman, whilst I deal with the cord and that. And you might fetch me up some of that water you've been a-boiling, and I 'spec' Milady could do wi' a nice cup o' tea.'

Foxy sniffed at the use of the title but she did not care what anyone called her, not today. She had a son and soon she would have a waist again, too. And the thought of a cup of tea was sheer bliss. She watched Mrs Bottomley lethargically as she did her various tasks, then took the tea from Mrs Waughman and sipped, sipped . . .

'She's wore out,' a voice said from a long way off, and the cup of tea was taken carefully from her sagging grasp. 'She's laboured long an' hard, now's the time for 'er to rest. Settle 'er on 'er side, Mrs Waughman, whiles I bath the child.'

And Foxy slid contentedly into slumber.

In the early hours of the morning Mrs Bottomley left and Foxy lay like a queen amongst her pillows with the baby, neatly night-gowned, in the crook of her arm and gave audience. Mr Allsop and Mrs Waughman came in first, Mr Allsop beaming from ear to ear, his eyes bright with triumph.

'You've done well, Miss Foxy, very well indeed,' he said. 'A beautiful little boy – Nurse was sorry to have missed the moment of birth but she said you and Mrs Waughman managed excellently.'

'Aye; I never seed a baby born afore; 'twas quite unusual,' Mrs Waughman admitted. 'All them little fingers and toeses an' that . . . an' what a gurt bellow 'e give when I smacked 'is little bum.' She looked down at the baby, lying against Foxy's breast. 'Nice little chap, ain't 'e, Miss Foxy?'

Foxy smiled. She looked down at the face framed in the cream-coloured shawl which, Mr Allsop informed her, had been worn by Mr Laurie and by his father before him, and saw that the baby was a miniature of John, unmistakable, delightful. 'He is lovely,' she said, and was aware of the softening of her own voice. 'He's the image of his father!'

Allsop began to smile and then, to Foxy's surprise and consternation, he ducked his head and she realised there were tears in his eyes. 'Yes, he's a real little Clifton,' he said, and Foxy was guiltily aware of how nearly she had given her secret away. 'Mr Laurie was fair when he was born; kiddies often are, I believe. And now I'd best telephone for the nurse who's coming to look after you both until you're out and about again. She's only in Gloucester, not too far to come.'

'Right,' Foxy said lazily. 'Well, I know I've had a sleep but I could do with another. What's the time?'

'Five o'clock,' Allsop said readily. 'I'm ready for bed myself and I'm sure Mrs Waughman feels the same. I'll leave a note for the staff.'

'Right; could you put the baby in his cot for me, Mr Allsop?'

Allsop came nearer the bed. 'Indeed I could, I'd dearly like to hold him,' he said, his voice creaky with an emotion he could not control. 'I'm proud of you, Miss Foxy, and so will Mr Laurie be, when he hears.'

'And I'm proud of my son,' Foxy said softly. 'What'll we call him, Mr Allsop? I rather like the name Edward.'

Allsop took the baby from her and stood, cradling the child in his arms, looking down into the small face as though he could never have enough of the sight. 'Edward is nice, Miss Foxy; how about calling him Edward Allen? After Lady Clifton? It is a family name.'

'Fine,' Foxy said. Weariness was beginning to catch up with her again and she longed for sleep. 'Oh, by the way, the nurse was awfully good to me, though she wasn't around for the birth. I'd like to buy her some chocolates or something, just to say thank you.'

'Of course; I'll see to it as soon as I can be spared to drive into Ledbury,' Mr Allsop assured her. He laid the baby tenderly in his cot and pulled the blankets up. 'There you are, Master Allen,' he said. 'All warm and cosy. You and your mother can enjoy a nice, long sleep now, after your labours.'

Madrid had changed. The bomb damage was dreadful, of course, but there was another, deeper change. It was hotter, shabbier . . . more hopeless, somehow, Laurie thought as the lorry trundled along the Calle de Alcalá. Yet that was not the whole story. And presently, when he was set down, he was able to pinpoint the change more accurately.

People were no longer happy. The last time he had visited the city there had been taverns, small bars, restaurants, all doing good business. The poor had been desperately underpaid and over-worked but a great many of them, living from hand to mouth, were still happy people. The war had changed all that; now the people were pale and hungry, they jumped at sudden noises, they dodged into doorways when a car back-fired or a dog barked and they were deeply miserable.

But not Mirri. Laurie knocked on the door of Leá's small house and Mirri answered it. She was eating bread and cheese and for a moment she just stared, jaw frozen, hand halfway to her mouth. And then she gave a breathy little crow, spraying him with wet breadcrumbs, and fell into his arms.

'Laurie, Laurie, Laurie! Oh, how wonderful to see you – how the uniform suits you! Oh, I knew you would help us . . . things have been very bad here but with the help of the International Brigade we fought off two fascist attacks . . . oh Laurie, I am so happy!'

She took him indoors, introduced him to her old nurse, someone she described as a foster-sister and a couple of friends. They insisted that he join them at their meal, but when it was over Mirri took him for a walk round the streets, and they found themselves alone at last.

They had walked up into the old part of the city where a great deal of damage had been done by the bombing, but Mirri knew where she was going. She went confidently through the tiny, narrow streets, until they came to a high but crumbling wall. She led him right along it until they reached a hole at ground level no more than a couple of feet high. She dropped to her knees, then looked up at him, her dark, expressive eyes full of laughter.

'Come on, Laurie, here we must crawl!'

He crawled after her and found himself in a tiny fairyland. The house which had once owned this garden was a ruin, but the garden itself, and the little summerhouse, were perfect. The garden was mostly paved, and the raised beds were a riot of colour. The flowers and shrubs had taken over, banning weeds, nettles, briars so that little had to be done to keep the garden in excellent order. In the summerhouse there was a comfortable couch along one wall and a low table before it. There were magazines and a sewing basket, even a piece of embroidery lay on one of the chairs. Wicker furniture, lavishly cushioned, was scattered casually about, and there were ornaments along the window-ledges and pot plants in niches and blue glazed tiles on the floor.

'I found it ages ago,' Mirri confided. 'I've brought a few of my own things and I come here at least once a week to water the plants and keep it tidy. The house is no good but I call this place . . .' she gestured around her, '. . . my own little home. It's quiet and private, you see, and Leá's house is so crowded and noisy now.' She sat down on the couch and patted the cushion beside her. 'Please sit down and rest; I would make you tea, but there is none. However, I always keep a bottle of lemonade in the cupboard – would you like some?'

'No,' Laurie said baldly. He put his arms round her. She was no longer soft and cuddly, melting against him. Now she had a whipcord quality about her, she was strong, spare. All the baby softness had gone, banished by the war and by her work. It made him feel sad, yet he smiled and kissed her gently on the top of her shining head. 'Dear Mirri, you even *feel* different in my arms, but I love you just the same.'

She drew back a little, looking up at him seriously. 'You can't love me the same because I'm a different person and so, I imagine, are you. We shall have to get to know each other all over again, Laurie, when the war's over.'

'Yes, there's a good deal of truth in what you say. But Mirri, my dear, I'm here to arrange for you to go home. To my home, in Herefordshire. I have a good friend taking care of the house for me, she'll welcome you, as my staff will. I shall feel very much better about you when I know you're safe at Clifton Place and not risking your life in Madrid.'

She shook her head at him, smiling indulgently.

'There, you see, how little you know me! This is *my* war, I'm fighting for *my* people. I'm a militiawoman, a member of the armed forces and proud to be so. I can't just walk away whilst they need me and I can't let them go to hell with the Nationalists, for that's what would happen, if Franco won.'

'But I'm here now, sweetheart. I'm fighting the war for your sake,' Laurie pointed out, though even as he said it he knew it wasn't true. Once, it might have been, but not any more. He'd seen terrible things, heard about worse ones. This was his war now, his fight. He would stay as long as he could, as long as there were enemies to fight, and he would do it whether Mirri was in Madrid or safe in his beloved Herefordshire.

'One fights one's own war,' Mirri said. The light was draining from the sky and in the dusk her face looked old, wise, the soft roundness of cheeks and chin quite gone now, the hollows and planes much in evidence. I believe she's less pretty but more beautiful, Laurie found himself thinking. She's an El Greco girl now and she's right, she's a stranger to me. My Mirri was a jolly, selfish little thing. This one ... ah, this one's quite different. And she won't be rescued; how do I handle this?

Mirri solved it. She turned in his arms and kissed him passionately on the mouth, then pulled away when he would have deepened the kiss.

'We must go now, Laurie,' she said a little breathlessly, getting briskly to her feet. 'I have a dear friend – Josefa, you've met her – who thinks that free love is everything. She has a dozen different young men each month and weeps over them all. I'm not like that. I can't do two things at once, I can't love and hate at the same time. Right now I work very hard at hating the Nationalists and I have become good at it. I need that hatred, because one day it may keep me alive. When the war is over, then perhaps I shall be able to love again. But until then we're companions in arms, not lovers. Do you understand?'

Laurie followed her out of the perfect garden through the hole in the wall, then straightened himself up and took Mirri's arm.

'I nearly understand,' he said cautiously. 'But one thing I have to say, darling Mirri. When the war's over, whether it's a good result or a bad one, will you get in touch with me? And if there is ever a time when you feel that further fighting is useless, if you aren't needed or wanted any more, then will you let me know? Write to me at home, because I'm bound to get back there, and anyway I keep in touch, and I'll come for you, carry you off home with me. Will you promise me?'

She was touched; her big eyes filled with tears and she smiled and nodded, then blew her nose vigorously on a tiny handkerchief.

'I promise. If things go badly, or if they go so well that I'm no longer needed, I'll write to you. And . . . thank you, Laurie.'

Later, back at the front, Laurie caught himself wondering whether he wanted to receive such a letter from Mirri, asking to be taken to England. She had seemed so – so *foreign* somehow, so very different from the girls back home. But then he chided himself; any girl would be changed by what she had gone through, by what she must still endure. He was fortunate to have won her love; now he would wait until she turned to him.

It was, after all, the only thing he could do.

Twelve

The kitchen was hot, so Foxy had opened the back door and as she, Allsop, Mrs Waughman and Edith had breakfast, wafts of warm summery air and birdsong drifted in from outdoors.

Edith was the latest addition to the staff. She was a sort of nursery maid – that's to say, she looked after Allen, helped Mrs Waughman in the kitchen and did the things which Foxy was least handy at. She knitted baby bootees, fashioned bibs out of pieces of old towel and soaked dirty nappies in a bucket in the kitchen and then washed them. She was only eighteen, younger than Foxy, but she had a sort of down-to-earth good sense which made her seem older than her years and she and her mistress got on well.

Foxy sometimes wondered why it was that everyone called the baby Allen instead of Edward, but it didn't really matter to her and oddly enough, he seemed more like an Allen than an Edward, anyway. He was such a love, so adorable! He had recently started to smile and she spent ages trying to persuade that wonderful look to spread across his small, fair face, and knew that she was not the only one. Allsop doted on the baby and was often to be found hanging over the high-backed old pram, cooing besottedly.

Edith was proud of working for Miss Foxy up at the Place, though she had shown signs of wanting to address Foxy as 'milady'. Foxy had taken fright at that.

'You promised, Allsop,' she had said threateningly. 'I had to agree to let you tell people, but you said it was to be a – a sort of open secret. And nothing's an open secret if people call me Lady Clifton when you and I know I'm no such thing. If it goes on I'll – I'll take the baby and go somewhere where I'm just Foxy Lockett again.'

It alarmed him, frightened him into agreeing that he would talk to the staff. And you had to give Allsop credit; from that day on Foxy had been Miss Foxy again and no silly nonsense about bobbing a curtsey in the corridor, either.

'Would you like another slice of toast, Miss Foxy?' Edith said now. Mrs Waughman made a cooked breakfast but Edith always hopped up when her eggs and bacon were eaten and made toast beneath the old-fashioned grill.

'No more toast, thanks, Edith,' Foxy said now. 'I'm going out this morning. I'm taking Allen for a walk in his pram.'

'Be you goin' to the village, Miss?' Mrs Waughman asked hopefully. She was always after someone to do a bit of shopping, get her herbs, spices, a few oranges. She loved cooking and enjoyed setting before them food which they would praise her for.

'No, not this morning.' Foxy straightened her shoulders. 'I'm going over to Bees-wing Farm to see Mrs Hoverton. She's not met Allen yet and I'm sure she'd like to see him.'

Because he's her grandson, the sentence should have finished. But it must not, of course. And anyway, if she knew Mrs Hoverton the thought of a bastard grandson would not exactly fill her with joy. One day she might have to know – well, one day she would have to know – but until that day dawned, Allen would just be her shameful bastard offspring so far as Mrs Hoverton was concerned. Unless she'd heard the rumours of a secret marriage, of course.

'Would you like me to run you round in the pony-cart, Miss Foxy?' Allsop asked now, looking anxious. 'It's an awfully long walk and you've not been out and about all that long. It wouldn't take but half an hour, and I could come over for you again later.'

'No thanks, Mr Allsop, I'd rather walk. It's good for me and for the baby, too. I daresay Mrs Hoverton will offer me a bite of lunch, and perhaps she might drive us back by pony-cart. There would be plenty of room for the pram if she used the big one.'

Allsop acquiesced, seeing that she had made up her mind, and Foxy began to prepare for her walk. But she was secretly dreading meeting the Hovertons after so long, particularly the farmer's wife.

What'll I say if she asks me outright? Foxy worried, putting on her coat and straightening Allen's pram-cover. She had sold the little ring Laurie had given her to buy the pram, not wanting to take the money from the estate, and since she had been wearing the ring on a chain round her neck no one had noticed it had gone. She did not worry over what Laurie would say, however; he would understand the need, and John, she assumed, would be relieved. He had never approved of her accepting the ring.

Foxy leaned over the pram and smiled dotingly at her son. He was awake and looking jaunty in a pale blue woolly beret and matching jacket with nice blue leggings on his fat little legs and Edith's latest offering – blue bunny-bootees – on his fat little feet.

No one else has ever dared to ask me straight out if I'm married to Laurie, Foxy's worried thoughts continued, but Mrs Hoverton's known me since I was a little kid, she could ask and I couldn't possibly snub her. I don't know that I want to lie to her, either. Oh drat it, why is life so complicated?

'All ready, Miss Foxy?' Allsop leaned over the pram and made a most unbutlerish noise; a sort of coochy-coo. 'Our little lad's looking very smart, aren't you, Master Allen?'

'If he answered you, that *would* be smart,' Foxy said, preparing to push the pram out into the yard. 'I notice you don't congratulate me on *my* appearance, Mr Allsop, and I put a lot of thought into this get-up.'

'You always look smart, Miss Foxy,' Allsop said with considerable untruthfulness. 'I like you in navy and white.'

'It's a good thing you do, because it's still the only thing I've got that fits me,' Foxy said with unimpaired cheerfulness. The neat navy skirt and jacket with the white piping and the sailor collar had been bought for a few pence at a village jumble sale when, shortly after Allen's birth, Foxy had realised she was not going to get her 22-inch waist back without effort. Now, the skirt was a bit big in the waist but a couple of safety pins saw to that, and it was comfortable, the buttoning jacket coming in useful since she was still breast-feeding.

'Breast-feeding's unfashionable, ladies say it spoils your figure,' Edith had said, only to be told sharply that breast-milk was cheap and that Foxy's figure had never been any great shakes anyway. Edith, blushing, had said that she, personally, believed strongly in mother's milk and had only repeated a remark she had heard another woman utter. Foxy had grinned at the girl and told her she was forgiven but Edith, she knew, would think twice before she made such a remark in future.

'Whoa, horsie,' Foxy said now as she pushed the pram carefully across the cobbled yard, out under the arch and into the lane. 'If I bounce you, Allie love, you'll throw up milk on your nice blue cardigan and then what will Edie say to me?'

Allen gurgled and gazed with his big, dark-blue eyes, at the passing treetops. Foxy, walking stoutly, decided that worrying about the forthcoming visit was useless. Mrs Hoverton was too kind, as well as too polite, to tell her she wasn't welcome at the farm and besides, why should she not be? She might be officially a bad girl, but everyone knew that the hop-pickers were no angels, and Mrs Hoverton had been good to them year after year. Why should she change now?

Allsop was right though; even going cross-country it was a good four miles and Foxy's legs ached by the time she turned into the familiar farmyard. Allen had fallen asleep almost as soon as she started out, undeterred by the rough going, but she pressed on, bringing the pram to a halt right outside the farmhouse. She tapped on the back door and then, greatly daring, opened it a touch.

Mrs Hoverton was sitting at the table, drinking from a blue china cup. She was reading a letter, her face screwed up with concentration, a pair of glasses perched on the end of her nose. She did not hear the door opening and continued to read, so Foxy cleared her throat.

'Ahem! I did knock, Mrs Hoverton, but you didn't hear me . . .'

'Well, if it isn't our Foxy!' Mrs Hoverton jumped to her feet and came across the room, a hand stretched out. 'Nice of you to call, child. I hear you're managing very well up at the Place, whilst Laurie's away. As it happens, I've just received a letter from John, I was absorbed in it, that's why I didn't hear you knock. I don't know if he writes to you . . . ?'

'I've had a couple of letters,' Foxy admitted. 'Umm . . . shall I leave the pram outside, Mrs H? Only Allen's asleep, it seems a shame to wake him.'

'It'll be safe enough out there,' Mrs Hoverton said. She did not so much as glance at the back door, to Foxy's disappointment. She was still at the stage when she could not imagine any living soul not falling in love with Allen after one peep. 'We can have a nice, cosy chat . . . wait on, I'd just made myself a cup of tea, the pot's still hot, and I've scones barely cool from the oven. Come on in and sit yourself down; it's a long walk from the Place, you must be fair wore out.'

'It is a good walk,' Foxy said. 'But I came cross-country, though it wasn't easy getting over some of the meadows; they aren't ideal for pram-travel. Still, I managed.'

'Good, good.' Mrs Hoverton poured a cup of tea and carried it to the table, then went to the dresser where the scones were piled up on a tray to cool, took one, split it, buttered it and handed it to her guest on a small floral plate. 'Now! You'll hear from Laurie regularly, of course? How is my dear boy?'

'Doesn't he write to you?' Foxy asked, surprised. 'I know it's been difficult to write back, or was until he joined the Brigade, but surely he writes now?'

'I've not had a letter from Laurie for two months,' Mrs Hoverton said. 'I don't know for sure, but I think he's a little upset with me.'

'Upset? Why?'

Mrs Hoverton looked self-conscious. 'I'm sure I don't know. I'm as fond of Laurie as I am of John – goodness knows, they were both reared as my children – but ever since the breach, when Sir George simply snatched him away from us, there's been a – a sort of coolness, I think.'

'Not on Laurie's side,' Foxy said firmly. She knew that Laurie was extremely fond of both his foster-parents and would not hurt either of them for the world. She said as much, through a mouthful of scone, and Mrs Hoverton got up and went and helped herself to another cup of tea.

With her back to Foxy, she said, in a muffled voice: 'You're a good girl, Foxy. I don't know why . . . but you know how it is, Father and I had plans for John which he simply couldn't share, and John's always been close to Laurie so I suppose . . .'

'If you're trying to say that Laurie was upset with you because you and Mr Hoverton didn't – didn't take to me, you're wrong,' Foxy said, choosing her words with care. 'He likes me, of course, but you're his mother, certainly he thinks of you as such.'

'*Likes* you? Surely it must be a little more than that – I understand you have considerable power up at the Place, that you pay the wages, have control over the incomings and outgoings . . .'

Foxy, cursing herself, said awkwardly, 'Well . . . perhaps I put it badly. As you say, I'm doing my best to keep the Place running smoothly because that was what Laurie asked me to do. But even so, Laurie wouldn't judge you because you didn't take to me. If you see what I mean.'

'I think I see,' Mrs Hoverton said. She smiled thoughtfully and reached for a second scone. 'Well, well, so that's how matters stand!'

She thinks she's caught me out, that I'm not married to Laurie at all, perhaps not even particularly special to him, Foxy thought, and was surprised by her own annoyance. What right had John's mother to assume that she, Foxy, was the sort of girl who would sleep with a fellow just to get a job whilst he was away fighting?

'*Do* you see, Mrs Hoverton?' she said therefore, in a rather belligerent tone. 'Perhaps you do, but it seems likelier that you don't. What I was trying to say was that Laurie loves you. I don't come into it. What there is between Laurie and me is private, personal.'

Mrs Hoverton's hand was carrying a buttered scone to her mouth; it stopped in mid-flight. Mrs Hoverton cocked her head to one side, her eyes, bright as a robin's, fixed on the younger woman.

'How foolish I am, now you've taken offence,' she said. 'I didn't mean to upset you, my dear, I'm far too fond of you for that. I'm really sorry if I spoke out of turn – there! And now shall I tell you how John is? I know you and he used to be such good friends.'

'Yes, do,' Foxy said with a cordiality she was still far from feeling. 'I expect you know that he and Laurie met at gunnery school in Spain? Only I daresay the course must be almost over by now, so they'll be going back to their companies any time.'

'John's already left,' Mrs Hoverton said. Her face had seemed calculating to Foxy but now it was wiped clear of all expression save that of a helpless, sorrowing love. 'I worry about him so much, because he was such an aggressive little boy, so determined always to fight for the underdog. I can't see my John letting anyone else go into danger when he was there to go himself. And he's gone back to that dreadful valley . . . it's just outside Madrid and the fighting's very hot there. John doesn't say so, of course, but I do read the newspapers.'

'I know. I worry about both of them,' Foxy said. Mrs Hoverton probably hadn't meant to be nasty, she told herself, it was just natural curiosity. She thought if she gave me a hard time she'd discover the truth about Laurie and me, and all she got was a polite brick-wall. And now she had lowered her guard and was showing Foxy the worried mother beneath the practical, efficient farmer's wife. 'It's a vile war – I don't know which side is worse, but if half the stories are true . . . well, I just want our boys to come home.'

'That's how I feel,' Mrs Hoverton said. 'Can I persuade you to stop for a bite of dinner, love? Mr Hoverton would love to see you . . . I could drive you home afterwards, in the pony-cart.'

Foxy had thought she wanted the invitation, now she realised she did not. 'Thank you, but I shall have to get back,' she said with false regret, rising to her feet. 'It's been lovely; perhaps I could come back again, when I have more time?'

Mrs Hoverton stood up too; there was genuine regret in her expression now, genuine kindness in her eyes. 'I shouldn't have questioned you the way I did,' she said simply. 'You didn't like it and I don't blame you. But don't you think you could forgive me? Stay for dinner and let me take you home afterwards?'

'Of course I forgive you, but I have to feed my baby,' Foxy said gently. 'And change him, too. Babies are a great responsibility, Mrs Hoverton.'

As she spoke she turned to the back door. Mrs Hoverton went ahead of her and opened it. 'Ah yes, the baby.' She leaned over the pram, pulling back the covers a little way. 'My, isn't he like Laurie was as a baby? But you wouldn't know that, of course. Not so dark, though . . . I wonder if he'll have your hair colour one of these days, Foxy dear? . . . but still very like.' She reached out a hand and stroked the petal-soft cheek. 'What a little love,' she said softly. 'How I wish . . . oh look, he's waking up!'

'If you don't mind my feeding him in your front room, then I suppose I could stay,' Foxy said gruffly after a moment during which the unknowing grandmother cooed to the child. 'Would – would you like to hold him?'

'Oh, I would,' breathed Mrs Hoverton. She leaned into the pram and plucked the child out, cooing to him all the time, then held him for a moment against her cheek. 'How soft his skin is – I'd forgotten how soft! Now you must come indoors, little man, so that Mummy can change you and Gran can watch.' She turned to Foxy, her eyes very bright. 'Since I think of Laurie as my son, naturally, I think of his child as my grandson,' she said simply. 'But I have no right . . .'

'It's fine by me,' Foxy said. 'But please, Mrs H, don't mention the baby to Laurie – or to John, for that matter. I've not said anything because it would be a sort of blackmail to get Lo back, and I won't descend to such tricks. He – he'll come back when he's ready.'

'I see. Very well, I'll say nothing. But my dear, I don't want to worry you but the child is heir to a great estate. Wouldn't it be fairer if he had a father as well as a mother? Should something happen to Laurie . . .'

'It's all right; we've made provision,' Foxy lied. She gently detached the baby from Mrs Hoverton's grasp and began to undo her jacket. 'Will it be all right if I feed him now? It won't take me more than twenty minutes.'

'Yes, of course. Did you bring a clean nappy? I've probably still got some upstairs, from the days when John and Laurie were small. You can imagine what a heap of the things two babies needed . . . and how I hated washdays!'

'I brought a couple of clean ones, one muslin, one towelling,' Foxy admitted. She twinkled at her hostess. 'Just in case we let bygones be bygones and you asked me to dinner!'

The pony-cart made short work of the journey which had taken Foxy most of the morning, so it was just about time for what Allsop always referred to as 'afternoon tea' when Foxy, having waved Mrs Hoverton off, pushed the pram back into the kitchen. Mrs Waughman, peeling vegetables at the sink, informed her that Edith was redding up the nursery and Mr Allsop was cleaning and jointing two rabbits which Fletcher had brought in.

'Did you 'ave a good day, Miss?' she asked, as Foxy began to take the baby out of his pram. 'I 'spec' Mrs 'Overton took to the little feller, eh? Women do love babies. I do meself.'

'Yes, thank you, it was a nice day,' Foxy said primly. 'Can you keep an eye on Allie, Mrs Waughman, whilst I go and tell Allsop we're back? Are the rabbits for dinner tonight, incidentally? Because if they are, I'll just nip down to the garden and pick some herbs – what do you need with rabbit?'

Foxy was proud of her tiny herb garden, but Mrs Waughman shook her head. 'Don't need no 'erbs, Miss Foxy, 'cos I sent young Edith down for 'em an hour since. But I wouldn't mind a few redcurrants, if there's any on the bushes.'

'I'll look,' Foxy said. She took the colander from its hook by the sink and left the house, going through the yard, across the side lawn and into the kitchen garden. She and Allsop had decided to make the kitchen garden their business since Hector was getting too old to manage the formal garden and the vegetables too, and Foxy found she enjoyed weeding, seeding and harvesting her crop. Now, she went to the currant bushes and picked a dozen or so fine strings, dropping them into the colander, then walked slowly back along the narrow, box-edged path, eyeing the neat rows of vegetables but thinking deeply.

One moment she thought that Mrs Hoverton knew the baby was John's, the next she was equally certain she did not. To be sure, Allen was fair-skinned and blond, but he was too young to show a strong resemblance to anyone, or so Foxy told herself. It was true that on first looking into his little face she had seen John mirrored there, but that was shortly after the moment of birth. Since then he had begun to alter subtly, to look less like – well, less like a sort of reddish caricature and more like a child. And colouring aside, so far as Foxy could see he was just a baby, though a very attractive one. Putty nose, big blue eyes, blob of a chin, fluffy, pale yellow hair . . . no, it just wasn't possible that Mrs Hoverton should see a likeness to anyone at all. Had she not remarked how like Laurie the baby was? That, surely, proved that all babies resemble each other.

Slowly, she returned to the kitchen. She handed the colander and its contents to Mrs Waughman, who made contented noises and said that there was nothing like redcurrant jelly to turn roast rabbit from an ordinary meal into a feast, and then went in search of Allsop. She found him in the butler's pantry. He had finished skinning and jointing the rabbits and was arranging a great many pink, scarlet and dark red roses in an enormous crystal bowl.

'We're back, Mr Allsop,' Foxy said, entering the room. 'How lovely those roses look – are we having visitors?'

'No, not today, but I'm practising, you might say, because after a christening it's customary, Miss Foxy, to give a tea. Godparents will of course be invited, and various others. Mrs Waughman has already made the cake, though it is not yet iced.'

'Christening? But I'm not having a party after he's christened; I didn't even know he was going to *be* christened,' Foxy said, alarm sharpening her voice. 'Really, Mr Allsop, you can't just push me the way you want me to go, you know. Because I'm not married to Laurie I'm in an invidious position anyway. I refuse to make it worse by going through the charade of a christening, let alone a party.'

'It's expected, Miss,' Allsop said reproachfully. 'Even if the boy was just – well, just a village by-blow, if you'll excuse me using such language in your presence – he would be christened. What would the Reverend Chamberlain say if you announced you did not intend to christen your son?'

'I don't know,' Foxy said sulkily. 'And frankly, Mr Allsop, I don't care. I haven't been to church since Allen was born, and I didn't go much before, come to that. Why should he expect me to christen Allen?'

'Because everyone has their babies christened, everyone halfway decent,' Allsop said sharply. 'And because Mr Laurie would be distraught if he knew you were contemplating not christening his son, regardless of whether the child was born in wedlock or not. I agree, reluctantly mind, that perhaps it might be a mistake to have a big party, but I think you must have the godparents back to tea, and the vicar and one or two personal friends.'

'I *can't*,' Foxy wailed. 'Mr Chamberlain might ask me about the wedding; I can't lie to a vicar! Well, I suppose I could, but he might find out and – and excommunicate me or something.'

'He won't do any such thing. He's far too vague and woolly,' Allsop pointed out. 'He probably thinks he married you and Mr Laurie himself; he's getting so old and doddery he forgets who he is half the time, let alone who others are. Now come along, Miss, be sensible, then we can start to plan times and dates and so on.'

'But – but I haven't got any personal friends,' Foxy said desperately. 'I only know the staff here, the Hovertons, a few farmers and their wives and the Bees-wing farmhands. Oh, and I'd like to ask the nurse – I think she lives in the village, so she can easily pop over. She was awfully kind to me when I was so silly and frightened. It's no use asking Auntie Bea because she won't come; she's too busy with her boarding house.'

'There you are, then, you have a great many personal friends,' Allsop said triumphantly. 'The staff would all come, naturally, and the Hovertons. You make a list, Miss, and we'll send out proper invitations as soon as the Reverend has given us a firm date.'

'Well, all right, but I don't like it,' Foxy muttered. 'I'm living a lie, Mr Allsop, and it's you that's making me.'

Mr Allsop tutted. 'Living a lie indeed, Miss Foxy! How *extremely* melodramatic. All you're doing is anticipating what is to come, in order to make your son's life easier. Now run along and make me a list of the people you wish to invite, if you please. We haven't got all day, I want this christening performed before Master Allen's so old that he walks into the church unaided!'

A few weeks later Foxy emerged from the church feeling, if possible, guiltier than ever over the deception she was practising. Around her, people murmured nice things about the baby, asked after Sir Laurie, chuckled over the fact that Master Allen had squalled loud enough to release a hundred devils when he found himself unexpectedly doused in cold water.

Everything had been arranged by Allsop, of course, and no one had murmured a word about such a christening being a trifle over-elaborate for the illegitimate son of a one-time hop-picker. So well had Allsop done his work, using the tools of rumour, innuendo and a pretence of total frankness to spread the story he wanted spread, that there had not been a person in the church who did not believe him or herself to be attending the christening of the legitimate son of Sir Laurence Clifton.

It had called for a great deal of organising and downright hard work, too. Allsop had made lists, sent out invitations, planned, spent money, whilst Foxy had told him grandly that he might do as he wished since she was washing her hands of the whole business.

'Very well, Miss Foxy. Now the cake is made and decorated – no, Miss Foxy, you may not see it, since you would be bound to want to alter something – and the food is prepared. We couldn't run to champagne . . .'

'Thank God!' interposed Foxy fervently.

'. . . But I have a good white wine chilling in a bucket down the well,' Mr Allsop continued coolly. 'And Mrs Waughman washed the christening gown in milk and pressed it with a cool iron and it looks just as it should – it's very old, you know. The Reverend Chamberlain has all the details written down, which is just as well, otherwise you might find your son rejoicing in the names of Phillipa Mary, and since you very sensibly asked Mr and Mrs Hoverton to be godparents and they are good people, you will be respectably turned out. Master Allen, of course, will look just as he ought; old lace is old lace. Now is there anything else?'

Assuming that Allsop was referring to the christening gown when he mentioned old lace, Foxy hoped he was right. The gown had been used for generations of Clifton young, Allsop told her, but putting a small boy in coffee-coloured lace seemed a bit pansy to her. Still, she had faith in Allsop; he undoubtedly knew how to do things properly.

When the service began she knew she had been right to leave it to Allsop, save for one small detail. She had been astonished and angry when Mr Hoverton, holding the baby in his arms and reading from the piece of paper thoughtfully provided by Allsop, announced that the child's names were Edward Allen Laurence St John.

But reproaching Allsop never got her far so she contented herself with a glare to which he responded with a look of such polite puzzlement that she almost forgot herself and laughed aloud.

And now, outside the church, she was greeting her guests and sorting them out between the various cars. The Hovertons, as godparents, would take her, Allsop and the baby back to the house. Mrs Waughman and Edith had left the service unobtrusively before the end so that Hector could return them to the kitchen to add final touches to the christening tea.

Foxy was wearing a coffee-coloured dress and jacket, with

brown shoes and a pair of brown silk gloves. She felt smart and sophisticated, she felt like Lady Clifton, but she still gave Allsop a vicious nudge when she got him in the back of the Hovertons' dark-blue motor car.

'You've been and gone and done it now!' she hissed indignantly. 'How could you saddle the poor kid with all those names? I mean – St John of all things, as though he were on a crusade or something.'

'It's pronounced "Sinjun", as if you didn't know, and Cliftons are always called Laurence St John or St John Laurence; I thought you knew that. The other names are the choice of the parents,' Allsop said mildly. 'Folk would have been most surprised if he'd been called anything else.'

'Well, but . . . Ah, that reminds me,' Foxy said, wisely changing her grievance in the face of Allsop's reasonable reply. 'I asked you to invite the nurse, you said you had – but where was she?'

'Wasn't she there? Probably she had a confinement to attend,' Allsop whispered soothingly. 'I assure you, Miss Foxy, that I would never flaunt your wishes.'

'Unless it was for my own good,' Foxy hissed. 'And why was that other awful woman invited? That Bottomley person? I saw her peering at her prayer book and singing flat.'

'Mrs Bottomley is the nurse, and you said to invite the nurse,' Allsop said patiently. 'So why are you grumbling?'

'Oh, she isn't the nurse, she's the midwife. No, I meant the nurse, the one who came in first but left when Mrs Bottomley arrived. Late, of course. She was awfully nice, that nurse, I'm sure I've seen her around the village but I don't know her name. You know, Mr Allsop, you went and fetched her and she stayed with me almost up to the birth.'

Allsop frowned.

'I went into the village, but I brought Mrs Bottomley back, her assistant had already left for another case. I didn't actually see her at all, I hadn't realised she had come on here. What did she look like?'

'She was quite tall and very slim and she was wearing a blue dress with a white collar and cuffs. She had nice dark-brown hair, done in a low bun thing on the back of her neck, sort of old-fashioned, I thought. She had blue-grey eyes and she wore a very pretty ring, I think it's called an opal. A shimmery, greeny-blue stone.'

There was a long silence during which Allsop stared out of the window and Foxy stared at the back of his head. Then he spoke.

'A nurse. A nurse wearing an opal ring,' he said thoughtfully, still keeping his voice low in deference to the Hovertons in the front seats, though they were talking animatedly about mutual friends met in church. 'Unusual. However, I fear I misunderstood you, Miss Foxy, thinking you meant Mrs Bottomley, and I'm sorry for it. As for young Allen bearing the family names, as I've already said, it was expected by those who know the Cliftons. I had no choice but to add them to the other names. Why, Sir Laurence would have insisted on it had he been present.'

'Don't change the subject . . .' Foxy began, just as the car turned in between the tall stone gateposts and Mrs Hoverton looked over her shoulder, smiled dotingly at the baby and addressed Foxy.

'Wasn't little Allen good? Will you take him out of his christening gown as soon as you get indoors? Only it would be so dreadful if it got marked or torn. Mr Allsop was saying it's probably two or three hundred years old.'

Foxy answered politely and then turned to ask Allsop again just who he thought the woman was, but he was busy telling the Hovertons all about the christening gown, how the lace was handmade, the satin specially purchased in Paris, and he went on talking to them, calmly but persistently, until they arrived at the house.

After that, it was all go. It was not a big party by Clifton standards, Foxy supposed, but even so she was kept busy until the last guest had left. And even then there was Allen to bath, change, feed and put to bed before she could go downstairs and tackle Allsop on the subject uppermost in her mind.

Mrs Waughman was washing up and Allsop was wiping, his black tail coat discarded, his striped shirt sleeves rolled up, a voluminous green apron protecting him from flying suds. Foxy, entering quickly, thought what a domestic scene it made, then remembered that she was still cross with Allsop. He took too

340

much on himself, that was the trouble. How she was going to explain away christening her child Laurence St John, when she knew all the time that he was a Hoverton, she could not imagine, and saying that it was all the butler's fault would not go down well in any company.

But it had happened, and there was nothing she could do about it. What she wanted to know now was the name of the woman who had been with her right up to her baby's birth. Allsop knew a lot more than he admitted, she was sure of it from the protracted silence which had greeted her question and the fact that he had turned his head away rather than look her in the face.

Accordingly, she went into the kitchen and picked up a tea-towel. 'Let me help you,' she said briskly. 'Mr Allsop, I'd like a word when you've finished here.'

'We're almost through, Miss Foxy,' Mrs Waughman said, clattering a fistful of tea-forks onto the draining board with a wet and wrinkled hand. 'If you want a word wi' Mr Allsop yur, jest you go ahead. I'll finish the rest meself, no bother.'

'Thanks, Mrs Waughman,' Foxy said gratefully. 'I'll go to the study, Mr Allsop, and wait for you there.'

She guessed that the butler would want to remove his apron and don his jacket before leaving the kitchen and so it proved. Five minutes ticked past, then Allsop appeared in the splendour of his tail coat. He stood before the desk, looking over her right shoulder, very wooden and correct.

'Yes, Miss?'

'Who was the woman I mistook for a nurse? I think you know, Mr Allsop.'

There was another silence, then Allsop said: 'She used to work here once, Miss Foxy. I daresay she wandered in and heard you call out. She was always a very thoughtful young woman.'

'Oh,' Foxy said, taken aback. She did not know what she had expected to hear, but it wasn't that the young woman had once been employed at the Place. 'What was her name?'

'I don't recall, Miss Foxy. Was that all?'

'No, it was not! What was she doing, wandering around the building? Where is she now?'

Allsop removed his gaze from whatever it rested on and looked full at Foxy. His eyes were dark with foreboding. 'I could be wrong.'

Foxy repressed a wild desire to scream and hit him. If there was ever a master of prevarication it was the man who stood before her. 'Who, *you*, Mr Allsop?' she said frostily. 'Wrong? You astonish me.'

Mr Allsop actually smiled, though it was a fleeting expression. 'It's not unknown, Miss Foxy,' he said. 'I am the last person to claim I'm infallible.'

'Right. We've got that sorted out. Then what was the woman doing, wandering around the Place? And where is she now?'

There was a pregnant silence. The butler spoke.

'She – she must like the old place. She's often here. She – she – ' He stopped speaking but continued to stare steadily over Foxy's shoulder. 'She lived here once,' he said slowly. 'A long time ago.'

'You're trying to tell me she's a ghost. I don't believe it for one moment,' Foxy said, trying to sound scornful and self-assured whilst the hair rose gently on the nape of her neck and cold shivers ran down her spine. 'She was no such thing, she was just an ordinary young woman, I couldn't see through her, her head was on her shoulders not under her arm, she wasn't pale or ill-looking, she was just ordinary, like I am.'

Allsop nodded. He looked supremely unhappy. 'Yes, Miss, so just let's leave it that I can't tell who the young person was, shall we?'

'No!' squeaked Foxy. 'Allsop, I'll ask you once more and if you prevaricate again I'll – I'll take the baby and go and live with the Hovertons, as a housekeeper or something. Mrs Hoverton says Laurie's like a son to her so she feels Allen is the next best thing to a grandson, which means she could scarcely deny me a roof over my head. Now! Who is she?'

Allsop spoke immediately; clearly the threat of leaving the Place still held good so far as the butler was concerned.

'Lady Clifton,' he said.

'Please don't call me a name to which I'm not entitled,' Foxy began angrily. 'It doesn't make things any easier if you persist . . .'

'The late Lady Clifton,' Allsop said. 'Now are you satisfied, Miss Foxy?'

*

John was sitting in a patch of shade under an olive tree, reading his latest letter from Foxy. It was evening, and the worst of the sweltering heat was over but even so, as he frowned down at the sheet before him, sweat dripped off his nose and plopped onto the page.

'Want a game of poker, *Teniente*?'

John looked up; Vicente Trujillo was a good young man, a natural soldier, and normally John would have joined in the game willingly enough, for pay mounted up for the International Brigade. Even on the princely sum of five pesetas a day one could scarcely help saving, because there was so little on which to spend the money. Poker with one's men, who had homes and families desperate for every penny, helped to spread spare cash around a bit. But Foxy's letter was complicated and important; he needed time to think about it, time to read it over and over.

'Sorry, Trujillo; later, perhaps.'

'Right, *Teniente*,' the boy said good-humouredly. 'It is good to have letters from home; I love it when my sweetheart, Lidia, writes to me.'

He wandered off and John began to read the letter over again, his eyebrows shooting up towards his hairline as he did so. Foxy had told him about the baby shortly after the christening. She had realised that if she did not mention it, someone else was bound to do so. The farmhands occasionally penned a card to him, his mother wrote weekly, so the chances of Foxy keeping her secret were few and far between.

He had been pleased, of course he had. The trouble was, England seemed so far away, so – so *unreal*, somehow. The vivid image of Foxy which had helped him through his first months in this most foreign of lands had dimmed almost imperceptibly until she was just a picture postcard, a girl who had made love with him very sweetly, a soft, pliable red-haired creature of passion and warmth who would undoubtedly have married him by now, had things been different.

His little son was a complication he could not come to terms with and, to be fair to Foxy, she did not want him to try to do so. '*Allen seems just my child, it's as though no one else was involved,*' she had written, almost apologetically, when she told him about the baby. *'Allsop is delighted with him and your parents love him dearly, but that's because he's a very attractive little boy. I simply adore him, I'm happy just to be his mother, it worries me not at all that no one, save me, knows the truth about him. So please, dear John, don't think of acknowledging him or doing anything rash, like coming home. We are managing very well, Allen and I.'*

But in this letter she had admitted that, when John did come home, there would be complications.

'Everyone thinks Allen is Laurie's son,' she wrote. *'Even your mother, John. So I'm wondering if it might not be best if we go away when you come home? Otherwise, and this is my only original idea, Laurie and I will have to have a big fight and I shall have to storm out, with the baby under my arm, and then marry you and let people say it was on the rebound. What do you think?'*

If he was honest, John thought it was all a bit melodramatic, a bit absurd. Why should everyone assume that the child was Laurie's, just because Foxy was living at the Place? Everyone who knew the three of them knew Foxy had always liked him best, knew his parents had more or less forbidden them to marry. Surely it was self-evident that the kid was his?

But the truth was that it simply didn't seem important. Who fathered a baby and who didn't was scarcely a matter of life and death, and this war was all about just that – life and death. I might be killed tomorrow, John thought impatiently, and that would solve one problem. Or Laurie might be killed, which would solve another.

In the time John had been in Spain he had seen countless people die, had heard of the deaths of thousands of others. He could not imagine going home again, being ordinary, farming the land. Here, the steady march of the seasons which he knew and loved so well back home did not happen. The gentle dying fall of autumn was unknown to them, as was the subtle rebirth of spring. The soldiers frequently remarked that the weather either froze the balls off you or burned them off; half-measures were unknown. John had watched the locals gather oranges in February and olives in August, but none of it seemed to bear any relationship to the crops he harvested back home. He watched peasants hand-hoeing the fields, ploughs being pulled by oxen, little boys stone-gathering, bent old women in universal black milking a skinny cow or a mean-eyed goat, and could not believe that this was still happening. Spain seemed stuck in biblical times, unaware that for the rest of Europe the twentieth century had arrived.

And the desolate landscape of the battlefields did not help, because one front is very like another once the fighting becomes fierce. Sunbaked earth, untidy trenches which constantly collapse because of the nature of the soil in which they are dug, aerial bombardment from the sky which is almost impossible to guard against, and the barrage from the enemy's big guns. These were all problems which John, now acting lieutenant, or *teniente*, in charge of a company of 150 soldiers, had to face on their behalf daily.

And he had soon realised that so long as he could make England seem like a distant dream, he could enjoy what he was doing, see it as a challenge and a crusade. Fascism with all its faces was abhorrent to him and although he very soon realised that the Republicans pulled in different directions, argued constantly, weakened their own cause by their bickering and did great wrongs to their own people, he fought for them. Simple peasants who had never been able to lift their heads deserved better than the likes of Franco; they deserved a chance.

So John wanted to win the war, and that meant sticking to his guns. He and Jack were together still, but Frankie had been wounded at the battle of Brunete and invalided home and Laurie had gone ahead of them, with a bunch of recruits, to defend another town which had stood out against the fascists.

'We'll meet up from time to time,' he had said as he and John, after a very happy week at the officer training school, went their separate ways. 'At least I'm official now – I've written to Mirri and Mum and dear old Foxy, giving them my address – so I've had mail, and wherever they send me in future I'll continue to receive mail and parcels and proper medical treatment if I'm ill. You've no idea what a relief that is!'

'I can guess,' John told him. 'I felt pretty uncomfortable alone on Gloucester platform until I met up with Jack and Frankie. You must have felt a hundred times worse.'

'A thousand,' Laurie said with a rueful grin. 'Because I'm not like you, John, willing to throw myself into anything that's going. I'm the solitary type.'

'Not any more you aren't,' John had pointed out. 'This whole business has changed you, bro; you'll never dither again, you'll just go for it.'

'Like you do, you mean? Perhaps. But we're still different, John, with different aims. There are times when it isn't enough to be doing my duty by my men, trying to win this war. I simply want to be back in Herefordshire tackling my own particular problems, and if I could go without losing face, I might do just that. But I don't think you would, would you?'

'Probably not. I've made too many friends, seen too many good men die. No, I'll stick around until we've either won or lost altogether. Not that we shall lose, of course.'

'Of course,' Laurie had echoed. 'You'll write to me when you've got a moment?'

'Or come and see you, if we're posted anywhere in the same vicinity. So long, Lo.'

'So long, Johnny. Take care.'

They had parted lightly, easily, but John had known a considerable sense of satisfaction just because he need no longer worry over Laurie. He knew where his foster-brother was and could find out how he fared. In wartime, that meant a lot.

Laurie knew about the baby, but seemed completely indifferent. He feels like I do, John told himself; it isn't a life and death matter so it isn't important, and besides, Foxy's probably exaggerating. There's absolutely no reason for anyone to assume the child is Laurie's get just because she's working at the house! Would they? No, of course not, he comforted himself. Laurie's got it right.

'*Once I'm home we'll sort it all out,*' Laurie had said comfortably in his last letter to John. '*Folk will soon see the error of their ways when I take Mirri back with me to Britain, and then you can storm in and grab your Foxy and carry her off, old fellow. Never fear I'll try and stop you; I'm very fond of the girl, she's done me a good turn, but that's the extent of my involvement with her.*'

So having decided that Foxy was probably panicking over nothing, John folded the letter and got up off the ground. She was a good kid, Foxy Lockett. She was doing Laurie a good turn, keeping his house in order whilst he was away, and his own mother had spoken highly of her. When I do go home, and tell everyone we're going to get married, they'll not worry over who fathered the kid, he told himself. These things happen all the time, I daresay. It isn't as if she and Laurie were married – that would make things difficult, because I daresay there hasn't been a divorce in our family, let alone the Cliftons', for a hundred years. But a bit of pre-marital bed-hopping – well, that could always be put right by a nice church wedding. Well-known fact.

And John strolled off to get himself a meal before returning to the front at the end of his twenty hours off.

Mirri, Josefa and Jacinta were sitting on the parched grass in one of the small garden squares in the city centre, off-duty for once and trying to relax. The three of them spent most of their spare time together since Inma had been badly wounded whilst defending the city the previous winter. She had been sent to Valencia and had not returned, though she had written to say she would probably be doing office work in future at the headquarters of the Communist Party.

Furthermore, though the Nationalist army had scaled down both its air attacks and the continual shelling of Madrid, enormous damage had been done both to the city itself and to morale. The air raids, almost always carried out at night now, were heartily dreaded and the shelling, though it seemed most of the shells landed on the poor area of the city which was already almost flattened, still increased the toll of dead and injured.

Mirri, Jacinta and Josefa, being part of the militia, knew, too, that the war was not going well elsewhere. Franco had taken the industrial north and a great many Republican soldiers had gone over to him after his victory, disgusted by the lack of support they had received and the contradictory orders, filtering as they did through Russian advisers, which they felt had led to defeat.

'They are traitors, they disgust me,' Mirri had stormed as she and Josefa listened to the wireless set in the hotel which was the militia headquarters for as long as it remained standing. 'How can men do such things?'

But Jacinta, who was a communist and totally dedicated to the cause, was noncommittal. And that evening, when they were at home, with Leá cooking them a meal of beans and rice, she told Mirri that she despaired of their leaders.

'They won't pull together; they would sooner see our Republic crumble beneath the heel of the fascist dictator than let one faction or the other have their own way over the tiniest detail. People like that will finish us off more quickly and neatly than a thousand Francos or a million fascist troops. I begin, at last, to despair, little sister.'

Mirri had been horrified to hear the girl she looked up to and trusted talking in such a defeatist fashion, but the following day Jacinta said she had been unduly pessimistic and exhorted Mirri to work like a slave and prove to everyone that militiawomen could do anything a militiaman could do. And as the days passed she appeared to regain her usual conviction that they would win the war. So Mirri followed suit and tried to hide her own unease.

'Only another month or six weeks of this heat and we'll all be shivering again,' Jacinta observed now. She was industriously knitting what looked like a scarf though the colours – pink and white – seemed distinctly unmilitary.

'Who's that for?' Mirri asked. 'What brave comrade is going to be fool enough to wrap that object round his neck?'

Jacinta was a poor knitter; she scowled at her friends, grinning at her efforts, and rolled the scarf defensively round the needles. 'It's for me. I can wear it under my battledress when we're in the trenches. Or I might give it to Leá. She feels the cold, poor darling.'

Leá's little house had been totally destroyed by shells but, with the stoicism showed by so many in a similar position, she had simply commandeered another tiny scrap of a house, wedged between two larger ones. Because the girls were able to bring her their rations she – and they – fared a great deal better than most of the population but even so, the little woman spent hours every day searching for food and, when she found it, preparing and cooking it. Horse meat, donkey, goat, were all luxuries now. Mirri some-times suspected they ate cats and dogs, but she never voiced the thought. With provisions trucks so rare and the peasants keeping well clear of the city you ate what you could when you could, just to stay alive.

Mirri finished the last of her bread and olives, sighed and rolled over onto her stomach. It was breathlessly hot and she was bored and restless. For a week now nothing had happened, even the shelling had ceased, and after so much fear and danger the sudden cessation was bound to be hard to bear. She had heard about the defeats in the north, the awful, pointless slogging-match at Brunete, but it was hard to understand why they had happened or whether they were, in fact, as important as some people thought.

In Madrid they had beaten back the fascist troops in five or six weeks of intensive fighting, and everyone said that whoever held Madrid held Spain. If you believed that, then what did the north matter? And you never knew when Franco's army would return to make Madrid its objective once more. So the girls continued to man the trenches, to keep their rifles loaded and well-oiled, even for what was, at present, merely a watching and listening brief. Attacks can develop almost overnight, their officers told them, and the girls, who knew as well as they did that the uneasy peace would suddenly end, nodded and almost – not quite, but almost – wished something would happen, just to break the monotony.

Earlier in the year, men on leave had come into the city on furlough, but what with shortage of food and the generals' distrust of uniformed men not known to them, plus the fact that so many had been killed, a good deal of such leave had been stopped. Indeed, a curfew was in force – after 2100 hours only accredited military personnel were allowed on the streets – and most of the bars and cafés closed early because there was very little beer, wine was in short supply and coffee was a luxury only seen, it was said, by combatants. Which meant that men on leave could find better places to spend their time than in a big, dirty, war-weary city.

'Are you bored, little Mirri? Then why not write a letter to your man; he's at the front, isn't he? Men at the front love to receive letters,' Jacinta advised. 'Or go and see if you can buy some lemons; Leá makes such marvellous lemonade, if she can get hold of sufficient sugar or honey. And lemons, of course.'

'There must be millions of lemons on the trees in Seville and Valencia,' Mirri said wistfully. 'Do you know, there's a rumour that our masters are deliberately not bringing food into the city? One of the militia told me it's because Madrid, as it stands, with a great many extremely hungry people, is more of a liability than an asset. They think Franco won't attack because if he held Madrid he'd have to feed everyone.'

'I thought they were going to murder all the men and rape all the women and then set fire to what was left,' Jacinta said. Earlier in the year hysterical and terrifying stories had been deliberately circulated concerning the atrocities inflicted on their prisoners by the fascist army. 'Remember that fellow by the Puerta del Sol? The stories he told made my flesh creep. But I wouldn't mind a drink. Why don't we all go and see if we can scrounge some coffee or lemonade out of someone?'

'Because we're resting, for once,' Josefa said lazily. She was polishing someone's belt buckle. Mirri leaned over and flicked it. 'Whose is that?' she asked. 'Not another feller, Jo?'

Josefa grinned. Despite her sturdy stature and square, plain face she always had a new fellow on hand. Jacinta said, without malice, that it was because she was too generous, but Josefa didn't seem, to Mirri, to give much away. Apart from a few small tasks such as polishing a belt buckle, cleaning a pair of shoes or darning a torn shirt, she did very little for her swains. She allowed them to buy her blackmarket cakes or sweets and take her to a theatre or a restaurant, but other than that it was just long walks and quite a lot of hand-holding.

'No, not another feller,' she said now, continuing to polish. 'It's the same one. That Norwegian. I like blond men.'

'Don't know any,' Mirri said. She pulled a pale thread of grass and began to chew the stalk. 'Does he give you fags?'

'Sometimes,' Josefa admitted. 'Why? Have you run out?'

Mirri had never seen a woman smoke until she joined the militia; now she enjoyed a cigarette whenever she could get hold of one.

'I have no connections, no *enchufado*,' Mirri said dolefully. 'Give me a little cigarette, darling Josefa, and when I am next in the money I'll repay you.'

'A uniform means you are *enchufado*,' Jacinta pointed out. 'The military can get anything they want, you know that.'

'Then let's go and get some smokes,' Mirri said, jumping up. In the blazing heat her energy was amazing but though Jacinta groaned she got up as well.

'Everything but cigarettes, because there aren't any,' Jacinta remarked as they set off. 'Still, we can go and talk nicely to the men. They get a ration whenever there are any available. Pity your boyfriend doesn't know you smoke; he could send you some.'

'I wouldn't take cigarettes from a soldier at the front,' Mirri said automatically. 'I wonder what he's doing now?'

'Sweating,' Jacinta said. 'Have you noticed, the International Brigade sweat much more than Spaniards?'

'Oh, phooey! Last winter you said the Italians froze to their guns and died without firing a shot which showed they were effete southerners, and then someone here told me the same thing had happened to her young brother. Everyone suffers the same when the temperature soars or drops.'

'No, but they say the International boys go into battle naked to the waist,' Jacinta said, widening her eyes. 'If that isn't decadent I don't know what is. Our men keep their shirts on!'

'I wouldn't have minded being naked to the waist myself at noon,' Mirri observed. 'Except that my shoulders would probably burn.' They had reached the Calle de Alcalá, with the Gardens of the Ministry of War on their left and the Cibeles Fountain before them. 'Where shall we try for lemons?'

'Well, nowhere here,' Jacinta said, looking up the vast, tree-lined street, and then peering into the blue sky. 'Let's cross over.'

'After the tram,' Mirri said, catching hold of her arm. 'Honestly, Jacinta, you still cross a street as a peasant crosses a field. One of these days . . .'

'There are so few trams now that I never think about them,' Jacinta said. 'Anyway, whenever I come out onto one of the main roads I'm busier looking for shells or enemy aircraft than for trams. However, I've survived the Moors and the German bombing from the air, so I don't intend to be mown down by one of our own vehicles.'

'They usually shell us at nights; but you're right, it's become instinctive to look up before crossing an open space,' Mirri agreed. 'No doubt it will be the death of us yet – jay-walking whilst avoiding enemy fire!'

The three girls crossed the road and hurried on their way, reaching their destination in good time. The lemons were easy to

351

buy, but the block of hard, grey-looking sugar came from under the counter and was handed over with a black look. Mirri felt guilty, but Jacinta said they worked hard and needed drinks.

'Who would have got the stuff otherwise?' she asked. 'It's all blackmarket or *enchufado*, we're agreed on that. So why should some fat old Russian or one of the top brass who want lemons to slice into their whisky as a little extra get what means a lot to us? Don't feel guilty over depriving them, little sister, militiawoman is a proud title and we've earned it by hard work. And now let's go back to HQ, to see what our duties are to be for the next twenty-four hours.'

They strolled back to the mansion which had been requisitioned by the army and went into the empty, echoing front hallway and over to the notice board.

'We're on roadblock guard,' Mirri said with disgust, as they stood in front of the cork board with the day's duties pinned up on it. 'A waste of time and energy; because of the curfew the only people liable to pass will be military, on official business.'

'Or spies,' Jacinta reminded her. 'Come on, let's take these back to Leá, get her to make the biggest jug of lemonade she can manage. And we'll take a jug of it along to our road block, then we can have a drink from time to time.'

'It's Allen's first Christmas but he's too little to understand much, so I want our people to have a good time, even though it means sacrifices for us,' Foxy told Allsop as the two of them polished a huge silver salver and a silver teaset until they shone like mirrors. 'I know selling these things is a sacrifice, Mr Allsop, but without it we can't possibly hope to help the tenants and see that their kids have a good time. I don't have to tell you what a bad year it's been.'

It had indeed been a bad year. Of the ten tenants who farmed the land owned by the Cliftons, no fewer than six had gone to the wall and two had been unable to pay a full year's rent. Cheap imports, the real need for higher wages and a wet spring followed by the driest summer for years had contributed to their downfall and Foxy, unable to do a thing to help, could only watch as the families moved out.

'They can stay . . . there's no point in them leaving,' she had cried when the first tenant was declared bankrupt. 'I know they can't pay the rent – the estate can wait.'

The trouble was, it wasn't just that they couldn't pay the rent. They couldn't make a living and in order to thrive the farms needed modern equipment and better stock which neither the estate nor the tenants could afford.

'They're moving into the cities, to go into munitions factories and places like that,' Foxy said despairingly. 'What a dreadful change for them – if only I could help! When Laurie comes home I'm sure he'll reproach me for managing his affairs badly and letting his tenants leave.'

'It isn't your fault, Miss Foxy, and anyway, you can't have people sitting idle on Clifton property when someone else might be able to make a go of it. Besides, we'll maybe let them to someone with a bit of cash,' Mr Hawkings said comfortingly, when Foxy went to see him to discuss the dreadful state of affairs. 'The Depression isn't letting up, not yet. But it can't be long, these things never last. They go in cycles and this one has, in my opinion, almost had its day.'

That had been in September; now it was nearly Christmas and not one of the farms had been re-let though the remaining tenants were still managing to pay at least some of their rent.

'I don't disapprove of selling the silver, Miss Foxy,' Allsop said now, polishing away. 'The Lord above knows Sir George sold as much stuff as he could whilst he was able to do so, and we survived that. The Cliftons, thankfully, have always been hoarders. Why, if we were to go through the attics I daresay we'd find two or three silver tea-services every bit as good as this one.'

'Oh, Mr Allsop, you're such a comfort,' Foxy said, admiring her face in the side of a fluted silver teapot. 'If it wasn't for the trust in the offing I don't know what we'd do, though. The home farm is coming on, but it'll be a long time before it pays its way. And the rain's done for most of the winter cabbage we sowed, you know. Though the sprouts look like being nice in a month or so.'

'So long as Mr Hawkings can forward us a trifle now and then on account of the trust, we should get through somehow,' Allsop said. 'Now about this Christmas party – are you sure you want to have it, Miss Foxy? No one will be surprised if you do nothing this year, what with Sir Laurie fighting in Spain and you having your own little boy to think of. Because if you really want to help the estate workers (and most of them are ex-estate workers, come to think) it will mean more going than the silver tea-service.'

'We should never have had that expensive christening, with that huge tea for people who eat huge teas every day of the week,' Foxy said sadly. 'But I never thought so many farms were in a parlous state. I mean look at Bees-wing; they're flourishing.'

'Yes, but they've done better than ever with the hops,' Allsop pointed out. He picked up the cream jug and began to rub it vigorously with his polishing cloth. 'Folk thought Mr Hoverton was mad when he put Willard's Patch to hops, because it's a huge field, but he took good care of the plants, kept clear of downy mildew when it struck almost everyone else in the area, and made a great deal of money.'

'I wanted to try hops,' Foxy muttered beneath her breath. 'But John said the outlay was too big and Mr Hawkings agreed. Still, at least we've not bankrupted the place. Not yet.'

'Nor we shall, whilst I'm around to prevent it,' Allsop said grimly. 'Now, Miss, do you want to hold this party or do you not? Because if you do, I suggest you climb the second flight of stairs and take a look in the second room along.'

'I'll go at once,' Foxy said. 'And tomorrow I've got a meeting with Mr Hawkings. I – I suppose you wouldn't like to come along?'

'Drive you into Ledbury, you mean? Certainly, Miss, I'm sure I can be spared for an hour or two.'

'No, I meant attend the meeting,' Foxy said impatiently. 'I feel I must know where we stand with so few rents coming in and I think you should know, too. I comfort myself with the thought that Laurie's trust will come to fruition anyway next year – but can we last till then? I'm already telling myself that Mr Hawkings is bound to suggest that we let Cyril go, though I'm sure he won't suggest sacking Hector. And what about Fletcher and the others? And the girls who help with the housework? Mr Allsop, for the first time since Laurie left, I'm truly scared!'

*

354

'Retire Hector and Carruthers. I know they've worked on the estate all their lives but they can keep their cottages, since you won't be employing anyone in their stead. The pension they'll receive isn't large but Hector and his missus must have put something by, they've no children, after all. As for Carruthers, he must be well over sixty-five and he and his wife have a grand garden there. Besides, the estate will be generous in the matter of rabbits, trout from the river, fruit for bottling and jam-making, I'm sure. They'll get by, Miss Foxy, which is about all you'll be able to do until the trust is paid to Sir Laurie.'

Foxy and Allsop, sitting side by side opposite the solicitor at his big, leather-topped desk, exchanged quick glances. It was all more or less as they had expected, save that the money invested, which they had assumed to be steady, was not. Mr Hawkings did not say he had invested unwisely, nor that Laurie had done so, and Foxy supposed that the investments might have gone back to Sir George, but whoever was responsible there was no point in querying it. What can't be cured must be endured, Allsop was fond of quoting. Now she could see his point.

'And shall we be able to get by, Mr Hawkings?' Foxy said hopefully. 'I don't know what our outgoings are . . .'

'Wages for staff, food for same. Cost of the telephone, rates and taxes, running of the car, feed for animals, vet's bills, doctor's bills, a small amount of interest on the money borrowed from the trust fund,' Mr Hawkings said. 'You'll have to dispense with the services of the village girls, but I daresay you won't mind that. And I really think you should consider getting rid of the nursery maid. A cook, of course, is essential because she will save you money by making bread, bottling fruit and so on. However, incomings are small. Probably incomings could be set against animal feed and vet's bills.'

'We can't get rid of Edith,' Foxy interposed firmly. 'She's the nursery maid and she's worth her weight in gold. We don't pay her much, nowhere near as much as she's worth and anyway she's Mrs Waughman's right-hand woman, she's endlessly useful in the kitchen as well as in the nursery. Why, if it wasn't for Edith I wouldn't be able to do the books or work in the kitchen garden or anything!'

'Hmm. The telephone, then?'

'Oh dear! Suppose we need the doctor for Allen in a hurry? Or suppose one of us is taken ill? It's such a help, Mr Hawkings, especially with Laurie so far away. Isn't there any chance of letting one of the farms?'

'There's been no interest as yet. Folk aren't even wanting to buy – not that you'd sell, of course. Well, you couldn't. Mr Laurie – I mean Sir Laurie – is the only one who can do that and then only under certain circumstances. The car, then? It's not an essential expense, is it?'

'No. The car can go,' Foxy said decisively. 'And we'll eat less, won't we, Mr Allsop? But we're going ahead with the Christmas party. We've sold a very ugly silver tea-service . . .' an involuntary gasp of protest from Allsop was completely ignored, '. . . and a pair of horrid little chairs all covered in woodworm which we found in the attic.'

'Heirlooms,' Allsop said in a hollow voice. 'Doubtless we were cheated; they're probably priceless. The way that dealer pounced on them . . . he wanted the oil painting which hangs above the sea-chest in the yellow bedroom, but I put my foot down, Mr Hawkings.'

'It's a horrid, cheap reproduction,' Foxy said defiantly. 'Of some sour-faced fellow . . .'

'It is a very fine portrait of Prince Albert as a young man,' Allsop said. 'It is worth a great deal of money, far more than that dreadful little man has ever handled. Why, during Sir George's time at the hall I actually hid it, told him he'd sold it whilst in his cups! I trust, Miss Foxy, that you aren't going to force me to behave similarly.'

'No, of course not,' Foxy mumbled, going pink. 'I wouldn't sell anything without consulting you . . . I did ask you about the chairs.'

'That's true, you did. And I was sure it was all right until that man began almost drooling over them,' Allsop admitted. 'Sorry, Miss Foxy. It was as much my fault as yours – if we were cheated, that is.'

'I don't think we were cheated,' Foxy said. 'But dealers never pay more than they have to. Next time . . . oh, but I do so hope there isn't going to be a next time! Still, Christmas is saved. We may not be able to splash out, but we'll be all right. We'll get through until spring, and then with a bit of luck either Laurie will be home, or we'll let the farms.'

'And the trust ends on his twenty-fifth birthday, which isn't far distant,' Mr Hawkings said. 'Of course the money can only be released to Sir Laurie himself . . .' his voice trailed away and Foxy smiled at him a trifle doubtfully. She sometimes suspected that he knew her relationship with Laurie was only that of friendship but was saying nothing because it would have made a bad situation worse.

She frequently wished she had not lied quite so convincingly to Allsop over the matter of Allen's paternity, because she had no intention of profiting from the situation. If Laurie were killed she could always disappear. But in the meantime, soldier on, Foxy Lockett, she told herself bracingly as, with mutual thanks and promises of support, the two of them left Mr Hawkings's office. Be thankful that the war you fight is just a small, personal one, with financial ruin at the end of it if the last battle's unsuccessful. Hundreds of miles away, in the country she always thought of as sunny Spain, Laurie and John were fighting a grimmer war, with the possibility of a far more violent end always with them.

Foxy shuddered and shook her head to dispel the terrifying thought. She buttoned her coat and pushed her hands deep into her pockets, then she and Allsop strode briskly down Church Street and turned into High Street. A light dusting of snow had fallen, giving the houses and shops a picture-book appearance, and even Dapple and the cart looked festive with the pony's breath steaming and the cart itself white-rimmed.

'Well, that's over, Mr Allsop; at least we know where we stand,' Foxy said brightly. 'Shall we go and spend some money on Christmas fare for the party?'

It was Christmas eve. Mirri was mounting a roadblock and though the skies were clear it had snowed heavily during the course of the afternoon. The bombed buildings, the cobbled street and the pavements were hidden beneath a blanket of white and the soldiers and militiawomen on duty walked up and down just to try to keep warm, stamping their feet and blowing on their hands.

It was bitterly, unrelentingly cold. Mirri wore her uniform, every spare bit of clothing she possessed – which was not saying much – and had a thick, hairy blanket across her shoulders and tied at the waist with string.

Beside her, Josefa, similarly bundled, was whistling tunelessly between her front teeth and trying to knit the first of a pair of black woollen mittens – she was using wool sent in one of the parcels – when she stopped short suddenly and put a hand on Mirri's arm. 'What was that?'

'A plane.' Mirri listened, her ears by now accustomed to the different engine notes. 'Oh hell, it's a bomber . . . one of theirs.'

The road was blocked so that they might stop strangers, or people driving unauthorised vehicles. A waste of time and energy, Mirri thought crossly. They had been here all day and had seen no one who did not look cold, hungry and depressed – in other words, just like all the citizens of Madrid. And what was more, no one wanted to get into or out of the city, or not by this route, at any rate.

'Better get under cover,' one of the soldiers said gloomily. 'You go first, girls.'

There was a dug-out to the rear of the roadblock; not much protection if a building fell on it, but better than nothing. Having got the girls inside the men followed, then dropped the sacking curtain. God knew what good it might do, but at least it gave one the illusion of safety. And the soldiers were right, there was no point in standing about in the open street with bombs falling.

They heard the long whistle, then the *crump* of the explosion. Not too near. As they cowered in their miserably inadequate little dug-out they heard the wail of a frightened child, the scolding voice of a woman. Mirri popped her head out from under the sheet of rusting corrugated iron which was the roof.

'Get into the third house on the right, dear. It's got a good, deep cellar,' she shouted. The woman, bundling an old couple and two small children in front of her, turned towards the sound of Mirri's voice, her face a pale blur in the darkness.

'Thank you, comrade,' she called breathlessly. 'The children won't hurry, they want to watch, and my *madre* is very afraid. Third house on the right, you said?'

'That's it . . .' Mirri was beginning when another bomb fell, closer this time. Even in the darkness she saw the big building crumple, go down on its knees in a flurry of dust. 'Hurry,' she exhorted the woman. 'Hurry!'

The woman scooped the smallest child up in her arms. Mirri struggled out of the dug-out and ran to help her, seizing the old woman by the hand and putting her other hand to the old man's elbow.

'This way, let's see if you can run,' she encouraged, and the old couple tottered and slid through the snow along beside her, the old man wheezing and coughing, the old woman uttering the high wail which, earlier, Mirri had assumed to be a child crying.

They reached the house and Mirri ushered the little family inside and down the stairs. She went as far as the cellar door, opened it, shouted to the man nearest the doorway – for the cellar was crammed to capacity – that she had another family for him, and shut the door on them. She was running up the stairs just as another explosion rocked the house, making her feet tingle, even as the air rushed from her lungs, the pain of it doubling her up for several agonising moments.

Presently, she tottered up the rest of the stairs, gasping for breath in the thick, dust-laden air. Then she stood for a moment in the empty doorway – the door had been burned for fuel long since – and stared out at the square.

It wasn't really a square any longer – that was to say, it was no longer surrounded by the broken teeth of buildings. The side opposite where she stood simply wasn't there any more. A settling, creaking sound told her that buildings were still collapsing, or might collapse, in the next few moments. She had better run back to the dug-out . . .

She was halfway across the square before she realised that the dug-out had gone. Disappeared. There was absolutely no sign of it. Disorientated, she stared around her, then told herself to be calm, to think. She had been in the third house on the right, opposite the dug-out. She and the small family had made quite an appreciable path through the snow; the dug-out should be just *there* . . .

Nothing. Just piles and piles of brick and rubble, beams and dust, covering up the white blanket of snow.

Be calm, Mirri ordered herself; she was trembling and her chest ached with a deep, continual pain. She could not understand what had happened but she thought she knew, now, where the dug-out had been. She went as quickly as she could across the square, a hand to her sore ribs. The house nearest the dug-out, a four-storey building, had collapsed in on itself, and a few bricks and tiles, nothing more, were scattered across the top of the dug-out, hiding it from a casual glance. With a deep sigh of relief, Mirri shouted.

'Josefa! Ramón! Pedro!'

No answer. Not a groan, not a whisper. Desperately, Mirri began to clear the tumbled rubble, until she could see that the corrugated iron had slid forward and down, hiding the entrance. She felt sure her companions had followed her out, had taken shelter elsewhere, but she lifted the iron a little way and peered inside.

There was something . . . she reached forward and pulled, then gave a small scream as the thing came easily, too easily, out into the open.

It was an arm in a tattered blue sleeve. Just an arm. And the hand on the end of the arm clutched fiercely at a pair of needles from which hung a bloodstained woollen mitten.

Thirteen

'The Republicans took it and couldnae holt it. Now they expect us to tak it an' gie it back to them! Och, an' I'll tak a bet it's a miserable bluidy hole anyway; there's no' a decent town left in Spain if you ask me.'

The speaker, a short, red-headed Glaswegian, poked his head above the trench for a moment, then drew it back down again with a disgruntled mutter.

'Weel, sor? How lang do we stay here? We dinna ken where the fascists are, but there's on'y the five o' us, and one machine-gun. Shouldnae we see where the rest o' the comp'ny are?'

John and four members of his company were crouched in a narrow trench, their Maxim poking a round black eye threatening in the general direction of the enemy troops, whilst around them one of the worst blizzards they had so far encountered howled and snow built up on the mud beneath their feet, the soil around them and on their wet heads and shoulders. John had only recently returned to the front from a stay in hospital; a bullet wound in the leg made him limp even now, but the doctors had assured him it would mend.

'Jock's got a point, sir,' a scruffy young Welshman, with lank black hair and eyes dark as the pits he came from, said apologetically. 'Not a bite we've 'ad for twenty-four hours, either. Any chance of some grub, is there?'

John grinned at him. The boy's skin, warm and tanned in the summer by the unaccustomed Spanish sun, had gone the most peculiar shade of green but his cheeky grin and unquenchable optimism hadn't altered one jot. He had come here to show them buggers where to get off, he had told John when he first joined the

361

company, and he'd bloody stay until they'd done just that; eh, mun?

'We don't have any grub here, Eifion,' John said regretfully. 'But you're right, not much point in sitting in a hole like this. There must be a barn, or a deeper trench, or . . .'

'Ware!' it was Jock, his hand flapping desperately at them as he tried to get behind the machine-gun. 'Someone's comin', sir. Geddown, you stupid wee buggers!'

Eifion, who had bounced up to take a look, bounced down again. There was a flush on his sallow cheeks now.

'I seed shadows, mun,' he hissed close to John's ear. 'Bloody great shadows . . . it could be them Moors, out to . . .'

He broke off. The men approaching were talking as they scuffed along, their voices thin against the blizzard. Jock swung the Maxim round, a hand lovingly caressing the firing button. The men were only yards away when John grabbed Jock's hand, forcing it back.

'Let it alone, man. They're carrying wounded; it's probably our own side.'

'It'll be too bluidy late if they get any closer,' Jock muttered. 'It's no' English they're speakin', sor – we'd best fire.'

Sammy and Luke, the two remaining soldiers who had been huddled up together in the bottom of the trench, sat up, moving cautiously, trying to get their heads above ground without being seen.

'They're speaking Spanish,' John said after a moment's attentive listening. 'And they're dressed in rags; they're ours. You have to admit the fascists wear pretty tidy uniforms.'

It was true that the ranks of the Republican army had ceased to care what they wore, provided they were covered. A soldier thought himself lucky to get a battle-dress top; he would wear any trousers he could find. And boots, in the Spanish battalions, were prized possessions; most of the soldiers wore rope-soled sandals which did not even begin to protect their feet in such ferocious weather conditions. The International Brigades, on the other hand, had somehow managed to keep their uniforms more or less intact even after getting on for two years of war.

'Is there a password?' someone hissed. There were grins all round at that. The International Brigades were by now uneasily aware that their Spanish counterparts were not, by nature or inclination, soldiers. When they were afraid they fired first and asked questions second, if at all.

'Just get down and stay down,' John advised. 'Jock, if you touch that button . . .'

The aggressive little Scot sank onto his haunches. In the gloom of the storm John saw the brief flash of his teeth as he grinned. 'Awright, sor,' he whispered. 'An' if they cut us tae pieces, we'll all know who to blame . . . sor!'

The approaching men, straggling along now, looked likely to bypass the trench. They were indeed carrying wounded and two of them were helping a third. John was sure, now, that they were Republicans, but even so he did not call out. Two of the men carried rifles; too many mistakes had been made, too many soldiers had been shot by their own side. He had no desire to add to their number. He kept very still and watched them pass and when they were just shadows in the driving snow, he turned back to his men.

'Right. We'll follow them, try to keep them in sight. That way, perhaps we'll get back to wherever our HQ is – if we've got one anywhere within walking distance.' He turned back as the men began, stiffly, to move. 'And keep *quiet*; we aren't the only ones who can't tell friend from foe in this.'

The five of them stumbled out of the trench and began to walk in what they sincerely hoped was the direction of the rest of the army. John, with feet so cold he couldn't even feel the throbbing wound in his calf and an enormous thirst, found himself wondering how Laurie was faring. He was here, somewhere on the Teruel front. I'll see if we can meet up, once things are better organised, John told himself. We're not going to get into Teruel again, though; might as well make up our minds to that. Still, there will be other opportunities.

And then he remembered what his commanding officer had told him when he came to visit him in hospital. Rob had been gaunt and worried, although it was before the taking of Teruel and the subsequent losing of it.

'I don't like the way things are panning out and that's the truth, my boy. The Spanish communists in Tarazona shot the man who

363

had done more than most to win this war, without compunction or a second thought,' he had said. 'And when Bill asked them why they said they'd done it because he was an anarchist. Because he might have betrayed them. And that little man – he was only little – had been spying for the Republic, sending back invaluable information. He'd been caught, eventually, and tortured by the fascists but he'd not told them anything at all. To get away he'd jumped out of a third-floor window and walked a hundred miles with a gammy leg in terrible conditions . . . and my *God*, when he reached the Republican commanders they bloody *shot* him, whilst they were still telling him what a first-rate fellow he was. I tell you, John, there's no hope for us with people like that in charge.'

If it wasn't for the fellows I'd get out, John found himself thinking now as he limped onward through the snow. If it wasn't for the likes of Eifion and Jock and the ordinary Spanish peasants who've fought beside me I'd walk out of this hellhole and never come back.

'You awright, sir?' Jock had realised he had fallen behind and now he fell behind too, putting a hand beneath John's elbow to help him along. John was shamefully grateful for the support and slowed for a moment, dragging the stingingly cold air into his lungs, bending to ease the ache in his back caused by the unnatural position of his wounded leg.

'I'm all right, but my leg's gone numb. It keeps twisting so my foot hits the ground at the wrong angle. Sorry, I'm holding you back.'

'Not at a', sor, not at a',' the young Scot said soothingly. 'I just dropped back a wee way to tell you there's a barn ahead and a fire, wi' men round it; someone's just spoke in English, what's more, I heerd 'um wi' my own ears.'

John straightened up and began to limp forward once more. 'That makes it worth going on, Jock. If you'll just continue to lend me an arm we'll make it in no time. A fire may well mean food!'

Laurie knew John had been wounded and envied him that wound right now. John, you're a lucky old devil, tucked up in a hospital bed with a pretty nurse beside you, he thought to himself as he crouched by his gun, his men strung out beside him. You won't be hiding behind a bloody great rock with the remains of your friend Arny, smashed like a puppet by a direct hit, on your right and a dour, terrified Spaniard on your left, shuddering with cold, firing his rifle, *crack, crack,* sitting back and shuddering with cold once more.

They had been here for what felt like weeks, but Laurie had lost track of time. The Brigade had been called in when it became obvious that the Spaniards, who had taken Teruel, could not hold it. They would have to fall back on prepared strongpoints . . . but in the falling back many lives would be lost.

It was a hopeless task, and everyone involved must have realised it. The fascist air force came over whenever they felt like it, machine-gunned the fellows on the ground, dropped their bombs and blew the men to bits, and then returned to their bases. The Republican air force no longer existed.

And in the face of superior gun-power, bigger and better tanks, a more disciplined force, the Republican retreat began. So Laurie, crouching in a little ravine, with snow-capped rocks all around him, waited for the next rush and wondered how long it would be before the order to retreat came once again.

The shelling was dreadful; the roar of cannon and the clatter of machine-guns never stopped and scarcely a minute passed without a shell bursting near. 'They've found our measure,' Casares said, raising his voice above the cannons' roar, the clatter of machine-guns. 'Any minute now . . .'

He was right. Shells were bursting all around; fragments of rock were hurled twenty feet into the air, the snow disappeared, clouds of earth fell on the men taking what cover the ravine offered. Laurie decided they would have to move. He got to his feet and shouted: 'To me . . . back to that plantation . . . come on!'

Even as he shouted there was a tremendous explosion, like nothing he had ever heard or experienced before. He felt his coat torn off him as though it were paper, felt himself rise up in the air. *I'm dead and being taken up to heaven,* he thought. *It's not as bad as I expected, dying.*

And then the pain hit him and he knew he wasn't dead. He felt a rock smash against his head and for one scarlet, agonising second he saw, in his mind's eye, what he had given up; Clifton Place on a

365

sunny afternoon and Foxy, in her old blue dungarees with her bright hair pulled back from her face, standing on tiptoe to pull down a hop bine. Then darkness came down like a muffling blanket and he knew no more.

Retreats are agonising. When John and his depleted company found the rest of the army they hung grimly on to their weapons and did their best to counteract the withering Nationalist fire, performing feats of bravery and endurance well beyond the call of duty. But their best was not enough. They were forced further away from Teruel by the constant bombardment, a hail of tracer bullets from the aircraft swooping and diving on them, and by the tanks, the bombs and the huge numbers of well-fed, well-kitted-out Nationalist troops. Ill-equipped, ill-clad and starving, the Republican army didn't stand a chance of recapturing the little town which they had fought so valiantly to take and then to hold.

'They're pushing us towards the sea,' John said to Jack, when they met momentarily as they manoeuvred their depleted little companies into the same gully. '*Our* officers know what they're doing; if only the generals in charge of the Spanish battalions could say the same!'

'Oh, they'll tell their troops we're taking up a defensive position between Teruel and the coast, you mean,' Jack said with a grin. 'The Republican generals will tell us they chose to do this for some reason or other and we have to nod and smile and say how sensible. Not that we've any choice in the matter, we're outgunned, outmanoeuvred, outequipped, if there is such an expression.' He lowered his voice. 'We're fighting for a lost cause, *amigo.*'

'I believe you're right. I'd get out of it, quit, but how can we leave good fellows to certain death? My men are excellent soldiers, they're brave and resourceful. The Britons have fought like lions, but the Spaniards are as good, when they're well-led. But without me . . . I don't know.'

'You should have gone home to Blighty when you left the hospital,' Jack said. 'You've still got one helluva limp.'

'Yes, but it'll mend. When spring comes, perhaps.' John grinned at Jack's sardonic look. 'Oh come on, winter can't last for ever – can it?'

They laughed, then went back to their own companies, promising to meet up the next time there was any sort of cessation in the bombardment.

Two days later, John was making his way across terrible terrain when a sniper opened fire on them. John motioned to his men to scatter behind various boulders and stunted bushes, then threw himself down behind a small, snow-covered hump in the ground and steadied his rifle on top of it. He watched until he saw the sniper's gun flame as he fired, gold against the blue dusk, and then he took careful aim.

The sniper toppled out from behind the boulder that had hidden him. John saw him for a moment against the snow, saw the scarlet mess that was his face, then he dropped to the ground, arms flung out, and lay still, a dark cross on a white ground.

John went to stand up and as he moved he knocked the snow from the hump on which his rifle had rested; he saw that it was not a hump of snow but a man, stiff, stark. John frowned down at him, at the grey-white skin, drawn tight over the high cheekbones, at the dark hair stiff with ice, at the droop of the amused and self-mocking mouth.

It was Jack.

Losing Jack hit John hard. Inside his head he kept thinking that there must have been a way to save him, that he should have suggested they both leave the battlefield. Anything which would mean that cheerful, long-suffering Jack was still here.

But thousands had died, many of them British, American, and French as well as Spanish. It isn't just Spain's war, the lads of the International Brigade had said, it's the war of every man who believes in freedom of choice, in democracy. We're fighting against fascism, not just against Franco. The wicked fairy never triumphs and the devil always gets his just deserts, it's bound to happen this time, too – isn't it?

But they were all beginning to suspect that this story was not going to have a fairytale ending. As John and two of his men dug a grave for Jack, John found himself thinking again that there could be only one end to the struggle, and that was the wrong end. Jack had come here in good faith, to fight to see right done, and he was dead. Others, thousands of others, had died – would die. But right would not triumph. Through petty selfishnesses, stupidities, bigotry and blunders the upper echelons of the Republican Party had let their people down and were losing the war.

If I'd known Jack had fallen I could have got him out of it, even if it meant both of us deserting, John told himself grimly. Jack had been wounded but John thought the cold had probably killed him, and the fact that no one had found his body until it was too late. If only we'd stayed together, John told himself, there might have been something I could have done. We came here together, we should have left together. And he filled in the grave with boulders, made a little cross out of a piece of fencing and at last stood by Jack's grave and grieved for the death of friendship, the death of hope.

Next day, a day of fearsome cold which penetrated the stoutest boots, the thickest overcoat, the company found themselves in the thick of battle with the Nationalist army actually charging down amongst them. Above them the sky was clear and a watery sun shone. John, screaming instructions and encouragement to his lads, levelled his rifle, took aim and fired repeatedly. Men fell, but more came on. John stepped behind a rock to reload, stepped out, saw a grey-clad soldier no more than ten feet from him, fired, watched his enemy stand, stagger . . . keel slowly sideways. But there was another behind him, coming on fast. Fear was gone in the heat of action. It was like target-shooting at the fair with an added sting in the tail; him or me, me or him. John swung the barrel to the left, squeezed the trigger . . . and heard the empty click, knew he was out of ammunition once more. Swiftly he dropped on one knee to reload and as the bullets began to slide smoothly into the breach something heavy hit him hard and suddenly across the head. Stunned and sick, he lay behind a boulder whilst the fighting surged over him, surged back. He got a confused impression of legs, bare feet, boots, cracked shoes, old-fashioned puttees. There were shouts and screams, rifle fire, cannon's roar, then someone pushed hard against him, cracking his head on the boulder. John passed out.

*

He came to himself to find that he was alone, the only living person on that snow and blood-streaked hillside, with the sky at that particular stage of evening which is at once wistful and romantic, deep blue overhead with stars pricking out, pale green towards the horizon, with flame and rose outlining the distant hills.

For a moment he simply lay still, trying to get his bearings, to make out what was happening. The quiet was incredible; he got to his knees and thought for a wild moment that he had gone stone deaf, for the hillside was littered with bodies and, most horrible of all, bits of bodies. But not a sound broke the stillness, not a voice nor a shot. No plane marred the perfect arc of the sky; an observer who could not see the broken bodies, the spent cartridges, the blood, might have thought it a peaceful scene.

And then he heard it, and knew he was neither deaf nor dead. It was birdsong. The singer began tentatively, a liquid trill which swelled by slow degrees into a paean of praise for the beauty of the sunset, the clarity of the light, the brilliant cold of the air. John looked round him, at the tumbled limbs, the young, open faces, the blood-boltered snow, then he looked up at the bird, ascending into the deepening dark of the sky.

The bird sang and sang as though it were performing before a huge and appreciative audience and John, the only listener, stood in the snow amidst the quiet dead and wept, and the tears froze on his cold cheeks.

Much later, when it was fully dark, he made his way up the hill, down the other side, and across a small valley. Behind the next hill, he thought dully, he would find HQ and the men who had survived. If he could just find the strength to climb the next hill . . .

And then, halfway up the next hill, in a fold of land, he found a filthy little cow byre. Still feeling stunned and disorientated by the blow on the head and the horror of finding himself the only man alive on the battlefield, John went into the byre like a somnambulist, hands held out before him as though to ward off evil.

It was wonderfully warm in there, and the occupants, two skinny cows, turned to stare at him with their mild brown eyes. Milk! He could still milk a cow and God alone knew how long it was since he had last eaten or drunk. His mouth was foul, his tongue cleaved to the roof of it with thirst and exhaustion. He knelt in the thin, dirty straw and tried the udder of the nearest cow and clean, sweet milk squirted out onto his knees.

Trembling with eagerness he milked her, first into his cupped hand, then directly into his mouth; he lay beneath the cow's meagre bag, tugging on the teats, laughing when he directed the stream into his eye by mistake. Recovering not only his strength but his sanity, beginning to come out of the nightmare of loss and, strangely, of rejection, which had been his when he came round to find himself alone.

The cow was grateful for the relief of milking, John was farmer enough to be aware of it, so he took a few desultory mouthfuls from the second cow, but he was beginning to feel weariness overcoming him and the cows, their warmth and their sweet breath, were making him long for sleep. Healing sleep, he told himself, curling up on the straw right under the first cow's constantly moving jaws. If I can sleep I'll forget the terrors and the bodies and the dreadful, insidious smell of violent death. If I can sleep . . .

He awoke knowing he was no longer alone. He opened his eyes with the utmost care and caution, and saw, beyond the cows, three men. They wore tattered fragments of uniform; they were Republican soldiers. He listened to their talk. They were Spaniards and had come from the battlefield and despite their appearance they were intelligent men, discussing what had been happening in an informed and sensible way. They spoke of 'afterwards' and John realised that they were already accepting defeat, planning what to do when the purple Republican stripe on their national flag would be replaced with the Nationalist scarlet.

They did not know he was there, he realised that. They thought themselves alone in this snug spot. If they had known he was awake and could understand almost every word they said they would, he supposed, have guarded their tongues.

Listening, he soon realised that they were in trouble with their own side, the Republicans, and feared reprisals from their own people as much as they feared what would befall them if the fascists triumphed. One, the leader, had killed a man he had long hated, who had dishonoured his family in some way. But the dead man had influential friends in high places; the leader knew 'they' would not let the matter rest.

'And we're in no better case, when it comes down to it, eh, *amigo*? Sorotto saw the colonel rape his sister and the colonel knew he was seen; I sold my uniform and my dead comrade's rifle for a bite to eat. Yes, we're unpopular, and that's putting it mildly.'

The one John thought of as the leader laughed bitterly. 'Between the devil and the deep, eh? Now what about him? We could leave him here when we go tomorrow.'

The leader was a black-bearded, hard-eyed giant of a man with a scar running across his cheek from right to left. For a chilling moment John thought the man meant him, then he realised that there was another man, lying on the straw. The three were clustered around him now, looking down.

'Finish him off.'

The second speaker was a light-haired, fair-skinned, ascetic-looking man. Young, tight-lipped, humourless, with a fanatical gleam in his pale eyes, John thought. He shifted a bit until he could see the third man, a short, gipsyish-looking fellow with broad shoulders and high cheekbones. He probably came from Asturias, John guessed; Asturians often had that almost Russian look. By God but he'd fallen into strange company; they were a sinister trio. The three witches in Macbeth, crouched round their cauldron, could scarcely have given a more frightening impression.

'Why? He's one of us, even if he is a foreigner. The International Brigade fought well; this one fought well for all I know. If we get him back to a hospital he might fight well again.'

The tall man snorted a laugh. 'What? With smashed feet? I say finish him off, for his own good as much as ours. He'll be no use to anyone like that.'

He raised his rifle with its fixed bayonet. John heaved himself to his feet and lurched towards them. He could not have frightened them more had the dead suddenly come to life; they all stepped back, jaws dropping, faces paling. The light-haired one crossed himself twice, very quickly, a priestly gesture.

'Comrades, what talk is this of killing?' John said in Spanish, approaching the group. 'If this fellow is near death . . .'

He looked down. This time the shock stopped his breath in his throat, stopped him in mid-gesture, almost stopped his heart. Then he looked up, at the three men all staring at him as though he were an apparition. He was being given another chance! He had not been able to do a thing for Jack, but this – this was different. This had to be different. Because the man lying in the straw, with his feet just a tangled mess of blood and splintered bone, was Laurie Clifton.

An hour later, he knew what he must do. He had heard the three plotting, which in ordinary circumstances would have been enough to kill him. But they wanted, above everything, to get away to another country, start afresh. The leader was Nante, the Asturian Pérez, the light-haired one Sorotto. Apart from Sorotto, who worried John, he thought the others would probably keep their word.

'This man is my foster-brother, he's an English lord; Sir Laurence Clifton,' John explained. 'We are very close, and I won't stand by and see you kill him. I know you could kill both of us, keep us both quiet for ever, but what would be the point? Besides, I heard you talking. You want a new life, and a good one. What can get you that good life?'

'Money,' Nante breathed. 'Pesetas . . . no, pesetas will not be good for months, maybe years. Francs. Or your pounds.'

John nodded portentously. At his feet, Laurie groaned deeply and moved his head. Nante's bayonet jerked convulsively. It was not that he wanted to kill Laurie, but neither did he want to spare him. All he wanted, right now, was a way out of all this for himself and his comrades. John realised that Nante knew they could not deliver the wounded man to safety so probably it seemed better to give Laurie a quick, clean death than to let him rot here.

'Yes, English pounds. And my brother here is rich. He could give you money and not miss it.'

'But he's wounded; he may not recover. If you try to succour him, he'll only hold you back. If he dies, who gets the money?'

That was Sorotto, his voice light, unemotional.

'A distant cousin. Not me. But if you would help me to get my

372

brother to a doctor, then I would lodge him somewhere safe and go to England. Bring you back enough money to make the three of you rich.'

It was all he could think of but he knew, as soon as he looked at Nante's face, that the idea had taken root. The enormous man frowned down at Laurie.

'Get him to a hospital? Yes, that's possible. Not for me, I'm too noticeable, but Sorotto and Pérez look like a hundred others. If we stole a truck, put him in the back, we could get him as far as Barcelona, even. There's a big hospital there.'

'How far are we from the army, here?' John said eagerly. 'I can steal a truck. I'll need it to get to the coast, to France, perhaps. I can be over to England and back in no time. And if Laurie's still alive . . .'

'No. No good.' Sorotto shook his fair head, smiling silkily. 'Once he's in hospital he's no concern of ours; it won't be our fault if he dies. The bargain is we get him to a hospital, then we get you to the coast. And you bring the money straight back to us or your brother dies.' He grinned suddenly, coldly, his eyes lighting up with that fanatical flame which John had glimpsed before. 'Even in a hospital a man can die,' he said lightly. 'If you renege, I can promise you he'll die slowly – and horribly.'

John's stomach turned but he merely said stolidly, 'You'll get the money, I give you my word. But – you'll wait? You'll do nothing for a month?'

'Three weeks,' Nante said, clearly trying to regain control of the situation. 'And Sorotto's right; we can kill but we can't promise your brother life. That is in God's hands . . . that's to say, in the hands of the doctors,' he added hastily.

'Good. Then shall we say a hundred quid?' He added the value in pesetas, but all three men shook their heads.

'Not enough,' Pérez said in a thick, Asturian accent. 'We need a new life, not a new pair of trousers! I have a wife, seven children . . . they have scarcely a mouthful of bread between them. You said a good life,' he finished accusingly.

'I meant a hundred quid each,' John said quickly. He saw the small Asturian's eyes widen slightly, then narrow. 'I think there is just sufficient money for that . . . but it is a large sum – an immense sum.'

'Good. But you must bring back as much money as there is available,' Nante said. 'There are ways of finding out if you're lying to us, keeping something back. A rich man, you say . . . this is, after all, the only chance we'll ever have to lay our hands on real money.'

'I can't give you more than Laurie's got,' John protested. 'I don't know the extent of his fortune. However, I'm confident that I can raise £300 from Laurie's estate – there's a trust, but it ends when he's twenty-five and his birthday's in a few weeks' time. So I should be able to get you the money though it will leave Laurie penniless.'

'But alive,' Nante reminded him. He went to the door, then nodded as if satisfied. 'Go with Sorotto and steal a truck,' he commanded. 'Be quick. Your friend is losing a lot of blood.'

John looked down at Laurie's feet, black blood oozed through the rough bandages which he had bound shudderingly around the ripped flesh and protruding bones earlier. Laurie hadn't regained consciousness at all; was he dying? Could a man survive such wounds? But he straightened his shoulders; this was a chance he must take and at least Sorotto was going with him. The others were, he thought, trustworthy enough.

'Come on then . . . what's your name? Clifton?' Sorotto said, making for the door. Outside, the snow had stopped. The moon was shining on a still, deserted landscape. Somewhere the peasants who owned the two cows were lying, dead, in the ruin of their little hovel, struck by the bombardment. Pérez told John they had found them and the ruined cottage and he had then led his companions to the byre which was still standing in a nearby field.

'No, Laurie's a Clifton but he's my foster-brother, not my blood brother. I'm John Hoverton.'

'Right. March then, Hoverton. We've no time to waste.'

Sorotto led him out into the freezing night. Stars twinkled above their heads, the moon's round eye gazed down upon them. Without even a glance behind them the two men set off, side by side, feet silent on the carpeting snow.

It was a decent truck and John had managed to purloin some cans of petrol, too.

'If we're caught we'll be shot,' Sorotto said. 'Stealing from your comrades is despicable. I shall say it was you, naturally. I had no part in it, you forced me to join you in the cab.'

John grinned and nodded. 'That's right. And of course they'd believe you, with your honest face. Does that make you happier?'

'I wouldn't mind seeing you with a bayonet through your belly,' Sorotto said in his light, cold voice. 'You wouldn't grin then.'

'Probably not. Keep watching for the byre, will you? I'd have thought we should have been there by now.'

'It's always further than you think . . .' They were bouncing over open country and now Sorotto stiffened and pointed. 'That's it! See, against the woodland?'

John narrowed his eyes in the greying dawn, then nodded.

'That's it, all right. Hold tight, I'll have to go through this hedge, though it's thin enough.'

They trundled to a halt in front of the byre and John knew a moment of chilling fear; suppose Laurie had died in his absence? He had been away three hours.

But the door swung open and the two men appeared. They were carrying Laurie on a plank of wood and loaded him into the back of the truck without a word. Then Nante and Pérez came round to the front.

'Out,' Nante said curtly. 'In the back.'

John obeyed immediately. He ran across the snow and climbed over the tailboard of the truck, falling to his knees beside Laurie. His friend was breathing heavily and there was a blue line round his mouth. John took off his coat and laid it over Laurie's body, then leaned against the side of the truck and managed to get Laurie's head onto his lap. It comforted him when Laurie made a muttering protest, though he neither opened his eyes nor seemed aware of what was happening to him.

The truck lurched into movement and John bent over his friend.

'You're going to hospital, they'll sort you out,' he said in a heartening tone. 'Not long now, old fellow!'

In the end, Sorotto and John took Laurie in to the big military hospital in Barcelona. The pain of moving had brought Laurie round twice, and once John had persuaded him to have a drink of milk – he had filled his canteen with it before they left the byre – and Laurie had taken two mouthfuls, which was something.

The hospital, used to wounded men, crammed Laurie on his stretcher into a busy ward and Sorotto had a word with the nurse. He and John stood by the bed, looking down at Laurie.

'I told her I'd visit regularly,' Sorotto said. 'I told her he was my *teniente*, and very well-liked.' He gave a nasty little trill of laughter, the first laugh John had ever heard him give. 'She'll be surprised when he suddenly disappears as soon as he's fit to move, but if I leave him here you might think up some trickery to get him back to England without paying your dues. And a fit man will be interested to know why he's dying, whose fault it is.'

'I'll be back,' John said shortly. He was turning away when a hollow-eyed man in the opposite bed, who had been staring curiously at them, said: 'Is that feller there young Clifton? Sir Laurence Clifton, I should say? Well, well, well! My parents often talk about him, though I only met him a couple of times, when he moved back to Clifton Place to take over from his old man. Not long before the war, that was. You'll be a comrade in arms, I daresay?'

'I'm his foster-brother,' John said, glad he had told Sorotto the truth. What a wonderful piece of luck, though, meeting someone who knew Laurie! 'John Hoverton. I don't think . . .?'

'Albert Rudge. I don't think I've met you, but I know your father . . . he's quite thick with my old man. You farm over at Bees-wing, don't you? I'm a close neighbour of Laurie's. Who's your friend?'

It had never occurred to John to wonder if Sorotto spoke English but he raised his brows at the light-haired man beside him. 'He's in my company. He's . . .'

'Manuel Talavera of the International Brigade,' Sorotto said smoothly. 'At your service, Mr Rudge.'

The man in the bed laughed, then winced. 'What a magnificent name . . . makes Rudge sound most awfully lightweight. Nice to meet you, Talavera, and you, Hoverton.' He propped himself up on one elbow and peered across at the still figure on the bed. 'I say, poor old Laurie, he looks in bad shape. My goodness, I hope for all our sakes that he makes it – my father's land marches with his, you know, so we've all been looking forward to Laurie getting at that trust. It's at least ten thousand pounds I believe.'

Beside him, John heard Sorotto give a muffled gasp. Cursing his bad luck now at finding a man who knew Laurie on the ward instead of thanking his stars, John tried to laugh it off. 'Ten thousand pounds? That can't be right, old boy. One thousand pounds more like.'

'No, I tell you m'father assured me it was at least ten thousand pounds,' insisted Rudge. His lean cheeks were flushed and even the slight effort of leaning up on his elbow seemed to tire him, for he flopped back on the pillows, breathing heavily. 'At least ten thousand pounds,' he repeated as soon as he could speak again. 'The uncle owned a brewery, you know. M'father says young Clifton will have enough to put the place to rights and still have a nice little sum left over. Some fellers have all the luck.'

'I don't call it lucky getting your bloody foot blown off,' John said bitterly. 'I'm off now . . . come on, Sor . . . Talavera, I mean. We've got work to do.'

'You'll visit?' Albert Rudge called weakly. 'Come back and see me, and your foster-brother.'

John made noncommittal noises but Sorotto turned round at once, smiling his cold smile.

'I'll be in every day,' he said menacingly, or it sounded menacing to John. 'I'll want to make sure that a man worth his weight in gold is fit and well for when the money changes hands.' As they left the ward he turned to John. 'And don't forget, your foster-brother won't be here when you return. I'll have him somewhere close, somewhere safe. But somewhere secret. You'll not see him again until I have the money, *all* the money, counted out to the last centavo, in my possession. But don't worry, a man worth his weight in gold will be cherished, until you return, or I know you've broken trust.'

And he isn't referring to the trust, it's my speedy return he's thinking of, John told himself miserably as they hurried down the long corridors and out into the sparkling, sunny afternoon. What a stupid, loud-mouthed bugger that Albert Rudge is – if only he knew what he's done! What was more, his thoughts continued, they'll kill Laurie now from sheer spite if I don't come back with all the money, because I lied to them in the beginning. Oh God, help me to help Laurie! Hawkings *must* be prepared to hand over the money in exchange for Laurie's life. And dear God, let me get back here in time!

Despite his fears, John got back to England in slightly less than a week. After a good deal of pleading, Sorotto drove him across the border into Portugal and down to the coast where John bribed a fisherman, with promises since he had no cash, to take him to a port where he might get a ship for England.

In the port he found the British consulate and told his troubles to a small, bewhiskered aide who tutted at him, gave him clothing and sufficient money for his journey home and asked him, rather pathetically John thought, to return by some other route.

'The Portuguese are eager to please General Franco and the Nationalists, especially since they are sure that Franco will win,' he explained quietly. 'And it is thought to be undiplomatic to be seen to assist those British nationals who have been fighting for the Republic. If you can come in by another route . . .'

John promised he would do his best. He would have promised anything to anyone to get on his way, so that he might reach England quicker.

His ship docked in Southampton on a day when the English weather seemed determined to show that it could compete with northern Spain any day. As the ship came slowly alongside the quay it hailed, the hailstones so big that going down the gangplank was a tricky business. Halfway to the station the hail turned to bitter rain which, by the time John had boarded the train for Ledbury, had turned to snow. He reached Ledbury station to find that the snow seemed to have set in but it wasn't far to Church Street so he set off at a brisk pace, eventually dripping his way up the stairs to Mr Hawkings's office, the melted snow running down his threadbare overcoat and dripping from his peaked cap. If his parents knew he was home he might be delayed, if he went to the Place Foxy would expect . . . God knew what she would expect, but it was not that John would leave again, almost as soon as he had arrived. She might plead, beg . . . his mother would certainly do both if she saw him limping up the drive to Bees-wing, so it was best to get the visit to Hawkings over first.

He nearly gave Hawkings a heart attack, though. He walked into the office and told the girl he must see her boss at once and then, when she said primly that Mr Hawkings had a client with him but she would be happy to make him an appointment John just limped past her desk and opened Mr Hawkings's door.

The client was an elderly farmer whom John knew well. He turned, face expressing outrage, which changed to blank astonishment when John addressed him.

'Mr Cutler, I'm most awfully sorry, but I have to see Mr Hawkings on a matter of the utmost urgency. Life and death, in fact. Do you mind . . .?'

'Who are you, sir? And how do you know my name?' Mr Cutler blustered, very red about the gills. 'Marching in here without so much as a knock when I've a private appointment with my man of business . . .'

'Life and death, sir,' John reminded him. Mr Cutler had got ponderously to his feet at John's precipitate entrance and now John took him by the elbow and propelled him, still protesting, to the door. 'It's Sir Laurence Clifton, Mr Cutler. I'm here on business connected with *his* life – or death.'

Mr Cutler stared. 'Who are you, sir?' he repeated. 'I don't . . .'

'John Hoverton,' John said impatiently. 'Is it the beard? I can't think I've changed all that much in a couple of years!'

'John Ho . . . my word, I'd never have known you,' the old man said. 'You went off to fight that Franco feller so they told me. Well, boy . . . you aren't a boy any longer, that's plain.' He saw John's involuntary movement and hastily headed for the door. 'Don't worry, John m'boy, I can take a hint. And it's good to see you alive and well. I'll pop in again in an hour, Hawkings.'

John took the chair just vacated by Mr Cutler and grinned across the big desk at Mr Hawkings. 'Afternoon, sir,' he said civilly. 'You've met me a couple of times over farming business but we've not had much to do with each other in the past. Yet you know Laurie well and it's Laurie I've come about. He's in hospital in Barcelona and in very grave danger, too. Let me explain.'

He had rehearsed what he must say all the way from Spain to England so he told the story well and quickly, leaving out everything which he considered non-essential, but even so Mr

Hawkings could not, at first, take it all in.

'Sir Laurence is gravely wounded and in hospital, and a ransom is being demanded for his life?' he said incredulously. 'But – but I read my papers, Mr Hoverton, and I was under the impression that Barcelona is still in Republican hands.'

'It is. Sadly, his life is threatened by three Republican soldiers.'

'I don't understand,' Mr Hawkings said in a baffled voice, shaking his head at his own stupidity. 'Tell me again and this time, let me have the entire story, right from the beginning. Then, perhaps, I will understand better.'

This time, John did not attempt to edit the story in any way. He saw that to do so would not help his cause. He told Mr Hawkings about the battle for Teruel, the terrible conditions, the way the fortress town had changed hands, the retreat. He told him about the finding of Jack's body, his own distress that he had not been able to prevent his friend's death, the blow on the head he had received which had resulted in his being left for dead when the Republican army retreated still further.

The scene in the cow byre he painted with especial care this time, making the point that the three men, though intelligent enough, were in bad trouble and would, but for his intervention, have killed Laurie then and there. Then he explained how he had bargained for Laurie's life, and how, in the hospital, a man called Albert Rudge had given the game away, had actually named the amount of money which Laurie could now command, since his twenty-fifth birthday had come and gone while he lay in hospital.

'Sorotto, or Talavera, I don't know which, if either, is his real name, heard. He said right away that if I came back with less than the £10,000 which Rudge had mentioned then they would kill Laurie. Mr Hawkings, these are desperate and terrified men. I must get back to Spain with all speed and I must have the money with me, or none of us will ever see Laurie alive again.'

'I . . . see,' Mr Hawkings said after a long silence, during which he frowned down at his blotter and John rasped at his bearded chin and gingerly touched the wound on his forehead where he had been hit in the snowy gully. 'You want me to release the money to you, on Mr Laurie's behalf, I take it?'

'Yes,' John said baldly, adding: 'Please,' as an afterthought.

'But what will Sir Laurence say to that? Surely he would not give up his inheritance.'

'Oh no, I expect he'd far rather die,' John said sarcastically. 'And Sorotto wouldn't just kill him, you know, he'd . . .'

'All right, all right, I understand,' Mr Hawkings said hastily. 'But ten thousand pounds – how can I take such a vast sum and simply hand it over when the estate is in such desperate need of money spending?'

'Are you prepared to risk it? Are you prepared to let Laurie die and then explain to his heir why you can only hand a part of the trust over to him?' John asked coolly. 'I don't think I'd relish either prospect, Mr Hawkings.'

'No, no, of course not, I'd not thought . . . and the need is urgent, you say? Mr John, could we not send troops . . . diplomats . . .'

'It's impossible to tell anyone, send anyone, because of the state of the country . . . there's a war on, Mr Hawkings! Besides, I can't think of a better way to spend ten thousand pounds than to save a life. And even if we could involve the authorities, Laurie will be taken out of that hospital just as soon as they dare move him,' John said. 'They aren't fools, Mr Hawkings, they must know we could try something of that sort. I am to go back, with the money, and only when they have seen and counted the notes, will I be told where Laurie is.'

'He might be dead by then,' Mr Hawkings said uneasily. 'We might be paying over the entire trust for – for a corpse, Mr John.'

'We might, but we shan't. I shall retain the money in my own possession – and I'll be well-armed, Mr Hawkings – until I see that they've kept their side of the bargain.' John leaned over the desk in an agony of worry. 'Mr Hawkings, you must release the money! Surely I have every right in the world to demand that you save my foster-brother? I swear to you if something goes wrong, if we don't get Laurie back alive and well, then I'll spend the rest of my life paying the money back. When I inherit Bees-wing I'll sell it and all the money shall go to the Clifton estate. Will that do? If you want me to I'll swear it on – on my mother's life.'

'I'll get the money,' Mr Hawkings said. His voice was low, his eyes dark with worry. 'He's a good young man with more than his fair share of troubles already, and you're a man of your word, John.

It may take a little while, but you shall have the money in ten days' time.'

'That won't be soon enough,' John said dully. 'I must begin making my way back to Barcelona in a week and I've a long trek before me. Mr Hawkings, there must be a quicker way.'

'There may be. Come back here in two days and I'll tell you how I've got on. Are you going home, now?'

John nodded wearily.

'I am. No point in hanging around Ledbury, spending money I haven't got. I'll go home to Bees-wing.'

Ada Hoverton was overjoyed to see him, wept over his limp, the wound which could be seen just beneath his hairline, his skeletal thinness, but she coddled him and made him eat everything she could lay hands on and, best of all, she understood his burning need to return to Spain.

'I love you all the more for taking the money and going back to all that horror to save my other boy, my son Laurie,' she said earnestly when John had explained his errand. 'Whilst you're here you must eat well and drink lots and lots of milk, to get you up to your proper weight again. And you must take great care when you leave, because you'll be carrying a fortune on your person and there are wicked men about. And John, my dear, you must fetch Laurie back home, to the people who love him, and then you must think of yourself. Your dad and I – and Bees-wing, for that matter – need you. We aren't getting any younger.'

'You're a spring chicken, and Dad's another,' John teased her. 'But you're right. Spain is over for me. Next time I come back it'll be for good.'

The local doctor, who had brought John into the world twenty-five years earlier, came up and tutted over the wound in his leg, gave him a healing ointment for the gash in his forehead, then patted his shoulder and advised him to 'stay at home, lad, and let foreigners fight their own wars'.

John grinned and said he'd think about it, but four days later he was on a cross-channel ferry, heading back the way he had come. The money was in large-denomination notes, packed round John's skinny frame in a canvas and leather money-belt. He was fitter, if no fatter, and a reliable little revolver nestled in the pocket of his greatcoat. But his anxiety showed in his jerky movements, the way he constantly turned his head, keeping watch in case he was being observed, and in his reluctance to move away from any solid object which would defend his back.

He reached Barcelona on the eighteenth day and went straight to the hospital, half hoping, half fearing, to find Laurie still in the bed. But Albert Rudge assured him that Laurie was a lot better, had been wheeled from the ward in a borrowed wheelchair by 'your friend, Mr Talavera'.

'Did he leave any sort of message?' John asked, trying not to show too much eagerness. 'I'd really like to catch up with them again.'

'Oh, yes, there was a message. They've gone by rail, I think, to Figueres.' He lowered his voice conspiratorially. 'Señor Talavera wants to get Sir Laurence over the border as soon as possible. I would not be surprised, judging by the way the war is going, if he goes, too. And why not? This is no place for anyone. When my lung-wound has healed enough for them to move me I shall be sent home, thank God.'

'Good, glad to hear it,' John said. 'Did he say whereabouts in Figueres? It's a sizeable town.'

'The fort, wherever that may be,' Albert said at once. 'I've never visited the town so I wouldn't know, but he seemed to think you might.'

'I do,' John said, foreboding striking his heart. That dreadful place in whose deep cellars the walls were dark with the blood of rebels, traitors, striking miners and anyone else unfortunate enough to rouse the ire of those in power. 'Thanks, Albert.'

He thought it unlikely that Sorotto had taken Laurie anywhere by train, they would have travelled, no doubt with Nante and Pérez, in the stolen truck. But he would have to use the train, which was probably why Sorotto had mentioned it.

John went and saw the ward sister before he left the hospital; she was a pleasant, middle-aged Frenchwoman, rushed off her feet, but pleased to be able to give him good news.

'The *teniente* did well,' she said enthusiastically. 'He was not able to walk, of course . . . one of his feet had to be amputated, no doubt you were told? . . . but his great friend, Señor Talavera, wheeled

383

him away in a chair. He said he hoped to take the *teniente* to France, where he might wax fat on butter and goat's milk. We laughed at that, and the *teniente* said he could scarcely wait, since the Señor 'Overton who had sent for him was as dear to him as a brother.'

John swore beneath his breath. It had not occurred to him that Laurie would need persuading to get him out of the hospital without a scene. But of course, his own name was a password, as Laurie's name would have been to him had he heard it in similar circumstances. And to find himself in that old, bloodstained fort with three rogues . . .

'Thanks, Sister,' he said, however. No point in letting anyone else know what the situation was. 'And . . . the *teniente* was really much better?'

She considered, head on one side.

'He should not have gone,' she said judicially at last. 'But he was eager to see this 'Overton and his friend promised to take good care of him.'

John left the hospital and made for the railway station at top speed. All the fears which he had spent so much time in subduing were coming to the surface once more. Hideous visions of Laurie in those deep underground cellars, with an amputated foot and a wheelchair and Sorotto, damn his cold eyes . . .

He reached the station and was told that the first train going to his destination left next morning. There was no point in returning to the hospital or, for that matter, to the town, so he slept on the platform with his gun pressing comfortingly against his side. He slept well, too, considering the deep sense of dread which haunted him.

He reached Figueres the following day, as dusk was falling. He went straight to the fort, abandoned now by the military, and was immediately spotted. Pérez was on watch.

'*Ola, amigo,*' he said, coming to meet John as though they were old friends, a hand outstretched, a beam almost splitting his face. 'We said, Nante and I, that you'd come, and within the time limit, too. You have the money?'

'I have,' John said gruffly. 'And my friend?'

'Your friend chafes at your absence but otherwise he is well. Come, you shall see him.'

He led John into an inner room where Nante and Sorotto sat playing cards. Laurie was lying on a makeshift bed in one corner. He was asleep and John studied his pale, dark-shadowed face. He looked ill, but not as dreadful as he had looked when John had last seen him.

'He's all right; we keep our word,' Nante said negligently, lounging to his feet. 'Did you keep your word, Englishman?'

'I did. Do you want to count the money now?'

'Every centavo,' Sorotto said. 'I will count it. Bring it to the table; Nante, keep an eye on the Englishman; Pérez, keep guard.'

John shook his head. 'No. You should all three watch the count, or who knows? Sorotto might say I hadn't brought the right amount.'

Sorotto's pale eyes flashed and his hands tightened into fists but before he could speak Nante, who had been standing by Laurie's bed, returned to the table and sat down again.

'The Englishman is right; we should all watch the count,' he said. 'Not because we don't trust one another, but because it's what is right. But Pérez, stand back and have your rifle ready in case of treachery.'

'My brother's life is worth more than the money,' John said mildly. 'But carry on.'

He dragged a chair across the room and sat down by Laurie, fingering the revolver in his pocket. It was loaded, the safety-catch off; if Sorotto did try to claim the money was insufficient, or if he simply tried to kill either of them, John was determined to take at least one of the trio with him. And he knew it would be Sorotto who would leap for his gun first.

But in fact the count went well. There were astonished looks when they found that, far from the few hundred pounds they had expected, there was much more than that amount, but though John saw Nante give Sorotto a very penetrating glance, nothing was said. Finally, with the money in heaps on the table, Sorotto turned his head.

'Very well, the bargain's complete. We're going to cross the border into France tonight. You?'

'We'll wait,' John said. 'Laurie's not fit to leave yet.'

'Please yourself.' He turned to Nante. 'How much food have we got left?'

'What there is we'll leave,' Nante said curtly. 'For all that money . . . why is there all that money, incidentally?'

He stared at John, who stared back.

'Ask Sorotto; I'd be quite interested to know why he didn't confide in his partners, myself.'

'In case you reneged, of course,' Sorotto said scornfully. 'Why else?'

'Doesn't make sense, but . . . think about it,' John said encouragingly to Nante and Pérez, both staring from him to their friend as though watching a tennis match. 'It'll keep you busy as you climb the Pyrenees, no doubt – unless you intend to catch a train now that you're in the money?'

'Us? Offer English money without being questioned, suspected?' Nante said, grinning. 'No, we'll walk for a bit.' He jerked his head at the other two and they began to move towards the old and battered door but before they reached it, Nante turned to John once more. 'We got on well with your friend; he's a nice fellow. We wouldn't have harmed him.'

'No? What about Sorotto?'

'Him neither; we wouldn't have let him.' That was Pérez, grinning, snapping his fingers, obviously excited by the money and by the fact that they were on their way at last, after what must have been a fairly nerve-racking couple of weeks. 'He's a nice *hombre.*'

John grinned back. 'You're right. But watch your friend. A third of ten thousand pounds sounds a lot, until you consider the whole.'

Pérez's smile faltered, but Nante opened the door and ushered him firmly through it.

'You're thinking of thieves falling out, eh, *amigo*?' he asked cheerfully. 'It won't happen, we've been together too long. *Adiós!*'

The other two echoed the farewell, then the big wooden door shut behind them and John and Laurie were alone in the dirty little room with its straw-strewn floor and its unglazed slit of a window.

Fourteen

Spring had come to Madrid, but it was a harsh and unforgiving spring. Indeed, even the warmer breeze, the sunshine, seemed hateful to Mirri, for now she had no one to share it with. Josefa had died in the dug-out that awful night and the next day, when Mirri had returned to the little house squeezed in between the two big ones, it was to find that the whole front of the building had been sheared away by a direct hit.

When the building had been struck Leá had been sitting in the downstairs room with Jacinta, engaged in some simple household task. The blast had sucked Jacinta out through the huge hole in the wall and thrown her down like a rag doll on a pile of rubble. Mirri had thought her unharmed, her beautiful, lively face untouched, her body apparently unwounded. But she was dead.

'It's blast; it kills without a mark,' one of the troopers told her when he came upon her trying to revive the girl. 'What are you going to do about the old lady?'

There was little she could do; Leá had somehow managed to convince herself that Jacinta had run out of the house and escaped the blast, that she was alive and well somewhere, and as soon as she was able to hobble she simply disappeared.

Mirri had returned to the house a couple of nights later, calling out cheerfully to her old nurse that she had brought a sack of rice, some sausage and some dried tomatoes as well as a bottle of olive oil, only to come face to face with a tiny, wrinkled old man who assured her, nervously, that he had been invited to take over the house by Señora Leá.

'She's gone to live with her daughter,' he told Mirri nervously, as the two of them met in the rubble-strewn hallway. 'She called out to us, explained who she was, said there was a back room and a good, deep cellar and would we like to move in? She said her daughter had left home hurriedly and told her to follow as soon as she was able. We were happy to find a roof beneath which to shelter, even though it's been terribly damaged. But the cellars are sound, just as the *señora* said.'

'I see,' Mirri said. 'Well, I'm afraid you'll have to share with me, because I've always lodged with Leá and I've simply nowhere else to go.'

The old man's eyes brightened. 'A militiawoman, under the same roof as me and my family? That is an honour indeed. Do you eat at headquarters or will you be coming home for meals? My wife is an excellent cook, one of those women who can make a feast out of almost nothing.'

'I eat once a day at home, and bring my rations here,' Mirri said, almost smiling for the first time since Jacinta's death. She knew that it was her rations which would ensure her welcome, not her physical presence. 'We are fed by the army during our shifts, of course.'

'Of course,' the old man echoed. He held out a gnarled brown hand. 'Fidelio Amarante at your service! And you are . . .?'

'Miryam Rodriganez, better known as Mirri,' Mirri told him. 'If I bring you my rations, and any extras I can get, will your wife cook for me as well as for the family?'

'Certainly, certainly,' Fidelio said, rubbing his hands. 'It will be for us all a great pleasure.'

So Mirri settled into the cellar with the Amarantes and began to feel a little less lost. But as day succeeded day and the situation in the city did not alter, Mirri's enthusiasm for the war and its outcome began slowly but surely to drain away. Jacinta's cheerful determination and Josefa's comfortable convictions were no longer here to fuel her own belief in the Republic. Even when the warm and sunny weather returned and Fidelio managed to patch up the house so that they could use some of the rooms, she felt permanently cold and permanently afraid. If only Laurie would come, she found herself thinking. If he was to come now then she knew she would go away with him, back to England. It wouldn't be running away, it would be sensible, because she knew when the

Nationalists took Madrid she would be killed, and there could be little doubt, now, that they would take it. It might not be this year, it might not even be next, but the day would come and then they would all die, anyone who had fought, or even thought, for the Spanish Republic.

She had told Laurie that she was doing a good job for her country, that she was happy and did not want him to try to take her away from Madrid. This was no longer true, but Laurie's letters had suddenly stopped and though she had written, there had been no reply from him. In her secret heart she thought that he must have been killed as so many had been killed before him, and once or twice she had caught herself thinking that, even if he was alive and was to walk into Madrid this very day, he would scarcely recognise her. She knew she was disillusioned and war-hardened, knew the conflict and her losses had changed her completely from the naive, trusting youngster with whom Laurie had fallen in love to a politically aware woman who had grown cynical and detached after almost two years of war.

But she was dreadfully afraid, now, that Laurie would not come. I'll wait a month, she decided, once she and the Amarantes had done the best they could with the house and were settling down amicably in the place, and then I'll really think about moving away from Madrid. What good am I doing here, after all? I'm not saving lives or even killing fascists, I'm just manning stupid roadblocks and sitting in stupid trenches waiting for someone to take a pot-shot at me, or I'm cowering in a cellar. What's the *point* of it all? Too many good people had died already, why add one more name to the dreadful tally?

Still. She would give it another month. She did not know what she would do at the end of that time, she simply thought that she would make a change. And until then she would go on as before, manning roadblocks, keeping watch on the enemy from the trenches in University City, serving at the officers' club two or three times a week. She did not intend to grumble, or confide in anyone how lukewarm her adherence to the Republican cause had become. Perhaps, she thought vaguely, time would heal the wound in her belief as it would heal a wound in an arm or a leg; if so, she hoped such healing would come soon, before it was too late.

So Mirri behaved as though her life had some meaning and was not a hollow mockery of what it had once been, and bided her time. And the war rumbled on with the news always bad, the spectre of defeat always nearer. Sometimes it seemed to Mirri that all Spain was holding its breath, doing nothing, only waiting. But she was not in Aragon when the Republican army broke and fled for no cause that anyone could put a finger on. She did not understand the significance of Franco's gains, which had divided the country in two. She did not realise that, after Ebro, it would be Madrid.

'John, you should never have come back! You're a deserter, you know, so whichever side gets you, they'll kill you. You've got to get away, whereas I'll be safe enough. I'm wounded too badly to be useful, no one's going to bother to kill me because they'll think I'm all but dead anyway.'

Laurie, bearded now and hollow-cheeked from suffering and lack of food, spoke with all the authority at his command, which was not much. He had come round twenty-four hours ago to find himself lying in a tiny, filthy room, on straw, whilst John bathed his face with a hank of sheep's wool soaked in water, and tried to feed him with bread and hot Oxo. His only emotion, then, had been relief; John had found him, he would be all right now, but as soon as he had some food inside him and had thought, he had realised that John should have been with his brigade, that his first loyalty, according to army tradition, was to his company, no matter how shot-up and scattered, and not to his foster-brother.

And then, of course, they had talked.

John had explained briefly that the three men who had taken him from the hospital and brought him here were not friends, precisely. They had ransomed him.

'For what?' Laurie had said, weakly amused at the thought. 'For the tenner I left in the bank in Lisbon? Or for my uniform?'

'Nope. For real money. You're twenty-five now, Lo, a big boy. You've got the trust, or rather . . .'

'Really? But they couldn't have had that; Mr Hawkings would never give it up.'

'No, not under normal circumstances, but this was a bit different. Mr Hawkings didn't want to have your death on his conscience so he – he got the money together. I went over to Ledbury and brought it back within the stipulated period, then your gaolers went, leaving you and me here, together.' John paused. 'You were up in the old fort but I brought you into the village as soon as you could be moved and paid for the use of this stable, just for a few days. I trundled you in on a handcart and you slept like a child all the way. The villagers are good people, but . . . you know the fellows who brought you here? Well, one of them, Sorotto, would have killed you without compunction if I'd returned empty-handed. The others were all right, but Sorotto was an animal; in short, *not* one of the good cowboys.'

'No. I never did like him much,' Laurie had said drowsily. 'God, my right foot hurts!'

John patted his shoulder. 'Yes, I know, but in a couple of days, when you're stronger, we'll get you out of this.'

Laurie had not, then, completely understood. Pain and hunger, bone-weariness and shock, had anaesthetised him to a certain extent. But now, twenty-four hours later, his mind was sharper, and the facts were beginning to mean something. John had been out of Spain, without anyone's permission, for almost three weeks. And on his return, what had he done? He had come straight to the aid of his foster-brother, completely ignoring his responsibilities as a *teniente*. The Republican army was already suffering badly from desertions; they would love to make an example of a British officer, if they could lay hands on him.

'John? I said they'd shoot you as a deserter if they caught you. Look, I'm all right here, I'll survive somehow. You could bribe someone to take me back to Barcelona, perhaps. Only you must get away!'

John had been making them a meal; he had brought dried and tinned food back from England and there was still enough left to keep them going, he said. Now, he was stirring one of his concoctions in an empty corned-beef tin, over a tiny, smoking oil-stove. He turned and grinned at Laurie.

'Don't worry, we're both going. I thought we'd leave at dawn tomorrow, if that pleases your lordship.'

'Ha ha,' Laurie said weakly. 'And how am I to travel, my good man? I've not so much as put my feet to the ground yet.'

'By handcart,' John said briefly. 'I am going to drag you, enthroned on a handcart, right across the Pyrenees.'

'Oh John, you're quite mad! Look, I'm a dead loss . . . have you managed to get hold of some crutches? You said you'd try and I am a bit better. I'll have a go with 'em, then maybe in a few days . . .'

He flung aside the blanket, went to swing his legs round so he could get up, and gave a deep, agonised groan. He stared down at his legs, at his crushed and mangled left foot and at the right leg, which finished at the knee.

For a long moment Laurie said nothing, then he lifted his eyes from their contemplation of his injuries and looked across at John.

'When . . . what . . .?'

'They amputated in Barcelona; there was nothing else they could have done,' John said gently. 'But they've done the best they could with the other one and they say you should be able to walk, with the aid of sticks or crutches, once you've . . .'

'I'm a bloody cripple! A one-legged freak! *Un cojo*, half a man! And you want to take me back to England, to be pitied, talked over in hushed whispers round Herefordshire tea-tables! I'm better off here, where at least *un cojo* who has lost a leg in the war can beg for his bread. Whilst I'm in Spain no one need know, there'll be nobody to say *Poor old Clifton; have you seen him? He's a cripple – awful, isn't it?* Besides, if you leave me here then once you're out of the way I can finish myself off with a bullet through the brain – if someone doesn't do it for me, that is.'

John gave him a long, steady look, then tipped the contents of his corned-beef tin into two tin mugs. He walked over to Laurie and pushed him roughly back against the heap of dirty straw, then covered his legs with the blanket once more.

'There are others a thousand times worse off than you, old son; men blinded, deafened, men with no arms, no legs . . . so don't let's go through the self-pity thing. It's bloody hard luck, I don't deny it, but at least you've got a home to go to, a country that isn't being torn apart by civil war and someone to give you a helping hand until you're fit again. So how about counting your blessings and eating some of this so-called stew, instead of sitting there pitying yourself?'

'There, you see? All I can do is . . .'

'Laurie, I'm warning you! Count your blessings, old fellow, and try to eat. You'll need all your strength for the ordeal ahead. We're leaving at dawn tomorrow.'

He pushed a mug into one of Laurie's hands and a chunk of bread into the other. The smell coming from the mug was savoury and despite himself it brought the water rushing to Laurie's mouth. But he was still appalled by what had happened to him – how had he not known? He put the bread down and then stood the mug on the floor beside it. He tried to be sensible, but he was filled with bitterness and dread. A cripple! How could he face them, at home? Everyone thought he had been mad to come, but if he had returned with Mirri tucked against his side, a whole man, then they would have understood. And what about Mirri? She would have no use for a one-legged man, *un cojo*, even if he was rich. So I'll never marry, he thought despairingly, I'll never lead a normal life, not now.

But the word 'rich' had reminded him. He scowled across at John, determined to know the worst, to lay bare the truth, however unpalatable it might be.

'Well? How much of the trust money's gone, then? Just what did you bring back to those three greedy bastards, Hoverton?'

He saw the colour leach from his friend's face, then rush back in a tide of crimson guilt. But John faced him steadily, nonetheless.

'A good deal. But money's only money, old fellow, and you've still got . . .'

'They found out how much it was, didn't they? They demanded it all, didn't they? And you, you soft bugger, you handed it over. Go on, admit it; you've made a pauper of me, haven't you?'

John sighed and shrugged, then nodded slowly.

'Yes, I suppose I have. I didn't mention any sum, apart from anything else I didn't have a clue how big the trust was, I told them I'd bring them three hundred pounds and they were well-pleased. But Albert Rudge was in your hospital ward, remember? He spilled the beans, never knowing, of course. They took most of it; Laurie, I had no choice, Sorotto would have . . .'

'Killed me; I know it and I wish to God you'd let him,' Laurie said thickly. 'Oh, I wish to God you'd let him!'

And with one quick, convulsive movement, he turned and buried his face in his pillow of dusty hay.

John left the stone building and stood outside in the yard as the sun slowly inched down the sky, flaming to scarlet the plain below and the softly undulating foothills of the Pyrenees. He understood some of what Laurie must have felt, but there was a deep, desolate ache inside him, an ache due partly to a sharing of Laurie's pain and partly to guilt. He should have managed to keep back some of the money, he could have lied, got counterfeit notes from somewhere, done something, anything other than meekly hand over Laurie's fortune. But time had been so short and he had been so desperate to save Laurie's life . . . it seemed hard, now, to be told Laurie didn't want his life, would have preferred to die.

And it isn't true, either, John reminded himself stoutly. He dipped a chunk of the coarse, dark-brown bread into the thin stew and chewed it dutifully. If he was going to drag Laurie over the Pyrenees on a handcart – and he was – then he needed all the strength he could get. No, it wasn't true that Laurie wanted to die. He had been shocked and disgusted to find that his leg had been amputated, horrified to hear that the ransom which had been paid for his life had been most of his inheritance, but he would come round. He would learn to walk again, he would begin to enjoy life . . . once they got back to Herefordshire everything would be different.

He stayed out in the yard until the darkness was absolute, then returned to the shed. A moon hung in the sky outside, big and pale and cold, and illumined Laurie where he lay sleeping. John walked over to his friend and looked down. The mug was empty, the bread had gone, and scratched in the earth floor were what looked like . . .

John bent and peered. A twig lay nearby and Laurie had used it to scratch a message.

'Sorry, J. L.'

John found his eyes filling with tears; Laurie hadn't changed, not really. Right now he was coming to terms with losing a leg, believing that he would lose his lover, hearing that the money on which he had relied had gone. But underneath he was still Laurie and one day he would look back on this night and marvel at how he had thought himself better off dead.

John crossed to his own small patch of straw and lay down. He did not expect to sleep much, but he had better get what rest he could. Tomorrow looked like being a pretty tough day.

Presently, against all his expectations, he slept.

In the grey dawn they set off, Laurie blanket-wrapped and silent, shivering with cold, John with his own blanket round his shoulders and the rest of their possessions piled at the foot of the handcart. No one came out to see them off as the cart rumbled up the dusty village street and all too soon they were beginning to climb.

When the sun rose and turned the mountain-tops pink they stopped for a breather and something to eat. They were quite high now, and could look down on the little town below them. Smoke curled up from a chimney, and people, small as ants, emerged into the street, going about their business. Laurie, taking the chunk of flat bread and the few olives held out to him, said humbly, 'Thanks, John. Sorry about last night. It was the shock.'

'Doesn't matter,' John said. 'I – I read your note. We're going to have to keep our eyes peeled for water, though I filled every container I could find. Perhaps you could do that, old boy.'

'Course.' Laurie sat up and tugged at his blanket, freeing his legs. He looked at them with distaste, but lying to one side of them were the homemade crutches which John had paid a villager to fashion for him. Laurie laid a hand on the smooth wood. 'Shall I see how I go?'

John hesitated. He felt he ought to encourage Laurie to do as much as he could but on the other hand they were on rough and rocky pasturage and a fall might make things worse. Accordingly, he shook his head.

'Not yet, old boy. Ground's too rough. Wait till we stop this evening, when we've made a bit more headway. When we reach France, of course, you'll find it much easier going.'

'All right,' Laurie said.

John glanced at him uneasily; he was being far too co-operative, meek, almost. It was a far cry from the Laurie of the previous night. But he finished his own meal and stood up, seizing the handles of the cart once more. His arms were trembling still from the strain of pushing and pulling the cart and though he would never admit it, a couple of times on the steeper slopes he had thought his heart would be torn from his body with the effort he was forced to make. He had heaved at the cart with all his strength, fighting its natural desire to trundle downhill, and was beginning to realise what a task he had set himself. If Laurie could walk, or scramble rather, for short distances, it would undoubtedly help a lot. But he dared not risk a tumble. So for the time being they would continue as they were.

'I'm going to push on the flat bits and pull on the steep slopes,' he said rather breathlessly presently, turning the cart laboriously and heaving it as a pony might, up a narrow and stony track. 'It saves on energy.'

'Sure. But no point in going too far today,' Laurie said presently, his voice sounding thin and small in John's pounding ears. 'The next time you come to a flattish bit, let's camp.'

John agreed and continued to strain on the handles of the cart. *I'll get him to France if it kills me,* he began by thinking, but soon it was *I'll get him to France if it kills us both* as the gradients steepened and the stretches of flat ground lessened, for Laurie was pale and silent once more, obviously suffering a good deal of pain as he was bounced and bumped up the stony weathered track.

But John kept on. Somehow, with frequent rests, he made the top of the first peak before dusk. Then the two of them sat in the gloaming, not saying much, staring out over the great plain beneath them, at the lights of Figueres far below.

'Downhill tomorrow,' Laurie said presently, as John wedged the handcart into a rocky niche so that even if the weather got bad his friend would be at least partially sheltered. 'Can you get in here, too?'

'No. But there's another niche a few feet away,' John said soothingly. 'If you need me, call. I'll be with you in no time.'

'Right,' Laurie said meekly. 'Sleep well, old chap. You've had a pretty grim day.'

John chuckled. 'No. The grim days are behind me now. When I was trying to get to England and back . . . now that *was* grim! This is a picnic by comparison, so sleep well yourself.'

'I will.'

But even before the sky lightened with the dawn, Laurie was awake. He got himself out from under the cart, not without difficulty, and then got up on his knees. He fumbled for the crutches, and after a good deal of grabbing and swaying, actually gained his feet. Then, with the crutches jammed into his armpits, he took two wavering and uncertain hops, swinging his stump and using his good foot.

It was not easy; it was hard, damned hard. But in the hour before dawn, with the utmost care and quietness, he practised diligently, and by the time John stirred Laurie could swing himself for a few steps, though his good foot, which wasn't that good, really, hurt so much when he balanced on it that he came near to giving up.

But he remembered the wheeze in John's chest after a steep climb the day before, the waxy pallor of his face, and he persevered. He must be able to take some of the weight from John's shoulders, he simply must!

'Downhill's easy,' John said jubilantly as they set off after a breakfast of more bread, olives and a small piece of smoked sausage each. 'All I have to do is make sure you don't career away from me and smash my lovely handcart on those perishing rocks down in the valley.'

It was harsh terrain, though, uninhabited not only by man but by most other creatures, too. Occasionally they saw a yellow-eyed, skinny goat or a vulture circling but other than that they saw nothing and no one. And though John declared that downhill was easy, it proved not to be the case at all. He found himself having to use all his strength to stop the handcart from simply snatching itself free and bouncing down the boulder-covered hillsides. By evening he had wicked blisters all over his hands and even his stout boots had not altogether saved his feet from damage, and Laurie, whilst not complaining, did mention that he'd got wood-splinters in his fingers when unexpected jolts had caused his clutching hands to slide along the rough wood.

'We're a couple of crocks,' John said wearily as he slowed the handcart after a heart-stopping scramble up a goat-path no wider, in places, than ten inches or so. 'Ah well, we've got this far so we'll spend the night on this little plateau, I think. There aren't any suitable crevices but we can lie against the rock.'

'What about wolves?' Laurie asked uneasily. 'Don't they live in the mountains?'

'Don't know. No one mentioned wolves to me when we were talking about going over the Pyrenees,' John assured him. 'Come on, one short sharp tug and we're there.'

They reached the plateau and Laurie sighed with the sheer bliss of not being in motion. John wedged the handcart with a couple of large stones and flopped onto the rocky ground. 'Phew! I hope we see a stream tomorrow or we're going to run short of water.'

'We're bound to find a stream as we go higher,' Laurie said. 'And there'll be snow, I fear. They say it never quite goes from the tops.'

'Well, at least it will be cooler; I must sweat out every spoonful of water I drink and more. And I'm pretty damned tired,' John said. But he got to his feet nevertheless. 'I wonder what those birds are doing?'

'Which? Oh, them. Kites, aren't they? They're a long way off and pretty high up, something – or someone – has probably fallen over an edge, and they're anticipating a good meal.'

John shuddered. 'Yes; there was a nasty moment earlier in the day when I thought you and your carriage were about to go for a fly. But it didn't happen, so there's no point in worrying. I'll make up some of that dried soup stuff with the last of our water, shall I?'

'No need. Let's just have bread and olives and a drink of water,' Laurie said wearily. 'Then we can try to sleep.'

Laurie, practising very early each morning, was getting almost proficient on his crutches, though he recognised that, on the sort of terrain he and John were crossing, a man on crutches would be little or no use. But today, as the dawn greyed the sky in the east, he had managed to circumnavigate the small plateau twice and was feeling extremely pleased with himself. When John woke and saw him he gave an involuntary cry of alarm, scrambling to his feet before he recognised Laurie.

'Lo, what a devilish fright you gave me,' he said reproachfully. 'I'd been having a lovely dream, all about food and pretty women, and then I wake up to find you looming over me. But how marvellous, you're actually getting about. Well done, old boy!'

'Thanks,' Laurie said. 'Want to watch me go?' Without waiting for a reply he set off, keeping to a steady pace, and went neatly round the plateau, wheeling to a halt before John's startled gaze. 'Well? What d'you think?'

'You've worked a miracle,' John said solemnly. 'But you'll have to get back on the bloody handcart for a while, my son. We've a long toil up and a dreadful slither down to face before there's a chance of another drink and you know how it is, when you've no water, then your thirst just grows and grows.'

'Right,' Laurie said. 'But when we get into the foothills perhaps I can walk for a bit then.'

He knew he sounded wistful but he couldn't help it. The handcart was terribly dangerous and horribly uncomfortable and he was terrified that dear old John would have a heart-attack or something, lugging his burden up the sort of inclines which were best left to mountain goats.

'Perhaps you can,' John said. 'We'll set off now, and we can chew our ration of olives as we go.'

They found a stream on the evening of the third day. It tumbled down a rocky defile, clean and fresh, with patches of grass on its banks here and there. They drank deeply, then filled their water bottles, and then, with a backward glance or two, set off once more.

The mountain ahead of them loomed black and white-capped. 'We'll go over its shoulder though, not its head,' John explained. 'You can see the path . . . it's high, but it can't be as bad as it looks. We'll need to find shelter tonight, a cave if we're lucky.'

That sounded reasonable, until they lost the path. Or perhaps they didn't lose it, it was just too narrow for the handcart and too steep, as well. At any rate John found himself pulling the handcart over ground so rough that not even a saint could have stood it.

Laurie, white-faced, shouted to him to stop and rolled off the handcart and onto the ground.

'You can't do it, old fellow,' he panted when he'd got his breath back. 'And what's more, I can't, either. I'm going to try to crawl up this next bit. You'll do it all right without my weight on the cart.'

And for a couple of hundred yards the two of them battled against the mountain, and as it grew dusk, against the cold. Above them the snow, looking dirty and menacing, capped the mountain-top. On their level nothing grew, no bird flew, not even a vulture. And they saw no cave, no sheltering boulders, nothing but rocks and the snow above them.

'We'll have to stop here,' John panted at last. 'There isn't much shelter and there's a storm brewing by the look of the clouds, but we've gone far enough. We'll drape the biggest blanket over the handcart and we'll both squeeze under there somehow. We'll make it till morning that way.'

They did, but it was an eerie and unforgettable night. The storm hit them a couple of hours after they had made camp, and despite the covering blanket and the sturdy little handcart they both found their teeth chattering as the snow and sleet lashed against them. But apart from huddling together like a couple of puppies there was little they could do, so they drank a mouthful or two of water, ate the last of the bread and olives, and then simply hunched up, backs to the blizzard, and endured.

At some time during the night John must have fallen asleep for a few minutes, for he certainly dreamed. In the dream he and Laurie were making their way through a narrow mountain pass with towering crags to their right and a deep and awesome drop to their left. Laurie was on his handcart, John was pushing, and suddenly Laurie leaned over the abyss and said in a conversational tone: 'Well well, look who's here!'

John obediently looked . . . and saw a ghastly sight. It was a man, eyeless, with the blackened flesh of the long-dead, crawling up the sheer face of the rock towards them. He saw John looking and waved a skeletal hand. 'You've come, you've come,' he said in a creaking, falsetto voice. 'How *delightful* to see you, my dear boys, how truly delightful! I didn't die in my bed, as I realise you know, but has anyone told you I was murdered, thrown over a precipice as I slept? Ah, the ingratitude of one's nearest and dearest never fails to amaze. Dreadful, what the young can do to one.'

John gasped; although totally unrecognisable, he knew it was Sir George and so did Laurie.

'Hello, Father,' his foster-brother said. 'How's hell?'

'Not so good, lad; not so good,' the ghastly figure of Sir George said mournfully. 'But I'm on my way up, as you can see. Yes, I'm on my way up!'

And before John could speak or move, Laurie had said jovially, 'Oh no you're not!' and had put his good foot right in the middle of Sir George's chest and pushed. Sir George, with a dreadful cry, went bouncing down the cliff and as he went his screams echoed hollowly around and around and around and around . . .

And John awoke. His heart was hammering in his chest and sweat had run down the sides of his face and soaked his shirt-collar, but at least he now knew it was nothing but an extraordinarily vivid dream. What was more it was no longer black night, he could see a lighter patch in the sky to the east, and the storm had eased, though the wind still howled fretfully around the bare crags above their heads. John inched the blanket away from the handcart, conscious of the sleeping weight of Laurie against his back, and saw that the snow was piled up round them but that it had stopped snowing. He clambered out of what had become, during the course of the night, quite a warm little nest and stretched, then glanced up at the mountain still left to conquer. Birds, either vultures or kites, he could not tell which at this distance, circled up there, and behind them he could see a small patch of very pale, ice-blue sky, and even as he watched one of the birds gave a screeching, haunted cry.

So that was what made me dream that beastly dream, John thought to himself, unpacking the camping stove from beneath the bit of canvas which held their belongings safely to the foot of the handcart. Well, whatever they've got up there, it's unlikely to be Sir George! And with that he lit the camping stove and put a tin of water on to boil, then produced a small bar of chocolate and a handful of porridge oats. He had been saving the chocolate for an emergency and in view of the fact that they had no bread and no olives and must, he felt sure, be almost over the Pyrenees, it

401

seemed appropriate enough to celebrate.

When the porridge was made John sliced the bar of chocolate into slivers over the top in lieu of cream or sugar. Then he woke Laurie, who came crossly back to consciousness, rubbing his eyes and complaining that he'd been dragged back from a wonderful dream in which he had all the legs he needed and the services of his favourite filmstar, the blonde and busty Mae West.

'Sorry, old fellow,' John said remorsefully. 'But personally, I had the ghastliest nightmare and couldn't wait to wake up. And unless we start descending soon we're in trouble since we've almost no food left.'

'How much is almost none?' Laurie said, tipping porridge and chocolate into his mouth with considerable enthusiasm. 'I say, this is really good.'

'Almost none is about a spoonful of oats, the same of dried beans, one more powdered soup and that's it,' John said, examining his rucksack. 'Still, if we keep on slogging that should see us down into the foothills of France.'

'I dreamed of Kendal mint cake,' Laurie said wistfully. 'Why didn't you pack a bar or two of that, old fellow? It keeps you going in the mountains for days. Still, there you are, some people have no foresight.'

'True. I apologise for my stupidity. And for giving you a kick up the posterior to get you moving, which I shall do in ten seconds if you aren't perched on the handcart by then.'

'No point; it's scramble-time,' Laurie said gloomily, eyeing the tiny, ladder-like path up which they had to adventure. 'I'll go ahead, then if I fall you can catch me. And you drag the cart. I'd tell you to tip it over the edge, but . . . sorry, what have I said?'

John, who had shuddered violently, patted Laurie's shoulder and began to tie their possessions on the handcart.

'Sorry, it was just that nightmare I was telling you about. Tipping over edges came into it. Are you fit? Then start crawling.'

It was a long and dangerous haul. Right at the top, where the wind whistled so loudly that conversation was almost impossible, they rested. And up here it was flattish, so Laurie, ruefully regarding his scraped and bloody knees, hoisted himself onto his crutches for a bit of practice. He was deeply tired, but the journey down would be easier than the journey up and anyway, it had taken them so long to reach the summit that it was doubtful whether John would let them go very much further tonight, especially since he had spotted what looked like a cave only thirty or forty feet below them.

So round the summit Laurie went, then returned to sit on the edge of the handcart. John was lying, face down, on the rocky scree. Laurie could not see his face but he knew if he could it would be drained of colour, the eyes ringed with the black of almost total exhaustion. He glanced down towards the little cave; if he could get there under his own steam it really would save John a gruelling thirty minutes or so. And presently, when he stopped near John again, he heard a small, curling snore emerging from his foster-brother's mouth. He grinned; that was good, John could do with the rest. And he could have a go whilst John slept, then if it was too much for him he could claw his way back to the handcart and pretend he had been snoozing, too.

He was about to set off when he saw the birds again; circling just below him. They were bigger than they had seemed, definitely vultures, or something similar. Huge wings, long, bare necks . . . they were descending now and then, then flying up again as if afraid. Laurie stayed where he was for a moment, looking down. If there was something dead and disgusting on the path he did not much want to encounter it on his crutches, far less find himself buzzed by a very large and indignant vulture which thought he was horning in on a good meal.

But the path wasn't too steep at that particular point and he could, if necessary, crawl down it. Don't be a ninny, Laurie, think of what John's had to do, he adjured himself, and set off.

Ten action-packed and terrifying minutes later he reached the little plateau with the cave on one side of it. A vulture as big as a turkey was doing what looked like a macabre dance over something near the cave, its giant wings outspread whilst another, only slightly smaller, made darting dives at the first bird. It was all very well telling yourself that the vulture was one of God's creatures and couldn't help its odd appetites or its weird habits, Laurie thought, but when you were this close to one revulsion stepped in.

'Bugger off, you ugly bastards,' Laurie shouted. 'Go on, dance the fandango in someone else's backyard, we need that cave for . . . Oh, my God!'

The vultures rose, in a series of ungainly hopping runs, and were airborne and, oddly, beautiful. And behind them they left what was undoubtedly a man.

Laurie made his way over to it. He rolled the still figure onto its back, the words he had been about to utter dying in his throat. The man was very, very dead, and it was easy to see why. He had not fallen over a cliff nor had he been attacked by vultures – not whilst he lived, at any rate. He had been shot neatly through the centre of the forehead. And he was Pérez.

'As soon as I saw Pérez I guessed we'd find Nante, too,' John said later as they made their painful way further down the mountain.

Nante had been shot, though his wound was in the back of his head, and he had been lodged in a small gully halfway down the mountain. Too weak to dig graves, John and Laurie had simply piled rocks and boulders over the corpses and left them. 'I knew Sorotto was a natural-born killer, someone who enjoyed killing,' John panted as they continued down the stony little track. 'And as I said, three hundred pounds or so sounds a lot until you think of ten thousand pounds. I just hope and pray that Sorotto's well ahead of us, that's all. I don't fancy meeting him round some dark corner now that we know what we know.'

'Nor me,' Laurie said fervently. 'Do you think he lured them into the cave and shot them there? But if so, why was Pérez on the plateau?'

'I imagine because a shot's difficult to miss, especially in a narrow little cave like that one,' John said, having considered the matter. 'I'd guess that Sorotto shot Nante, who was the biggest and most fearsome, probably whilst he slept, and tipped him into the gully. Perhaps the shot woke Pérez, who managed to get out onto the plateau. But it's only conjecture, of course, and to be frank I don't want to know. Especially since Sorotto's the only one who can tell us what really did happen.'

'Yes, I see what you mean,' Laurie said thoughtfully. 'Any curiosity I may have harboured has just died; I don't want to know either. He must be well ahead of us by the state of the corpses.'

'A week or more, hopefully,' John agreed. 'Look, old fellow, would you mind camping down under the handcart again tonight? Only this path's too damned steep for my liking, I'm terrified I'll put you over the edge despite the bright moonlight. Next time the path zigzags we'll pull as far away from the drop as possible and snug down.'

'Suits me,' Laurie said laconically. 'I wonder if we'll meet a friendly goat which will let us milk it tomorrow? I could murder a . . . oh, sorry.'

'Quite. Even the thought of murdering a mug of milk makes me think of those two poor stiffs. But food, now; what've we got left? Some water and those dried beans. Well, I suppose we could chew on the beans, it might stop our stomachs actually keeping us awake all night.'

'There's a bend coming up,' Laurie said as John's toes dug frantically into the loose, gravelly surface of the path. 'Swing us over . . . that's fine. We'll be all right here till morning.'

'And tomorrow, please God, we'll see the fat lands of France spread out before us,' John said devoutly, wedging the wheels with a couple of large stones which he had brought down from the plateau for that purpose. 'Grab the small blanket and I'll drape the big one; we'll be snug enough under there, though at this altitude we may get sleet again.'

Despite John's foreboding, they did not have another storm and next day, as they negotiated a tricky bend, they saw France. The foothills ran down from the bare mountain crags into folds of tender green, melting almost imperceptibly into tended fields, rolling meadows, the tiny squares of cottage gardens and little farms, all stretching out before them like a promise of paradise.

'What a magical sight,' Laurie breathed, sitting up on the handcart and shading his eyes against the brightness of the morning sun. 'That's the sea over there, isn't it? How blue it is!'

'How it glitters,' John said. 'Imagine, in a few days we'll be on that sea, in a clean ship, with food in our bellies and as much as we like to drink. Life isn't so bad, eh, old fellow?'

'It's been worse,' Laurie said. 'Those poor chaps, John! I know they helped to rob me, but they had so little, you couldn't blame them trying to get something for themselves. Besides, you said it was only Sorotto who heard about the amount of the trust and insisted on having it all. I bet Nante and Pérez would have been happy enough with a hundred quid each.'

'They'd have been happy enough just with their lives, that's the sad and dreadful truth,' John murmured. 'Why in God's name didn't Sorotto just decamp with the money? He could have got clean away with a few hours' start.'

'Because that wasn't his way,' Laurie reminded his friend. 'Once he'd made up his mind to have it all he wouldn't dare to risk them following him, challenging him. It would be the same if he knew we were alive and had got across the Pyrenees. Well, it would be the same if he thought we were after him. He'd kill us without a thought, you said so yourself.'

'True,' John said. He had been sitting on the edge of the handcart, but now he stood up and squared his shoulders. 'Off we go then – France and freedom, here we come!'

Foxy couldn't believe it at first when Mr Hawkings told her that John had been home, taken the trust money, and returned to Spain.

'But why did you let him? What's he going to *do* with it? And why didn't he at least come in and see me?' she said wildly, staring at him across the desk as though he were personally responsible for what had transpired. And indeed she felt he was, at that moment. 'I've done my best for the estate, I've kept my part of the bargain, what more could I have done?'

'He took the money to ransom Sir Laurence,' Mr Hawkings said gently. 'So it was not for the monetary benefit of either of them, but for Sir Laurence's life. Mr John was in a tearing hurry because the men who were holding Sir Laurence said the money must be paid over in three weeks or he would be killed. And Mr John knew very well that one of the men was a killer who would have slit his prisoner's throat with pleasure, given the slightest excuse. So you see, there was no choice, as such, in the matter. It was either pay over the money or see Sir Laurence die.'

'I see,' Foxy said dully. 'Then what do we do now, Mr Hawkings?'

'We wait, Miss Foxy. The two young gentlemen are making their way home at this very moment, no doubt. Sir Laurence has been wounded, I don't know how badly or the nature of the wound, so that may delay them further, and I don't know whether it's occurred to Mr John, but officially he's probably posted as either dead or a deserter, so I hope most sincerely that he doesn't fall in with any troops of either persuasion.'

Foxy blanched and Mr Hawkings held out a comforting hand.

'It's all right, Miss Foxy, I'm sure they'll get home in a few weeks and then we can talk about what to do next. You've done an excellent job, Sir Laurence is going to be absolutely delighted with you, so you'll have no worries on that score. And money isn't everything, as I'm sure you know. At least you'll have your . . . your . . . at least you'll have Sir Laurence home once more, safe if not completely sound.'

Foxy murmured conventional agreement with this sentiment, but she was terribly worried. She and Allsop had been limping on from month's end to month's end, secure – they thought – in the knowledge that sooner or later Laurie would be back, and they would have sufficient funds to commence their various schemes for the improvement of the estate. Now, with no money, the future looked grim. But it won't affect me, Foxy told herself, because when John gets back I'll go to Bees-wing with him, I won't be needed here, then. As for the home farm, well, Laurie said he'd give it to me and I'm sure he'll do so. But if he can't afford to hand it over, so what? Mr and Mrs Hoverton will just have to get used to the idea that their precious son has married a penniless hop-picker!

As for Laurie, he had been wounded but would doubtless make a complete recovery, so she need not worry about him. All she actually needed to do was to see to her little son and wait for the boys to come home. Only then would they be able to untangle the web of lies she, Allsop and the boys themselves had woven.

Foxy had gone into Ledbury on the bus when Mr Hawkings asked to see her, leaving Allen in Edith's tender care, and when she came out of Mr Hawkings's office it was to find a fine, drizzling rain falling. Part of her, the farming part, was pleased because a fine rain penetrates and they had had a couple of very dry months. Another part, the housewifely part, was annoyed, because she had left a line of nappies blowing in the stableyard. And yet another part was disappointed because she had been looking forward to a wander round the town and some leisurely shopping and the rain would spoil all that.

But rain or no rain, she would have to think very carefully before she went shopping. What money she had might have to last longer than she had ever anticipated. And she realised, belatedly, that she had no way of knowing whether Laurie had ever managed to find his Mirri, whether he would be returning with her, or whether he and John would come back by themselves. And John might have to return to Spain once he had left Laurie at the Place.

It would be madness to go back, though, Foxy told herself defensively, walking quickly along the street and heading for the bus stop. The drizzle had turned into a positive downpour, with rain driving into the earth like stair rods, and Foxy turned up her coat collar and tried to shrink down into it as she walked. It isn't as if the war is any concern of his really, her thoughts continued, and it's going most awfully badly, according to all the wireless and newspaper reports. He really shouldn't risk himself when everyone says the Republicans can't win. Besides, he's got a son; he should come back and settle down now, for Allen's sake if not for mine.

She reached the bus stop and glanced hopefully up the road. Just as she turned her gaze back to the nearest shop window, she heard the bus's engine roar and saw it coming down the flooded road, a bow-wave preceding it. The driver saw her and drew in to the kerb.

'Hop aboard, Missie,' he roared. 'Lovely weather for ducks, eh? We'll all 'ave webbed feet be teatime if this goes on!' Obeying him, Foxy tried to tell herself once more that Laurie's predicament was no concern of hers; if he was penniless that was something he had to face. All she had to do was to remind him he had promised her the home farm, take the deeds and go to John.

But a pall of unhappiness had settled over her and was not to be easily shifted. It was not until she was upstairs in the nursery later that evening, bathing Allen in the oddly shaped baby-bath on its wooden stand, that she was able to throw off her depression, and even then she knew her happiness was a transitory thing. The baby, crowing and splashing, could take her out of herself but once he was fed and bedded, her thoughts would turn back to Laurie's problems – and her own – and she would feel all the old insecurity and unhappiness rushing back.

Money! What a curse it was, especially if you did not have it. But Laurie still had a great deal of property and his health and strength. No doubt he would manage perfectly well without her – and she must be allowed to go to John now, they had their own future to think of.

But all through the evening and even after she sought her own bed she worried about Laurie.

When Laurie and John reached France they should have been able to relax, but Laurie's mangled foot, which had been used constantly as the terrain grew easier, began to throb and burn. John unwound the bandages one evening when a glance at his foster-brother's face showed that Laurie was almost certainly running a temperature, and found the wound suppurating, with thin red lines running up from the worst of the gashes as far as mid-calf.

'We'll find a hospital,' he said firmly, gently replacing the bandages and throwing away the filthy, stinking dressing. 'This needs the sort of cleaning up which only professionals can give.'

And he was grateful that he had insisted when, upon their arrival at the nearest small town, Laurie began to talk wildly, his face flushed and his voice slurred.

'He's running a high fever,' the hospital doctor said when John managed to get Laurie inside. 'He's strong, there's no doubt about that, but the wound's septic and I fear the infection may have entered his bloodstream. Forgive my bluntness, but do you have money?'

'Enough,' John said. He was devoutly thankful, now, to Sir George for their sojourn in France after leaving school; his grasp of the language, though rusty, was still good. 'Can you cure him, Doctor?'

'We can treat him, which is all the most exclusive hospital in the world can do. You'll stay in the town so you can be near him?'

'If I may.'

'Good. Go to Mme Foix at No. 16, Avenue Marceau. She will give you bed and board and will not cheat you. And come back here in . . .' he consulted a wristwatch, '. . . in about four hours. By then we shall be able to tell you more of your friend's condition. He is just a friend?'

'That's right,' John said. He had no wish to have to go into yet more detail about his relationship with Laurie. 'We come from the same town in Herefordshire.'

'I see. Very well, *monsieur*, go now and return at six.'

John went back to the ward to explain to Laurie that he was going to get himself lodgings and found Laurie, looking absolutely dreadful, apparently sleeping. There was a nun sitting beside the bed and she smiled at John, plainly sensing his worry though he did not speak.

'When he wakes I'll tell him you've gone for a wash and brush up and some food,' she whispered. 'The doctor is a good man, he'll do his best for your friend. If God wills it, he will doubtless recover.'

John smiled, thanked her and left, feeling a little easier. He was sure Laurie was in good hands and getting the best care possible and he knew that his own nursing was nowhere near good enough. I should have realised he was doing too much, he castigated himself as he walked down the Avenue Marceau, searching for No. 16. I probably caused the whole thing by letting him hop along beside me on his crutches from time to time, but I thought he needed some mobility, some exercise. I had no idea it could do him harm.

Mme Foix proved to be a small fat Frenchwoman with snapping dark eyes and a full, scarlet-lipped mouth. She was neatly dressed in black with her dark hair in a bun on the back of her neck and she welcomed John to her home and showed him to a small, scrupulously clean bedroom and then, downstairs, to a slightly larger room where, she said with a shrewd glance at the state of him, he might repair for a meal every night at seven o'clock save that she would prepare him a snack now, whilst he made use of the jug and ewer in his room.

Her English was excellent and almost unaccented. John paid her the very modest sum required and went back to his room. He found a small tablet of soap and a thin towel and enjoyed the luxury of a strip-down wash, horrified by the amount of grime he removed from his person. That over, he brushed his hair, dislodging a goodly amount of dried grass and leaves which he had somehow managed to accumulate, and then glanced at himself in the mirror. What he saw shocked him to the quick. Haircut and shave tomorrow, he told his reflection grimly; you can't walk through a small French town looking like a Spanish brigand, far less pay regular hospital visits!

He went downstairs and Mme Foix met him in the small, dark hallway, with a tray. She went ahead of him into the dining room and unloaded from the tray a dish of steaming chicken and vegetable broth, a blue china bowl of freshly baked rolls and a pat of dewy yellow butter.

'That should last you until seven o'clock,' she said with an indulgent glance at the eager way he sat himself down. 'There is a bottle of good white wine on the sideboard; I'll pour you a glass.'

'You are very good,' John said, tasting the soup. 'And a wonderful cook as well, Madame.'

She bridled, shooting him a coy look.

'So all my visitors tell me. Well, young man, eat up, and when you've finished perhaps you could bring the tray and your crockery into the kitchen? We don't have many house rules but I'd best explain to you what they are and how they affect my guests.'

The meal was soon over, and all eaten, too, for the white rolls seemed heavenly to one who had eaten nothing but coarse unleavened bread for weeks. John had a modest half-glass of wine, afraid that it might go to his head after such a lengthy abstinence, but he thought it an excellent vintage and planned to buy some for Laurie in a day or two.

When he had eaten everything he wiped his mouth on the napkin provided and carried the tray down to the kitchen, which proved to be a large, stone-flagged room with bunches of herbs hanging from the ceiling, an immense oven dominating most of one wall and a great many religious pictures everywhere. Mme Foix welcomed him in, put his dirty crockery into a bowl of water to soak, she said, and then bade him sit down whilst she talked.

The house rules turned out to be simplicity itself. There was a visitors' book in the hall with four columns. Each evening, when a guest came in for the last time and did not intend to go out again, he signed his name in his column. Thus, in theory at least, the last one in knew he was last and so could lock the front door with the key always left in the lock for that specific purpose.

'Some people give keys out like confetti,' Mme Foix said disapprovingly. 'I prefer this method. And because I want to make life easier for us all, I do ask for punctuality at mealtimes. Breakfast is at eight o'clock sharp, luncheon at one p.m. and dinner is served at seven. In your case, however, because you have a friend in the hospital, I will merely ask you to tell me what your commitments are, so I can cater for you around them.'

'You are very good,' John said humbly. 'Are there any more rules?'

'No women in the bedrooms,' Mme Foix said promptly. 'On a Sunday some of my gentlemen like to lie in, and this is perfectly acceptable provided they tell me at what hour they will eventually arise. And don't expect breakfast, of course,' she added. 'Hot water for washing is available from six thirty in the morning until a quarter to eight, and in the evenings from six until seven.'

'Fine,' John said, rather dazed by such a rush of information. 'What about baths?'

'There is a public bath-house not a hundred yards down the road,' Mme Foix told him. 'And the laundry calls on a Monday. I don't do washing for my guests.'

'I see. And since the clothes I stand up in are all I possess, I think perhaps I had better go out and buy some bits and pieces. Can – can you suggest a suitable shop, Madame?' John asked.

'Go to M. Douvaine, on the Place Mairie,' his landlady advised him after a moment's thought. 'Doubtless your friend will need a nightshirt, a toothbrush, soap, and perhaps cachous to sweeten the breath? The clothing you may purchase from M. Douvaine, the other things are available at the pharmacy of M. Cherisy, on the Rue du Bois-sabot.'

Thanking her, John took his leave and walked to the Place Mairie, which was at the centre of the town. It was a pleasant spot with trees around the square and the shops small enough to be friendly. He would try to get Laurie a striped nightshirt, John decided, which would look more like English pyjamas but would be easier for nursing a wounded leg and foot. And now that his landlady had mentioned it, he realised how wonderful it would be to clean his teeth properly, with paste, instead of scrubbing at them with a worn and bare toothbrush.

The sun was shining as he came out of the gentlemen's outfitters and John felt comfortably full of chicken broth, new-baked bread and self-confidence. His landlady had recommended an excellent shop and he now owned a couple of shirts, a tie and two pairs of thin cotton socks as well as the striped nightshirt and a towel. He sang beneath his breath as he walked; things were looking up, he no longer felt quite so desperately worried about Laurie. He would just pop into the pharmacy for the rest of the things he needed and then he would go back to the hospital and give the little nun the nightshirt and toilet things.

The pharmacist was quick and obliging and John found a pointing finger can, on occasion, be as good as a grasp of the language. He paid for his purchases and hurried back to the hospital, hoping that Laurie would be awake and able to appreciate that he was now safe and in good hands.

The ward in which Laurie lay was quiet and sun-drenched, the patients mainly sitting out on the long balcony which ran along the south-facing side of the room. Laurie was in a partitioned-off section of the ward at the far end and John hurried along there, tapped and entered.

The doctor was standing at the head of the bed, talking to the small nun; they both looked grave, but they turned as John entered and the doctor said, 'Ah, it's our patient's friend. Nurse, will you stay here whilst I have a word?'

The nurse nodded and smiled and John gave her the brown paper bag with his purchases in it, explained what they were and then followed the doctor back into the main ward. As soon as they had left the small room the doctor turned to him.

'Monsieur, your friend is very ill indeed. I have asked for a surgeon from a large neighbouring hospital to come and see him in the morning. I can't say for certain until the surgeon arrives, but I fear it may be necessary to amputate your friend's left foot. The infection is severe and may otherwise prove fatal.'

John spent a restless and miserable night, totally unable to come to terms with what was happening to Laurie, and next morning was first down to breakfast and then could not eat what was put in front of him.

'They say Laurie may have to have his left foot amputated, and he's already lost the right one,' he told Mme Foix miserably as she served him with hot croissants, honey and more of the dewy butter pats. 'He's always been a very active bloke; he took the loss of his right leg hard.'

'So would any red-blooded man,' Mme Foix said, pouring milky coffee into a large white cup. 'Eat your breakfast; you're going to need all your strength if you are to give your friend the support he will want.'

John picked up a croissant, smeared it with butter and ate it absentmindedly, then took another. 'Yes, but what am I to do if they say I must give my consent to the amputation?' he asked miserably. 'I don't know this surgeon at all, how do I know that cutting Laurie's foot off is the right decision?'

Mme Foix considered, small head cocked to one side.

'He is a surgeon, you are not,' she observed after some thought. 'I am a cook and you are a soldier. If I told you that a broth needs a good bone stock to start it off, would you take my word for it or would you cast around to make sure I hadn't got it wrong?'

'Why, I'd take your word for it,' John said at once. He had eaten the second croissant and was buttering a third. 'You're a very good cook, Madame.'

'Well, at any rate I am a cook. If you meet this surgeon and don't trust him then you can always ask for a second opinion, but I am sure that the doctor is anxious only to do what is best for his patients. It is his opinion, remember, that your friend may die of blood poisoning if the foot is not surgically removed. If the surgeon who has come to examine your friend agrees with him can your opinion count, in such company?'

It cheered John considerably because he realised at once that she was right and, in the event, his opinion was neither sought nor taken. He went round to the hospital to find Laurie's bed empty.

'They're operating,' the little nun said, taking his hand and shaking it gently up and down. 'The surgeon is a good man; your friend could not have a better. Come back tomorrow; this evening he'll not be conscious enough to know you.'

'Very well,' John said, his voice trembling. 'Only I'd like to come back this evening, if you don't mind. Laurie and I were raised as brothers; he's very dear to me.'

The nun gave him a penetrating glance, then nodded slowly. 'Very well, otherwise you will probably imagine things to be much worse than they are. Come back at ten, when we are settling the patients for the night. Mr Clifton may be round by then.'

John spent the rest of the day walking round the town in a daze of apprehension. He found a river and fed the swans with bits of bread which he bought from the local baker. He practised his French on some school children who practised their English on him, and then he went back to Mme Foix's house and pushed her excellent cooking from one side of the plate to the other.

His fellow guests eyed him sympathetically but said very little. They were all French and had almost no English. Mme Foix bustled in with a bowl of fresh fruit and tutted at his uneaten food, then with the kindness which he had already realised was part of her nature, returned with a cup of chicken broth and stood over him whilst he drank it.

Ten o'clock saw him already outside the door of the ward, trying to peer in through the tiny glass panes in the swing door afraid to go in for fear of what he might find.

'Monsieur Hoverton?' The nun, seeing him hovering, emerged from the ward. 'Your friend is in a good deal of pain and has been calling for you. He's in a private room now – will you come with me, please?'

'Of course, Sister,' John said and followed her along the corridor and into a small, whitewashed room with an oil lamp burning beside the bed. Laurie lay on the bed with a tube leading into his arm and a cradle over his legs to keep the blankets off them. His face was pale and his eyes dark-circled yet he lay quietly enough.

'The fever has left him,' the nun whispered. 'Sit by the bed; if you need me, ring the bell. I won't be far away.'

John sat down in the chair she indicated and watched Laurie's chest rise and fall with his breathing. And presently, as he watched, Laurie's dark lashes lifted slowly and his gaze began to scan the room. John leaned forward and touched the thin brown hand where it lay on the coverlet.

'Lo? It's me, John.'

The eyes moved slowly, as though the owner of them was too tired even to look around, then fastened on John's face.

'Johnny? Where's this place?' It was a hoarse, slurred whisper.

'It's a hospital. You've had an operation, old fellow. How d'you feel now?'

Laurie grimaced. 'Awful. Can – can I have a drink?'

There was water in a jug on the side table and an empty glass. John half-filled it and raised Laurie tenderly with an arm round his shoulders. Then he held the glass to Laurie's lips. His friend took two quick, feverish gulps, then lay back, and John lowered him to the pillow.

'How was that? Nice?'

Laurie nodded weakly. 'Very nice. God, I've had some terrible dreams. I dreamed . . . but now you're here it'll be all right. You won't let them do anything I don't want, will you? Tell them they mustn't do anything to my other foot.' He gave a weak smile but his eyes were dark with remembered terror. 'I dreamed they cut the other foot off, too, and I couldn't bear it if that happened. You won't let them, will you, John?'

John, with tears in his eyes, shook his head. 'No, old fellow, I won't let them do anything you don't want. You know me – stubborn as a mule, just like you. Would you like another sip of water?'

Laurie sighed deeply and slowly shook his head.

'No, no more water. I'm bloody tired, old chap. I suppose you – you couldn't just hold – hold my hand for a moment, just so I know you've not gone away? I'll sleep if – if I know you're still there.'

'Easiest thing in the world, since I'm going to stay here for a while,' John said. He moved his chair alongside the bed and took the thin, hot hand in his again. 'In fact, if it's all right by you, I'll stay here tonight. I can sleep just as well on this chair as I did under that wretched handcart.'

Laurie muttered something, then his eyelids drooped and he slept.

But two or three times, during that long night, he awoke with a cry, to grip John's hand with all his strength and to beg him, sometimes with tears, not to let them cut off his other foot.

Fifteen

'It would have been nice to have come home in September, when the hop-pickers would have been busy, and the bines would have been in full fruit,' John said as the train chugged across the rolling downlands in the late October sunshine. 'But at least the trees haven't lost their leaves yet and the colours are glorious.'

Laurie, swathed in blankets and still pale and hollow-eyed from his sufferings, grunted.

'Aren't the colours marvellous, Lo?' John prodded gently. 'Isn't it wonderful to be home, or on the way home, at last?'

'Yes,' Laurie said flatly after the pause had stretched and stretched.

John sighed and took out the newspaper which he had bought earlier. Laurie had been ill for so long that, even now, talking was an effort, but it wasn't that which made him so difficult, it was his whole attitude to his disability. He blamed John, the surgeon, even the little nun who had nursed him so devotedly, for his condition and he refused to look on the bright side because he said it didn't exist.

At first, of course, he had not realised the nature of the operation which had been performed on him and when he finally found out that his left foot as well as his right had been amputated he had gone into a kind of shock, where the news had to be repeated to him at painfully short intervals, and then he had simply refused to discuss his state. He told John frankly that he would sooner be dead than the way he was and though the hospital had fitted him with artificial limbs he refused to wear them; instead he crawled around the ward, to the annoyance of one or two other patients.

'We're sending him home because unless his attitude changes

there's nothing more we can do for him,' the doctor told John. 'He's far from well, but maybe he'll find it easier to accept his condition in England, amongst his own people. I'm sorry we've not done better by you both.'

'I'm afraid Laurie's taking it really hard,' John said gruffly. 'Sometimes I could break his neck . . . he simply won't listen to reason or make the best of things, and he keeps laying blame, mainly on me. I don't know what they'll make of him when I get him back to England. You wouldn't think it was the same bloke who left Herefordshire a couple of years back.'

'Time heals; give him time,' the doctor said quietly. 'As for being the same bloke as you say, he is not, of course. War and grievous wounds change more than the condition of men's bodies; they change the landscape of men's minds.'

And now, sitting in the train as it clattered through the golden autumn countryside, John remembered what the doctor had said and reminded himself, as if he needed reminding, that he must be patient, that time, the great healer, must be given a chance with Laurie. He looked across the carriage at his friend, huddled in his corner, and tried a grin. Laurie did not respond.

'As soon as we get to Bees-wing we'll have a socking big cup of tea and a slice of one of Mum's rich fruit cakes, shall we?' John said hopefully. 'Only perhaps you had best go straight to bed, Lo, and have your cake up there. It's been one hell of a long day.'

'I suppose.'

'We'll leave a bath until tomorrow,' John went on thoughtfully. 'Then, if you feel fit enough, we'll drive round to the Place and you can have a talk to Foxy and Allsop about how things have been going.'

For the first time, Laurie showed a little animation.

'I'm not going back to the Place. I'm never going there again. What's the point? There's nothing I can do, not now the money's gone.'

'Yes, but it is your home, Lo,' John said, trying to sound sensible. He was just grateful they were alone in the carriage. Other people, who did not know what Laurie had been through, could not possibly understand. 'Besides, you'll want to chat to Foxy . . . she's worked awfully hard to keep the place running for you.'

'Well, she can stop,' Laurie said flatly. 'I've no use for it. I shall sack the staff and close the house, that's all I shall do. And ask Mum if I can stay at Bees-wing until . . .'

'Until what?' John said, hoping for a reasoned and sensible reply. 'Until you're better?'

'Until I'm six feet under,' Laurie said grimly. 'That's all I've got ahead of me and you must know it.'

'John sighed. He unfolded his paper and spread it out. 'Don't talk like that to Mum and Dad though, or they'll be dreadfully upset,' he said helplessly. 'Come on, Laurie, you know Mum and Dad will love to have you to stay, but you'll get sick of kicking your heels at the farm in a week!'

'Kicking my heels? Oh, that's rich, that is! Why, if I *could* kick my heels . . .'

'I'm sorry, it was an unfortunate choice of phrase,' John said humbly, trying to quell an insane desire to laugh. It wasn't funny at all, it was sad, but for some reason he longed to give a huge guffaw. It's been weeks and weeks since I laughed out loud, he realised wonderingly. Well, thank God once we get home I'll be able to laugh again without offending his lordship!

'Unfortunate,' Laurie was muttering. 'Bloody unfortunate when it's you that's a cripple, you that's not got a penny to your name . . . how could I possibly earn my own living without being able to walk? Even if that girl had got Clifton Place up to scratch I couldn't keep it there like this!'

'Of course you could!' John said bracingly. 'But don't worry about it now; when you're better . . .'

Laurie snorted and John, defeated, dived behind his paper once more. Best to say nothing at all, he told himself, when he's in a mood like this. Best just to wait and see. But he had always hated waiting, action was much more his style.

So for the rest of the journey the two young men remained silent, John reading his paper and Laurie simply staring out of the window whilst the train clattered on towards its destination.

Foxy was building up the compost heap, layering in a judicious mixture of dead leaves, household waste and manure from the home farm, despite a good deal of non-cooperation from a frisky and fractious wind, when she thought she heard Mrs Waughman shout.

Time for a cuppa, she told herself thankfully, but nevertheless she loaded her barrow with the fallen leaves which threatened to bury her vegetable garden completely and pushed it along the neat brick path. As she passed the green door, she thought, she could put her head out and see if Mrs Waughman was really telling her it was time for a break, or whether it was just wishful thinking. She approached the doorway, but whilst she was still several feet away, Mrs Waughman's head appeared round the edge of the door frame.

'There's a feller at the door askin' for you,' Mrs Waughman said, trying to capture several wisps of grey hair which were blowing all round her face. 'I told 'un you were out yur but 'e looked so 'elpless like I said I'd give 'ee a shout.'

'Oh, all right,' Foxy said, standing her wheelbarrow down with some relief. 'I could do with a cuppa, Mrs Waughman; is the chap in the kitchen? And is he selling something?'

'I dunno if 'e's sellin' or no,' Mrs Waughman said doubtfully. Foxy, who could tell a seed merchant's traveller at fifty paces, sighed. Mrs Waughman, she thought, would have difficulty telling men from women if the former didn't wear trousers and the latter skirts. 'Still, 'e never said 'e were sellin'. An' I put 'un by me, in the kitchen. Might as well wait wi' me, I thought. I give 'un one of my new-baked scones.'

'Oh well, he must be all right, then,' Foxy said. Mrs Waughman would never have offered one of her famous scones to someone she didn't trust. 'I do love your scones, Mrs Waughman, especially when they're still warm from the oven. I shan't be a tick, I'll just empty this barrowload into the compost.'

She tipped the leaves onto the heap, shovelling them deep into the hot heart of it, and then dusted her hands together and set off for the kitchen. The kitchen garden, which was her pride and joy, was actually beginning to pay for itself and to produce sufficient fruit and vegetables to feed them all, so the compost heap was going to boost production, according to old Hector, at any rate.

Foxy went straight into the kitchen and over to the sink. The man was sitting up at the table, eating a scone. He grinned at her, a flash of white teeth in a brown face, and she registered vaguely that he did not look like an agricultural traveller as she held her hands under the jet from the big brass tap.

'Afternoon,' she said cheerfully with her back to him. 'I'm Foxy Lockett and I'm running the farming side of the estate for the owner at the moment. What can I do for you?'

She turned as she spoke and the man was shaking his head sadly. She saw that he was blond-haired and dark-skinned, that his chin was a good deal lighter than the rest of his face which seemed to indicate that, until quite recently, he had worn a beard, that his clothing was cheap, flashy-looking somehow . . . then he spoke.

'Foxy, you can't look me in the eye and say you don't know me any more! Or can you?'

His voice hadn't changed, but everything else had. She stood there, water dripping off her finger-ends, and simply stared, incredulous. He was taller, broader, yet gaunt, somehow. And much, much older. Not just two years but decades older. He made her feel young and gawky and stupid, like a baby bird still wet from the egg.

'John?' He had fathered her child, the bright little boy at present being wheeled round the estate by Allsop, to give her time to get at the garden. Foxy remembered how she had adored John and envied anyone close to him, and then how she had lain in his arms and begged him not to leave her. But he had gone anyway, because his brother needed him, because he wanted adventure. And now he was back and as foreign to her as it was possible to be. A big, raw-boned man with haunted eyes and a weary smile. A man, not an idealistic boy.

'Well? Am I John or aren't I?'

He meant it as a joke, but Foxy shook her head, genuinely puzzled. 'I don't know – I wouldn't have recognised you, you're so – so different! Is it really you?'

He stood up and came round the table. Mrs Waughman, entering the room from the scullery with a bowl of potatoes to peel, stopped short. Foxy moved towards him as though she could not help herself, but she did not want to get too near. Two years . . . oh, but so much water had flowed under the bridge since that night when she and John had made love so tenderly! She had been so certain then, but she was certain no longer.

'Foxy? Come on, sweetheart, give me a hug and tell me you're glad I'm back!'

For a second it was just John and Foxy and in that second she shot across the room and into his arms. They hugged briefly, John bent and kissed her equally briefly, then they stood back, both, Foxy was sure, embarrassed by the moment of closeness. He smells funny; odd and foreign, Foxy told herself. And he feels funny too, not strong bones and cuddly flesh, not the half-demanding, half-supplicant lover she had known. He was a stranger to her and his body was a stranger, too.

'Well, bless me, is that Mr John?' That was Mrs Waughman, mercifully placid as ever. 'I'm sorry, sir, but I can't deny I din't reckernise 'ee! There, now sit down, both of you, an' you shall 'ave more tea an' scones. Miss Foxy, she do enjoy a nice scone or two.'

It made them laugh which broke the ice a bit and Foxy remembered that no matter how he felt, John knew he could not come to her here as a lover. She was supposed to be in love with Laurie, and until they could untangle the web, that was how she must behave. Accordingly, in a voice which she strove to make ardent, she said: 'John, it's wonderful to see you, but why isn't Laurie with you? Don't say he's ill again?'

'No, he's not ill exactly, but he's still at Bees-wing. He's been quite severely wounded. He asked me to say nothing about the nature of his wounds, but in any case you'll see him tomorrow. Foxy, he's – he's not himself. He told me he would never return to the Place but my mother's talked to him and he's agreed to give it a try. So I'm bringing him back tomorrow.'

'Good,' Foxy said, again trying to sound eager. 'We'll have so much to talk about! Oh, is there any news of Mirri?'

'None. Look, we must all talk, but not yet. I came over chiefly to break my promise to Laurie, because you and Mr Allsop, at least, must know in advance that . . . that . . .'

'Go on,' Foxy said encouragingly. 'Mrs Waughman is the soul of discretion.' She turned to the other woman. 'You can keep a secret, can't you, Mrs Waughman?'

'Aye, that's right,' Mrs Waughman said, buttering scones. 'Do 'ee take sugar in tea, sir?'

'Yes, please. Two lumps. Foxy, my dear, Laurie's had both his feet amputated.'

There was a shocked silence. Foxy stared helplessly at John, not knowing what to say, and Mrs Waughman's buttery knife was suspended in mid-air.

'Oh dear God, poor old boy,' Foxy said at last. 'How's he taking it, John?'

'Badly,' John said briefly. 'But I'm hoping, when he gets back here, he'll see that there's some point in wearing his artificial legs and learning to walk. At the moment he's just ... just stopped trying. He's not interested in anything or anyone, he blames the world for what's happened to him and he wants, in a way, to hurt the world by ... well, by giving up, ceasing to exist.'

This time the silence was longer, until Foxy said uncertainly: 'I'm glad he's coming home, but what will he expect of me, John? I'm no nurse, I don't have the patience, and Allen takes up an awful lot of my time. We had a nursemaid, but she left, we couldn't afford to pay her properly.'

She expected John to look round, to light up, to demand to see his son, but he just nodded gravely.

'Yes, I suppose a baby does make quite a lot of work. Well, I think you must try to interest Laurie in life, Foxy. If you can do that then we're away, but if you can't ...' he shrugged. 'I just don't know how it will end,' he finished.

'Mirri? Couldn't she ...?' Foxy said, mindful of Mrs Waughman's listening ears. 'Look, John, there are business things I should discuss with you; if you'll just come to the study with me for a moment ...'

'Of course,' John said. He followed her out of the room and into the study, then sat in the visitor's chair whilst she took her accustomed place behind the desk. 'I take it you want to talk about Mirri without your housekeeper hearing?'

'More or less,' Foxy said. She realised suddenly, with a jolt of the heart, that John did not want to be alone with her. He was tapping his fingers on his knee, looking thoroughly uncomfortable. It was a relief in a way to see that she was as much a stranger to him now as he to her, but it was also a sort of insult. As if I'd leap into his arms after so long, and with so much between us, she thought crossly.

He's safe – and so am I! She took her place behind the desk and raised her eyebrows. 'Well? What's happened to Mirri?'

'Mirri was in the women's militia, defending Madrid. It's almost impossible to get letters anywhere specific, but when she did not answer one particular letter, Laurie enquired and was told that several units of the women's militia had been moved out of Madrid to other places where their services were needed. He knew he could get news of her from Madrid if he could get there, but getting there proved much more difficult than he had imagined and now, he fears she's dead. Anyway, he thinks she would have no time for a man without feet.'

'He shouldn't prejudge her,' Foxy said crisply. 'John, about the money. Mr Hawkings says there really isn't *any* left, apart from a few hundred. He has various suggestions to make to Laurie which might help, but he won't discuss it with me. And most of the work I've done has been on the home farm . . . I suppose I can scarcely expect Laurie to hand it over to me as we agreed, when the poor fellow's got no trust, no money at all coming in. But I haven't taken a penny in wages for months, though the Place does pay for my keep, and Allen's.'

'He'll pay you sometime,' John said defensively. 'Or I will . . . I'll take over the farm, you know, when Dad and Mum retire, then I'll be able to give Laurie financial help. I'll see you get wages until then, and the value of the home farm in time even if Laurie simply can't . . . but there again, he might prefer you to take the property.'

Foxy stared. But it had been her dowry, the gift which would make her acceptable to the Hovertons as John's wife! He could not have forgotten all that, surely?

'What's the matter? Oh, I know it won't be for a few years, perhaps, but won't you want to go back to Cambridge, once Laurie's got himself sorted out and is in command again, at the Place? I always thought you'd go ahead with your degree, when we came home.'

'Do the last year of my degree, with a toddler under my arm? I don't think that would be very acceptable,' Foxy said, at her driest. 'I suppose Laurie might employ me as an estate manager, though. I'm good at it, and as you already know, I'm cheap.'

The last remark was meant to be a double-edged sword, but John did not rise to the bait.

'Oh, I'd forgotten the child. Well, I can't answer for Laurie, but I know, when he thinks about it, that he'll acknowledge his debt to you. And you won't hold it against him that he can't pay you back immediately, Foxy? I know you – all sharp words and quick retorts but soft as marshmallow underneath.'

'Was I ever like that? I don't think so. But look, we'll have to talk about the child. I've not . . .'

'I'll pay you whatever you think is necessary,' John said quickly. 'But I can't acknowledge him – or you. Not yet. Not until we've got Laurie sorted out.'

'I haven't asked you for money,' Foxy began, and found she was speaking to an empty chair. John had simply got up and walked out of the room whilst his last words were still ringing in her ears. Foxy sat very still for a moment, staring at the swinging door. Then she hit the desk very hard with clenched fists – and began to laugh.

Of all the things she had imagined, this was the strangest. That John, whom she loved, who had said he loved her, should treat her so! Yet she acknowledged that he had changed beyond recognition so that they were virtually strangers – perhaps he was the more straightforward of the two of them in simply stating calmly that he could have nothing to do with either her or the child until they had sorted Laurie's affairs.

He's fallen out of love with me, Foxy found herself thinking quite calmly. And the truth is, I may well have fallen out of love with him. Only he must have known how he felt for some time, whereas for me it's only happened today, so it's still strange to me.

And presently Foxy, too, got up and left the study, walking calmly back into the kitchen as though her life had not just suffered a major change of direction. Mrs Waughman was peeling potatoes at the sink and Mr Allsop was lifting Allen out of his pram. They both turned to smile at her as she entered the room.

'All right, Miss Foxy?' Allsop asked. 'The young gentleman has been good as gold, in fact he fell asleep coming back; I do hope it doesn't mean he'll wake at six tomorrow morning.'

'Hello, you naughty young gentleman,' Foxy said, taking the warm, wriggling body of her son out of Allsop's arms and giving him a kiss. 'Thanks for keeping him amused, Mr Allsop, I got a tremendous amount of work done in the kitchen garden, nearly all the leaves are cleared. And we had a visitor whilst you were away, didn't we, Mrs Waughman?'

'That's right,' Mrs Waughman said after a pause for thought. 'Miss thought 'e were a traveller, but 'e weren't no sich thing.'

'It was John – John Hoverton,' Foxy said. 'They're back, Mr Allsop. John's bringing Laurie back home some time tomorrow. I must warn you that he's – he's been very badly hurt, but . . . isn't it wonderful that he's coming home?'

Across Allsop's face there broke a genuine beam of pure joy; there could be no doubt that he, at any rate, loved Laurie truly.

'Tomorrow? Oh, Miss, and his room not ready, nothing prepared, no special food got in . . . what time will he arrive? Can I go shopping? But young Master Allen's in cracking form, he said "moo" and "baa" when we passed the cows and the sheep, that'll brighten Mr Laurie's eyes!'

'I daresay you're right,' Foxy said. 'Mr Allsop, Laurie's lost both his feet.'

There was a dreadful pause; Foxy, watching Allsop's face, saw it age and grow grey before her eyes. But then, suddenly, his expression brightened.

'How terrible; truly terrible. Poor Mr Laurie, however will he bear it, and him so active always? But once he's back in the saddle things will change here, you may be sure of that. We'll put our heads together and we'll find a way to get the estate running properly. Mr Laurie will think of something, you'll see!'

And in the face of such cheerful optimism Foxy found she was incapable of disagreeing, of bringing the indispensable Allsop down to earth with a reminder that the trust money had gone and that a man who could not walk would be more of a liability than an asset.

'You're right, Mr Allsop,' she said, therefore. 'Come on, we'll go and see if there's any decent wine left in the cellar – there might be a bottle of champagne tucked away somewhere, you never know!'

Next day, they came. Foxy, with Allen in her arms, met them at the front door, Allsop hovering. Laurie looked absolutely terrible, grey of skin, hollow-cheeked, none too clean, with lines of pain and misery carved into his thin face. He made no attempt to greet anyone, though he kissed the baby's cheek and Foxy's when she more or less thrust herself and the child upon him. Then he shook hands with Allsop as though they were strangers, hunched down in his wheelchair and simply left them. Oh, he sat there, drank the coffee which Mrs Waughman made – the champagne remained in the butler's pantry; even Allsop could not help but realise that the last thing on Laurie's mind was a celebration – and nodded once or twice, but whilst with them in body, his spirit was far away. Bitter, brooding, he sat in the wheelchair, hunched forward onto his blanket-wrapped knees, staring at – what? Was he seeing the plains of Spain where he had received his terrible wounds, or the great mountain range that he and John had crossed? Or was he seeing the small, vivacious face of Mirri, the girl he loved and had lost? Foxy did not know, she simply found herself wishing, fervently, that John would take him back to Bees-wing with all speed, because she could not cope with such deep, intense animosity and unhappiness.

She acknowledged the animosity though she could not understand it. Did he hate them because they were able-bodied and he was not? Was it because of the wild rumours which had linked her name with his, made him the father of her child without the pleasure of begetting? She only knew that, when he thought she was not watching, he eyed her with deep, brooding dislike.

Just before lunch was to be served she escaped into the kitchen, ostensibly to tell Mrs Waughman not to forget to bring in a small dish so that she might let Allen eat with the rest, but really to buttonhole John who had left the room to use the downstairs lavatory.

'John!' she hissed as he emerged. 'Here!'

He looked as though he would have liked to ignore her, but he sighed and came over to where she hovered by the study door.

'What? I don't want Laurie to think we're whispering about him . . . you must have noticed how edgy he is!'

'Edgy? He's not edgy, he's too busy hating me and despising you,' Foxy hissed desperately. 'John, you can't leave him here, you just can't! If you do, I'll run away, I swear it. I told you before I didn't have the temperament for nursing and now that I've seen him . . . John, I'm plain scared! He's not with us at all half the time and the other half he's – he's plotting something awful, I know he is. Take him back to Bees-wing, please. Oh John, if you ever loved me, or thought you did, take him back!'

He looked astonished, then uneasy. She had said out loud what he was trying to forget, that he had loved her once, and bringing it out in the open had clearly hurt and worried him. These *bloody* men, she thought furiously, they go off to fight their wretched stupid wars without a thought for the people they leave behind and they come back a mass of contradictions and inhibitions and strangenesses and expect a woman to nurse them and pity them and take back a man who isn't the man who went away, who could turn round and murder her in her bed . . . John had loved her once, but his love had died. He expected her to accept this, to deny her own love and to go on facing him, pretending he meant nothing to her. It was impossible, too much to ask – but he asked it without compunction, without a thought.

'Take him back?' John said incredulously now, ignoring her frantic reminder of their love. 'I can't do that, Foxy, this is his home! It's taken me hours and hours of pleading and threatening to get him to come back here at all, but now he's here he must stay, he really must. He's got to take responsibility for himself, other-wise he's lost.'

'But John, the way he looks at me . . . and I've got the child to think about. Please, please take him away!'

'Foxy, listen to me! You've got him all wrong, he doesn't hate you – why on earth should he? He hates humanity, perhaps, but he wouldn't hurt anyone. What will help him most is to be away from me, partly because he holds me responsible for the amputation of his right foot, and partly because he thinks I should never have paid the ransom. Once he's away from me he'll soon begin to be his old self again, I'm sure of it.' For the first time he came towards her and touched her voluntarily, taking hold of her shoulders, looking earnestly into her eyes. 'Do you remember the old Laurie, Foxy? The boy with the lock of black hair always dangling over his eyes, so that he kept jerking his head to get it back? The boy who took on this barn of a place and his pig of a father and did his best for both of them? He's still there, Foxy, underneath. If only we can uncover him he can live again!'

But the words left Foxy cold. He had the nerve to ignore what had happened between them, to ignore their son, and to demand that she take on responsibility for the man he had saved, apparently against that man's will.

'Do it yourself!' she blazed at him. 'Do it yourself, you bloody arrogant Hoverton! Don't expect me to take on your burdens!'

John gasped and might have replied, but at that moment a voice spoke to them both.

'Lunch is on the table, Miss Foxy, Mr John, and Mr Laurie's going to need a rest afterwards. I've prepared the room next door to yours, Miss Foxy, so you can keep an eye on him if he wakes in the night, needs anything, but what about Master Allen? He's a good boy, but if he wakes from his afternoon nap and shouts as he sometimes does, he's bound to wake Mr Laurie, and Mr Laurie needs his rest.'

'Then you'd better unprepare the room . . .' Foxy was beginning crisply, still in a white-hot rage, but John laid a hand on her arm and jerked his head meaningly towards the butler. Allsop was standing in the doorway to the white drawing room and behind him, a shadow moved uncertainly; Laurie had wheeled his chair up behind Allsop and could no doubt hear every word.

'. . . Unprepare the room and put Sir Laurie a little further off,' Foxy finished smoothly. 'How about the room beyond the blue room? The rose room is quite a way from Allen, and it overlooks the side garden, too, which will be nice in the summer.'

'Very good, Miss Foxy,' Allsop said, giving both of them a forbidding glare. He must have heard them quarrelling and come out to stop them upsetting his master, Foxy realised. 'Ah, Mr Laurie, allow me.'

He seized the chair and wheeled the hunched figure out of the white drawing room and into the dining room and Foxy and John, chastened, followed meekly in his wake. In the dining room Allen was already sitting in his highchair, banging on his tray with a spoon. Allsop slid the small dish with its border of yellow ducks in front of him and spooned a revolting-looking concoction into it.

'Vegetable soup and some nice groats, Master Allen,' he said, as though the apple-cheeked baby had demanded to know what he was being offered. 'You'll enjoy that. And there's some lovely sieved plums for your dessert.'

Foxy happened to be looking at Laurie as Allsop spoke and to her pleasure and astonishment Laurie's dark eyes suddenly flared with wicked amusement and a smile curled his mouth. It was brief, it came and went like summer lightning, but it gave her hope. Perhaps John was right, perhaps all Laurie needed was to be in his own home again and he would 'come back' as John had put it.

'Roast potatoes, sir? You always did enjoy Mrs Waughman's roast potatoes. She does them with a little bit of bacon fat, I do believe, which gives them an extra bite.'

'Thanks,' Laurie said dully. He did not look at Allsop as he spoke and presently, when they had all been served, Foxy felt his eyes on her again. He was giving her that dreadful, baleful look once more, as though . . . as though he hated her.

I can't stand it, I'll run away, Foxy said wildly, inside her head. But already a tougher, more practical Foxy was telling her that she would do no such thing. Laurie owed her; she might not be able to get what she was owed at once, but she'd get it in the end. And in the meantime, since she and Allen could not live on air, she would stay here and do her best to turn the situation to her advantage.

'It isn't right, Mr Allsop. Mr Laurie just messed 'is food about, an' that's no way to treat my cookin'.' Mrs Waughman, washing up, was almost tearful. 'What's more, Mr Laurie, 'e needs feedin' up, but 'ow can we do it if 'e won't eat 'is vittles? You should ha' told 'im straight to eat up.'

Foxy, drying the dishes, felt for Mrs Waughman. That lovely meal, which they had all worked so hard over, had been wasted so far as Laurie was concerned. He had picked at it. John, on the other hand, had eaten everything on offer, even accepting a second slice of Mrs Waughman's famous cherry pie and ladling on the custard as though it grew on trees. It had plainly never occurred to John that food had to be paid for, or grown, or both. Rich bloody farmers, Foxy thought angrily, swearing – internally – for the second time that day.

'I will have a word with him,' Mr Allsop said now. He was

preparing a tea-tray, having taken Laurie up to bed for a rest. He had promised to wake him in an hour or so with a cup of tea and some of Mrs Waughman's homemade butter shortbread. 'But possibly it was the excitement of homecoming ... or perhaps, when one has eaten sparingly for some time, it becomes difficult to eat normally once more.'

'John seems to have managed it,' Foxy said nastily. 'I thought he'd never stop eating! Did he say when he'd be back?'

John had seized the opportunity offered by Laurie's nap to run away, or that was how Foxy saw it. At any rate, when she came downstairs after putting Allen down for his own after-lunch sleep Mrs Waughman told her placidly that John had left and had said to say cheerio to her.

'No, Miss, 'e didn't say when he'd be back. And as for 'is eatin' too 'earty, I like to see a young feller enjoy 'is vittles,' Mrs Waughman said repressively now. 'Mr John's 'ad a 'ard time an' all, Miss Foxy. Did you see 'im go short on one leg?'

'Short on one leg?'

'He limps,' Allsop explained. He was folding a linen napkin into a fan to place on the tea-tray, working with loving attention. 'No doubt you didn't notice, you were too busy watching Sir Laurie. It's the result of a bullet wound, I understand.'

'Oh, that,' Foxy said. 'He doesn't limp much, though.'

'No, not much. Will you take Mr Laurie's tea up, Miss, or shall I?'

'I will,' Foxy said, trying not to show her reluctance too openly. You are supposed to be in love with the chap, she reminded herself severely. He's supposed to be Allen's father, furthermore, and he's taken damn-all notice of my little chap so far. Of course it was understandable if you knew the truth, but the truth, right now, was best kept under wraps. Especially since John looked all set to deny paternity should it ever come to that.

'Very good, Miss. I've done the tray but I do think Mr Laurie needs the rest so perhaps you might take it up in an hour, shall we say?'

An hour later Foxy, tray-laden, went quietly up the stairs. She paused outside her bedroom door to peep at Allen, who was in fact completely invisible, a tiny bump under the coverlet and one small outflung hand being all that was on view, and then continued on to the rose room. Outside the door she paused to adjust the tray on her hip, went to knock, then changed her mind. Damn it, she wasn't a servant here, she wasn't even paid a pittance, let alone a wage. And since it was commonly supposed that she and Laurie had made Allen together . . .

She pushed open the door slowly and cautiously. Laurie lay on his back, dark eyes fixed broodingly on the ceiling above his head. She wondered if he had slept at all or if he had been lying awake all this time, waiting for someone to come and help him up. She came fully into the room and put the tray down on the bedside table.

'Come on, Laurie, your tea and biscuits,' she said cheerfully. 'Sit up and look lively, I haven't got all day.'

He turned his head and looked at her. 'Leave it there, would you?'

His tone hit Foxy on the raw. Instead of leaving the room she plonked herself down on the bed and shook her head.

'No, I won't leave it there, I'm going to sit here and pour you out a cup of tea and then I'm going to watch you drink it, and eat at least two pieces of Mrs Waughman's shortbread,' she said deliberately. 'You hurt her feelings at lunchtime, you know. She spent hours preparing that meal and you couldn't have eaten more than a couple of mouthfuls.'

'So?'

'So that's no way to treat people,' Foxy said angrily. 'What's happened to you, Lo? You used to care about people's feelings, you hated it when some rich old gent kicked a dependant in the teeth, now you're doing it yourself. Why?'

'I can't kick anyone anywhere. Perhaps you've forgotten, my dear girl, but I've got no feet, which means no kicking, either,' Laurie said acidly. 'Pour the tea and go, would you? To be blunt I'd rather have your space than your company.'

'Well, that's hard luck, and you'd better get used to having me around,' Foxy said. 'I live here; I've lived here for ages now without being paid any wages, I've got a small son to support, and I'm going to go on living here until you either pay me what you owe or die and leave me the estate. What do you think of *that*?'

It surprised a reluctant bark of laughter out of him and for a moment, just a second or two, Foxy saw the old Laurie looking out of the new one's embittered eyes. But then he was scowling again and the shutter of indifference had come down, hiding any emotion save anger or boredom.

'Just because I've got no feet, because I can't help myself, can't get away . . .' he began, but Foxy attacked him at once.

'You've got no feet, I grant you that, but you can help yourself and you can get away, if you want. John told us you've got artificial ones but you won't wear them. It's your choice, Laurie, but I tell you after a month or two of me you'll learn to wear those wooden pegs just so you can toddle away from me and get some peace!'

What happened next surprised them both. Laurie reared up in bed, reached for the tea-tray and upended it, sending tea, biscuits and china crashing all over the floor. Foxy, burned by flying liquid, shrieked, then leaned over the bed and boxed Laurie's ears, only to find her wrists caught and held in a tight, vengeful grasp.

'How dare you hit me, you little vixen! By God, I'll teach you to lay hands on a defenceless man . . .'

'Defenceless? Who started it? Who behaved like a spoilt brat and threw tea all over me? And you've smashed the breakfast set which Mr Allsop got out of the china cabinet specially to please you. You're an out and out bastard, Laurie Clifton, and if you don't let go my wrists I'll . . . I'll . . .'

'You'll do what?' jeered Laurie, gripping her wrists more tightly than ever. 'Go on, do something, show me what a termagant you really are!'

Foxy gave him a look of burning contempt, bent her head and bit his hand as hard as she could. Laurie gave a roar and released her and she spun across to the opposite side of the room, flushed and angry, but smiling triumphantly.

'See? It takes more than brute strength to keep me in my place, Laurie Clifton! And now I'm going downstairs to have my own tea and you can bloody well starve for all I care!'

She was out of the room and flying along the landing when Allsop stepped out of her bedroom doorway. He had Allen comfortably settled on his hip and he was smiling.

'Well, Miss Foxy, I reckon you're going the right way about it – you'll have Mr Laurie behaving reasonably in no time. Nothing takes a man out of the sulks quicker than a good old quarrel. Who threw the china?'

'He did. He's broken everything and it's all over the floor, the best breakfast set, the one you got out of the cabinet,' Foxy muttered. She was suddenly aware that tears of rage streaked her probably dirty cheeks and knew her chest was heaving with angry sobs. 'He's a – a – '

'He's a very sick young man, and he was born in wedlock; I was there at the time,' Allsop said with a faint smile. 'Now you take young Allen downstairs, Miss, and get yourself a nice cup of tea and some cake. Allen's got some rosehip syrup waiting. I'll see to Sir Laurie.'

'He'll probably chuck the rest of the tray at you,' Foxy said resentfully. She wanted sympathy, not someone telling her it was good to quarrel with an invalid.

'I think *not*, Miss Foxy,' Allsop said imperturbably. 'Oh, make another cup of tea, will you? If you'd be so kind as to bring it to the head of the stairs, with a couple of pieces of shortbread in the saucer, I'll see it isn't thrown around again.'

'Bet he won't drink the tea or eat the biscuits,' Foxy said ten minutes later, handing the cup and saucer over outside the rose room door. 'Not that he'd throw it at you, Mr Allsop – he wouldn't dare.'

Allsop, taking the cup from her, chuckled. 'Nor he would, Miss; I've known him since he was a small boy, that's why. Now you run along and start getting Master Allen ready for his bath. Mrs Waughman's got supper in hand. I think I can safely say that you can leave Mr Laurie to me.'

Laurie lay in his bed and watched the cold November rain falling on the garden and wondered what was happening to him. All the time John had been lugging him towards his home, come to that, almost all the last year he'd spent in Spain, he had longed with real passion to be back here, in Clifton Place, Herefordshire. He had imagined everything, from a triumphant homecoming to the

434

things he and John would do once they'd settled in. Riding horses, spending money on doing the home farm up, going to market together to buy young stock . . . some of his happiest moments, in Spain, had been spent thinking about his home.

But then he had lost both feet, which meant there were a great many things he could not do. And then he had seen Foxy again. Standing in the hallway in a short-sleeved white blouse and her blue working dungarees with the baby on one hip. Smiling, shiny-eyed, yet a little doubtful. And in one vivid, painful leap of memory, he had gone back to the moment on the battlefield when he had thought he was dying, when he had realised what he had given up to come to Spain.

Herefordshire. The orchards rosy with fruit, the bines heavy with the creamy, papery hops, the sheep under the trees, their wool furred with a heavy dew. In his yearning mind he had seen the kilns, their pointed russet tops stark against a pale-blue autumn sky and the gipsy caravans, brightly painted, making their way along the lane at Bees-wing, heading for Winford's Acre. And Foxy. Standing between the rows, with her bright hair haloed out round her thin, freckly face, a smile hovering. Sitting on the kitchen doorstep, shelling peas, swathed in a huge white apron. Digging in the kitchen garden, turning to shout to him, laughing, showing her amazingly white, slightly crooked teeth and the pointed tip of her tongue.

For years he had told himself she was John's girl, that he and she could never be more than friends. That Foxy herself would not want anything warmer than friendship from him. Once he had fallen in love with Mirri, furthermore, he recognised his feelings for Foxy as an infatuation brought about because he admired John and she was John's choice. Besides, Mirri was hauntingly beautiful and Foxy was not. No one could see the two girls together and still think Foxy pretty, even. He knew all these things were true, so why did the mental pictures of home contain Foxy so frequently? It was strange that despite having seen Mirri more recently, it was Foxy's face which had danced before his inner eye, Foxy's voice he had heard, Foxy's slim, practical body which he longed to hold in his arms . . .

There, it was out! He had been in love with Foxy for years, but had kept the forbidden emotion under wraps. And now, because he was a cripple and because she was John's girl, he hated her. She had everything. The baby, the affection of all the servants, including Allsop, and John himself of course. Oh, she and John hadn't seen much of each other since their homecoming but that's because of me, Laurie told himself with sour triumph. They can't sneak off for afternoons of love because John feels guilty for handing my money over to those murderous Spaniards, and she feels guilty because . . . well, because she must have known how I felt. And John's too busy in the afternoons to come over to the Place and she's got the baby, she can't just go off any more. What's more, if she had any humanity she should pity me, but does she? Does she hell! She bosses me about and gives me slant-eyed looks and tries to turn Allsop against me. She hates me and I bloody well hate her, the hard-faced little gipsy!

There was a tap on the door and Laurie lay very still. He would pretend to be asleep, he wouldn't give *her* the satisfaction of knowing that he had been lying here, thinking.

'Mr Laurie? I've brought you some tea and a piece of Mrs Waughman's apple cake. I'll put the tray on the bedside table and help you to sit up, shall I, sir?'

Laurie's heart, which had speeded up and seemed inclined to hop about in his chest, steadied. Allsop. Of course, *she* wouldn't bring his tea-tray up any more in case he threw the tea over her! As if he'd done it on purpose – as if he would. Still, there were compensations in having her living at the Place. He could watch her when she wasn't looking; he liked that. She moved nicely and of late he had noticed a wistful look in those grey-green eyes which could turn so hard and cold when she was angry. He liked that gentle, wistful look; it wasn't directed at him, of course, but he could pretend, couldn't he? And he liked her kid; dear little chap. For all I know he is my son, he told himself, taking the teacup from Allsop and sipping the hot tea. She can't say we've never shared a bed, because we jolly well did, even if it was only in friendship.

'Apple cake, sir? Master Allen's going to have a tiny piece when Miss Foxy gets him up, presently. It's made from our own apples, out of the top orchard. Miss picked a basketful only yesterday.'

He could see her now, scrambling up into the tree, hair in two long, untidy plaits falling over her shoulders, apples stowed away about her person, grey-green eyes bright with the excitement of scrumping.

'All right. Thanks, Allsop.'

'And when you've done, sir, I'll help you to get up. Miss Foxy wants to go into Ledbury next week after Christmas things. I thought you might like to accompany her in the pony-cart, even if you can't actually walk around the shops as yet.'

His heart gave a delighted little lurch, but he told himself not to be a fool; she wouldn't want him and God knew he didn't want her! It was the child, it would be fun to go shopping with the child, to buy Allen some small toy for Christmas.

'No, she'll do better without me,' he heard his voice saying, and admired the indifference in his tone. 'The cake was good; tell Mrs Waughman, would you, Allsop? And now, if you'll give me a hand, I'll come downstairs in time for dinner.'

For the next few weeks, things continued stormy up at the Place. Because it was expected of her, Foxy fetched and carried for Laurie to a certain extent but drew the line at more intimate nursing.

'He doesn't want me to see him undressed,' she said defensively the first time Allsop suggested that she should give him his bath. 'It would embarrass him dreadfully – and me, as well. I know you think ... well, I know before ... but he's changed, and I don't mean his disability, I mean he's *changed*. I don't know him any more and to be honest, I don't like him very much, either. And he hates me – the look in his eyes sometimes is really frightening – so don't expect me to do things like helping with his bath. It's bad enough having to talk to him about the estate instead of just going ahead and doing what's needed. It's not as if he's interested, either. He enjoys snubbing me or disagreeing with me, that's why he insists on being consulted.'

'He will be interested again, one of these days,' Allsop said placidly. They were in the study, deciding what crops would bring in the most money. 'Give him time, Miss Foxy, give him time. The old Mr Laurie's there, all right, just waiting for the right moment to emerge. Every now and then I see him looking out at me with the

437

old grin, the old sparkle. Then he goes back in again, but it's proof he's still there.'

'Oh, phooey,' Foxy snapped. 'He may emerge, as you call it, for you, but I don't believe he ever will for me. Look, this is supposed to be a discussion of estate business, so let's get on with it, shall we? I want to talk about hops. I know Laurie didn't approve years ago, I know John said it was too expensive, but I still want to make Long Meadow into a hopyard again. They're a crop which may be pricey to rear, but they pay you back a hundredfold if you get it right.'

'It means such a big outlay, Miss,' Allsop said worriedly. 'It's not like buying twenty ewes and putting them to the ram in the hopes of twins all round, or getting a large packet of cabbage seed and spreading manure an inch thick . . .'

Foxy laughed. 'Mr Allsop, you're wonderful, you can always make me see the funny side,' she said. 'And you'll never let me forget the cabbages, will you? But can't you understand? Ewes and cabbages are new to me so I jump in with both feet and take a chance, and sometimes things work out right – you must admit the cabbages are magnificent – and sometimes they don't, like the ewes not all having twins. But hops are different. Hops are something I really know. And the Hovertons would help me with young stock, advice, loans, I know they would. Even John would help, if it was hops.'

'Then we'll put it to Mr Laurie,' Allsop said at last. 'But don't blame me, Miss Foxy, if he just says no. It'll mean extra workers, extra equipment, all sorts, and Mr Laurie's still feeling his way.'

'I won't blame you,' Foxy said, and made her plans. She did not intend to sound Laurie out for the first time with Allsop standing by. She meant to tell Laurie on the sly as soon as she got a chance and threaten him into compliance in any way that occurred to her.

That afternoon she watched Allsop heaving the wheelchair up the shallow stairs, then went up behind him, to tuck Allen in for his afternoon nap. Allen was at his most charming, laying his face against hers, cooing to her, patting her cheek with one fat, starfish hand. But one of his round cheeks was suspiciously pink and Foxy was not surprised when, upon being laid tenderly in his cot, her son hauled himself up on the bars and began to whine.

'You're cutting another tooth, honey-chile,' Foxy cooed to him, smoothing his curls with one hand. 'Mummy will rub something nice on your poor old gummy-gum-gum. Then you can go to sleep and I can plant Swiss chard.'

She went and rummaged in her underwear drawer and presently produced, rather guiltily, a small bottle of rum, filched from Allsop's jealously guarded supply some weeks ago when Allen first began to have teething troubles. Quite a little, rubbed on the enflamed gum, seemed to help, and since she felt she needed her sleep and also some time to herself during the day, Foxy usually applied a drop when the baby was restless. She dreaded to think what Allsop would think of her if he ever found out, however, and never revealed how she managed to get him to sleep when Allsop had predicted a wakeful night for them all.

'There you are, you juvenile soak,' Foxy said now, rubbing the alcohol onto Allen's swollen gum. 'You'll soon drop off and Mummy won't be long. When the seedlings are all set out in neat rows I'll come in and sing you a nice song and get you a lovely bottle of rosehip syrup and a nice hard rusk to chew on.'

She left the room to the sound of Allen's indignant shout and waited at the foot of the stairs until the shout faded to a mumble, then she went into the kitchen where Mrs Waughman was washing up after luncheon and Allsop was frowning over his accounts.

'I'm going to work for an hour or so,' she said to the room in general. 'If Allen bawls you'd better call me, but hopefully, he'll sleep now.'

Allsop nodded and continued to add up a column of figures, Mrs Waughman advised that there would be a cup of tea on the go at four, and Foxy left them to it and trotted across the yard in the increasingly wintry wind. Thankfully, most of the leaves were now off the trees and making themselves useful in her compost heap, but she usually took a brush to the paths to clear up strays a couple of times a week and was doing so now when it occurred to her that she had left her bedroom door open. Laurie, despite many protestations, had actually begun to sleep in the afternoons; it would not help their relationship along if Allen woke him.

Sighing, Foxy propped the brush up against a convenient gooseberry bush and set off back to the house. Lately, Laurie had begun to show an interest in Allen, sometimes even smiling at him or asking him a simple question, but Foxy had not encouraged it. What was the point? Sooner or later, when Laurie was in a bad mood, he was going to deny that Allen was his child simply out of spite. And once that happened, though she had no illusions, any longer, that John would take her in, she would have to leave Clifton Place.

So she crossed the yard, slipped in by a side door and made her way through to the hall and stairs. She listened at the foot. Silence. Still, better safe than sorry, she would just nip up and close her bedroom door . . .

She stole up the stairs and went quietly along the landing, paused outside her door . . . and heard a noise from within the room, a sort of subdued chuckle. Damn, he was awake then, but not in pain or cross, apparently. Perhaps if she shut the door very, very gently he wouldn't notice and would continue to play happily.

But she couldn't resist a peep. Little darling, chuckling away to himself, no doubt conversing with Teddy, or Golly, or one of his other toys. She put her head round the edge of the door – and gasped.

Laurie was sitting on the floor with his legs spread out, and sitting between them, obviously playing some sort of game, was Allen. In the stunned moment for which she simply stood and stared, a thousand questions assailed Foxy's mind. How had Laurie got here? How had he got Allen out of his cot? Why had he done such a thing? What were his motives? For it seemed to her that Laurie did nothing any more without a darned good reason.

Then two emotions, fear and jealousy, stepped in. She rushed forward and plucked Allen from his companion, clutching him defensively to her hammering heart.

'He's s-supposed to be asleep, not playing,' she stammered. 'What do you mean by taking him out of his cot, Laurie? And how in God's name did you get in here?'

Laurie swung round, his face flushing guiltily. 'I didn't wake him, he woke me,' he said defensively. 'He was crying, so I crawled through and got him out of there. Bloody cot, it's more like a prison, you should have seen him with his mouth square-shaped and one cheek all red, clutching the bars and pressing his wet little face against them. But as soon as he saw me he smiled,' he added. 'So of course I got him out of there.'

'You had no right,' Foxy blazed. Fear and jealousy are strong and disturbing emotions. 'He's my son, you had no right . . .'

'My son, too,' Laurie snapped. 'Mine too, don't forget! He needs a father as much as he needs a mother and now he's got one, so don't you try to interfere between us, you sharp-tongued vixen, or you'll find yourself out on your ear whilst my son and I get to know each other better.'

Foxy could only stare. His son? *His* son? He knew very well whose son Allen was!

'Don't be silly,' she said slowly, all anger dying but curiosity rearing its head. 'What on earth makes you say a thing like that? You know who fathered Allen.'

'Do I? But I don't know any such thing, my dear. If it was John, as you tried to make us believe, then why isn't he more interested in the lad? He's not so much as chucked him under the chin and he's here often enough, almost every day. He doesn't take much notice of you, either.'

It was true, of course. Foxy felt her own face flame. 'He – he doesn't love me any more,' she said uneasily. 'But he knows, he must know, that I've never played him false.'

Laurie's dark brows rose. He looked cynically at her.

'Never? Not even when I came to you in the dark of the night, got into your bed, put my arms round you . . . Don't say you've forgotten our night of love, Foxy Lockett!'

Foxy stared at him and he stared straight back, his dark eyes serious now, neither cynical nor judgemental. Did he believe his own words? He had come to her room, he had been in great distress, but there had been no night of love, and he must know it. Foxy didn't know much about men's sexual drives, but she did know a bit about her own, and her one experience with John had, for many months, tormented her with a desire for more. She was certain that Laurie could not have possessed her whilst she slept – that was the stuff of fiction, not real life!

'Well? What have you got to say for yourself? I daresay the truth is that there were other men beside John and myself, and you don't really know who Allen's father is.'

'I do know,' Foxy said in a low, choked voice. 'But it doesn't matter, Laurie, it really doesn't matter. Allen's my little boy and I can give him all the love he needs. You or John or – or the baker's man, it really doesn't matter. Allen's all mine.'

Laurie suddenly fell across the floor and Foxy incautiously took a step towards him, the child still in her arms.

'Are you all right? What's the matter?'

He reached for her, grabbed her calf. His fingers were like bands of steel, they hurt. Foxy rocked unsteadily and cried out.

'Laurie? What is it?'

'Put the baby into the cot,' he said, his voice low and grim. 'Go on, put him back.'

She popped Allen into the cot and realised her mistake immediately; Laurie's other hand promptly grabbed her other leg and he pulled her hard towards him. Foxy tried to resist but she was caught off balance; she fell to the floor and promptly found herself grabbed by the hair. She tried to struggle, but Laurie rolled over on top of her, squashing the breath out of her. He looked savage, dangerous.

'So you'd deny me the right to play with my own child! I've got little enough and you'd deny me that! You think I'm just a useless cripple, don't you? Someone you can send off to bed in the afternoons like a naughty child, someone to be humoured when there are people about and bullied when they aren't. Well, you're going to learn your mistake, you're going to treat me with more respect in future.'

He reached for the neck of her blouse and ripped; buttons popped and bounded across the room and Foxy shrieked and hit out, landing a good punch just below his right eye. He swore, then laughed breathlessly and heaved at her gardening dungarees. They were thin, much-worn cotton and tore with a sound like a chain-saw.

'Laurie, leave off,' Foxy yelled at him. 'What the devil do you think you're *doing*? Oh, I'll kill you when I get up!' His face was suffused, furious, but he said, speaking jerkily as he continued to drag at her clothing: 'I'm going to rape you, you nasty piece of work, you ginger-headed tease! Then you won't think me of no account!'

Suddenly it was serious, not just a fight but something more. The baby was staring at them through the bars of the cot, eyes and mouth round, lower lip beginning to tremble. Foxy stopped struggling and turned her head to look up at her tormentor.

'Please, Laurie. Think of Allen. He mustn't see either of us behaving like animals.'

He went very still. Then he rolled off her without a word.

Animals. The word stopped him dead in his tracks. He got off her and then somehow managed to sit himself up. He looked at her, at the blouse hanging off one shoulder, at the torn dungarees, at her stomach, streaked with blood where he had scratched her in his efforts to get her clothes off. She had come into the room with that glorious mass of flaming hair tied back from her face with a piece of narrow ribbon; now her hair hung in witch-locks round her countenance, the ribbon gone. Her small, pale face with the big green eyes and the scattering of freckles was tear-streaked, and even as he watched she knuckled her eyes in a childish gesture, spreading dirt.

He was breathless still, his body's urges clamouring, but the hot and vengeful rage was cooling, shame was flooding in. Why on earth had he behaved like that? He had fantasized that the child was his but he knew, really, that Allen was John's son. He had said to himself, *but suppose we had made love, that night I spent in her room?* and even though he knew they had done no such thing, it had comforted him to believe the baby was his. It made him feel more normal, as though there was a future for him, as though someone would love him for himself one of these days.

She was on her feet now, leaning into the baby's cot, taking one of the blankets, wrapping it around herself sari-fashion. Then she turned and looked down at him, her small face puzzled, all the anger and jealousy gone, just as his own anger had disappeared the moment she stopped fighting him. He thought she had never looked lovelier, gentler.

'Why, Laurie? You hurt me, you know.'

He nodded, ashamed. 'Yes. I'm sorry, I don't know what came over me. The truth is, I've been coming through in the afternoons for a game with Allen quite a lot the past couple of weeks. I – I don't need the rest like I did, and I suspect he doesn't, either. So we – we amused each other, you could say. And when you came and snatched him away from me, I saw red. It was as if – as if you were saying I'd never be normal, never have a kid of my own, never know a woman's love . . .'

He stopped speaking. He could feel his eyes filling with traitorous tears, his mouth working. He ducked his head so she wouldn't see this sign of unmanly weakness but she did not seem to mind. She knelt down in front of him, took his hands in a soft, warm clasp. The big green eyes which could look so cold, or flash with such white-hot fury, were gentle now, brimming with tears, as his eyes had been. She leaned forward and did something she had never done before; she put both arms round him and drew him gently close, so that he could feel the softness of her breasts against him, smell the sweet perfume of her skin. Then, very slowly and gently, she began to kiss his face, her lips moving sensuously across his skin until their lips met, fused . . .

In her arms for one breathless, heart-stopping moment, he knew complete and utter happiness. He strained her close, desperately eager, knowing that for the moment all the friction between them, all the hurt, was being gently healed by their kisses. He touched her reverently, and she touched him, and then they drew apart and smiled, and he saw her eyes were still cloudy with tears and love.

Love? But she didn't love him, she hated him, she'd said it enough times! And he didn't love her . . . did he?

'Can you crawl back to your room or shall I bring the chair?'

She whispered the words against his neck, curled up against him now like a cat, warm and purring.

'I can crawl. But I'm awfully comfortable here, on the floor.'

She laughed softly. 'So am I, but for what I feel sure is to come I need a nice, soft bed and no small spectator.'

His heart bumped urgently and other things, more basic things, began to happen. He looked at her and saw she was serious, that she was offering herself to him with love, not with pity. But he had to make sure.

'I'm a cross-grained, detestable cripple,' he said beneath his breath. 'And you're a brave and wonderful girl. But you don't have to . . .'

She put a small, work-roughened hand over his mouth. She was smiling. 'You're just Laurie, just my Laurie,' she crooned. 'You've come back to me, just as you were. Come to bed with me, Laurie, and we'll make each other better. We've both had a hard time, now we can help each other.'

He went with her, through into his bedroom. She walked, he crawled. As he crawled he told himself that he would get used to those bloody wooden legs if it was the last thing he did because he did not intend to crawl whilst his woman walked.

His woman! His thoughts turned fleetingly to Mirri, to the little, dark, dimpled girl he had told himself he was in love with. It was just because I couldn't ever have Foxy, he realised now. Poor Mirri, what a good thing she never knew she was second best! But then they reached the bedroom and he heaved himself up on the bed and lay there, watching with hot and hungry eyes as Foxy took off the blanket and then the remaining garments he had left her. Naked, she went over to the dressing table and brushed out her glorious hair with his brushes, then came back to the bed, lifted the covers and slipped inside. She lay close to him, cool against his heat, and put her arms round his neck and let her small, pink-tipped breasts rub gently against his broad chest. She massaged his neck, then down across his muscular shoulder blades to the tender small of his back, and as her hands worked lower, so their bodies drew closer and closer yet.

'Foxy, my dearest girl, are you sure . . . Because any moment now it'll be too late to draw back,' he said urgently at last, moving his mouth away from the soft skin of her breast. 'I won't mind, I'll understand.'

She laughed breathlessly and kissed him, then pulled back; her green eyes narrowed into wickedly gleaming slits.

'I'm sure. If you tried to escape now, I'd go mad,' she whispered. 'You're about to be mine, Laurie Clifton, and I am going to be yours whether you like it or not.'

He laughed too, and manoeuvred her gently into position.

'I like it,' he whispered. 'Oh Foxy, *how* I like it!'

'Well? Are you going to come to the Christmas fat-stock sale? John says it's the best place to pick up a decent heifer at this time of year, and we could really do with at least one more to put in calf.'

Laurie grinned at Foxy across the oval walnut table in the small breakfast parlour and inserted another spoonful of groats into Allen's hopefully gaping mouth. With their new, open relationship Allen had become a shared joy; if Foxy fed and changed him at breakfast, Laurie undertook the task at lunchtime and so on throughout the day, though Laurie, as yet, was only a delighted spectator when the bath was brought out. Foxy had offered to let him have a go but he was afraid, he told her, of inadvertently drowning their son and heir; as yet he would stick to drying the small, wriggling body with one of the big white bath towels.

And the small breakfast parlour was where they ate their breakfast now, *en famille*, as Laurie put it. It was cosier than the big dining room and more convenient than the kitchen, where Allsop was doing one task and Mrs Waughman another, making meals noisy affairs which did not always suit Foxy, Laurie and the child.

'When are you going to get wed?' Allsop grumbled to Foxy whenever he caught her alone, which was not often, these days. 'It's plain Mr Laurie's getting better and better, his depression seems to have lifted, he's using his artificial legs, taking over the books, telling us all what to do, so why don't you marry and put things right for Allen?'

'It's too soon,' Foxy had said. 'He seems ready, but he can't be sure, not completely. Oh, Mr Allsop, I wish he *did* want us to marry, but he hasn't asked me, you see. And even the most forward girl wants to be asked!'

Allsop sniffed. 'If he's not said a word by Christmas I'm going to ask him outright if he doesn't think it's time he made an honest woman of you. Besides, you've the child to consider; he'll be at school in another few years!'

'And perish the thought that anyone might call him a love-child, even if that's just what he is,' Foxy said, grinning. 'Believe me, Mr Allsop, I wish . . . but it's Laurie's decision.'

But now, sitting in the small breakfast parlour with Allen squeaking and dribbling groats and Laurie eating cold boiled eggs – whoever fed Allen always ended up with cold food – Foxy repeated her question. 'Laurie, do listen! Are you coming into Ledbury for the sale?'

'I'd like to,' Laurie admitted. 'But isn't John going with you?'

He still, Foxy thought ruefully, seemed to have some sort of a grudge against John, though his grudge against herself had disappeared from the moment they had become lovers. Ever since he had treated her with loving kindness, teasing her, arguing often, but with an undertone of friendship which not the most violent quarrel could quite take away. But perhaps he would settle down with John, too, given time. John had done so much for him, it was tremendously unfair, especially now, when Laurie was so much better and John was still unstinting with help and advice over all their plans, particularly those concerned with the home farm and its management.

'He said he'd come with us to the market if we needed him. It's up to you, really.'

He looked at her with an expression in his eyes which she could not interpret. Then he said slowly, 'John's awfully knowing about Herefords, though. Perhaps you'd better go with him.'

'All right,' Foxy said. She had a good reason for not encouraging Laurie to accompany her, though she did not intend to tell him that! She meant to go into Ledbury with John but to stay in town without him in order to buy Laurie's Christmas present. It was to be hop setts, which she and Fletcher intended to plant in Long Meadow, ploughed for the purpose. She had used all her savings and had borrowed a little money from Mr Hawkings, against the estate, but she did not intend to say a word to either John or Laurie until it was too late for them to object. 'Then will you keep an eye on Allen? He's always good with you, you lucky blighter!'

It was true that Allen adored Laurie and was usually good in his company and to her secret surprise, Foxy hardly ever thought, now, about her child being John's son. Somehow, Laurie had claimed him and John's one contribution, on that long-ago night, seemed of little importance compared with Laurie's loving care. Allen was talking quite a bit and had referred to Laurie as 'Dadda' as soon as he could get his tongue round the word. If he thought about John at all, it was as a visitor and a not particularly welcome one at that.

'I'll beat his little bottom if he isn't good,' Laurie said, pulling a face at Allen and reaching out to rumple the child's soft, fair curls.

'What's the arrangement about the sale, anyway? Is John coming here?'

'No, we're meeting in Ledbury, at the bus stop,' Foxy said.

'Yes. Well, you go with him, Allen and I will keep each other amused.'

John came in from the milking, had a hasty breakfast, and told his mother that he was taking Laurie and Foxy to market. He went up to his room and changed from his working clothes into a tweed jacket and flannels, and wondered whether Laurie would come with them this time, or whether he would find yet another ingenious excuse for remaining behind.

John could not settle down to the life he had once thought ideal for him, hard though he tried. He did his best to forget Spain and the war which was still raging all those miles away but sometimes the thought of men he'd known battling on without him was painful, and at other times he remembered Mirri, the girl Laurie had loved, and he blamed himself bitterly for not making a push to find her. Yet frequently the sheer unfairness of Laurie's grudge against him simply made him want to quit; to walk out of the farm and away from Herefordshire and start a life somewhere else. Anywhere else.

It was almost worse when Laurie suddenly began to get better, to show affection towards Foxy and the child, because John felt unbearably guilty. Why could he himself not love Foxy as he had once loved her? Why could he not play with the child, take him on his knee, read him stories and comfort him when he felt poorly? It was unbearable knowing that he could have done so with Foxy's blessing had he wished to show such affection, but the plain, unvarnished truth was that his love for Foxy had died in Spain, and he had never really even thought about the child they had made that night. And now, because he was ashamed of his own feelings, he told himself that he didn't *know* Allen was his get; Foxy could have been with anyone, anyone at all, including Laurie. Allsop was convinced that Allen was Laurie's son and perhaps he knew a thing or two that John did not. Probably the reason that he no longer cared for Foxy as he once had was because he sensed she had been unfaithful. But he could feel nothing for her any more, not even friendship, and though he constantly reminded himself how good she had been over taking care of the estate and giving up her degree it did not raise one iota of honest affection in his heart.

Sometimes John thought that though Laurie had been wounded on the outside, he himself had been wounded just as badly, inside his mind. Some softness, gentleness towards women, had been almost surgically – and painfully – removed, and he could not function properly without it. Though he longed for Laurie's trust and affection yet he himself had none to spare. He found himself resenting Foxy, her quick wit, her sense of humour, the way she flung herself wholeheartedly into every exploit, because somehow she had dodged round Laurie's sharp and prickly guard and found the old Laurie. He could not do it. Laurie was now perfectly polite to him, sometimes friendly, but never, never close. The warm brotherly love which they had shared had gone, cooled, died. And no matter how hard John tried he could not resurrect it.

But life had to go on. John picked up his Burberry, for it looked like rain, and went down to the kitchen. His mother, baking bread, looked up as he entered the room.

'You meetin' young Foxy later on? Nice li'l boy she's got there. Tell Laurie we'd like to see him when he's got a moment, talk over the new stock he's buyin' and so on. What's more, I want to know when the weddin's planned for. I need a new hat, nothing fancy, but something smart. I've seen a navy one with a bunch of pale blue feathers – real pretty, but stylish, too.'

'I thought they were married,' John said mildly, mindful of the gossip which had been going the rounds since Allen's birth. 'I thought they got married before Laurie left for Spain.'

His mother gave a disbelieving snort. 'You thought no such thing, John Hoverton! 'Tes what they always says when they'm in love an' the child beats the bann-readin', then they marry later. But we go along with it, see, rather than have the child called names.'

'Oh,' John said lamely. 'Well, perhaps when Laurie's better . . .'

He began to walk towards the back door; the trapped feeling was back again because Laurie wasn't going to marry Foxy, there had never been anything between those two except, latterly, for friendship. Laurie had been quite impatient with her when they'd

449

been kids, and though he appreciated what she'd done for the estate and seemed fond of the baby, that was all, there was nothing more. So sooner or later there was going to be some explaining to do and he, John, did not intend to have any part of it.

'Laurie is better, he's a changed person,' his mother said from behind him. 'I can't understand the boy and that's a fact. If ever I see two people wantin' each other it's they two, yet will he name the day? Puttin' it off time and again, and for why? I can't tell, but when he comes here I'll give him a piece of my mind, dilly-dallyin' over something so important. That little lad needs a father . . . he'll be in school in a couple of years . . .'

The back door shut. Crisply. John sighed at his own rudeness but did not go back into the kitchen to apologise for cutting his mother off in mid-flow. He simply could not bear to hear her chewing over the strangeness of Laurie not wanting to marry Foxy when he knew damned well that he ought to be the one to propose marriage to the girl. He could imagine how Foxy's face would light up if he went over there this morning and said: 'Look, old dear, let's get hitched; I know you were never unfaithful to me, we loved each other and made a baby together, so surely we'll be all right again, once the knot's tied?'

His mother would be pretty pleased, too. She'd always wanted a grandchild, she would be delighted to learn . . .

No! He couldn't, wouldn't, do it! When he looked at Foxy now, or at the child, he felt nothing but a faint distaste and a great, echoing emptiness.

Resolutely, he strode to the stable and backed the car out, then roared off up the lane. He owed Laurie, Laurie himself had made him aware of it. John still felt that he could have done nothing about the amputation of his foster-brother's right foot, but the ransom money weighed heavily on his conscience. Surely he could have done *something* to keep at least some of the money? But no, he had been too scared of missing the deadline and had simply handed every penny over to Sorotto and the others.

He was saving the small amount of money his father allowed him – farmers' sons are invariably badly paid on the grounds that, one day, they will own the whole shooting match – to pay for any equipment or supplies which Laurie might need as time went on, but that did not amount to much. And in the meantime, he would go with Foxy today – and Laurie too, if he turned up – to buy the heifer they wanted. He knew Foxy was interested in making a hopyard but could not encourage her. The expense, the equipment and above all, the labour, would simply sink them, he was sure of it. But he would help them to build up a decent dairy herd and would lend any equipment which they would need and would hope, humbly, that one day, Laurie would forgive him for losing him his fortune and giving him his life.

Sixteen

The letter arrived on Christmas Eve morning. Laurie met the postman halfway down the lane and took the mail from him, stuffing the whole lot into his pocket, assuming they were all, as usual, bills. He was feeling pleased with himself because he had managed to walk this far, admittedly with the aid of his crutches, and he could see the bus stop ahead. The letters, he told himself, could wait.

He had been vague about where he was going over breakfast but Foxy, absorbed in preparations for Christmas, hadn't been pressing and Allsop, who was in on the secret, merely cautioned him to 'get a taxi if you find yourself overtired, Mr Laurie, and come straight back home.'

Laurie said he would, but he did not intend to do anything so feeble if he could possibly help it, because he was going into town to buy Foxy a present. He was not sure just what he would buy, but he had extracted some money from the estate and meant to get her something pretty. Something to show her how he felt about her, if that was possible.

Standing at the bus stop, he wondered about a ring. She had recently told him about selling the ring he had given her, had explained, with tears, that she could not afford to buy Allen a pram and knowing how necessary a pram was for her child, she had sold the ring.

'But I hated doing it, my darling Laurie,' she assured him earnestly, lying in the curve of his arm on his bed after they had made love. 'And that was before I knew how much I loved you; I hated doing it because it seemed such a betrayal. I sold it to the shop in New Street – one day, when we're rich, perhaps we might buy it back.'

So a ring seemed a good idea, but she might think he was trying to trap her – which he was – into a permanent relationship and he really didn't have much to offer. They were lovers, and not only that, they were close friends, but was that enough? Of course it wasn't. I know full well, Laurie reminded himself, that Foxy and John have been in love since they were in their teens; how could I hope to win her in the face of that long, fond relationship? It had gone sour on them since Spain, allowing him to step in, but if John beckoned . . . would she go to him? Leave Laurie, the Place, their life together? He did not know for sure.

The bus rumbled to a halt beside him and the conductor, with a beaming grin, hauled him and his crutches aboard, informing the passengers that it was 'Sir Laurie, sneakin' out to do his Christmas shoppin' just like all us men do, come Christmas Eve.'

Laurie grinned at them all, admitted that the conductor wasn't far out, and went and sat by Mrs Fletcher, a sensible, down-to-earth woman who cleaned up at the Place from time to time. She spent the journey advising Laurie to be sure to take a look in at the market, since there would be some rare bargains today.

Getting off the bus wasn't easy, but once again with the conductor's friendly help he managed it and Laurie swung off towards the market. He bought some bits and pieces, then went into The Feathers to decide what to do about Foxy's present over a drink. A small piece of jewellery, perhaps? A locket would be nice . . . but whose photograph would she put inside? Probably Allen's, he thought, and realised that so far as he knew Allen had never had his photograph taken. Would it be awfully cheeky to put in a photo of himself?

Yes, it would, he decided ruefully, and put his empty glass down on the table before him; should he have another?

He dug his hand into his pocket for money and felt the letters. Might as well read them whilst he was sitting down; if they weren't all bills he might have the courage to spend a bit more on Foxy, buy her the ring he longed to give her, perhaps.

They were not all bills. In between two familiar brown envelopes he found it; small, filthy, smeared with rain – or tears? – a letter with a Spanish stamp. And Mirri's handwriting on the front.

It was awful how his heart sank. He had believed her dead, he had been sad, but he had put her completely out of his life, out of the reckoning, too. His brief infatuation with her had died because it had only been infatuation, not love. And now, like a skeletal hand from the grave, she was reaching out for him, wanting something from him. He knew it as soon as he saw her round, childish writing on the envelope.

Unwillingly, he tore the envelope open and spread out the single sheet. He looked for the date; 12th December 1938. It had not been long getting to him then, all things considered. He turned the envelope over and saw, by the postmark, that it had been posted in Madrid – did that mean she was still in that city?

He turned back to the letter, his heart bumping unevenly in his breast. He had so longed for news of her, yet it had come too late! He had fallen deeply in love with Foxy, he wanted to make his life with her and even should that prove impossible, he knew he would never again believe himself in love with Mirri.

He began to read the single sheet.

Dear Laurie,

I don't know if you will ever read this, I don't even know if you are still in Spain, or even alive, but I felt I must write. I am alone now and very unhappy. There is much hardship in the city and almost no food. We are always hungry. I would have stayed here, been a good Republican, fought for my country, but I've been wounded so I am not so useful. The fascist army is very strong, their air force bomb us all the time and the guns never stop. My friends are dead. I think I will die soon; certainly when the fascists come they will kill me. Many are fleeing but I have nowhere to go, no one to take me in. I know I said once that I would not leave, would not go with you, but that was long ago, I was younger and more foolish then. Now I wish I might come to England, Laurie! We were so happy there, do you remember? Up in the hills, with the sun slanting through the trees and the city spread out below us, so beautiful? When they come one must wear a dark-blue shirt and tell many lies. I do not have a dark-blue shirt. I know one should die well for one's country, but I'm very frightened, Laurie. If you read this, please come.

Mirri

Laurie sat at the table with his empty glass before him and felt the tears form in his eyes, spill over, run down his cheeks. The letter blurred, cleared, blurred. What a desperate, naked appeal! But he would not be much use to her with two wooden legs and crutches! Yet how could he not go? It was scarcely her fault that he had fallen out of love with her and the appeal touched not only his heart but his pride, too. How could he ignore it, simply continue with his own life, knowing that a young girl had appealed for his help and he had, by his silence, denied her?

Miserably conscience-stricken by the sad little letter, all the pleasure of buying a gift for his love left him. He bought her a tiny, cheap locket in the end, but it was pretty, and hung on a thin, gold-coloured chain. She would understand when he showed her the letter that at least he must send any money he could scrape together . . .

Money wouldn't help. If only there was someone he could send in his place, someone who would get her out for his sake!

John. John would do it. He knew John so well; there was no fear, now, of his being shot as a deserter since the International Brigades had been disbanded. He would simply be a traveller, someone going through Spain on business. Something like that, anyway. But could he ask John for such an enormous favour? Was it fair?

But John had everything; looks, personality, his health and strength. And Foxy's love, if he wanted it. The deep, unbearable jealousy which had attacked him from the moment he and Foxy had made love to each other had, if anything, grown worse as their closeness grew. The fear that one day, she would leave him for John, made sleepless nights hideous. So why shouldn't he ask the unaskable of his foster-brother? One day, he and Foxy would leave Laurie out in the cold again, so why shouldn't John work for Foxy by clearing Laurie's conscience over Mirri?

All the way home on the bus, on the walk through the damp, December lanes, he gnawed at the problem like a dog with a bone, but inside him, the conviction was growing. John would go. He, Laurie, no longer loved nor wanted Mirri in the way he once had, but he was perfectly prepared to pay to get her here and to look after her until she was able to look after herself. And

John owed him; why should he not pay the debt in the only way he could?

By the time he walked in through the front door, his mind was made up. He would show John the letter. That was all he needed to do, just show him. After that it was up to John.

'Look, tomorrow's Christmas Day, so I think you ought to go round to Bees-wing before we serve dinner to see the Hovertons and wish them the compliments of the season. Actually, I more or less told John you would. They were awfully good to you, Laurie, when you were a kid. And you could give John his Christmas present.'

It was evening and Laurie and Foxy were decorating the hall and setting up the tree. Foxy had found a couple of boxes in the attic, full of old-fashioned baubles, artificial icicles, tiny glass birds and miniature teddy bears with grumpy, Edwardian faces and stiffly jointed limbs. Having garlanded everything available with holly and large bunches of mistletoe Foxy was carefully hanging her newly acquired treasures on the clean-smelling branches of the newly dug fir-tree. She thought Laurie had been a bit quiet since his trip into Ledbury – he had told her he'd gone in to buy some small extras for the baby – but dressing the tree and decorating the dining room had cheered him up and now, thought Foxy, the time might be ripe to try once more to heal the breach between the foster-brothers.

'Present? What present? I thought we were only buying for Allen, because of our cash situation.'

'That's right, but what you're going to give John won't cost a penny.'

'What? Not winter cabbage!'

They laughed. Foxy's excellent crop of winter cabbage was appearing so constantly on the menu that Laurie had asked why she didn't donate it to the local hospital, or possibly mail it to the Chinese – anything rather than be condemned to eat it daily for the rest of the winter.

'No, not winter cabbage. Forgiveness. It won't cost you a penny, but John would value it more than anything money could buy.'

*

Laurie picked up one of the cross little teddy bears and perched it on a branch. He did this with great concentration and care before he spoke and then he mumbled, with his head turned away: 'Can't. Wish I could, but . . . oh hang it, Foxy, he's got everything! And – and what he hasn't got now he'll have, in the end.'

'That's not true, Laurie. He's deeply unhappy. Can't you be generous?'

'No.'

Laurie watched her face change and his heart sank. He wanted to be generous, to forgive John for having been Foxy's lover, but he just couldn't. Even knowing that he intended to ask his foster-brother to go into danger for him didn't ease the gnawing jealousy which attacked him every time he thought of John. John was tall, blond, handsome – able-bodied as well. John had no doubts, no uncertainties, he had never suffered from such things. He knew Bees-wing Farm was the best place in the world to be, knew that he himself was its master. He strode his acres without a single fear to haunt him, because he understood the land, his crops, his animals. Laurie, who had wanted to be a dreaming academic but had found himself saddled with an encumbered estate, a crumbling mansion, had tried to do well by it and look where that had ended! He had been half-killed in the war and had got himself into the hands of unscrupulous men so that the estate had been forced to ransom him and beggar itself. And the girl he loved should have been given the home farm as her dowry so that she could marry John and go off to Bees-wing where, no doubt, she would have made his foster-brother the happiest man on earth.

But instead, Foxy had made him whole, given him hope, a future, even a son. They shared Allen, they shared Clifton Place, they shared their bed and they joked and fought and loved as any other couple might, with never a thought of his disability or her first love.

Thinking back, Laurie knew that he had forgiven John for handing over the ransom money the second that he and Foxy had become lovers. As for his legs, they no longer mattered, even the pain was lessening day by day, and he had known all along, really, that John could no more have saved him from amputation than flown to the moon.

So it wasn't the old grudge that he clung to now, but a new one. John and Foxy, Foxy and John, it had been like that for years and years, with Laurie, indulgent and uncomprehending, watching from the sidelines. And now he himself was centre stage and he would not, could not, give it up, hand John the prize. Yet he knew he could not hold Foxy against her will, either – a fine predicament.

He loved her. Oddly enough he was sure she loved him, too, but then he remembered John, godlike and golden, smiling and gentle, and knew it was asking too much to expect Foxy to stay with him when John, and Bees-wing, beckoned. She would go, any girl would; she would take Allen, and he would be alone, the way he had been after his father had reclaimed him.

'Any more teddies in that box, Lo? I've saved the severe little angel with the real hair for the top of the tree. What about candles? Only I'm nervous of fire. But wouldn't they look pretty?'

She was rooting through her own box, her face flushed, her eyes bright. He knew she was enjoying every moment and suddenly love burned in him and desire crackled through him, sweeping aside apprehension over the future, his certainty that John would win her, everything.

He swung over to her on his crutches, then leaned them against the tree and put his hand out, cupping the nape of her neck, drawing her towards him. She looked up and read his expression and he saw the pink deepen in her cheeks. But she came willingly into his arms, snuggling her face against the side of his neck.

'Oh sir, this is so sudden,' she murmured with mock bashfulness, and butterfly-kissed his cheek with her long, light lashes. 'Shall we go upstairs, make sure the baby's really sleeping?'

'Definitely. But we'd better finish here first, I suppose.'

She glanced around, then up into his face. 'We've finished, more or less. Let's go into the kitchen and I'll make us a hot drink and plead exhaustion and say goodnight to Mrs Waughman and Mr Allsop. And then we can go to bed.'

'Love you,' he whispered, as they drew apart and began to head for the kitchen. 'You're my favourite girl, Foxy Lockett.'

'And you will go to Bees-wing in the morning? They love you so, Laurie, and Allen and I will have you for the rest of the day.'

Her cheeks were still delicately flushed, her eyes brilliant in the faint light from the oil lamp. He was seized with a desire to please her, at whatever cost.

'I will. And I'll tell John it's all right, and mean it. I promise, sweetheart.'

'Oh, Laurie!' She stood on tiptoe and kissed him on the mouth, then drew back. 'You are so kind . . . bless you, my darling!'

Later, they lay in his bed and made love and Laurie fell happily asleep, only to waken in the early hours when she slid quietly out onto the linoleum and padded to the door. He sat up.

'Where are you off to? Come back, you've let the cold in!'

She laughed softly but opened the door.

'Can't. Mustn't shock people. We're not married, after all.'

It was two or three in the morning, and very dark. His courage should have been at a low ebb but for some reason it was not. It was, after all, Christmas morning!

'Foxy, will you marry me?'

The words came out loud and clear, though the anxiety behind them was barely hidden. Suppose she laughed, said no, told him not to be a fool? But he should have known her better.

'Oh . . . Laurie, I'd love to marry you!'

Even in the dark he could see the pale oval of her face, the white flash of her smile.

He could not go to her, could not jump out of bed and sweep her triumphantly into his arms, but he tried. He forgot everything but the desire to hold her, to kiss her, to tell her she'd made him the happiest man on earth. He swung his legs out of bed and suddenly she was beside him, pushing him into bed once more, clambering in after him, all breathless, laughing, probably crying a little, too, for her voice, when she spoke, wobbled. 'You mean it? You truly want to marry me?'

'More than anything else on earth,' Laurie said, cuddling her into his arms. 'Dear God, I never knew I could be so happy!'

And it was true, because lurking in the back of his mind, ever since he had decided to show Mirri's letter to John, had been the thought: if he goes to Spain he may never come back. I won't need to worry that Foxy may discover she loves him best, because he won't be here. I'll never feel jealous of him again.

But now, that jealousy had evaporated like dew in sunshine. He knew Foxy; she would never lie for any sort of advantage. She had said she would marry him, she had said she loved him. For some reason that he still could not fathom, she had fallen out of love with John and into love with him. He put his arms round her and cuddled her close and revelled in his new-found security and content.

'Good morning, sir.' Allsop crossed the room with his usual soft, rapid step. 'A merry Christmas to you, sir. I've brought your tea a trifle early since . . .'

He had swished back the curtains as he spoke and now he stared, openly astonished, at the bed. With its two occupants. Both lazily smiling at him.

'Good morning, Allsop,' Laurie said demurely. 'Merry Christmas to you, and thanks for the tea. But we could do with another cup.'

'Morning, Mr Allsop, merry Christmas,' Foxy said mischievously. 'I never thought to see you astonished, but you do look rather surprised.'

'Oh, Miss . . . Mr Laurie . . . does this mean . . .' Allsop's usual poise had deserted him, he was stammering and red about the gills, the tea-tray clattering between his hands.

'Well yes, it does,' Laurie said graciously. 'You may think it's all a bit back to front – the honeymoon preceding the ceremony, for instance, but we despise conventionality, don't we, my dear?'

'Oh, definitely. Look, chuck us the tooth-glass, Mr Allsop, and I'll drink my tea out of that,' Foxy said. 'Has Allen woken up yet?'

'Well, he's awake, Miss. Playing, I daresay. I heard him babbling away to himself . . . only I thought 'twas to you he spoke, naturally.' He put the tea-tray down on the bedside table and headed for the door. 'Shall I get him up, Miss, and bring him through? There are several small presents awaiting his attention in the breakfast parlour.'

'No, better not. I'll go and get him up myself and get both of us dressed, because Laurie's going over to Bees-wing later to wish the Hovertons the compliments of the season and I'm going to give

Mrs Waughman a hand with the Christmas dinner.' She started to pull back the covers then seemed to recollect something and pulled the sheet up again, reddening. 'I'll just have my tea first,' she said loftily, as Laurie sniggered. 'Thank you, Mr Allsop.'

'You'll have to stop calling him *Mr* Allsop when you're Lady Clifton, you know,' Laurie said presently, sipping tea. 'He was stunned, wasn't he? But most awfully pleased, of course. Well, my love, where and when? We'll have to do it on the q.t., what with one thing and another, but I suppose banns still have to be read and so on?'

'Unless we make a bolt for the border,' Foxy said, bright-eyed. 'I don't know much about such things but I'm very sure Mr Allsop does. We'll consult him over breakfast!'

'I love Christmas morning breakfast, even though if I eat too much I have to miss out on the pudding, later,' John said as his mother piled his plate with kidneys, bacon and two golden-eyed eggs. 'Even now, when I'm too old for surprises, I get that sort of glow, just knowing it's the 25th of December.'

'Remember the year you and Laurie had your first bikes?' Bill Hoverton said, spiking a fat pork sausage on his fork. 'Eh, that were a good Christmas, I tell you. You and Laurie rode and rode and we had to shout you in for your dinners ten or twelve times, and when it rained, after, you went and rode in the big barn and Laurie's front wheel punctured on a nail and then and there the pair of you got out your repair kits and a bowl of water . . . we laughed, didn't we, Mother, to see the two of you, so serious, dipping the inner tube in the water, happy as Larry when you saw some bubbles! I were watchin' your face, lad, and for two pins you'd have shoved a nail in your own tyre for the fun of mendin' it. Isn't that right, Mother?'

'You would,' confirmed his wife, nodding. 'More toast, son?'

'No thanks, Mum. A farmer's work is never done . . . we got the cows milked early but I just want to check the sheep. They're not due to lamb yet, but better safe than sorry. And the walk will do me good.'

'Well, didn't you say Laurie was coming over for a drink later? Why not walk up to the sheep then and meet him halfway? Go on, lad, treat yourself to another cup of coffee.'

'Just one more, then,' John said, handing over his large white china mug. 'Foxy said she would be busy with dinner, but she thought Laurie would probably come over. He'll probably come in the trap.'

'Aye, probably. Any chance of them buying a car again?'

John's heart sank as it always did when money and Laurie were mentioned in the same breath. 'Not yet, they need every penny they earn to keep the Place going,' he said. 'It's awfully cold out, so will you mull some wine for when he comes?'

'If he comes,' his mother said a trifle grimly. 'It's like harnessing the wind to get him over here, these days. I don't know what we've done wrong, I'm sure – first he wants to live here for ever and never see the Place again, then he never comes near us!'

'He's coming to terms with things,' Bill said comfortingly. 'Don't 'ee worry, my dear, every time I see Laurie he's more like the lad who went off to Spain and less like . . . well, less like the fellow who came back, put it like that.'

'And he will come,' John said, getting to his feet. 'Tell you what, he'll be in church, I expect, so we could offer him a lift back here. I'll run him home again in time for his dinner.'

'So you're coming to church?' his mother said with some surprise. 'Well, that's a turn up for the books as they say! We're honoured, and so will the parson be, let alone astonished. I thought you'd gone off church services, after Spain.'

'Oh, well, it is Christmas,' John said. 'Anyway, I like the carols.'

When he had gone his parents smiled at each other with understanding and affection.

'Knew he'd begin to come round, act more natural, like,' Bill said. 'I don't know much of what happened to the lads over there, but it wasn't anything good, you may be sure of that. Haunted, that's what they've been. But they're coming out of it, slow but sure.'

'Thank God,' Ada murmured, beginning to clear the breakfast things away. 'And now if only Laurie can see that our John's no threat to him, perhaps they'll start acting like brothers again!'

'Is *that* what's been bothering Laurie?' Bill said slowly. 'You're a shrewd woman, Ada. But why should he think John is a threat?'

'Because at one time, John and Foxy were . . . close. But I warned the boy off and he took heed,' Ada said. 'In a way, I wish I hadn't; she's a nice girl, really. But she'd never ha' done for our John, though it seems she's ideal for Laurie.'

Bill laughed. 'Managing puss, you mean. And is that what Laurie needs?'

His wife laughed too, but nodded. 'That's right. Now John wants a girl he can take care of, whether he knows it or not. Come along, Bill, are you going to stand about here all day, or are you going upstairs to get changed?'

The first person John saw when he entered the holly-decorated church was Foxy. She was sitting next to Laurie in the big old Clifton pew, with her bright red-gold head close to his dark one. If I didn't know better I'd think they were lovers, John told himself. He did know they were getting on well now, though it seemed to him that they quarrelled constantly, sometimes over the most trivial things. But at least that awful, brooding bitterness with which Laurie had regarded everyone seemed to have begun to fade. Everyone said he was becoming more like his old self, and John hoped they were right. But towards himself, Laurie's dislike and bitterness seemed as strong as ever. If only I'd been clever enough to have kept some of the money back, John said to himself for the thousandth time, then I wouldn't feel so bloody guilty, I'd tell him where he got off, make him see I couldn't have saved his leg. But Laurie was always the clever one, I was always just the farmer's boy, just old Hoverton who plodded on somehow.

It was a good service. John and Bill Hoverton sang at the tops of their voices, whilst Ada piped away beside them. And when the congregation had shuffled out, after handing over their hymnals and prayer books, he saw Foxy again, waving vigorously as she tore past the lych-gate on Laurie's old bicycle. 'Going home to get dinner on the go,' she shouted to them. 'Laurie's just having a word with the vicar.'

'We'll go on, dear,' Ada Hoverton said when Laurie did not immediately appear. 'You'd best go and see if Laurie needs help. You've got room in that dreadful little car for him, haven't you?'

John's beautiful sports model, his pride and joy, had never met with his mother's approval, but now he grinned at her, nodding. 'Yes, there's plenty of room, his crutches can go in the boot. We shan't be long I don't suppose, Ma, so put the punch on.'

They always had punch on Christmas morning, in the big china punchbowl which had been in their family for generations. And Ada served hot sausage rolls on a dish which was equally old and cheese straws in a fat pottery vase with holly round the rim.

John stood and watched his parents drive off, then turned back to the church. Laurie was standing in the porch with the vicar but even as John started down the long path, the two men shook hands and Laurie began to swing himself towards the lych-gate. He saw John waiting and smiled.

John smiled too, uncertainly. From here, it had almost seemed as though Laurie meant the smile, as though . . . but it must have been a trick of the light. Laurie could not so easily give up his grudge, could he?

'John, old son!' Laurie balanced carefully, leaned his right-hand crutch against his side, then held out his hand. 'Merry Christmas – and I'm sorry!'

'Sorry? For what?' John said uncertainly, shaking his foster-brother's proffered hand. 'You are coming back for a drink, aren't you? Mum and Dad will be awfully upset if you can't . . . though I'll understand, of course,' he added hastily.

'I'm sorry I've been such a selfish, whining bastard for so long,' Laurie said cheerfully, tucking his crutch back into his armpit and heading for the gate once more. 'And of course I'm coming back for a drink, I wouldn't miss it for the world.' They reached the gate and Laurie went through it and stood alongside John's car, parked right outside. 'Well? Are you going to accept my apology and try to understand what drove me, or are you going to snub me something rotten and tell me to go to the devil?'

John couldn't believe it. After months and months of facing up to Laurie's bitterness and dislike, this sudden volte-face seemed too good to be true. He blinked across at his foster-brother just as a long ray of pale winter sunshine illuminated them both.

'Oh . . . the latter, naturally,' he said. 'Laurie, what's happened? Why are you apologising for what I'm sure you couldn't help.'

'But I could. I behaved abominably and I hurt the people nearest me worst, I know it. But somehow, yesterday I – I saw what a rat I'd been and I wanted to make up. Foxy said I ought to forgive you and suddenly I saw, clear as clear, that you were the one whose forgiveness I ought to be begging for, not the other way around. I knew all along that you couldn't have stopped them amputating my foot, and I knew, too, that you'd given me my life by fetching the ransom money and handing it over. So I'm sorry I was such an ungrateful bastard, old chap, and I hope you'll forgive me.'

'Me, forgive you?' John bent and unlocked the door, then hugged Laurie hard. Laurie hugged back and then they drew apart, both embarrassed, John thought, by the unexpected emotion they felt over the reconciliation. 'I knew all along that you'd come to yourself soon enough . . . God, what a Christmas present! Why, you old son of a gun, I've come close to topping myself these past few weeks! Only I was sure you'd let me off eventually.'

'Let you off? Fool!' Laurie tossed his crutches into the back of the car and lowered himself cautiously into the small bucket seat. 'My God, what a damned uncomfortable vehicle; not much point in taking a girl out in this!'

John swung the starting handle and then raced round and squeezed behind the wheel. 'Haven't tried. Haven't wanted to. And now, Lo, how's everything going up at the Place?'

'Everything's going pretty well, thanks,' Laurie began, then reached into his jacket pocket. 'Hang on a moment, before you move off. I've had a letter I want you to read. It came yesterday morning. It's from Mirri.'

He handed John the letter.

John took it and began to read. Halfway through he turned and looked at Laurie, expecting to see his foster-brother almost in tears, but Laurie was looking at him, his expression serious but certainly not sad. John read the rest of the letter, then went back to the beginning and read the whole thing through again. Only then did he hand the single sheet back to Laurie and rev the engine.

'Oh Laurie, the poor kid! But you can't possibly go . . . Someone must, of course . . . if you would trust me, I'd go like a shot!'

'I had thought . . . wondered . . .' Laurie began, but John was already planning. I could go to France and cross the Pyrenees again, he told himself. She'll still be in Madrid, the city's besieged, so she won't get out in a hurry. I'll find her, tell her I've come from Laurie, bring her back here . . .

Laurie was talking though, so John tried to listen. Laurie was saying he had never been so happy, that he had not realised marriage was even on the agenda, that he had assumed with the loss of his legs, that girls would simply discount him as a marriage prospect . . .

I've just got to bring her back, he's relying on me, John thought happily. And if she's alive still, I can do it! Poor old boy, I thought he'd lost all interest in the girl, but now, because she's written, he's a different person. Oh thank God for Mirri, because this letter from her has brought good old Laurie back from whatever dark land he's been travelling through. I'll be proud to go and winkle her out of Madrid, bring her back to dear old Laurie . . . and it'll be action again, not just watching the corn grow and the hops run up their strings! I've missed action almost as much as I've missed Laurie and now, with a bit of luck, I'll be having both!

'. . . not going to tell anyone else, of course, not even your parents,' Laurie was saying. 'And it will take a while, I realise that, to plan things out, get the banns read and so on. But John, old man, I can't tell you how marvellous it feels to know you're loved, when you've managed to convince yourself that it'll never happen. I don't mind telling you, I never expected to be so happy again.'

'That's marvellous, old fellow,' John said heartily. 'And I'd much rather you didn't breath a word to anyone, particularly my parents. You know how they worry.'

Laurie agreed, shooting a puzzled glance at John. John grinned at him.

'Sorry, talking at cross-purposes. I meant it wouldn't do to tell them that I'm going over to Spain to fetch your Mirri out, because they wouldn't realise how easy it will be, they'd simply read the papers and believe I was in the thick of it and in deadly danger.'

Laurie nodded. 'Of course. John . . . are you absolutely sure? I feel such a worm having to ask you, especially when I'm so happy myself, but I've no one else to turn to, and I wouldn't be much good, peg-legging it across Europe on my crutches!'

John turned the car into the Bees-wing farmyard, cut the engine and reached for Laurie's crutches. Then he jumped out of the car and went round to the passenger side.

'Don't worry, old fellow, I'd do anything for your happiness, you know that. And go on with your wedding plans; it'll give you plenty to think about until I – we, that is to say – get back.'

'I will. And . . . John, old chap, I'll never be able to thank you for what you're doing for me. You're one in a million.'

'That makes two of us,' John said huskily. 'Ah, here comes Mum to give you a Christmas kiss; not a word, remember!'

The punch was a big success, the sausage rolls delicious and Laurie, totally at ease now he and John understood each other, was unable to resist whispering to Mum that unless he was much mistaken, there would be a wedding in the family before too long.

'But since we were supposed to have got married before I left for Spain it's going to be very quiet and some way from here,' he confided. 'Oh, Mum, it's what we both want, we're so happy!'

'I'm so happy for you,' Ada said, giving him a hug. 'What a Christmas, eh, Lo? Tell me, what did you buy Foxy?'

'A trumpery little locket on a chain. But as soon as I've got some money she's going to have a ring . . . a really good one, Mum.'

'You won't need money, love,' Ada said, surprised. 'All you need is to tell Mr Hawkings; there are family jewels in the bank vaults in Hereford, you know. Oh yes, your mother had some pretty rings, and some brooches and that. They can't be sold, I grant you, because they're Clifton jewels, to be handed down, but they're yours, like, to give to your future wife.'

He gaped at her; there was no other way to describe it. 'Really? Are you *sure*? I can't wait to see Foxy's face when I tell her – I gave her a cheap little ring before I went to Spain but she had to sell it to buy Allen a pram. She's a good girl, Mum; she cried when I gave her the locket, she was really thrilled.'

'I believe you. She *is* a good girl, Lo, just right for you.' She paused, looking at him thoughtfully. 'She and John thought they were in love once, years ago. They were all wrong for each other and I told him so, because I knew they wouldn't suit , and he backed off, thankfully. But was that why you and he seemed to have lost your friendship, when you first came back from Spain? I did wonder, but it seemed . . .'

He nodded, shamefaced. 'It was. But that's all behind me now, I shan't envy anyone or be jealous of anyone ever again, I don't think. Foxy's all I ever wanted, and I never dreamed I'd be lucky enough to win her. Now that I have, I'm in seventh heaven. Even not having feet doesn't matter a jot.'

Ada gave him another hug. 'You're a good lad. And now, young Laurie, I'll call John to take you home or Foxy will think I've kidnapped you. I know too well what it's like when you've cooked a good dinner and the man of the house doesn't turn up to eat it!'

John told his parents he was going to visit a group of French friends from the International Brigade; he showed them the envelope which had held Mirri's letter fleetingly, then handed over the letter of invitation which he had written himself, using his left hand to hold the pen instead of his right.

'Funny writin',' his mother commented. 'None too well-educated, these Frenchies. Well, go if you must, John, but don't be too long away. Foxy's going to be needin' help when spring comes.'

'She won't. She's got a good grasp of what she needs to do and I've told her to come and ask Dad if she gets in a fix. She will, too, or Laurie will. He's a prince to what he was three months ago. But I'll be back long before spring – I just want to see the fellows, that's all.'

'Aye; you've been restless for a while, now,' his mother commented, placidly knitting. 'Best go and get it off your chest; then you can settle down.'

'That's right. I'm leaving Saturday,' John said. 'Can someone run me into Ledbury for the train? Only I don't fancy leaving the car there for a matter of weeks.'

'Your dad'll want to see you off,' Ada told him. 'You might bring back some of that goat's cheese your dad likes. And a bottle or two of decent wine.'

'I might bring back more than that,' John said thoughtlessly, and had to parry some difficult questions as a result. But he went to bed that night well-pleased with himself. Whatever they might think of

468

his actions, they would never dream he'd gone back to Spain!

"Tes my belief he'll mebbe try to slip back over the border,' Ada told Bill grimly in bed that night. 'He's not been himself since he came home; it's almost as though he lost something there, and wants to get it back.'

'Not that money, I hope,' Bill said sleepily. 'It were on his conscience, poor lad, and 'tes clear he'll never see that again. But he's headed for France, love, not Spain! No one would want to go back into that blood-bath, not voluntarily. Not again.'

'Mebbe not,' Ada said doubtfully. She brightened. 'And our Lo's gettin' wed, Bill! All on the q.t. of course, but he good as said it were on the cards any time now. He's a good lad, our Laurie. He deserves a good lass and he's got one in Foxy.'

"Tweren't what you said when John fancied her,' Bill said sleepily. 'But there you are, what's right for one's wrong for another; I've heard you say that time and agin.'

'I talk sense, but I do talk it often,' Ada admitted rather confusedly: she had had a long day. 'Hope the weather don't close down on the lad; he'd not be best pleased to have to put off his trip.'

Outside, the wind howled and snow fell in soft flurries against the window panes.

"Twon't last,' Bill said hopefully. 'Night, my love. Gi's a kiss.'

Laurie had showed Foxy the letter when everyone else had gone to bed on Christmas night. She had read it and wept.

'You loved her once,' she had said at last, mopping her wet eyes. 'Poor little thing, how unhappy, how abandoned, she must feel. And you showed the letter to John?'

'Yes,' Laurie said, not elaborating. Foxy sniffed, blew her nose, then smiled.

'He'll fetch her back,' she said confidently. 'John's like that. He wouldn't leave a puppy down a rabbit-hole, let alone a girl in a war. He'll bring her home.'

'I believe he will,' Laurie admitted. 'I didn't have to ask, either. He offered.'

'But . . . if she comes here, won't she expect you to marry her?'

'No, of course not. John will explain that I'm going to marry you.'

'Oh. That's all right, then. What did John say when you told him?'

'He was pleased for us, he said so,' Laurie assured her. 'There isn't a jealous bone in old John's body, lucky chap.'

'True. Shall we go up, now? It's been a long day.'

And next day, Laurie had gone over to Bees-wing again on some pretext and had given John the letter.

'It doesn't give much away, but you'd better have it. You can show it to her when you find her, so she knows you come from me and are a friend. And it might be best if you just mention the marriage, so she knows how things stand.'

'Right,' John said, taking the letter and stowing it carefully away in an inner pocket. 'I probably won't see you again before I leave, old fellow, so wish me luck.'

'I do,' Laurie said fervently. 'And I wish to God I was fit enough to go with you.'

It was not until several days later that John, reading the letter for the twentieth time, realised something very significant: Mirri had not once said she loved Laurie, nor that she was longing to see him again; far less had she mentioned marriage.

But surely, she would not have written to Laurie had she not still loved him? Thinking about it, he remembered she had not known into whose hands the letter might fall, so she would scarcely have vowed undying love. Once she was with Laurie again John was sure she could not fail to love him, regardless of his disability. Nevertheless, it cost him an hour's sleep before he realised that fretting would get him nowhere; the important thing was to reach Spain and find Mirri. Once he did that, he could make her understand.

It took John until mid-January to get as far as the Pyrenees because despite everyone's hopes, the dreadful snow in Britain had fallen just as fiercely in northern France. And this time, when he reached the foothills, he hired a guide. Jean Douleurs, a thin little whippet of a man with long dark sidewhiskers and droopy eyelids, pronounced himself delighted to get John across the mountains, especially when he saw John's equipment; climbing boots, sturdy hooded jackets suitable, the Army & Navy Stores in London had told him, for tackling the Arctic, and long, baggy skiing trousers, to say nothing of a hefty haversack well-laden with dried and tinned goods.

'I hope to bring a friend out with me,' John said rather guardedly. 'A friend who's got caught up in the war by accident. That's why I've brought a second set of foul-weather clothing. Is there anything I've forgotten?'

He had a folding primus, pitons and a hammer, a full hip-flask (brandy, naturally, he had said, filling it back in The Feathers, with the landlord looking on, uncomprehending but appreciative) and several bars of the Kendal mint cake which Laurie had yearned for not so long ago.

'You are well-equipped,' Jean Douleurs said. 'It is unlikely, even in this weather, that you will need the pitons, because I shall lead you through the passes, but better safe than sorry, eh? When do we leave?'

'Tomorrow morning, at first light,' John said at once. 'My friend is in Madrid; so I have a good journey ahead of me once I reach La Mancha.'

'Of course; and they are having a terrible winter in Spain,' Jean told him. 'You will find much hardship, much misery. And there is the war, of course,' he added, eyes bright under their drooping lids. 'One cannot ignore the war.'

'I mean to try,' John said stolidly. 'The war is not my concern; I'm just an Englishman travelling in Spain.'

'And you did not get that limp in a war? Well, I believe you, *monsieur*, but thousands would not.' He held out a hand, ironic laughter curling his long, mobile mouth. 'Until first light, *monsieur*.'

It was tough going, even with a guide who knew his business and the right equipment. It took them two days to reach the foothills on the Spanish side of the Pyrenees and then John took Jean's hands in his, bade the little man Godspeed, and thanked him from the bottom of his heart.

'I wouldn't have made it without you,' he assured his companion. 'I've never tackled the mountains in winter before; they're fearsome.'

'Aye, you could die and never be found up there,' Jean agreed sombrely, raising his voice above the howl of the wind. 'But you did not die, *monsieur*, and you will come home, surely, by an easier route? The mountains are not good for little girls who are worn out by the war.'

They had talked of John's quest, sitting round their tiny primus in the shelters Jean had made for them, and Jean had embarrassed John by telling him that few would risk a war to save someone else's girl.

'But Laurie and I are as brothers,' John had said haltingly. 'Besides, he could not go himself.'

'Even so, many would think it too great a favour to ask. But you'll succeed, *monsieur*; I can read a man's face and there is determination in yours, and something of stubbornness, too.'

But that had been talk over the primus stove, with the shelter round them; now they stood on the bare mountainside looking out over the great plain of La Mancha whilst the wind tugged at their clothing and ever and anon sleet was hurled into their faces with enough force to cause pain.

Now, John agreed that the mountains were not suitable for a girl and said that he and Mirri would try to get home by sea, then he stood and watched Jean out of sight before turning to face the snowy plain below. Way, way out there, was Madrid. And how was he to get there? He smiled to himself as he set out on the long downward slope. He would walk; there was no alternative.

There was no food left in Madrid. Cats and dogs had disappeared from the streets months ago and enterprising street urchins were selling rats on the Plaza Mayor to those who had the money to buy and whose hunger was sufficiently strong to stomach the small, strong-smelling carcasses.

Mirri, no longer of much use to the militia because her right wrist had been smashed and she could not even hold a rifle let alone fire it, lived in the underground, alone amongst the family groups. She had tried cellars, odd corners of bombed buildings, even dug-outs, but one's best chance of survival was other people's warmth.

But the cold got everywhere. The wind was bitter, and it brought the snow right into the shattered city so wherever you went the wind and the snow would find you, making it impossible to keep dry and equally impossible to be even a little warm. But in the underground, with a couple of hundred people huddled into one small station, it was just possible not to freeze.

Outside, in the wide, once-beautiful streets and squares, the trees had gone. Those which the starving citizens had left had been cut down recently by the militia; they needed hot food, even though it was mainly coffee made from toasted barley grains and a small quantity of poor rice or beans. And Mirri was not entitled to share the militia's rations any longer, nor did she wish to do so. As Franco's troops got nearer and nearer to the city it became more and more dangerous to wear a red shirt or khaki clothing. Soon after being told she was no use to the fighting forces, in fact, she had managed to exchange her uniform for a shabby grey blouse and a pair of dark-brown trousers, both garments removed from the bodies of the dead.

She had found the corpses in an abandoned, shell-shattered house on the outskirts of the city, a young girl of twelve or thirteen and a boy a couple of years younger. They had lain, hunched up, as though to conserve what warmth there was in their thin, starved little bodies. By them was an old peasant woman, rocking herself, keening out her misery.

'They died of eating earth,' the old woman had wailed, tears coursing down her seamed, filthy face, after Mirri had helped her to dig a shallow grave for the children. 'I told them not to, but they would not listen – they were so hungry! And I shall die too, very soon. But take the clothes, if they'll fit you. Franco's butchers may let you live if you have ordinary clothing instead of that uniform.'

They fitted because Mirri was so thin, now. Thin like a bone, with no roundness, no femininity. She had seen her reflection in a metal door down in the underground and had been fascinated and frightened by her hollow cheeks and lustreless hair, with her bones showing through her frail, transparent skin, and her eyes, dark-rimmed, making her look afraid even when she was not. She had written to Laurie weeks ago, without any real hope of a reply. She had turned down his offers of help when he had first made them, why should he help her now? But the truth was, she supposed him dead. Why not? Everyone she loved was dead, Leá, Jacinta, Josefa, Inma . . . the list stretched like a ladder up to heaven, although she no longer believed in heaven, and hell was right here, in Madrid.

She had written to Laurie because . . . because it was like stretching out a hand in the dark and groping for the hand of a friend. She knew Laurie would still be her friend, no matter what, and just to pretend to speak to him, which was what the letter amounted to, had given her, for a moment, hope. Perhaps she would live, perhaps she would not simply die of the hunger which was killing fifty or more people in the city each day, now. Perhaps there was a miracle just around the corner for little Mirri Rodriganez, who had done her best for her country, had manned the trenches and fired her gun until the fascist bullet had put a stop to all that.

But she didn't really believe in miracles, in her heart. She wasn't even afraid of death, not any more. There would be a moment of terrible pain, she supposed, and then warmth, and darkness, and no hunger ever again. That was not so bad, was it?

Sometimes she thought it might be an idea simply to lie down in the snow and wait for the cold to kill her quietly and gently, without fuss. Yet somewhere within her was another Mirri who said, stubbornly, that she was too young to die and too full of life, and hope. That this was a terrible time, but it would pass. That she must endure, do her best to remain alive, and the good times would come again.

John picked his way amongst the rubble, his warm jacket marking him out immediately as a foreigner amongst the starving, pathetic citizens of Madrid who shambled along pressed close to the tumbled buildings or dived into doorways to escape the soldiers and vehicles which seemed to rule the snow-littered, shabby streets. But they were proud people, the men and women of Madrid; no one tugged at his coat, begged, made any demands on him. They went their own way, eyes huge, black-shadowed, mouths tight. Most wore a purple armband to show their allegiance; John found himself hoping sincerely that they had a bit of scarlet and gold ribbon by them: the whole world knew the Republicans were beaten and the Nationalists had won, but the

Republican leaders seemed reluctant to admit the truth and blazing from every wall, every hoarding, were posters demanding that the people of Madrid should fight on. Starving men don't fight, they die, an old man had said to John the previous night, in a tiny, straw-filled room at what had once been an inn. Now there was no food, no drink, not even a bedroom, just the old stone stable and the straw.

There had been no attempt to keep John, or anyone else, out of the city, though, which was useful. He had taken the advice of an elderly man who went into the city regularly to sell, on the black market, a few vegetables or a hare.

'Come with me, *señor*,' he said. 'We must avoid the University City, because that's where both sides have dug their trenches, but we'll walk quietly round and slip in by a little back lane; no one will challenge us.' John had seen people coming and going – they were still running the trains, for God's sake, to and from a besieged city! – and had thought, hopefully, that this augured well for his getting out again, with Mirri beside him.

Once in the city, he saw that troops were everywhere; armoured cars tore past, horns honking. The military were nearly as ragged as the citizens of Madrid but they must have been given rations of some sort, he supposed. At least they had *alpargatas*, rope-soled sandals, on their feet; the poor of Madrid, despite the bitter weather, went barefoot.

He approached a soldier and asked where the militiawomen were billeted. The soldier did not seem to understand. He was young, with long, greasy black hair and a squint and he looked at John as though he hated him.

John tried again. He spoke slowly, clearly, in his fairly basic Spanish, and the man's face cleared.

'Ah, the girl soldiers,' the soldier said, and grinned. 'They are everywhere, but they are of Madrid so they do not have billets. What is the girl's name?'

'Miryam Rodriganez,' John said. 'She's usually called Mirri.'

The soldier shrugged. 'I don't know her. Look, when the girls come off duty they have to walk along the Puerta del Sol to go and have a meal at HQ. You might see her then. Or they serve the officers food in the special officers' quarters, which are in the Calle

Echegaray. It's quite near the Puerta del Sol so you can kill two birds with one stone and visit both in a couple of hours.'

'Thanks,' John said. His coat was dirty and torn at the elbows, his ski-trousers speckled with mud and soaked with snow, but he still looked smartly turned out compared to his companion. He fished two squares of dark, bitter chocolate out of his pocket. 'Want these?'

The young face lit up, and the soldier's hand shot out at once and took the chocolate.

'Thank you, thank you! Good luck with your search, comrade!'

Mirri had begun to sleep a lot; too much. What with the cold and the gnawing hunger pains though, sleep was the only half-nice thing she knew, and even that could be dreadful, haunted by dreams so that she cried out and disturbed others.

The Nationalist air force wasn't bothering much with Madrid any more, though, which was a good thing. They knew they had won, they knew if they bombed the city they would bomb men and women who had no means of fighting back and no will to fight back, either. We're no threat any more, Mirri thought, looking around at her fellow-sufferers, all jammed together for warmth in the narrow station.

She had not eaten anything but a handful of beech nuts for two days. When morning comes I'll go to militia headquarters and explain that I can no longer fire a gun or be useful as a militia-woman, but ask if I might clean, wash up, scrub floors – anything for a bit of bread or some beans, she thought. They won't want me to die.

But when morning came a great lassitude had settled upon her. She stayed where she was, curled up in a corner behind a seat, and every time she opened her eyes very strange things happened; great, looming shapes rushed up at her, people with bulging eyes and huge foreheads leaned over her, boots, with no one inside, tried to kick her in the face. So, not unnaturally, she kept her eyes tightly closed, curled up even tighter, and began to experience a sort of dreamy other-worldliness in which she was safe and well and in a warm bed from which she might presently be taken in order to eat the meal that was being lovingly prepared for her.

But if she opened her eyes the illusion died, so she kept them closed. In a part of her mind she knew the day was passing, knew, bleakly, that if she did not move there could only be one end for her, but that was not enough to open her eyes, let alone move her cramped, rapidly numbing limbs.

And presently, without realising it, she slid from a light doze into a deeper doze, and from that into a state of limbo in which she floated, unknowing, in a semi-coma from which she might easily never wake.

John had done everything he had been advised to do; he had walked up and down the Puerta del Sol, round and round the small hotel on the Calle Echegaray, in and out of the surrounding tiny streets and alleyways, and though he had seen a great many young women he had not seen Mirri – or not so far as he knew. Since he had never met her, he did not expect to recognise her immediately, but Laurie's infatuated description of long ago had stuck in his memory; small and bright, with black curls, dimples and a tiny, crescent-shaped scar under her left eye. So he scrutinised every face, asked everyone he met whether they knew a girl called Mirri Rodriganez, and did not give up until darkness had fallen. Only then did he decide to go back to the inn and get a night's sleep before beginning his search all over again next day.

He had walked into the city centre first thing in the morning but now he decided to see whether it was true that the Metro was still running. He found an entrance, shouldered his haversack – he had not dared leave it anywhere, realising that its contents, even after his long trek, represented more than most of these poor devils saw in a month – and descended into the darkness.

Halfway down the flight the lights went on; dim little bulbs which just about lit his way. Others were stumbling down the stairs, which might mean the trains really were running or might simply mean that people slept down here to have some sort of shelter over them.

He reached the platform. He asked whether trains still ran and was told that they did, but intermittently, not to schedule.

'One will be along in a moment, though,' an old man in a black peasant smock informed him. 'I have come in from my village to speak to the right-hand man of Col Casado – a very great man. He will save us yet, you'll see. And I shall go back to my village on this train.'

'Good,' John said. He saw a seat, but before he could claim it, it was taken by a family who surrounded it, spreading a thin blanket across its wooden slats, talking to each other as they did so . . .

John was about to move further down the platform when there were exclamations and much activity around the seat. The mother of the family, stick-thin, with haunted eyes, called out that there was a body . . . would someone remove it?

'It's a girl,' she said, and even in her condition her voice softened with pity. 'Poor, skinny little creature, I think she's gone.'

John turned away; one did not stare at another's misfortunes, nor at a dead girl who could no longer turn away, cover her face.

'She's not dead, I don't think. We should take her to the hospital.' That was another voice; a man stared down at whatever lay behind the wooden seat. 'Anyone give us a hand? Pepe, fetch a couple of militiamen, they've got more strength than . . .'

John stepped forward; the girl was only a child, after all, he could see that much from where he stood. 'I'll help you up the stairs with her; she's so small I could probably . . .'

He stopped speaking, looking down into the small, deathly white face. Black, tumbled curls, a drooping mouth . . . these could have belonged to anyone. But beneath her left eye a small, crescent-shaped scar showed blue against her flesh.

No one noticed his hesitation and John covered it smoothly. '. . . I could probably carry her myself,' he said. 'I'm in no hurry, I'll take her.'

The man and the woman bent and lifted the girl and put her into John's arms. 'Take her to the hospital, comrade,' the man said kindly. 'The military will tell you where it is – you're a stranger here, no?'

'That's right,' John told him. 'I can walk to my destination when I've left her in hospital.'

They nodded and smiled, his poor Spanish no surprise to them; people from all over the world had fought for Spain, perhaps some of them had stayed true to their trust, remained in this gaunt and terrible land which was being torn apart by the warring factions.

John climbed the stairs, the girl light as a feather in his arms. He kept looking down at her, and now doubts crept in. Was this really Mirri, the girl Laurie loved? Her face was no longer heartshaped but simply small and thin, her cheeks were hollow, her mouth had the strange, fallen-in look of the starving. He did not want to hand her over to some hospital not knowing . . . but how to discover her identity whilst she was so obviously too sick to tell him anything?

He trudged up the last few stairs and into the snowy street. He saw a soldier and went over to him, indicating the girl in his arms with a jerk of the head.

'She's ill, I don't know what's the matter but she's unconscious, I think. Can you tell me how I find the nearest hospital?'

The soldier gave him directions and John shambled off and presently came to a sizeable building which did not look in the least like a hospital, save for the large red cross on the door.

'It was a gentleman's mansion,' the girl who sat behind a small desk in the hallway told him. 'Take her up the stairs, first door on your right. They'll see to her, if there's any point, that is. Do you know her name?'

'No . . . I thought she was . . . but no, I don't know her name.'

The girl nodded as if she'd heard the story a hundred times before and went back to the book she was reading. John carried the girl up the stairs and through the first doorway on his right, which proved to be a ward full of sick and wounded people lying on straw mattresses. The room was stuffy yet very cold and it smelt horribly of suppurating wounds and sickness. As John stood uncertainly in the doorway a nurse bustled towards him.

'Another one? Oh, she's not wounded . . . why, it's that little militiawoman who smashed her wrist last year; what's the matter with her now?'

'I don't know. She was in the underground, like this,' John said. His heart had lifted at the nurse's words. 'Do – do you know her name, Sister?'

'No, I can't remember . . . wait, wasn't it Mirri? Can't remember the rest of it, though. She's suffering from malnutrition and hypothermia, that's clear enough. Put her on that mattress, would you? I'll bring her a hot drink of some sort, though heaven knows what; we're short of everything here, as you've probably realised.

If you can get a drink down her she might survive.'

'Might?'

'She looks fairly far gone; starving, freezing, and despair itself are all capable of killing, or at least of causing death,' the nurse said severely, 'and this young woman has undoubtedly suffered all three. She has much in common with the majority of people in this city who have no *enchufado*, no significance to those in power. But she may survive. Will you stay with her?'

'Of course,' John said. 'She is engaged to be married to my foster-brother. I've come to Madrid to find her and take her home.'

Mirri swam back into semi-consciousness because someone was calling her name and something seemed to be pushing against her lips. She opened her mouth to answer, to say she was here, over here, and warm liquid invaded her mouth, making her first gasp and then choke.

'Hold on,' someone said in English. 'That was my last Bovril cube, don't spit it all over the floor.'

'Laurie?' Mirri whispered unbelievingly. 'Laurie?' But she still could not open her eyes, not properly; she tried, but the lids seemed unbearably heavy, far too heavy to allow her to look at whoever was holding a cup to her lips.

'Come on, Mirri, try to drink,' the voice said again. Mirri, swimming slowly up to the surface of full consciousness, realised that someone was propping her up somehow with an arm around her shoulders, that her head was lying on someone's chest. 'Just take a little sip, my love.'

She knew that rolling Herefordshire accent! Laurie tried to talk like all the others did at Cambridge, but he kept lapsing into his own warm dialect, she had teased him about it often. And yet . . . and yet . . .

She sighed and took a sip of the drink, and immediately she was in Cambridge, in Laurie's room with the firelight playing on the walls and Laurie crouching on the hearth, holding a toasting fork out to the flames with a round of bread speared on it, whilst she sat next to him eating buttered toast spread with Bovril.

She opened her eyes, knowing what she would see; the cosy, lamp-lit room, the prints on the walls, and Laurie, crouching before the fire. Instead, she saw her own pale, thin hands, a rough blanket, and a cup with wreaths of steam rising from it whilst in her nostrils was the delicious smell she knew so well. And when she moved her eyes she could see a man, sitting close so that her head rested against his shoulder, his strong, tanned fingers around the cup.

She turned her head properly round to look at him. Hair as yellow as a day-old chick, a strong, square face, blue eyes . . . not Laurie? *Not* Laurie, when she had been so certain, had heard Laurie's very voice in her ear not two minutes since?

She frowned up at the man who held her, trying to make sense of what she saw; Laurie's voice but another man's face? And then, in a blinding flash, she knew. The foster-brother Laurie admired so much and talked about all the time, John Hoverton! Laurie had said John was fair, very handsome, tall . . . it must be him, it had to be!

'John 'Overton,' she said in a thread of a voice. 'You must be John, Laurie's foster-brother. Why are you here and how did you find me?'

'Laurie sent me, told me you were in Madrid,' the fair-haired man said. 'I found you by chance, really. Did you get a letter, saying I was coming to bring you home?'

She could not shake her head but she said, 'No,' in her new, reedy voice.

'Oh. Well, he wrote, but I don't know what address he put on the envelope, come to think of it. You didn't give us your address when you wrote, you see, which made it harder. I've got your letter somewhere, Laurie gave it to me so that you'd know I was a friend. I was supposed to produce it as soon as we met, only the circumstances weren't quite as straightforward as Laurie had supposed they would be.'

He sounded amused. Mirri, sipping Bovril, warmed by the blanket and by the undemanding strength of his arm around her, smiled too and then took a good look at the face above her own. He was lovely! So golden and dependable, so strong and self-assured! But he wasn't Laurie, and she had appealed to Laurie.

'Why didn't Laurie come himself?' she asked. Not as though she cared much about the answer, but more from a sort of vague politeness, because she found she really did not mind. This John Hoverton was Laurie's good friend and would be good to her, that was what mattered.

There was a perceptible pause and then John said simply: 'He has been quite badly wounded.'

'Oh. And – and you are to take me back to England?'

'That's right, back to Clifton Place, Herefordshire.'

'If I want to go,' Mirri said. The drink was gone and it had strengthened her but she didn't mean what she said, it was simply an automatic answer, a sort of assertion of self.

'No, not if you want to go; whether you want to or not,' John said equably in his calm, pleasant voice. 'You're no use here, remember? You've smashed your wrist.'

She nodded uncertainly. 'Yes, I did. See!'

She held out the injured wrist. It had not healed well, the skin was all crumpled and purple . . . horrible. John leaned forward and enclosed her whole wrist in the palm of one of his broad, dependable hands. He held her tenderly. 'Poor Mirri. We'll make you better.'

At that moment she knew she would never doubt his ability to do what he said. If he said he would make her better, make her better he would. She nodded again, with more confidence.

'That would be nice. It's very ugly, all purple and chewed-looking. It used to be smooth and white, like the other wrist, but since that man tumbled into the trench on me and fired his gun at such close range it's been horrible. And I couldn't fire my rifle with only one proper hand, so they didn't need me in the militia any more.'

He made a sort of growling noise in his throat and for a moment the arm round her shoulders tightened, then he released her, laid her gently back on the straw pallet.

'Well, all that's over now, and as soon as you're well I'm going to take you home. Can you sleep for a little? Then later, when you wake again, I'm going to get you a small bowl of bread and milk. You'd like that, wouldn't you?'

'I'd like it *now*,' Mirri asserted hungrily, her mouth watering at the very thought of such a treat – she had not tasted either bread or milk since she had left the militia. 'I could eat a very large dish of bread and milk . . . a *huge* dish.'

John laughed, but shook his head at her. 'It's dangerous to overload a stomach which has been empty a long time,' he asserted. 'But you shall have your bread and milk just as soon as Sister says you may.'

'Oh! Do you have a sister here, then?' Mirri asked. It seemed very odd, but then everything had been odd today.

'No, not *my* sister, *the* Sister. You're in hospital, Mirri – didn't you realise?'

'No, I didn't,' Mirri said vaguely. Despite her conviction that she was able to eat bread and milk at once she was suddenly aware of a deep and demanding tiredness. She was so sleepy, so very sleepy . . . 'You won't go away? You'll stay with me now you've found me?'

She heard his voice even as she drifted into sleep.

'I won't leave you. I'll be back by your bedside when you next wake up. Sleep well, *niña*.'

Seventeen

Laurie had been delighted and touched with Foxy's Christmas gift of the hop setts, but the winter of 1938–39 was appalling, one of the worst in living memory. First the snow had lain on the ground for weeks and weeks, putting an end to any thought of serious work on the land, and now, as the snow melted, it had flooded low-lying agricultural land, roads and ditches, making field-work even less possible.

The setts were planted out despite the weather, however, and Foxy was determined not to be discouraged, so a couple of weeks earlier she had gone to a sale in the Bromyard area of Hereford where a hop farm was on the market and had bought, amongst other things, a collection of old cribs. And now, with the rain swishing down the gutters and gurgling along the overful ditches and the invaluable Allsop looking after Allen, she, Laurie and Fletcher were in the big barn, repairing their new acquisitions. Fletcher, who had never grown hops, was turning out to be a great help, reading up about the crop in his spare time and putting his new knowledge into practice whenever he could. Laurie, mending the sacking on their new-secondhand cribs, was bewailing his own stupidity in not taking more notice of what went on around him at Bees-wing Farm.

'I spent my childhood watching the men in the hopyards without really seeing a thing until September,' he said gloomily, sitting on a straw bale and watching Foxy and Fletcher scrubbing, brushing and re-hanging the wood and sacking of the cribs. 'And now that we're going it ourselves ... no, I apologise, now that you're doing it and I'm watching from the sidelines ... I realise what hard work it is and wish I'd noticed a bit more. In fact, if John was here he'd probably tell me off good and proper for not attending to what went on when we were kids.'

They had received a hastily scrawled letter from John, saying that he had found Mirri, that she was in hospital in Madrid and that, if all went according to plan, they should be back in England for the summer. Foxy, who knew very little about conditions in that country, could not see why John did not simply stick Mirri in an ambulance and carry her off, but Laurie had explained that to avoid suspicion John and Mirri would have to cross very large areas of Spain, almost certainly on foot.

At first Foxy and Laurie had planned to postpone their wedding until John's arrival home, but when the brief letter arrived Laurie said it was not fair on anyone to wait indefinitely so they decided to get married quietly as soon as work allowed, and to go away for a week to the seaside resort of Llandudno, in North Wales, whilst the invaluable Allsop and good Mrs Waughman ran the Place, and Fletcher and the other farm labourers kept the hopyard and the home farm running.

'Once the hops really get going we won't have any time off at all, any of us,' Foxy assured anyone who would listen. 'So we'll do everything we possibly can as it crops up, and take our holiday when we can see a quiet week approaching.'

Allsop and Mrs Waughman, and probably most other people, guessed that the week would be a honeymoon rather than a holiday, but they were too tactful to say so aloud, so Foxy and Laurie laid their plans, and a suggestion that the Hovertons might like to look after Allen had been greeted with scorn by Allsop.

'And what's wrong with myself and Mrs Waughman?' he had asked indignantly. 'Young Master Allen knows us a good deal better than he knows the Hovertons I think you'll find, Miss Foxy. And there's no better place for a little lad than his own home.' He slanted her an old-fashioned look. 'Especially when his parents are off on their honeymoon,' he ended acidly.

Feeling comprehensively snubbed and put in her place, Foxy had agreed, meekly, that he was right and had dismissed any thought of moving Allen from Clifton Place whilst they were away.

'Unless you think he might come with us?' she asked Laurie

half-hopefully, but Laurie had laughed, squeezed her, and shaken his head.

'No, my sweet, I don't think any such thing. In the nature of things we shall only have one honeymoon and during that week I don't intend to share you with anyone else, not even my son.'

And Foxy, loving him more with every day that passed, had said with a submissiveness foreign to her nature: 'Well, if you really would prefer it, we'll leave Allen with Allsop, then. He's got a real gift with kids, the old boy, don't you think?'

'I do. He's very attached to the little chap, and no wonder; Allen's a charmer, he winds Allsop and Mrs Waughman round his little finger. So he'll be thoroughly spoiled for a week and we'll come home and grumble at them when Allen insists on staying up late, drinking port and smoking big black cigars.'

'Fool,' Foxy said affectionately. 'I'm looking forward to being married to you, Laurie Clifton!'

'Ditto,' Laurie had said. 'I'm looking forward to hearing you called Lady Clifton, personally. And to finding out what your real name is!'

But now, in the big barn with the double doors open to let in what light there was in the grey, overcast sky, Foxy picked out another damaged crib and pushed it towards Laurie.

'Here, patch this one, would you, Lo? And as for you not taking in hop-lore as a child, it wasn't important at the time. You were going to be a dreamy academic and pay other people to look after your property, if I remember your plans correctly.' She pulled the next crib towards her and examined the sacking, her nose almost resting on the worn material. 'I wonder whether we ought to replace the bag part on this one? It's rotted right through on the left-hand side.'

'Just call me your sewing woman,' Laurie grumbled, picking up the big, curved needle threaded with coarse brown string and digging it vengefully into the sacking. 'Mind you, I always fancied myself as an artist, so perhaps I can be artistic with my needle instead of my brush!'

'Tell you what though, Lo, the Hovertons never bought second-hand cribs in their lives, I'll be bound, so you wouldn't have been able to help us to repair these even if you'd cut your eye-teeth on

486

crib-management, so to speak. Oh, this one's wonky, Fletcher. Can you do something about that leg, d'you think?'

Fletcher took the crib from her and examined it. ''Tain't the leg, Miss Foxy,' he said at length. ''Tes the rope what 'olds 'un together. I'll soon fix that.'

'Oh, right. Thanks, Fletcher. And tomorrow, no matter how bad the weather is, we'll have to check on the yard itself. I think we put the posts in deep enough, and of course the setts are growing at a fair pace, but I'd still like to make certain.'

Laurie groaned again and, catching Fletcher's eye, winked. The construction of the hopyard, which had been finally managed in January despite the thick snow, would have been impossible but for Mr Hoverton, who had driven over on his tractor, sniffed at their plants, and masterminded the erection of posts, wires and poles.

'Why? Uncle Bill said it was a nice piece of work, didn't he?' Laurie remarked, stitching away. 'Even though it's March the hopyard will be freezing cold and wet, you know.'

Foxy, in her turn, sniffed. 'Mr Hoverton said we'd done well weeks ago, after the floods. He'll expect us to check regularly, I know he will, and I can guess who'll get the blame if something goes wrong at this stage. Oh, I'm so *extremely* thankful that Long Meadow's on a steepish hill! If we'd planted on the flat – and lots of people do just that – then we'd have been helpless when the place flooded and all our setts would probably have rotted.' She turned and pulled a face at Laurie. 'And don't think I've forgotten, Clifton, who it was said only an idiot would plan a hopyard on a steep slope like that and wouldn't it be better to plant the hops on Stony Patch. If we'd done what you wanted . . .'

'Pax, pax! You're in a quarrelsome mood, Foxy Lockett, you just want to find fault!' Laurie pushed his mended crib towards her. 'What about that, then? Neat, eh?'

'Very neat,' Foxy said approvingly. She went and sat beside him on the edge of the straw bale and kissed his cheek, giving him a squeeze as she did so. 'Lovely fellow! Poor old Laurie, are you beginning to regret the hopyard?'

'Not for a moment,' Laurie said stoutly. 'You'll want to plough between the rows soon, I daresay. I'm a dab hand on that tractor, though I'll need you to work the pedal.'

'My lad can do that for you, Mr Laurie,' Fletcher said. After some initial grumbling, the staff had agreed to drop the 'Sir' in favour of 'Mr', which they had used all their lives and found came easier to their tongues. 'He'm only ten, but he'm bright enow for that.'

The pedal, which was a combined clutch and brake, was situated just behind the driving seat and should have made driving easier for Laurie, except that he found it hard to get his balance right when steering the heavy tractor and having to put an arm behind him to work the pedal. However, Foxy, perched just behind the driver's seat, could work it to Laurie's roared instructions and thought, privately, that the tractor gave him a freedom which, so far, he could not attain in any other way. They could not afford a motor car and even if they had been able to do so she did not see how Laurie could have driven it, though he talked vaguely about hand controls which, he said, were available to special order.

'Thanks, Fletcher, it would be a real help if your lad could do that,' Laurie admitted now. 'Can he come round to the Place tomorrow then, at about nine? That will leave Miss Foxy free to hoe between the plants – unless you'd rather try your hand with that great long prodger thing, fixing top-hooks, old girl?'

'Oh hell,' Foxy said, putting her head in her hands for a moment. 'Mr Hoverton said if we'd employ a man he'd guarantee to send one of his chaps over to show him what to do, and I never gave it a thought until you just now said. I do believe hops are the hardest things in the world to grow, I seem to spend all my time thinking about them. And we've got to string first, then brace the strings, and then later it'll be training the little buggers . . . no, Laurie, don't pretend to be shocked, little buggers they are and little buggers I called them . . . to crawl the right way up the strings. Mind you, there are always women who want a few weeks' work, and they'll make a better job of that than any man. But it does make me wonder if we were wise to decide on hops.'

'Hops are all I know,' mimicked Laurie. 'Remember saying that, sweetie? Much you *did* know, Foxy!'

'Don't remind me what a fool I was,' Foxy moaned. 'I thought I knew about hops . . . well, I do know about picking and so on, it's

488

just the enormous amount of work that goes into rearing the plants and making the actual yard itself that passed me by. Which, when you think we only came down in September and left in October, isn't surprising. But we'll do it, Laurie. We'll grow our hops, and get them into the kiln and out to the buyers . . . and we'll be rich!'

'We shan't, but I don't think that matters. What matters, frankly, is managing. Provided we manage, that will suit me fine.'

Foxy glanced outside at the steadily falling rain, and sighed.

'It will suit me fine, too. Only I'd like to think that Allen had a bit of security behind him.'

'Security's bad for boys; they need adventure and thrills,' Laurie said robustly. 'How much land will we put down to hops eventually, do you suppose?' They began to stack the cleaned and mended cribs up against one of the barn walls. 'Because we're going to need an awful lot more farm workers. How many labourers does Uncle Bill employ?'

'You should know far more about that than I possibly could,' Foxy pointed out. She picked up a sack and slung it across her head and shoulders. 'Come on, let's make a bolt for the house; Mrs Waughman will be making elevenses around now – and I'd like to check that Allen's all right.'

Fletcher, draping his own shoulders in a sack but knowing his trusty flat cap would keep his head dry, glanced up at the grey sky and announced: ''Twill be fine be dinnertime.'

Fletcher was usually right in his weather predictions so Foxy smiled hopefully.

'Good; then we'll go up to the hopyard as soon as we've had our elevenses and decide what needs doing next,' she said. She glanced lovingly across at Laurie, hopping puddles. 'One of these days you're going to chuck those crutches away, Lo, d'you know that? You're getting awfully good at pegging along on your wooden tootsies. I bet you could manage with a stick, come to that.'

'I probably could,' Laurie agreed rather breathlessly, as they hurried through the rain towards the kitchen door. 'But I'm faster on crutches; if it came to a race between the two of us, my girl, I'd win hands down.'

'Feet down, you mean,' Foxy said with a grin. 'Well, when the weather's a bit better you're on. We'll have a proper race and see who wins. And it'll be me.'

They arrived at the back door as she spoke and Laurie paused beside her as she struggled to turn the wet handle and reached across and rumpled her hair.

'We'll see, we'll see! Mrs Waughman, we're starving! Where's our pot of tea and your marvellous scones?'

On the first suitable day, Bill Hoverton sent Elias over to show them how to string.

'Monkey 'as to be rare long, to reach top o' poles,' Elias explained as they stood in the gentle, drizzling rain, watching him expertly guiding the string from the ground pegs to the airy height of the top hooks on the wire. 'An' thee mun't jerk nor leap, nor let 'un goo slack. 'Tes a trick, see?'

Laurie nodded, watching closely. 'I see. The string goes from the big ball in your cloth bag, up the hollow rod on the end of the stick, and you just snag it neatly over the top hooks and then down, through the peg.'

'Aye, I can see thee've watched well,' Elias conceded. 'And soon's I've strung a row, young Foxy, my Mabel and t'other wimmin 'ull come an' brace the strings wi' binder twine.' He turned to grin at Laurie, patiently plodding through the newly ploughed earth with his sticks and his huge wellingtons clagged with muck. 'An' after that 'tes hop tyin'. Tha'll need more wimmin to do that. Mus' 'Overton'll git thee a reli'ble lot what'll come right up to 'oppin'.'

'Good,' Laurie said absently. He picked up his own monkey, threaded the string as Elias had taught him, and began to tie the end firmly to its anchor-point. 'Well, let's see whether I really have got the knack, Elias!'

'Tha'll do,' Elias said after a moment. He wiped a hand across his brow, knocking a row of sparkling raindrops off the peak of his cap as he did so. 'Where's Mus' Allen, then?'

'Mr Allsop's taken him shopping, in Ledbury. They've got a list as long as your arm, but Mr Allsop wouldn't take the pony-cart and leave the lad with Mrs Waughman. Said he could stow most of the groceries in the bottom of the pram and the rest he'd carry. He thinks it's better for Allen to have plenty of fresh air, apparently.'

Elias grunted. 'I git fresh yur all day an' every day an' I canna say I think it ha' done me much good.'

'Oh, I don't know. You've done two rows to my half; that has to mean something.'

Elias chuckled; 'Goo you on, Mus' Laurie, that's 'sperience, not fresh yur.'

'And two flesh and blood feet, perhaps,' Foxy said, coming up quietly behind Laurie and kissing him explosively in his right ear. He squawked and teetered, then righted himself.

'Don't do that, I'm managing with one stick, did you notice?'

'And the monkey stick,' Foxy said, grinning. 'You really are shifting, Lo, for a beginner. And Fletcher's not doing badly, either. And I've braced string after string, so the wind shouldn't knock them about. Wouldn't it be lovely if the rain stopped, though?'

'It might, arter we 'as us dinners,' Elias remarked, stringing like fury. 'Often do, y' know.'

'It's mutton stew,' Foxy said longingly. 'Mrs Waughman makes a grand mutton stew. I've told the girls bracing the strings to come up to the house and eat their sandwiches in the big barn, and I thought we'd take them out something hot.'

'Them'll 'ave flasks, likely,' Elias said grumpily over his shoulder. 'They 'ont need no stew.'

'I meant a hot drink,' Foxy said with dignity. 'Don't be so mean, Elias. You'll get plenty of stew, don't you worry.'

Elias reached the end of another row and fastened the string, then walked to the next. 'Thou dunna want to start somethin' thee canna finish, Miss Foxy,' he advised. 'There'll be a ruck o' wimmin workin' yur before the month's out. Now come on, Missie, brace these yur strings!'

'I hope the wind doesn't change!'

It was a glorious blue day at the end of April and Foxy was working with the tying gang, disentangling any bines which had grown out of true and re-routing them, then ripping out any extra growth so that only two healthy bines now attached themselves to each string. Because of the intricacy of the task she was doing it with an inch of tongue protruding from the corner of her mouth, and now she stuck the rest of it out at Laurie, who was coming along the rows behind the tying gang, spraying Bordeaux powder to prevent downy mildew.

'Very funny! But it's terribly important to keep the bines on the straight and narrow, and in a couple of weeks it'll be time to fertilize again, so we want to get them straightened out before then.'

'Now straightening out a bine I've yet to see.' That was Florrie Perkins, a cheerful, apple-cheeked girl who had been working for the Cliftons, on and off, ever since they started the hops. 'They'm daddecky little devils, tha's the snag. I's afeared to snap a spike if I hurries.'

'Then don't,' Foxy advised. 'Take your time, Florrie, like I do. It may not be the hardest job in the world, but it's not one you can hurry, and at least we've got the weather today,' Foxy blinked round the hopyard, at the sun shining down through the goldy-green leaves, which hung, almost unmoving, in the breezeless air. 'No wind to blow away the Bordeaux powder, thank goodness, and no wind to snatch the bines down again before they've taken a strong hold of the strings.'

'Aye, I hate that,' Florrie said, reaching up to persuade a recalcitrant shoot to let go of its brother and climb the string, instead. 'Nothin' wuss'n puttin' 'em up an' then watchin' the wind blow 'em all down agin.'

'Nor there is,' Laurie said, puffing Bordeaux powder a couple of feet behind them. 'Sorry, did I get you? I'll let you get ahead again, shall I?'

'Go and see if it's time for a tea-break,' Foxy said longingly. 'I'm dry as dust – dry as Bordeaux powder, in fact. Is it eleven o'clock yet? It must be, I'm sure the sun's in the right position.'

'It's a quarter to the hour,' Laurie said, consulting his wrist-watch. 'And it'll take you at least a quarter of an hour to get back to the house. Only I thought you weren't taking an elevenses break today? I thought it was a longer luncheon-break?'

'Fancy you remembering and me not; then we won't have to go back to the house today because Mrs Waughman and Cyril are bringing jugs out,' Foxy said thankfully. 'It's such a lovely day that Allsop said he'd bring Allen out, too. And Uncle Bill's coming round later, to take another look, though he said he thought we'd got the idea, now.' She turned to Florrie. 'I tell you what, Flo, why don't you nip off and give them a hand to bring out the tea? It would be a break for you and it might hurry them up!'

'I don' mind,' Florrie said, delicately curling a sturdy little bine round its string. 'Shanna be long, mind. Mus' Laurie, why dunna thee tie for a bit if 'ee can git the knack?'

Florrie began to trudge back to the bottom gate along the ploughed furrows, calling out as she went that she were off to fetch 'levenses.

'I don't mind having a go at tying,' Laurie said, laying aside his powder dispenser. 'I imagine it's not difficult so much as fiddly. So since Florrie's gone off and I'm ahead with my task I'll do my best to keep up with you, Foxy Lockett.'

'''Tes women's work, kind zur,' Foxy said demurely, quoting the farmhands, who thought it infra dig for a man who laid hedges and dug ditches to do the fiddly, neat-fingered task of persuading a bine to climb a string. ''Ee woun't wan' t' do women's work!'

As she said it she remembered, with a little slab of dismay, the many times that Laurie, cursing his own inability to do some task, would say he was only good for women's work. But it had been many weeks since he had used the expression and now he cast her a long, amused look, then stumped past her, balanced himself on one stick and started to retrain a bine.

'It is fiddly, something you couldn't do if you had large, clumsy fingers,' he said over his shoulder. 'But I imagine, once you've got the knack, you can get up a fair turn of speed, can't you?'

'Speed! That reminds me,' Foxy said, moving briskly along to the next string and tearing out a third bine which was endeavouring to clamber over the selected ones. 'John's being awfully slow, wouldn't you say? He wrote ages ago to say he'd found Mirri and we've not heard a word since. Nor have Uncle Bill and Aunt Ada. Surely they must be well on their way by now, probably over the . . . what are those mountains called? Oh yes, the Pyrenees; they'll be over them, won't they? I mean winter's well and truly finished here, it's almost May, so it'll be really hot in Spain, I imagine.'

'Probably. But I don't know how far they've got . . . honey-chile, I've told you before, a country at war isn't like a country at peace.

John won't be able to get on a train or a bus because most of them won't be running and those that are will be crowded with troops. He was in the Republican army, no matter how you look at it, which means he could be in danger if he was picked up by either side.'

'Oh, Lo, but you said . . .'

'Yes, I know. The International Brigades have packed it in, so you might think at least the Republicans wouldn't want his blood. But once an army withdraws, that's it. I don't think a member of that army can just turn up again and expect to get any sort of welcome from desperate fighting men, unless he downs tools and joins them, of course. And Foxy, love, although we fought for them, I think both John and I knew that there were terrible wrongs being done on both sides. The Russians, and some of the Spanish Republicans, were killing innocent people for no reason. Look, I'm not trying to frighten you, but I want you to see that John will *have* to take his time and keep his head down. Otherwise he might never get home at all.'

Foxy straightened and gazed at him; she could feel her face growing cold and stiff. 'Not – not come home? Oh, Lo, but . . . it was my fault that he went! He – he went for us, didn't he? Do you think we ought to go after him, make sure he's all right?'

Laurie shook his head at her. 'Don't be silly, darling. I would be more harm than help and so, to be frank, would you. John's the most sensible, level-headed bloke I know, bar none. He'll come through, I'm sure of it, but he'll take his time. We've just got to learn to wait patiently, and that's always the hardest thing to do.'

Because it was such a lovely day, Allsop sat on the windowseat with the child on his lap and the window open behind him so that the breeze could blow the scents of wet earth and new grass into the bedroom. Allsop had a brightly coloured picture book spread out before him and he was reading aloud, slowly and carefully, a finger tracing the outline of each word as he pronounced it. And Allen, breathing heavily, was following the story, which he knew by heart, with close attention.

'So the little red hen and her chicks ate up all the lovely white bread and the naughty farmyard animals had none,' Allsop said impressively. He closed the book and held it flat on his lap. 'Did you like that story, Allen?'

'Ess,' Allen said definitely. He put a small and rather grubby hand on the book's bright cover. 'More!'

'More *please*,' Allsop suggested tactfully. Allen thought about it, then thumped the book again.

'More . . . please.'

'Very well, since you are such a good boy, we'll have just one more.' Allsop opened the book again and riffled through the pages. 'Which one would you like this time, young feller-me-lad? I'll turn the pages for you and you stop me on the story you want. How about that, eh?'

He began to leaf slowly though the book, but presently, looking at the child, he realised he had lost Allen's attention. Allen's gaze was fixed on the doorway, where the door was slowly swinging open in the draught from the window, and he was smiling the wide, innocent smile of the very young.

'Mumma?' he said rather uncertainly. 'Mumma?'

'Is Mummy out there?' Allsop asked. 'I think not, Mummy is busy today, teaching her new ladies how to persuade little hop plants to curl round their strings. I wonder if it's Daddy? No, we would have heard Daddy coming up the stairs, his crutches go bump, bump, don't they? It's the wind moving the door, only the wind. Now which story shall it be, Master Allen?'

But the child was now smiling joyfully at something just inside the doorway. 'Nanna!' he shouted triumphantly. 'Is Nanna!'

Allsop sat very still as the little boy appeared to watch someone cross the room, then the child beamed up at something – nothing – right in front of him and beside Allsop. With the door open the breeze increased, ruffling the pages of the story-book and then, lightly, lifting Allen's fair curls from his baby brow. Allen laughed, bounced on Allsop's knee, then turned to beam at him, his eyes sparkling with pleasure.

'Nanna,' he said again. 'Is Nanna.'

'Milady?' Allsop said, looking straight before him and speaking to no one in particular, his voice low and gentle. 'Is it really you, Milady? Isn't he a fine young fellow, then, your little grandson? And he's being brought up right here, at the Place, without any interference from anyone – I'm making sure of that. But I believe he can see you, though I cannot.' He sighed and looked down at the book again. 'I did it for the boy's sake,' he said obscurely. 'Not for any other reason than for the sake of the boy. You'd have done the same, if you'd seen what I'd seen. But there, you've always known, Milady, that I'd do anything on earth for you and yours. Anything on earth.'

He waited a moment, then turned back to the child and the book. He found a picture of three billy goats and a small, hump-backed bridge and addressed Allen.

'How about the three billy goats gruff, Master Allen? And you can take the part of the troll, and sing his song for me, since you've been so good.'

Towards the end of May, Laurie and Foxy decided they were finally in a position to arrange their wedding, and their week away. Foxy fancied mid-June, and Laurie agreed it would be nice, if they could just get everything done that should be done, and find time to tell the men and women who now worked for them what to do next. After some bad times, they were beginning to be cautiously optimistic about their beloved hopyard.

'We got the stringing done in good time,' Laurie said as he and Foxy sat side by side on the terrace in the new secondhand swing-seat which Laurie had bought at a closing-down sale. 'I'd never even been in a hopyard before when they were stringing . . . I was at school, I suppose . . . but now we could actually do it ourselves, at a pinch. And we've got a good team, the women who braced the strings had done it before, for other hopyards, but now they're glad of the work with so many farmers going to the wall. I reckon we could leave 'em for a week, in a fortnight or so.'

'The tying gang have done their second check, and I personally sprayed with Bordeaux powder whilst you picked off all the heads with downy mildew,' Foxy said thoughtfully. 'They've put down more fertilizer, and Fletcher rolled between the rows only last week. The weather's getting better and better though, so I reckon we'll have to keep checking for damson aphid. Mrs Stubbins said if we looked in the hedgerows we'd see how dense the little beasts were on the blackthorn, because it's only when they run out of that, that they take to the bines.'

'Did you look? How bad are they?' Laurie said lazily. 'I've got the tying gang coming back in a couple of weeks to spray with nicotine; Uncle Bill advised it.'

'I checked the hedges and there's still a bit of room. But I reckon in a fortnight we'll need your spray . . . and the ground will need working over so the earth can be mounded up over the hop-roots. We'll take our own cuttings for next year, remember, so we must encourage some low growth.'

'It never bloody stops, does it?' Laurie said cheerfully. The swing-seat had stopped moving and now he pushed at the paving with one of his artificial feet and started them rocking gently once more. He put a hand out and stroked Foxy's cheek. 'Look, love, I reckon the workers know what's expected of them and Uncle Bill says he'll walk the hops each day whilst we're away. He's quicker to spot trouble than anyone else I know. And sweetheart, if we leave it much later we'll be into high summer when there's a great deal to do at the home farm as well as with the hops. The burrs will be coming on the bines and you really do have to watch them then, Uncle Bill says, or you can lose your entire crop to the downy mildew.'

'Right. We'll put it in hand, then. Will you book us somewhere on the front, where we can see the sea when we wake up? Oh Lo, I'm beginning to get really excited – I actually believe it's going to happen!'

'I'll book the guest-house by telephone tonight. And I'll book the registry office in Gloucester and do all the other things. I wish old John were here, though. He'd be my best man in every sense of the word. Still, he'll be back as soon as he can, we all know that.'

'I wish he could be here as well, of course,' Foxy said. 'And poor little Mirri. I just hope she doesn't hate me for taking you away from her.'

'You didn't.' Laurie heaved himself up from the swing-seat and held out his hands to her. 'Come on, we've lazed for long enough, we must get instructions for whilst we're away sorted out and down on paper. As for Mirri, sweetheart, it was simply infatuation, puppy-love, if you like. She was unhappy with her language school and unhappier at home. She loathed her father and didn't much care for her mother, so naturally the first man who kissed her became very important to her. But now she'll be as changed as I am. She'll come here and meet the right person for her and live happily ever after; you see!'

It was a lovely wedding, though extremely quiet. Foxy wore a peach-coloured linen suit and a matching hat and felt immensely proud of Laurie in a dark suit and tie, garments he rarely wore, for a farmer's life is not conducive to suits and ties.

There were only five wedding guests – the Hovertons, Allsop, Mrs Waughman and Allen – because people were supposed to believe that Foxy and Laurie had been married for a couple of years, but though quiet, it was jolly. Mrs Waughman threw confetti, the Hovertons gave them a cheque which, Laurie informed his wife jubilantly, more than covered the cost of the honeymoon, and Allsop in a burst of exuberance foreign, Foxy was sure, to his nature, tied old tin cans to the bumper of the taxi which took them from the register office to Clifton Place.

Because Allsop and Foxy had done their best to get people to believe in the 'secret marriage' Laurie agreed, albeit reluctantly, that they should not broadcast the news of their real wedding, so after the marriage the wedding party returned quietly to the Place for a wonderful meal which Mrs Waughman had prepared before she left. Mr Hawkings joined them and admired Mrs Waughman's magnificent wedding cake which would take an army several months to devour. He brought champagne to toast the happy couple and Mrs Waughman became rather merry under its influence.

'Good luck, Sir Laurie, Milady,' Mrs Waughman, obviously primed, called out as they climbed into the taxi which would take them to Ledbury station to catch the train for Llandudno. And Allsop, with a prim smile, added: 'Have a good time and come home refreshed and ready for work once more.'

He was holding Allen and Foxy noticed that the child looked tearful, uncertain. She leaned forward and tapped the driver on the shoulder.

'Oh do stop for a moment! I forgot . . .'

The taxi driver obediently drew his vehicle to a halt and Foxy wound the window down feverishly and leaned out.

'Mr Allsop! Do come to the station with us, see us off! And – and bring Allen!'

Allsop, with the child in his arms, needed no second invitation. He hurried over to the taxi and got in beside Laurie and the three of them, with Allen interjecting coos and crows, discussed hops, heifers and related subjects until they reached the station.

'I've told the driver to wait,' Foxy said as the train drew in and she and Laurie hurriedly boarded and then leaned out of the window. Allen, wonderfully happy to be waving to a choo-choo, bounced up and down in Allsop's arms, tears and uncertainties forgotten. 'So you'll get a lift back to the Place, Mr Allsop. If you need us . . .'

'They won't need us,' Laurie said. The train pulled out and he sank back in his seat and pulled Foxy down beside him, then dug her in the ribs.

'Well, that's that – we're off on our honeymoon at last, Matilda! Oh, how we'd have teased you, John and I, if we'd known you were really Matilda Lockett! Well, sweetheart, you're Matilda Clifton now . . . how d'you like the sound of that? Or should I say Lady Clifton?'

They were alone in a first-class carriage, from which they would presently be ejected, Foxy was sure, by the guard, but at least it gave them some privacy for a bit.

'Lady Clifton! My Auntie Bea *will* be impressed,' Foxy said, leaning her head against Laurie's shoulder. 'It's odd, though. I'm not over-awed by it all, it just feels . . . nice. Comfortable. Even the Lady part.'

'Good,' Laurie said contentedly. 'I wish we could have written to John, though, and told him about it all. But he's never given us any sort of address and even if we'd thought to send a letter to the hospital, which never occurred to me, they won't be there by now, they'll be miles away, probably pegging it for England as hard as they can go. With Europe seething and war with Germany a certainty, they can't get home quickly enough for me. And anyway we'll tell him all about the wedding when he gets back.'

'Including how guilty I feel over a week in Llandudno, spending money we haven't really got,' Foxy said. 'Only now the cheque from the Hovertons will cover it, you say?'

'It will. They've been very generous.' He leaned his chin on the crown of her head, then hugged her again. 'Imagine, a whole week when we aren't working at top speed with eight or nine other people, coming home so exhausted that we stay in our own beds, get woken at five a.m. to milk cows or amuse Allen . . .'

'It will be nice,' Foxy admitted. 'Mrs Waughman is a wonderful cook, and we're terribly lucky to have someone to cook for us, but it'll be nice to sit down to a meal with just the two of us. Do you realise, Lo, that this is the first chance we've had to get to know each other without either John, or Allsop, or even Allen, around?'

'Good; so long as we don't talk about hops,' Laurie said with considerable feeling. 'Because I don't mind telling you, wife of my bosom, that your conversation palls when it's nothing but hops, hops, hops.'

Foxy snuggled against him and sighed.

'I won't mention hops until we're on the train home,' she promised rashly. 'Well, not more than once in twenty-four hours – would that be fair?'

Laurie smiled lovingly down at her.

'It'll do, Matilda,' he said. 'It'll do.'

It was a sunny day, and beginning to be hot. The curve of the Orme was shimmering against the blue sky and the beach donkeys had already started their day. Watching the small animals plodding patiently along the sand, harness jingling, the tiny children on their backs screaming, laughing, made Foxy think of Allen; how he would have enjoyed all this! But Laurie was right, they needed a break, and they would be back with their responsibilities weighing on them again soon enough.

Foxy glanced lovingly at her new husband as they walked along the beach, with the sea crashing onto the sand on their right and the beautiful curve of promenade and big hotels on their left. He was looking better than he had looked for ages, with colour in his cheeks and a sparkle in his eyes, and he had progressed to using sticks instead of crutches, though because of the nature of sand she was watching him carefully to make sure he didn't slip. They were deep in conversation, however, on a subject which fascinated them both.

'What I want to know is what's odd about the Chinese room,' Foxy said, bending to pick a shell out of the smooth, wet sand. 'It's years and years ago, but John was always the most practical, down-to-earth person, and he felt it. In fact, he felt it worse than I did. I just thought there was . . . oh, I don't know, something there which wasn't . . . wasn't *ordinary*. But it more or less attacked John – it not only blew out his candle, it knocked the candlestick out of his hand.' Foxy's eyes were dark with remembered fear. 'I didn't go in that room again for years . . . even when I moved into the Place I steered clear for ages.'

'I felt something, but it wasn't anything angry, it was just something full of sadness and – well, I suppose it could have been fear,' Laurie said, after a longish pause for thought. 'Perhaps it wasn't even fear, just deep unhappiness. But whatever it was, it's gone. In fact, I feel sort of wrapped round when I'm in there. That's why I told Allsop we'd sleep in there when we get home, and put Allen in the dressing room. Because it's a welcoming room, now.'

'I know what you mean,' Foxy admitted. 'I've never told you before, darling, but when Allen was born I was in that room and someone came to keep me company. A nurse, I thought, a lovely person. I wanted her to come to the christening and I told Allsop, but she wasn't there. Allsop asked in the village, but the woman I described wasn't the assistant nurse. Allsop said . . .' she hesitated, turning to look fully at him, feeling the breeze lifting her hair, knowing her puzzlement must show on her face. '. . . Allsop said that the only person who looked as I had described her had been . . . well, your mother, Lady Clifton.'

Foxy thought Laurie would scoff, but he did not. Instead, he motioned with his head for her to follow him and then led the way off the beach and up onto the promenade. He went to a wooden seat and sat himself down, then held out his hand.

'We need to sit down and talk,' he said. 'Come on, sit by me and we'll have a bit of a cuddle. The worst thing about still needing two sticks is that I can't hold your hand when we're walking.'

'You're getting better all the time; in a few months you won't need a stick at all,' Foxy observed, sitting down beside him. 'Then I take it you aren't going to tell me that Allsop's a silly old woman and I'm another? I almost wish you would, to tell you the truth. I mean, I've never believed in ghosts.'

'Nor me. But something very odd happened one afternoon a few weeks ago. If you remember, I was beginning to get about without my crutches, and I could go upstairs fairly well, provided I clung to the banister. I'd come back to the house to fetch our battle plan – you know, that exercise book we'd been using so we'd remember what we were likely to need, and when we were likely to need it – only when I reached the study I suddenly remembered leaving it on the windowsill in your room.

'So of course up the stairs I went, in my socks because I'd shed my boots outside the back door and without my crutches because I could use the banister more effectively. I reached the head of the stairs and realised that someone was in the ivory room so I paused, wondering whether to call out or whether to sneak in quietly, if Allen was asleep and just muttering to himself.

'I listened, and it was Allsop, reading to Allen. I know he sometimes reads him to sleep and felt I oughtn't to barge in so I was hesitating on the landing when I heard something very odd.'

'Listeners never hear good of themselves,' Foxy said wisely. 'Was he telling Allen what a worm you are?'

'Certainly not! No, but Allen was sort of crowing, obviously very pleased about something, and then I heard Allsop begin to talk, but not to Allen. To someone else.'

'What did he say?'

'He said something about Allen being a fine fellow, and then he said . . . I can remember this bit because it was so *odd* . . . he said, *But I believe he can see you, though I cannot.* And then he added that he'd done it for the boy's sake, and finished by saying he'd do anything on earth for "you and yours, Milady," whatever that might mean.'

'Very odd; creepy, in fact,' Foxy said. 'I can remember when I thought Allsop was a bit creepy, actually. I don't now, I just think of him as a tower of strength, but I used to be rather scared of him. He knew so much and never seemed at a loss. Of course I was only a kid then, but you know how it is, and he is very awe-inspiring in a quiet way. I wonder what he meant . . . *he can see you, though I cannot*? Can children see ghosts, Lo?'

'I don't know, and anyway I don't think I believe in ghosts. But I'm beginning to suspect it may be quite important to believe in this one. Because if there is a ghost, I really think it must be my mama.'

'Ye-es, but why? She was happy at Clifton Place, wasn't she? I mean I know your father was pretty horrible when we knew him, but surely that was because of her death? Surely he was just . . . just weak and embittered because he'd been left alone? That's what I always thought, anyway.'

'I don't know,' Laurie said slowly. 'But I tend to think that it was her unhappiness which we felt so strongly in the Chinese room. It *was* her room, and she did die there.'

'In that bed?' Foxy shivered. 'No wonder I didn't like going near it, then.'

'Nor me. Yet when I came home, after Spain, the room felt quite different. I've been in a couple of times, I sometimes do a bit of sketching in there, and Allen's come in once or twice and he seems perfectly at home.'

'You've been sketching, again? Oh, Lo! But why didn't you tell me?'

'I don't know; I've always felt a bit ashamed of my painting, as though it was a girly sort of thing to do. My father more or less said that real men didn't paint, you know. Foxy, it's taken me simply ages to work it out, but I wouldn't be at all surprised if – if my father didn't have something to do with my mother's death.'

'Oh, Laurie, that's absurd,' Foxy said at once. 'Why on earth should he hurt your poor mother? She was no threat to him, and anyway, he must have loved her; she'd given him the son he wanted.'

'I know. But I asked Mr Hawkings how she had managed to tie her money up so that I couldn't touch it until I was twenty-five, and Sir George couldn't touch it at all. And he explained about the trust . . . and told me that Sir George had expected to be able to use the money freely after his wife's death. I pricked up my ears at that, you can imagine, and asked him why, and he said that firstly Sir George had assumed all her money would go to him as the next of kin, and apparently even after he was told her money had been left in trust, he thought that as my parent he would be able to use the money for my upbringing, etc. So you see, he thought he would benefit from her death.'

'I see. I didn't know. But he had lots of money in those early days, didn't he? He splashed it about, Allsop's told me several times.'

'Yes, he did. But my mother's money was a lump sum, the money Sir George took from the estate was largely from sale of lands and so on. My maternal grandfather was only a farmer but his brother had become an extremely rich brewer, and left him everything, house, land, the brewery, everything, when he died. So, when my grandfather died, he left it to his only child, my mama. Apparently, my mother sold up and put the money into the trust, because I suppose she knew she wouldn't be able to hold out against Sir George if he simply demanded cash. And then the baby – me – was born, and very shortly afterwards she died.'

'Why did Sir George wait until you were born? Why not kill her as soon as he knew she had inherited the money?'

'I don't really know the answer to that one, Foxy, but I imagine it was because, once they had a child, Sir George thought it would be plain sailing to take the money in the child's name. If she'd died before I was born the money, I take it, would have gone to her cousin's boy, down in Paignton.'

'And you honestly think he – he killed her? But people would have suspected, surely?'

'I don't know. She'd just had a baby, Sir George was going round telling everyone he had an heir, praising his wife to the skies . . . she wasn't strong, probably a pillow across her face in the dead of night . . .' Laurie shuddered. 'I'm not saying it did happen, but it's what I've begun to believe may well have happened. Why else would my father never go near that room, never mention her name, except when he was too drunk to know what he was saying? And once I moved into the Place I very soon realised that he – he hated her as much as he hated me. I heard him, over and over, curse her and the trust she had set up.'

'And do you think he committed suicide, then? Only the doctor was sure it was just an accident.'

'Well, no, I don't think it was suicide. Nor do I think it was an accident. Do you remember we thought the telephone wires must be down? Good old Allsop sent for the telephone repair man, only the chap couldn't find anything wrong but the telephone seemed to right itself, since we were then able to get the doctor?'

'Yes, I heard about it,' Foxy said. 'I wasn't around, but I heard.'

'Well, I think it's quite likely that Allsop tinkered with the phone after he'd given the old boy a bottle of whisky and shoved him in the lake,' Laurie said frankly. '*I did it for the boy's sake,* he said at one point, when he was talking to ... well, let's say when he thought he was talking to my mama. And to be frank, if Sir George had continued to spend money he hadn't got there wouldn't have been much estate left for me to inherit. The trust couldn't make good cottages and farms which Sir George had sold. So, you see ...'

'Allsop cares very much for the estate, and the Cliftons, doesn't he?' Foxy said. Her heart was beginning to thump like a trip-hammer in her chest and her mouth was dry. 'Dear God, Laurie, do you realise what we've done? We've left Allen in the care of a murderer – and if he knew Allen wasn't heir to the Clifton estate, if he knew he was just the bastard son of a local hop-grower ... why, he might do anything!'

'But he doesn't know. He can't know,' Laurie said uncertainly after a moment. 'Besides, he loves Allen, you know he does. We would both trust Allsop with our lives! And this is all conjecture, darling, guesswork. I could be totally wrong, both my mother and Sir George could have died perfectly natural deaths.'

'Yes, but dare we take a chance when it's Allen who's at stake? Lo, if Allsop starts poking around in my room he might find those letters ... God knows why, but I kept John's letters telling me how he loved me, how he'd marry me when he got back from Spain and could acknowledge the child. I meant to burn them once you and I ... oh, Lo, we must go back! Or should we ring the police, ask them to look after Allen for us until we get home?'

She was on her feet, clutching his arm, the chill of terror turning her blood to ice in her veins. She seized Laurie's hands and tugged feebly, trying to help him up, then felt the world tipping crazily around her ... and felt herself falling, falling ...

'Of course I'm all right,' Foxy said weakly when she came round to find herself slumped on Llandudno promenade, with a white-faced Laurie bending over her. She got shakily to her feet, still feeling as though her nice, safe world had suddenly tipped upside down. 'I'm sure I simply fainted from sheer panic – but we must go home, Lo! Let's not waste time going back to the boarding house, let's go now!'

'Oh my love, I'm sure you're panicking without the slightest cause,' Laurie said, helping her to her feet and assuring the people who had begun to form a small crowd around them that his wife was quite all right and had just found the heat a trifle exhausting. 'But if it makes you feel better I'll hail a taxi!'

The taxi driver took them straight to the railway station, only to find that they had an hour and a half to wait before the next train left.

'Then we'll pack and pay our bill and leave,' Laurie said. Foxy could see that now she had drawn her terrible conclusion he, too, could not wait to get home. 'But I'm sure you're wrong, Allen will be quite safe. As I said, I'd trust Allsop with my life. Only . . . I'd feel happier if we could just make certain.'

They rushed back to their lodgings, paid the bill and packed, Laurie explaining to the proprietor that they had telephoned home and heard that a close relative was ill.

'Lies pile on lies,' he said as they reached the railway station for the second time that morning. 'Where's it going to end?'

'I'd tell the hugest lies in the world if it got us back to Clifton Place quicker. Oh Lo, we never should have left him,' Foxy mourned as they got into the carriage nearest them when the train drew into the platform. 'What sort of a mother am I, to leave her little boy with – with someone I don't really know at all, just to go gadding off on honeymoon?'

'You wanted to leave him with the Hovertons, but Allsop persuaded you to leave him at Clifton Place, instead,' Laurie reminded her. 'It's my fault, I should have realised . . .'

Foxy put her hand over his mouth. 'Don't! No point in blaming ourselves or each other. Just will the train to go faster . . . to get there in time!'

There was no one to meet them of course, but they caught a taxi which took them straight to the Place. They bundled out of the vehicle and Foxy dived at the front door, pushing it open with an impatient hand, then turning towards Laurie who was hurrying along with his stick doing yeoman service.

'Lo? I'm so frightened!'

'No need.' He dumped their suitcase in the hall, then took her hand and led her through towards the kitchen. 'They'll be having tea, I expect. You'll take one look at our boy's smiling face and then you'll stop worrying.' He lowered his voice. 'Just how, now I come to think of it, would Allsop explain away the sudden death of a perfectly healthy little boy?'

'He'd say he'd been poorly for a day or so . . .' Foxy began as they reached the door. She pushed it open impatiently. 'Ah, Mrs Waughman, we're home!'

Mrs Waughman was standing at the Aga, stirring a bubbling saucepan. She frowned at them, then smiled uncertainly. 'You 'ome already, Sir Laurie, Milady? Well, there, I s'pose Mr Allsop rang you to come back bein' as 'ow Master Allen's not so well?'

'Where is he?' Laurie said baldly. Foxy felt his impatience, his fear, and even in her own highly charged state, was glad he shared her feelings so completely. Allen might have been his own flesh and blood from the whiteness of his face, the little shake in his voice.

'Who, Master Allen? Why, he'm up in 'is cot; Mr Allsop's seein' to 'im. Master Allen's been poorly all day, he'm . . .'

'Come on,' Laurie snapped and fairly dragged Foxy across to the stairs. At the foot, he gestured her to go ahead of him. 'Go on, hurry! I'll follow as fast as I can.'

Foxy ran up the stairs two at a time. She tore across the landing and charged at her bedroom door. She flung it open and stared at the empty room, totally flabbergasted, then turned to Laurie, who was just reaching the head of the stairs.

'They aren't here, Lo, the room's empty.'

'Try the Chinese room, love. When I sent the postcard earlier in the week I said we were going to sleep there, with Allen in the dressing room . . .'

He did not finish the sentence since Foxy turned and flew further up the landing, then stopped short. She opened the door of the Chinese room so slowly and carefully that it did not make a sound and then she stood in the doorway, staring.

Laurie came up behind her and stood there too, a hand on her shoulder, looking into the room.

Allsop was sitting on the bed with Allen enthroned on his lap. He was holding out a teaspoon, full of blood-red liquid, and he

507

was saying in a firm but affectionate voice, 'Come along, young feller-me-lad, just you swallow this lovely pink drink and you'll sleep like a little log; trust old Allsop to see you right.'

He leaned Allen back in the crook of his arm and brought the teaspoon round . . . and Foxy and Laurie fell into the room, Foxy knocking the teaspoon out of his grasp so that red liquid splashed on Allen's white cotton sleeping suit, on the bedspread, on Allsop's dark trousers.

'No!' Foxy gasped. 'No, you aren't to give him that stuff!'

Allsop looked totally astonished. His thin grey eyebrows rose up and up until they almost touched where his hairline would have been had he not been almost bald in front.

'It's all right, Milady. I decided not to telephone you after the doctor had been this morning, because Master Allen is so much better. But he's cutting a big back tooth and he's running a temperature, so Dr Pready gave me a bottle of medicine to ease the pain and help him to sleep.' He glanced from face to face. 'I don't, myself, agree with over-medication of the young,' he said smoothly, 'but since this medicine seems to soothe the pain I saw no harm . . .'

'Where's the bottle?' Foxy said sharply. 'Have you put anything else in it?'

Allsop frowned. 'What are you saying, Milady? You aren't suggesting I'd do anything to hurt Master Allen?'

Laurie closed the door and went and sat on the bed beside the older man. He took the baby from him and handed him to Foxy.

'Give him his medicine, darling, and tuck him up in his cot.' He turned to the butler, still staring, white-faced, at the child. 'Allsop, how did my mother die?'

'Pardon me, Mr Laurie?'

'And how did my father die, Allsop? Who gave him the whisky which may have caused him to fall in the lake?'

'Sir Laurie, none of this is relevant to the fact that you burst in here and snatch the child, whilst Miss Foxy . . . I mean Milady, naturally . . . stares at me as if she thinks me capable of . . . of any vile thing. Your mother died when you were two weeks old, she'd not fully recovered from your birth, I don't know what was written on the death certificate but I don't see . . .'

'I think you do,' Laurie said. Foxy had taken her son into the small dressing room and could be heard talking quietly to him as she put him into his cot. 'I've suspected for a long while, Allsop, that you might have assisted my father to drink that whisky; I believe you probably pushed him into the lake.'

'That's a very wild accusation, Mr Laurie,' the butler said evenly. 'And not one, I think, which you would care to utter in a courtroom.'

'No. Because frankly, if my father hadn't died when he did, I doubt very much whether I should have had any inheritance to come back to . . .' he broke off, almost smiling at Allsop as light dawned. 'That's why you did it! Because I'd threatened to stay away from Herefordshire altogether rather than share a house with Sir George, and you love Clifton Place and you knew very well that the old man would have ruined the place, legally or not, in a twelvemonth once the hope of getting the trust money for his own use was gone.'

Allsop gave a small nod and an even smaller smile. 'Well, that's your theory, Sir Laurie. But you didn't think for one moment, surely, that I had anything to do with your mother's death? Why, I would no more have harmed a hair of her ladyship's head . . .'

'No, I'm very sure you didn't hurt her. I think my father killed her, to get at the trust,' Laurie told him. 'I can't prove it any more than anyone else could at the time, but it's what I believe. What do *you* believe, Allsop?'

The butler nodded. 'I share your belief, sir,' he said. 'I have no sort of proof, but I've always thought he at least hurried her end. She had been very ill, you know, with a chest infection.'

'I knew she'd not been well,' Laurie admitted. 'So that was it; a chest infection which turned into pneumonia when . . . he was cunning, you have to grant him that.'

'He never came into this room again, not willingly,' Allsop said, more to himself than to Laurie. 'Not until that last night. And then he didn't know what he was doing, of course.'

'No, of course not,' Laurie said. 'What happened?'

'I gave him the whisky; said I'd found a bottle in the cellars, tucked out of sight. He didn't care where it came from, so long as he got his nose stuck into it,' Allsop said in a flat voice. 'When he'd drunk three-quarters of the bottle I brought him in here . . . he was terrified! He saw her, you know,' he added conversationally. 'I

509

knew she was still here, but I've never seen her. Only ... only sensed her. But he saw her. His face went the most horrible purplish-grey colour, and he just turned and ran for the door. He stumbled down the stairs – I thought every moment he'd break his neck – and out of the side door. I followed.

'He didn't go to the lake, not on his own legs. I wheeled him there in the wheelbarrow, looking sick and mumbling a lot of rubbish about how he'd hated her – her, who was worth a thousand of him! When we reached the lake I just tipped him in and he sank like a stone. I returned the barrow to the elm avenue, from whence I'd removed it, and went back to bed. And slept well, Mr Laurie; better than I'd slept for many a long night.'

'You *did* do away with him, then!'

Allsop looked indignant. 'I did no such thing! He was vilely drunk, but he was a strong swimmer. I was very angry, I admit it; I meant to bring him round in no uncertain fashion. It wasn't my fault that he refused to try to swim, even. Why, it isn't even deep there ... and there was no water in his lungs, the doctor said so.'

'No; he died of a heart-attack,' Laurie said, remembering. 'And I suppose you'll tell me you did it for the sake of the family? You're loyal, Allsop, I'll say that for you.'

'The family? Which one? Do you mean the Cliftons?' Allsop sniffed scornfully. 'Jumped-up nobodies, the Cliftons, until 1754 they didn't even own property, or nothing substantial, begging your pardon, sir, for my frankness. My lady was an Allen, a very old family, they could trace their ancestors back to the Conquest, you know. Now she was a proper lady ...' he smiled for the first time, '... like your wife, sir.'

'But Foxy isn't ... well, we don't even know who her father was,' Laurie said, very confused. 'Which ... which was why we thought you might do Allen harm. I'm sorry for thinking it, but ... but ...'

'Oh, Miss Foxy isn't nobility, but she's clever and hardworking and a credit to us all, sir,' Allsop explained. 'Besides, my lady wanted her boy to be happy and she'll make you happy, will Miss Foxy. And Miss Foxy's seen her, too – when she was in labour with Master Allen my lady came to her, comforted her. All I wanted, ever, was my lady's happiness. And now all I want is to see you and Miss Foxy and Master Allen secure and in control of Clifton Place. Not because you're Cliftons, begging your pardon, Mr Laurie, but because you're my lady's son and Mr Allen is yours. So I hope you won't ever accuse me of wanting to do the youngster harm, sir.'

Laurie took a deep breath. Foxy had come out of the dressing room and had been listening for some while, so he glanced across at her, eyebrows raised. She nodded. Neither of them could let Allsop go on believing Allen to be Laurie's child; not after all he had told them. 'Allsop, I'm afraid that Master Allen isn't . . .'

'Isn't your get, sir, if you'll excuse the expression? No, I rather fancy Mr John was responsible, wasn't he? I don't think that matters, certainly my lady won't love him any the less for that, and certainly I couldn't think more highly of him were his father the king of England himself. Because he is your son, wouldn't you say? An adoptive son is legally one's heir, if one wishes it to be so.'

'Allsop, you never fail to surprise me,' Foxy said from the doorway. 'And we were fools to think you'd harm any of us, regardless of race, creed or colour. Tell me, why did your lady marry Sir George? And why did you come here with her, and then remain after her death?'

'She married Sir George because her father did not care for the very ordinary young man with whom she fell in love,' Allsop said. 'So she married him on the rebound, and to get away from her dictatorial parents. I came to work here shortly after she herself arrived because she told me Sir George would be advertising for a butler; I answered the advertisement and easily obtained the position. I was to be a – a friend in court, you might say. And I stayed after her death because I knew she would want me to look after Mr Laurie, despite the fact that for many years he only visited and did not live here.

'And now, sir and madam, if you'll sit with Mr Allen until he goes to sleep I'll go down to the kitchen and lay two more places for supper.'

'I wonder who the *ordinary young man* was whom Mr Allen the brewer didn't approve of,' Foxy said sleepily a week later, as she and Laurie lay in their brand-new bed in the Chinese room. During their hurried visit to Clifton Place halfway through their honeymoon – they had returned to Llandudno the following day – Laurie had told Allsop to sell the fourposter, which had proved to be a valuable piece of antique furniture, and the butler had replaced it with a comfortable modern divan. 'Whoever he was he can't have had much gumption; he should have thrown her over his saddle bow and ridden away with her.'

'Perhaps, in a way, he did,' Laurie said after a moment. 'I don't suppose he had any money, do you? Perhaps he was in no position to support her.'

'You think your mother's true love was Allsop, don't you?' Foxy said bluntly. 'You think he followed her here because it was the only way he could be near her.'

'Don't you?'

Foxy chuckled. 'I did wonder. Because if there's one thing I always thought . . .'

'What?' Laurie said as the silence stretched.

'Oh, nothing. Just that I wish we'd never doubted Allsop, and yet I'm glad we found out what he did. It's certainly a very strange, rather sad story.'

'You weren't going to say that at all,' Laurie said accusingly. 'You were going to say you'd always thought I wasn't very much like Sir George to look at, weren't you?'

The silence this time was an astonished one. Then Foxy prodded him in the back with a stiffened forefinger.

'I never said that! Why, I'm sure you're a Clifton through and through!'

'Are you? Personally, I think it's something that we'll never know for sure. But you must admit, the old man never treated me much like a well-loved son and heir, did he? Perhaps he had his doubts.'

'Perhaps your mother said something of the sort to him, and that was why he put a pillow over her face – if he did,' Foxy suggested. 'Gosh, what a weird thing love is, Lo. Like a disease which makes you do things you'd never do without it. I mean, can you imagine poor Allsop wheeling that barrow over that shocking ground, pouring sweat and scared someone would pop out from behind a hedge? I find it awfully difficult.'

'I agree. And I'm not sure he was motivated by love, precisely.'

'He was!' Foxy said stoutly at once. 'Love for his lady's child, that's you, and a desperate urge to make sure the old man didn't drive you away from Clifton Place.'

'Oh yes, I agree with you, then. That kind of love is a bit different from the kind I meant.' Laurie put a hand on the nape of her neck and drew her close. 'What a good thing you and I haven't caught the love-disease,' he said. 'If we had, I daresay we'd make awful fools of ourselves.'

'Awful fools,' Foxy agreed, a laugh trembling on her lips. 'And now we'd better go to sleep because tomorrow we've got to apply the nitrogen; Uncle Bill says any later and the hops will be too green and we'll get a poor price. Isn't it wonderful how much we've learned since we first planted the hopyard, Lo? I mean I'd never even *heard* of a monkey until Mr Hov . . . I mean Uncle Bill . . . shoved one into my hands and showed me how it guided the strings up the hop-poles. I just hope the men Uncle Bill is lending us to work the kiln are as good as all the others he's recommended because if it's possible, I know less about drying hops than any other part of the process!'

'Don't worry, Uncle hasn't let us down yet and I don't think he's going to start now,' Laurie said sleepily. 'And now we really must stop talking; the alarm will be going off before we know it, and it has to be muffled fast, before it wakes Allen.'

'He loves the little dressing room,' Foxy murmured. 'Oh, Lo, we're so lucky – I hope to God John's getting on all right. I wish he'd write.'

'Me, too,' Laurie told her. He thought apprehensively that they were so close their thoughts often got entangled and he just hoped she did not know how desperately worried he was growing over John's non-appearance. But there was nothing he could do. Except pray. He put his hands over his face quietly, in the dark, in the old, childish gesture, and began, in a whisper so low that it was almost inside his head.

'God bless all those I love and all those who love me and please, God, take care of John for me. Bring him and Mirri safe home. Amen.'

Superstition? He did not know, but after his prayer, he slept.

Eighteen

John sat on an outcrop of rock and watched the heat haze shimmering over the plain below him, though it was early in the morning still and the sun had only been up two or three hours. Behind him, in the small stone shepherd's hut, Mirri slept. John dug around in the pocket of his worn jacket and found a cigarette. He got out his matches, lit the cigarette, and blew smoke towards the mountains.

It was late July and he had begun to think, at one time, that he would have to stay in Spain indefinitely because Mirri had been so gravely ill.

He had believed her to be very much better, too, otherwise they would not have moved on. The hospital in Madrid had told him she could now manage a short journey so the two of them had taken to the hills, making their way to a tiny village where John had friends who had somehow managed to come through the war alive and get back to their own place.

There, in the warm sunshine of early summer, Mirri had begun to look like a young girl again, instead of a starved and sick old woman. But despite John making her eat as well as they could afford, and seeing that she rested in the heat of the day, she remained painfully thin. And to keep her mind active he talked to her in English until she could converse properly again in that language, he laughed at her, teased her, told her all about Beeswing Farm and about Clifton Place and the surrounding countryside. She became cheerful at last and livelier with every day that passed and John had been sure his treatment was working, thought she was gaining strength daily.

When he was sure she could manage the journey they set off for the Pyrenees. Spain was in a confused and dreadful state, with the Nationalists the victors but with law and order still to be settled. A man with a gun is law and order so far as he himself is concerned, and John, though he was armed, dared do nothing to upset the Nationalists who strutted the streets, guns at the ready, burst into houses unprovoked and demanded to see papers, hustled young girls off to 'answer a few questions', and released them after long and sometimes terrible interrogations.

But the two of them kept their heads down and their mouths closed. They spent as little money as possible and drew no attention to themselves. They both wore thin and ragged clothing and spoke nothing but Spanish when they were in company and it worked, because no one challenged them.

Then Mirri stumbled one day on what appeared to be a smooth and dusty road and fell over, and when John went to pick her up, teasing her that she must have fallen over her own feet, she was unconscious. He took her to a small hospital in the nearest town and she was laid on a dirty straw pallet whilst the doctor examined her.

'She has pneumonia and probably tuberculosis,' the doctor told John briskly. 'She's been malnourished for a very long time and this has given her no resistance to disease and very little will to live. She may recover, or she may not. We can keep her here and try to clear the pneumonia, but the other . . .' he shrugged, '. . . the other needs treatment which we cannot give. To get such treatment you will have to take her out of Spain, to France perhaps, or Switzerland.'

'Make her as well as you can,' John said. 'I'll take her to France as soon as she can be moved.'

But in the end, he moved her because he dared no longer leave her in the hospital. The bullet wound in her wrist had been remarked upon by one or two of the nurses and though they seemed pleasant girls, one of them at least talked proudly of how her father had been a captain in the Nationalist army, and how well he had known General Franco.

So here they were, getting nearer the border day by day, with Mirri listless and coughing badly, occasionally having to stop, putting a thin hand to her heaving ribs. John was careful never to hurry her, to tell her always that they had all the time in the world, but even so she must have known there was urgency. She needed treatment soon, John was sure, before the disease simply burned up her skinny little frame.

He smoked his cigarette down to a stub, then ground it out on the rock and turned to look back at the shepherd's hut. Mirri had woken and stood in the doorway, looking past him, at the distant mountains and the plain between. He smiled at her with real affection; he thought her the bravest person he had ever known, for not one grumble had ever passed her lips no matter how weary she grew.

'Mirri! Good morning, little one. Did you sleep well? I'll catch a goat presently . . . you'd like some goat's milk? I'm afraid there isn't much else, but the old woman gave me half a loaf and said we might milk one of her goats if we could catch it.'

Mirri smiled at him.

'Yes, I would like some milk,' she said, her voice very small and thin. 'Bread and milk is easy to swallow.'

He nodded and came over to where she stood.

'You look better today; you've more colour in your cheeks. We'll move on later, then, if you feel you can walk a little.'

Mirri had been standing in the doorway for five minutes, watching him, before he turned and saw her. He was so kind, and so beautiful. She wished she was still beautiful, just so that John would get pleasure from looking at her, but she knew she wasn't. Her limbs were like sticks, her colour had a waxy pink brilliance which did not suit her and to save the pain of breathing, she had hunched her shoulders forward until her shape was almost deformed.

But you would never have known it from the warm way in which John looked at her! And he had grown stronger and more beautiful yet, seeming to thrive on the outdoor life which had dragged Mirri even further down. His hair, gilded by the sun, was white-blond, his skin was warmly brown, which made his blue eyes seem bluer than ever. If only I were well, Mirri told herself over and over, I would be so happy just being with him. But I'm not well, I'm ill, and I hold him back. If it hadn't been for me he'd have been home months ago, working on his farm, talking to Laurie, helping people at home instead of wasting his time with me.

Because quite a lot of the time she really did know that John was wasting his time. Yesterday morning when she woke there had been blood on the straw pallet by her mouth. This morning she had coughed blood again. Dark, odd-looking blood. And the cough had wrenched at her lungs with such pain that she had nearly cried out.

But not quite. John must not know. She knew he wouldn't leave her, not whilst she lived, but she knew, too, that he would insist on staying here longer, trying to get her fit before tackling the mountains. And Mirri had grown wise these past hard years. In Spain she would never get better, she would just get worse. But if she could get over the mountains, into France, then perhaps someone really could cure her, make her well again. That was what one part of her mind thought; the other part had dark thoughts which had to be banished so that she could smile at John and show him a brave face. And meanwhile, if she could get to France . . .

It would be wonderful to be well. To breathe without pain, to walk without effort, to talk without breathlessness. Sometimes she thought about England, because if she ever reached it she would be well, but she didn't think about Laurie, not any more. She couldn't even see his face in her mind's eye, the only face which swam constantly behind her closed lids was John's – gentle, golden, always kind.

John turned towards her and Mirri smiled at him and felt a cough rising up in her chest and refused to let it roar out, not whilst he was looking at her. Only when he had turned away to cajole one of the goats into letting him milk her did she cough into her hand . . . wiping away the splatter of blood quickly on her rusty black skirt.

She saw the mountains getting closer and was forced to tell John that she mustn't talk, mustn't laugh. She had no spare breath, she must put all her effort into getting there. He had started putting a strong arm round her waist, almost carrying her, and now he said they would rest for longer . . . but she shook her head. Every step was pain by the end of the first hour, but she plodded on. As she continued to walk she realised that John was almost lifting her off her feet, but she still ached dreadfully, even his arm around her hurt her brittle bones. Yet she never thought of giving up, turning back. In her mind the hills were beginning to mean safety, and health, and – and a tomorrow. She must reach the hills!

It was days before they gained the foothills and by then the heat was another enemy; John decreed they would walk by night and rest during the day, but the heat, and sheer exhaustion, prevented her from sleeping. She simply lay awake all the long, hot daylight hours, trying to prevent the cough bubbling up in her throat, spilling out at last with bright blood . . . giving her away.

But they did reach the foothills. And when morning came and they sought the shelter of a small copse, John simply took her in his arms and lay down with her, holding her close to his chest. His beautiful face was grave, but when he saw her looking at him he smiled.

'Poor little Mirri, how very brave you've been and how very hard you've struggled to keep up with me. I'm sorry if I've made you walk when you needed to rest, but from now on, I'm going to carry you. Heaven knows, you weigh no more than a little bird, so it won't be much effort. Now put your head on my chest and cuddle up and we'll both be asleep in less time than it takes to tell!'

And with his arms around her and his broad chest beneath her cheek, Mirri fell into a deep and dreamless slumber at last.

John tried not to move, to keep so still that he would not wake her. He thought he had succeeded, and fell asleep at last himself. When he woke it was dusk and he put a hand on her brow to wake her.

Despite the heat of the day, which was still slowly ebbing, her brow was cold.

He could not believe it, at first. He called her name, shook her, hugged her, but she responded not at all. He looked into her small face and saw peace there, and knew she was dead, yet still he could not accept it.

'I'll carry you over the mountains,' he said, his voice ragged with grief. 'You won't have to walk, little one, I'll carry you every foot of the way!'

Nothing. He was alone.

He buried her in the copse, because there was nothing else he could do. Did I know she was dying? he asked himself as he dug and dug with only a stout branch ripped from a tree for a spade. Reason told him he must have known – he had seen the blood, understood its portent – but he had simply been unable to accept what reason told him. Getting Mirri back to Laurie had become his main aim in life, and then taking care of Mirri, loving this courageous girl, had simply taken over. Of course he hadn't loved her in the way Laurie had, he had only known her sick and weak, someone whose whole dependence was on him. No, he had loved her as he loved all poor and helpless things, and his rescuing of her would have been the only joyous and wonderful action to have come out of the bloody civil war.

Oddly, though, he found he was not dreading telling Laurie that his girl was dead. He knew that Laurie would not have been able to love the Mirri that he, John, had known. Laurie wanted a woman who was his equal, someone with spirit and a sense of adventure, not a girl whose need to be succoured overwhelmed all other aspects of her personality. No, Laurie would not have loved this Mirri, so from his point of view her death, though sad, was not the tragedy for him it might once have been.

John laboured on as the heat of the day faded until the grave was deep enough. Then he wrapped the small, skinny body in the blanket which had been Mirri's, and lowered his burden into the grave. He kicked and shovelled the earth back into the hole, then rolled a couple of boulders over it; he did not want dogs or wild pigs digging here.

He said some prayers. They weren't the prayers for the dead which he should have remembered, but snatched lines of poetry, some verses of a psalm, a hymn which Mirri had sung before she fell ill. And the hotch-potch seemed, in a strange way, more appropriate than real prayers. Then he threw the stout branch deep into the undergrowth and set off, towards the great humped shape of the Pyrenees. He did not look back, but looking up, his eyes were still blurred with tears. Mirri had longed to reach the mountains, believing that if she could once get across them she stood a chance of being cured. It was a fantasy, but the sort of fantasy she needed to keep her going, day in, day out, a hope as frail and elusive as that which keeps a man going in mountainous terrain – the peak you are climbing is always the highest, always the last – until you reach the summit and see, stretching before you, peak after peak.

He walked fast and presently realised with a jolt of guilt that he was enjoying walking fast. He immediately slowed, then speeded up again. It wouldn't help Mirri if he was caught here, trying to get out of Spain, with a Nationalist bullet wound in his calf and a British revolver in his pocket. But when he reached the first peak he turned and looked down across the Spanish plain, towards the little copse where Mirri lay, peaceful at last.

'Goodbye, little one,' he murmured. 'I'll never forget you, but I need to remember you with joy, not sadness. So I'll remember you in hospital in Madrid, when we first met, and you told me you could eat a big, huge bowl of bread and milk right away – now!'

He turned away, to the descent which awaited him, to the peak on peak which stretched before.

The kilns were being cleaned and prepared for the picking which was now no more than a month away and whilst the men laboured, Foxy and Laurie drove the tractor between the hop rows and checked the hops, which were now right at the top of the poles and could only be examined either by a man on stilts or by Foxy, standing up on the bar at the back and steadying herself on Laurie's shoulders.

'Can't look for wilt like that,' Bill Hoverton said, puffing away on his pipe. He had walked up to the yard and met them as they finished their inspection and ran the tractor into the shippon. 'You're movin' too fast, on a tractor. You want to be on foot.'

'Why on foot? Wilt's easier to spot than other diseases, because the whole bine snuffs it and dies,' Foxy pointed out, but Bill shook his head at her.

'You try spottin' one dead bine in that tangle of green,' he said, pointing the stem of his pipe back towards the hopyard. 'You want

520

to go along real slow, on foot, starin' at every single stem; that'll tek you a time, but 'tes worth every minute.'

'Tomorrow we'll do it,' Foxy said, getting rather stiffly down off the tractor and holding up her hands to give Laurie some assistance. 'Come on, Lo, we'll go and have a look in the kilns, see how they're getting on.'

'Mind they check the chimneys,' Bill said mildly, 'We 'ad a 'splosion one year 'cos of an old owl, caught in the chimney. They've got to be clear or you'll have trouble.'

'We'll make sure they check, Uncle,' Laurie said soothingly. 'Come in and have a cup of tea. No news, I suppose?'

Everyone was worried about John, now. There had been no word from him and the news coming out of Spain was all bad. Europe was in ferment and despite Chamberlain's 'Peace in our time' speech of the previous autumn, no one had much faith in Britain's ability to keep out of what was happening across the Channel.

'No. Nothing yet,' Bill grunted. 'Still, you know John. Hates letter-writin'. Happen he'll turn up without a word, grinnin' from yur to yur.'

'Probably,' Laurie said. 'Perhaps he'll come back for the picking. That 'ud be good, to have the three of us picking in the new yard come September.'

'Four,' Foxy corrected. 'He won't come back without Mirri.'

'Oh . . . yes, four,' Laurie said. 'I keep forgetting Mirri.'

It took John longer to walk through the Pyrenees than he had expected, considering that summer was very much with them, which meant no snow, just the great, bare brown summits. But the rivers were threads, to be eagerly sought out, and he missed Mirri.

He followed the same path he and Laurie had taken nine or ten months earlier, because it was the one he knew, so he was reminded of that terrible journey, with Laurie riding on the handcart, every step of the way. He missed Laurie badly, more even than he missed Mirri, and realised how glad he would be to get back to England. Yet he had thought, once, that England was boring, had found it difficult to settle down.

Not any more. I'd rather be bored in England than excited

521

anywhere else in the world, he thought grimly. And though he wasn't bringing Mirri back with him he could tell Laurie truthfully that he had done his very best.

After three days, he realised he was very near the spot where he had buried, to the best of his ability, the bodies of Nante and Pérez. He was on the path just below the plateau and the cave when the storm came upon him. A summer storm, with a twisting gale-force wind which picked up what little topsoil there was this high in the mountains and whirled it around his face in a hateful, dusty fog. He clung to the path for a little, then decided, since night was falling, that he would make for the plateau. He could shelter in the cave either until the sky cleared and the moon came out, or until morning came.

The plateau was swept bare, desolate. Nothing moved, no vulture hovered, no eagle soared on the wings of the mighty wind. John went on hands and knees into the cave, then got out his blanket and some of the hard ship's biscuits which he had brought with him. He had a drain of water left in his flask and he drank it, then put the biscuits away again. They were too hard and dry, he would leave them until he found another stream. He sat up for a while, staring out at the storm, then he wrapped himself in his blanket, lay against the wall, and very soon, slept.

John awoke when the sun's rays crept into the cave, warming him, telling him the nighttime chill was behind him. He sat up, yawned, rubbed his bristly, bearded chin and after a moment, shuffled to the entrance. He looked out on the morning, and it was early, and cool up here on the high mountain-top.

I'll scramble down a bit further and find that stream, John told himself, folding his blanket and laying it on the top of his knapsack. Then I'll have a drink, eat a couple of biscuits, and be on my way. He ducked his dead – the entrance was a good deal lower than the cave itself – and was about to go out when it occurred to him that he had never seen the back of the cave. Was it very deep? He did not think so, but nevertheless he turned and walked into the cave, away from the cool, sunny morning and into darkness.

The cave got lower and lower. He could see, ahead, that the roof was no more than a foot or eighteen inches from the rock floor.

There was something . . . not water, surely? But there *was* something, on the floor of the cave at the very back.

John bent as the roof got lower and shuffled forward. He put out his hand . . . and it was the body of a man, lying on his back, with the front half of him almost wedged into the lowest portion of the cave. John gave an enormous shudder and leapt back, cracking his head sharply on the roof.

The pain made him think. Had the fellow been trying to escape from something, or someone, and got wedged in there, to die? It seemed unlikely, but . . . I'll leave him, John decided. I've done enough burying of bodies to last me a lifetime and anyway, this chap is probably no more than bones by now.

He frowned down at the body in the dimness. There was something . . . with rough distaste he seized the man by the legs and pulled. The body was disgustingly light and slithered towards him unexpectedly easily. Probably because the cave was dark and cool, it did not appear to have become a skeleton, in fact the body was that of a youngish man. John crouched down and looked at the face. Grey and cold, with the mouth fallen in and the eyes shuttered, he still knew it.

Sorotto. Or Talavera. The killer, the cheat, the sadist. Dead. John looked, but could see no wound, no obvious cause of death. He supposed that one of the others, in dying, must have fired a pistol and wounded Sorotto mortally . . . but he did not intend to examine the corpse for a bullet-hole. What he intended was to get out of here, to get back into the clean sunshine, to leave this hateful, hated man to the only sort of peace anyone could give him, now.

He was on his hands and knees, about to leave the cave, when he remembered the money-belt. It couldn't still be around Sorotto's waist, surely? He hadn't noticed it . . .

He went back. Shrinkingly, he opened Sorotto's coat and saw what remained of the money-belt and what remained of Sorotto. Rats or vultures had disembowelled the body and the money-belt had disintegrated where the air and the rodents had been able to reach it. But across Sorotto's back the long pouch was intact.

John opened the pouch. He took out the money, the large-denomination notes which he had last seen being counted, by candlelight, in a stable. He stared, incredulous. The rats had had a good deal, but there was still quite a bit left!

John sat back on his heels for a moment, almost unable to take it in. Sorotto hadn't got away with any of the money, and he, John, had been the first person to find the body – and the small fortune in the money-belt. He would have something for Laurie, after all. Quickly, almost furtively, he began to push the remains of the money-belt and its contents into the front of his shirt. Then, calm now, he fetched his knapsack and without a backward glance, left the cave and began to descend the steep, treacherous little path. For the first time, he felt he was on his way home.

Today was the first of September and so today the hop-pickers were arriving. The gipsies in their caravans had come, and girls and boys on bicycles from the local schools. Folk from Hereford, more from Brum, the Welsh from their narrow valleys. It made no difference that Clifton Place had not employed pickers in living memory; the advertisements went in, the ill-written, ill-spelt replies came back, and now picking was in a fair way to starting.

'War or not, it don't mek no difference, they'll still come,' Bill Hoverton had said and now Laurie and Foxy, standing together by the gate, could see it was true. Old ladies, younger ones, children. Not so many men since a good few had already been called up. And all the paraphernalia they brought with them... hopping boxes, small items of furniture, beloved toys, bedding, clothes...

Ada Hoverton had advised over who should go where.

'Put the Welsh together in the big barn; they like to sing, of an evening, and it's a beautiful sound,' she said. 'And the Brummies are hardworking and tidy, so let them have them old stables; the roof's good, I noticed that. The youngsters will go home each night, the locals, I mean, and those from Hereford will be comfortable in the outhouses; they'll have first go at the lavvy in the coachman's house.'

'We're starting at eight tomorrow morning,' Laurie said cheerfully to anyone who asked. 'And my wife will be bringing supplies round later. Just bread, cheese, potatoes, that sort of thing. Milk's already in your quarters – and we'll be up at the house if you need anything.'

'Will it be all right?' Foxy asked that night, as they lay in bed. 'It's easy to talk about the picking and the pickers, but I can remember fights, feuds, all sorts. And folk arguing about the rate, and marching up to the farm to pester your mum when they said picking was harder than she thought. I could see them sizing us up out there, seeing how young we were, how – how *green*, Lo. But we can't afford to be cheated, we're already in debt, we'll need to pay the bank back as much as we possibly can so they'll back us next year, too.'

'We won't be cheated,' Laurie said drowsily. 'Don't worry so much, pet. There's always Allsop.'

'So there is,' Foxy droned, already half asleep. 'He'll talk to them if they try to bully us, won't he? He'll tell them where they get off.'

'That's right, he'll tell them. Now go to sleep or it'll be morning and you'll still be lying there, worrying.'

He waited. No reply came. Laurie propped himself up on one elbow and looked down into his wife's face. Correction; his wife's sleeping face. Her mouth was a little bit open but her eyes were tightly shut and her breathing had deepened.

Laurie lay down again, and smiled to himself. Presently, he slept.

The next day dawned misty but with sunshine quick to draw up the mist, looping it up like scarves to reveal the river and the cattle in the fields, hock-deep in it. Foxy got up as soon as she woke and ran over to the window.

'There's a gipsy picking mushrooms on what used to be our front lawn,' she remarked, trying to scratch a gnat bite between her shoulder blades and performing some fairly unusual contortions in order to do so. 'Oh, and he's got a really draggly dog with him.'

'I wouldn't mind mushrooms for brekker,' Laurie said, from the bed. 'I wonder if Allsop will compete with a gipsy? He often does nip out early and get the little button ones because he knows we like them.'

'Well, there's no sign . . . yes, there he is! Immaculately clad as ever, only he's wearing wellies. Hey ho, we'd better get a move on, because we've still got cows to milk and beasts to feed even though it's the first day of hopping.'

'Right,' Laurie said, pushing back the bedclothes with considerable reluctance. He sat on the edge of the bed, reached for his wooden legs, and began to strap them into place. 'I'm going along to the bathroom as soon as I'm mobile, so do you want to wake Allen?'

'Not particularly, but . . .'

'Mumma? Dadda?' The small voice sounded extremely cheerful. Foxy padded over to the dressing-room door and opened it.

'Yes, sweetheart? Mummy's here.'

'Allie come out?'

Without looking into the room, Laurie knew that the baby would be standing on tiptoe, both arms up, stretching towards his mother. Poor Foxy, with so much to do, and no nursery maid yet. They simply could not afford one, though it meant that Foxy, who was such a hard and natural farm worker, was frequently occupied with the baby. A nursery maid would have been wonderful, but when you get right down to it, money really doesn't matter, Laurie told himself with deep content, stripping off his nightshirt and running cold water into the handbasin. We are so lucky! If John would come back I reckon we'd be completely happy and not many people can put their hands on their hearts and say that.

Hot water would be nice, too, his thoughts continued, but that was a commodity which would come when it grew colder. He couldn't fetch water up the stairs but Foxy could, and would in the depths of winter. In the meanwhile, washing in cold wasn't so bad. It made you feel not only fresh and clean but wonderfully righteous as well, which had to be good.

Laurie scrubbed himself, then made his way back to the Chinese room and dressed in his oldest clothes; hop-picking was not for the well-dressed man, what with nettles, the prickly bines, the black stuff which oozed off the hops . . . old clothes were what everyone would wear.

Whistling a tune beneath his breath, Laurie continued to prepare himself for the day ahead. He thought of the many times that he and John had done this together, in a ferment of excitement because the pickers had arrived and the picking would start in less than an hour. Then, he had just enjoyed the excitement but now he had to think of so many things! The rate, the booker, the cribs, the

526

busheller, the drier . . . how on earth had he thought that he and Foxy could cope? Even with the inestimable Allsop, could they possibly get through this, the first harvesting of their hops, without some major calamity?

'Lo, breakfast's on the table. Allsop's going to deal with Allie today so we can both be in the hopyard. Fletcher's down there already, setting things up, and Elias has got the book out and he's standing by the gate, eating a beef sandwich and getting ready to tell the families where to pick.'

Foxy's voice floated up the stairwell. She must have dressed like lightning whilst he was in the bathroom and gone down ahead of him. Serves me right for dreaming, Laurie told himself, leaving the bedroom and heading for the stairs. And I wanted to be out early, this morning, to watch it all beginning, so in future years I could tell my kids how we started up the Long Meadow hops. He voiced the thought to Foxy when he reached the kitchen, where Mrs Waughman greeted him absently from her place by the stove. Foxy laughed at him, then reached up and pinched his chin.

'Don't worry, you know how slowly everything starts the first day! It'll be ten before they pull the first bine and by lunchtime you'll wonder what we got so excited about. I nipped over just now to take a look though, Lo, and I was so proud! The sun on the bines, the cribs all out and standing ready, the sounds from the gipsy encampment floating to me on the breeze . . . it was wonderful.'

'So's mushrooms, bacon and fried bread,' Allsop commented, coming into the room with Allen trotting along beside him, clutching his hand. 'So's a hot cup of tea and toast and marmalade. And so are your lovely groats, Master Allen,' he finished enticingly.

'H'obble groats,' Allen said automatically. 'Me have mush'ooms an' flied blead.'

'That kid's got Chinese blood in his veins, I swear it,' Laurie groaned. 'Fried bread, Allie. Say fried bread and you shall have a piece.'

'Flied blead,' Allen said hopefully. 'Mush'ooms, Daddy?'

'Well, we'll see. Ready to dish up, Mrs Waughman?'

'Yes, Mr Laurie,' Mrs Waughman said. She had long ago given

up the unequal struggle of trying to remember that Mr Laurie was now Sir, and Miss Foxy was Milady. 'Will you 'ave a negg, an' all?'

Foxy spluttered but Laurie said yes please, he would have an egg as well and would Mrs Waughman like to fry one for Allen, too, whilst she was about it. Allsop made disapproving noises but he managed to sound indulgent at the same time so Mrs Waughman broke two eggs into the pan and put plates on top of the hob to warm.

'I won't have a fry-up, thanks,' Foxy said presently, when Mrs Waughman enquired as to her wishes. 'I'm getting fat. Besides, you know what it's like in the hopyard on the first day, you're never still for a moment. I'll have a good lunch . . . what are you staring at me for, Lo?'

'Oh, nothing,' Laurie said, gobbling fried bread. 'I just wondered why you thought you were getting fat.'

Foxy giggled and shot a quick glance at Allsop. Laurie reached across the table and squeezed her hand. 'Go on, admit it!'

Allsop, who had been preparing Allen's breakfast in a small dish with a picture of a cow jumping over the moon round its rim, stopped short, frozen, one hand holding a fork, the other the knife with which he had been cutting Allen's fried bread into small squares.

'No. You admit it,' Foxy said. 'I thought you said . . .'

'We think we're having a baby, Mr Allsop,' Laurie said. 'Another baby, I mean. Foxy hasn't seen the doctor yet, but . . . well, we're pretty sure.'

Allsop's knife and fork began to move once more, slicing fried bread, and his smile spread and spread until it could almost have been described as a beam.

'Well, that's the best news you could have given me! Another baby, Miss Foxy, and just at the right time for Master Allen, too. He needs a companion. Congratulations to you both.'

'Oh ah, that's nice news,' Mrs Waughman said ponderously, coming over to the table and putting Allsop's plate down before him. 'When's it comin', Miss?'

'Next March, I think, when Master Allen is a little over two and a half. Hopefully, by then, we may be able to run to a nursery maid again because I want to put another hopyard down this winter and it's hard work; it takes both of us all our time, doesn't it, Laurie?'

Allsop tutted.

'The truth is, Miss Foxy, you'd rather be outdoors than in,' he said roundly. 'Oh well, each to his own, I suppose.' He plucked Allen up and settled him in his highchair, fastening him in. 'Come on, young fellow-me-lad, you wanted egg and fried bread, now let's see you put it away!'

John got off the train at Ledbury station and thought how very quiet the town seemed after the hustle and bustle of a Europe preparing for war. He didn't have much luggage and wondered whether to ring the Hovertons and get someone to meet him, but he decided against it and went out into the road, hailing a taxi.

He had money, of course. The first thing he had done on reaching France was to change one of the big notes for more manageable cash and now he was on fire to get to Clifton Place. It would be grand to see Bees-wing and his parents again, of course it would, but he couldn't wait to see Laurie's face when he produced the money.

'Where to, sir?' the taxi driver asked. He stared at John, no doubt wondering who this large, unkempt-looking stranger was. John grinned at him. He had travelled in the other man's taxi many a time, especially when he and Laurie had been bound for local dances when they were in their late teens.

'To Clifton Place, I think. And I see you don't recognise me with my beard,' he said cheerfully. 'It *is* you, isn't it, Mr Bream? I'm John Hoverton behind all this hair.'

'Well, Mr John, I don't know when I bin more amazed,' the driver said, with the air of one who takes amazement for granted. He handed John into the back, then went round and climbed behind the wheel. 'You an' that brother o' yourn ... allus goin' orf an' comin' back diff'rent. Mind, young Laurie ... Sir Laurie, I mean ... has settled down nicely. A wife an' fam'ly does that for a feller.'

'A *wife*?'

'Oh ah, Sir Laurie married that young Lockett girl; she's Lady Clifton now. They've got a nipper an' all,' the taxi driver assured him. 'I drove 'em to the train for the 'oneymoon. They went to

Llandudno. But they've been back a good while now.'

'But didn't you say they had a nipper?' John said with a touch of mischief, having digested this unexpected piece of information. He wondered how Mr Bream would explain that one!

'Oh ah ... well, they say as 'ow the young people got married before Sir Laurie went off to Spain; the 'oneymoon was a sort of 'oliday to mek up for not 'avin' an 'oneymoon before,' Mr Bream explained conscientiously. 'But o' course the truth is, they 'ad the babby first, then the weddin'. 'Tain't unusual as you know, Mr John.'

John sat back in his seat. He thought of how hard he had tried to bring Mirri back for his brother and how totally unsuited he had thought them. But ... Foxy? Little Foxy? Laurie had married Foxy Lockett? They had pretended, of course, but it was just expediency, and when he and Laurie had got back from Spain Laurie had really detested Foxy.

Whilst John thought this over no one had spoken a word but suddenly Mr Bream turned round in his seat and grinned.

'Good weather for the 'oppin', eh, Mr John? They started this very mornin', so you ha'nt missed much.'

'Oh, at Bees-wing, you mean,' John said. 'I'll go over and give them a hand later.'

'Well, no doubt they're 'oppin' at Bees-wing,' Mr Bream acknowledged. 'But I meant at Clifton Place. First year they're done it, an' all. I drove past earlier – I were tekkin' a fare over Stoke Edith way – an' there they was, a-pullin' the bines in the new yard. 'Twas a purty sight.'

'Yes, of course, the new yard,' John said. What next, for God's sake? Mr Bream would probably inform him presently that Master Allen was starting university next week and that Mr Allsop had taken up rugby football!

'Will I drop you off at the yard or the house?' Mr Bream remarked presently, in the middle of a long description of hopping when he had been a young 'un. 'I dunno who'll be at the 'ouse today; they'll mostly be in the 'opyard.'

'Drop me there, then,' John said obligingly. 'It's not too far from the house, I take it?'

'Nobbut a step.'

'Right.' John, who had leaned forward in his seat during the conversation, leaned back and looked out, at the green grass on the verges, at the russet fruit in the orchards, at the dark gold of a field of late-ripening wheat. He smiled; he was beginning to realise that he had reached home at last.

'Goodness, Mrs Honeywell, your Dora picks as fast as a grownup – how old did you say she was?'

Foxy was picking at the Honeywell crib whilst Laurie picked with the Coppings, because it was good policy to get to know your workers and there was no better way of getting to know them than picking with them.

'Near enough eight,' Mrs Honeywell said. 'Not bad for a littl'un, is she?' She beamed fondly down at her small, skinny daughter, who was stripping a bine with all the efficiency of a long-time picker and tossing the burrs into an upturned umbrella, being too small to reach the crib. 'Mind, she's been givin' a hand for a year or two, now. And wi' my Bernie off wi' the army, learnin' to be a soldier, I can do wi' all the help I can git.'

'Where did you pick before?' Foxy asked. 'I don't remember you at Bees-wing, where I picked until I grew up. But I'm sure we've met before, haven't we?'

'Oh aye, Milady, at the dances in the village hall,' Mrs Honeywell said rather shyly. 'I picked for Ramages till this year but that were wi' Bernie's fambly, his mam and his aunties. Seein' as how he's not wi' me this year though, I thought I'd try a change. An' when Tess 'ere – she's Bernie's brother Ted's wife – saw the advert, we decided to sign on.' She was a neat, attractive woman in her late twenties and now she gave Foxy a knowing little grin. 'We thought it 'ud be more fun, like, to git away from the old'uns for a bit.'

'Lucky for us,' Foxy observed. 'Because of the war in Europe and the Germans invading Poland, most of the fellows who would normally sign on are either in the forces or waiting for the signal to join up. So the rest of us will have to put our backs into it before the weather changes, and that means working Saturdays, I'm afraid.'

'It did say in our letter. If it 'elps, I daresay no one minds missin' a Sat'day off. 'Sides, we don't usually pick in the rain, not heavy rain, so we'll get us days off,' Mrs Bernie agreed. 'I've never knowed a hop season what didn't bring on the rain. An' it's not quick, pickin' in even the lightest shower.'

'It's hateful, and let's hope we don't have to do it,' Foxy said, stripping the last burrs from her bine and standing back. 'You're doing us proud, you Honeywells, many thanks. We'll be stopping work for a tea-break any minute now, they'll be bringing the tea-urn down, so . . .' she broke off. 'Who's that? Oh my God, it's . . .'

She did not finish the sentence but simply turned on her heel and ran like a deer towards a tall figure, standing in the gateway to the hopyard.

'She fair flew,' Mrs Bernie observed, her quick fingers pausing in their work for a moment. 'Nice, ain't she? Hope nothin's gone wrong.'

'She's got 'er arms round some bloke,' Mrs Ted said. She wiped her sticky hands on her sacking apron and reached for the next bine. 'Now Sir Laurie's there with 'em. They're all a-huggin' as if they 'adn't seen each other for years!'

'They probably haven't,' Mrs Bernie said prosaically. She fetched another bine from the pile the pole-puller had cut down just as a cry of 'Clear 'em up!' was heard from the busheller. Mrs Bernie looked critically into their crib. 'We're doin' awright . . . eh, Dora, love, that brolly's all but filled; ain't you a good gel, then?'

The family group began feverishly clearing the last bine and finished just as the small procession, with the tractor and trailer behind, came into their row. Mr Fletcher, as busheller, clambered over the trailing, de-burred bines to measure the hops into his cane basket, the booker came behind him, to fill in the picker's card and his own book with the measured amount picked. And the pole-pullers with their sacks open and ready waited for the measured hops to be tipped inside.

'You're doin' well,' Mr Fletcher observed when he had measured their hops. 'Easy pickin', would you say?'

'Not bad at all,' Mrs Bernie said. She enjoyed him asking her that, as one hop-picker to another. 'It'll be good till the dew gets heavier, then the first hour's mucky work.'

'Pray for dry, Mrs Honeywell,' Mr Fletcher said. 'Did Milady mention we'd be pickin' a seven days' week, 'cos o' this war they reckon we're gettin' into? She did? Good. Right, fellers, the next house is . . . Jeffreys.'

The men and the tractor and trailer trundled past. 'No point in startin' to pick again till we've 'ad our tea, eh?' Mrs Ted said hopefully and almost as she spoke they heard the shout and saw, at the end of their row, the tea-urn trundle past on a wheelbarrow. Mrs Bernie straightened thankfully from her self-imposed task of picking up and cribbing the few hops which the men had dropped.

'You're right, Tess,' she said. 'C'mon, Dora love, us'll enjoy a cuppa wi' everyone else. March!'

'John! We've been so dreadfully worried . . . have you been home? Your dad was here earlier but . . .'

Foxy gave John a hard hug, then stood aside as Laurie swung round the corner, dropped both his sticks and hurled himself at John.

'John! My God, we've been frantic, especially now, with all of Europe gone mad! Are you all right? I can't believe you're here!'

'I'm fine,' John said. He felt fine, too, with the smell of the hops in his nostrils and his friend around him, sun-tanned and happy. 'What's all this, then? I distinctly remember advising against a hopyard until you could afford the equipment. I see you took my advice!'

They laughed, bless them, Laurie aiming a mock punch at his chin, Foxy pinching his arm.

'Yes, but we need money pretty badly, old fellow, and it seemed the best way,' Laurie said. 'We're in debt to the bank of course, but what farmer isn't, these days? Farm prices have slumped, but a good crop of hops will always sell.'

John felt Laurie's hand gripping his arm; gripping it as though he needed the physical contact to assure him that John was really present and not just a dream. Wait till I show him what I've brought home, John thought, and grinned affectionately down at his foster-brother.

'And you've married Foxy here! I wish I'd been around for the wedding, but I've brought you a present, of sorts.'

Foxy had been standing quietly, smiling at both of them. Now John saw her face flush, almost painfully.

'Is it Mirri, John?' she said. 'Where have you hidden her?'

John opened and shut his mouth. Then, with difficulty, he said: 'I left her in Spain, Lo. She – she wouldn't come any further.'

He looked at Laurie. He saw relief in his brother's eyes, then Laurie said: 'Oh well, so long as she's all right. But why did you delay so long, old chap? We expected you months ago!'

'Mirri was . . . she was very ill,' John said painfully. 'She had tuberculosis, Lo. She died.'

For a moment Laurie looked stricken. His face bleached beneath its tan and his eyes looked haunted. 'The poor kid! John, I had no idea, she seemed so strong and – and self-sufficient, somehow. When did she die?'

Foxy had moved up, to stand close to Laurie. He turned towards her and her arm slid round his waist. She said to John, 'Lo was very fond of her, but they had grown apart. Poor girl! Did she suffer much pain?'

John stared at the good red earth of Hereford beneath his cracked boots. 'I think she did, though she was immensely brave and never complained. But she longed to get out of Spain, to find a hospital somewhere which could cure her disease. Other than that . . . well, she was too ill to think about much else.'

'Poor girl,' Foxy said again. 'Did you tell her Lo and I were getting married?'

John frowned. 'No. How could I? The last time I spoke to Laurie he was full of marriage talk, but that was when he thought I was bringing Mirri home. He kept asking me to tell her about the marriage . . . but I never did. There would have been no point, as it turned out.'

Laurie was frowning too, staring up at John and squinting against the brilliant sunlight. The pickers were thronging past now, heading for the tea-urn, and John moved to one side, back against the bines, to give them room to pass.

'Marriage?' Laurie said slowly. 'But that was Foxy I was talking about, not Mirri! I was telling you to tell Mirri I was getting married, because I felt it only fair to let her know. My God, John, how could I have guessed you'd misunderstood?'

'Well I'm damned!' John said. 'What a mess. But it doesn't matter a jot, not now and not then, even. Mirri never mentioned marriage, she scarcely mentioned you, Lo, to tell you the truth. I think she was desperate when she wrote, but desperate for a friend, not a lover.'

'Then you don't think I let her down? Thank God,' Laurie said devoutly. 'It's been on my conscience ever since you left that I never should have asked you to go, John, but . . .'

'I'm glad you did, old fellow,' John said. He could feel a smile beginning and shoved his hand into his knapsack, feeling for the money-belt. 'Because handing that huge sum over to Sorotto has been on *my* conscience ever since it happened. And if I'd not gone to find Mirri I'd never have found . . . this.'

He had wrapped it in a square of white cotton after counting the contents many, many times. Now he watched Laurie slowly unfolding the cotton, staring at the canvas and leather pouch, undoing it with trembling hands, bringing out notes . . .

'Lo! Oh darling Lo, John's brought some of your money back!' Foxy gasped. 'Oh John, I can't believe it! I never grudged his losing it, not once we knew how we felt about each other, but life will be so much easier with a bit of cash behind us! Oh, John . . . tell!'

'It's a long story,' John said. He fell into step beside Laurie as his foster-brother began to walk, with the aid of his sticks, over towards the gate. Foxy pushed her hand into his elbow and John laid an arm across Laurie's shoulders and thus linked, they made their way up towards the house.

'We like long stories,' Foxy said contentedly. 'How much money is there, John?'

'More than half. Oh, and Sorotto's dead, Lo. I found the money actually on his body.'

'My God, so you fell in with that rogue again – be thankful you haven't got a bullet in you, old fellow. But you must ring Mum and Uncle Bill as soon as we get back, let them know you're safe. And you must meet Allen; he's walking, talking, all sorts. And Allsop will be delighted that you're okay.' Laurie paused. 'It'll take weeks to tell you all our news, and longer, I daresay, for you to tell us what you've been through. You'd better start now, before we reach the house, because Allen chatters like a magpie once he starts.'

'All right,' John said readily. 'I'll start with my climbing up into the Pyrenees that first day . . .'

He remembered it well, could see it, in his mind's eye, clear as clear. Reaching the top of the first peak, turning, looking back at the foothills below him, at the tiny copse where Mirri lay. He remembered her bravery, her determination, and the frailty of her. He remembered the beauty of her large, luminous eyes, dark-rimmed in her small, white face. He even remembered the feel of her in his arms, the lightness, the way she clung.

'And when you'd looked back the way you'd come, what then?' Foxy asked, and John realised that he had fallen silent for too long. The other two were looking at him, Foxy with impatient affection, Laurie with more understanding than John wanted or needed. The dead, he reminded himself, are over and gone; life is for the living.

'Well, then I turned my face towards the heights and saw the mountains stretching ahead, peak on peak . . .